The Best Seller

Arunabha Sengupta

ISBN: 145380398X
ISBN-13: 9781453803981

Praise for Big Apple 2 Bites
by
Arunabha Sengupta

This is the story of every young Indian who finds himself in the world's greatest landscape... The writer's exuberant prose regarding this martial art made me think of learning it too... Sengupta has very rightly captured the middle-class mentality of the Indians in the US...The writer has dealt with topics as diverse as software, religion, racism, philosophy, emotions, fate and globalisation. The novel is racy and the language is simple...The writer brings to the reader the scents and smells of America...Interesting read

- The Sunday Tribune

Honest portrayal of society ... fresh perspectives on almost everything from the very mundane to the most lofty.

- Deccan Herald

The hallmark of the story and one that distinguishes it from many others is that it is written entirely in the second personApart from a deep insight into the work of a process consultant, the story also makes one realise the misconceptions about other cultures and their norms and values which still rule in spite of globalisation. Well worth reading

- The Dawn

Mumbai version of Bartleby the Scrivener. Thumbs Up

- Work the Globe

Humour in every page

- The Asian Age

Reads like a Dream

– P.Lal, Poet and Founder, Writers Workshop India

A most refreshing sense of humour

– Shyamala Narayan, Book Review India

To
Profsky
The Lotus in the World of Slushpile

Acknowledgements

A novel of this size and span could not have been completed by an author as temperamental as me without events and incentives to spur me on.

Thanks to all who have been instrumental in shaping the events that have shaped the story and devising the incentives that have brought it to conclusion.

In all the falsehood and chance that surrounds the so called real world, one can read plenty about it in the pages that follow, I always count the blessings of having found the truth in the form of Rumela. It is an added advantage when the truth in question plays the part of proofreader, editor and critic.

It was a delight each time when my daughter Meha looked at the screen of my laptop and discovered names of places she has been to. It is moments such as these that make the toil of over five hundred pages meaningful.

My heart goes out to the small, select and splendid fan club who waited patiently during the long, long gap between the publication of *Big Apple 2 Bites* and this novel. I do hope their vigil and encouragement will be rewarded.

And finally, heartfelt gratitude to Professor Lal for not only being a mentor who bears the torch in a world of fickle flicker, but also for the permission to cast him as a character in the story.

Part I:

Asset Substitution Problem

I

"The Amsterdam skyline looks like assorted chocolate cake. I always feel like taking a bite."

Throughout the journey back from Alsmere, Subramanium's delicious imagery sweetened Sandeep's lips into a smile. When they got off the NS Intercity at Amsterdam Zuid, however, the visual diet on offer was predominantly liquid.

The suit-clad herd, tongues lolling out, collectively clopped to the Heineken run modern day watering hole.

Endless arguments, dry discussions quickly sunk into temporary oblivion of thirst quenching amber. Talk flipped around from gloomy contracts, cost containment and constraints to infinitely more cheerful premises of biking, rowing and hockey. The summer beamed with a genial smile. In short, it was an unusually sunny Friday afternoon in Amsterdam. The year during which great banks tottered and fell.

Walking across the WTC courtyard, Subramanium soaked in the atmosphere.

"There is something about Europe. Quaint old towns or modern cities, there is always a character. I never seem to have enough of it."

Sandeep nodded, observing the eager executives as they made a synchronised beeline for the weekend heralding beer.

"I wonder if this is the root cause of the crisis," he mused. With a sharp movement of his hand he clutched his teacher's Chinese tunic, pulling him back on to the pavement. "Careful now, this is continental Europe. Always look left."

Subramanium adjusted his cotton attire, checking for possible rips.

"Thanks, son. But, be gentle with this thing. It's my best suit."

They made their way across Strawinskylaan to the tram stop, the older man carefully peering towards the correct side.

"What it is with you and the Chinese suits," Sandeep laughed. A couple of years back, he would not have taken the liberty. For close to one and a half decades, following the archaic principles of traditional martial arts, his *karate* and *tai chi* teacher had been beyond questions. However, this was their second foreign trip together. A brief one week camp in Bangkok the year before, followed by this workshop in Netherlands. Tentatively, the barriers of anachronistic etiquette had given way to a rewarding peek at the man behind the black belt and the sash.

The man in question, half a century's martial arts experience under his reputed belt, chortled. "I don't have slant eyes and yellow skin. If I am to be taken seriously by Europeans as a *tai chi* instructor, I have to be packaged in oriental wraps."

He took one last look at the spirit sipping salarymen.

"How does it feel to walk away from all this?"

Sandeep followed his master's gaze across Zuidplein. Chairs and mug laden tables encroaching on to half the pedestrian path. Suits, ties, laptops, handbags and beer mugs. The Dutch work force sprinkled here, there, everywhere with Chinese, Japanese, Koreans, Indians, Surinamis and Pakistanis.

"It's a bit late in the day to ask the question, even to oneself. Honestly, the moment I look beyond the suits and into the eyes, I feel relieved."

"You miss the money?"

"Freedom has a price."

"Probably your book will make you a millionaire."

Sandeep chuckled as Tram number 5 approached with a clang.

"We keep forgetting that rich authors are outliers. The majority are either earning their wages as waiters or proudly poring over their collection of rejection slips."

∾ ∾ ∾

As student and teacher boarded the Tram, a dignified head glistened amongst the weekend welcoming crowd. Bereft of any serious vegetation barring a few scholarly wisps, the crown in question belonged to K. Ramesh, Vice President, European Operations, *Axiom Consultants.* Having a conversational drink with him was his client Dave de Boer, CEO, Operations and IT Division of the HMH Bank.

"Netherlands produces 266 different varieties of beer," the banker observed. "And Belgium 270."

The VP beamed.

"If anyone asks me what I did while the market was going slow, I'll say I tasted the different brews of BeNeLux."

"Yes, and waited for the next boom."

The sentence was intoned casually, but it cut Ramesh to the quick. The Dutchman had turned back to his drink, with the quiet satisfaction that follows caustic quips. The cumulative din of hundreds of conversations started getting on the VP's nerves.

"You're eking a living out of your Anglo Saxon legacy, Ram, but you're also limited by it."

Ramesh peered into his mug and wondered if this merited a reply.

"Could you elaborate on that?"

Dave de Boer laughed.

"Nothing personal, Ram. I may be guilty of generalising, but you Indians are getting everywhere because of that one legacy handed down by your colonial overlords. The English language. They taught you to be clerks. In every business sector that demands a pen pusher, you do a great job. I will accept that. There is no number cruncher like the Indian to run the Project Management Office. But, you know what your problem is, Ram? You can't think by yourselves."

Ramesh racked his brain for a face saving response. It was true. All that *Axiom,* in the guise of consultants, had managed to get hold of in HMH was a bunch of PMO positions.

"You can copy and paste documents and processes. You will mug and preach Sarbanes Oxley and Lean Six Sigma. But, show me something original – some idea not clerically copied from the West or Japan. Something purely ...," the CEO brought his mouth close to Ramesh's ear. " ... purely Indian ... Can you think of anything?"

Severely short of hair, Ramesh bristled to the best of his ability.

"Whenever I think of you, I am reminded of Bollywood, Ram. The same model. Hollywood success stories and popular hits copied, pasted and packaged with an Indian stamp. You are good at that, but at little else. I believe even your constitution is nothing but a patchwork of the French and the Irish ..."

"We are not whatever the British made us, Dave," Ramesh said, breaching the Golden Rule of always agreeing with the valued client. "We are a nation of heritage, thousands of years of learning and the oldest philosophies...."

Dave de Boer laughed and patted Ramesh on his back.

"Forget ancient history. Show me in modern currency. In Euros," he said, twisting the knife in the rawest wound. "I am sorry, Ram, it's Friday evening. I have to go out there and live."

He downed the remaining amber of his mug and got up.

"And let me know if you come up with a *Gandhian* remedy to this mess we have got into."

He left the exact change for his drink on the table and walked out into the weekend. Left alone, Ramesh fought to digest the parting words with his pint of beer.

From all around him came bursts of noise resembling choked motorcycle engines – sumtotal of drink laced discussions in Dutch.

"I would recommend Hermaans. Start with *Beyond Sleep.* If you enjoy it, you can come back and pick up *Darkroom of Damocles.* The other book I'd recommend is *The Assault.*"

"Harry Mulisch?"

"Right," Jeroen, the brown haired young man working in the American Book Centre, was full of helpful enthusiasm. "People tend to go gaga about his *Discovery of Heaven,* but it can put you off as easily. It's safer to start with *De Aanslag.* I'm afraid that needs to do as starters. We Dutch are not great writers."

"I don't believe that," Sandeep disagreed. "It's more likely that you have not really marketed your Literature across the globe, like we Indians are doing now. It is impossible for a country of your aesthetic sense and large bookcases to be without the writing gene."

Jeroen laughed. "We don't have a Shakespeare or a Dickens in our ranks, anyway."

Sandeep picked another book from the local Literature section.

"What about this?" he asked. "The travel book I am carrying recommends it as a good account of life in the Red Light District."

Jeroen shook his head.

"That will give you the statistics of her genitalia, if you are into that sort of thing, but it is definitely not something I'd classify as a good read."

Sandeep laughed. "I guess one should not go by reviews."

"Definitely not. They can be purchased. Is there anything else I can help you with?"

"I was wondering if you had something by Dario Fo."

"Dario Fo? I don't think we do. But, tell you what. If you take 1,2 or 5 to Liedseplein, there is the Theatre and Film Book Shop with an excellent collection. You can try there. I see your friend has also found something."

Subramanium had joined him with a couple of books from the fitness section. Jeroen carried Sandeep's pile to the cash counter.

"Will you look around some more, or should I start billing?"

Sandeep smiled.

"Go ahead mate, before I manage to inflict destitution on myself."

Jeroen laughed.

"I know what you mean."

"There is a quote by a fascinating Bengali author from our land. No one can turn a pauper from buying books. I guess times have changed."

"You bet they have. Now people become paupers from making too much money. These are times to shake up our basic beliefs."

∾ ∾ ∾

The Indian gentleman was approaching the dreaded borderline between youth and middle age – perhaps a bit too early compared to the active Dutchmen. As he sat quietly with a beer on one of the chairs laid out for the summer crowd of Leidseplein, his eyes followed the animated afternoon crowd with something more than casual curiosity. A pencil in his hand notched tally marks onto a notepad. He wondered if the exercise would be easier with an iPad and smiled to himself.

Two hundred and thirty people had passed from right to left in the last fifteen minutes. A staggering one hundred and six of them had been talking on their cell phones. Fifty seven more had been either texting or playing those curious digital games. He did not even count the hordes of people wired with earphones, listening to music on iPods, iPhones or their cutting edge derivatives. He had also observed at least two people reading on hand held Kindle devices.

He lowered his pencil. Enough data to take him through the weekend. His eyes fell on the leaflet announcing Boom Chicago's new show – *Upgrade or Die.* The punch line read *iPhone therefore I am.*

Dr. Suprakash Roy burst out laughing.

∾ ∾ ∾

"*Yang style Tai Chi Chuan,* by George Salinas," Subramanium held up an illustrated volume. "I know the guy. Trained with him for a few years. I used to spend a lot of time in Hong Kong those days." He chuckled. "Played me a mean little trick. He knew getting to be the first non Chinese instructor certified by Sifu Wong would be a unique selling point. I was somewhat ahead of him in that direction. He talked Sifu into taking a few days off, accompanying him on a trip around Mainland China. In the mean time, my funds ran out, my visa expired. I had to go back. So, he got the honour – a couple of years before I could return and complete my training."

They sat in the courtyard of Spui, digging into their takeaway packs of Nasi Goreng. Around them residual ripples of the merrymaking of Leidseplein trickled in, footsteps dispersing across the cobblestones towards the Dam.

"It's magnanimous to buy his book, *Sensei*." As he had started off as a student of *karate* under Subramanium, Sandeep used the Japanese term for teacher. Students of *tai chi* preferred *Sifu.*

Subramanium laughed. The remnants of rat race.

"This is a pretty good book. And I know he's authentic, a master. A lot of my students may find it helpful."

A smile touched Sandeep's lips as he looked at the imposing chocolate brown buildings across the Singel. The paternal mode of address indicated that the preachy strain in the master was about to be unleashed.

II

Text message sent at 5:35 AM

Stillness of the morn
Weights clank in the multigym
Modern solitude

Text message received at 5:37 AM

Dead tired post long night
Stupid text beeps shatter sleep
What's your problem dude?

Dr. Suprakash Roy looked at the chronologically ordered text messages on the Blackberry. His gaze was expressionless, cultivated through the years of professional practice.

"Do you recall the phone number of the guy you exchanged the messages with?" he asked.

Perched on the canal side bench, his cousin was confused.

"The number is in the message details. Also in the sim memory."

"Do you remember it?"

"For God's sake ... no I don't."

"Ah ...," the doctor smiled. "You called me up about three times today. Twice, I may add, when I was in my bath. Do you remember my number?"

Pritam fidgeted. "No. Why do you want to know?"

The doctor became even more curious.

"What about your own number?"

"This is a new number for use in the Netherlands."

"Yes, but you have been staying here for over a couple of months, haven't you?"

"Come on Sup-da," Pritam threw an impatient pebble into the Rijn Galgewate. "Don't you have anything else to say? You keep looking at the messages and ask stupid questions."

The psychiatrist followed the trajectory of the small projectile.

"Careful. There are a lot of ducks here."

"Eh?"

"Your pebbles may hurt one of the birds. People in the Netherlands are very sensitive about that sort of a thing."

In his own professional circles, Pritam Mitra the consultant had a reputation for being unflappable. Hostile clients and imbecile superiors notwithstanding, seldom had anyone seen him lose his practised smile and smooth persuasive eloquence. There were rumours, albeit unsubstantiated, of a sturdy, well stacked folder once hurled at him by a disgruntled employee of a Manhattan financial institution. It had taken place during the findings presentation of one of his early assignments. Even the unorthodox use of office stationery in the nascent days of his career had failed to wipe the smile from his face. Nor had it succeeded in taking the edge off the gentle reasoning of his voice which recommended rationalisation of fifty percent of the work force.

However, seasoned pro that he was, he displayed chinks in the armour of his celebrated calm.

"I come here seeking your professional advice and you talk about ducks?" he fumed. "This is Leiden, a university town. With a fully functional student community born and brought up in this nation of beer guzzlers. Are they always in the best of behaviour? Will throwing pebbles into one of these godforsaken canals raise a frigging eyebrow?" He paused and looked at his elder cousin. "Do I have to lie down on a couch for you to come up with some constructive comments for a change? Excuse me."

They were interrupted by the ringtone of Pritam's phone. While the consultant tried to use his professional skills to get out of an unwanted conversation, the good doctor sighed. Not without reason. Wronged on several counts. In the short barked telephone communication of the morning, his younger cousin had not mentioned that his professional expertise would be in demand. It had seemed a natural rendezvous of first cousins, chancing to cross paths at the other side of the world. Besides, sadly, not too many people, even among the well read and educated, knew the difference between a psychiatrist and a psychoanalyst. A psychiatrist did not use a couch, unless he actively specialised in the Freudian science. Lastly, what was he supposed to infer from a visibly agitated cousin who showed weird lines of poetry?

Dr. Roy, however, was intrigued by the Blackberry. This was the fourth time his cousin had been interrupted by its ringing. There had also been twangs of incoming emails and beeps of arriving text messages. When he had arrived at the agreed place of meeting, the consultant had been reviewing a power point presentation on his hand held gadget. And he had used the same device to show the peculiar rhymed messages, vaguely hinting at problems.

"Right now, all I can detect is a touch of insomnia," he remarked when Pritam had managed to nip the conversation short. He had been looking forward to dine at one of Leiden's many delectable restaurants, but his cousin in his frame of mind was not the ideal companion across a dinner table. "Do you constantly stay online with that phone of yours?"

"Yes, I do. Goes with the job. And you are right about insomnia," Pritam agreed. Bicycles shuttled about on the cobblestoned banks of the canal and he looked at them with disapproval. "I haven't slept a wink these last couple of days."

"I can make that out ... if someonelike you is desperate enough to try writing Haikus in the wee hours of the morning, something must be wrong. I didn't know you were into writing. Or going to the gym at five thirty."

Pritam shuddered.

"I am not into writing Haikus," he replied.

"No?"

"Definitely not. Nor any other sort of poetry. I hate the guts of writers."

"The lines you just showed me? Were they forwarded? Side effects of Blackberry addiction?"

"A momentary indiscretion – temporary insanity. I am paying the price for it. I'll never write anything else in my life – except assessment reports and cost cutting strategies. Excuse me."

The doctor nodded gravely as Pritam proceeded to skim through a newly arrived email. The sun was still high in the sky even as the clock in the distant tower showed half past eight. A year in Netherlands had still not accustomed him to dinner under the sun.

"For a moment I was really worried about you."

"Oh yeah? I thought you were more worried about the ducks."

"That too ... I was getting the impression that the years of advising clients to lay off their old hands had got on your conscience. You are unable to sleep with the body-count of jobless fathers, weeping mothers, starving kids growing on your conscience ..."

"You do know how to cheer people up, don't you?"

Suprakash Roy bowed. He was seven years older than his disgruntled cousin, but their relationship had always been open and friendly.

"One tries to please."

Although thirty nine, the doctor's scholarly habits, looks and attire made him look half a decade older. Pritam Mitra, on the other hand, looked his age – and the recently acquired grey hairs had come as a relief to him, lending an aura of wisdom to his arguments as a consultant.

"Don't you shrinks ever learn bedside behaviour?"

Dr. Roy frowned. He did not like being referred to as a shrink. Besides he was getting hungry, in spite of the persevering sun.

"Care to tell me something more about your anxiety? Less cryptic perhaps than a couple of haikus?"

Pritam pushed his fingers through his hair.

"I really don't know where to begin."

"The beginning, in most cases, proves to be adequate."

"Avoid these pseudo witty clichés," Pritam snarled. "Leave that to the consultants. It all started when I went into this Toko shop...Excuse me." He irritably glanced at an incoming call and barked."I'm kind of busy, could you please call back? Thanks."

"What shop was that?"

"Toko ... it's run by a Pakistani family and they sell Indian food and spices ..."

"The world is a strange place," Dr. Roy observed with a sigh. "You know, most of the Indian restaurants in London are owned by either Pakistanis or Bangladeshis. I have a Lebanese colleague who says it is similar with Lebanese food, most of those restaurants abroad run by Syrians and Egyptians."

In a crisp sentence, acutely wanting in degrees of decency, Pritam told his cousin what he could do with the Indian restaurants in London. For good measure, he added as corollary what could be done with their Lebanese counterparts in other regions of the world.

"And if you agree not to interrupt with your geopolitical analysis of the world of cuisine, I will go on with the sequence of events. I was in Toko at five minutes past two one afternoon – when this girl came in and looked at the television."

At the introduction of the fairer sex, Dr. Roy smiled to himself. A bit of a late bloomer, this Pritam. However, if he remembered the precise moment of meeting a girl – down to the exact minute – he was probably going through a delayed juvenile phase. His money would be on late adolescent infatuation rather than Obsessive Compulsive Disorder. He heaved a Freudian sigh of relief and waited as a reflective smile touched Pritam's face.

"And the television was showing live feed from one of those websites which stream cricket matches. India was playing Australia at the Wankhede . The girl looked at her watch."

Incoherence, agitation and a marked tendency towards ignoring social decorum. Attention Deficiency Disorder was growing among professionals who had reached a certain level of seniority. With mails, phone calls, text messages creating havoc on the working memory.

"Why don't we take one thing at a time?" he asked. "There is an Argentinean restaurant I know of. And ... I think it will be wise to switch your cell phone off for a while."

∾ ∾ ∾

Birla Mandir, Kolkata

"Nārāyanam namaskritya naram caiva narottamam
devīm sarasvatīm vyasa tato jayamudīrayet
We begin the 245th reading of the Mahabharata."

The motley group of thirty odd people settled down for an hour of reading by the tall elderly scholar. The clear, composed voice reverberated across the room.

Majority of the audience were elderly, but some young faces were scattered here and there. Most listened attentively, some fingering beautiful cloth bound volumes of the Indian epic. Some nodded off.

III

Abundant beer and smoky haze. Aside from that, however, the *Laurierboom* was very different from the other bars of Amsterdam. No loud music, no television screens showing football matches or music channels. Quiet, hushed, cerebral discussions. A warm glow spread through the premises. People sat in clusters, pairs of eyes following the movement of wooden pieces and pawns on varnished chess boards as some of the patrons settled down to friendly games of various degrees of seriousness. The standard of the games was the highest to be found in bars. This establishment in Jordaan was proud and homely, and some of the best club players of the land of Max Euwe assembled for a relaxing game.

In one warm corner of the bar, clutching a hardly sipped mug of Grolsch, Sandeep sat fighting a losing battle. He had picked on a tall, scholarly Dutch guy with a bald head and a thick moustache. Within a few minutes he had regretted it. Playing Ruy Lopez, one of the few openings that he remembered passably well, he had managed to progress stutteringly to the middle game till a double pawn and a restricted bishop had slowly suffocated him. This has been followed by the two knights of his opponent combining to bring about a quick finish to the skirmishes. In the return match, he had responded to his opponent's king pawn opening by advancing his queen bishop pawn. The resulting Sicilian affair was embarrassingly one sided. After a dozen moves, he had lost a pawn and there was a gaping hole in front of his king.

Not too many people watched their game, preferring more evenly matched encounters. Sandeep glanced up to notice a couple of bored Dutch faces and a pair of curious eyes belonging to a young girl who looked Indian.

Even as the white bishop advanced diagonally, coming to rest in a crucial square hinting at a double threat, Sandeep's eyes unmindfully swept around the room. If Dr. Suprakash Roy had been there, he could have detected a sub-conscious attempt at locating the probable escort of the owner of the curious eyes.

His hands hovered uncertainly over the knight and his bishop pawn, and after moving the latter one square, he pressed the clock and looked up again. When he looked back at the board, the Dutchman had dealt crippling blow to his queenside, something he had neither anticipated and nor had any idea of countering. His knight was helplessly under threat.

After a few furtive trains of thought, Sandeep offered his hand. He had had enough hammering.

"Wish you a pleasant stay in Amsterdam," his opponent said in that endearing Dutch accented English.

Sandeep smiled and got up. His place was taken by one of the Dutch spectators.

He looked at the girl and smiled.

"Hi," he said.

"Gave up your kingdom for a horse?"

Sandeep laughed. No hint of accent, but the Indian roots were unmistakable.

"Well, it's more of a case of a tide in the affairs of men taken backwards."

It was the girl's turn to laugh. A loud confident chortle rather than the usual girlish giggle.

"Not much argument for losing one shaft and shooting his fellow of the self-same flight?"

Sandeep enjoyed this Shakespearean counter thrust.

"It is more to do with 'if the injurer is weaker spare him and if stronger spare thyself'."

Familiar and funny within the first few exchanges, Sandeep liked the conversation. The girl was tall – by Indian standards, of course appreciably dwarfed by the towering Dutch damsels. She wore a white blouse with a light blue jacket and blue jeans. She seemed to be in her mid twenties, younger than him by some years. However, Sandeep knew he did not look thirty one. He moved closer and caught her eyes which sparkled with fun as she spoke – spontaneity that endeared or alarmed depending on one's openness to emancipation. Sandeep felt a rare thrill.

"In non-Shakespearean words for a change, I am Sandeep."

The girl took the offered hand in a firm grip.

"Too bad it's not Anthony or Cassius ... we could have continued in the same vein. Shruti."

"What's in a name?"

"That's cliché. Have you ever tried calling a rose a *gezelligheid*?"

"Or a tulip to give it local fragrance?"

"Rose still happens to be the national flower of Netherlands. By the way, you left your beer on the table."

Sandeep raised his finger to his lips.

"Let's hope no one notices. I'm not too fond of beer. If Dutch authorities get wind of that, they may cancel my visa. But you've got to order something to play in this place."

"I guess you can order coffee."

"I was not too sure about that. I mean this is a bar after all and ordering coffee might have looked stupid."

"Not in this country. Coffee's always acceptable."

They looked at the keen tussles in the other tables.

"Who are you with?" Sandeep asked.

The girl shot him a quick look. The eyes were alive. The curious upward tilt of the nose could be regarded as a blemish, but to Sandeep it seemed to be an icing on the layers of her obvious attractions.

"Why do you assume I am with someone?"

Sandeep liked the sharpness of the voice, the edge with which the challenge was thrown in the air.

"I was just wondering ... coffee seemed such a good idea I was thinking whether you could join me ..."

Shruti shrugged.

"Would you like a game as well?"

"A game? A game of chess?"

She grabbed an empty table.

"So not only does coming into a bar unaccompanied lie beyond the boundaries of the Indian female, but also a game of chess ..."

Sandeep was groping for the correct move even before the game.

"Er ... eh, no ... I mean, I am not one of the archetypical Indian males you come across ... Why, I idolize Judith Polgar and ... well ... Kaneru Hampi."

"Remembered the name in the nick of time."

"Well, I also strongly propagate the idea that chess was invented by Mandodari ..."

"Ravana's wife?"

"The same. Compensating perhaps for the trials of being married to one of history's blackguards."

"You think Ravana was a villain?"

"Well, mythology puts him down as a demon king ... who abducted Sita ..."

"What if I say that mythology could have told a different story had he won the war?"

Sandeep considered this.

"That's interesting."

"Rakshashas ... Well there's a theory that Rakshashas were actually Rakshaks or guards."

"So manufactured consent worked even in the mythological era."

"It sure did."

"Maybe this injustice drove Mandodari to chess."

"Or maybe the women of Lanka found it a better pastime to slashing and killing each other."

"I should have seen that coming. How would you like your coffee? With or without milk?"

"With."

"Sugar or no sugar?"

"No sugar."

"Explains your figure."

"Thank you. But I do have lots of sweet dishes."

"Explains your charm."

"Don't overdo the charm part yet."

"Clock or no clock?"

"I beg your pardon?"

"I'm talking about the game?"

"Spare me the clock. I am neither that good nor serious."

The game was well contested. Shruti proved to be an imaginative player, although not very sound in the basics of Giuoco Piano. The middle game was hard fought and although Sandeep held on to the small material advantage of a pawn, Shruti's double bishop balanced things out. After half an hour, Sandeep offered draw.

"So, chess is not the domain of men alone, is it?" Shruti asked as she accepted the offer.

"Never has been."

"Not all Indian girls come into chess bars accompanied by cerebral male escorts."

"Accepted," Sandeep nodded. "And not too many pretty girls open a conversation quoting Shakespeare."

Shruti raised an eyebrow.

"And if they do, they limit themselves to 'What's in a name' and 'To be or not to be'. The clichés."

"Do you throw about your compliments like idle wind that impresses me not?"

Sandeep thought for a while.

"I do have eyes to wonder and don't lack tongue to praise."

"And do you pick Indian girls to compliment or do your flirtations span across international borders and put the Dutch dames at peril?"

"Well, most of them are close to eight feet tall. One would need a telescope to detect whether they are pretty or not."

"So your chivalry is indeed restricted to domestic lasses?"

"Mostly out of optical limitations."

"One does not need great eyes to see that Dutch girls are gorgeous."

Sandeep laughed and paid the bill.

"I do admire them, their obvious attractions packaged in leggings and bicycles, hockey sticks and giant earrings any self-respecting cat can leap through. However, there are logistic impediments to chivalry. You can politely offer to carry a heavy bag for an Indian lady. However, in the case of a Dutch girl it makes no sense. Most often she can manage the bag and the chivalrous guy along with it with biceps to spare."

"So left to yourself you would rather keep the women demure, docile and fragile."

"Delicate would have made an apt alliteration."

"So, what's your considered counter?"

"I find it amazing how you turn all my appreciative allusions into chauvinistic sentiments."

"That's because *I* find it amusing how you try to wriggle out of the sticky situations with your ready wit."

"I will praise any man that will praise me."

"Would you rather have me bury you than to praise you?"

"I would rather you bury the hatchet. Let me make it clear once and for all. I am all for the emancipation of women, of them entering bars alone and proud, of enjoying analytical activities. That too ladies of all nationalities. And I am next to none in my admiration for the Amazons and the Valkyries. However, as Gratiano says, we will end this discourse after dinner."

He bowed and made way for Shruti to lead the way.

"Dinner? Who said anything about dinner?"

"It was I. In such a night as this the sweet wind could have gently kissed the trees and the moon could have shone bright but for the infernal hours the sun stubbornly keeps in these parts. I was wondering if you would join me for dinner on my last night in Amsterdam."

Shruti hesitated.

"When Lorenzo would say those words, most often Jessica would be bathed in sun light coming through the oculus on the ceiling of the Globe Theatre. I can take heart from there," Sandeep continued. "However, it's an open offer. You can accept or refuse. I am not assuming affirmation out of chauvinistic prejudice. Nor am I trivializing the female freedom of choice ... I just think our conversation is too magical to abandon abruptly."

Shruti made her way out of the bar.

"It may be a bit tedious to continue along the same lines without plunging into plebeian pits from time to time."

"Plunging into plebeian pits ... you outdo yourself, my lady. May I apologise for being imprudent enough to suggest an alliterative alternative a while back?"

"You are provisionally pardoned, your choice of dinner may earn you the unconditional. What about this being your last night in Amsterdam?"

They walked along Laurierstraat, heading for the Dam.

"In a manner of speaking. I will return in a couple of weeks. But I need to get my visa renewed."

"So you will be back in no time?"

"Right."

"So this is not your last night in Amsterdam?"

"Truthful manipulation. For your gracious company."

"I find you incorrigible, but yet strangely not unbearable. I assume you are renewing your visa from India?"

"Yes. Delhi probably, but it can also be done from Kolkata if I am to believe some people."

"Are you going to Kolkata?"

"I am."

Shruti made a tut-tutting sound with her tongue.

"I know another guy who's going to Kolkata tomorrow."

"Oh is it? Must be the same flight."

"Probably. I was supposed to meet him today to ask a favour. But a colossal idiot gave me the wrong address." She turned and looked at him. "You know why I went over to watch your game?"

Sandeep shrugged. "A ruggedly handsome Indian guy in a bar full of Dutchmen. Probably the princess in you saw the proverbial knight in shining armour."

"A knight who loses his knight to the Dutchman and thus the game?"

Sandeep smiled. The wit elated him.

"High hopes," Shruti continued. "It was because from a distance you looked like him."

"James Dean?"

"No, the colossal idiot I was talking about."

"Ouch. Must be my retarded twin brother separated at birth ..."

"I don't know about your being twins ... you are not identical, just a superficial similarity ... But I won't argue about his being a retard. He gave me this address. One of those artist alleys of Jordaan. And I took the trouble of going there early in the morning, to be sure of collaring this guy. And I found out he had given me the address of a studio ..."

Sandeep stopped. "Studio?"

"Yes. One of those studios of some yuppie new artist. And obviously it was locked. There was no one around to ask. Only two guys in glorified pyjamas doing some intricate *tai chi* manoeuvre."

Sandeep put his hand up, in an urgent gesture for his new friend to stop. "*Tai chi.*"

"Yes, you know, the Chinese movements ..."

"I do know the Chinese movements ... Was it by any chance a small street neighbouring the celebrated Ninestraatjes?"

There was confusion in the confident face of Shruti. Her nose, with that endearing tilt, seemed to be sniffing for some explanation.

"It did border the nine streets. How on earth ..."

"Madam, you have done grave injustice to my doppelganger. Everything makes sense now. He sent you to the right place. I am temporarily sleeping in an artist's establishment – or his studio."

"How has that ...?"

"And one of the two guys you saw in the glorified pyjamas doing *tai chi* was none other than yours truly. You had been looking for me."

Shruti gaped.

"You are *that* Sandeep?"

"Yes, and you are *that* Shruti as well."

Shruti shook her head.

"That cannot be."

"It certainly is. I can vouch that I am Sandeep. The very one. And you are the girl who looks at her watch at five past two in the afternoon when she sees a cricket match being telecast in a Pakistani store."

Shruti stared.

"Let's stick to old reliable Shakespeare and his antecedents who had a clear concise tale to tell. The stream of consciousness stuff is not really my cup of tea. Although Professor Lal says a great deal of good things about James Joyce. What exactly do you mean? Why are you ... or rather ... how are you Sandeep when you are staying in an artist's studio? Why were you doing *tai chi?*"

"I can understand your confusion if not the logical flow of your questions. I was doing *tai chi* because I have always done it ... ever since I was twenty...that makes about eleven ... well forget that. I happen to have come to Amsterdam for the sole reason of participating in a *tai chi* workshop. And I am staying at the studio because it belongs to an artist and my friend whom you saw in glorified pyjamas is an apprentice to this artist ... The good man allowed me lodging for free if I could rough it."

"Why on earth do you have to rough it?"

"Because I am broke. Or very close to being one."

"But aren't you a consultant?"

"Am I a consultant? Well, you do ask a lot of questions."

"Yes I do. I hate mysteries – unless they are written by Agatha Christie, or preferably Dorothy L Sayers."

"Without starting another sex war, why do you think there are such a lot of female mystery writers?"

"Stop it ..."

"And some of them pretty ordinary ... Dorothy L Sayers and Agatha Christie of course were peerless, but what do you think of Ruth Rendell. And say, Mary Higgins Clarke?"

"That too ... you quoted Shakespeare. Not only the plays but also a frigging sonnet. And you claim to be a consultant ..."

"Pardon me, but as Shaggy would have put it, *it wasn't me*. It was Pritam who made the claim."

"You don't like beer and you produce alliterations at the drop of a hat."

"Madam is kind..."

"And from your backpack, I see the corner of Pablo Neruda's *Love* sticking out."

Sandeep smiled. He lowered his backpack and retrieved the offending volume.

"I got it for 2 euro from the Boekenmarkt at Spui today. That's the diversity of Amsterdam. You can buy twenty minutes worth of love for fifty euro ... or can get it for a life time for as little as two ...Ouch."

Shruti had kicked him on the more sensitive part of his shin.

"Explain."

"It's a long explanation ..."

"I expect it to be. A so called consultant who is broke and reads poetry and plays, does not like beer, does *tai chi* and lives in an artist's studio ... out with the truth."

"Don't you think that is a lot to explain, ideally discussed over some hot dinner? I know of this wonderful Vietnamese restaurant ..."

Shruti scowled.

"How on earth are we going to eat in a restaurant if you are broke?"

Sandeep smiled.

"Is there a better place to go Dutch?"

IV

Mail from Ajay Yadav to Axiom_HMH team
Subject: Musical Soiree
Sent 8:32 PM

Dear All,

Axiom HMH is going to conduct a musical soiree on Monday from18-30 to 19-30 hours. Madhu says there will be a lot of talented musicians. Many of the senior HMH members are also going to be there.

Although on the face of it an event of entertainment, I would expect everyone to turn up, since this is an event through which we are building our Axiom brand image.

Thanks and Regards,
Ajay Yadav
Account Manager – Axiom HMH

Mail from Madhu Deb to Axiom_HMH team members other than Ajay Yadav
Subject : FW : Musical Soiree
Sent : 8:34 PM

Dear All,

The soiree is by no means compulsory. Please feel free to bunk if you have plans for the evening. :-)
But I do guarantee a lot of entertainment.
The proceeds of the lucky draw is going to CRY for the education of homeless Indian children.

Cheers,
Madhu
Senior Manager – Axiom HMH

Mail from Trisha Das in reply to Madhu Deb's mail
:-) I will attend but thanks Madhu-di.

Email from Simon van der Wiel
To: De, Amrita (Axiom), Paul, Trisha (Axiom)
Sub : Fw : Musical Soiree

Don't you guys ever stay off your official mails?
I guess Ajay means that if we don't turn up for this we'll have to face the music. :-)

Simon

Email from Amrita De to Simon van der Wiel
Sub: Re: Fw: Musical Notes

No. The show will be on Friday. You need to go there to listen to the music.

Thanks,
Amrita

Email from Simon van der Wiel to Amrita De
Sub: Sub: Re: Fw: Musical Notes

"Face the music" is an expression, which approximately means to face the consequences. Never mind.

Cheers.
Simon

Email from Amrita De to Simon van der Wiel
Sub: Re: Fw: Musical Notes

Sorry. Did not know.

Thanks,
Amrita

Mail from Ajay Yadav to AxiomHMH team
Subject: New Member
Sent: 8:45 PM

Dear All,

As you know, HMH is co-hosting the Crisis Control Conference to be held next week at the ING Amsterdamse Poort building. Pritam Mitra, Principal Consultant of Axiom Core Consulting group, will be one of the speakers. He is very senior and you can benefit from the paper he will present at the conference. It is of primary importance that his presence is utilised to the maximum in terms of interaction with the top management of our clients , so that we can project ourselves in a different role at HMH during these hard times. I would expect each one of you to extend as much help as possible to him, bw allowing.

Although on the face of it an event of entertainment, I would expect everyone to turn up, since this is an event through which we are building our Axiom brand image.

Thanks and Regards,
Ajay

Mail from Amrita De to everyone except Ajay Yadav
He copied and pasted the last part from the last mail.

Mail from Trisha Paul to everyone except Ajay Yadav
Trust him to mess things up.

Mail from Madhu Deb to everyone except Ajay Yadav
Stop it, you lot :-) :-)

Mail from Simon van der Wiel to all except Madhu and Ajay
Don't you guys ever sleep?
What is bw? Back waters? Belgian Waffles? Bantam Weight?

Mail from Gunjan Das to all except Madhu and Ajay
It can also be West Bengal backwards.

Amrita De to all except Madhu and Ajay
Can it be Brick Wall?

Trisha Paul to all except Ajay
It's band width, for god's sake.

Chat between Simon van der Wiel and Trisha Paul

Trisha: Had a question.
Simon: Good to see u online, Apple Cheeks
Trisha: That's not my name
Simon: Don't u guys ever switch off ur official mails?
Trisha: Not many do. Madhu-di asked whether u can perform during the soiree.
Simon: Ever since Gurfunkel left me, I pledge by the Sound of Silence
Trisha: I had to get that one off Wikipedia. Please keep things simple.
Simon: I'm not sure I'll make it to the soiree.
Trisha: U saw Ajay's mail. U're supposed to.
Simon: I'm not too sure that I'm supposed *2 do anything beyond my 36 hours.*
Trisha: Ur presence is important.
Simon: The Dutch face of Axiom in HMH? U do know that I am half American, don't u?
Trisha: I am not the one u need to convince.
Simon: I'll handle shifty eyes. That is to say I will forget him and his mail. This new guy. Pritam. Is he a big shot?
Trisha: He comes with a reputation.
Simon: He looked young
Trisha: Yes, he did.
Simon: Seemed tense and in a hurry
Trisha: Did not notice that
Simon: Yes, he was ... I saw him trying his best to cut short the meeting when Madhu was being her hospitable best.
Trisha: Madhu-di takes care of everyone who lands here.
Simon: Good soul.
Trisha: She's de best.
Simon: As long as she doesn't start discussing that son of hers.
Trisha: Don't be mean
Simon: She entrusted me with the responsibility of being his buddy.
Trisha: Good 4 u.
Simon: I am not so sure about that.
Simon: What's a buddy supposed to do, anyway?
Trisha: Show him around the office, accompany him to lunches, introduce him to clients, get him help with bank accounts, with the chip knip, show him the departmental stores, the bars ...
Simon: Hold on. Departmental stores, bars, restaurants – why should a colleague need help with those?
Trisha: People new to Netherlands need help
Simon: I don't care much for the buddy system. He is over 18, should find things for himself.

Trisha: :-)
Simon: Is it the Axiom consulting wing which rationalises workforce of clients?
Trisha: I guess so.
Simon: So, that's what shifty eyes means by positioning in these hard times? This new guy's here to advise HMH to sack their internal people.
Trisha: Probably
Simon: Ur conversation style is so reminiscent of Sly Stallone
Trisha: I don't understand ... Google tells me Stallone talked in monosyllables, is that what u mean?
Simon: Can Google ever be wrong? Why are u online? Isn't hubby at home?
Trisha: He is working today
Simon: What is it with u guys? Why do u work weekends? Why do u want to stick around with colleagues after office hours? Introduce buddy systems? Does it give u a kick?
Trisha: We can't afford 36 hour weeks. U keep hearing Ajay saying all sorts of things about the troubled times, we have to put in the extra bit ...
Simon: bs
Trisha: That's ur version of cryptic abbreviation? Like bw?
Simon: Not that cryptic. Fairly commonplace. I ought to write a biography of shifty eyes. I'll call it "Shivers down my what?"
Trisha: As usual didn't understand. Am no good at puzzles.
Simon: Why don't u exchange notes with the legions of broken hearts who tried to unravel your puzzle and suddenly found you married?
Trisha: I was never an enigma. The easiest girl to lead on.
Simon: Were u?
Trisha: Yes. Even someone as simple as Mangal led me on far enough to get me married to him. Bye. GNSD
Simon: And what on earth is GNSD
Trisha: My cryptic abbreviation. Good Night Sweet Dreams.
Simon: U2 Apple cheeks
Trisha: That's not my name
Simon: I am just calling u... not biting into them
Trisha: Stop it.

∾ ∾ ∾

London

In his Haymarket office, K. Ramesh looked at his laptop and shook his head. The chain of mails that had snowballed into this horripilating proposal for cost savings told him an eloquent story. Sitting in the plush chair and looking out at the greyish English skies, Ramesh wondered whether the infernal Dave de Boer had not hit the problem surrounding the Indian professionals in the nub.

He had mailed Sudhakaran, head of the Core Business Consulting group, asking for an alternative approach for reducing costs. It was to be prepared without referring to any of the standard industry processes – totally original, bearing the stamp of innovation.

The communication had erupted into a sequence of delegations and conference calls, most of them late at night. The trail of mails made it abundantly clear that busy senior managers had passed the burden of thinking to busier managers who had in turn passed it on to even busier junior managers and the objective had been traded around in a fierce electronic version of Chinese whisper.

At some point a document had been prepared as a stop gap measure to thwart the flow of sinister escalations. Different proposals prepared throughout the chequered history of the consulting wing had been put together with the rustic crudeness of a sledgehammer. Somewhere during the course of evolution, industry standards had been ripped off by untrained hands, leaving undeniable traces and crude footmarks. Diagrams had been modified and mutilated, tables had been converted to text. The patchwork was a useless blob of conflicting, clichéd methods, barefaced in plagiarism, embarrassing in the lack of the rudiments of thought.

He felt like someone who had set the cat among the pigeons and had ended up collecting bush loads of poop.

V

"Never become personally involved with your patient," Suprakash Roy had learnt during his formative days as a budding psychiatrist. He had absorbed his lessons well. Cousin notwithstanding, the advanced symptoms of unexplained *dysphoric* fear notwithstanding, he bit into his sirloin steak with gusto. As an independent observer he would have diagnosed himself as *parorexic*. He was hungry.

Pritam brought his knife down on his medium rare rump steak with violence bordering on antisocial personality disorder.

"You were talking about the girl who looked at her watch," psychiatrists were not supposed to egg their patients on, but then, this was just his cousin.

"Yes, I was. And then you started to talk about Argentinean steak houses. Is it normal for you to think of dead meat when your patients are about to open up?"

Dr. Roy subtly reminded him that he was not his patient in the strictest sense of the word.

Pritam responded colourfully that going by the the strictest sense, the word *human* did not include diehard admirers of bovine flesh .

"So the girl looking at her watch is supposed to be significant?" the medical man changed the subject tactfully.

"Yes, and had you been thinking about it rather than cows running across the Pampas, you would realise why. You remember that I told you it was five minutes past two?"

Dr. Roy nodded.

"That made it thirty five past five in India."

Suprakash made the time zone calculations and concurred. "That's true. Given the incident took place in summer."

"The incident did take place after the cut off date. Still don't get it, do you?"

There was a pause as the doctor reached for the baked potato and thought about the tricky poser.

"I am afraid I am a bit confused. What exactly am I supposed to get here?"

Pritam looked heavenwards. On the decorated ceiling of *La Boca Steakhouse,* a painted cow ran across the top of the restaurant pursued by a lasso wielding, sombrero clad cowboy on a horse. "*Think.* For a change, think about it. I told you there was a match being shown on the television in the store."

"Yes, some sort of a cricket match ..."

"It was not some sort of a cricket match. It was a Test Match between India and Australia, being played at the Wankhede Stadium, Mumbai. You realise that it was odd ..."

"True. Cricket on TV in Netherlands is really strange ...However there is an English place in Leidseplein where I had the fortune to dine with a colleague from Oxford and they did show county matches..."

Pritam interruption was short, crisp and anatomical.

"It's not that. Why don't you get it? Neither did Sandeep. Haven't your grey cells been exercised in a while?"

With a solemn face the doctor added Narcissism to the increasing list of potential problems. A grandiose self image leading to contempt for the intellect of peers.

"Five thirty five is a bit late for a cricket match to continue in India, don't you think? Sun doesn't shine till eleven in our part of the world." Pritam remarked, his knife almost banging against the plate.

"Ah, yes ... A bit late ..."

"And there was a puzzled look in the girl's eyes when she glanced at the Television and then at her watch," Pritam continued, his voice losing some of its razor sharp irritation to make way for pleasant reflection. "She knew that it was late for a day of Test cricket. I am sure you'll agree that it was a good indication that she had been following the match."

Suprakash was somewhat more conservative about conclusions drawn from circumstantial evidence. However, experience had taught him to agree with men of questionable mental stability, especially when armed with steak knives. He wondered whether he should have committed gastronomic blasphemy by choosing McDonalds over authentic Argentinean steak. At least the cutlery under the Golden Arches was plastic.

"Is it not fascinating to find a girl so much into cricket? I mean not one of those screaming twenty-twenty fans, but one who followed Test Cricket – the real thing ..."

Dr. Roy considered this. "Among Indian girls, yes ... however you won't believe me when I tell you that a large proportion of my elderly female patients in Kolkata were very much into Test Cricket. They were bored of life, and to pass the long lonely hours during the day, Test Cricket is the ideal television sport. And in this part of the world it is not such a strange thing to find a girl inclined towards sports. Dutch girls are as much into sports as guys ... they play football, hockey ..."

"Bugger the Dutch girls."

Suprakash Roy stopped, a thoughtful expression on his face. As a true apostle of Freud, pleasant thoughts on similar lines had often crossed his mind. However, put in crude terms like that, the words lacked attraction.

"And screw your elderly female patients in Kolkata," Pritam drove the point home.

Dr. Roy winced. Even ignoring the Hippocratic Oath and medical ethics, it was a ghastly thought.

"The girl was into cricket. And that *is* fascinating. On top of that she was damn good looking."

So his cousin was indeed in love. It was a weight off his chest. Love did bring forth strange afflictions. Besides, Pritam was over thirty two now and still single. When he had landed in Utrecht on his consulting assignment, Suprakash had received several calls from his aunt, the consultant's long suffering mother. She had entreated him to hammer some sense into Pritam, to talk him into getting married. While the good doctor had no intention of forcing his cousin into a hasty decision – if the matter solved itself, he could claim credit as a worthy counsellor in the family circles. He smiled.

"Wipe that smirk off your face, you have mayonnaise all over your lips," Pritam snapped. "Yes, I was interested in the girl ... but that's not what the problem is."

The good doctor sighed. "Go on."

"I approached her. She was indeed knowledgeable about cricket. Not only that, she was as sharp as she was good looking. You see, there is a wit about her ..."

"I get it, go on ..."

"You know me ... I love cricket, that's my only diversion in life. I have dreaded relationships because I keep having this recurrent thought of having to fight for the remote with Tendulkar nearing a century and my partner wanting to watch one of those pathetic *saas-bahu* serials or moronic reality shows or one of those tiresome talent competitions ..."

"I guess if you wait for another two or three years, Tendulkar will have retired ..."

Pritam's next retort was accompanied by the knife waving about for emphasis, and it shut the older man up completely.

"That's the most ridiculous suggestion one can expect to hear."

"Well ..."

"Sachin can play for another ten years if he wants to."

"Mmm ... yes."

"My mother would kill you if she heard you postponing my match making by another couple of years ..."

"Of course."

"So, shut up."

"Quite so."

"I was fascinated by the girl. We talked and decided on a date ..."

"That's good."

"She wanted me to pick her up in a rented car in front of the Victoria Hotel and drive around the Dam Square, head towards Prinsengracht and ultimately have dinner in Leidseplein."

Dr. Roy raised his eyebrows.

"That doesn't sound very romantic. I mean driving to the suburbs, Zaandvoort, Keukenhof Gardens and so on are great. But, central Amsterdam and the most chaotic part ..."

Pritam nodded.

"I know. Constructions everywhere, tramlines, millions of pedestrians, countless dogs on infernal leashes and those crazy bikes ... I have driven for years in Kolkata, but this was real hell. Add to that a substantial percentage of my monthly pay shelled out just for the parking space – which by the way was about ten kilometres from the restaurant."

"Not the best idea, was it?"

"Well, I don't know," Pritam looked dazed. "She specifically wanted me to drive through the craziest part of the town. And later on, on *gtalk*, she told me that it was the best test of a man's patience."

"Ah, I see ...," the doctor was impressed. Also strangely interested. "So tell me, was your interaction more in real life or in these chat sessions and exchanges of sms?"

Pritam shrugged.

"I don't know ... these days one can always stay in touch with the internet and the cell phone."

"Precisely."

"Precisely what? I don't see what you're getting at. I was talking about the idea of hers to test my patience."

"Yes, that seems to be very original."

"Isn't that fascinating? I mean this sort of out of box thinking towards relationships ..."

"Out of box thinking?"

"Yes, damn it, it's a technical term we consultants use a lot. Going beyond the normal. Innovation and all that," Pritam waved his knife irritably, and his cousin hastily nodded his comprehension. "It became clear to me that this was *the* girl. And I had passed the test of patience set by her..."

"Indeed?"

"Yes, I did. Get rid of that sarcasm in your tone. My conduct all through that drive through hell's alleyways was most charming. In normal circumstances I am a patient person, goddammit."

"Quite so. You know, patient has a different meaning in my book."

"Witty, aren't you? I would have been a picture of patience, like the Dalai Lama, even when faced with someone as infuriating as a steak eating psychologist."

"Psychiatrist," corrected his cousin. Not too many people knew the difference, he thought again, sadly. Anyone could become a psychologist these days. Most infuriating of them were the social working volunteers trained in two-week crash courses.

"Shrink. Whatever. I would have been patient even now, had it not been for my stupid urge to share my experiences with Sandeep."

He paused to dab his mouth with the napkin. Suprakash looked at him over his glass of Mojito.

"This is the second time you have mentioned Sandeep. Do I know this gentleman?"

"You have met him. And he is not a gentleman. I have my doubts whether he is human ..."

"You seem to have this doubt about a lot of people."

"A considerable percentage of the people I am interacting with right now. But you have met this guy. He was with me in college. He used to hang around with me a lot about ten years back. You know, the sporty guy into Karate and all those oriental martial arts ..."

"I seem to remember. He used to go out for runs in the morning while you and the other guy, Aveek, would sleep off your night's liquor. He was the guy who always looked fit."

Pritam grunted.

"He was not the only one who looked fit. I was not so bad myself."

The plates were removed from their table by a Hispanic waiter. The sharp steak knife taken out of the equation, the doctor became a bit more vocal in his arguments.

"But, Pritam, you always had your fondness for beer. I wonder whether you ever ran more than a hundred metres in your life – except every now and then to get from one board room meeting to another ..."

"You are not too good at being funny, do you know that?" Pritam stopped his cousin from pursuing a detailed analysis of his sporting life. "And it may be news to you that this Sandeep and I once came second in a college fete."

"At a relay race?"

"No, at a Separated at Birth contest."

"What contest?"

"Separated at Birth. You entered the contest with a partner and the pair who resembled each other most won."

"You seriously had games like that?"

"Yes. And we resembled each other. And still do – to a certain extent...," Pritam clutched his forehead with his fingers. "This is complicated."

"What is?"

"You see, Sandeep happened to be here on a *tai chi* seminar..."

"On a what?"

"*Tai chi* seminar. Another of those oriental martial art forms. We contacted each other through the class of '98 mailing list. We met in one of the sports bars in Rokin and I poured my heart out. You know how it is, when one is getting into a relationship ... or trying to ... and he meets a close friend from the past ..."

"True."

"And he started giving me peculiar advice."

"Such as?"

Pritam waved his Blackberry.

"These haikus. He asked me to develop the poetic dimension of my nature. He explained the structure, the syllables, the rules... Asked me to get into shape by going to the gym ... not that I was out of shape, though. And when, puzzled by a major dilemma, I sent him this haiku that fatal morning, you see the response..."

Suprakash nodded gravely, suppressing the ready smile at remembering it.

"He is one of those snakes from the Biblical paradise."

"Snakes, Biblical paradise," Dr. Roy repeated aloud. "I wouldn't have put you down as one with a gift for allusions."

"I have to know something of the Bible for my clients. Most of them are white Americans who go to church every Sunday. I had a junior make me a deck of twenty slides of the essential quotable aspects."

"I see. Professional hazard?"

"Yes. But the point is that Shruti was all set to go on a backpacking tour across Europe. Covering a chunk of Europe largely under the Schengen zone. She made it clear that I was most welcome to join her ..."

"Wow ...So you'd get to know her in the Biblical sense?"

"No. Part of the deal was to keep it platonic. But, think about it ... This fascinating girl, the amazing locations of Europe. I had also finished my assignment. I was thinking of changing my job. A three week break was right there in front of me. After which I could submit my resignation and join this great firm in New York City."

"Doesn't the financial crisis make it difficult for you to change jobs at will?"

Pritam managed to approximate a self satisfied smile.

"We are consultants. We thrive in these situations."

"You make clients pay you and break even by rationalising?"

"To some extent."

"So what was the problem?"

Pritam sighed. "There was this weeklong seminar on cost reductions that stood in the way."

"Weeklong seminar on cost reduction?"

"Yes, a joint venture of six major financial institutions of the Netherlands ... You know, ING, Rabo Bank, ABN AMRO, HMH ..."

"They arrange a seminar on cost reduction? That too for a week? Isn't it a self defeating exercise?"

"The banks want experts to advise them on crisis control."

"And you are one of the experts?"

"Well yes, I am one of the people whose papers were accepted for this prestigious event."

"So your writing skills extend from Haikus to academic papers. You just went up a couple of notches in my regard. I guess you get paid for it."

"Yes, obscene amounts. The companies can sponsor that with the salaries of half a dozen people they lay off based on our papers."

"How do you sleep at night? And how do you call it a prestigious event with a plain face?"

"The world says so. It works in multiple ways. We are the commodities that the organizers sell. A lot of companies register to carry away some pearl of wisdom that will help them reduce cost. They pay through their noses to send executives to attend the event. Everyone is happy. The organisers get a lot of money. The executives do their networking. The speakers get paid and also earn a lot of brownie points."

"What points?"

"Brownie ... I was also supposed to meet the chairpersons from ING and HMH as a networking strategy of our company. And I obviously had to do some networking within the conference."

"Networking seems to be a focal theme."

"It is."

"Are there official sessions known as networking?"

"There are."

"Doesn't it make you sick?"

"No it doesn't. You make me sick. The world runs on networking."

"Once people believed it was love that made the world go round. Those with a more scientific bent of mind put it down to gravitational forces."

"No, it is networking. Why, man, aren't you on Linked In?"

"Linked In?"

"Linked In. The Social Networking site for professionals. The meeting place of the knowledge industry."

"I am not on Linked In but it fascinates me in a different way. Now, what exactly is a Knowledge industry?"

"You are not on Twitter as well, are you?"

"Well, not really ... "

"Man, you live in the Freudian age. Anyway, it doesn't matter. What matters is that it was supposed to start a couple of days into Shruti's travel plans."

"So work spoilt your romantic plans?" the problem sounded pretty simple to Dr. Roy.

"There never were any romantic plans. I knew that this dream European tour would be one of the best experiences of my life that never took place."

"Nice way of putting it. I think love has kindled the dormant poet in you."

"But then I called Sandeep by sending these Haikus and talked it over with him. He spoke ... like a man possessed. He told me of my approaching middle age, accelerated by the long hours and gallons of alcohol shared with my colleagues and clients. About the limited probability of ideal matches in the industry – the way I would spend the remaining years running and running to catch up with the sun while it would be rising behind me ... Stop the infernal humming."

"It's Floyd."

"Stick to Freud. And then he became even more passionate. He warned me that this wonderful, unique girl would fritter out of my life like one of the short-lived flashes of beauty. What was that he said ... yes, like a fair woman's glance from beneath her veil ... I did not quite know what he meant but got the gist. He ruthlessly pointed out the likely result of all this. How I would be forced into choosing one of the cookie cutter girls who were my peers – due to lack of choice, with limited exposure to the world that lay beyond the long hours in the company."

"I get the picture."

"Oh, I hate these authors."

"Is he an author?"

"Yes. He is here researching his book – some novel he is writing."

"You just told me that he was here attending a *tai chi* seminar."

Pritam sighed.

"It is complicated. He went on, saying that due to the lack of choices, combined with the dreaded double edged deadline of my age and my mother, I would in all probability get married to a fellow consultant who would talk about vision and mission statements at night," Pritam shuddered. "That was when he got me. I was scared. I visualised my wife in bridal attire, waiting for me, the embroidered *saree* pulled across her face, her demure eyes focussed on a Business Proposal. I could even see the company logo on the title page, could hear the cell phone ringing as the client partner wanted to have a conference call with both of us just as, you know ..."

The doctor nodded with sympathy. He had been well grounded in the Freudian concepts.

"Yes, I understand. So, he convinced you to go on this trip with your lady love ... and you are scared that you will lose your job?"

Pritam sighed again. His face, as he paid the bill, was one riddled with multiple emotions.

"It goes much deeper than that," he observed.

VI

Sandeep ordered Bahn Bao, Pho, Diet Coke for himself and Tia Maria for Shruti.

"Is life worth living? It depends on the liver," he observed. "So, no more than a peg a day for me."

Shruti looked unimpressed.

"It won't peg back my quest for truth"

"My teacher says that the skyline of Amsterdam looks like a platter of cute chocolate cakes."

"Neither cakes nor ale will divert me. Consultant to a broke tai chi student hobnobbing with artists in Jordaan. Is this a story of rebirth?"

"Don't you think births and rebirths will make the conversation too *laboured*?"

"This is becoming too *painful* to *bear*."

"I was not *expecting* that."

"I guess there will be *pregnant* silence from now on till you *deliver* your story."

Sandeep bowed.

"You have the last word. It seldom ends up this way."

"Even word play isn't strictly a male domain any more, is it?"

"This has been an educational evening."

"We should be the masters of ribbing, having supposedly been created out of Adam's rib."

"Why then are there so few female humorists in the annals of English Literature?"

Shruti wrinkled her upturned nose.

"If intentional, it's one of the most nauseating puns in history. You are plumbing the lowest depths of humour."

"But the funny bone can be found at the end of the humerus."

Shurti burst out laughing.

"You sure are stretching the radius of our repartees."

"Let's stop before we make laughing stock of the entire anatomy."

"Yes, and you supply some answers."

Sandeep sipped his diet coke. The restaurant was close to the Dam square and a curious mix of people thronged about.

"It really impressed me when I heard that you had asked poor Pritam to drive you around this part of the city."

"Don't you think that's the ideal test of patience?"

"True. So, Pritam is going on this tour with you."

"Yes."

"Lucky guy. Where do you intend to start?"

"Germany. Berlin. Pritam was quite obsessed with Paris, but I stuck to my original schedule."

Sandeep sighed.

"Yes, you know how it is. People fantasise about the Eiffel Tower, the Arc de Triomphe. Paris is supposed to be the romantic capital of the world."

Shruti nodded.

"I understand. But, this isn't a pleasure trip. I intend to use this for my dissertation."

"As far as I gathered from Pritam, you are associated with the University of Amsterdam."

"Yes, I am working on my doctorate in Political Science."

"I wonder how Pritam withstood that piece of information. I would have expected him to scurry for cover like a startled rabbit."

"We haven't really discussed my subject in detail."

"What is your specific area of interest?"

"The negative effects of the European Union. Particularly the refugee problem faced with the upheaval of the countries of the eastern bloc."

On getting to know her identity, Sandeep had put an unwilling lid on his salvo of compliments. After all, Pritam was his boyhood chum and one had to follow the code. However, during a fleeting moment of weakness, he wondered whether his dear friend was at all compatible with this intriguing girl. He leaned back and looked at her.

"You think there are negative effects?"

"Monumental ones."

"Are you one of those who view EU as an Anglo Saxon move to destroy the east?"

Shruti laughed.

"No. That's for conspiracy theorists. But there are shortcomings, especially if one focuses on the Eastern European countries. But we are digressing. And my intuition says you are doing it purposely. What is a consultant doing in Amsterdam staying at an artist's studio and attending *tai chi* seminars?"

Sandeep sighed.

"It's a long story."

"Going by what we ordered, we have a long meal ahead of us."

"Aren't you one of those die hard antagonists of talking while eating?"

"Quite the contrary. Nothing so appetising as dinner-table discussion."

"Where do you want me to start?"

"May be not as early as David Copperfield. But somewhere during your university days, so that I can keep track of your career path."

Sandeep shook his head. "That's difficult. My career path is more like an intricate web of small roads and lanes, by-lanes and alleys."

"Why don't we try to trace your locus?"

Sandeep could not let loyalties hold his urges in check any more.

"Locus. Fascinating. Your figures of speech have touched subjects as diverse as Literature, Physiology and now Mathematics. And you have not even started out on the Socio-Economic and Political scenarios, which, I understand, are your forte. So, let us start following my locus. Did Pritam mention anything about my being a classmate of his?"

Shruti shook her head. "No. He said you were a fellow consultant."

Sandeep nodded gravely as he caught the whiff of aroma from Shruti's drink.

"We did our masters in Mathematics together. From the Indian Institute of Technology. Following that, Pritam did his MBA. I started out in IT. Is that early enough? I have not exactly been David Copperfield, but neither have I been Holden Caulfield."

Shruti blinked.

"I don't get it. I mean, I've met all sorts of IT people from India. One cannot help doing so nowadays."

"True. You cannot throw a brick without beaning an IT specialist squarely on the head. The Geometric Probability of the inviting thought is close to 95% across the world."

"There. I can see that you did your masters in Mathematics. But, I have not yet met a consultant who has even heard of Catcher in the Rye, forget playing on the Copperfield-Caulfield relationship. Add to that Shakespearean allusions and Pablo Neruda sticking out of the bag. Girls are slightly better though. I have met some avid readers among female professionals. But, what is your secret? What's going on?"

Sandeep nodded.

"I understand. I have battled on those very grounds, there are scars all over me. I joined the industry in the heydays of Y2K. When one could not walk past an IT company without an attempted ambush by the Human Resources. Within two years I was suffocating. There is a period in life when all the faculties are at their peak. Creative juices, mental sharpness, physical prowess, the liberal flow of libido. And it struck me that I was spending those best years of my life making changes to COBOL code. There were things I wanted to do that suffered from lack of time ..."

"Like *tai chi*?"

"Karate, *tai chi*. I still managed to keep training. Especially at the overseas martial arts schools – something made possible by my foreign placements. But I missed writing..."

"Writing?"

Sandeep nodded and paused as the waitress served them.

"I desperately wanted to write. I had always dreamed of being a writer. I was working on a few ideas. Wanted to pen them down as a novel ..."

"Writer?" Shruti seemed thoughtful. "That does make many pieces fit. Before you continue, could I ask you a question?"

"Certainly."

"Are you behind those bad haikus I keep receiving from Pritam?"

"I influence them, yes. Compose them, no. I just asked him to be creative."

"Do you ever consider the consequences of your action?"

"Believe me I suffer as you do, if not as much. He is in the habit of sending me some of his compositions . I will think twice before influencing someone else ..."

"A lesson learnt ... Pray, continue. You were just voicing your angst as the unfulfilled writer."

"During 2001 and 2002, I was in New York City. Things were not so rosy any more in the IT world. There was a slow down. Not nearly as bad as this one, but the US economy had fallen off the chart. The 9/11 did not help ... People were losing jobs the moment you took your eyes off them. That was when some young men I knew in the media decided to start a new venture. I sort of gave up my job."

"Without being laid off?"

"Right. I watched my teammates being sacked – or let go as the Indian companies preferred to put it. And I had this butterfly of life trying to force itself out. I resigned. It was a great feeling. A sort of self sacrificing hero who took one for the team. It relieved a lot of people, who combined to fill in my gap. Actually, if I had not resigned, I would have been sacked anyway. COBOL was getting on my nerves. I did not do myself any favours by asking my manager to look for an MF-COBOL CD in the Natural History Museum. You know, the type of black humour that gets labelled as attitude problem by insecure managers. I returned to India, dropped my things in Kolkata, went to Delhi and joined this group of young journalists."

"Wow."

"Well, it did sound great at that time. It was a team of investigative journalists. Have you heard of a paper called *Uproar*?"

"Of course," Shruti's spontaneous excitement was infectious. Her eyes sparkled. "The sting operation specialists. Were you associated with them?"

Sandeep chuckled.

"In a manner of speaking. For five long years, we did their investigations for them. Set up and conducted the sting operations. Remember the case of the Mumbai politicians caught on tape talking to the lynchpins of the underworld?"

"Vaguely ... Yes, there was something quite sensational at that point of time."

"We had set it up. I had written the script. The execution was carried out by two of our team mates. There was only one *Uproar* journalist who took part in the operation. That was one of the more successful ventures, because we got paid for it ... Two years after the assignment, and about sixty percent of the promised amount, but we did get paid. My American dollars were almost gone by that time. It came as a great relief when we saw the money. We also did a couple of other assignments for a television channel which paid well. For a while things were smooth. Then we ran into trouble."

Sandeep paused to enjoy a fleshy piece of crab.

"You seem to have led an interesting life."

"Depends on the liver again. Most of it was like struggling with backs to the wall. I loved being creative, making up scripts for real life, got a kick out of it when the targets took the bait and fell into the trap. But then, at the end of the day, you need the money. And that was where things went wrong. We worked on four more projects for *Uproar.* The sandalwood smuggler in Tamil Nadu, the terrorist links in the Maharashtra cabinet, several exposes in Gujarat during the riots and the Australian tourist who was linked to child prostitution. You seem to remember all of them ..."

"Of course. They are some of the best known sting operations of the last few years. At least in India."

"Right," Sandeep laughed. "Being a political science graduate you are likely to remember most of them. The tragedy was that we were the ones thinking up these stories, planning them, executing them. And it ended up making Mayank Manhas a god."

Shruti looked at Sandeep with curiosity.

"That man puzzles me."

"Doesn't he?" Sandeep sounded bitter. "He is a champion of the masses. A great crusader for truth. Well, he was too caught up with the big picture of truth to pay attention to nitty-gritty like payment of dues. He made a packet out of his book, but we did not get a penny. I have never come across anyone who read the novel, but it was touted as the most important Indian work by the Costa Rican Nobel prize winner. *Gibbs Everlasting* published it."

"I haven't read it. Tried to glance through it in a bookstore once, but never went beyond the second page."

Sandeep allowed a frown to touch his forehead for the first time during the evening.

"That Costa Rican is his boozing buddy. Some things that really take the cake is influenced by ale."

Shruti made a face.

"And he did not pay your team?"

"He still owes us around twenty lakhs."

Shruti whistled.

"And that's not all. For a publication touted as the people's paper, there were a lot of things not quite right. You know, Mayank Manhas set this paper up with the help of some known big wigs of the society, each of whom paid a lakh and became a founder member. The paper was allowed to become a propaganda machine for some of them. There were numerous other things, including digging up dirt from the past lives of any other channel or paper that tried its hand at sting operations. But, this is my story and not *Uproar's.* We were starving. And one by one the members were forced to join more fruitful vehicles in the media world. As for me, I was neither a journalist, nor an IT person ... I was in a strange situation."

"And what happened to your writing?"

Sandeep chuckled again.

"That's an even longer story."

"That's something that piques my interest even more."

There was a pause as they looked at each other. Suddenly without any fathomable reason they burst out laughing.

"Well, let me put it this way. I completed a novel and started hunting for publishers. Soon I realised that writing is one of those peripheral skills, nice to have in a writer," Sandeep paused for effect. If he had expected Shruti to show surprise, he was disappointed.

"Rejection slips?"

Sandeep nodded. "Right. It would not have been so bad if I had not obtained foolproof evidence that the manuscripts, sample chapters, the painstakingly compiled approach letters and the customised synopses were not even glanced at. Add to that the type of *literature* that was flooding the market. After some time I got down to writing another novel. I have one completed and one semi-completed novel in my hands right now."

Shruti tried to keep up with the flow of information.

"Where does consulting come into the picture?" she asked.

Sandeep smiled. "The locus is getting complicated, right? Sometimes I get confused myself. We come to the beginning of 2007, the band of investigative journalists forced to disband. Only the founder of our group, a guy named Kailash Nayak, is still following up with Mayank Manhas and his henchmen for the outstanding amount. I am left on my own with limited savings. For a couple of months, I did some odd jobs like teaching Mathematics and taking private *tai chi* lessons. It was then that I was rescued by another phenomenon of modern times – the blog."

Shruti was almost done with her dinner. She stared at the young man in front of her with amused curiosity.

"The blog?"

"Yes, the celebrated weblog."

"Someone read your blog and hired you?"

Sandeep laughed.

"It would be more probable for some publisher to actually read my manuscript. It was another amazing turnaround."

VII

Blog of Simple Simon at blogspot.com
Tags: Corporate, Cultural, Carnal

When I talk about my parental, environmental and occupational background I generally leave confusion in my wake. Dutch father, Irish mother, Oregon upbringing, Amsterdam job, Indian employer and colleagues, Dutch client – it is complicated.

To the Americans, with their compulsive categorisation of people into winners and losers, I daresay I give the impression of being one of the latter. Who would fancy answering to Indian bosses anyway? Majority of the Americans are liberals, with firm conviction in global equality irrespective of race, ethnicity or sex. Unfortunately, this open-mindedness is more often than not garnished in the dressing of condescension.

However, the shortcomings of my adopted countrymen aside, there remains a speculation, pretty strong even in my own mind, that my employment owes less to professional competency and significantly more to my Dutch name. Not so much the cosmopolitan *voornam* but the van der Wiel that follows as infix and *achternaam*. I am an interface often doubling up as an interpreter of nuances. In their own quiet and populous ways, the Indians are infiltrating the world and its industries. I am an insignificant yet useful pawn in their onslaught.

There happen to be some sensualists in my sphere of social and electronic acquaintances, most of them on my mailing list, who are curious about a solitary facet of my official circumstances. With the proliferation of Bollywood the world over, and the dominance of the Indian damsels in competitions involving heavenly bodies of the planet, one question that I face quite often is – *how are the Indian girls.* Seldom is it a polite inquiry about the well being of my fair colleagues. More often than not the expectation involves a mathematical analysis of curves, figures and face values. When I reveal that most of the colleagues I deal with are women, their eyes flash and electronic smileys drool in excited anticipation.

I have faced so many objective questions about some of the rather private attributes of these wonderful women that I have decided to place the details in a private mail to my mailing list once and for all for the admirers of Indian beauty.

I know as well as the rest of the aficionados that the standards are high. Aishwarya Rai is long past her Miss Universe days, but continues to dazzle us with her on screen appearances, while the controversy surrounding *Big Brother* actually enhanced the absolute nirvana that can be grabbed in a palm, namely, the waistline of Shilpa Shetty.

In the corporate world, however, the Indian lady lags significantly behind in such matters.

It is a defining facet of this culture that the entire work force swears by busy schedules and long hours. Most of them dangle sixty hour weeks as medallions around their necks. And even beyond the premises, office is not entirely forgotten, the line between work and personal lives is remarkably fine. After the stretched office hours, they tend to stick together, cooking for each other, living in the same apartment complex, often sharing rooms and talking shop long into the night.

This leaves very little time for exercise. The absolute lack of concern for the physical, well approaching callousness, is surprising to say the least. In spite of being ladies from the country of the stunning glamour girls, ignoring the robust athleticism of the Dutch girls that they see around them, their years of experience as professionals can generally be deduced mathematically as a function of the girth of their waistlines. Physical exercise to these people is a domain that can be accessed by free souls, a tiny percentage of the unmarried section of the populace, who do not have the heavy burden of running the Project Management Office of a department of the Bank while taking care of their families.

I apologise for sounding critical. I understand that these long hours at the cheapest of rates is the USP behind the global infiltration of the Indian. One has to work at becoming indispensible. So, necessary or not, it is perhaps sacrilege to leave the office premises before the last of the clients is already digging into his dinner. But this does leave some solid deposit around the midsection aided and abetted by some prehistoric notions about food habits and physical culture.

As mentioned, I sent my private mailing list a mail today outlining the attractions my job offers in the fairer way, detailing the charms of all my female coworkers. Unfortunately, the piece is unsuitable for posting in a public blog.

Mail from Simon to his mailing group
Subject: A touch of lass

Apart from the highest head of our small account in the bank, whom I would classify less as human and more as a personification of anxiety, and a particular creature who falls in the uncertain fringes between the genders, the other four of my co-workers are of the fairer sex.

Among the four women who share the cubicles with me, two are considerably young, in their mid to late twenties. Of them Amrita is the only one who is single and, probably therefore, the only one reasonably slim. However, it seems to be more a result of malnutrition brought about by unscientific diet than healthy living. She is small, dusky and seems to be a dreamy sort, quite friendly and helpful in the limited interactions we have had. The exchanges could have been more frequent and fruitful had her English vocabulary not been limited to around fifty five words, resulting in blank, uncomprehending stares at every utterance of more than two syllables.

Trisha, the other young belle of the group, is a chubby cheeked, lively sort who has been married for a few months. She looks pretty comely with her smart dress sense, would have been quite attractive if her nose had not resembled a buzzer and her post marital contentment had not started to generously redraw the contours around her midsection. She is quite a joy to converse with occasionally when she becomes witty and unrestrained. But these ventures are generally short lived with her frivolity jumping into a chastity shell whenever the subject becomes remotely flirtatious. She comes across as someone who has not yet bitten into the forbidden fruit, a characteristic I find in a lot of Indian girls at work and elsewhere. However, whether this dietary restriction is the result of inherent innocence or has been edited out of the menu card with calculated deliberateness is something that still eludes me.

Next comes my favourite in terms of personality. Lahari is in her mid thirties, and following the above mentioned laws of corporate corporeality, she is corpulence personified. She had been good looking in the limited years of her first youth, if the framed photograph of the her wedding day is anything to go by – and the semi fossilised charm still peeps through sometimes, from beneath the fast and furious accumulation of flesh. However, she is the one least apologetic about her weight, blaming it on her passion for good food – a fanatic who devoutly bends over her dishes to worship the gods of cholesterol four times a day. She has a one year old and is the only one to show immense disregard for the policy of staying beyond normal working hours. She also happens to be the only member within the group who has not asked me probing questions related to the existence and attributes of a girlfriend. She has a wonderful singing voice, delighting us in many of our trademark and tiresome social get-togethers. Her one shortcoming is her laughter, which has a grating effect on the softer senses and is accompanied by manoeuvres of her bulk which remind me of mouse over operations on a glitzy web page.

The first thing one notices about Madhu Deb is her zest for fellow feeling, although my uncharitable thoughts often put her obesity slightly ahead. But, whichever way one looks at her small, rotund form, with the round, smiling face and smartly trimmed hair, one cannot fail to notice the cheery bonhomie. One can almost think of her as the reason why Julius Caeser had instructed Anthony to let him have people around him who were fat. Caeser, of course, had specified *men*, but the ancient times had been notoriously full of male chauvinists and the Roman general had probably been too smitten by the proportionate charms of Cleopatra to bother about fat ladies.

She is an excellent manager – taking great pains to make sure that employees have a good life in these distant shores. To do this, she keeps herself updated about the personal life of each and every individual and offers her help in any sort of problem. This pays enormous dividends. There are weak moments, when I equate her with some of the exotic Halloween samples found in Goebbert's Pumpkin Patch, Greater Chicago, but she remains the one person everyone wants to work under, talk to and be with.

While one can casually overlook her conviction that she continues to carry the self proclaimed charming beauty of her first youth even after stepping quite firmly into her early forties, her only other shortcoming is also endearingly human. She has this maniacal urge to stretch a fifteen minute conversation into an all day event by touching upon every topic under the sun with a major bias for her son, Hidori. However, she is the smiling face of our company and embodies the brand essence of cheerful service.

I am wondering whether or not to include the other colleague into this analysis. Gunjan, after strict scientific tests, may still be detected to bear the Y chromosome, but I will continue to have more than a strong suspicion of otherwise. Much of the feminine side of his nature is borne out by his passion for gossip and whining, which exceeds that of all the ladies put together. Apart from this, with his small fragile frame and positioned paunch, he resembles someone just about to step into her third trimester.

There have been several crude queries in the past few weeks from friends, mostly of robust American upbringing, wondering who among my female colleagues is the easiest to fornicate with – I understand the more universally accepted expression is 'screw'. Given the compulsive urge to ingratiate himself to occidental people, I would put the last member on my list, Gunjan, as the foremost candidate.

I hope that I have managed to paint an accurate picture of the effeminate perks of my employment. My American acquaintances will now be more convinced of my membership in the category of losers, what with bearing Indian bosses and not even making *ends meet*. However, that is how the terrain lies and we can proceed to more important reflections in my future public blogs and private mails.

Cheers
Simon

VIII

No one knows for sure whether, when questioned about the phallic shape of his favourite addiction, Freud had really said, "Sometimes a cigar is just a cigar". But there is no doubt that he regarded smoking as one of the greatest and cheapest enjoyments the world provided. Walking his talk, he inhaled the fumes of about twenty a day.

Suprakash Roy attributed his love for postprandial fag to sub-conscious emulation of the Viennese legend. However, not really fancying a Freudian morphine induced death while combating mouth cancer, he limited his daily intake to one.

Now, having exhaled a luxurious cloud, he walked along old Singel.

"You invited him to sleep in your apartment? Why exactly ...?" he was somewhat confused. Pritam had refused the proffered cigar and now drew agitatedly on his Camel.

"He's at present living in the artist quarters of Jordaan, sleeping in one of the studios. He has been researching his novel for much of the nights.I thought it would be the decent thing to allow him access to a proper bed during my working hours."

"Novel? I guess I know the location he is researching most of the nights."

"I don't. I hate the guts of writers and their works."

"Oh yes ... You have aired similar sentiments earlier. What exactly does he do these days?"

"Till a couple of months back he used to be a personal blogger of a Vice President of a multinational bank."

For the first time since his formative days of smoking, Dr. Roy almost choked on his cigar.

"What was that?" he coughed.

"He was the personal blogger of a Vice President of a multinational bank."

"What is a personal blogger?" there was a distinct increase in animation.

Pritam sighed.

"I asked him more or less the same question. It seems that this VP had hired him to write his blogs."

"His personal blogs?"

"Yes. Or rather his official blogs. You see all these big guys have to publish their blogs nowadays. They are expected to have this informal blog in which they communicate the latest vision and mission ...," Pritam shuddered. Words linked with ominous memories. "And this guy couldn't write for toffee as Boycott would put it. So he hired Sandeep."

Suprakash blew a ring and looked thoughtfully as it disintegrated.

"How interesting. What was his designation? Chief Executive Blogging Assistant?"

Pritam's answer was impatient.

"How does that matter? Obviously there was a different role and designation on paper. Chief Marketing Advisor or Technical Analyst. But, his job was to write blogs for the top boss. And that's not really surprising. It's fashionable nowadays. And necessary. Every uneducated politician in India has blogs to get the votes of GenX. Do you think those illiterate idiots write their own blogs? It's an industry ... at least it will grow into one."

The good doctor closed his eyes and thought about it. He could see his professional chamber of the future. Frustrated creative writers, the sweat of their brows used to polish the halos of the society's celebrated half witted hoodlums. Sparks of creativity borrowed to light up superficial crowns.

"And he got his break as a writer from there, did he?"

Pritam shook his head and kicked a pebble.

"No. He's still waiting for a break. And he did something outrageous to lose his position as the blogger of the big boss. But, we are not discussing his life here."

The older man sensed the irritability in his cousin, subtly moving out of the range of his cigarette wielding hand.

"So what happened when you asked him to sleep at your place?"

Pritam grunted. "I was doing him a decent favour out of the goodness of my heart. And when I came back and rang the bell, I got the shock of my life ..."

"You made your living as a ghost blogger?" Shruti sat on one of the Amsterdammertjes, or little Amsterdammers. They were small metal poles constructed to prevent parking on the pavements. Sandeep sat in front of her on a bench along Kloveniersburgwal. The quaint narrow gables stood out with unique Amsterdam charm against the final rays of the day.

"Yes. The pay was decent. There are a lot of writers doing that nowadays."

The merry atmosphere of the NieuwMarkt showed no signs of calling it a day. The red light district was a stone's throw away. In spite of the dubious reputation, it was one of the prettiest parts of the city, and one of the safest.

"There are a lot of people in high and mighty positions of different organizations who need to come across as smart, suave, witty leaders. Communicating with charisma. And then you have this phenomenon called blogging. Suddenly it's fashionable for all these powerful men to have brilliantly written corporate blogs of their own. It's become their main vehicle to reach out to people. In most cases, however, the creativity in these individuals is restricted to the domain of procreation. Whenever they have taken up an inspired pen other than for the purpose of impregnation, it has been to set the seal of their signatures on lucrative business deals. Now, how the hell are such guys to post literary gems in blogosphere?"

"So they hire talented writers."

"Well, they initiate the hiring process. Left to themselves most of them wouldn't be able to distinguish between Shakespeare and Harold Robbins. One of the top requirements is to recruit a ghost blogger with a sense of humour. They make their underlings onboard such unfortunate creatures. Again, left to themselves, they may read through all the ninety four books of P.G. Wodehouse without smiling. So, judging sense of humour is also better off delegated."

People walked in and out of the by-lanes that led into the celebrated De-Wallen. The visitors included the surreptitious prospective clients to merry bustling families. Amsterdam was a strange amalgam of cohabiting diversity and tolerance. There was even a kindergarten on the fringes of the district. A television channel had interviewed some of the kids, asking them what they thought the ladies in the windows were up to. The children had replied that they were *selling kisses.*

"I guess with humour and writing skills, you were ideal for the job. So blogs build their leadership image?"

"Other than that it's the in thing. Corporations promote blogs and encourage people to exchange ideas, in the process keeping an eye on things and throwing and testing their own ideas as well. It works as a propaganda machine as well as a documented grapevine ..."

"Documented grapevine?"

"Promoting free, unrestricted blogging with corporate reward schemes actually ensure that blogs replace a chunk of unofficial gossip in the organisation. So, it's information control under the guise of knowledge sharing, idea generation, collaboration and all those synonyms of bovine excrement. And if you have a crisp, chiselled, funny, visionary blog by the leader, you use this same machinery for propaganda."

"Cool. You seem to know the ins and outs."

"Well, I was inside the system, and now am out of it."

"What was your designation? Executive Ghost Blogger?"

"I was called Senior Consulting Executive. My job description included vague jargons such as synergy, innovation, knowledge harvesting. But, the sole purpose of my role was to write blogs for this obnoxious orang-utan who was a VP of the Bank."

Shruti nodded. "I will take a course in avant-garde alliterations from you. But, didn't the colleagues come to know that you were the one writing the pieces for the big boss?"

"I had to sign a non-disclosure agreement coupled with some vague intellectual property clause."

"And how was it writing masterpieces for this guy?"

"For this semi-living embodiment of literary impotence? Well, it was a trade-off. After coming here I do find it strangely analogous to the window displays, but then the job did pay ... and gave me the financial security to continue writing. Working for *Uproar,* in contrast, was like putting your card into a defective ATM. Besides, I did not make any attempt to write masterpieces. I enjoyed myself. Wrote spoofs."

"Spoofs?"

"Right. For example, the big boss's blog was launched with great fanfare. I had written a small three liner for the occasion. *To blog or not to blog, that is the question. Whether 'tis nobler in the mind to suffer the slings and arrows of outrageous market, or to take up the mouse against a sea of troubles and by blogging circulate them?*"

Once again Shruti laughed loudly, and Sandeep liked it. Much better than giggles.

"And did you receive accolades?"

"At first I received a mail from the moderator who had flagged it for revision. This was a young girl just out of college. She had copied and pasted the text into Google and obtained matching results. She wanted me to provide the reference URL."

"Reference URL for Shakespeare?"

"You heard me."

"So when I tell you that a consultant and Shakespeare don't go together, I do have a strong case."

"Mind you, I was in a bank. Only my designation hinted at consultancy. However, after I had stepped over such literary potholes, the blog grew popular. It would have become more celebrated if the incorrigible imbecile had not started believing that he wrote them himself. The moment he got the inkling that it was a great boost to his fan following, he decided to review the pieces – insert his dreadful ideas ... in fact he even went to the extent of indulging in ghastly wordplays."

Shruti frowned.

"That must have been awful."

"Yes, when he interfered it was indeed infuriating ... but it was his blog after all. It was fun too. I mean I got a kick out of the spoofs."

"I am dying to hear them."

"Here is one of the first ones for the great gargoyle. *It is a truth universally acknowledged that a successful man in possession of a good department must be in want of a blog.*"

"Did Jane Austen's spirit pay you a visit?"

"No, but stirrings in her grave were recorded on the Richter scale. Anyway, ghosts don't need to fear ghosts. I continued to write. Made the most tedious events of the financial world sound literary, exciting, funny ... almost like the blurb of a best seller. In my own way, I paid homage to all the great writers. *Whether I shall turn out to be the hero of my own department or that designation shall be held by some other employee these blogs must show...*Made him sound almost human. *For a long time, I left office early ...* Made him charismatic and nonchalant ... After he had acquired a company on a summer shopping spree, I wrote *It was love at first sight. The moment I saw the company I was madly in love with it. ...*"

"That's a Heller of a line"

"I made him sound funny too. When the Satyam boss was taken into custody, I wrote *Someone must have slandered Ramalingam Raju, for one morning, without having done anything truly wrong, he was arrested.* Worked like Metamorphosis. The blog soon became enormously popular, more than the dumb dinosaur had ever been. The hit rate was going sky-high. I even got an achievement award. But, then, he started taking a personal interest. And you can imagine how disastrous that can be."

"*Mr. Bigshot said he would write the blogs himself?*"

"Not so Woolfish. He just wanted to review and approve whatever went out. There were too many people reading *his* blog. Blogs had become his face, his identity. I even wrote one with the title *Blogito Ergo Sum.* He did not leave the review to one of his sensible managers any more. He started poking his nose, telling me to change this and that ... putting words in my mouth ... or rather *his* mouth."

"Quaint expression. In this newfangled line of work, it must be an occupational hazard."

"Imagine a ghost being haunted by his live self. When I was about to write about a complicated topic, I started by saying *I have never had more misgivings in starting a blog...*"

"Well, I am foxed by that one."

"*Razor's Edge*. Somerset Maugham. But, he told me to change it to something like 'having hesitation while putting my ideas on the financial situation on my blog'. It redefined commonplace. Soon my borrowed genius was being stifled, being bored to death by the blunt instrument on his shoulders."

"Bored to death by a blunt instrument. That should be patented as a unique hashed metaphor."

"He blatantly murdered the converted efforts of the great authors one by one, with metronomic precision. Punching his own words to eliminate Tolstoy, Kipling and Poe. It was like pouring champagne into cod liver oil. What's worse, he tried to insert his own brand of humour – at least what he thought was funny. Before a scheduled speech I wrote, *Under certain circumstances, there are few hours in life more disagreeable than management talk.*"

"Henry James!"

"Exactly. And he changed it to *Under certain circumstances, management talk can be avoided, but there is a chance you might miss something important even as you put in your best effort for the bank.* And to add insult to injury, he added a smiley to that."

"Criminal," Shruti observed thoughtfully.

"As time went on, I protested , argued, pleaded and but he kept intervening, doing his best to hack my flowery offerings into a ghastly jungle of boredom. And soon he got feedback that his blogs were losing their edge. That's another side of the documented grapevine. Everyone could reply to his posts. While earlier a secretary used to sort through the responses and read him a filtered extract, by now he had become used to glorious ghosted glory."

"Another of your gems."

"Sensing plummeting popularity, he took me to task. Told me I was not putting in my best. Even went to the extent of saying that he had had to correct my work in recent times."

Sandeep gripped the arm rests of the bench in agitation. Reaching across, Shruti patted his arm.

"Must have been terrible."

"Right. And then I rose up to a new challenge. I had started hating his grumpy guts. I took to writing stuff that would go way over his bean. Things that sounded impressive, but vague and if read thrice or more, pointed back towards him. And the ploy worked. I ended a particular blog on annual review with Kurt Vonnegut's *All this happened, more or less.* When the topic was stagnant market, I wrote like Beckett. *The sun is shining, with no alternative, on nothing new.* Some well read employees started enjoying it again. A smaller percentage, but the numbers improved. The idiot saw that things were working and I gave him enough hints to lay off my back. So he did. I even started writing his speeches for him. *One morning when I woke up from uneasy dreams, I found myself transformed into a giant CEO.* He loved that without realising what a perfect pest he was. The ones who had read Kafka loved it more. With things becoming smooth once again, I had this wild urge to strike back. At all the wrongs done to me. By *Uproar*, by the semi-literate readers of the publishing monoliths who sent rejection slips without opening my manuscript package, by this syphilitic CEO who had the audacity to overwrite my manipulated masterpieces."

"Syphilitic CEO. This is a turning out to be a master-class on indigenous alliterations."

"Thanks. The great man inspires me to unchartered unpleasantness. So, in due course, I went berserk. When there was a huge profit, I wrote *This is the story of what an employee's patience can endure and what a man's ambition can achieve.*"

"*Moonstone?*"

"Close enough. *Woman in White.* This got unprecedented popular response and earned me a warning from the pretentious porcupine. By this time, he had killed so many inspired trans-creations that I was at the end of my artistic tether."

"It's funny that you use trans-creation. Or serendipitous."

"I don't know what you mean. But, right now I am exorcising myself of this exalted excrement, so I will continue. The moment he lowered his guard, I described the bank as *A squat grey building of only sixteen storeys.* This went unnoticed and unappreciated. No one even commented on the reference."

"I am afraid, neither can I... Sounds familiar, but ... Is that Orwell or Huxley?"

"The latter. *The Brave New World,* no less. The hideous hedgehog did not even find it remotely offensive. He thought it was flattering. I was frustrated. Misconstrued into malapropism. Finally, I described the belligerent baboon's workplace in explicit words. *Far out in the uncharted backwaters of the unfashionable end of the Western Wing of the Second Tower lies a small un-regarded yellowish man. Orbiting him is an utterly insignificant little organisation whose ape-descended life forms are so amazingly primitive that they still think financial spreadsheets are a pretty neat idea.* This became huge. The popularity charts exploded. I was sacked."

"Left to hitchhike across the galaxy," Shruti sympathetically patted Sandeep who sat with a reflective look on his face. "That must have been real bad."

Sandeep shook his head.

"I don't know. I was so sick of working there, dealing with this colossal chimpanzee every day."

"I tend to detect a hint of bitterness in your voice. I guess your novels speak about all this?"

"To some extent ... in fact, to a large extent ..."

"Truth, as you know, is stranger than fiction."

Sandeep shrugged.

"I seem to have led an interesting life. Although, not always financially rewarding."

"And what happened after that?"

Sandeep got up and stretched. He had a flight to catch the next morning. Reason beckoned him to bed, but the conversation wanted to linger.

"I came to Amsterdam."

"How? Why?"

"My *tai chi* teacher travels to Europe every year to teach in Germany and the Netherlands. He is funded by the European Taichi Association. These guys paid half the fare for an assistant instructor. That was me. I managed to pay the remainder, because as I said, my efforts at ghosting for the coat clad catastrophe were well paid for."

"I wish I had a pen. I wonder how many of these expressions I will remember. So all this while, through your multiple professions, you had kept learning *tai chi.*"

"Yes. And to a lesser extent, I also kept up my *Shotokan Karate.*"

"I would love to analyse your curriculum vitae."

Sandeep shuddered.

"Don't even think about it. My CV confuses everyone. It is even more difficult to prepare than a synopsis. By the way, you know agents and publishers want solicitations and synopses before they look at your manuscript ..."

"Yes, I have heard of that."

"Think of James Joyce writing a synopsis of Ulysses."

Shruti chuckled. "Well, we can go into that later. It's too good a subject to touch superficially. But, now, I want some answers. So, after your *tai chi* lessons, you stayed back in Amsterdam."

"Yes, this second novel that I am on the verge of finishing, has some chapters set in Amsterdam...Actually, after coming here, I thought that Amsterdam was a good backdrop for the final part. I am calling it the *Dutch Gambit.* I guess that explains my visit to *Laurierboom.*"

"Much more than the quality of your chess."

"Enchanted. One of the *tai chi* students is an artist. He found me a place without rent. So I stayed back."

Shruti looked thoughtful.

"Well, you have clarified almost everything, but two pieces don't yet fit."

Sandeep smiled. Two American girls walked by leaving a strong whiff of marijuana.

"Are you bent on unravelling the mystery? Can't it remain as something that will be an enigma to draw you back to me ever after?"

Shruti shook her head.

"I will die of curiosity."

"Why? You're not feline in any respect except in the athleticism of your gait."

"My catlike gait makes me give chase whenever I smell a rat."

Sandeep looked at her with twinkling eyes.

"So, what are the two pieces that steal your peace of mind?"

"Do you want me to keep up the repartees by giving you a *piece of my mind*?"

"You want to postpone the peace of mind for a war of words?"

Shruti laughed aloud again.

"Let's get down to the explanation. I will have to think out of my skin to keep up this standard."

"That shouldn't be too difficult. In addition to a razor sharp mind, you do have minimum skin-fold thickness."

"That's the most peculiar compliment I have ever received, if it was indeed a compliment. I would love to read your stuff."

Sandeep bowed. "All you have to do is wait a couple of lifetimes. I increasingly have the feeling that fickle fame will come to me posthumously, if at all."

"Now tell me, how are you managing the funds to go back to India to get your visa renewed and to get back here? Air tickets are not cheap. And why did Pritam say that you are a consultant? Was it just to avoid going through your complicated employment history?"

Sandeep got up and started to walk westward towards Jordaan.

"The answers my friend are linked. And you are the pebble that sent ripples across the great ocean I am to cross twice in a few days. " he began.

IX

"What do you mean by that?" Dr. Suprakash Roy, before switching to psychiatric research in the Leiden University Medisch Centrum, had run quite a successful practice in North Kolkata. In his professional experience he had come across all sorts of wierdos. But, his cousin's latest statement hinted at identity disorientation and fugue that startled even the hardened veteran in him.

"You heard me," Pritam replied looking at the night sky which had finally stretched its pall over them. The air had grown chilly and the disgruntled consultant swore. "Damn. There should be a law about summer temperatures here."

"Thank your stars that there is no rain," the doctor reminded him.

"Ah yes. Four seasons a day. As I said, when I rang the bell and the door opened, I saw my own damn self staring back at me."

Dr. Roy sighed.

"Could you elaborate on that?"

"That blasted Sandeep had carefully altered his looks in subtle ways ... had turned out to be so very much like me that I almost ran away ... He had cut his hair to my length, had gelled it straight. He had done something to the eyebrows, to the clothes that he wore ... I told you we had won the second prize at a Separated at Birth contest ..."

"But that was more than a decade back, in your college days. This guy, as far as I have heard from you, keeps himself fit, while you ..."

"While I what?" The aggressive challenge in the voice made Dr. Roy rephrase his statement.

"Well, you must have been trying to make up for all the long sedentary hours, late nights, beer and other varieties of alcohol ... you write haikus about the gym in the early morning, after all ..."

"I said that was temporary insanity."

The doctor felt around for the right words.

"Was the visit to the gym also temporary insanity?"

Pritam grunted. "Sandeep pushed me into it."

"He seems to have been a major influence in your life."

"He is a scheming snake."

"I believe you already used this comparison."

"I'll use it again."

"Could you elaborate? I mean we were at the point where this scheming snake had started to look like you. That makes him more of a chameleon. What was he playing at? And how did he manage the beginnings of a rather substantial paunch?"

Pritam picked up a pebble again.

"I don't have a substantial paunch."

"Easy with the pebble."

"He did not have to put on a – er – rudimentary paunch. He somehow managed to make his face resemble mine. Few minor adjustments here and there, and the effect was miraculous. It seems he has done this sort of a thing during his days as an investigative journalist."

"You said he worked as a blogger."

"He had been an investigative journalist before that. He has also worked as a software engineer for some time."

"And he is also a martial artist?"

"That too."

"How does he manage all these things?"

"Chameleons can ...They are good at supernatural powers. Remember those ghastly snake movies of Bollywood – 1950's to 1990's."

Dr. Roy was not very convinced with the reptilian explanation of versatility. Nevertheless, he let it pass.

"He convinced me that he could look like my passport photograph."

The good doctor almost asked why any sane person would want to accomplish this quite unenviable feat.

"And I was convinced. He took me inside and discussed it at length. He told me to relax with a bottle of excellent Jamaican Rum. Which, incidentally, I had been saving up for the weekend. "

"Are you up for some drink now?"

"Well, I need something strong."

Dr. Roy pointed at a cosy looking bar frequented by students. They walked towards it.

"First of all, he pointed out that I was thirty two ..."

"It is not a bad thing that, you know. Age is relative. Five years from now, when you are thirty seven, you will reflect how good things were when you were thirty two"

"Shut up."

"Eh?"

"He said that if I waited any longer, my cheeks would become more pudgy, my hair greyer and my waistline wider. Don't smirk."

"I wasn't smirking ..."

"He told me that I would always get marriage proposals from the traditional match making circles because of my NRI status and my substantial income ..."

"You mean online matrimonial sites?" the doctor asked, interested.

"Maybe ... He also added that some interesting samples of the female species, for example Shruti Rattan, would no longer be willing to be seen within miles of my vicinity. Those were the exact words of the snake."

"Did he hiss them?" the words were said before Suprakash could stop himself. The pebble followed a fast, parabolic path and missed his nose by a whisker.

"He pointed out that I would be likely to end up with a bride who switched the channel to Indian Idol just as Tendulkar was latching on to a full toss four short of his fiftieth test century."

Dr. Roy shook his head doubtfully as they ordered beer.

"50th century? It's possible but remotely so. You see, I follow each and every match here on Cricinfo ..."

"We are not discussing cricket."

"Quite so," the good doctor wondered if the large can of Heineken had been a good choice after the recent brush with the pebble. He would have to be more careful in his choices of food and drink with his cousin around.

"He also dwelt considerably on the issue of the women colleagues and their voluminous asses, repeating the vision and mission theme."

"And you saw the company logo yet again. Did it appear in your mind as a glimpse of a web page ...?"

"Worse. After I was shit scared of the future, he showed me the alternative path. A month of romping about the beautiful cities of Europe with the most interesting woman I had ever come across, beautiful, intelligent, cricket loving ... he spoke about being up there in the Eiffel Tower with her, looking over the romantic capital of the world, wowing together as the same tower sparkled for the hourly ten minute every night, bobbing up and down together on the gondolas in Venice ..."

"I wouldn't have believed you were capable of such imagery."

"These are the words of the snake ... I remember all of it by heart ... words with which he spelt my doom. He talked about walking hand in hand along the cobblestoned streets of Prague's magical old town and floating on a boat along the blue Danube from Budapest to Vienna. He talked for about half an hour, so covered Germany, Austria, Norway, Sweden, Denmark, Greece, Spain and Portugal as well. At the end of his speech, I was almost weeping."

"I don't quite like the direction this is taking ..."

"And then, having made me drink half a bottle of Captain Morgan, he told me he would sacrifice himself on the altar of my love."

"He would go around Europe with Shruti?"

"Shut up," Pritam shuddered at the ghastly thought. "He said that he would present the paper for me while I went about Europe enjoying a romantic vacation."

Dr. Suprakash Roy managed to fight down an incredulous expression by falling back on professional experience.

"You agreed to that?"

Pritam sat down on another bench beside the canal and took a long draught of his beer.

"I did put up a fight."

"A fight?"

"I mean, I did play the devil's advocate ... but, by then my words were slurred. He pointed out that this was a part of the world where no one knew me. Which is true. I have joined *Axiom* in the USA, I will go back there after this. In all probability I will be joining a new firm. I was working out of Utrecht for another client and no one knows me in Amsterdam. I recommended so much downsizing in that company that the CEO will probably have to double up as the receptionist. So, no one from that organisation will attend this event. ... Somehow, the snake managed to get all this information out of me ... He said that for a friend he could hold fort for a week at any conference. He just needed to go back to India and get his visa renewed, which he would obviously do at *my* expense."

The two men looked long at the lights of the Leiden Medisch Centrum on the other side of the canal. For the first time, the doctor was really worried.

"Pritam, tell me you didn't go through with this."

Pritam threw the beer can into the canal with a jerky movement.

"He said that he had played different roles when he organised sting operations. He said that a profession like consultancy was a piece of cake. He had impersonated military men, power brokers, the personal assistants of ministers, weapons buyers and pimps ..."

"That's an odd mix."

"He masterminds sting operations."

"What an idea, putting your profession at par with the ones he spoke of."

"Well, the only one I could identify with was the pimp. I told him that I had no doubt he could, with some luck, get through the registration process, but there were several loopholes in his plan. He could reach the podium – what after that? I was going there to speak of the role of a change agent during financial crisis …"

"A what?"

"A change agent – one who accelerates changes. An euphemism for the downsizer as he put it. It is a professional's job. I told him that anyone would find out that he was not a professional. Pritam Mitra is a famous consultant. It would be the funeral of my career. And he said that was exactly what he wanted it to be. Just like a funeral. People would sing my praises – not one bad word anywhere, only I would not be there … Stop chuckling."

"I was merely appreciating the sense of humour."

"You were, were you? I explained that the process of Organisational Development and Change involved complicated theory. A Change Agent had to deal with Unfreezing, Changing and Refreezing with proper evaluation of Empirical Rational, Normative Re-educative, Power Coercive and Environmental Adaptive People. I talked about McKinsey's 7S, Lewin's Change Management Model and Kotter's eight step model, of ADKAR and Dynamic Conservatism, of the Formula for Change, of the Six Change Approach … I became quite theoretical, trying to show him how out of depth he would be in fielding questions."

Dr. Roy massaged his temples.

"And what did this friend of yours say?"

Pritam sighed. "He emptied the remainder of the bottle of Captain Morgan on my head."

Suprakash smiled with content. He was growing to like the young man.

"What are you smiling at?"

"Was I smiling? Must have been a grimace… What a horrible thing to do? Excellent Rum too. I love Captain Morgan – especially with Coke. However, a most interesting case, I must say. What happened after that?"

Pritam sighed.

"He said something about my needing a break from the professional rat race … doing something meaningful and exciting rather than networking. In the unlikely outcome of our being hounded by the Interpol there would be a full and unconditional confession on his part which would lay the blame solely on his shoulders. And then this odd thing happened. I looked at him, and from every facet of his appearance, one word almost broke free – *bohemian*. Somehow my train of thoughts focused on a page of Lonely Planet's *Europe on a Shoestring* – an article on the real Bohemia, in the heart of The Czech Republic, accessible through the wonderful Schengen Visa, a part of a possible Europe trip with an interesting young woman. I started thinking."

"A curious connection. Your cognitive map must be interesting."

"Please, leave jargon to the consultants. The conference would come and go ... and soon I would be back in New York, in another company. Could I afford to ignore this heaven sent opportunity of winning a wife like Shruti to present a paper for which anyway *Axiom* had the Intellectual Property Rights? He told me to think of twenty years from now. I would keep taking away the jobs of husbands, fathers and single mothers. With passing of time, it would not amount to anything but bank balance and a guilty conscience. But, this one flight of fancy, one crazy adventure, would make my whole life worth living. It struck home."

"You are kidding."

"Mind you, I was sozzled by then. We actually discussed the pros and cons. We even did a Failure Mode Effect Analysis ... A way of finding all the ways that a particular project can fail."

"You *must be* kidding ..."

"I am not ... I was also sick and tired of the last few weeks. Working with Dutch clients, discussing the same things over and over again in endless meetings. I wanted to get away from it all. However, in the end I was convinced that this was madness. It would be the end of my career."

Dr. Roy heaved a sigh of relief.

"So better senses did prevail?"

"Yes," Pritam sounded crestfallen. "But, after a couple of days. By then Sandeep had talked me into it and had already gone and met the chairperson of the conference."

"What?"

"I told you. He impersonated me. Using my alcohol induced words as sealed agreement. HMH Bank is one of the hosts of the event and there is a small *Axiom* team within it. He knew I was supposed to meet the senior people of this account any day. He used my official id card to get into the premises and met the managers of the *Axiom* account. He informed them that he would be back within a week to speak at the conference."

For a long time Dr. Suprakash Roy sat without a word.

"And you played along?"

"He did that while I was having these screwdrivers drilling through my skull in the worst hangover since college. He claimed that it was thoughtful of him to get introduced given the circumstances ... For the sake of my romantic plans."

Dr. Roy's cigar had burned down without being aided by too many puffs.

"I am starting on this trip with Shruti next week. There is no way this can be called off now. The euphoria of adventure has gone out of the window with the hangover. I can't sleep. The tension is killing me. I have walked him through the presentation dozens of times. He may be able to talk to the slides, but I don't quite know how he will handle the questions. And the networking ... well, as long as he doesn't get it into his head to do the networking for me, it is sort of okay ... I am leaving the company anyway. But suddenly it seems that the Axiom account in HMH is publicising the paper ... for the brand image and all that. So, there might be some senior people from ..."

Dr. Roy looked at his cousin with hardened eyes.

"I am a doctor who can help the sick, even the insane," he declared. "But, my specialisation does not extend to the stupid. And this is by some distance the most idiotic thing I have ever heard of in all my dealings with mental cases."

∾ ∾ ∾

"That's so awfully good of him."

Sandeep sensed a combination of light and warmth inside, a feeling commonly experienced by the likes of Mother Teresa, spread through him.

"He's a great chap."

"He seemed okay. He cursed only once while driving around Dam Square."

"He has his qualities."

"You should write his blog for him once in a while."

Sandeep winced.

"Maybe. I'll stay off blogs for some time, though."

"Or a couple of decent *haikus* from time to time."

"Maybe."

"So good of him to arrange for you to take over his job while he's on vacation."

Sandeep smiled.

"Yes. He really wants to go on this vacation. He wants to ... er ... get to know you."

"That's kind of cute."

"He always fancied girls who know their cricket."

"You never know which of your hidden talents will in handy."

"Especially with such great guys as Pritam. The moment I told him I wanted to stay on in Amsterdam for a while, hunting down literary agents and using office stationery, he thought up this brilliant solution."

"Office stationery?"

"Yes ... my agent hunting for my second novel has become stationary due to the huge amounts of postage involved. What with manuscripts, first three chapters, first five chapters in some cases, synopses and self addressed stamped envelope, sent to publishers and agents across UK and USA, the postage cost alone is enough to make an author starve. My contribution to the slush pile has been reduced to a trickle from the lack of a functioning financial engine. I intend to make off with loads of office stationery during the conference."

"How good of Pritam to recommend you to take his place in the conference."

"As I said, he is a capital guy."

"Do you know anything that you are going to say?"

"Of course. I will present a paper."

"And they let anyone do that? Even if it is such a ridiculous conference, they should have some filtering criteria..."

"My paper got selected because I was recommended by the great Pritam Mitra, and probably they rejected all unsolicited manuscripts ... especially the ones without a self addressed stamped envelope. Maybe the synopsis was a screening criterion."

"It's called an abstract in the academic circles."

"Whatever."

"But it was great on the part of Pritam."

"Of course. He's a swell chap. That's about the tenth time you mentioned it. Becoming a tad tedious."

"Too bad I can't have such fun exchanging literary quotes with him."

Sandeep hesitated. By now he was fully into doing his friend a good turn.

"Well, he does read ... although the subject may be off the beaten track of Literature."

"Oh does he?"

"Well ... I can guarantee he has read Steven Covey."

"I don't think I am acquainted with Mr. Covey's works."

"Good for you. Let us see. What else might he have read? Jack Welch, George Soros, Donald Trump, Malcolm Galdwell, Ricardo Semler ..."

"I suddenly feel incredibly illiterate. Will Thomas Friedman be common ground?"

"As long as the world remains flat, it might work. But, nothing from Beirut or Jerusalem."

"What a pity. But, I must bid you good night."

They had reached the Westermarkt tram stop. A stone's throw from the Anne Frank House.

Sandeep hesitated, trying to think of something to say.

"That's a pity too. Must you?"

Shruti nodded.

"You have an early flight tomorrow."

"Without resuming our recent repartees on chauvinism, will you manage on your own?"

"Yes. I won't need a black belt to escort me."

"When shall we meet again? In thunder, lightning or in rain?"

"Do you say that because it was unusually sunny today for Amsterdam? Or are you trying to call me a witch?"

"A witch in the lines of Fleur Delacour."

Shruti laughed loudly again.

"That's a magical compliment. Since you will be returning soon, we can meet as soon as the hubble bubble's done ... when the backpack's been undone."

"I hope for Pritam's sake that's not 'ere the set of sun'."

"We will talk about the exact hearth later. Maybe through emails and sms?"

Sandeep fished out his cell-phone and they exchanged numbers and mail ids.

"For someone as broke as you, you do yourself well with accessories."

"That's one of the reasons for my being broke. And I have recently come into riches, with our large hearted common friend being the benefactor. I am being paid a hefty fee for this conference. Good enough to continue for a few more months in Amsterdam, hunting down agents and publishers."

Shruti stopped.

"Ah, that reminds me. The reason why I had gone to meet you in the first place ... Can you take a package back for me? To Kolkata? I could post it from here, but it would be frightfully expensive and I wouldn't want it to land up in some wrong hands."

Sandeep bowed.

"To use a much hackneyed expression, your wish is my command."

Shruti dug into her backpack and produced a thick packet.

"If you can courier it once you are back, it would be great ... However, if you want to take it to the addressee yourself, I can guarantee it will be worth the effort and more."

Sandeep read the address printed on the package.

"Professor P. Lal. 162/92 Lake Gardens. Is this the same Professor Lal who is so eloquent about *rakshashas*?"

"That and much more."

"Would he be the same Professor Lal I am thinking about? The father of Ananda Lal?"

"The very same."

Sandeep felt the parcel.

"By any chance, is this a manuscript?"

Shruti waved her hand.

"No big deal. Just something I wrote over the last year or so ..."

"I will be damned. Are you an author too?"

Shruti shook her head.

"Not a serious one ... I don't hunt down agents ... "

"But, hey ... I have talked to you for the last couple of hours ..."

"Three to be precise."

"See, that's what I mean ... I can feel it right here that whatever you have written will be a delight to read."

"Clairvoyant critic?"

"Are you sending this to Professor Lal for a review?"

"Well no. Find out for yourself when you reach Kolkata. Tot ziens."

Taking a step towards him, Shruti opened her arms and they hugged.

"Have a safe flight."

"Thanks," Sandeep's loyalty was temporarily transfixed by touch. His feelings for the mutual friend for a moment quivered on the verge of jealousy, making him wonder whether a dull, dreary consultant was really someone who deserved a European vacation with this extraordinary girl.

By the time he had re-stabilized his wavering views and tottering knees, the subject in question had crossed the street and was moving away towards the tram stop.

"Welcome ever smiles but farewell goes out sighing," he called, but was not too sure whether Shruti heard him.

Part II:

Ethics and Fundamentals

X

Lake Gardens, Kolkata

Sandeep called from his cell phone as he stood outside the dilapidated kiosk. The name *Book Nook* stood out in exquisite calligraphy.

Sunil Pillay answered on the twelfth ring. Experience had made Sandeep sceptical about the man's sobriety, regardless of the hour. At ten in the morning, he expected half a dozen pegs of neat whiskey already thrown down the garrulous gullet.

"Dada, how are you?" the voice greeted him jovially. Sandeep bit down the vitriolic response that rushed to the tip of his tongue.

"Hi, Sunil ... Could you give me an update?"

"Patience, friend. It's being done."

"Patience ... indeed. How poor are they that have not patience. Add to that being fleeced off by an unscrupulous ..."

"I have not stolen, my friend. Your book is receiving the finest packaging and will be available from Starmark, Crossword and the leading stores across the country ... Give me some time. Unforeseen circumstances, mate. But, it will be done. I trust you have talked to other authors of *Amphibian* ..."

Sandeep had to admit it. He had called up and emailed different authors. All had maintained *Amphibian* got the books to the stores and did a decent job of packaging, editing and getting reviews. The Indian publishing industry was a crazy place.

He took a deep breath.

"How many days, Sunil?" He knew he sounded harsh. He meant to.

"Chill man. It's almost done. Patience."

"I don't mind being patient if you keep your promises," he snapped. "You promised a forty day timeline. That way, I could have had the volumes in the stores two months back. I have returned from Amsterdam. I was there to attend a *Tai Chi* camp. Practitioners from all over Europe had assembled. It's probably news to you, but *Tai Chi* plays a major role in the novel. It was a perfect marketing opportunity. To make it available across the clubs of Europe ..."

"Sorry man, this has never happened before," Pillay sounded curiously like an answering machine. He had said sorry too often.

"Apologies do not help, Sunil. I am leaving for Europe again in a week. And I have splendid connections with the *Tai Chi* clubs there. As things stand now, I won't be able to take some volumes with me ..."

"How many copies do you need?"

"Twenty would be good enough to start with, but please don't promise if you can't deliver. This has happened too many times."

From the other end of the country, Pillay laughed.

"Have faith in us, dada, we're doing our best. I promise to send across twenty copies by Sunday. You can write it down."

Sandeep sighed.

"I'll believe it when I see it Sunil."

~ ~ ~

"Take a seat, if you can find a place," the voice that rang out from inside was dignified, yet tinged with humour.

The moment he had entered through the blue gate beside the kiosk, it was apparent that he was expected. The doorman had responded to his name with a smile one can get only in India. There was a rumble of expectation in his stomach. In the last few days, he had read a lot about the Writers Workshop. There was quite a lot of information on its exquisite website.

He had come down to the kiosk to submit Shruti's manuscript with the intention of a seeing a lot more. The swapped identities had greatly enhanced his purchasing power. He was notorious for his profligacy in bookshops.

However, as a bookshop, it turned out to be unlike anything he had ever seen. A cubby hole in the proprietor's own words, congested shelves contained the product of authors across half a century, in volumes that were works of art, things of beauty. Covered in hand-woven *sari* cloth of lustrous colours, the titles embroidered in gold *zari* script, laid out by the virtuoso calligraphic talents of the publisher himself. The slight imperfection from being hand bound, hand set and embroidered, made them delightful to touch.

There were many titles Sandeep wanted to browse, having discovered them on the website. *The Complete Plays of Asif Currimbhoy, The Gitanjali transcreated in English* by Joe Winter, the first edition of *Mappings* by Vikram Seth – published by the

Workshop before he went on to become the author of *The Suitable Boy* and *Golden Gate*. There was also an exciting new novel set in the software world during the Y2K days.

However, the most intriguing had been the works of the publisher himself. The Indian classics transcreated into English. *Dhammapada,* all the *Upanishads,* the *Bhagavat Gita* – the message unadulterated, the verses simple and the poetic rendering intact. The most amazing being the four decade project of transcreating the entire *Mahabharata* of Vyasa, verse by verse, *sloka* by *sloka.*

He had also been fascinated by what he read about *Lessons,* the one of a kind memoir by the poet. After two hours of enthralled browsing in the cramped and distinctly user unfriendly interiors of the kiosk, he had allowed himself the purchase of a copy.

He had laid aside Hermans, Gide, Pessoa and the other recently acquired European greats, as well as the fascinating volumes on Organisational Change thrust upon him by a visibly apprehensive Pritam. In spite of its considerable thickness, he had read *Lessons* within a night. The lyrical language was a lesson in itself.

Lessons had been written after the Professor had been snatched back from the jaws of death following a mystery illness in 1989. While there were snippets describing his experiences in the United States before and during the illness, including perhaps the most lyrically artistic description of voyuerism, most of the book was a homage paid to famous and not-so-famous people who had been associated with him all his life. It was so unlike any other memoir Sandeep had read.

"I wonder why Professor Lal, with the versatility of his pen, had to open his own publishing establishment," he had asked Shruti in an email.

The response had been cryptic. "You can gauge the reason once you meet the man."

Curiosity mingled with half honed journalistic instincts had found him in the huge study of 162/92 Lake Gardens. He looked around … there were piles and piles of books everywhere. High up near the ceiling, in shelves that ran around the room, on the ground, piled up in tantalizing balancing acts, on the table … or what he approximated to be a table through the expanse of elegant, enticing editions.

"I tell myself, and more often I tell my wife, that someday I will organise this place," the tall man was in his late seventies, seated in the middle of an ocean of crystallised thought. "I have a very general idea of what is where. I know this section is for Literature, that for Philosophy. But, please take a seat."

Sandeep took a while to find a chair free of books.

"So you are the young man who brought Shruti Rattan's manuscript from the shores of the West?" he asked. There was a twinkle in his eye. "Or should I say dykes?"

"Yes," Sandeep laughed. "She is a friend. She wanted to know if there was something else you require."

Professor thought for a while.

"I don't think I need anything else. She has sent the manuscript, also the floppy."

"Floppy?"

One of the eyes of the Professor had been lost in a cricketing accident of his youth. The other one remained as intense as ever. Now it looked confused. "Yes, the modern marvel of the computer age ..."

"I think she sent a CD ... a compact disc."

"Is it? Oh well, it is all the same to me. It's too late in the day for me to become computer savvy – isn't that the expression? I don't touch the machine there," he pointed to an antique piece in the far corner of his room. "My granddaughter reads all my emails to me. Also writes my replies."

Sandeep looked around the room. There were all kinds of books on the shelves. The floors were taken up by Writers Workshop volumes. There were posters on the wall, of W.B. Yeats, of Tagore ...

"You may not be computer savvy, but Writers Workshop has a most fascinating website," he observed.

There was a smile on the serene face.

"That's another miracle of karma. I have been associated with so many wonderful people who have helped me with the Workshop from time to time. It is the work of one of the young authors of Writers Workshop. And it is amazing. The magic of the web. People from all over the world visit the site, and I get orders every day."

Sandeep wondered. The site was static, without the basic features enabling e-commerce.

"But, Professor, how do you get the orders? I saw no provision for ordering online."

Professor Lal laughed. "Thank God for that. We are not equipped to process online orders. The address is available on the website. People mail or call for books. That's enough for me."

He paused. "You know, my binder, Atoar Hossain, is the third generation of his family working for me. And these books have been displayed the world over just for the unique binding. He can't manage more than 150 copies a month. He doesn't want to either. So, even if there is technology to bring in more orders, we won't be able to meet it."

He sat musing for a while before waving his thoughts away with a dismissive gesture of his long fingered hand.

"But, what brings you here? Shruti Rattan. She is a wonderful writer. Full of curious insights. Presented in fascinating forms."

"She is a wonderful girl," Sandeep agreed.

"She must be. The musings on Europe are so delightful. It must be great for you young people to be able to travel around. You did say you were leaving for the lowlands?"

Sandeep laughed.

"Yes, I am. I wanted to meet you before I left. I can't really say that there is any particular reason, but Shruti spoke so much about you, I read so much from the web site and then I also read a copy of your *Lessons*. You see ..."

"Ah, I see you are trying to find a justification. I assure you there is no need. To an old man, visitors are always welcome. And you have done your bit for the workshop by being the messenger. Making the delightful pieces available to me. The one who makes the message available is of great importance. Just think of what the *Mahabharata* would have been without Sanjaya narrating the war."

Sandeep smiled. Something in the atmosphere of the room was intoxicating.

"Besides, we would not have the great epic unless it was borne down by a series of messengers – ones who repeated the *slokas*. From memory. It was strictly oral rendition. And one wonders how all this intricate weaving of *karma*, the magnificently complicated story line, so many diverse characters, without loose ends, managed to transpire in such succession."

"What about the story of Vyasa dictating all that to Ganesha?"

The Professor laughed. "Who wrote it down with a broken bit of tusk? That's something inserted later. There was no concept of books at the time of Vyasa or the Mahabharata. Surprised? Do you know that there is no Sanskrit word for book?"

Sandeep thought for a while.

"What about *pustak*?"

"That's Farsi. The same with *boi* or *kitab*. The closest one can get is *grantha*. And that means compilation, not really a book. You see, if you get down to the nitty-gritty, you come across a lot of surprises. We are so used to the concept of a book, we had to create the sub plot of Ganesha taking dictation from Vyasa."

"Maybe after a couple of millenniums we will rewrite that version with Ganesha being the content writer of a divine website, Vyasa supplying him the material, the functional specifications, through heavenly FTP servers." Sandeep wondered if he had just trivialised the great epic, but the Professor laughed.

"Of course. Who knows? The web is so fascinating. It's like a wonderland."

"I read the article *Profsky in Wonderland.* It's by the same person who designed the Writers Workshop website."

"Arunav," the Professor laughed indulgently. "Very talented, versatile. My only fear is that he may be sidelined into fringe literary activities. But, you know, talking about the web ... I spoke to you about the incoming orders..."

"Right."

"There is a book called *Mrityunjaya – the Death Conqueror*. It's by Shivaji Sawant."

"Yes, I know. I read about it on the website."

The professor pointed his long index finger.

"Well, there you go. You sense the magic. It's a new age *mayajaal.* Connecting people's lives. But, Shivaji Sawant. In Marathi literature he is a household name. And this story about Karna is one of the best novel adaptations of Mahabharata. It is a book worthy of the Nobel Prize. I read the Hindi version. My Hindi is not that strong, so I got together with Nandini Nopany and had the entire book transcreated into English. And when we took it to Manny Manekshaw of the *Walrus Publishers,* you know what his question was? This top boss of the publishing monolith asked us, 'Who is Shivaji Sawant?' We had no choice but to get it published through the Workshop. For so many years it lay there in the kiosk, without selling a dozen copies a year. And now. The magic of the web. I am getting orders every day, from all over the world. Two copies here, four copies there ..."

As he listened, some of the bitterness of recent times tinged the euphoric energy.

"This Manny Manekshaw," he started.

"Yes, the head of *Walrus Press.*"

"You know that he has published his own novel. *The Purple Apple Mansion.*"

"Yes, I have heard about it. But, I have not really read it."

"That's good for you. Eminently avoidable. However, tell me something. *Walrus Press* publishing Manny Manekshaw. Doesn't this qualify as self or vanity publishing?"

The Professor waved dismissively.

"Vanity Publishing ...it doesn't really make sense. Let me tell you something. A group of writers and I started the Writers Workshop. Why? Because people would not publish us. What was one to do? Without alternative publishing one is at the mercy of these publishing monoliths. Like *Walrus.* I don't know about Manekshaw's book, but most of the instant successes are pulped by the end of the year. Modern day publishing is nothing but book dumping. It's a racket out there."

The words of Shruti suddenly made sense. One could not picture Professor Lal haggling with the bookstores to stock some of the Writers Workshop books, to place them one on top of the other near the entrance in spiral formation. That was for MBA whizkids turned into so called authors.

"It's your choice. What does your *dharma* tell you to do? Which path to choose?" Professor smiled. "I believe you are an author yourself."

Sandeep hesitated. He had not said anything about himself other than his forthcoming trip to the Netherlands.

"Well, I've been associated with authors for half a century. I can almost sniff them out," Professor continued.

Sandeep looked at the smiling face.

"I would not call myself an author. A writer, yes. My first novel is being published in a defined but ever expanding time frame ..."

Professor laughed. "That happens in India. Who is the publisher?"

"*Amphibian Books,*" Sandeep replied.

Professor pondered.

"I've not really heard of them. But, come to think of it, being an amphibian goes a step further than being a walrus, doesn't it? Makes it more adaptable."

"Well, it is run by a gentleman – to be precise, a man – called Sunil Pillay."

"Well, it's good to know you are being published, though I have not heard of the publisher or the man behind it. Just make sure that your works are not pulped," the Professor said. "We don't have any distribution, but we do not pulp any of our books. Any book published by the Workshop is always available. Another thing. Don't let them edit your work. You as the author know what you wanted your work to say. No editor can read your mind."

Sandeep cleared his throat.

"Professor, could you spare a word of advice for a new author?"

The Professor shook his head.

"You are asking someone who has stayed clear of mainstream publishers through his life," he replied. "Do you really think it is advisable to ask for my advice?"

Sandeep nodded. "I am going to Amsterdam on a new assignment, a role I have never played and never thought of playing. My sole intention of going there in a new garb is to hunt down agents and publishers, you know, to be in close contact with the lands of literary opportunities – namely United States of America and the United Kingdom."

He paused and looked around him.

"I have read *Lessons.* It was unlike any other memoir I have ever read. I wanted to spend some more time sampling books from the Workshop. But, time won't permit me. I have to gear up for the ridiculous role I will be playing there. So, the least I can do is to ask for some parting advice."

He was reminded of the words from *Profsky in Wonderland.* "*Knowledge and culture bound in volumes, filtered by a great mind, assimilated for three quarters of a century, packed into one large room, spilling into the corridors outside and the landing of the staircase. I wanted to be a bookworm who could start devouring the cover of the first volume and not stop till the back flap of the last . . . Could I cut off a slice of the environment and take it back with me? To use it as spiritual air freshener, a mental sieve to clear the mind clouded with the soot and stain of the corporate world?*"

The Professor seemed to be in a dilemma. "I am not really in favour of advice. Every individual is blessed with a *dharma* that is specific to him. My way may not suit yours. And look at what mayhem was caused when Arjuna succumbed to the advice given by Vasudeva-Krishna."

He smiled.

"However, if you insist, I can tell you what I have learnt in my life. You want to be an author? Make sure that you live long."

"Pardon me?"

"I started transcreating the Mahabharata in 1969. Now, towards the end of the first decade of the twenty first century, I'm getting these reactions. There have been doctorate degrees thrust on me. Television channels are starting to telecast my Mahabharata readings. And the Workshop? After half a century, there are people across the world coming in to study and research it. People from the Ivy League. So, that's my advice. Live long. When you do something for a sufficiently long period of time, people sit up and start to notice."

This was not quite what Sandeep had expected. Inexplicable, curious. But, even *Lessons* had been insightful in unexpected ways.

The Professor took up a small thick volume and quickly wrote something in it. He extended his arm and Sandeep found himself looking at a beautiful pocket sized volume of his rendering of the *Bhagavad-Gita, the Final Fully Revised Definitive Transcreation.*

"Well, as far as advice goes, I can give this to you. But please remember that it raises more questions than answers. And sometimes it takes recourse to brainwashing and magic."

Sandeep took the book in his hands. Inside, in exquisite calligraphy, Professor had signed his name and offered his best wishes.

"And if you are wondering how to live up to this new role, this new garb as you put it, you can pick up a copy of the *Virata Parva* of the Mahabharata from the kiosk. As I keep saying, the Mahabharata has all the lessons that one can learn."

Sandeep walked out of 162/92 with a feeling he had only known after long hours of *Tai Chi* training.

XI

"Thank heavens I decided on tinted windows," the ageless man remarked as he finally found a way past his partner's skilful hands and managed a palm heel strike to his ribs. "They are not strictly legal, you know."

The traffic was in dynamic standstill. The last five minutes had witnessed a couple of energetic turns of the keys in the ignition – born more out of hope than purpose. Not a car had moved on the Airport Road of Bangalore.

Sandeep was conscious of the intense internal sweating that accompanied such sticky hand – *chi sao* – sessions with his master. Having found his way past his student's defence, S. Subramanium rested his hands on the steering wheel. One of the lessons he had successfully imparted during their ten year association was the continual pursuit of art regardless of the constraints of life. This was the first time the *sifu* had engaged in a focussed lesson in the front seat of a car while stuck in traffic, but it did not surprise Sandeep. Constraints can come in many forms – spatial, temporal, continual or temporary. It is always possible to walk on the path, or drive along.

"This is good news indeed," Subramanium remarked. He had the local inhabitant's knowledge of the probable wait time in the deadlocked rows of vehicles, and also the serenity to withstand the minutes and – sometimes – hours. Sandeep often wondered if the man was as calm in his private thoughts. The veteran continued. "A martial artist has to travel. Otherwise he soon ends up knowing everything."

The car moved forward a few inches. The Manipal Hospital lay to their left while the looming form of the Leela Palace came into view on the other side. Sandeep smiled. He was used to the remarks of the master. A few wrinkles beside the eyes and his weather beaten face hinted at his advanced age – which remained as much a mystery to him as the S preceding Subramanium. From the anecdotes of his encounters with renowned figures of the *karate, tai chi* and *yoga* worlds, he could not be less than sixty five. Sandeep knew Subramanium would continue to travel, thus unmasking enormous limitations of the knowledge gathered over half a century. Unlike so many of his students, who had become stagnant with satisfaction within half a decade.

"I wonder how long I will be able to continue in Europe," Sandeep sighed. "I'll try to stick around for a few weeks ... There's my novel to take care of ..."

Subramanium smiled.

"A man of many talents."

"A tailor made candidate for the Jack of All Trades ..."

"Master one ... master just one ... or try to master ... and if Jack did not become a master of any but kept trying, I'd say he was successful."

"It's the journey and not the goal."

"Yes, and Bangalore traffic teaches you that there is no other way. I'm glad for you, boy ... I was glad when you went to New York ... I had hoped you would go there more often and train further with Chen Yang. Although going to YMAA was not my recommendation ..."

Sandeep smiled. *Tai chi* could be a systematic exercise for holistic well being, with the slow, graceful and indigenous movements. However, each of the steps could be converted into exceptioanally effective martial applications. Subramanium had always limited his lessons to the art of well being. It was a perpetual puzzle to Sandeep. According to him, as a serious *Karateka*, the old master should have been, like him, extremely interested in the esoteric martial techniques of separating the tendons, and sealing the breath.

While in New York, he had dutifully attended the school of Chen Yang – an instructor descending from the direct line of the founder of the Chen style *tai chi chuan*, Chen Man Ching. Subramanium had trained with him during his travels to China early in his life. However, in the weekends Sandeep had made off to Yang's Martial Arts Association in Boston to pick up the martial applications taught by Dr. Yang Jwang Ming. Subramanium had not shown any reaction when he had come back, apart from a hint of a smile. To this day Sandeep was not sure whether he had been offended.

Now, he saluted his instructor by placing his fist and palm together. Having taken *karate* lessons first, he was more comfortable bowing with his hands beside his hips... but, in the car, as just taught by the teacher, physical, circumstantial constraints notwithstanding, the art has to go on.

"To be honest, I loved the six months of training. But, then, when I came back here, I had no one to train with. I still remember the concepts, the moves, but the practice has been limited. And after all these years, Sifu Schmidt's classes at the seminar ..."

Subramanium touched his foot lightly on the accelerator and the car edged forward.

"Sifu Schmidt is a master of the martial applications."

Sandeep knew from his experiences at the seminar in Amsterdam that Subramanium was not too bad at the techniques himself. He remained silent.

The older man looked at him and laughed.

"Don't hold anything against me, boy. I teach *karate* as a combat art. Yoga as a form of meditation. *Tai chi* too is a form of meditation for me, meditation in action. To my inner self, I am not an instructor in the *Tai Chi Chin Na.* I have a minor academic interest, that's all."

One of the rare few in the world who enjoyed his profession.

"May I remind you what minor academic interest in people like you can amount to?"

At last the row of cars moved forward and the speedometer crossed 20.

"I could not do justice to your youthful passion for the applications, my boy. I know that life is long ..."

"Well, it sure needs to be. You are the second person who has said so on this visit."

"Believe me, for a passionate martial artist, during the course of life, doors will open. Just as it opened for you ... Circumstances took you to New York. Next, when everything came to a standstill you managed a trip to Amsterdam ... and even in this crisis, you have managed to land up there again. Try and attend some of Sifu Schmidt's camps. If possible try going to his school on weekends. He has frequent seminars all over the country. Germany is close enough to the Netherlands and with the Schengen Zone and free borders ... you see everything is working for you. It may be your chance to hone your skills in *tai chi chin na.* Opportunity has knocked ... "

"Opportunity has not really knocked. Someone else knocked and when the door was opened slightly in response, opportunity surreptitiously slipped in."

Subramanium took a left and entered a narrow street.

"I am used to your peculiar professions. So, I am not surprised. But, all I'll say is make use of the opportunity to the fullest. Europe will open new doors in your studies."

Sandeep sighed.

"I had dropped in a martial art store in Amsterdam ... there were such beautiful *shenza.* And also some exquisitely carved long swords. There is no way I can get those into India."

Subramanium shook his head. "It will cost you ten times to bribe the customs officers. "

Sandeep nodded.

"In this country you have to make do with handmade wooden swords."

Subramanium looked at an oncoming bullock cart and skilfully manoeuvred his Santro into another by lane.

"There are some broad-swords available at the Sports Authority of India complexes. Result of *wushu* being included as a demonstration sport in the Asian Games."

Sandeep shuddered.

"I've seen them. Lethal instruments. A minor cut and tetanus is inevitable."

With a laugh, Subramanium brought his car to a halt in front of a Chinese restaurant.

"Joseph Wong, the owner, is my student."

"I know, I have eaten here a couple of times...."

Sandeep's cell phone started ringing as he was about to get out of the car. He looked at the caller id and smiled at Pritam's Amsterdam number. With a slight flick of his thumb he pressed the reject button.

"We just have time for lunch and the trip back to the airport," Subramanium remarked as he walked into a dark, spacious restaurant decorated with Chinese lanterns and laughing Buddhas. A couple of waiters in plain dress bowed deep with bright smiles of recognition at the master.

"A six hour trip to Bangalore just to meet me is madness," the master said. "But knowing you, that's not abnormal." He sat down at a table for four, paused a while and smiled widely. "And, Sandeep, believe me, I am really touched by your gesture."

Sandeep relaxed with his head resting on the back of the wooden chair and laughed.

∾ ∾ ∾

Emails between Sandeep and Sunil Pillay

Dear Sunil,

You hardly have any idea how much of a struggle it was to key in 'Dear' at the start of the mail. I waited for the copies of the books, knowing fully well that you would let me down. And you did not disappoint me. You don't keep your word, but you are pretty consistent at that."

Sandeep

Dear Sandeep,

Sorry Dada. This has never happened before. It seems your book is jinxed. I will definitely send you forty copies to your address in Antwerp.

Sunil

Dear Sunil,

I am going to Amsterdam and not Antwerp. At least try to make the false promises believable.

Sandeep

Dear Sandeep,

We are doing our best. Please don't lose your faith on us.

Sunil

Part III:

Idiosyncratic Risk and Hit

XII

Blog of Simple Simon
Tags: Indian work culture, professional and personal lives

As I have mentioned earlier, from my name to my job, from my culture to my nationality, from my expected outlook towards life to the one demanded of me by my colleagues, I am a wretched soul with an identity crisis.

Born to a Dutch father and an Irish mother, by some queer joke of fate, I am an American citizen. And although I grew up on a steady diet of American culture (pardon the oxymoron), I was recruited by an Indian multinational primarily because of my fluency in spoken Dutch.

Strange things are expected of me, being employed for & in an Indian organisation, where the demarcation between work and life becomes fuzzy to the point of non-existent.

Case in point – what took place today. I have been asked to practically babysit a senior consultant who has grown out of diapers for about three decades. They call it the buddy system, and by the looks of it, it promises to be a round the clock affair.

Strangely, the others seem to find it normal whereas I can't tolerate sticking to colleagues after office hours. With the Albert Heijns, Bijenkorfs and Bulldogs all around Amsterdam, who needed me to point out shops, stores and bars. Banks and bars? Well, in Amsterdam it's as much a laugh as finding sex.

But, being a Dutch speaking American citizen with an Irish parent , employed by an Indian firm, what else can I expect?

Mail from Simon to his Mailing List
Subject: Baddie Buddy

I have given an inkling of what took place today in office in my rambling domain, namely the blog. However, the particulars are more sinister and intriguing –

and obviously not fit for the eyes of curious colleagues with corporate conscience. So, followers of my workplace stories, it is back to the mail format.

My immediate boss, Madhu, at her zestful best, walked into my cubicle early in the morning and planted herself there, intent on discussing the intricacies of American Presidential elections.

Now if Madhu plants herself in your cubicle, it is one of the challenges of the job to dislodge her. For one thing she weighs considerably more than what the doctor ordered. Add to that the magnitude of her opinion, which takes contradictions, counter opinions and even concurrence in its stride, with the steadily acquired managerial expertise of never listening to anyone. She enforces her views, sparing no gory detail, while nimbly moving on to other complicated matters and considered, inconsiderate opinions. The final nail in the coffin for neglected work and interest quotient is hammered in when all the diverse topics ultimately converge to Hidori, her four year old son. Conceiving at a late age has its drawbacks, which include burdening underlings with the most vivid details of the singularly mundane activities of the child. Here the deviations to other subjects stop, and in mathematical terms, the discourse converges and progresses ad infinitum until fate (read cell phone) brings relief from unknown corners.

Today, she started with Barrack Obama, moved to the minute details of the life and times of Colin Powell, and proceeding along the dark path (culturally insensitive pun) moved to Toni Morrison (whom I dare say I have not read. Neither has she if my intuition does not deceive me), *Roots* (Alex Haley, which thankfully I have read, and can detect that she has not), and Chinua Achebe (whom I have not heard of, let alone read and I will be surprised if she has). As I had feared, the talk turned to what young people should read, and with one practised laddering act, she started recounting everything Hidori has read or has been read to in his four long years of life and what he is expected to read in the next sixty or so.

By this time my cubicle had turned into a general place of rendezvous, with the apple cheeked Trisha, the dark, cheerful Amrita and the grumpy faced Gunjan joining in. Madhu adapted to each new addition with the practised efficiency of the seasoned rambling boss. I was internally gasping for air, all my senses crying out for a quick peek at the NFL scores to neutralise the thirty minute discourse. The others hung on to each and every word of the informal knowledge sharing session. I had almost started praying for the first time since the eve of my Scholastic Aptitude Test, when relief came in the unexpected form of our Account Manager, Ajay.

This particular fellow gives me the impression of being in a constant state of fear. He hardly answers a question without looking with worried eyes at all possible corners of the room and beyond. I have never quite fathomed his reasons for such shifty eyed movements. He always makes me uneasy, willingly or unwillingly casting the shadow of impending doom.

Today, however, his arrival was a blessing. Spotting Madhu in my cube, he crept in looking as he habitually does, like an errant dog caught in the act of toppling a garbage can.

His arrival had the immediate effect of stopping the Hidori saga. Soon, young feminine charm of the gathering withdrew. Trisha and Amrita, connecting eyes, hastily murmured about things to take care of and disappeared. Gunjan stayed back, obviously eager to eavesdrop into managerial discussions.

Ajay started speaking of the imminent arrival of the consultant, Pritam Mitra. This guy seems to be a high flying executive. His paper has been seriously hyped by the Axiom senior management to HMH and Ajay was quite shaky because he had not heard from him in three days.

Gunjan nodded sagaciously, observing that a man of Pritam's seniority should have the professional sense to inform in advance about his arrival.

Ajay added that some of the mighty celebrities of *Axiom* were coming in from all parts of the Netherlands to attend the all important presentation, including K. Ramesh, the Vice President of Continental Europe operations. As usual, he looked as if he perceived a probable chain of events leading to his loss of job and his being sent back to India, ears drooping, tail in a weak, undecided low hanging curve between his legs.

Only Madhu Deb remained unflustered. She had a brief conversation with someone on the phone and informed us that the consultant was in Frankfurt and his flight would land in Schiphol in another hour and a half. She had just spoken to the taxi driver who was strategically stationed to pick him up from the airport. Once she had sent Ajay back to his room, one of the dozen or so layers of tension peeled off his face, she turned to us and expressed wonder at her having to think of all the logistics.

Gunjan nodded sagaciously again, this time observing that a man of Ajay Yadav's seniority should not display his misgivings so openly, likely as it were to affect the morale of the team, especially in these trying financial conditions.

There being a brooding threat of the return of the Hidori chronicles, I had just got off my seat in a determined dash for the men's room, when suddenly Madhu reminded me of having been designated the 'buddy' of this new hotshot consultant. He was a senior resource after all, and a local person to show him around would be absolutely necessary. Especially the shops, the banks and the bars.

She asked me to be sure to give him a call at his hotel in the evening to find out whether he required any assistance.

After this she bounded off, singing a loud greeting to another unfortunate soul about to be burdened by the Hidori saga.

Well, so I am left with this novel role of a babysitting buddy. Cross cultural trials and tribulations that come with my choice of work environment. But, as I said in my blog, what else can such a mixed up employee expect?

Cheers
Simon

∾ ∾ ∾

Text Message from Sandeep to Shruti
India to West
Words cloaked in embroidery
Long Fingers show way

Tell me something though – how many readers will your work reach through WW? Will it ever reach book shops and get reviews?

Text Message from Shruti to Sandeep.
Great Haiku. Your friend has somehow stopped his dreadful haikus due to something that keeps him worried.

I write for myself, not others. The size of the footprints does not matter as long as I have walked.

Email from Sandeep to Shruti

Got your sms.

The other side is fighting for shelf space with the best selling literary works by film actors, pop stars, wrestlers and semi-literate management graduates, hundred rupee best sellers in tapori English, wives of CEOs suddenly turning authors. But in return, you do build a nice little collection of rejection slips. . . . . We are sorry your submission does not fit our publishing plans right now. We wish you success in your literary journey. Or,to make things exciting, our publishing calendar is full. And you can make out that they treat your work with respect, they have zealously restrained themselves from tampering with your efforts by opening your manuscript.

Then there is someone like Professor Lal, who has to make do with his own publishing institution. In spite of his brilliance and erudition. Or is it because of it?

But, you seem to be a free spirit, blissfully untouched by such frustration. A touch of Satori.

How's your Europe tour shaping up? I think you are to leave tomorrow.

∾ ∾ ∾

"What the hell is Doblin?"

Sandeep, who had unfortunately pressed the answer button, sat in the waiting lounge of the Frankfurt Airport and blinked.

"What the hell is what?"

"Doblin. Something to do with an Alexander thing." Pritam Mitra sounded on the edge.

Sandeep tried to think. In his subconscious mind he had expected the caller to be Shruti responding to his email. His childhood friend's voice had not really been a happy substitute. True, he did feel a trifle sorry for him after the brief bitter conversations of the last couple of days, almost always ending with Sandeep heartlessly disconnecting the line.

"Could you please elaborate?" he asked. "Why are you working on crazy cryptic crosswords when you must be gearing up for your European Escapade?"

There was a grunt from the other end followed by the sound of running water.

"I am already into the tour. I am calling you from the toilet of the train."

"How romantic in a double-o-seven way. So, how are the toilets of Thalys? Is the water in the cistern tinged with *les parfums francais*?"

"I am not in the goddamned Thalys. It's ICE."

"Right, you're on your way to Germany. Can we call it the ICE breaker?"

There was a pause after which a gloomy voice reached him from behind closed lavatory doors.

"My partner prefers the mayhem capital of the world to your romantic one. We have just crossed Emmerich, on our way to Berlin."

"Wow."

"Shove your exclamations ..."

"Quite. So, you are going the other way, are you?"

"Yes. In more ways than one. We are about to stand face to face with the fascinating history of the Cold War, the World War bombings and the Holocaust. That's what my travelling companion is raving about. It is like writing one of those History tests yet again, with complicated Geography that keeps changing with time and wars. She is so delightfully passionate about bombed cities. She wants to visit every place graced by an explosion. She wants to start with Berlin and continue to some place called Dresden ..."

"You haven't heard of Dresden?"

"Is it well known?"

"It was bombed to smithereens in the Second World War."

"That explains her interest."

"You have to bear with it. She is a student of Political Science. I take it you haven't read Vonnegut's *Slaughterhouse Five*."

"I haven't heard of it, neither have I heard of Vonne-whoever-the-guy-is. Ah yes, I understand. Intellectual types, you know what's going on in the real world and also in the world of Literature. The last few centuries at your fingertips. So, answer me, what is Doblin?"

"What is this peculiar word you keep repeating like a metronome?"

"Doblin, for God's sake. Something to do with this place in Berlin called Alexander-something. Our hostel is supposedly right next to it. That's another thing. Even if I offer to sponsor her accommodation in one of the more comfortable hotels, she insists on youth hostels with dormitories. Separate dormitories for sexes at that. Anyway, I know Dublin is in Ireland, but have never heard of Doblin. I can't even look it up with you having pinched my blackberry."

Sandeep thought for a while.

"Did she mention Biberkopf?"

The response was loud.

"She mentioned about a thousand names of that sort. Names full of consonants with one or two vowles thrown in as an afterthought. We were discussing the Warsaw Pact. I had looked it up on Wikipedia before the trip to impress her. I almost lost face confusing the Convention and the Pact."

Sandeep chuckled.

"She is certainly interesting. You can learn a lot from her."

"Let me take baby steps, Sandeep. Let me learn about this Alexander thing first."

"Well, I guess she was referring to *Berlin Alexanderplatz*, a novel by Alfred Doblin. Set in Berlin, around the Alexanderplatz district."

"Is it something to get excited about?"

"It may be, if that's your thing. Alexanderplatz during the time of the novel was the heart of Berlin's night life. As far as I know, after the Second World War, things changed. It became a major centre of GDR's redevelopment, with the TV tower and all that. And later, after the fall of the Berlin Wall, many of the buildings and structures were renovated. It's actually one of the places where you can see the old East and the young West side by side …"

"Fascinating, isn't it? Side by side? How do you know all this? Is it supposed to be general knowledge of normal people?"

"Well, I visited the Alex, Pritam. I had read up about it."

"You did, did you? I keep forgetting. You're not normal. Normal people don't travel on swapped identities. They don't think consultancy and sting operations are interchangeable. So, you've been to Berlin too? And your precious Alex. I'm sure you found Paris beneath your dignity."

"Well, I won't say that … After all Paris was the home to Proust, Gide and Celine."

"Celine Dion?"

"Er, let's just say that I did not have the funds to visit Paris. I've been to Berlin. Our *Tai Chi* team went there for a day. I understand how a place like that, with all the history, the communist flavour along with the consumerist icons will appeal to a girl like Shruti …"

"You understand, do you? You'd have loved this trip … You know where she wants to go apart from this damn Alexander place?"

"Well, I think I can guess. East Side Gallery, Checkpoint Charlie, Topographie of Horrors, Stasi Museum, Jewish Museum, Humboldt University…"

"Do you guys communicate on twitter? Or is it telepathy?"

Sandeep laughed.

"I was just trying to think of places that might interest her."

"You missed out the Holocaust Memorial and all the other sites remotely associated with the World War or the Cold War, most of them to be covered on walking tours when the sun is right up there. And, oh, did I mention the romantic getaway to the Sachsenhausen Concentration Camp?"

"I would have mentioned them too." He did not dare add that he found the itinerary fascinating.

"The Zoo, the aquarium, the Tiergarten with the beer drinking expanses, Unter den Linden, the Postdamerplatz shopping paradise … these hold no attractions for her. Neither do the art museums, where at least you can get away from the sun. And she intends spending an entire afternoon walking along the East Side Gallery…"

"Many people do that Pritam. It's a fascinating place. Artists from the world over …"

"What's so great about grafittied walls? There are plenty of them in India."

"Well, this is somewhat different …"

"The only difference will be the lack of stench, no one will probably pee on the walls here – I would have, if I was not worried about the cops and the complications of my officially presenting a paper in Amsterdam while being accosted urinating in Berlin. Why, one election in Kolkata and you get all the wall art you want."

"Sounds like you are having a whale of a time."

"You know the biggest problem? If I suggest an alternative, she says I am free to go around as I please. She will happily go off alone and join me in the evening."

"Emancipation, my friend."

"Well, the tour has just started. I'll definitely crack the morbid socio-political shell around her. The tension of having left my job on the sacrificial altar, on the non-existent shoulders of a scheming snake ... this should pay off somehow."

"Go for it, mate."

"Are you already in Amsterdam?"

"No ... in Frankfurt. Am on my way, don't worry."

"You can still take a flight back."

"No, my conscience won't let me."

"Conscience. Why don't you send a mail saying you are sick?"

"I'm sorry. A promise is a promise. I cannot let you down."

"Can't let me down, can you? Why have you changed the password to my *Axiom* mail id?"

"I have to check my – or rather your – mails, don't I? Relax. Don't take your focus off the job at hand. Concentrate on Shruti."

"Are you sure you can handle the presentation?"

"Piece of cake."

"Don't make yourself visible ... appear for the presentation and then scoot as soon as possible."

"I've already started looking for the Harry Potter invisibility cloak on eBay."

"Stop kidding around. You remember what to do in case of a difficult question?"

"Oh yes, don't worry."

"Repeat the same thing over and over again until the guy stops. Else tell him you will take it offline."

"It's a perfect science."

"Or ask him to think whether it is the right question."

"Also an art."

"Go over the presentation at least thirty times the day before you present it."

"You can count ... on it."

"Practise in front of the mirror."

"Do you really do that? Doesn't it nauseate you?"

"Shut up. Don't send emails from my account unless absolutely necessary."

"Of course."

"Don't flirt with girls ... I have a clean reputation."

"What do you take me for?"

"A snake. A lecherous snake at that. Don't draw any attention to yourself."

"I will take special lessons in camouflage from a certified chameleon. Being a snake myself, I just have to ask around in the reptilian brotherhood."

"Avoid the *Axiom* team members like plague."

"You sound like Polonius."

"Who?"

"A guy in Hamlet who was big on parting advice. Why don't you exchange notes with Moses about the ten commandments? I am on the verge of carelessly brushing my finger on the cancel button."

"Stop ... stop. Don't do that. Another thing. This damn European history, geography and current affairs ... This is getting on my nerves."

"Quite. I understand ..."

"I don't know what the Lisbon Treaty is. And I don't care. I don't give a damn if Polish and Czech presidents are dragging their feet over it."

"Klaus and Kaznysci."

"Whatever. Don't show off. Could you do me a favour? Could you send me a couple of slides – I mean slides as in a power-point presentation – which more or less tell the entire story of European politics?"

With a sad smile Sandeep disconnected the line and put his phone on silent.

Mail from Simon to his mailing list
Sub: What's up Buddy?

I know it is late and I have to be in office tomorrow, but my net-conscience will not allow me to sleep till I have cleared the name of the new Indian consultant.

I had not really been too kind to him in my blog and my thoughts, with the impending courtesy call in the evening nagging me at the back of my mind.

Grudgingly, with infinite distaste, I finally picked up my phone and called him at half past six. The voice that answered after the sixth ring sounded pretty confused.

When I informed him that I was from his office, he took a long time to respond.

"Office? Which fucking office?"

I realised my lack of thoughtfulness. I had not taken into account the three and a half hour time difference and no doubt, tired from the long flight, the poor fellow was already in bed.

I apologised just as he found his bearings and informed me that as I had supposed, he had fallen asleep and could not quite make out where the devil he was.

I informed him that I was supposed to be his official buddy.

"What is that ingenious oxymoron supposed to mean?" he asked, winning my eternal respect.

When I explained to him that I was supposed to accompany him to lunches, show him around the office and generally ensure that he had everything that he needed, from office stationery to inside information about grocery stores, banks and bars, I distinctly heard him choke.

"Is it absolutely necessary for you to be my designated haemorrhoid ?" he asked after a slightly uncomfortable silence. Unaccustomed to such expressions from Indian colleagues, I searched for an answer. His next question was more cryptic.

"Do you have a price?"

Obviously, I asked him to clarify adding that I was expected by the company to play this role.

"How much will you take to get off my back and leave me alone?" He added that if I left him to himself, after pointing out exactly where he could access the office stationery, and resisted my burning compulsion to accompany him to bars and Albert Heijns every waking moment, he would swear to my bosses that I had been as inseparable from him as a piece of sticking plaster. He even offered to buy me a round of beer if I promised a lack of zealous effort.

Needless to say, I was delighted and thanked him profusely, not hesitating to voice my opinion about the ridiculousness of this so called best practice. I welcomed him and wished him luck for the presentation of the paper.

He must have dozed off even as I was speaking for he wondered which f***ing paper I had in mind. When I said that celebrities of *Axiom* had been lined up to fill the front row, dignitaries including the Vice President of Continental Europe, he gave the impression of being puzzled that the continent had its own designated Vice President.

It was great to find such an accomplished consultant indulging in light hearted banter even when jet lagged and sleepy. I did not want to disturb him any longer and hung up, a huge weight off my shoulders and a recharged smile on my lips.

Some of my colleagues are turning out to be unconventional enough to be interesting. An encouraging sign.

Cheers
Simon

XIII

"Good morning, Pritam, this is Madhu Deb," the booming voice bursting with bonhomie hit the aspiring author smack between his eardrums. Sandeep's groggy reaction was one of a shell-shocked rabbit caught between the aural equivalent of headlights. "I hope I didn't wake you up."

Sandeep clutched his temples and followed it up by squeezing the bridge of his nose.

"Sorry to dash your hopes, but you did that to perfection."

There was a brief period of silence. Sandeep tried to recall who on earth Madhu Deb was. The voice over the cellular network sounded vaguely familiar.

"I am so sorry, Pritam, I understand you are jet lagged," Madhu Deb sounded apologetic. "I know your paper presentation is tomorrow and if you want to go back to sleep, please pop back in bed by all means. I just wanted to find out if you would be attending the conference today."

The image of the woman behind the flamboyant fellow feeling floated fuzzily into Sandeep's sleepy surface of consciousness. Something short, beaming and bloated. He had met her on that fateful day he had trotted up to the HMH premises to introduce himself as Pritam, leaving his consultant friend to battle the after effects of one and a half bottles of Jamaican rum.

There had been two of them. A shifty eyed man in his late forties and this friendly fleshy female half a decade or so younger.

The former had been brisk, taking fifteen minutes to welcome him and point out the importance of the paper and how it could differentiate *Axiom* as a service provider in the huge HMH organization. For some reason his eyes had kept hastening to the door, the laptop and sometimes behind himself in fast, furtive glances, as if expecting unpleasant surprises around every corner of space and time.

The latter had consumed a couple of hours in an elaborate attempt to get to know him, but had not really gone beyond introducing herself. Within seven minutes or so, Sandeep had learnt that she had started out as a consultant herself and had spent a considerable period in the United States. After those seven minutes, Sandeep had stopped listening – being vaguely aware that the conversation – or monologue – had centred predominantly around a kid named Hidori.

Now as he listened with sleep deprived ears, he deduced that it was this self-same superior, with the full force of friendliness unabated.

"Er . . ." he hesitated. Pritam had advised him to avoid the management. Today would be the first day of the conference, and he thought he would slip in at some point of time to get an overall idea of the proceedings. "I think I will drop in sometime later during the day."

"That's perfect," the voice boomed back. "There will be *Axiom* people around. If you spot one of them just pass the message that you are here. I will come by. But, there is no hurry."

"Um. . . quite. Sounds good."

"I thought of asking you to join me for lunch, but I . . ."

"Er, no . . . I . . . I am kind of fasting today."

"Fasting?"

"Er, yes. Helps me get the old biological clock ticking."

"That's nice," the voice was tinged with good humour now. "I should try that sometime. Although the first thing I do on reaching a new country is to try out their cuisine."

Sandeep looked longingly at the bed. The event organisers sponsoring the stay had put him up at the Novotel. The hotel bed was comfort itself wrapped into a six by six frame.

The lady continued. "That's somewhat of a constraint here, though. Dutch food is not really well known for variety. I take it as a blessing that my son has adjusted to the local food . Hidori is ..."

"My ... my phone is ringing ..."

"Is it? But, I am talking to you ..."

"Yes. It's the hotel phone. I guess it's my wife from India. I have to cut you off ... sorry about that."

"Wife? I did not know you were married."

Sandeep put the phone down and massaged his temples.

The clock showed fifteen minutes past nine. The infernal female.

After a few brief, futile attempts to go back to sleep, Sandeep got up and switched on his Compaq Presario. The painstakingly compiled spreadsheet listing all the promising agents and publishers across the great countries of USA and UK stared back at him. He had consolidated the information from the Writers Handbook of the year, with colour coded cells denoting the degrees of promise.

He had based his list on a number of factors. Acceptance of emailed-ed query letters, probable time to respond, with supposed attitude towards new authors being the top priority. There were other factors too, depending upon the preference for particular types of fiction, Diaspora centred novels, someone remotely Indian among the names of the listed agents of the company. He now sat down and zeroed in on four of the most encouraging.

He followed this by pulling up his prepared query letter and creating four copies addressed to the different agents. Minor modifications – in some cases major ones – were required due to the contrasting interests specified by the agent web sites and the Writers Handbook.

The next step was to prepare the synopsis. He had already prepared a generic outline. Now, he went through the steps of making four copies – each altered in subtle ways to meet the demands and the profiles of the agents. The *hook* had to be different, the *storyline* had to be presented in diverse ways to fit the style of existing authors these agents represented, to make one's novel seem as close to their expertise and expectations as possible. In some cases, it was also necessary to mention why the book was likely to be a winner in the contemporary market. One had to list the success of similar works. These basic steps were outlined by the numerous books and web sites listing guidelines for new authors.

All this was painstaking work. The hours passed by, and by the time the four sets were ready, Sandeep was famished. As he sat with the frozen dinner at half past three in the afternoon, he reviewed the four sets meticulously. According to the several books and web sites he had referred to, the actual writing of the masterpiece was about 10% of the work. The real challenge started after that.

As he ate, he surfed the net in search of book reading sessions in local stores. This was another *valuable* piece of advice picked up from the instruction manuals for unpublished authors. Get to know the authors. If their style matched yours, go up to them and get friendly. Most of them would not grudge sharing the names of their agents. And if you got lucky, some of them could also refer you to their agents and publishers. A more fruitful relationship might end up in the author's accolades on the back cover of your book.

By the time he had mentally gone through all the recommendations available for his breed, provided by the authors of these bestselling books on producing best sellers, he became distinctly aware of his jet lag.

He clicked the desktop shortcut to minimise all the windows– the query letters, synopses, first three chapters in some cases, first five chapters in others, three sample chapters in still others, the spreadsheet of short listed agents and publishers, and the Googled up responses for book reading sessions in the local English language book stores in and around Amsterdam. The green landscape of Windows XP appeared from behind the minimised windows and he stared at it to try and regain some semblance of sanity.

Swallowing the micro-waved spaghetti and meat balls, his mind, numbed by the long flight, disturbed sleep and the editing of the last few hours went into a reverie. Soon, his imagination was playing him tricks. On corners of the wallpaper appeared healthy spotted cows and lazily elegant horses, grazing alongside quaint windmills. In short, in his semi conscious mind, the familiar European landscapes merged with the Windows XP desktop. As the focus returned and the windmills stopped rotating, the imagined cows and horses disappeared from the screen, Sandeep found himself thinking of Amsterdam followed by Berlin, Dresden, Prague, Bratislava, Budapest … Soon, he was going over the email received the previous night.

Nations small, diverse
Economy staggering –
Europe – enigma

If you think that's too much realism for a poetic form about abstract realisations of the soul, I am sorry. But, I find Europe fascinating in a lot of ways which are more social and historical than scenic. I agree Basho would have cut through the greenery of the landscape with the delicacy of an ikebana sensei with seventeen exquisite syllables. However, much as I enjoy the sights as the train rushes through one colour of green to the next, with quaint towns scattered around old churches, I find the natural beauty too perfect to pen down with interest. Not a blade of grass out of place! It is the imperfection in the world that produces the greatest art forms. The long fingered Professor once mentioned an old Chinese saying that readers like to discover six printing mistakes in a book. I'd rather look at the interesting blemishes than fascinating flawlessness.

So, how are your literary adventures shaping up? Are you finding time to write, now that you are back in the rat race?

Best wishes,
Shruti

~ ~ ~

Blog of Simple Simon
Tags: Crisis, Industry, Corporation, Brand, Soul

Is Crisis an industry?

In the curious consciousness of the business world, this would be a profound thought. Somehow, this relentless quest for making more and more money, which has, in my opinion, landed us in this financial soup, has been reformatted by the corporations into something along the lines of eternal strife for knowledge, truth and God.

This is nothing new. Modern day business barons have somehow managed to embed the illusion of a soul into their ruthless ventures. A pretty ancient principle called the Brand has reached ridiculous proportions today. Products, which ultimately anyone can manufacture, has taken the back seat, and the brand has become far more important. The value, the conscience of the corporate identity, that extra component which can only be termed spiritual.

For example, the Nike president Tom Clark, who also doubled up as the sneaker shaman, spoke of keeping the magic of sports alive – the inspiration of sports allowing us to be reborn constantly. It was much more than selling shoes.

In this setting of corporate transcendence, it is quite natural for the facade of interpretations of the financial crisis to include pseudo metaphysical diversions. The rampant reactions of the so called pundits of the markets – none of whom foresaw this slump – range from intelligent afterthoughts to philosophical ponderings. A huge cult seems to have grown out of the worship of the Money God, and like any other civilization, they seem to be developing their own religion, philosophy, rules and value system. Or is it value laundering, the washing of the dirty soul corrupted by the pursuit of material wealth?

Enough of my philosophical digressions.

The reason for all this rambling is that out of the compulsion of being the official buddy of our new consultant, I had to spend a considerable amount of time and energy sitting through presentations by the high and mighty of the financial world. Everyone had formulae for dealing with the crisis, converted into gimmicky slides and presented with the seasoned composure of consulting professionals. I kept listening to half the things that were being said while looking for my elusive buddy, who, according to our Senior Manager, would be turning up sometime during the day. Thankfully, two others shared the task. All of us were wearing our blue *Axiom* shirts as instructed, with the company logo and the Brand statement – *Service is Axiomatic.*

The objective of our search, however, remained elusive. I had sat through too many financial expositions and by the time a certain gentleman in a crisis defying tuxedo started speaking I was already wondering whether or not we were converting the crisis into an industry.

I was listening with some interest to the arguments of the speaker. Every natural or man-made phenomenon with considerable publicity, according to his view, ultimately bowed to the rules of economics and ended up becoming a marketable commodity. Soon it spiralled out of control of the individual and the organisation and became an extension of itself modelled passively by its consumers. He argued that even the financial crisis, because of the tremendous hype and the associated apprehension surrounding it, had already become a marketable entity around which industries were starting to grow.

Unfortunately at this point of time, with the slides becoming more technical with an increasing gamut of jargon, my attention wavered and I walked out of the room. The remote likelihood of all this banter leading to something concrete remained blissfully unexplored.

Mail from Simple Simon to his mailing group
Sub: The Unusual Indian

As I walked out of the conference room alluded to in my blog, I walked into a new experience which promises to be unusually exciting for a mundane corporate world.

Outside, in the large lobby, Amrita was engaged in animated discussion with someone seated hidden behind one of the pillars. Walking in their direction, I saw the renowned *Axiom* consultant for the first time. He was sitting with a laptop on his knee, a mop of unruly hair on his head, the pillar almost strategically chosen to hide him from public view. He looked quite young and as I approached them from the rear, I could see Amrita bubbling with laughter at something he was saying.

" ... I really have to ensure that I modify all my material so that I no longer understand them, you see," I heard him saying as I came within earshot. " ... else I won't really fit into this conference. I also need to test the presentation on a couple of hardcore insomniacs. If I can't get their eyelids heavy within the first sixteen and a half seconds, I must consider myself unprepared – going by the current standards. This involves a lot of work ... and I really cannot afford a long familiarisation talk ..."

Accustomed to regular conversations with my friendly young female colleague, I could vouch that she was not following much of what was being said. She is quite an intelligent girl, but as far as her English is concerned, she has her limitations. But nevertheless, she was enjoying the sarcastic humour.

She glanced up at me and smiled widely.

"This is Simon," she pointed. "He's my colleague from *Axiom*."

The consultant turned around and stood up. He had an uncommonly strapping, athletic build for an Indian professional. Given his experience, I had already budgeted for a proportional paunch, but he could easily pass for a sporty twenty five year old.

"Ah," he responded in recognition, pointing with his index finger. "Haemorrhoid."

"No, he is from *Axiom* only," Amrita hastened to correct his misconception. Poor girl. She must have heard the word for the first time in her life. I could not help but chuckle and Pritam joined in.

"Of course. That's axiomatic given he is my designated buddy," he laughed.

Amrita's smile remained on her face, but her eyes confessed confusion. The experienced professional patted her shoulder.

"Never mind. I just meant that we know each other. We have spoken on the phone. I already owe him a beer, but he has to earn it by sticking to our agreement and not to my back."

It was a bit too cryptic for Amrita. Trisha on the other hand would have enjoyed the exchange, although, I dare say, she would have pretended not to have understood much of it later on.

"As I was saying to your friend out here," Pritam continued. "I have to work on the presentation ..."

I smiled. "To make it fit in?"

"Yes. Make it sufficiently incomprehensible from the third slide onwards. I also have to test it on a couple of ..."

"Insomniacs."

"Right ... You are real quick on the uptake. "

"Some of the presentations are a bit different though," I added. "I was listening to this one on the Crisis being an Industry, and before it became a tad too academic, I was able to follow pretty well for the first dozen slides or so. Interesting topic, don't you think?"

I noticed a perceptible change in him. He became guarded, choosing his words carefully.

"Not much room for discussion there. A five day seminar on crisis control ... Isn't that an industry?" He looked at my nametag. "Simon van der Wiel. But from your accent, I could have sworn you were from the west coast."

I laughed.

"I grew up in Oregon."

"That's cool. No Henry Higgins, but I am pretty good at accents."

I laughed again, but added in a whisper. "Keep it to yourself, though. I have been recruited primarily to be a Dutch face – and tongue – for the company."

Both of us turned towards Amrita while laughing at our own jokes, and Pritam deliberately changed the conversation to include her.

"To get back to what I was saying, it is extremely important that I change the presentation ... and for that I need time. I can't afford a couple of hours for getting to know people of the account and that sort of . . . thing ..."

It was a pretty undiplomatic thing to say to rank juniors given the standards, protocols and brand consciousness professed by the organisation, but there was an earnestness that was infectious. Amrita, I could make out, was already a big fan.

It was what he said after this which made my day.

"I know you guys are here to report back to the head quarters whenever you spot me dead or alive ... and given some of the presentations that I sampled, it would be a fifty-fifty affair, with a slight but distinct edge towards the morbid," he checked himself again, noticing the vacant smile of Amrita. "But, could you do me a favour and be somewhat late in sharing the good news ... If some weighty footsteps do grace the conference because of the tidings ... news, that is, ... please convey that I left the premises immediately as they entered. You see, there are things in life one has to attend to. At this juncture of my life, although I love little kids – in the strict non-paedophilic sense – I am slightly apprehensive about listening to minute by minute updates of the chequered life of a four year old."

As I could not stop myself from laughing out loud, the exceptional man turned to paraphrase it for Amrita.

"Your manager likes to talk about her son. I will keep a day aside for her sometime later – considerably later – but today I prefer to go to the hotel and work on my presentation."

Amrita giggled with her hand near her heart. We all have been ravaged by the Hidori stories.

"You can count on us," I said, beaming.

"Incidentally, why is he called Hidori? Odd name."

I winced. It had been explained to me in graphic detail about seven times going by the last count.

"They wanted to name him Misha after the mascot of the Moscow Olympics. But, a cousin of Madhu had a son when she was a couple of weeks from delivering, and named her child Misha. So, Madhu and her husband picked the next mascot that came to their mind."

The consultant nodded. "I see a well prepared answer. And a hint of pain. No wonder you have been subject to the explanation once too many."

I was becoming a devoted fan with every passing minute.

"So, I'll see you tomorrow," Pritam said and shook hands with us.

We were about to leave when he called me back.

"Simon, a word."

I went up to him and saw him trying to push his laptop into a satchel full of books.

"Are you coming to the presentation tomorrow?"

I informed him that I was.

"Could I trouble you to get me some company stationery? .... I would require about a dozen large envelopes capable of holding around sixty A4 sheets."

"Of course."

"Can you bring some postage stamps as well?"

"Would you like to have *Axiom's* Fedex and TNT numbers?" I asked, slightly puzzled by the request.

"That would be great," he was genuinely pleased. "Really appreciate it."

All through the way back to the HMH building, Amrita kept recounting the many hilarious quotes that we had been blessed with.

During my stint in the company I have realised two things.

One, the Indian organisations are hierarchical to the extreme. The reporting lines and the chains of command are almost sacrosanct. So very different to the Dutch way.

Secondly, the limited number of Bollywood films I have watched out of interest or recommendation, and the discussions I have heard among my Indian friends and colleagues about them, all seem to point towards a certain fascination for the anti establishmentarian icon.

In my opinion, this enchantment is a direct result of the hierarchical structure of the society.

Right now, I could make out the two principles working to convert Amrita into an admirer of this unconventional newcomer.

At the same time, I can't deny that I myself found the approach of the senior consultant really refreshing. I hope he is not serious about making the presentation dull ... because I will be there for the session and I have witnessed the potential of something really interesting.

Cheers
Simon

∾ ∾ ∾

Dear Sandeep,

Thanks for considering me. After careful consideration, I don't think my agency is the right one for your novel – The Dutch Gambit.

Please note that the decision is not a reflection of the quality or the literary merits of your work.

Wishing you all the best for your literary journey.

Yours sincerely,
Joe Snider

That was quick, thought Sandeep as he changed the colour of the row listing the Snider Literary Agency in his Agents and Publishers spreadsheet to grey. One day for a rejection slip through email. He wondered if the agency used an auto-responder. So much for careful consideration.

XIV

The phone rang early in the morning as Sandeep was about to step into the grasp horse's tail position of the long form. It did nothing to brighten his mood.

The view out of the window was one of the worst that one could bargain for in Amsterdam. Wet gloomy weather aside, Rai was unlike the beautiful city in every possible way. The picturesque canals and the quaint brick architecture were conspicuously absent. Neither had he a view of the winding Amstel.

The previous evening had been spent in preparing more synopses, query letters and blurbs for more agents. A long telephone call had followed during which Sunil Pillay had done his best to explain his failure to deliver copies of the book before his departure. When at half past ten he had finally tried to go over Pritam's presentation, he had surrendered to sleep after a brief one sided skirmish.

He grabbed the cell phone and barked an unfriendly hello into it.

"Who the hell is Billy Pilgrim?" demanded the ruffled voice of the man he was impersonating.

Sandeep blinked.

"Is this a coded message? Have you actually got entangled in the cold war?"

From the neighbouring country, Pritam snapped back. "This is no time for wisecracks. Who the hell is he?"

Sandeep inhaled and exhaled in the method prescribed by many of the soft martial arts.

"If you don't mind my saying so, your timing for practical jokes leaves much to be desired. You may not realise it, being miles away from the scene, but I do have to make an important presentation today."

In an elaborate sentence etched with colourful vocabulary, Pritam said that he knew b*** well that he had to f*** make a f*** presentation.

"And I bloody well hope that you are going to pass that half hour without hitches and get the hell out of there. Now, tell me who is Billy Pilgrim."

Sandeep sat on the bed.

"Are you in Dresden?"

"It's our next stop."

"Do you remember our talk about *Slaughterhouse Five?*"

"Slaughter what?"

Sandeep sighed.

"*Slaughterhouse Five.* Kurt Vonnegut's novel about the Dresden bombings ..."

"Blasted bombings. The whole country seems to have a fascination for bombs."

"Well, I would not exactly put it that way ... But, Billy Pilgrim is the main character of the book."

"So that's the hue and cry about Billy Pilgrim. She referred to him about twenty times during dinner...and all I could do was smile like an idiot. The internet kiosks at the hostel are always occupied, so I couldn't even wiki it. I am sharing my room with a bunch of Estonians, who wouldn't really be delighted if I woke them up and asked about this precious guy. Have the two of you read all the books that have ever been published?"

"No. I definitely haven't read *The McKinsey Way*. So how was the concentration camp?"

"I am living through it. And after a scorching afternoon at the Sachenhausen, after going through all the scintillatingly gruesome stories of the holocaust, seeing the prison cells and hospitals and burials and baths, I returned to Berlin and mixed up between Estonia and Slovenia. Add to that her penchant for biking and walking in sweltering heat. Not for her the air conditioned hotel rooms or shaded hop on hop off bus trips. She has driven me within striking distance of a heat stroke."

"Enjoy yourself."

"Now this Billy Pilgrim thing is the last opportunity to score some points and redeem myself. Could you tell me something more about him?"

Sandeep thought for a while.

"Well, he could travel through time for one thing."

"He could, could he? I wish I could do the same and change the events. At least the part of going ahead with this ridiculous scheme. Who writes this crap?"

"Kurt Vonnegut, as mentioned. It's a modern classic."

Pritam grunted.

"Are you ready for the presentation?"

"I will manage."

"Spend the half hour and scoot from the vicinity. Have you interacted with the people from *Axiom?*"

"Only with a couple of junior resources. I've avoided the senior management like the plague."

"That's good."

"And oh ... I forgot to mention. You are married."

"What?"

"You are married. You received a call from your wife yesterday morning."

"What on earth are you talking about?"

"Sorry buddy, but I had to say that to get a persistent senior manager off my back. All in your best interest, mind you ..."

There was a long pause. Sandeep could sense Pritam grappling with the piece of information. He felt sorry for his friend. Going through a taxing socio-political and literary examination in the guise of romance, this sudden change in marital status was not exactly welcome news.

"Sandeep, I ..." for a few moments Sandeep braced himself for the most telling of verbal onslaughts. However, when communication resumed from the other end, it was a miraculous change for the better. The voice was friendly, relaxed and cheerful – a transformation so remarkable that it had even changed its sex.

"Hi Sandeep, I had no idea that you were available on the shelf for conversation."

The gloom surrounding the atmosphere, the view, the fate of his first and second novels and the impending threat of the conference suddenly lifted. There was glorious sunshine and chirping song birds everywhere.

"Hi, my fair lady. How is your continental campaign shaping up?"

"Having a great time myself. Can't say the same for your friend, though."

"I gather as much from the poor soul. Why make him hop through hopeless historical hoops?"

"Astute alliteration, I must say."

"You inspire me to greatness. Why make him plough pitifully in political playgrounds?"

"You outdo yourself."

"Why lead the lover-boy through literary labyrinths?"

"You do know lover boy has a different meaning in Amsterdam."

"Why tie him in knowledge knots involving Berlin Alexanderplatz and Billy Pilgrim?"

There was the familiar lilt of loud laughter which warmed the cockles of Sandeep's heart.

"Knowledge knots ... that's an alliteration of some distinction. Is it the pronounced n or the spelt k that should be considered? The beauty of it is that it is valid both ways. However, to answer your quaint queries, there is always the risk of giving secrets away to a sympathiser of the opposite camp."

"I am a neutral negotiator in this curious cold war."

"Remember, I am trusting you here in a big way. There are roads he can take ... The choice is his. And he cannot deviate from his professional path of the consultant. He cannot admit lack of knowledge about anything."

"His *kula dharma.*"

Shruti laughed again.

"I see the influence of our long fingered friend. What about you? Have you adjusted to your current *dharma*?"

Sandeep thought for a while.

"I guess you showed me the way."

"And what exactly does that mean?"

"Choosing one's own path. The Professor was singing praises of your writing skills."

"He is too kind. What about you? Any response from agents?"

"Yes. I am developing a scintillating collection of rejection slips."

"What about your previous novel?"

"It's beginning to resemble the moon mission. The launch date keeps getting postponed."

"Keep your fingers crossed. And don't talk about the absurdity of cross fingered writers."

"I may have to limit myself to footnotes."

"Something will turn up."

"A la Micawber."

"Yes ... whenever it seems to be the worst of times, it also is the best of times. As Dickens said in the Tale of Two Cities."

"As long as one keeps his head. A tad difficult in the times he described in the book."

"We won't stop unless our cell-phones run out of battery. Or my travelling companion runs out of patience. He is standing here waving his arms and legs, doing a fairly decent impersonation of an octopus. Why is he agitated?"

"Probably he feels like the ancient mariner."

"What do you mean? Oh, I see ... I can't help him there, though."

"Can you go easy on the European Political scenario stuff?"

"Does he keep using you as a dial in Google service?"

"He has reason to be under a lot of stress. On top of that some joker changed his marital status in his company ..."

"I don't think he will allow me to carry on any longer ... Here he is – all yours."

The voice changed back into gruff, edgy, tense and threatening.

"What do you mean by my marital status ..."

Sandeep sighed and brushed his thumb against the cancel button.

~ ~ ~

Emails between Sunil Pillay and Sandeep

Dear Sandeep,

Sorry for the delay, but attached is the cover art work of your book. Please let me know if it looks good.

Sunil

Dear Sunil,

What you have sent is the image of a cartoon version of one of the more complicated positions of kama sutra. Enjoyable although it undoubtedly is, and uplifting in some crude sense and sensuality, it is definitely not what I would like to see as the cover illustration of my book.

Sandeep

Dear Sandeep,

Sorry for the mix up. Here is the real thing. Forget the previous one – a joke sent by a friend.

Sunil

Dear Sunil,

In recent times I have been quite critical of you – and justifiably so considering the interminable delays encountered and the carefree promises that you've been prolific at not keeping. But, the cover work really rocks. I love it. Give my regards to the designer and illustrator.

Now, could you please go ahead and finish the process of publication?

Sandeep

Mail from Simon to Mailing List

Sub: The Undercover and the Economist

After today I can look back at this turbulent period of financial history and say that I did play a part – a part few can probably claim to have played.

I never imagined office life – the same life that I have been leading for a year or so –would suddenly change into something this interesting. And this unorthodox.

I was already at the conference theatre of the sprawling Amsterdamsepoort building of ING when Madhu tugged at my sleeve.

"Where is your buddy?" she asked in a loud stage whisper. I could see the front row of the auditorium, where an almost apoplectic Ajay stood, wiping his brow. Beside him was K. Ramesh, the head of the Continental Europe operations of *Axiom*. It was just twenty minutes to the scheduled start of the presentation by Pritam Mitra and he was nowhere to be seen. It seemed that both Madhu and Ajay had called him up several times, repeatedly coming up against a Dutch voice message.

I went out of the hall and tried his number. Pritam answered on the second ring.

"Hi Simon."

"Where are you?"

"I am at the Bijlmer Arena ... getting off the train. I will take ten more minutes."

I met him at the lobby of the reception, handing over the stationery he had asked for along with the Fedex account number of *Axiom*. He looked pretty dashing in his suit and tie which looked brand new.

"What a building," he exclaimed. "It starts at one end of the block and goes on and on and on. If Shakespeare had seen it he would have used the setting for a sequel of Hamlet . Only Hamlet would have been called Hans or Joost or Jaap. And all Laertes would have to do was to go to another wing rather than all the way to France. Sorry for being late. Actually I had to take a few print outs in colour."

I told him that Ajay would soon have cardiac arrest if he made him wait any longer.

"Pretty strong argument for vanishing altogether. Why is he so worried?"

"Because K.Ramesh is here."

"Who is K. Ramesh?"

I laughed at his pleasantry. However, after a minute I realised that he really had no idea.

"He is the Vice President of the Continental Europe operations of *Axiom*"

"Why do I have a vague feeling that I have heard of him?"

"He is important in *Axiom*. Almost everyday there are newsletters and mails about him."

"I don't read them. Life is short. I would rather spend my numbered reading hours on Dickens and Dostoyevsky"

"I mentioned him once, remember? During our first conversation – when you had just landed."

His face cleared.

"Ah yes, that had moved to one of the remote unused corners of memory. Why is he here?"

"For your presentation. Watch out ..."

Pritam had stumbled on something, and took some time to steady himself.

"I'd say that someone as important as this Ramesh should have better things to occupy his time."

"He seems to see this as a business opportunity. Crisis control paper at a prestigious conference and all that."

"Aha!"

He was on the verge of adding something when Madhu came out with the big smile on her face and the perpetual bounce in her stride.

"There you are," she approached my buddy with characteristic bonhomie and had wiggled around the offered hand to grasp him into a hug. The consultant looked more than a little disconcerted.

"I didn't know you were married," she continued.

There was a pause while Pritam looked around the room. Something in his gaze suggested a wistful longing for the pillar of the previous evening.

"Er ... it's a recent development. We've just gone through the legal formalities, the social function hasn't taken place yet."

Madhu laughed.

"I guess that was the main reason for your making off to India for a week."

"Um ... you could say so. Seems to fit in."

"Was it arranged or love?"

As so often happens in my conversations with the good lady, I could see Pritam gasping for air.

"Uh ... Love marriage hastily arranged."

"Wow. And what's the name of the lucky girl?"

For a moment the face of the consultant turned blank, as if all his faculties had suddenly decided to go on a synchronised strike. As Madhu hung on to his lips, expecting the answer to her million euro question, the man himself seemed to grapple with some unseen foe within the recesses of his mind. With Amrita and Trisha joining in during the last bit of conversation, the erstwhile bright pair of eyes scanned the growing number of faces with a vacant gaze. The silence was embarrassing.

Suddenly light peeped through in those eyes. The unseen mental foe seemed overcome. The faculties called back with urgent summons. The face, animated with inspiration, looked at our expectant gazes with a hint of a smile as the lips parted to utter one word.

"Shruti."

"Congratulations," said the leading lady, followed by the minor ones.

There was a trace of bewilderment as he shook the offered hands.

"All the best for the presentation," Amrita offered.

Ajay approached us with Ramesh by his side. More important hands were shaken.

"We are counting on you," Ramesh beamed at him. Pritam reached for a glass of water. He ended up spilling most of it on his new suit. I wondered if it was a case of nerves. But, people in his profession made presentations all the time.

Even though in the organisation structure of an Indian company Trisha, Amrita and I are insignificant small fry compared to the greater piscine echelons represented by Madhu, Ajay and Ramesh, we were all representing *Axiom* and, therefore, sharing the same space and breathing the hallowed air as the high and mighty. This enabled me to hear snatches of the conversation that went on between Ajay and Pritam.

"I sent a couple of mails asking for the deck that you are going to present."

"Deck? All I have is a presentation. And I am not really going to present that."

There was an uncomfortable silence.

"You see, the directors in Bangalore will want a report on the event including the full presentation."

"That is difficult."

"We have the IPR on any academic paper that is produced by employees ...The bosses will be ..."

Madhu had by now engaged herself in a loud and jovial discussion with Ramesh. So, the rest of the conversation was washed away by the rollicking sound-waves. However, within a couple of minutes, Pritam was back beside me.

"Simon, you are my official buddy, aren't you?"

"Yes, still says so on paper."

"I need your help."

"Sure."

He pulled me away from popular earshot to his favourite spot behind the pillar.

"Ajay wants me to send the exact details of whatever I present."

I nodded.

"You can send him the presentation, can't you?"

"There is no presentation."

This was a real shocker.

"Eh?"

"There is one, but I don't know what's in it. It's complicated."

"Someone else made it for you?" I asked. It always happens in the rarefied upper strata of the organisation.

"Well, that's one way of looking at it. Forget it. The bottom line is that someone has to record what is being said."

I did not like it.

"You want me to take notes? I am not too good at it."

"Nothing of that sort. Here, look." Like a wizard, he produced a cellular phone from his pocket. He pulled up the display and it became three times as long.

"A bit dated if you consider the latest models, but still a very powerful video camera," he continued. Even as I tried to draw some sense into what was going on, he was already showing me how to operate it. "Just press this button to start recording. The camera is right on top and there is no telltale light. So, if you put this in your pocket, and keep the aperture of the camera unconcealed, you can capture the entire presentation without moving from your place. Now go ahead and sit in the middle of the first row. Whenever you need to focus on some other thing, you can use this touchpad. Trust me, I have done this sort of thing."

I wondered whether he was serious.

"Of course. Simon, there is a time and place for rhetorical questions. Now let me fix this up for you."

The authority in his voice made it difficult, but still I protested feebly.

"Are you sure it's legal?"

"Are you sure that's the right question? Think about it."

"What do you mean?"

"I can't say for sure, but relax ... there is very little probability of this being allowed, so it will be fun."

"But ..."

"There's plenty of battery and the memory stick runs for one hour and five minutes. We will be done way before that."

With this reassurance, he left me with this cloak and dagger stuff and walked towards the podium.

The casual disregard for convention was infectious. It took me about five seconds to let the growing excitement disperse whatever ethical doubt had bubbled up from the seat of conscience. I hurried to take my seat as recommended by this extraordinary consultant.

The entire blog post that I have posted today this is based on the video recording carried out from the pocket of my coat. There are a few observations I have inserted, but most of the text comes directly from the resulting mpeg file downloaded on to my laptop minutes after the session.

Cheers
Simon

XV

Blog of Simple Simon posted at 8:09 PM

Tags: Financial crisis, philosophy, puzzle

What follows is the transcript of the talk given by Pritam Mitra of Axiom at the conference on crisis control in Amsterdam.

Ladies and Gentlemen.

I am here to talk about the role of an agent of change during the severe financial slump. And I intend to live up to the title – at least for this session.

I have brought about changes already, having arrived here for a presentation without a slide show.

(Audible reaction. Members of *Axiom* look around uncertainly.)

There will be no graphic, no picture more eloquent than ten thousand words. I am here to take oratory back to the classical age. When gizmos had not taken over the power to communicate. When the knowledge of the world had not been limited to the confines of power-point slides. When great works that still stand out in the traditions of the major cultures of the world as mythology and classics were handed down from generation to generation by word of mouth, stories told and retold. Continuous narration in simple language when the listener could not ask the narrator to wait while he glanced at the footnotes.

I see that this revelation has already had the effect of making you sit up and take notice. That is my intention. The hours of making the presentations, browsing the net to come up with the correct pictures, using the overhead projector and laptop, all have their associated cost components. And when talking of ways and means to reduce costs, why not start by slashing these very basic expenditures?

(Seated in the second row, the CEO of HMH, Dave de Boer, , laughs audibly. The atmosphere of the entire hall became exponentially lighter – the far reaching ripples of the important laughter echoes in every corner, parting the tensely pursed lips of the *Axiom* contingent into hesitant smiles.)

I am here to talk about how to expedite the change process that has to be performed, in spite of the difficult decisions that often have to be rolled out. I guess people expect me to talk about Change Management. I am expected to speak about Unfreezing, Changing and Refreezing, of McKinsey's 7S model, Lewin's Change Management methodology , Kotter's eight step system, of ADKAR and Dynamic Conservatism. The last time I heard someone speak about these theories, a bottle of excellent Jamaican Rum was emptied over his head. Captain Morgan if I remember correctly. Neat.

(The audience burst out laughing. Dave De Boer joins in too, and by induction the Axiom team.)

And let me tell you that theory is not going to help you here. No dogma will assist you other than the time tested way of looking at the problem objectively and finding ways to solve it – and before that, deciding whether or not you really want to solve it.

The solution to the problem lies not with the process of implementation but with the people. And the problems are genuine.

During rationalisation, one sees before oneself colleagues and friends, coaches and protégés, leaders and reportees, trainers and trainees, lunch mates and buddies. There are planners of one's work and the implementers of one's plans. One sees well wishers and team mates. One sees his very own colleagues gathered together to fight for survival. Then one's fingers fail oneself, the Thinkpad slips from one's grip. One's logic quivers. One is confused. One sees ill omen. One sees no good at snatching jobs from one's own colleagues and friends. One goes through this process of change and feels that he doesn't want to work anymore. He does not want euros.

What use is the euro when the very people for whom one used to wish success and happiness are the ones standing here, ready for the struggle for survival? They are the ones who have sacrificed their family and personal lives for all of us. Friends, trainers, seniors , leaders, PMO and analysts. The decision makers don't want to snatch away their jobs. What pleasure can there be in snatching away the jobs from trusted team members? It is a crime to snatch lives from the worst of enemies. So, is it right to take away the livelihood of our trusted colleagues?

Why change the ways of the past? Why unsettle our world by taking on roles other than what we are used to? These are people we have worked with for years. Why take their jobs away for the sake of supposed increase of revenue? We are ready to kill our own friends, our habits and ways of working because of profits that the organisation covets. Is it desirable? Much better if the changing winds in the organisation blew us away, and we ceased to work rather than working in the new fangled ways, breaking the trust of our own people.

(A faint hint of a smile touches the lips of K. Ramesh. In a nervous reincarnation, it finds reflection in the other lips of Axiom.)

However, the ideal change agent shows the way. He makes it clear that this sort of doubt is unprofessional. There is wisdom in such words. The true professional mourns neither the employed nor the jobless. It is not as if anyone was not without a job at any point of time. Professionals only dwell in the garb of their jobs. When jobs are taken away, they just change over and attach themselves to the next garb that comes their way. The spirit of professionalism lives on as one moves from job to job.

The question for change is more complex.

People change, work force changes flitting from organisation to organisation, everyone strives for the fifteen minutes of fame that catapults him to the next level in the organisational hierarchy. How in this environment is it possible to ensure non-selfish, non-attached work that will better the performance of the organisation?

The answer is to understand that everything changes. The people, the managers, the good times, the bad times, they come and go. The recession that is so big now will also be a thing of the past, just like the honeymoon eras of free market and dot com boom came and went. People move from organisation to organisation. Processes change with each passing fad that happens to be the current buzzword – TQM, Basel, Sox, CMMi, Six Sigma whatever. What remains unchanged, or should remain unchanged, is the unwavering vision of the company. With vision steady enough to withstand the lures of the good times and perils of the bad times, an organisation gains the strength to withstand the movement of the times, of passing buzzwords, of economic fluctuations and of attrition.

When someone tells me that this is my friend, the person with whom I have worked for the past six years, and now you tell me to cut off the long relationship, is it easy or correct to say do it for the organisation?

No, there is no such simple answer and no correct answer either.

At any decision making moment, there are four paths that can be followed.

(K. Ramesh now breaks into a silent bout of laughter. His face is full of amusement. He is clearly enjoying the proceedings immensely, stealing an occasional glance at Dave de Boer. The decision has been made for the company contingent. Top managers laugh in unison, in a peculiar corporate variation of Follow the Leader. I am somewhat inexperienced in management theory, but something remarkable seems to be taking place)

The first is the personal decision for the benefit of the individual. After all, an organisation is the sum total of different individuals. It will cease to exist without the members.

The second way to consider is the one of organisational benefits, the ways for the organisation to win in the situation.

The third way is the way of the contemporary buzzwords, what fads like Six Sigma or TQM recommend as course of action in such situations.

The fourth way is the way of values. What would be the most ethical path to choose in terms of organisational values?

All four ways are possible and there is no clear answer as to which is correct and which is not. The secret is to have a clear and unwavering organisational vision, and to decide on the correct way. The options are always available to the individuals performing the different roles and they have to exercise the choice in the way that they perceive to be the absolute best in view of all the information available.

(Ramesh cannot control himself any longer. He breaks into a guffaw which is echoed hesitantly by the company people. Some of the members of the audience look at us with surprise, but the dignified look on the Vice President's face reassures them.

"Empowerment," he observes and the CEO of HMH turns and nods. Everything is win-win from then on.)

Only if there is a very steady vision, are people – ever changing flux of people in view of job hopping and attrition – bound to choose the best path for the organisation without looking for personal benefits.

However, there is no guarantee that the prioritisation of the way will be correct every time and losses will not be incurred periodically. Each such loss needs to be followed by analysis and assessment and redefining of the process and vision.

(Ramesh is almost in splits now. For some others, the anxiety, temporarily assuaged by the superior's merriment, has now completed a full circle and returned to the primordial state of fear. It is the unusual reaction of his superior which makes them uneasy now.)

Have a strong assessment. Engage an expert if necessary. And have the results before you. And it is up to you to make the correct choice.

Mere knowledge won't help you unless you act upon it. By choosing not to act, you cannot attain equilibrium or perfection. The truth is that it is not possible to be still and in a state of inaction. The forces of crisis or good times, in short, the force of the industry, makes you act.

It will be the agent's job to talk to you and give you all the insights into the current situation. But, the choice of action will be yours. There will be no recommendation.

At any time choosing your own way, however misguided, is safer than choosing to follow the recommended way of others. It is the change agent's job to provide the guidance so that you can choose well.

He ended on this note and there was applause which can be best described as puzzled yet cheerful. The talk had been short and there was something in the speech apparently flavoured with wisdom and freedom that people liked. An esoteric quality surrounding the contents and the way they had been said. There were smiles on the faces of the bank bigwigs. This in turn seemed to please everyone.

Ramesh's good humour about the speech had made it a hit among the *Axiom* management. In fact, by the end of the day, I heard people saying that they had been witness to one of the best presentations ever made. The spurious making of a corporate legend.

Sandeep made his way to the rear of the room where Simon stood away from the crowd.

"Dude, I trust you got the whole thing."

Simon nodded.

"I did. You seem to be an expert in this sort of thing. Did you train as a covert secret agent?"

Sandeep smiled mysteriously.

"This *is* cloak and dagger stuff. You heard me up there, I am an agent ... change agent."

"There was a sort of philosophical quality to your speech."

"It *is* philosophical, Simon. It is the corporate song."

The hairless crown of K.Ramesh moved about scanning the hall and Sandeep moved to his favourite spot behind the pillar.

"Buddy, I need your services once more," he whispered. "Do you know of a strategic by lane along which one can get out of this building unobserved?"

Simon laughed.

"Well, you can keep walking back along this corridor and soon you will lose your way. This building is a maze. Walk for a sufficiently long time, and you will find a staircase somewhere. You won't be unobserved, but there is very little chance of meeting the same person twice."

Sandeep nodded in appreciation.

"Sound advice. Full of robust principles of geometric probability. You know what I think? There is no financial crisis. The money just got lost in the building, no one has managed to find it. They just need to look in all the corners. There are only about thirty thousand of them."

As the balding crown edged closer, Sandeep slowly stepped backwards as suggested. A few quick and creeping steps later, he was running along the cobblestoned streets of the Bijlmer shopping complex towards the station.

Text message from Sandeep to Pritam
The presentation went off well. Will send you the recording. Relax and enjoy.

Text message from Pritam to Sandeep
Now get the hell out of there. P.S. Who is Nabuko?

Text message from Sandeep to Pritam
I guess you mean Nabucco. It is a gas pipeline connecting Europe to Central Asia's gas rich area via the Balkans. Just a suggestion. No harm in confessing that you don't know.

Text message from Pritam to Sandeep
<Some counter suggestions resulting in response to the above, deleted to maintain levels of decency>

Text message from Amrita to Sandeep
It was a wonderful presentation. Touched my sole.

Text message from Sandeep to Amrita
Do you mean soul, or are you implying that I spoke of shoestring budget?

Text message from Madhu Deb to Sandeep
Great speech ... Everyone impressed. But where are you? Ramesh wants to have lunch with you.

Message from the cellphone provider of Sandeep in response to Madhu Deb's call.
"Het telefoonnummer kan niet worden bereikt" (The telephone number cannot be reached.)

Part IV:

Extension Swap

XVI

Thanks for considering me but I am no longer a literary agent. Please check *http://www.thereverse-makeover.com* *for details. Wish you success.*

– Rachel

After reading the short response to his emailed query letter, it was out of sheer morbid curiosity that Sandeep clicked on the hyperlink.

The Reverse Makeover is a brilliant first novel by Rachel Kelly.

Starting out as an editor, Rachel evolved into a successful literary agent. However, she has now metamorphosed into a popular novelist and is also the author of The New Author's Guide to Getting Published – The Rachel Kelly Way. She does not function as a literary agent any more but can be sought for advice as a professional speaker available for seminars catering to aspiring authors. She also conducts creativity workshops – some specifically geared for the female author.

The Reverse Makeover *is the story of a bookish med school sophomore, a bit of a nerd, who undergoes a personality makeover when she meets the coach of the university hockey team. However, she has to stop in the process of blossoming into a complete woman from a bookish academic and undergo a reverse makeover when her boyfriend has a disabling accident in the field, falling back on her academic brilliance to ensure rehabilitation and the necessary psychological assistance to guide the love of her life back into the rink.*

It was of course a New York Times Bestseller. According to the *Washington Post, "A brilliant achievement."* According to *New York Times "A sentimental journey into relationships etched with wit and pathos."* According to *Chicago Tribune "An important book."* . . .

Sandeep pulled out his spreadsheet of agents and publishers and proceeded to the next couple of names on the list. He checked their websites for updates before going through the rigmarole of tweaking query letters and synopses.

He had collected print outs of the next set of query letters, synopses, first three chapters, first five chapters, three sample chapters as required and was sorting and putting them into the hopeful envelopes – handed over by Simon – when the telephone rang.

He looked at his own cell phone – silent ever since the ominous luncheon proposition and wondered who could be calling his hotel room.

"Hello," he barked into the phone.

A dignified voice with a South Indian accent responded from the other end.

"Hello, Pritam. This is Ramesh."

Sandeep frowned.

"Ramesh? As in K. Ramesh?"

"This is he."

Sandeep wondered if putting the phone down would cost his childhood friend his job.

"It's good that you are in your room, I just wanted to get together with you for a couple of minutes. Can I come up?"

"Are you actually in the hotel?"

"Yes, I am calling from the reception. In truth, I am on my way to Schiphol. I need to fly to Budapest tonight. However, Madhu and I thought of catching up with you ... Sorry?"

"I asked if Madhu Deb is also in the hotel?"

"Yes, we are in the lobby."

Sandeep wistfully looked at the window. He could make out the drain pipe running down beside it, invitingly hinting at a calculated jump from the ledge ...

"Please come up," he said.

∾ ∾ ∾

"You didn't stay for the rest of the seminar," Madhu Deb's tone was not really accusing, but hinted at a required explanation. The faint hope of being in an unpleasant dream from which he would wake up safe and alone had disappeared with the important arrivals.

"I had to wind up a couple of things. You see, I'm going on leave immediately ... for three weeks," Sandeep offered as the bald headed VP and the chubby Senior Manager settled down.

"The CEO of the Operations and IT department of HMH did want to meet you," Madhu Deb observed. "He was pretty impressed with the speech – as in fact all of us were."

Ramesh nodded, his eyes on Sandeep.

"Yes, a lot of people wanted to talk to you," he remarked. "And it included me."

Was he being ticked off for leaving the premises without putting in sufficient time for networking? Was this a rap on his borrowed knuckles, or was it something more serious?

"I guess meeting one super important person is better than none," he offered weakly with a hesitant smile. Madhu Deb looked startled. Ramesh gave him a long look before chuckling.

"And I guess I am the luckier of the two super important persons."

He got up and moved towards the table. The Bhagavad-Gita presented by Professor Lal lay there, resplendent in the gorgeous saffron cloth binding. The Vice President took it and leafed through.

"Actually there were a couple of client queries ...," Sandeep offered.

"Sure, but you could have stayed. I know you were just supposed to make the presentation, but with Ramesh coming all the way ... Your cell phone was also off ...," Madhu Deb was on the verge of sounding unpleasant when Ramesh broke in.

"*Karmanye vadhikaraste ma phaleshu kadachana, ma karma phala hetur bhurmatey sangostva akarmani.*"

The other two looked at him, startled.

"Pritam. You did your job exceptionally well during the presentation ... and did not wait to reap the fruits. You were not interested in the networking that could result out of this. Of course, knowledge is superior to the ritualisation of process, as you aptly demonstrated in your talk. And meditation is superior to knowledge. Renunciation of the fruits of your labour is superior to meditation. Is that the philosophy you not only preach but practise?"

Sandeep slowly translated the rhetoric and thought about it. He was not too sure if he could make sufficient sense of the Vice President's words. Nor could he decipher where this was leading.

"I can't say I've found peace through the renunciation of fruits ... ," he observed.

Ramesh laughed. On the sofa, Madhu Deb sat looking baffled, her natural poise and command over the situation unable to come to her aid. She put on a neutral smile and busied herself in surveying the room.

"I don't know how many of the gathering got what you meant, Pritam. But, one thing was clear. The *Gita* has universal appeal." He waved the saffron volume in his hand.

Madhu Deb looked at the Vice President with a questioning smile.

"Why are we talking of *Slokas* and the *Gita*?"

Ramesh chuckled. When he looked at Sandeep, there was a twinkle in his eye.

"One of the downsides of reaching a position as I have, Pritam, is that you come across reverence and agreement without passing through the quality toll gates of knowledge. Madhu, I guess you must have understood that the entire speech of Pritam was a brilliant adaptation of the *Bhagavad Gita*?"

Sandeep marvelled at the way the Senior Manager took it in her energetic stride.

"Oh, well, of course. Now that you point it out, the parallels are even more striking."

Ramesh sighed and shook his head. "Anyway, I have discussed it with Madhu here and also with Ajay. I also had a one on one with Dave. I have a proposition."

Twice Sandeep checked himself. He stopped short of asking who Dave was, but only just. And with admirable self control, reined in his opinion about Ajay Yadav. Now he braced himself. Ramesh went towards the window and looked out at Amsterdam.

"This is the West. Concrete and steel, great highways and glittering buildings – riches and plenty, going for grabs and being respected as the go-getter..."

Sandeep interrupted him. "I'd say your observations would be more suited in the United States of America ... As far as Amsterdam is concerned, there are not too many high and mighty buildings. The soil won't allow it. And most Europeans are hardly go getters. They are the most laid back people I have come across. Amsterdam traditionally is not very eager in its display of pomp and glory. Architecture here is aesthetic while being utilitarian rather than symbols of great power. Comes from never having been ruled by a major power ..."

Ramesh nodded.

"I agree. The Dutch are egalitarian, following the strong principles of embarrassment of the riches. Partly because of the Calvinist influence. No showy stuff even from the royalty. But the fact remains that the image of the west in our minds is one of success, discipline, go getters and glitter. And that is why we take the methodologies and the processes of the west to be gospel. We design our consulting around the processes and practices that have been developed by them. We learn what they have designed and then sell it back to them. As long as we stick to this way of thinking, we will remain mere vendors and nothing more."

Sandeep followed the man apprehensively, trying to gauge where all this was leading, how the synchronised fates of Pritam and himself would dangle from the great man's imminent vision.

"We put the GE, the Motorola, Starbucks ... all these brands as the prophets of the industry. We stop just short of worshipping Jack Welch and Peter Drucker, devotedly following the McKinsey model. We are good at learning and tweaking and reselling. But, we will remain fringe players – a huge population of fringe players with passable knowledge of English, but nothing more. Look at the Japanese ..."

"Eh?" Sandeep looked vaguely around to find Madhu Deb taking a casual walk around the table where he had stacked his books.

"Look at how they have their Lean Systems, the Toyota Way. Their own models of Kano, Shingo, Iacocca. They were the only ones to challenge the business of the Western world because they created their own models ... did not borrow, tweak and resell western models like we continue to do."

"They are good at making their models accepted by the world," Sandeep ventured, guardedly. "For example, look at Judo and Karate. We are from the land of Kalaripayyat, but have we been able to market it?"

Ramesh's eyes twinkled.

"Exactly. We have all the systems with us. Why do we have to idolize people from Adam Smith to George Soros when we have our own Chanakya and his Arthashastra ... Our original industrialists are never put on a pedestal, but they are no way inferior to these western demi gods."

"We do have Amartya Sen now," Madhu Deb said absently, leafing through *The Assault* by Harry Mulisch.

Ramesh sighed. "What I am driving at is that we have a solid system of processes and standards internally developed through ages by our culture. There is huge potential that lies untapped. And the moment we come out with Indian knowledge, apply it to the industry and make it work, we will be players in our own rights. We won't need to learn a process designed by the Carnegie Melon University and teach it back to the Western go getters. We can bring a paradigm shift in the way businesses operate by making our riches of knowledge available, commoditised and applicable. We need to design our own processes by going back to our roots, not copy the west as we are so good at doing, from our films to our constitution."

Ramesh paused. Sandeep could see sweat glistening on his crown. He had worked himself up to a passionate climax.

"Just like the concepts of the Art of War that is now adapted into so many business processes, there is huge wealth of Indian wisdom that is waiting to be translated ... and that is what I really liked about your speech Pritam. You touched upon McKinsey model, the Adkar and all the Western models of change and then chose to quote Gita line by line," he smiled. "For a moment it seemed like plagiarism ..."

"I doubt whether Vyasa still holds the copyrights," Sandeep offered. He was still unsure whether it was just a congratulatory visit.

Ramesh burst out laughing.

"Pritam. You need to postpone your vacation ..."

"What?"

"I have already talked to Dave de Boer. HMH is very interested in a series of sessions by you which will make their organisation ready for change... You okay?"

"Quite. A touch of cramp."

"Of course, we are not charging them. To get anything financial on paper from the Dutch will require months. This is a model of relationship. Do you know the *Europe on a Shoestring* tours?"

Sandeep shook his throbbing head.

"I haven't managed to climb up to that financial category."

"Right," the great man laughed, misreading the spin in the statement, but nevertheless finding it hilarious. "I will advise you to take a walking tour with them. They start every day from the Dam Square at one in the afternoon. A very interesting business model which actually gets better in times of crisis. They don't charge anything. And offer the best tours."

"I intend to do that. I am on a holiday after all ..."

"Postpone it Pritam. I have done this big favour to Dave. Managed to get him in time just before his vacation. Beyond expectations – like our brand essence. Offering the services of a star speaker, a hugely expensive one, for free. He has to return the favour. It will lead to opportunities. Dave said the secretaries will arrange for biweekly sessions with the IT Banking staff. Nothing much to do other than formulate your theories and talk."

"Er ..."

"And during your stay, you and I will frame a proprietary process out of this. Indian process solutions for the financial crisis – preventive measures based on oriental wisdom. The time is ripe. The world is crying for new processes. After this utter rip in the entire financial fabric. You have it in you, Pritam. And I see the danger of all this potential for original thinking being shoved into the background to fight our regular fires in the celebrated ad hoc way of the Indian professional. This arrangement will give you the peace and quiet to build on your ideas. You and I can produce something that will create waves. A revolution."

"Er ..."

"We will talk about it. Also, you need to travel to Prague to conduct one more such session. For internal *Axiom* Europe senior management. You sure you are okay?"

"Er ..."

Ramesh looked concerned.

"You need some water. You don't look too good."

"No ... I'm fine ... What I want is this vacation."

"We'll arrange for it. Madhu told me all about your wedding... What's the matter?"

"Nothing, really ..."

Sandeep had slumped down heavily on the bed. For a few minutes nothing made any sense. Within the organisation, fame seemed to be snowballing towards him. Just the thing Pritam and he did not need.

"The main thing now is to ride the wave that has been created. You see, if I had told anyone that I would manage to land a consulting assignment in these times of financial crisis with HMH, people would have laughed at my face. But, we have got you into HMH, based on your presentation today. From here to a full fledged assignment is nothing but a matter of patience. There are no low hanging fruits in this BeNeLux area, one has to be patient. I have sown an expensive seed, and it will give me golden fruit. If you want, we can get your wife flown here for a European honeymoon."

Sandeep gripped the edge of the bed-sheet till his knuckles were white.

"Ramesh, these guys are on the verge of losing their jobs. If I bullshit them with the Gita, I can get killed."

Ramesh laughed. "Don't worry, I have thought about it. These guys have social security. There is a complex system of benefits. Job loss hurts, but not to the extent it does in India. All you will be providing them is some diversion, and believe me, the ones who attend will do so for the fun. The Dutch love intellectual stimulation. They are tolerant of new ideas, being raised for generations on three pillars of faith. They are liberal as long as you stay within limits and don't step on their toes. They allow cannabis but no hard drugs, see what I mean? One cannot be the centre of the Western world of trade for centuries, and still not be liberal. They also support Euthanasia. But, I must be going now. It was great meeting you. And we will work together. I am looking at something phenomenal here, changing the way people look at the industry and processes. I had heard a lot about you, but I never realised the originality behind the standard consultant. Madhu, he will be yours to take care of for the next three months."

The old faithful Madhu Deb smiled brightly.

"I have a task force to do exactly that."

"And anyway, the Dutch calendars are always full. I don't see you getting too many people into the room too often. There won't be too many meetings. The key is to place you here as an investment, and while you are here we will collaborate."

The VP stepped out of the room, leaving Sandeep to battle his strong emotions. The earliest he could get away was in a couple of days. He had intended to stay on in Amsterdam, maybe use the studio in Jordaan as before. But, this was serious. He had to steer clear of the vicinity, out of the enterprising reach of the visionary K. Ramesh and his henchmen, return the borrowed identity like a library book and go back to his struggle.

That was what it was all about. Struggle. A strange development – with some likely benefits to his literary ambitions as a by product, but something he had to side step. What if he sent a mail from Pritam's mailbox claiming illness? Or some medical emergency of his newly wedded wife?

∾ ∾ ∾

Email from Professor Lal to Shruti

Dear Shruti,

The technological marvel of the Internet fascinates me into a fervour. I suppose a growing kid nowadays learns to send emails before writing letters and wonders what on earth a postage stamp is. But, to me it is a continued sense of wonder that we can correspond with written words at the rate of the instantaneous even as you have no fixed address of brick and mortar, keep shuttling across the borders of the excellent concept of European Union. Even if it is just to ask after your health or to let you know in passing that the proofs are ready. And indeed they are and I have posted them to the address of your friend as you had asked me to.

Keep well,
The Professor

∾ ∾ ∾

Madhu Deb re-entered the room just as he was about to get up and close the door.

"Are you okay? Do you need something to drink?"

"I need sleep."

"I understand Pritam," she winked at him.

He started. A meaningful wink. What on earth did this gesture mean? He was struggling with more than his share of created problems – he had no time for obscure gestures of dumpy women. And even as he kept looking at her, Madhu Deb said something with an air of secret mischief that took the wind out of him.

"Or do I call you Sandeep?"

Whatever sanity was left in Sandeep now blew away in a fuzzy turmoil of fragmented tension. His first thoughts were of the smartly dressed police force that he had seen in the Amsterdam streets, sticking to memory because of some of the sexiest lady cops across the world. And nowhere had he come across a force so fond of going around on bicycles. Was it a felony that he had indulged in? Impersonating someone else in a seminar and quoting the Gita? Could he be imprisoned for masquerading as a liberator of the banking world, for pretending to be an expert on the antidote of credit crisis, for trivialising a sacred text into frivolous interpretation? Were the prison cells in Europe as bad as the ones across the Atlantic? Did one get sodomised by big black men in congested coops made famous by hundreds of prison movies?

"Sandeep Gupta. I don't think it is too good as a pen name, though."

For a full minute Sandeep's feverish mind grappled with the mysterious labyrinths the new statement seemed to trace.

"And you are a man of many talents. You have worked as an investigative journalist too, have you?"

"Well, between this job and that ..."

"And you are also a martial arts instructor?"

"Are you a clairvoyant?"

Madhu Deb held something in her hand. Slowly things fell into place. For someone with a background in investigative journalism, it had been an unpardonable amateurish oversight. But, then, he had always supported the team with his ideas and planning, seldom going out in the field and playing out the roles he had painstakingly designed.

The lady had been looking at the print out of the cover illustration of his first novel *Doppelganger Days*. Emailed to him that morning by Sunil Pillay and printed out from the *Informatie Centrum* of the hotel. During the recent conversation with K.Ramesh, it had been lying on the table by the sofa, accessable through curious casual saunters around the room. Below the back page blurb was a flattering photograph and a brief life sketch of his humble self.

"You look even better with curly hair," Madhu Deb observed.

"Th-thanks."

"Did you get them curled or is it natural and you have straightened them for some reason?"

"I ... er ... "

"Is the book out in the market?"

"Uh ... no, it'll take another week or so."

"No wonder you were so creative. At last I have someone to talk to about Literature."

"Talk about literature?"

"An author among us. Congratulations ...."

"I ... I don't want to make it public, if you know what I mean. That's why I use a pseudonym, you see ..."

Madhu Deb laughed.

"Relax, your secret is safe with me. I would really like to talk to you in detail about this ... but, now I have got to see off Ramesh. See you in office tomorrow."

"Office?"

"Yes. Obviously. We have to make plans of action."

Madhu Deb bounced her way out of the room, proclaiming that it was a pleasure to meet such a talented young man. Sandeep, having locked the door, collapsed on the bed, head clutched between his palms, the web of confusion almost a physical entity in front of his throbbing temples and hazy eyes.

Lake Gardens, Kolkata

Email read out by young Shuktara Lal to her grandfather, Professor P.Lal

"Dear Professor Lal,

The volume of Bhagavad-Gita that you graciously gifted me has not only advised a confused young man in a strange land, it has also allowed him to fit into his new role with élan. In fact, it was the paraphrased version of the first three cantos that I used as my first major presentation in the low lands. And would you believe it? It was touted as a grand success, with only one man in the crowd seeing through my maha-*plagiarism and, even after that, interpreting it as innovation.*

Thanks are due to you, because this is the first time I have managed to go through the Gita without being tied into knots by obscure footnotes.

However, I am on the verge of what promises to be profound suffering as a result of this so called success. My professional life has just become busier than ever and this involves a trip to Prague to spread the word of Lord Krishna – in other words, to speak about my novel approach towards customer presentations. This is contrary to my scheme of things, scooping out massive chunks of time that I would have liked to spend in hunting down agents and publishers. But, on the other hand, it may enable me to prolong my stay in Amsterdam.

Regards,
Sandeep

Email dictated by Professor P. Lal to his granddaughter Shuktara

Dear Sandeep,

What are you up to? The Western World has been through enough episodes of largely unnecessary violence in recent times. And yet you preach the Bhagavad-Gita to them? Is not one Kurukshetra

enough, that you urge a war ravaged world to follow the lessons of Vasudeva-Krishna in the sinful kali-yuga?

The Bhagavad-Gita is meant to be gone through at 'one go', with intermittent returns as many times as our dilemmas decide for us. Did not Vasudeva-Krishna speak all of it in one continuous vein? And was Arjuna supposed to ask his sakha-guru to wait and pause while he looked at the references?

The success and the suffering that you mention are supposed to go hand in hand. Krishna says this in the Karma Yoga, Canto 3 of the Gita. The world is your wish fulfilling cow. It will give you what you want and with it, the in-built opposite. You get what you want and then you have had it. Out on the other side of the world, I wait to see what holds in store for you once you get what you are looking for.

Keep well and please do tell,
The Professor

XVII

Blog of Simple Simon
Tags: Pomp, Jargon, Mediocrity, Laws of Globalisation

My continuing role as the official buddy has been dubbed LESSON – Logical Extension of SeamlesS ON-boarding. When you scratch the surface of this pompous piece of rhetoric it actually means continuing to point out bars and shopping malls to the new member. The maniacal euro pursuing corporate organisations not only try to manufacture a common soul by propagating brand values. They also develop their own poetic version of the mundane for that soul to be uplifted.

However, critical as I am, this microcosmic world has its uses. Concocted philosophy in form of brand values, laboured poetry in the garb of elaborate euphemisms, pseudo science in the guise of innovations, petty politics in the cloak of relentless back biting, ersatz society under the mask of people living virtually in each other's homes long after office hours, frequent musical soirees with the inbuilt sham of philanthropy through small change associations with NGOs masquerading as an apology of culture – all these have their utility.

What if some shifty eyed account manager, for example, had not reacted with jerky gestures at every sneeze of the client? What if some senior manager had not sung her cheery greetings and made her domineering presence felt across the length and breadth of the client organisation, threatening all and sundry with the next instalment of family stories? What if everyone had been free spirits like me?

Would then a bunch of largely mediocre people have found a satisfactory life abroad? A life that many of their friends and family were proud and envious of. The truth is that every business has to run in accordance to its own rules. If the more sensitive and intelligent of the lot get disillusioned at the contrivance, they have the choice of playing along, getting out of there or becoming an entrepreneur-visionary like K.Ramesh seems to be.

Mail from Simon to his mailing list
Sub: Existensial Dilemmas and Survival Strategies

LESSON notwithsanding (see my blog post published a minute back for the cryptic abbreviation), I am more than glad to be the re-designated haemorrhoid of this entertaining consultant. I am also pleased that he will be working with us for a while – and there will be a series of his talks. Like a man eating tiger, the taste of blood in the form of the hidden camera stunt had me craving for more.

When the good lady made the announcement during the weekly team meeting, I was not the only one to be excited. Seated directly in front of me, Amrita looked positively delighted. The interaction with him on the eve of his presentation had obviously left both of us impressed.

Gunjan dutifully informed that he had seen the man in question check into his apartment early in the morning and had helped him with his luggage. This, translated by the backbiting dictionary, meant that the famed consultant should have been in the office long back.

The appearance was ultimately made at noon, and he promptly popped in my cubicle. His greetings were hearty enough, but a trifle apprehensive. His first concern was again the office stationery about which he seems to possess a strange obsession. I dutifully showed him the cupboard where stocks of envelopes, pens and pads were stored. There seemed to emerge an excited gleam in his eyes as he surveyed the supplies.

His next task was to accompany me to the coffee machine for a quick session on what he termed survival strategies.

"Buddy, you are officially entitled to help me, aren't you?" he asked.

I replied that I was.

"Since I have to spend more time in the account than was originally budgeted for– and the key word here, mind you, is budgeted – I have been removed from the hotel and asked to occupy a corporate apartment in Amstelveen," he informed me. "Tell me, do all the *Axiom* employees live in the same complex?"

I thought I detected a distinct quiver in his voice.

"Are you talking about the apartments of Maarten Lutherweg near Sportlaan?"

He started at my fluent Dutch pronunciation.

"If you do mean Martin Lutherweg and Sportlaan, yes."

I nodded with a lot of sympathy.

"Yes. The company rents a lot of apartments in that area. So, most of the *Axiom* people working for clients like Rabobank, ING, HMH, ABN AMRO stay there."

He took a while to digest it.

"Everyone in the BeNeLux region, I guess?"

I laughed. "Nearly all working in Amsterdam. I presume you have been given a separate apartment."

This time a shudder did run over his frame.

"Do people have to share apartments too? With colleagues?"

I nodded. "Yes. But, I thought you knew that. However, with your seniority you must have been given a single apartment."

He became thoughtful.

"Yes, but Gunjan knows where it is – and seems pretty adept at making himself at home anywhere."

I understood his emotions completely, having been subject to similar invasions.

"Is there a way to shoo him away?"

I shook my head sadly.

"Not that I know of. Even if I excuse myself to go to the toilet, he generally waits till I get back."

He shuddered again.

"I hope he does not accompany you to join the act?"

"Thankfully not. He waits."

"Irrespective of the type of call you allude to?"

"Well, I don't think I've ever been that explicit, but I guess it wouldn't matter."

I could make out that he was shaken.

"I can't afford to have him as my honorary room-mate. I have work to do. Things that cannot be done perpetually in the bathroom. Who else lives there?"

I told him that I did not really know people of the other accounts. "From HMH, Amrita and Trisha do. Lahari lives in Amstelveen too, but in Zonnestein."

A thought seemed to occur to him so alarming that he almost spilt his coffee.

"And is one faced with the spectacle of Hidori and his mother on a regular basis?"

I patted his shoulder reassuringly.

"No. They live in Amsterdam. Near Station Lelylaan."

He heaved a sigh of relief.

"Small mercies. There may be a God after all," he observed. "What about you? Where do you stay?"

I informed him that I lived in Utrecht.

"You commute to Amsterdam every day? Isn't that a problem?"

I replied that most of the Dutch people commuted into Amsterdam from other cities. It was just a twenty minute train ride from my place. It gave me the time to catch up on my reading.

"Right. It's a small country. Ambling unmindfully for too long might land one in Belgium. You read a lot do you? I hope you have the good sense to keep that information to yourself?"

I asked him what he meant.

"Never let Madhu Deb know. Else she will soon be discussing books with you ..."

The painful expression on his face told me that he had already been there, done it.

"I know how you feel. When did she corner you?"

"About an hour back. As soon as I entered office. We talked about Ayn Rand and George Eliot. And of course ended the conversation with a thirty five minute session on Hidori."

He took a long sip.

"What about this lady? Do you have any secret escape method when she comes for you? Is there a trapdoor leading to a tunnel in your cubicle?"

I regretfully answered in the negative.

"The only thing to do is to wait for her phone to ring."

"But that's beyond our control. Unless we call the phone ourselves and that is not an option. What if we call each other?"

I thought about it.

"I call you when she is ..."

"Yes. We will watch out for each other ... The moment the conversation tips slightly and there is the ominous sign of Hidori being spilled into the discussion, we reach for the panic button. If the one on the lookout is in hearing range, he calls anyway. If not, the affected makes an emergency call, and the ally rings back. Deal?"

I loved the idea.

"Deal."

"Remember, that's what buddies are for. The others. Don't they find it troublesome? How do they take the crap?"

I shrugged.

"After all, she is a nice lady. She fights for her team. And people think spending more time with the boss keeps them in mid season form for the rat race."

"Netherlands is the last place for rat races, buddy. It's always raining cats and dogs."

I laughed. And it was now that he said the words that have been playing on my mind ever since.

"No one has ever become a stallion by winning the rat race."

I loved this new buddy of mine.

XVIII

Amsterdam

Blurb on the Back Cover of Doppelganger Days

Arun lands up in Manhattan as an engineer on business visa and then gives it all up to stay on as an illegal immigrant, intent on picking up the finer points of *tai chi chuan.* He works in a Chinese Restaurant and spends all his spare hours training in the martial art – getting injuries treated in a free dispensary run in a New Jersey Gujarati temple. However, when he falls for Nadira, a struggling Pakistani singer, he questions his decision and yearns for the comfortable life that might have been. Thus begins a double life, with indigenous identity thefts, enthralling escapades and peculiar pursuits through the world shattering days of the 9/11, Afghan and Iraq wars.

The novel deals with issues that are important, morose and with far reaching effects, terrorism, politics and racial discrimination in the modern world – but, nevertheless, it is related with humour in every page.

Sandeep Gupta is a writer based in Delhi, India. He has been a software programmer, an investigative journalist as well as an instructor in the martial arts of *Karate* and *Tai chi chuan.*

Mumbai, India

Mail from Sunil Pillay to Sandeep Gupta

Sandeep-dada,

There are a couple of reviews of your book in Mumbai Midday and The Asian Age. We do deliver our promise as long as you keep trusting us. I am shipping ten copies of your book to your address in the Netherlands.

Thanks,

Sunil

Review of Doppelganger Days in **Mumbai Midday**

Doppelganger Days by Sandeep Gupta is a novel that deals with issues that are important, morose and with far reaching effects, terrorism, politics and racial discrimination in the modern world – but, nevertheless, it is related with humour in every page.

Review of Doppelganger Days in **The Asian Age**

Doppelganger Days. Author: Sandeep Gupta. Paperback 275 pages. Rs. 225.

A novel set in New York City that deals with indigenous identity thefts, enthralling escapades and peculiar pursuits through the world shattering days of the 9/11, Afghan and Iraq wars.

The novel that deals with issues that are important, morose and with far reaching effects, terrorism, politics and racial discrimination in the modern world – but, nevertheless, it is related with humour in every page.

Amsterdam

Mail from Sandeep Gupta to Kailash Nayak
Sub: Plagiarism Galore

Hi Kailash,

Forget books. Even reviews are plagiarised, and that too from the blurb on the back cover. I am sending you the links of two reviews of Doppelganger Days *in national dailies. Along with it I am sending you the blurb of my novel. Judge for yourself.*

Please let me add– I was the one who wrote the blurb. It's always great to see one's words in print . . . however, there are exceptions.

Could you please check whether the book is available in Starmark and CrossWord yet?

Anything further on the Uproar front? Has Mayank Manhas and company coughed up the money?

- Sandeep

∾ ∾ ∾

Sandeep was thoroughly drenched by the time he completed his morning run. The Amsterdam weather blew with the wet winds of unpredictability. He paused in the field behind the apartment complex, lush green with the fresh layer of moisture, empty but for an enthusiastic Airedale Terrier and her waterproofed owner.

Having recovered his breath from the twenty minute run, Sandeep stretched and kept thinking about the reviews. The book world puzzled him. After the readers employed by publishers, now he knew how reviewers attached to the media dealt with the sweat and blood of authors. What about the general public? Did they read? They certainly did read the books sold with hype, and if they were supposed to like it, they did ... making the author another Caeser.

He shrugged and went through the karate *katas.* Starting with *Heian Shodan,* he went through the forms of the established sequence, completing the basic series, moving to *Tekki shodan, Basai Dai* and *Kanku Dai.* In the midst of complicated arm movements of *Jitte,* he made a mistake and stopped. Half baked training, he cursed. The more he flitted from one uncertainty in life to the next, his training continued to be sketchy. Soon the perfection achieved over the years would become rusty with neglect.

He stepped into the long form of Yang Style *tai chi chuan.* The smooth movements followed one another in the slow rhythm of his heartbeats. The rain beat hard into his face as he turned towards the wind, stepping into the *embrace the tiger, return to the mountain* position. And that is when he stopped. A few yards in front of him, watching with a pair of confused eyes, was the dark, drenched form of Amrita.

"Oh hi," he said. "I didn't know you were here. But, you're getting drenched."

She had just a cloth stitched tracksuit on her and it was soaking wet.

"I don't mind. I like the rain."

There was a soulful look in her eyes, probably brought about by her partiality for the rain.

"You are also out in the rain," she said with a smile.

"Me, yes, I am, but I cannot help it. It started pouring when I was a mile away from home. I had to get back."

"What is that thing you were doing?"

"Just some exercises."

"Was it karate?"

Sandeep shrugged.

"Depends on how long you've been watching me."

There was confusion in the eyes of the girl, and Sandeep hastily changed the language of conversation to Bengali.

"I was doing karate moves a while back. Now it's a different form."

"What's this form called?"

"Weird, isn't it?"

"No, it seems very beautiful."

Sandeep laughed.

"Well, properly done it is supposed to be graceful. By the way, I have to keep moving if I don't want to catch a cold. And I guess you will have to choose between running home and a running nose."

He had switched back to English and again there was incomprehension in the girl's eyes.

"I mean, I think you ought to get going if you don't want to sneeze all day long."

Amrita raised her eyes to him and let the rain plummet down on her upturned face.

"I don't mind catching a cold. I love the rain a bit too much. Don't you?"

Sandeep was not expecting the question. He wondered.

"I suppose so. I mean, getting drenched is fun. But sometimes a ringside view is more advisable than getting into the middle."

Amrita looked at him for a while.

"Yes, I know. My heart doesn't listen to advice."

Sandeep laughed and waved at her.

"See you in office if you don't end up sick."

He ran back to the apartment just in time to pick up the clamouring cell phone.

"What do you mean by three months?"

"I've explained, Pritam. I can't help it. This K.Ramesh wants to write a paper with me ..."

"What?"

"And there is something else they want me to handle. A series of talks for HMH bank."

"What?"

"I heard you the first time, old man. Relax, I am making you some money and fame. You keep having a good time. Congratulations, by the way. No conference has ever been this successful in the history of *Axiom.*"

"But how? I just copied and pasted several papers and internet articles. Why should the paper be such a hit?" Pritam sounded incensed.

"True, but it had nothing to do with your paper. I did not present it ..."

"What?"

"You keep repeating yourself, my friend. But, to get back to the point, I did not really have the time or inclination to read through the load of bull you had written. So, I copied and pasted ideas from a far more authentic source."

"Indeed? And what source was that?"

"The Bhagavad Gita."

"What?"

"This is the fourth time you said that, mate. You must see a specialist. The Bhagavad Gita, no less. And K.Ramesh was so impressed that he wants to write a process with me, driven by ancient Indian knowledge."

"The Bhagavad Gita?"

"Right. Your name is going to be etched in the history of consulting in golden letters."

"Yes ... yes, that's Sandeep, but ... I really need to talk to ... it's a catastrophe ..."

However, regardless of the need of the hour, enthusiastic determination and strong wrists won the day and Shruti's welcome voice came on the line.

"Did I hear Bhagavad Gita?"

"Yes, you did. Interspersed between a bunch of repeating monosyllabic questions."

"And how has our mutual friend exceeded my great expectations and managed to refer to that seminal work in these hard times?"

"You mean where the dickens did he pick up this forgotten treatise?"

"That's the million euro question even in this dreadful recession."

"I just told him that I have presented a paper ..."

"Ah yes ..."

"And it was a more or less plagiarised version of the Bhagavad Gita."

"Sounds wonderful. Why is he so upset by that? In fact why does every conversation with you upset him so much? But, I must speak to you later ... he wants the phone."

The voice once again transformed from the fun filled feminine to masculine moroseness.

"Are you bent on ruining my career?"

"Heavens Pritam, I have just informed you that your reputation has swelled. You may be up for a quick promotion."

"Listen to me. I don't want my reputation to swell. I don't want quick promotions. I am changing my job anyway. I want you out of there, do you get me."

Sandeep moved his thumb with a practiced flourish and disconnected the line.

∾ ∾ ∾

Mail from Kailash Nayak to Sandeep Gupta
Sub: Re: Plagiarism Galore

Hi Sandeep,

What do you expect? Reviewers will go through each and every word of your novel before writing the review? What use is the blurb then?

I checked the book stores you mentioned. Your book is not on the shelves yet. I called the distribution department of the Amphibian Books and was informed that it will take another month. Don't go by what Sunil Pillay tells you. Now that the book is ready, talk to the distributors directly about the dates.

*There is no payment from Uproar. I have been following it up on a weekly basis, but you know the f***ers.*

However, since we talked about book review and Uproar in the same breath, let me share something with you. Sushmita Chatterjee herself reviewed – can you beat it – Mayank Manhas' book, 'The Chemistry of Lust'. Imagine! Uproar reviewing a book written by their owner. Here are a few excerpts – Enjoy

By the way, for all the hype it created, I don't think this book sold more than a hundred copies world wide.

K.

Attachment with Kailash Nayak's mail

(Review of *The Chemistry of Lust* by Mayank Manhas published in *Uproar.* Written by Sushmita Chatterjee)

Steinbeck, Dostoyevsky and Marquez would have been proud of their tribesman – Mayank Manhas . . .

~ ~ ~

Leiden

Dr. Suprakash Roy took the call as he was about to step out of his office to grab a quick cup of coffee.

"Hi Pritam, are you calling from Prague?"

"No, I've just got off the train in Budapest."

"You are really seeing a lot of Europe."

"Not the parts I really want to see ..."

"Are you talking about Europe or being Freudian?"

"Screw your Freud."

"That would amount to homosexuality and necrophilia. Are you calling from your Blackberry?"

"How the hell does that matter?"

"Casual curiosity."

"I need your help."

"You surely sound terrible ..."

"I am having a tough time, Sup. I want you to go down to Amsterdam and meet Sandeep."

"Is that necessary?"

"You bet your *** it's necessary."

Dr. Roy sighed.

"I think we need to have a long call. Can you access Skype?"

XIX

Blog of Simple Simon
Tags: Drinking in Amsterdam, Gita retold

The hype that has followed the curious presentation of Pritam Mitra, my new buddy, has left me with myriad questions. The last of the questions was whether to post this in a blog or a separate mail. However, I decided that the interaction today with the famed consultant deserves to be shared with a wider public.

It is seldom that one stumbles across philosophy in the realm of filthy lucre. Yet, whenever I approached my friend for explanations, he responded with cagey frivolity.

"That's how it ought to be, Simon. According to a wise old man, the Gita is bound to raise more questions than answers."

Today, however, as we went about town in a rare fulfilment of my buddy role, I managed to make him open up about the concept, although in his own inimitable way.

We had started out in Haarlemmerdijk, browsing in the Het Paard Schaak en Go Winkel.

"I enjoy my game of chess, the battle of life played out on the board," my friend had confided. "The one recreation in which I have invested sparingly, without tipping the precarious balance of interests."

(I did not realise till much later what he meant by that)

So, I took him to the exquisite chess shop where he rapidly transformed into a child inside ToysRUs.

"Hold me by my coat tails, Simon, or I'll end up squandering my ill gotten gains," he caressed the massive collection of chess books, delicately fingering them as if they were antiques. Every chess board with carved pieces brought a delighted gleam to his eyes. "I already have a backlog of more than five hundred books. I can afford the money now, but even less time."

Ultimately he settled for the memoirs of Capablanca.

"This is how the buddy system should work. Remind me to log it as one of the more meaningful innovations. Insider's insights into sin city."

I asked him if he was agreeable to a short walk.

"In which case I can show you one of the more unconventional drinking places of the city."

Jay Garrido is originally from Aruba, gaunt and virile, bringing a new dimension to drinking to one's health. In 1978, he had found himself in the streets of Amsterdam at the age of 21, with more drugs and alcohol than blood in his veins. Legend has it that he was reformed by a vision of his grandmother showing him a feather. With the help of a friend, he set up a juice bar in Harlemmerstraat. Now in his fifties, he sold fruit and vegetable juice to customers, along with free words of encouragement to follow his liquid diet.

"Simon, my friend," Jay greeted from the dark interiors of his shop. He was hewing a coconut, peeling the white milky flesh for a customer. The stunningly beautiful yet homely American girl who assisted him flashed a smile of recognition. "Long time since the last detox."

My friend took to the place immediately. His eyes went over the rows of pineapples, oranges, coconuts, grapes, juicers and grinders, pausing a while on the proprietor and a trifle longer on his assistant.

"The virtuous version of wine and woman. Simon, you take the buddy system to new heights. Nothing like coconut milk as I debase the treasures troves of Indian wisdom."

More than once I had been down in the basement of the shop, where he grew wheat for the juice. The small green plants stood under lights simulating solar benefits, lovingly nurtured by the big man. As Pritam bent down to enter the cramped nursery, he was full of characteristic aphorisms.

"Speaks volumes for the modern world, Simon, where you have to go underground to do good for humanity."

On returning to the shop, he read the chequered life of the Aruban, proudly displayed on the wall. "God bless you, Jay. I will definitely have some of the wheat extracts, but nothing to beat coconut to start off. It's auspicious."

He turned mellower with every sip. We sat on the bench outside the shop, the merry crowd of Amsterdammers and tourists passing us by on the trendy street. The moment seemed opportune. So, I asked him if he would spend some time explaining the background of the Gita. He almost choked on his drink.

"I am the worst person to do anything of that kind, my friend. The English language is my medium. I revel in irony, understatements and cynicism that characterises it. Indian epics depict the thoughts, emotions and ideals of a more pastoral order. I am someone who can use the Gita as a frivolous tool, for meaningless inanitives like crisis conferences. But I lay no claims to doing justice through paraphrases, or coming remotely close."

The arrogant humility was infectious. I said that post conference I had done some reading up on the classic.

"A lot of people seem to have been influenced by it. Schopenhauer, Isherwood, Huxley, Emerson. I would like to know more. From what I read, it seems to be a dialogue full of advice – part of a bigger epic. A kind of Indian Sermon on the Mount."

The consultant shook his head.

"Sermon on the Mount? Gita is nothing remotely like it. It is a dialogue that takes place on the battlefield, with armies ready to plunge into the bloodiest of wars. Arjuna, who receives the advice, is not a monk, but a warrior by birth, training and circumstance. The lessons learnt and the doubts raised do not need renunciation of the world or monastic setting for application. That's why they are as effective even in the crisis ridden financial world."

"I have read about the battle. A showdown between the good and evil forces ..."

My friend corrected me again.

"Indian mythology does not paint the world in black and white, Simon. The cause of the war was convoluted. Both sides were full of great warriors, a lot of them virtuous. None were saints, most were sinners. As human beings are supposed to be. Circumstances forced them on different sides."

"Didn't Krishna, the god, the avatar, join the ones who had truth on their side?"

"Yes, but it was the choice of man. And Krishna participated as a charioteer. I would say he was the patron saint of Consultants."

I laughed.

"Aren't you afraid of blasphemy, my friend?"

"Blasphemy? Indian gods are sinners in their own right. Krishna loved good things in life. Women, wealth ... And he did not do a thing during the Mahabharata war except bring destruction to feuding clans through contradictory advice."

I mentioned that I could perhaps understand what he meant by irony, but could not start to appreciate the humour without knowing the background.

As the sun shone on the balmy day, the colourful people walked across on the street, Jay and his help poured glass after glass of varieties of juice, my buddy relented.

"The synopsis of the Mahabharata. Well, the first thing to understand is that the epic is a compilation of narratives. Strikingly modern after several thousand years. Give me a moment, my friend, let me compile a back cover blurb for you. Let the excellent juices augment my creative ones."

He closed his eyes and extended his head backward.

"The epic is a collection of eighteen volumes, the story of the descendants of King Bharata. Plenty of storylines and sub plots. I will just cover the main theme that led to the war. How should a blurb of the mammoth epic read?"

He opened his eyes again with a strange gleam of energy.

"When Pandu, the king of Hastinapur, dies in dangerous throes of sexual fulfilment, the Pandava brothers find their rights to the throne challenged by cousin Duryodhana, son of the blind caretaking king Dhritarashtra. As they grow up amongst fierce rivalry, they escape clandestine murder plots to go into hiding in the forests. When Arjuna, in the guise of a Brahmin, wins the sultry and sensuous Draupadi in swayamvar, they live in liberated polyandry … "

"Aren't you getting carried away? I realise I am easy to deceive, but …"

He stopped me.

"Believe me when I tell you, that's more or less how it goes. Pandu was cursed to a painful death by copulation … a strange interplay of karma, because he had mistaken a sage for a deer and had killed him just as he was on the threshold of ecstasy."

"In that case, how were the five brothers born?"

"Immaculate conception predating the Christ. That's one version. If the king had problems in getting it up, it was perfectly legitimate for hermits or gods to rise to the occasion and fill the gap … well, I told you I am not the right person for paraphrasing the epic."

"Could we go ahead with the story, without taking the back cover out of Harold Robbins?"

Fresh glasses of juice were served by the girl. Pritam's eyes followed her on her way back into the shop.

"Well, it gets to be more Ian Fleming. So, the hundred Kaurava brothers, led by Duryodhana, now know Pandavas are alive and well."

"Were the Kauravas also immaculately conceived?"

"Both the fathers of the Pandavas and Kauravas were. However, it might have been a case of self fulfilling fantasy played out by the author. Vyasa himself impregnated the royal grand-moms. The Kauravas, on the other hand, constitute the first documented record of test tube babies."

"You are kidding."

"I speak the truth. The Mahabharata contains everything that has ever existed. However, to carry on, Duryodhana relented by giving a small barren piece of land to the brothers, but they worked on it Israeli mode, converting it into a super city through alliances and construction contracts. They lived happily, visited by Krishna from time to time. Arjuna went on frequent marrying sprees.

"Duryodhana now arranged this game of dice – a true casino royal. Yudhisthira, the eldest Pandava, gambled away his property, his brothers, himself and ultimately their common wife, Draupadi. Speak of mortgage linked derivatives leading to crisis. Draupadi was disrobed in court, the template for future fashion shows. That too in front of the king, who missed out on the excitement, being blind. Bhima, the second brother, pledged revenge. The Pandavas were banished for twelve years and had to stay incognito for one more."

"No wonder they resorted to battle."

"Well, they did complete the thirteen years, full of action, adventure, intrigue and sex. Yet, when they returned, the throne was refused. Both the sides now went gathering forces through mergers, acquisitions, alliances and joint ventures – with some pretty neat recruitment policies. And then there was war. A gory eighteen day affair broadcasted ESPN style."

"Say that again …"

"The blind king had already missed out on the disrobing of Draupadi, but he wanted to catch the action of the war live. So, he recruited the services of Sanjaya, who narrated the eighteen days non-stop."

I was confused.

"It does seem to be a battle between good and evil."

"That's from the big picture as corporate gurus will tell you, painting things in black and white. However, when you go down to the resource level – character by character – there are so many interplays between circumstances and choices. There is no universal good and evil. Even the embodiment of Dharma lies through his teeth and resorts to gambling. That's what makes it a masterpiece.

"The general of the Kauravas was the grandfather of the warring princes, Bhishma the patriarch, a man who had pledged to serve the throne of Hastinapur, while simultaneously vowing celibacy. Bound by his own contracts, the personification of zealous self sacrificing corporate over-commitment, blessed and cursed at the same time with death by wish. Ultimately he lies on a bed of arrows, but still cannot die without seeing the end of it all and advising Yudhisthira on the art of administration.

"There is Drona, the commander of the Kauravas once Bhishma lies on his prolonged deathbed. He is the master teacher, who loves Arjuna, his best student. But, he is devoted to the throne, and cannot desert the Kauravas.

"There is Karna, the long lost brother of the Pandavas, probably the result of a juvenile fling, attributed to yet another immaculate conception. He is often portrayed as the tragic hero, generous to a fault, but devoted to Duryodhana. He is killed by Arjuna as he tries to pull out the sinking wheel of his chariot. On the advice of Krishna.

"The Pandavas win the righteous war through a number of deceptions, bending of rules, literal blows under the belt, ignoble warfare – all instigated by the consultant who makes the difference."

I chuckled.

"So, Krishna is a patron saint of consultants?"

"Yes, and the Gita is his manifesto. When Arjuna waits for the battle to begin, he asks Krishna, his charioteer, to take him to the middle of the battlefield, to take a look at the enemy. Seeing his elders, brothers, friends and loved ones, he is overcome with grief and refuses to fight. And then the consultant takes over. He brainwashes Arjuna through eighteen chapters."

I told him that in his blasphemous way, he was providing a great stepping stone to my understanding of the work. This inspired him to further details.

"Krishna at first takes the role of the harsh human resource guy, refusing to accept resignation. He reminds him of professional duty. He says that the body dies, but the eternal soul enters another being. So, it is not totally wrong to kill.

"When Arjuna is not convinced, he asks him to look at the bigger picture, work for the greater good, without attaching importance to the fruits of labour.

"Next there is a phase of self marketing as a guru. Krishna speaks of his experience as a consultant. How he comes into the picture whenever it is time to reward the good and punish the evil.

"When Arjuna asks whether it is better to resign or work, the master consultant nonchalantly tells him that work is worship.

"He teaches the confused warrior how to focus his faculties on the goal and nothing else. The goal in this case is the consultant himself. He is now gradually taking over the mind and free will.

"He teaches his student the path of knowledge, the knowledge again being limited to what he projects it to be.

"When Arjuna wonders about the material world and the ridiculousness of it beyond death, Krishna tells him of ways to obtain a retirement plan by focusing on him.

"He projects his multiple dimensions as an embodiment of every being, someone to call upon in all circumstances.

"He narrates how he is the supreme power of material and spiritual world. The brain of the warrior is clouded, and accepts the consultant as his guru.

"Having convinced his protégé, Krishna proceeds to dazzle him with a breathtaking presentation. It is here that he resorts to magic.

"Having numbed the mind, he talks about shoes and strings and sealing wax. The benefits of the process of devotion, the field and its knower, the nature and the nurturer, divine and anti divine nature, the three primary characteristics, qualities, about cutting through the wish fulfilling tree with a sword of detachment.

"Having confused him into believing that he is empowered, Krishna tells him to choose his path based on his own dharma ... subtly hinting at the way he has laid out for him.

"Tell me, can you think of a more successful consultant? In the end, Arjuna is convinced to fight, kill his friends and brothers, respected and loved ones."

He went into prolonged silence, probably reflecting on the exposition. When Jay stepped out to refill our glasses, he lifted his hand to stop him. "Amsterdam is notoriously short of free public toilets, my friend. Another glass and I will have to file for bankruptcy."

"So that is the Mahabharata in a nutshell?" I asked.

"The Mahabharata cannot be fit into a nutshell, Simon. The war ends with the ninth volume. It is followed by nine more, various sub plots, diversions, all linked together by a thread. Some of the lessons are indeed intriguing.

"Abhimanyu, the son of Arjuna, can charge through a particular enemy formation, but cannot break out of it. In the end he is killed in an unequal battle with seven great charioteers. Aren't we all in his place?"

He turned and smiled.

"You know what the greatest lesson of the epic is? After the all consuming war, Pandavas emerge victorious to find that they are the sole survivours save a handful. Who do they rule over in this kingdom of the dead? The entire struggle has been for absolutely nothing. Summed up by Shakespeare in one glorious line ..."

"Sound and fury signifying nothing," we chorused and laughed.

"Hope you have enjoyed the abridged tale told by an idiot," he signed off.

XX

Dr. Suprakash Roy loved the restaurant. *La Place* was slightly more expensive than *Vapiano,* but in return you were rewarded by the best view of the IJ River, garnished with the erudite sound of silence echoing from the eight floors of the Openbare Bibliotheek beneath the premises.

As he rolled his fork to entwine a number of noodles, the doctor looked at the pleasant faced young man who sat in front of him.

"Fancy meeting you here after all these years."

Sandeep nodded. After the brief telephonic discussion the day before, the psychiatrist had been a bit apprehensive about what to expect, but the hearty greetings had put him at ease.

"Amsterdam is a major hub of the Western world," Sandeep observed. "I guess that's why we keep running into acquaintances."

"I remember the three of you coming down to spend your holidays at our farm house. Pritam, you and that Aveek."

"Right."

"And where is the third guy of your team? Is he also lurking here somewhere?"

Sandeep shook his head. "I honestly don't know. He did not really complete college. Went off to one of those event management groups. That's the last I heard of him."

One of the more exquisite of Dutch beauties made her way across the floor of the restaurant. The two pairs of contemplative Indian eyes followed the fair footfalls till she disappeared behind the cash counters.

"Pritam did mention your weakness for women," the doctor remarked.

"Weakness for women?" Sandeep laughed. "I guess I am in excellent company. And you should know all about Freudian impulses. Neither am I the one romping around Europe, desirable damsel in tow."

Dr. Roy nodded.

"I wonder how desirable the damsel is right now. After you informed him that you were going to continue playing his part for the next three months, he suffered a major trauma. He is convinced that his job is all but lost."

"Why's that? Anyway he has another job in the bag. He should be elated. The presentation was more than successful. There are praises from the highest echelons of the organisation."

Suprakash never let disagreeable discussions get in the way of savouring food. He chewed reflectively on a succulent piece of chicken.

"I wonder what made you decide to continue. He is livid. He wants you to pretend illness and go back."

"I can't do that. I am hot property right now. The Vice President of Continental Europe wants me to co-author a proprietary methodology. If I feign illness, there is a good chance that I will be sent to Switzerland or London on company funds for quick recovery. The only way for me is to ride out this situation and get away as soon as the fad passes."

Dr. Roy looked keenly at him.

"Pritam seems to detect a hint of literary ambition beneath your noble intentions."

Sandeep returned his gaze with a smile.

"While I am here I will pursue my literary career. If you can call it a career yet. I will try to get hold of publishers and agents – if that's what he means. But, believe me, I can't help it. Sudden disappearance is not the solution. It will make his job all the more vulnerable."

The doctor shook his head. "How did he fall for it?"

"Love, actually."

"I understand that there was a definite degree of skulduggery involved with Captain Morgan playing a key role."

"He hasn't painted me in very good light ..."

"He thinks you are a snake."

"A peculiar analogy I can't quite fathom. The fact is that he got drunk ... and since he had already agreed to my proposal, I did the decent thing of going and meeting his colleagues."

"Have you rationalised or are you – to use another of Pritam's expressions – indulging in bull shit?"

Sandeep smiled.

"A little bit of both, my dear Higgins, like everyone else. Believe me, I am the one who is suffering now. I have to fly to Prague tomorrow with a lady whose idea of conversation is a six hour monologue on the life and times of her son."

The doctor sipped his bitter lemon.

"Ah yes ... I got wind of your Prague visit from Pritam as well. He was wondering if he should take the train from Budapest for the sole purpose of drowning your corpse in the Vltava."

"Indeed? I wouldn't have expected him to know the name of the river. But, then, this trip has been quite an education for him."

"I cannot really believe that you calculated the *Bhagavad Gita* stunt. That would definitely put you in the ranks of genius among impostors."

Sandeep smiled.

"I guess it was the cosmic connection of *karma*. Who told you about the *Gita*?"

"Pritam did. You have shared his password with him again and the emails are full of it. It seems to be a major discussion point. A new buzzword."

"Just think about it. *Gita* is the *new* buzzword. Let me assure you, the *Gita* stunt was pulled because I had not prepared the speech. I had to deliver the talk extempore. And the last thing that I had read was the *Gita*. It was my rotten luck that K. Ramesh interpreted it as the mother of all innovations. Anything remotely approaching the complexity of long division sums is considered an innovation in this industry. I have simply no way to get out of this without playing the part."

The doctor had come over from Leiden to meet this peculiar young man as a desperate measure – urged by the entreaties of Pritam. However, he was faced with a dilemma now.

"Tell me something, Sandeep. These emails and blogs that are going around propagating the success of your *Gita* stunt – how much influence do these have?"

"What do you mean?"

"I am thinking of the impression made in the *Weltanschauung* of a modern consulting company."

"The what?"

"Oh, pardon me ... I was referring to the world view ... You see, in my opinion, there is a separate world view for the people who spend most of their time in front of an electronically connected world. In a community which essentially lives on the Internet, how much do these mails and blogs mean?"

Sandeep gave this some thought.

"I would say it means a lot ... It literally means the world to them. For a lot of people the computer is the only way to know the world. Blogs and mails are the only way of communication. There is a lot of information out there, more easily accessible than ever before ... click of a mouse ... and a blog by a VP of Continental Europe really cuts through the clutter and makes them take notice."

Dr. Roy grew reflective again, this time without the culinary cause.

"Very interesting. You have had firsthand experience with this phenomenon, haven't you? You have worked as a blogger for a CEO or something like that."

Sandeep shuddered. "Dreadful memories. But, to answer your question, yes, indeed. I have worked as a ghost blogger."

"Why in these times do you still want to publish traditional novels? Why not just get your ideas across as blogs?"

The question confused Sandeep.

"The concepts are different. I mean, blogs are something everyone can have and there is the factor of reaching out to the reading public as well ... That is still conventionally achieved through brick and mortar bookstores and shelf space, where one has to fight it out with the latest literary prodigies like supermodels and WWF wrestlers. To ask a counter question, your curiosity really seems to have the whiff of professional interest. May I ask why you closed down your pretty successful chamber in Kolkata to come here and pursue academic research? You don't look the adventurous sort."

The doctor sighed.

"In the physical world, no. I am not really the one who will travel to the Stonehenge or the Eiffel Tower and try bungee jumping. But, the cognitive world is a very interesting terrain. And out there I am an adventurer. I felt pretty restricted in Kolkata. Chamber full of patients, and I saw each for half an hour or less. There was no scope to go deep into the mind. I had to restrict myself with medical treatment, removing the immediate symptom and hoping that it would not recur. There was no luxury to look at the root cause of the problem ... you understand?"

"To some extent perhaps ..."

"And I was interested in something else. Ever since the nineties, the world has changed. The internet has metamorphosed every single of our conformations, ideas and opinions of behaviour. It is a drastically new world we are dealing with, totally different world views ..."

"You mean you are dealing with the internet related psychological problems?"

"More than that. It is a new way of living, which does away with physical contact to a large extent. And also, there are these phenomena like the Second Life. Virtual Reality is less virtual and more real. Our standard conception of world view which governed our senses, responses, values, ethics and reactions, have changed so much into a conglomerate of the real and the virtual. It is increasingly a world where the laptop and the blackberry take precedence over the physical relationships between people. In this world, psychology needs to be studied anew – to remain meaningful within the new frame of reference ... am I boring you?"

"You interest me extremely. I am an author, remember? Rather a writer till the blasted Pillay manages to get the book to stores. Please continue."

"I am not referring to the Internet Addiction Disorder or indulgence in Cyber pornography which are recognised evils. Or other afflictions like semi-somnia where you cannot get enough sleep because of surfing late into the night or cyber chondria where you go to the diagnosis sites, find imaginary afflictions and map symptoms. These are known problems. What I am talking about are the changes in the general perception of the world."

Sandeep thought for a while.

"So, if someone tells you that the body movement that accompanies a lady's laughter reminds him of the effect of a mouse moving over an animated web page button, would that rouse your professional interest?"

Dr. Roy smiled. "Maybe. You see, through a small screen people are increasingly logging into an entire universe – parallel universes and beyond. There are reports of alarming percentage of time spent in front of the computer. If not, then staying connected through your cell phone. With twitter. I remember my schooldays. I used to travel to school by bus, a journey of about half an hour. That time was a period for contemplation, of thought. I could see passengers in the bus from all walks of life thinking."

"I also read a lot of books on my way to school."

"Sure. But shift yourself to a commute in the present day. What do you see around you? People hooked on to the various forms of gadgets. Either exchanging sms on cell phones, or surfing online, or twittering or simply playing all those curious Tetris like games. Don't you think that simply by looking at the commute time, a large portion of plain and simple thinking has been taken out of the lifestyle?"

Sandeep thought about it.

"That's one way of looking at it. If you look at the pages of history, people probably reacted the same way when the gramophone was invented, or the talking pictures and then the television came into the scene. And soon each of these became essential parts of the fabric of life."

The doctor smiled again.

"I am not interested in the pros and cons. I am not being judgemental or wondering whether things are moving towards the general good. I am looking on as an independent observer and my contention is that the way people live their lives and as a corollary, the way they think, are changing. The three dimensions of space have been phenomenally toyed with –with the world and beyond being locked up in a 10 inch screen."

Sandeep's eyes twinkled.

"Interesting."

"Think about the concept of time as well. Swatch is trying to promote a time zone free internet time for all the browsing population. So, there are serious indications that soon time will be a whole new system."

"The Sun is passé. We are ancient people still looking at a yellow star to guide our schedule."

"So, we are in a situation where the four Einsteinian dimensions of space and time are tampered with. This is different to the changes that took place in the last few decades, with the television and movies and branding and so on. The last ten years or so has seen a mutation in the way the new generation translates information. Change in pattern recognition, change in the awareness of the passage of time, the removal of social inhibition, the mental and physical aging process, mental imagery, dual coding of aural and visual senses – maybe there is another coding that needs to be added there for unique cyber senses... even interesting changes in language cognition brought about by the prevalence of internet. Let me ask you something. You do carry a cell phone. I know you do – you send some wonderful retorts to haikus sent by stupid consultants."

Sandeep laughed.

"Thanks. Glad you liked it."

"There are numbers you use frequently, don't you?"

"Yes."

"How many of those numbers can you recall?"

Sandeep thought about it.

"I don't think I recall even my own number."

"And think about yourself in your schooldays – when cell phones were still ..."

"I know what you mean. I could remember every number of close and not so close friends and relatives. It's something that I have thought about, really. The brain just decided one day to stop doing something that is redundant."

"That's how memory is affected in the digital world. You see where I am coming from?"

"It's fascinating, really."

"Would you mind if some day I go deeper into your profession as a ghost blogger?"

Sandeep raised his hands in a gesture.

"A pleasure. And I might be interested in talking more about your research. It is terribly interesting."

The psychiatrist laughed.

"Of course. I know you are an author."

"So we'll set something up. It seems I am going to be here for a while."

The remark brought a frown to the good doctor's brow.

"Yes, seems we can't help it. But, what do we do with Pritam?"

Sandeep's brows too knit themselves into a thought.

"True. He bit off more than he could chew ... and as far as I know, his romantic route has been too war ravaged."

Dr. Roy nodded.

"Berlin, Dresden, Krakow, Warsaw, Prague, Bratislava, Budapest ... I guess things are not going too well on the romantic front. The tension is killing him. The walks in the sun are playing tricks with his air condition honed senses, getting on his nerves. And add to that the guide attempting to tickle him with a feather in Prague."

"What?"

"Yes," the doctor said sadly. "It seems the guides were about to take a photograph of the group and asked everyone to smile. Since Pritam was not really being jovial, one of the guides tried to tickle him in the ear with a feather. Almost came to blows. I am afraid he will crack under pressure soon. Something you may not be able to comprehend fully, having never built a career over a decade."

Sandeep put down the fork and spoon and wiped his lips.

"I agree. But, his reputation has actually been enhanced. He was a reputed consultant. Now he is on his way to becoming legendary."

They stood up and descended down the stairs into the Bibliotheek.

"You know what fate awaits the legends. Recognition – in more ways than one. People recognise them. That is what he is afraid of now. And the apprehension that you will be exposed soon."

"It is difficult to be exposed when you are impersonating a consultant. Under the glossy cover, there is nothing but emptiness, colourless, odourless and tasteless. How can anyone detect fraud? In medical terms, a placebo would always work as well."

They had to lower their voice as they descended the many levels on the escalator. Both of them preferred it to the elevator, their united subconscious wanting to take in the reassuring collection of books – the persevering mementos of a pre-digital world.

"You and I know that. Pritam doesn't. He has built a successful world for himself and much of it according to him is because of his brilliance. And to an extent it is true ... you have to be brilliant at building on nothingness. I will do my best to reassure him, but he may still not be too convinced. I would recommend resetting the password."

They walked down the steps of the huge library and walked along the Oosterdokjes towards the Centraal Station. Dr. Roy lit a cigar.

"Freudian heirloom?" Sandeep asked, refusing an offered Havana.

"Yes, as long as I don't inherit the cancer as well. I would not recommend sharing the password. He will keep going through the mails and the anxiety will grow out of proportion. I will tell him to take a break, put his mind completely off work, the situation being under control and all that. I will ask him to enjoy himself."

"I doubt if that is an option on such a trip."

"He has to make a conscious decision and break the journey if necessary. Anyway, there was another thing. He says that you are getting pally with a couple of girls, exactly what he expected of a reptilian womaniser..."

Sandeep winced.

"He really called me that?"

"Yes. And things much worse. He spoke specifically of girls named Amrita and Madhu. It's apparent from your mails."

Sandeep laughed.

"Madhu Deb is the female who will be with me on the flight to Prague. She is a very jovial sort of person, who barges into your cubicle and mailbox uninvited. I can't help it. But she is in her forties and has a son she likes to discuss with a fervour approaching the fanatical. In fact, this flight to Prague is a constant source of trauma to *me* ... and has resulted in some lively literature on sms."

"Literature on sms?" Dr. Roy's professional interest was tickled.

"Yes ... and the other one, Amrita ... she's a fruity sort of girl. She tries sending me alerts when it rains. In Amsterdam it amounts to a twenty four by seven job."

"Ah ... but, then, why does this lady send you such alerts? Rain is for everyone, isn't it?"

"She did it once –by mistake she claims, but I doubt it. She followed it up with a misspelt apology mail. I became my charming self and said that even in error she had done me a service because I love the misty rain as much as the next person. Being born in June, rain and I are inseparable and all that nonsense. And since then she has taken on the responsibility of sending the rain almost as an attachment to her mails. She lies in wait for the first drop."

The good doctor paused in his tracks.

"You know, it is precisely this charming rhetoric that keeps my beloved brother awake at night. He said that this lady also sent you poems."

Sandeep shuddered again.

"Yes. And pretty ghastly ones."

"Ghastlier than Pritam's haikus?"

"You read Pritam's haiku?"

"Yes ... poetry on Blackberry. It was interesting ... a snapshot of the new cognitive world."

"To each his taste. The psychology of the text message. I dare say as far as depth of feeling goes, this girl is a notch above him. Scores higher on sincerity, has a sense of literary form. But Pritam at least spells correctly and doesn't make grammatical errors."

"Some of the young lady's poetry seems ominous to my cousin."

Sandeep shrugged.

"I spend the days trying to avoid Madhu Deb, preparing my series of Gita inspired speeches and wondering what to do about K.Ramesh's drive for self-actualisation. I spend evenings indulging in my hobby of collecting rejection slips. Whatever time is left generally goes after a guy called Sunil Pillay. I can't care less about an infatuated female. And anyways, I have already declared that I am married."

Dr. Roy nodded.

"Something that did not really endear you to Pritam."

As they approached the Centraal Station, they paused to listen to a Middle Eastern man playing the accordion. Sandeep could hear the doctor humming to himself as the catchy Arabic tune created a frivolous effect. He smiled.

"I am thinking how to help Pritam. It's a pity I can't treat his anxiety directly, but I will have to do my best. I have a plan. When do you leave for Prague?"

Sandeep winced.

"Tomorrow morning. Hey, you said you were interested in poetry on sms."

"From the academic point of view."

"I guess this will be really interesting ... I will forward a chain of poetic exchange ..."

"Not with the poetic lady, I hope ..."

"Spare me ... Nice girl, but not really my idea of a poetic partner. With Shruti."

"Shruti?"

"Yes."

"The girl Pritam is travelling with?"

"Yes. The same."

"You are exchanging poetry with her?"

"Fun ones."

"And you said that your wife's name was Shruti too, didn't you?"

"Er ... yes ... I did. I mean, the question was so sudden that for a moment all the female names in the world seemed to have been turned off from my immediate memory with the click of a remote. And after monumental struggle this one name surfaced from the depths of despair."

"Subconscious."

"Please don't attach Freudian interpretations to it ... As it is, I dread to think what Freud would have made of the Thai noodles that we just had."

They laughed.

"What plan do you have for Pritam?"

The doctor turned and faced Sandeep.

"Do you have a recent snap of your friend?"

"Recent snap?"

"Yes, something that shows his entire frame, not just his face."

Sandeep thought for a while.

"I don't think I have treasured any such photograph. But, I guess you will find some on Orkut and Facebook."

"Ah ... fancy not thinking of that. Okay, I will let you know our story tomorrow. For now, reset his password."

With a wave Sandeep left for the tram as the doctor stubbed his cigar and stepped into the station.

XXI

Exchange of text messages between Shruti and Sandeep, forwarded to Dr. Suprakash Roy.

Shruti:

On Trans-Continent flights there are no laws
Which protect the distressed from boredom's jaws
Hear the good lad's tale without any pause
Auditory organs lent for just cause

Sandeep:

Buckled to my seat
By hostesses of air
Talkative boss
In adjacent chair
Cotton balls or not
My ears will despair

Shruti:

Sadly...
Such Dejection
Won't result
In her ejection
From the plane
For u'll see her again
Being a royal pain

Refusing to be slain
By subordinate men

Sandeep:

Sigh...
That's cause for sorrow
For on morn of the morrow
Hostesses of air
Sultry or fair
Will walk the sky road
In strict read only mode
But I'll be in dismay
Listening all the way
With not a rhymed sms
To brighten my day

Shruti:

Surely...
A poetic drama's down the line
Divine comedy most truly thine
Trapped in the air
With lady boss fair
Emergency exits under repair

Sandeep:

My verse-atile friend
Take due care
Before you call
My lady boss fair
Maybe she once was
When airplanes were rare
And Professor Lal
Had a head full of hair

Shruti:

And horses had wings
And bosses no offsprings!!

Sandeep:

I hanker after the good old days
When sexes were seated in separate bays

Shruti:

Surely even then
Baywatch was possible
Barriers exist
To be rendered crossable
It all depends
And the means
Justify the ends

Sandeep:

All the bay that I can watch
Is vintage meat kept long in fridge
Pretty stewardesses saunter by
I feel like Mariner of Coleridge

Shruti:

No Shelley nor Blake
Had so much at stake
As pleasing a boss in air
Dungeons of sleep
Ever so deep
A waking man's despair

Sandeep:

Water or air
Ugly or Fair
Whatever the surface or charm
Pleasing one's boss
Is way too gross
Can do nothing but harm
I prefer to close
My eyes and dose
As to glory she yaps away
Again will I peer
When the end is near
In clear view is the runway

The doctor chuckled and dialled Pritam's number.

~ ~ ~

Budapest

Pritam answered the call on the first ring.

"Hi ... are you disturbing me? Not at all. I don't think that I am capable of being disturbed any more. In fact your call has given me the opportunity to tear myself away from the unending attractions of the Museum of Terror."

"Museum of Terror?"

"Yes. It is called the Terror Haza. You see, my travelling companion is so very into morbid stuff. There is a beautiful city, an awesome palace, the great Danube. And I have to spend my time being entertained by the gruesome display of devices which used to keep a tab on people during the communist regime."

"Not really enjoying yourself, are you?"

A heart wrenching hollow laugh followed from the other end.

"This is a sequel. We had spent an entire afternoon in the Communism museum in Prague. And there I almost made a colossal ass of myself by not realising the peculiar significance of the biggest McDonalds of the city being tucked away behind the museum of communism. God. It feels like – what's the French word?"

"Guillotine?"

"No ... it's a small two phrase word and very very French. Means something like the impression of having been through the whole damn thing earlier."

"Déjà vu?"

"That's it. You know, the only way I can see the Danube is by jumping into it. And it seems a positively brighter idea by the minute."

Dr. Roy wondered whether he should put this down as a Death Wish.

"Pritam, this is an international call. Listen to me, we have to talk."

"Hang up. I'll call you back."

"It's not the call charges that I want to cut short, Pritam. It's your self pity."

"My what?"

Dr. Suprakash Roy stood up. The time had come to take a firm grip on the situation.

"I have to tell you something very straight. You were the one who wanted to go on this trip with the wonderful girl ..."

"Wonderful ..."

"And you allowed yourself to be duped into an identity swap."

"I ..."

"And believe me, I met the guy yesterday. Also met some of the colleagues he works with – employees of your company. I got the impression that they never expected you, that is him, to be so accomplished. Things have really worked in your favour."

The doctor could sense his cousin grappling with his emotions at the other end of the connection. He carried on.

"I checked the situation. There is no way that Sandeep can get away from the three month assignment he is talking about without a face loss – or even a loss of job – for you. The top boss is pretty adamant about it. So, you have to live with it."

"But ... yes, I'll be back. No it's my cousin, and *not* Sandeep...," Pritam turned back to the phone as Shruti went back to her pleasant perusal of communist brutality. "You see, big brother, the snake has been impersonating me in Amsterdam and he has been carrying on long distance philandering with Shruti. But, is there no way out ...?"

"Absolutely none. The only way out for you is to play along and hope that this fellow does a good job. And he is doing an excellent job. Let me assure you, he is one of a kind."

"Isn't he?"

"And think about the money. Pritam, you make a ton. And this guy has agreed to a mere forty percent of the stuff he is earning for the time being ..."

"*Mere* forty percent? And *he* is earning, is he?"

The doctor took a deep breath.

"Pritam, he needs the money. And he needs the cover as well. And in the meantime, he is doing an excellent job to build your reputation further. I have talked to his colleagues. I have had a most rewarding conversation with a few of them, including your current supervisor, a lady who keeps talking about her son. I showed them your picture. The one in which you are playing golf in Philadelphia..."

"What?"

"Yes. The magic of social networking. It was on Orkut. And believe me, although you think it showcases the successful consultant, it also makes you look pathetically out of shape. Maybe it is more pronounced due to the setting, the golf links and so on. The mind tends to associate the incoming information rather than take the absolute ..."

"Shut up and continue."

"I was ..."

"I don't want a lecture on Cognitive Psychology."

The elder cousin was pained. After the trouble he had gone through, the attitude of Pritam irked him. True, he had not really talked to Madhu Deb or any of the other colleagues. But, he had thought the entire scheme up. Compared to Pritam, Sandeep had been a revelation. So curious about all that went on in the world.

"Okay. The point is that the photograph makes you look fat. I had printed it out and taken it along with me. I introduced myself as a doctor – did not mention the specialisation. I informed them that one of my colleagues was a dietician and he has been working on this revolutionary method of weight reduction ..."

"What?"

"Sandeep did mention you keep saying *what.* Maybe we can work on that together after this blows over. So, I explained to them that this is how you looked a few months back and had got into this tremendous shape following the prescribed diet of my colleague. But, there is a chance that if you do not follow the instructions of diet and regimen, you can slip back into your old shape."

"I ... I am not out of shape."

"Ahem!"

"I am not obese if that's what you mean. A few extra pounds maybe."

"Well, there is the problem of cognitive information processing once again. Think of yourself in contrast with Sandeep. That guy is an athlete."

"You seem to be his biggest fan."

"Well no. At present it is K. Ramesh who lays claims to that spot."

"God in heaven. But, I am supposed to look like him. That's how he can impersonate me ..."

Dr. Roy's tone was reassuring.

"Come now. He looks like your passport photograph. Not the rest of you. I fully appreciate the separated at birth contest, but a lot of things have happened since then. But, look at the beauty of the thing. Once this is over and you swap back your roles, you can just relax and tell anyone who asks that the diet and regimen are a thing of the past and you have switched back to your old self."

"I don't quite like the idea ..."

"That way no one suspects. And you can enjoy yourself. Here is what you have to do. Go slow, think slow. Whenever you start thinking of the negative effects of the swap, think again about what could have already gone wrong and hasn't. Think of all the positives that have come out of this. Why not treat this as three months of paid holiday while someone else works towards your promotion. Delay your new job. Spend some days in Paris, in Hamburg. The sinful cities. Get your mind off this. I assure you, this is the very best that you can do. In fact people crave for this sort of a thing."

"Hmph ..."

The heartfelt grunt summed it up.

"Paris. Hamburg. Let us get through this guided tour of the Cold War ..."

Dr. Roy steeled himself. Now he had to get to the second part of the plan.

"Ah, there you are. Who has told you anything about finishing this tour?"

"Eh?"

"You did not want to get married to someone who would talk about vision mission statements and business cases. Do you really want to go ahead and get hitched to someone who quotes Noam Chomsky and drops phrases like Perestroika and Glasnost at a romantic dinner? Whose idea of a kiss is something between Brezhnev and Honecker?"

Pritam was already clutching his temples.

"Spare me, big brother. Spare me the cold war jargon."

∾ ∾ ∾

Prague

From the IBM Thinkpad used by Manouk Kruif, PMO personnel, to jot down the meeting minutes of the high profile session for *Axiom* Europe Senior Management.

Paradigm Shifts in Consulting (oh yeah ?) ###@@@ 25th June.
Pritam Mitra (looks cool)

Presentation with no presentation ... (new level of crap. Plain lazy. No Manouk to make his decks???) Cutting costs by spending nothing on equipment and decks ... (so what about calling all these people to Prague for a meeting eh, wiseguy?)

\\
*************////////////////////////////////////

////////////////////////***\\\
\\\\\\\\\\\\\\\\\\\

///**************
*****\\\
************/////////////
///////////////////////////////////

Cool guy. Transcript mailed by Madhu on 17th June. (Use that for meeting minutes) It's the same bull.

????? Four paths for decision making??? NSEW? Maybe there's a GPS too.

Madhu goes hahaha ... she's a big fan.

Definitely something new.

Indian storehouse of knowledge to be leveraged. New offering. Why does it sound like old hat?

Q&A .... Not Slumdog Millionaire ... #$@P

****************>>>>>>>>>>>>>>>>>>******************

:-) :-(:-| Multiple choice
Prakash: Why was the presentation different from the paper submitted?
Cool dude: The only thing permanent is change. Everything changes. I am a change agent. In me people need to find change. (sounds like a new age guru)
Marco: Did you refer to any Body of Knowledge?
K.Ramesh (on Video conference from Budapest): In the present state of industry, we are the Walmart of knowledge vendors. We produce mediocrity by bulk and supply it cheap to the stores. When we mention body of knowledge the focus is on Body and Knowledge is nice to have. The paradigm shift – if that is to take place – is to make something out of the knowledge that exists in our country – complied though the ages and now moth ridden from being stacked in the unused

chambers of our library of inheritance. The knowledge reflected here stems from the country's philosophical opus – the Gita. (Zen Master speaketh.)
Shanthi: Can this be stored in the KR?
Cool Dude: What is KR? (Love it ... he's real cool)
Shanthi: Knowledge Repository of the company.
Cool Dude: Ah. The great suppository of information! (Was that intended? I guess it was.) Knowledge is boundless. Do you think it can be stored in the confines of a corporate website? (That surely is Zen)
Marco: What was the reference to the McKinsey method?
Ans: Let's discuss that offline. (I like this guy)

Madhu: Ramesh has found this particular method of imparting consultation particularly promising blahblahblahblahblah ....
Zzzzzzzzzzzzzzzzzzz

Dude checks his cell phone and says it's raining in Amsterdam ... guess what that piece of wisdom is meant to be.

*****************#########################))))))))))))))

Qwertypoiuyasdflkhhc

10:30 to 12:25 .... Lunch served yeah cool ...

XXII

Prague

The sun had painted Stare Mesto's exquisite cobblestoned streets in gold. Seated outside the *Bohemia Bagel,* Madhu Deb was having her second bottomless cup of coffee. When Sandeep arrived after a two hour training session at the Taichi Sokol Vinohrady in Riegrovy sady, he found her in a contemplative mood.

"There you are," the Senior Manager smiled as he took a seat in front of her. "I thought you would get lost in the splendour. An impressionable author."

Sandeep nodded.

"Prague is indeed the most beautiful city I have seen."

The fragile dam was broken. Pent up analysis gushed out in a practised deluge. There followed a clinical dissection of the wonderful cities of the world, some of which Madhu Deb had visited and some she had just heard of from different acquaintances. Sandeep was taken on virtual conducted tours across the world, from Sydney to San Francisco, from Moscow to Johannesburg, from London to Buenos Aires, from Toronto to Bangkok. As preface to these travelogues there were detailed descriptions of the different people who had narrated these experiences to the good lady, each one a dear friend and a sterling contributor to the society. These included, if he had not been guilty of imagining things in a daze, Michael Palin and Bill Bryson.

If Sandeep had not stopped listening in the early seconds of the second minute and had not been thinking about the crazy situation that life had landed him in, he could have collected material for at least half a dozen future novels. Novels that wielded the poetic license of deviating from strict facts with nonchalant bravado.

When his floating thoughts resurfaced onto the level of the conversation, Madhu Deb was earnestly talking about Hidori's reactions during their visit to Greece last summer. At some moment of distraction, the little fellow had sneaked into the subject.

"Samit did not know what to do ... you see, we are so different, Samit and I. He is one of the purely cerebral, exertion avoiding types ... while I have played every sport that has come my way."

Sandeep wondered what physical sports Madhu Deb had taken up in her youth and why they had done nothing to moderate her generous proportions. However, the lady in question had already moved on.

"I often wonder how we hitched together," she said in a reflective voice. "After all, we are as different as two people can be."

Sandeep had been thinking for a while that social norms expected him to contribute at least a word to what ostensibly was a dialogue. Now perceiving a small opening he jumped to get a word in.

"Perhaps that's how best matches work out. With the two people being different."

Madhu Deb smiled a wee bit sadly.

"Yes, it has its pros and cons. In a way, I am indebted to Samit. He travelled all the way to the United States when I was walking out of this turbulent relationship. I was a wreck and he just was there for me. We have had a wonderful relationship. However ..."

As she paused, Sandeep wondered if he had missed out on some important revelation about Madhu Deb's past life while daydreaming about the twists and turns of his own present one. What had suddenly elevated him into a trusted ear for the chequered past of the good lady?

" ... I don't really know if I have ever seen him as anything more than a very good friend."

She looked into her empty mug and asked the waiter for a refill.

"Relationships are not that simple, don't you think?" she looked at Sandeep and he managed to nod and mouth – "Yes, quite."

"Especially these days. How much of one's spouse does one see? Take your example. You got married, but ever since then you have been travelling."

On its way to his lips, Sandeep's coffee mug froze as he came to terms with this new development yet again.

"There are other people you interact with and meet more often than you meet your wife...I wonder whether the structure of society should be changed to suit the modern age."

Sandeep sipped his mug reflectively. The slight movement as he lifted the coffee mug hurt his wrist. He had been through a strenuous couple of hours with the Sifu at the Sokol Vinohrady. Some of the applications of *chin na* had been extremely effective.

As he rolled the strong brew inside his mouth, the hot liquid made him wince. The elbow of one beefy practitioner had connected pretty hard with the side of his jaw during a submission technique. He wondered if he had lost some enamel on his molars.

As his thoughts floated back into the space of the conversation again, he found Madhu Deb in the same reflective mood.

"Samit is a very nice person to have around, a good man to discuss Literature and music. As an intellectual companion I have nothing to complain ... why, he would have loved your session here."

Sandeep smiled. The session in Prague, with the half dozen *Axiom* representatives from Continental Europe, had been successful yet again. He had more of less repeated the same thoughts as in that epoch making talk in Amsterdam. And since it had already been touted as a successful benchmark, it had been accepted. Much like today's bestsellers. There had been a couple of complicated questions, but they had been handled with élan. And as taught over international telephone connection, he had taken the first opportunity to scoot from the meeting room. The promised offline discussions on some of the more complicated technicalities had not taken place. Madhu Deb had been a pliant supervisor. She had made the excuse for him when he had spoken of places to visit. After all, she had reasoned, an author needed his experiences.

Now the good lady was busy getting herself submerged in the sensual delights of a large chocolate brownie. Hidori supposedly loved brownies. He often helped himself to four or five while Samit and she had coffee. Did Sandeep want one?

Sandeep shook his head.

"No, thanks. There's some problem with my molars."

"Toothache? I don't think I need to be worried about the teeth until Hidori turns six ..."

"I think I've lost some enamel. The coffee has been hurting ..."

"How? Did you bite a spoon?"

Reluctantly, Sandeep recounted his accident at the *tai chi* class.

Madhu Deb was impressed.

"You found time to attend a class here, did you? I like that. Utilising every trip. Some years back I would have done the same ... Now, however, travelling with Samit is different. He is so sedentary. Hidori ..."

"Ouch ..."

It had not been planned. The hot liquid had really found its way to a nerve before the kid's name had popped up again. Madhu Deb for once stopped pursuing on her favourite topic.

"Is it that bad? Do you have a dentist?"

"Not in Prague."

"In Amsterdam?"

"I've to find out ..."

He did not know whether or not Pritam had a dentist.

Madhu Deb laughed.

"It's the writer in you, is it? Being so unconcerned about the worldly affairs? Samit, in fact, has the same attitude, but then he thinks there is a writer in him. One of his dreams which will never come true is to write a sprawling novel. But, he's too unenergetic. I wonder how Hidori ..."

"Ouch." Best practice revisited.

"Come on. You don't have to finish the coffee. Once we get back to Amsterdam we will do something about your teeth. I am sure our company has some ties with the dental agency I use..."

Sandeep, whose second cry of pain had been manufactured, was nevertheless suffering from that excruciating pain made possinble by exposed dental nerves. To him Madhu Deb's words seemed to be dipped in solace. For a moment he felt sorry for the unkind poetic exchange with Shruti.

"I'll make an appointment for you the moment we reach Amsterdam," the good lady continued.

Sandeep smiled.

"I can't really tell you how thankful I am. I had already surrendered myself to a diet of salami, cold boiled egg and karnemilk for the rest of my stay in the Netherlands."

The helpful lady laughed.

"Come on. Things are not so bad. I was thinking of something else. I need your help for that."

Sandeep raised his eyebrows eagerly. He would be happy to help in light of the lady's promised role in restoring his smile. To stay in the Netherlands without being able to say cheese was a frightening thought.

"You know I keep having these events for our team – something offbeat, something that is fun and promotes teamwork, keeps them interested and above all teaches them that life is a lot more than earning money ..."

A fleeting fear – a seed of doubt. Was it really a part of the job of a manager to teach the team how to live? What made her an expert on living anyway? But then, he had seen the team of Amrita, Trisha and Gunjan play apostles, clinging on to each word of the Hidori parables.

"I generally arrange these musical evenings – it also lets me do something for deprived children. But, I get the feeling that we could do with something else – something more offbeat – to add to the excitement."

Sandeep waited as Madhu Deb turned her round face and looked into his eyes.

"Would you mind conducting a demonstration tai chi class for the group?"

"Ouch," sipped Sandeep

ᔕ ᔕ ᔕ

Mail from Simon to his Mailing List
Subject: Walking the Way of the Warrior

An exhilarating experience. Entry into a world that seems fascinating and esoteric. And to think I had almost missed the summons.

We receive so many communications reeking of corporate bs from our senior managers, that more often than not I blissfully ignore them. It was only when Trisha came over for a chat that I became aware of the hidden facets of Pritam's character that had supposedly been unearthed by our exemplary leader.

"What sort of a buddy are you?" my chubby cheeked friend asked, with her characteristic mock aggravation. "You don't even know of his hidden genius."

"Well, I'm sorry, I didn't read the papers," I said.

Trisha rattled off the different qualities of the fascinating new guy. "He seems to be an expert in two different martial arts. Of course, that's on top of being a successful consultant. "

"Wow," I was impressed.

"In today's chill out session he will demonstrate tai ching chung or something like that."

I opened the mail from Madhu.

"It's *tai chi chuan,*" I corrected. "It's pretty popular in these parts. But, that's swell – and I don't mean your cheeks. At least we will have some fun for a change."

Whenever I speak about her cheeks Trisha comes back with a strong retort. She seems embarrassed by the chubby schoolgirl look they lend her in spite of my reassurances that it makes her quite attractive. As they indeed do, even making up for the snub nose and accentuating her aura of naiveté.

She was on the verge of saying something when there was a knock on the panel and the subject of our discussion stepped in. As usual he was carrying an apprehensive look on his face and a sheaf of papers in his hands – fresh from the printer.

"Well, *buddy,* I guess you have already read my obituary," he began and then broke off when he noticed Trisha. "Oh, hi."

"Obituary?" I asked, but Trisha had already returned the greetings and the consultant had taken full advantage of it to steer the conversation away from morbid topics.

"We were just discussing about today's martial arts demo," Trisha informed him, full of youthful enthusiasm.

He started visibly. "Has a date already been set for the funeral?"

I turned my monitor towards him. He glanced at the calendar invite from Madhu Deb and his jaw dropped. "Is there a direct flight from Amsterdam to Budapest?" he asked, and thereafter refused to throw some light on the peculiar query.

Trisha was full of her own questions. "Will you show us self defence techniques?"

Pritam shrugged. "I've just come to know of the session myself. I haven't quite decided what I am going to do. But, *tai chi* is more popular as an exercise system."

Trisha looked impressed. "There is so much to learn. Gosh, I don't know anything." She encounters the limitations of her worldly knowledge almost on an hourly basis and always confesses her ignorance unabashedly. It is an endearing quality. However, Pritam threw us a strange look and said, "It's better not to know too much, else one gets into trouble."

When the girl had left us, my official buddy collapsed in the second chair of the cubicle.

"Simon, do you have any passion or hobbies?" he asked.

"I do read a lot. I blog."

"I once worked as a ghost blogger. Or rather, a friend of mine did."

That sounded like a curious profession, but before I could ask him about it he wanted to know what else I did.

"I play the guitar sometimes, but that's confidential."

"Don't breathe a word of your reading to anyone either," he warned me. "Else you will soon be discussing the reading habits of Hidori."

I informed him that I had already been there, done it.

"In the next chill out session, you may be asked to read everyone to sleep."

"They find other ways of putting people to sleep. Have you attended meetings?"

"They are always on the lookout for new techniques. They call it continuous improvement. Or innovation. And of course, never let them know of your blog."

I smiled.

"I can't afford to. I don't really tell them too many things. You have a deal. In fact, I have not shared your expertise with hidden cameras as another facet of your multi-dimensional personality everyone is talking about," I said. "I guess you want it to remain that way."

He shook my hand.

"That's our little secret."

However, for someone so irreverent and disdainfully cynical, the session was a major surprise.

These events – most often an hour long and honestly not aloways the most exciting – are supposed to build a strong sense of teamwork. To an extent it does meet its goals, with the entire team being together for an hour away from the daily humdrum, with the vociferous cheerfulness of Madhu Deb and the friendly banter of Amrita and Trisha to brighten things up. The trick is to pick a spot as far from Gunjan as possible.

The details of the session can be found in my latest blog post. I won't really repeat the sublime levels of mastery demonstrated by Pritam. All I can say is that it was like listening to a Yanni composition live. With the positive caveat that one could engage in active participation.

In the end everyone was enthralled. Even Ajay Yadav seemed to go through the proceedings without taking time off to wonder about the safety of his job.

On the other hand, having kindled the sparks of interest in the graceful art in us, Pritam soon regained the air of apprehension. When Madhu wanted to know who wanted to learn *Tai chi* on a regular basis, a lot of hands shot up, including mine. But, the man responsible for all this enthusiasm was not that keen.

"*Tai chi*, or any other martial art, requires years of practice," he explained. "It is definitely not like one of the certification courses that you do in the industry. A couple of classes won't help you in any way. It is a continuous process that has to be perfected through years of dedicated practice. Unless one is prepared to make the sacrifices and is dedicated, it is not going to help. I will be here for only a few months. It is better if you can find a regular place to train … in Amsterdam…"

Madhu now declared the session over and asked the interested people to approach her so that she could work something out. Another of those initiatives right down her alley.

It was a distinctly nervous look with which my buddy nodded at me as I left the gym.

Curious aside : I ran into Amrita as I walked into the corridor. She was smiling and looking at Pritam from the doorway. In her eyes I noticed something more than admiration. It was a look which I have often seen in high school, although seldom directed towards me. A look of absolute infatuation, adulation and crush.

Cheers
Simon

∾ ∾ ∾

Blog of Simple Simon
Tags: Tai Chi, Chin Na

People who read these blogs call me a cynic. And to a great extent I am. With my peculiar American-Dutch-Irish-Indian legacy, and my somewhat strange yet commonplace occupation, I guess it is cynicism that keeps me going. There are opinions in the workplace world that the most damaging employee is the cynic. However, as long as I keep my mouth shut and reserve the posts of this private blog as the sole outlet for my pent up frustrations and feelings, I don't think I am too dangerous for the morale of the company.

However, with the arrival of this new consultant into the scheme of things, I have found myself becoming more and more prone to sharing my private thoughts with him. His quasi-philosophical paper may have swept many mighty figures off their feet, but when he speaks to me, his designated buddy, he does seem to have monumental disdain for the work that we do. In some ways a twin soul, easy to confide in matters of anti establishmentarianism and political incorrectness. My opinions seem almost eulogy in contrast.

Sometimes, his contempt for the fancy fabrication that we weave out of our ordinary offerings seems rather extreme. After all, this industry does provide bread – and also cakes and ale – to many, especially his countrymen.

The lesson life taught me today, nevertheless, is that one cannot afford to be hasty in categorising a fellow human being. I always have a problem with the American way of compartmentalising people as winners and losers. I have seen the management putting forward tags such as team-man, hard worker, employee with attitude problem ... I was also on the verge of labelling Pritam Mitra as an incorrigible sceptic with sweeping irreverence for the world . Things changed as we walked into yet another one of those chill out sessions organised by our senior manager, Madhu Deb.

We gathered there, including the Account Manager, to find ourselves taking part in a demonstration of *tai chi chuan.* The instructor was none other than this remarkable new addition to our group – Pritam Mitra.

The moment the motley group people of *Axiom* had assembled in the office gym, he started talking with a passion that I have seldom seen in anyone – in or out of the industry.

He started by asking us to follow his movements, which were slow, continuous and, to some extent, funny. He spoke of how the movement promoted the flow of energy along the meridians of the human body. According to ancient Chinese medicine, there were ailments that these sequences could cure. Grandmaster Chen

Man Ching himself was supposedly cured of tuberculosis at an early age by pursuing the art.

After speaking for some time about the exercise system, he started talking of the roots of *tai chi chuan,* how an old Taoist priest had analysed the movements of a snake and a crane in mortal combat and had developed this style of martial art. The basic principles were yielding, pliability and softness.

He proceeded to demonstrate how the slow movements could be used in the martial context. He asked me to be the volunteer and instructed me to strike him. When I threw an untrained punch, he moved with unhurried calm, going through the same exercise movements that he had shown earlier, in the process deflecting my blow, pinning my elbow and bringing me down to the ground. I am as tall as him, somewhat broader in built, but the way I was taken down involved minimal effort. It was a skilful, masterly demonstration. The corporate audience used to a largely sedentary lifestyle could not help but be impressed.

He spent the next few minutes talking about the philosophical aspects of the art, of how this exotic martial form had always been associated with the philosophy of Taoism, how the hard and soft aspects of it mapped to the *yin* and *yang* concepts, how it embodied meditation in action. Mind, body and soul exercise with the added martial dimension. He became highly lyrical and there was a glow in his face as he spoke.

There was something distinctly philosophical about the demonstration, as had been with his presentation a week earlier.

However, there was a significant difference.

During the presentation and afterwards, I had always sensed overwhelming flippancy about everything that he himself said, something that seemed to sneak its mocking head from beneath the outward seriousness. He was contemptuous about the very nuggets of wisdom he threw about with casual élan.

In contrast, there was a touching sense of conviction about the demonstration, a purity bred out of love, respect and dedication for the art. The earnestness of his speech and the perfection of the techniques had most of the audience rapt. In an industry thriving on empty words and superficial expertise, the display of sublime skill was a rarity.

Towards the end of the seminar, he spoke for some time about a discipline of Chinese martial arts called *chin na,* which I gathered was the science of seizing and controlling the opponent. He spoke of the way this specialisation could be used in tandem with any martial art, and how *tai chi* and *chin na* together formed a most potent combination. He even demonstrated a particularly painful wrist lock performed with grace and effectiveness on Gunjan. Whether the volunteer was picked up at random or by choice is something that will remain a mystery.

The great news is that, it has been more or less finalised that he will be taking more such classes – although I dare say he was not too enthusiastic about it. A new world has opened up for me and I intend to dive headlong into it in search of the enticing esoteric pearls of an exotic art.

Part V:

Compound and Open Interests

XXIII

Vienna, Austria

The photographs were the last straw.

Shruti was walking behind him, with a couple of old German friends who had suddenly popped up in Westbahnhof. Manuel and Andrea. What was infuriating was that she spoke to them in fluent German. Pritam, already struggling from the historical, political and socio-economical aspects of the tour, nursing a tender bottom from two hours of cycling, now found himself cut off from the linguistic angle as well. He had been weighing Suprakash's wise words of bringing a premature end to this torture when he noticed the photographs. They had been made into a collage on the board that acted as the guiding mast for the group of tourists taking the *Europe on a Shoestring* walking tour.

He could see himself in the two photographs, scowling at the camera in Berlin and Budapest. In a peculiar way, the caption on the collage stretched from his scowls from one to the other.

"Whatever your mood, you'll keep coming back to us" – the banner proclaimed.

Leiden, Netherlands

"Everything's under control," the doctor spoke into the phone immediately on answering the call.

"I'm on my way to Paris."

This piece of news brightened Suprakash Roy remarkably.

"Alone?"

"I am hitching on to a group of Indian backpackers. Three great, young software guys enjoying a vacation."

"And Shruti?"

"She's with two of her friends from Germany. They will continue on this tour of the war ravages. And they will speak in German ... much like your ruddy Freud."

Dr. Roy thought for a while.

"How are these new friends of yours?"

"Some of the best guys I could hope to know. One of them believes he is in Australia."

"Good for you."

"Another had his photograph taken in front of Mozart's statue and, all the while thinking that it was Napoleon."

"Excellent. I am glad for you."

"I doubt they know anything about world wars. Let alone there being two of them."

"I guess these are the guys brought in to replace people laid off in favour of outsourcing, as recommended by you?"

"Exactly. That's probably why I am so popular with them."

"What about the girl? How was the leave taking?"

There was a pause.

"Actually it was not too bad. She even kissed me on the cheek."

"Indeed?"

"She said that she was sorry that I did not have a good time. She also apologised for making me struggle with her political and literary allusions."

"And?"

"She said that this was a part of her preparation for dissertation as well as a vacation ... and it was best that I went away with friends and had a good time. She was very decent about it."

"Sounds wonderful."

"I'll take a break in Paris. And I've already started communication with the consulting firm in New York. They are okay with a three month delay."

Dr. Roy allowed himself a smile. His long distance behavioural therapy seemed to have cured Pritam of the panic attacks.

"You know the best thing about this? Whenever I start thinking of how Sandeep can screw up my career, I have some beer. And with these three wonderful guys around, that's enough."

"Great."

"You know Sup-da, you shrinks are losers. All your dopamine and anti-depressants and sleeping pills ... they are nothing compared to a mug of beer."

"Have you had a lot already?"

"Yes, and I will have more. The next time I am in Netherlands as a consultant, I will recommend the Vrije University to downsize by getting rid of psychiatrists, replacing them with these low cost software engineers who can be such wonderful beer drinking companions."

"I will keep that in mind."

"And I will ask the libraries to get rid of the books on psychology and replace them with crates of beer."

"Wonderful idea."

"In fact I can write a paper on it. Something that I will read out myself for a change. Heineken will sponsor me ..."

Dr. Roy sighed and disconnected the line. His profession definitely demanded listening skills, but it was important as well to know when to draw the line.

Mail from Subramanium Sensei to Sandeep

Dear Sandeep,

I understand your hesitation. You have too many things on your plate – but then you keep saying that you are a Gemini and so you are meant to.

I am glad you could attend some classes on tai chi chin na in Prague. You have often wondered about a possible way to develop your chin na skills, and now there it is in front of you. As long as you stay there, you can teach some basic tai chi to these people and can also sharpen your chin na practice.

I have no solution for your question on time. Time is limited to twenty four hours a day, and if you have to follow your goals of being a novelist and a martial artist, you will be stretched. But, it is not impossible. So many of the samurai were wonderful artists, writers, painters, calligraphists.

All the Best,
Subramanium

Mail from Sandeep to Shruti

My fair friend,

I wonder how your European exploration goes on. My personal journey in life becomes more and more interesting. The principal path is steadily becoming a conjectural, contradictory course, losing its way along adventurous alleys. These beckoning by-lanes often make me wonder if there is a path and a goal after all. Each alley comes with its own share of potential pitfalls. As our learned mutual friend would point out – everything has its in-built opposite.

Speaking of the professor, when I returned home tonight – delayed due to a tai chi class I am teaching every evening, and also an infuriating neighbour whose sole purpose in life is to whine his way into global depression, I found my postal mailbox full of surprises.

There was the customary rejection slip, this time from a literary agent in Manhattan, who after a lot of thought has decided that my book is not really something that matches his selling forte. Ah well, he at least used my SASE. I am yet to break the mystery of judging a book by a query letter, which stops a long way short of the proverbial mistake of judging it by its cover. But, this guy says he gave it a lot of thought – and he, I assume, is an honourable man.

The second package was a long awaited bunch of forty copies of my novel ultimately shipped by my publisher. I have been through the process of reviewing the proof online, going through the editing loops and also approving the cover art. But, even then, holding the final product in one's hand is an experience. In so many ways is a written book a labour of love. And while the electronic process of looking at the proofs and edited versions are quite like looking at the developing embryo in a USG, touching your produced book with your fingers is perhaps like holding the new born in your hands for the first time. Is it a sentimental allusion? I guess so, but I am indeed more than a little sentimental today.

Two extreme experiences in a writer's life being present simultaneously in my mailbox is odd enough, but there was a third dimension waiting in the wake. And I am as yet unable to decide whether it were my own paperback volumes or this third package which gave rise to a strange overwhelmed state of mind.

The package itself was beautiful, decorated with aesthetic creative calligraphy and design – something I have come to associate so readily with the Writers Workshop. I opened it to find a note written in the exquisite long fingered hand of the Professor which I reproduce here word for word:

"Sandeep, my boy,

Even as you spread the message of Janardana Krishna in the ivory towers of the west, your deeds are getting recognised in your forsaken backyard. I am sending you a copy of a 'review' of your book in the Statesman – which is not really a review in the authentic sense of the word, but is useful in its own way. I am eager to get my ancient, yet inquisitive, hands on your novel, but the young man I sent to the premier bookshops of Kolkata returned empty handed with the message that it was not in the stores yet.

What about your new novel? How far as it progressed towards the light of the day?

I am sending the proofs of the delightful collection of essays by your young friend, Shruti Rattan. As she steps from one great European city to another, keeping in tune with the unifying music of modern times, she has asked me to forward the package to you.

The Professor"

There are 246 pages of your writing, with the chapter names and the end markers etched gracefully by the carefully crafted strokes of the great man's Schiffer pen. Do I have the permission to plough through the proofs myself? Or do I respectfully hold on to them till you retrace your steps to the sin city?

The so called review, by the way, was a truncated version of the blurb I provided for the back cover. I envy your detachment. You don't really care what people think of your book. But, doesn't art always crave appreciation?

~ Sandeep

P.S. I came to know that my friend has finally decided that he was having an overdose of the cold war and has made off to the hottest sections of Paris to thaw himself.

∾ ∾ ∾

Amsterdam, Netherlands

The Dental clinic was only a five minute bus ride from Central Station according to the 9292ov website, but Madhu Deb insisted on driving him from the WTC office premises.

"I know you are a big boy, Pritam," she laughed, as she drove. "What I am worried about is the local anaesthesia that these people sometimes use. There is always a remote chance that one's particular physiology may react abnormally."

Sandeep had tried to open his mouth to argue that people the world over visited dentists every day without being confronted with vulnerable physiologies susceptible to the miniscule local anaesthesia. By then the helpful lady had already branched out to the diverse dental debacles of her near and not so near acquaintances across the breadth of her chequered career. By the time the topic had predictably converged to the unifying domain of Hidori, who had developed brand new premolars, Sandeep had rolled down the window and had half his head outside, gasping for air. He heaved a sigh of relief when they halted in front of the chamber beside Herengracht.

It was somewhat embarrassing to go into the clinic with a guardian in tow. Somehow Madhu Deb took on the figure of a bloated aunt in his subconscious. He approached the desk as the lady made her way to the waiting area.

The assistant who doubled up as the secretary was Chinese – with porcelain features and a sensuous mouth. Her name tag said Cynthia Wong. When she looked up, Sandeep wondered if she had been ripped out of the cover of a glamour magazine.

"Hi," he said. "Sand --- Pritam Mitra. I have an appointment ..."

"Em ee tay erh ah?"

"If you say so. One can't argue with looks like that."

"Ah ... ha-ha ... yes, you can go right in. The doctor is expecting you."

It was with some effort that Sandeep managed to detach his eyes from Cynthia and walk into the chamber.

The treatment took fifteen minutes, the efficient middle aged Dutch lady quickly filling the chipped molar with a metal cap. Madhu Deb beamed at him as he came out.

"You okay?"

"It feels all right."

He could make out that his speech was slightly unclear, with his left jaw still under the effect of the local anaesthesia. The supervisor, who had been flipping through a Dutch magazine, nodded knowingly.

"There, you see. The anaesthesia is still working. That's what I was talking about."

"It's just my jaw," Sandeep protested. "It is dropping... " He trailed off … the profile of Cynthia, back in the visible range, again had a strange effect on him.

"I'll take care of the payment," he said quickly and made his way to the desk. The assistant glanced up and flashed him one of those smiles that can make any red blooded man wobble at the knees.

"The charge for the filling is 77 euros. But, your insurance coverage will pay 50 of it," Cynthia started explaining. "You have to pay only 27. However, you have to pay the initiation fee to the insurance company or they are going to bill you for ….," she paused and looked at Sandeep, flashing another smile at his uncomprehending looks. A hint of mischief in the sensuously slanting eyes under the teasing arch of the brows. "Am I confusing you?"

"You are," Sandeep replied. "But, it's not the figures as much as the face."

"What's that?"

He must have been pretty difficult to understand in spite of his Don Juan flair –with half his face numb with local anaesthesia.

"You are just too beautiful for me to look at and listen to at the same time. The windows of my mind are not used to such multitasking."

She laughed and put her hand in front of her face.

"Does that make it better?"

Sandeep thought hard for something to say to match his previous flair of compliments, but the moment passed. That was the convenience of being a writer. You could think up a line for a week and put it in the mouth of your hero. But, in real life, moments pass. The chance goes untaken, while sensuous secretaries tear off receipts.

"This is for you to sign."

"The moment I can take my eyes off you I will."

She laughed again. Sandeep could make out that the girl was having fun, enjoying the attention.

"I can set up an appointment for you next Friday," she said.

"Is that a date?"

"Yes, for checking your broken tooth," she slapped his hand playfully.

Sandeep looked at her … in fact he wondered if he had ever taken his eyes off her. No one possibly could. What was a girl like this doing in a dentist's clinic?

"Well, go ahead and fix the appointment, but I have one condition."

"Sure, what condition? We can help you."

"I'll take some pictures."

She seemed confused.

"Pictures?"

"Yes. Deal?"

"Pictures of the filling?"

"No something more fulfilling. Pictures of an exquisite Chinese assistant of the dentist."

The girl was stranded between laughter and bewilderment.

"I don't know, really."

"Was that a yes or a no?"

She paused a while.

"Okay. Deal."

Sandeep shook hands with her, enjoying the harmless physical touch accompanying the flirting.

"Are you a photographer?" she asked.

"Not really. Do only photographers take pictures of exquisite beauty?"

She laughed.

"It must be my curly hair. You too have curly hair … maybe that's why you think I am pretty."

"Is my hair back to curly?" Sandeep looked at his reflection on the polished surface of the desk. "But yeah, it's the hair, the face, the eyes, the lips, the chin …," he caught himself before descending to lower depths of anatomy and decency. "Everything that combines to make you – you."

There was a tap on his shoulder and Sandeep turned to find Madhu Deb looking at him, patient aggravation on her face.

"Are you done with your philandering?"

He looked at her, a guilty feeling peeping through his eyes. For a brief moment, enjoying the fickle flirtations, he had forgotten about the kindly lady altogether.

That was cruel on his part, considering that she had taken the trouble to drive him all the way to the clinic.

"Eh? Sure ... we're done, aren't we? Is there anything else?"

Cynthia laughed. "I don't think so. See you next Friday."

As they walked out Madhu Deb shot him a mock look of disapproval.

"Quite a flirt, aren't you?"

"Eh? Not really. This was an exception. You see, one doesn't meet girls like that every day."

The lady shook her head indulgently.

"Right. She is also a model."

"Is she really? I was wondering why she was stuck in a dental clinic."

"She told me she is also working for a modelling agency, but it does not pay that well. So, a pretty young thing and our newly married role model is up to his tricks."

For a moment or two it did not make sense, but then he remembered his official marital status. He pursed his lips. Impersonation for a couple of hours was a professional skill acquired by investigative journalists. Playing a role day in and day out was a different ball game altogether.

"Er ... no, not exactly ... I mean, it's just minor flirtation," he laughed. His jaw was feeling better now. "Appreciation and wordplay being the key out here."

The lady smiled knowingly.

"Right. You're an author after all," she turned before putting the key into the door of the car. "But, you need not justify yourself to me."

"Uh ... it's not that."

"I believe as an author you are a student of human nature. And you know for sure that human beings are not meant to be monogamous."

A serious look had spread across her face.

"I ... I really don't know about that ...," Sandeep hesitated. The lady he had come to know as fun loving and cheerful seemed riddled by difficult thoughts right now.

"I ... forget the incident, it was just flirtation. Are you taking it seriously?"

Madhu Deb turned towards him with a wan smile.

"It's not that. I started thinking about something else."

They got into the car.

"It's sometimes that I get these uncontrolled thoughts, when I tend to remember a lot of things ... and then start thinking of life in general. And then for a while I kind of fall apart."

Sandeep was confused. He was not too sure about the cause and effect.

"Did I do anything ...?" he began.

"Of course not," Madhu Deb smiled and put her hand on his arm. "It's just these phases are often triggered by incidents which are quite trivial... But, forget it ... I have learnt to deal with it. Don't worry about me."

Sandeep was uneasy. He looked at the ignition. The lady had still not put the key there. She was waiting, getting a hold over herself.

"Are you okay?" he asked.

"I said, don't worry, Pritam," she looked away and composed herself. "It must be a surprise for you."

Sandeep wondered how to respond. In some cognitive quirk, he kept thinking of Suprakash Roy.

"Well, it seems you have some problems in your life. It's none of my business really, but apparently you seem to be such a happy, enthusiastic person."

Madhu Deb smiled sadly.

"Yes, I give the impression of being happy and enthusiastic, don't I? I guess I play my part well. But, believe me, things fall apart sometimes. They have fallen apart – I... I am living a patchwork life."

There ensued another pause which Sandeep found uncomfortable. He was not curious about Madhu Deb's personal life. In his experience, everyone had problems. And, while impersonating someone else, being the confidante of deepest secrets was not exactly an inviting thought.

It was a relief when she turned the key and the car lurched ahead.

"Driving in Amsterdam in a depressed state is not quite recommended," the lady joked.

He turned to thank her as she slowed down near Station Zuid.

"Please don't thank me. I kind of leaned on you for support today," Madhu Deb replied. "Remember your appointment next Friday."

Sandeep paused.

"I really don't know what problems you are going through in life and it's really none of my business, but if this takes your mind off the troubles for a while, it will be worth all the trouble of writing it."

He fished a copy of *Doppelganger Days* from his bag and handed it to her.

"Wow. Are you lending it or are you ...?"

"Consider it a gift. I mean, it's the least I can offer for ensuring that I don't have to live on karnemilk."

Madhu Deb beamed at him.

"Thank you ... for everything."

"It's a pleasure, really. I don't know whether anyone is going to read the book when it reaches the stores," he laughed. He did not have the connections to arrange the books in conspicuous pyramids in the stores, in the new arrivals area, in the manufactured best seller sections. It would be just another book on the common racks.

"It's not only that. Thanks for listening."

Sandeep wondered if he had been given a choice.

"And most importantly," the lady continued. "The *tai chi* classes are working wonders. It is a positive antidote to my depression."

"Well, it's a great art and has lots of benefits ..."

There was the sad smile yet again.

"True, but I understand the amount of trouble you are taking to teach us."

"I assure you, I have my own selfish motives. It helps me clarify concepts and continue training."

Madu Deb patted him on his hand.

"People will drop out ..."

"I expect them to. Come on, I have been in the martial arts for over a decade and a half. I know that for every sincere student there will be ten who will drop out after a couple of weeks."

Madhu Deb nodded and started the car. "I remain a sincere student. And I just wanted to do my bit by saying thank you."

XXIV

Excerpts from the series of talks given by 'Pritam Mitra' to the HMH colleagues. Reproduced from the mpeg files captured by hidden cameras on the person of Pritam Mitra's official buddy.

Whenever business declines and benches get overloaded the consultant incarnates himself in the annals of the organisation. The consultant has to come back time after time to protect the productive employees, to reduce non-productive assets and re-establish business.

Who realises the truth of the emergence and vision of the change agent, when he discards the role of a mere employee in the organisation, is not again employed as one. He becomes an entrepreneur. Discarding fear, family and friends. Absorbed in business and sheltered by it. Purified by corporate consciousness.

With all the expertise in financial markets, the gurus in your payroll and in the payroll of financial giants of the Wall Street and elsewhere could not foresee this slump. No one could predict it because the money god works in his own inscrutable ways. In retrospect, the cause and effect is easy to determine and explanations are aplenty. However, the truth is that when so many parameters are involved, we simply cannot predict.

So, who can predict what will happen tomorrow? Who can say whether the stocks will improve or go down further off the charts into the ground?

Our knowledge is obscured by ignorance, things that we don't know, cannot predict – and we human beings delude ourselves by thinking that we are in control. As long as ignorance misleads us, we will continue to be disappointed at not getting results.

The unsteady worker, motivated by the fruits of his labour, is trapped in the falsity and fickleness of the financial world. He is disturbed, distressed and disappointment-prone. He works for the future, setting target of rewards in front of him.

However, the unattached worker forsakes the fruits of his actions and works with the body, soul and intelligence, and gets purified by the action of working. He knows that while we see, hear, touch and notice, actually we know nothing at all. And this enlightened colleague is not fettered by the fruits of labour. He forsakes selfish attachment to his work. His serene mind conquers all the problems of life. He attains peace. And he is the most likely to survive.

∾ ∾ ∾

Blog of Simple Simon
Tags: Branding, Corporate Cosmology

Corporate consciousness – as I have mentioned in my earlier blogs –was introduced by the phenomenon of Branding. Soon it was a particular attribute that people were hankering for – which could not be put into tangible dimensions of the product. Just the brand name – Nike, Adidas, Tommy Hilfinger – marked up an otherwise commonplace commodity by unbelievable percentages. The miracle could only be explained in terms of a pseudo spiritual essence lent by the famed brand names.

While I have philosophised about this falsity of the corporation, I have seldom been witness to the heights of corporate cosmology that my current buddy is achieving through his series of talks. The moment he starts talking, he seems to throw restraint and caution to the wind and reaches a realm which hovers dangerously within the fuzzy intersection of wisdom and mockery.

Yet there is reason in his words, and the Dutch audience listen to him and cannot quite decide where and how to contradict, question and argue. At the same time, the Dutch are liberal people who have accepted philosophies and cultures from around the world. Part of this comes from seafaring adventurers from times of inception of the land who have played a peerless role in creating one of the most adaptable and spiritually vibrant cultures of the world by slow synthesis of thought around the world. And the average Dutch person is keen on intellectually stimulating thought. So, the talks generally end in a note of mutual respect and tolerance, back slapping and black coffee.

Mail from Simon to Mailing Group
Sub: Ageless Wisdom or Acerbic Humour

If you have read my blog already, you know what I was puzzling about. Today when the crazy consultant peeped into my cubicle on his way back from the printer, hands once again full of sheaves of print outs, and I asked him some pretty direct questions.

How much of what he spoke did he believe in?

He shrugged. "It is ancient wisdom, Simon. And it raises questions. They are not supposed to be answers by themselves. So, the question of belief and disbelief does not quite come into the picture."

In politically correct words, I told him to cut the crap.

"I am a bit confused, Pritam. You are earnest when you go out there and speak. And you are earnest when you teach *tai chi.* In both cases you philosophise. But, when you are in a *tai chi* class, you mean it. I can make out that you believe it when you say that it is a concept that has to be felt, when you say that one day it will suddenly make sense, when you say that it is a way of meditation in action as well as a way of life."

He smiled.

"And when I speak to the people of the Bank, I don't?"

"I am not too sure. I mean, I hardly see the same conviction. It is as if you know that you are indulging in bull shit of massive proportion ..."

"Bingo," Pritam interjected. "That's a great way to describe it. Bull shit of cosmic proportions. It is a manifesto to lead people to war. And it has been so across ages from mythological times."

I was not in the mood for cryptic answers.

"Pritam, let me tell you something. After a *tai chi* class, I always feel a satisfied glow inside me. And I am not alone. I know a few have left the class, but people like Madhu, Trisha and Amrita also tell me that they have similar experiences. It is drastically different in your talks. It sounds profound and a lot of people are impressed, but to me it seems you don't mean a thing. How can the same person philosophise in two different ways?"

"*Tai chi* is an art, Simon. Meditation in action."

"And Madhu Deb informed me – in a three hour session elaborately peppered with the Hidori stories – that the *Gita* is also a way of meditation. In fact, its various parts are called *yogas.*"

Pritam moved towards the panels and looked over the cubicle.

"I sort of understand your confusion, Simon. Let me try to explain it to you. When I speak of *tai chi,* I impart lessons that I have been through, in long painstaking ways. I have walked every bit of the way and know every bump and every flower bed one comes across. I have also experienced the holistic effect that the art has on your body and mind, and even the soul. But, when I speak of the corporate world, that's something I have only skimmed superficially."

I thought about his explanation.

"But, you are supposed to be a professional consultant."

He looked at me with twinkling eyes. "Am I?"

I pointed out that he was a well known figure in the world of consulting – especially after his paper presentation. Whereas, he was not really someone people knew of as a *tai chi* master.

He seemed to go into a trance on hearing my words. I was on the verge of getting worried that I had offended him when he turned towards me.

"Simon, let me tell you something I heard from my instructor."

I was excited. My short association with *tai chi* had already whetted my appetite for such tidbits of indirect knowledge.

"I learnt *Karate* and *Tai Chi* from Subramanium Sensei. I started with *Karate,* and that's why I don't call him *sifu* and call the place of practice the *dojo* and not something like *kwoon.* Subramanium Sensei is a fourth dan in Karate, an instructor of *tai chi* and also a teacher of *yoga.*"

"Wow."

"And he once told me that the best instructors of *yoga* that he has encountered, from whom he has learnt the most, are people whom hardly anyone knows."

He paused.

"Given the number of yoga instructors in India and abroad, that's a revelation, isn't it?"

Thought provoking indeed.

"What you essentially mean is that reputation has little to do with it."

My buddy shrugged.

"I don't know. I don't have the answers. Sensei had told me all this, and suddenly, when you asked the questions, I remembered it."

He might have continued, but just at that moment Madhu Deb bounded in with enthusiasm spilling out of her rotund form.

Too bad … we had just crossed the esoteric echelons of conversation.

Cheers
Simon

~ ~ ~

***Review of Doppelganger Days by Sandeep Gupta in* The Week**

Doppelganger Days Fiction Author: Sandeep Gupta Publisher: Amphibian Books Pages: 275 Price: Rs. 225

A contemporary novel set in New York City, *Doppelganger Days* deals with issues that are important, morose and with far reaching effects, terrorism, politics and racial discrimination in the modern world – but, nevertheless, it is related with humour in every page. It is also liberally peppered with *karate* chops, the author himself being an exponent.

This was something new. While the reviewer had not read the book, he had at least looked at his biographical sketch and extrapolated it to add an innovative sentence. Sandeep sighed as he made his way through the rest of the remaining literary agents and publishers in his list.

∾ ∾ ∾

The full exchange of emails between Sandeep, Kailash Nayak and noted Historian Laxmanchand Raha (reproduced in chronological order)

From: Sandeep Gupta
To: Laxmanchand Raha
CC: Kailash Nayak
Sub: Query from a new author

Dear Mr. Raha,

I am a new writer, just off the blocks with the publication of my novel Doppelganger Days by Amphibian Books.

I have read and enjoyed your historical analysis of the Indian Diaspora in the Americas – "The Other Indians of the New World". Since my novel deals with the Indian Diaspora of the New York and New Jersey area, I thought it would be of interest to you. I would also welcome any feedback that you could provide from the perspective of a historian as well as from the point of view of a knowledgeable reader.

I looked up the address on the Bangalore Yellow Pages of the internet.

<address>

Please confirm if it is correct. My friend Kailash (in cc) will send a copy of the novel to you – since I am currently in Amsterdam.

Thanking you in advance,
Sandeep Gupta

From: Laxmanchand Raha
To: Sandeep Gupta
Sub: Re: Query from a new author

The address is indeed correct.

From: Sandeep Gupta
To: Laxmanchand Raha
CC: Kailash Nayak
Sub:Re: Query from a new author

Dear Mr. Raha,

Thanks for the response. My friend in cc will send you the novel. Please let us know when you receive the same.

I will be awaiting your feedback.

Thanking you,
Sandeep Gupta

From: Kailash Nayak
To: Laxmanchand Raha
CC: Sandeep Gupta
Sub:Re: Query from a new author

Dear Mr. Raha,

I sent you a couriered package containing a copy of the novel Doppelganger Days by my friend Sandeep Gupta (in cc). It has been a week since then. I checked at the courier office and they informed me that it was delivered. Could you please inform us whether you have received it?

Thanking you,
Kailash

From: Laxmanchand Raha
To: Kailash Nayak
Sub:Re: Query from a new author

Yes, I got it.

From: Kailash Nayak
To: Sandeep Gupta
Sub: Fw: Query from a new author

*Look at the mail. It seems the a**hole got the bloody package four days back.*
K

From: Sandeep Gupta
To: Laxmanchand Raha
Sub:Re: Query from a new author

Dear Mr. Raha,

I understand that you have received a copy of my novel Doppelganger Days.
I am eagerly waiting for your feedback. Please let me know your views.

Thanking you,
Sandeep Gupta

From: Laxmanchand Raha
To: Sandeep Gupta
Sub: Re: Query from a new author

Thanks for sending me the book. I did not have your email id and could not respond.
However, I don't understand fiction at all.

From: Sandeep Gupta
To: Kailash Nayak
Sub: Fw: Query from a new author
Look at the mail below. What do you make of it?

From: Kailash Nayak
To: Sandeep Gupta
Sub: Re: Query from a new author

Forget him. Most of his so called historical writings are pro-establishment fiction. His collection of essays on cricket even more so – necessity since he has never played the game..

Waste of a copy.

I talked to the Starmark about the launch. They want us to finance it. They say that without proper publicity launches generally achieve no purpose. They will arrange for announcements in a couple of dailies, but the advertisement, snacks, the microphones and transportation of signed copies have to be arranged by us. They estimate around Rs. 10000.

K

Mail received by normal post.

Dear Sandeep,

We agree that the idea behind your novel – The Dutch Gambit – is interesting and the storyline has a lot of merits. We do believe that it has the potential to be a successful novel in the mainstream as well as worthy of critical acclaim.

However, ENC is at best a boutique publishing organisation, and the books that are published by our firm are handpicked by our members, and many of them have their own idiosyncratic favourites.

As of now, our publishing calendar is already full for the next couple of years. We strongly advise you to look for representation elsewhere.

Wishing you all the best for your writing career.

Yours truly,
Anne Stevens
Editor, ENC Publications

Mail from Shruti to Sandeep

Sorry for the late reply. I am in an Austrian village at the moment, one of those places whose hills are alive with the sound of music. However, the music of times has not quite resonated here and the inn I am staying in is blissfully spared the tentacles of the World Wide Web. I guess the correct term for such places still alive with the rhythm of the natural world is – offbeat. Quite a thought, that.

Congratulations... I don't really know the feeling yet, but I think I can attempt to understand the parental pride that you have described. I am longing to read your work, but not from a gifted copy. I fully understand the sweat and blood that goes into the process of creation and would like to read a copy by purchasing against the marked price.

When you see reviews like that, doesn't it seem like insult to the long, ardent and arduous labour that ultimately resulted in your book?

I wish you luck with your second novel. Now that the first one is published, will it help the fortunes of the ones that are to follow? I find the book trade quite mysterious in the murky, dark, film noir type of way.

As for the proof, I am not asking you to be the foster parent of my labour. I will pick it up when I am back. However, if you do find the time, please go through some of it and decide for yourself if you want to keep reading.

Pritam has indeed decided that he has had his fill of the conducted tour of twentieth century European conflicts. Much as I am sorry for putting him through this ordeal, after all it is not a pleasure trip but directly related to my dissertation. Till the last day, he remained a true professional – adept at filling up the holes in his knowledge with a truckload of bull shit. I have nothing but pity and a lot of affection for him, but he is not really my type by a long stretch of imagination.

Will return to Amsterdam via Hanover, Hamburg and Maastricht. Will see you soon.

~Shruti

XXV

Mail from Madhu Deb to Axiom Members of the HMH account
Sub: Salute in-house Greatness

Hi Team,

I have just finished reading Doppelganger Days by Sandeep Gupta (pen name of our own Pritam Mitra).

What can I say? It touches the soul. It is only after a while that I realised with amazement that the person who penned this amazing book is a colleague sitting right here with us.

I will urge each and every one of you to try to get hold of a copy and read it, if only to salute the multi-faceted personality among us.

Regards,
Madhu

Mail from Ajay Yadav to 'Pritam Mitra'
Sub: Fw: Salute in-house Greatness

Congratulations! Hats off to a unique talent. Wish you all the success.
Hope your assignment continues to be a success.

Best Regards,
Ajay Yadav
HMH Account Manager

(This mail was replied to all. The last line was an oversight, not removed after copying and pasting an original mail.)

Mail from Madhu Deb to 'Pritam Mitra'
Sub: Fw: Salute in-house Greatness

Additionally, I want to tell you something else. I know you want to get out of this daily monotony of the industry. A lot of us feel the same way. However, with your talent you have better chances of happy escape. If you do escape, please remember me as one of the less fortunate who walked a part of the path with you.

Also, I wonder what it is about you? Why do I talk to you about things that I never share? Does it come with being an author or is it something else that makes me trust you and cherish you as a special friend?

Regards,
Madhu

Mail from Trisha Paul to 'Pritam Mitra'
Sub: Fw: Salute in-house Greatness

Hearty congrats!! May you top best seller charts for years to come.

Mail from Gunjan Das to 'Pritam Mitra'
Sub: Re: Salute in-house Greatness

Congratulations, Pritam, keep it up.
- Gunjan
(This mail was replied to all)

Mail from Amrita De to 'Pritam Mitra'
Sub: Fw: Salute in-house Greatness

I am just happy for you. Can I have a copy of your novle(sic)?
(In Bengali)
If striving for golden sunshine is futile as reaching for the stars,
Let me at least bask in the silvery softness of the moon's reflected glory.

I know the bend in the river of your life will take you away – and with it this brief period of unknown joy.

However, let me not think of the future – but enjoy the moments that you and I have to share.

Mail from K.Ramesh to 'Pritam Mitra'
Sub: Fw: Salute in-house Greatness

Congratulations Pritam. Your creative flair was evident on the day of the presentation. I am dying to read this book. I love versatility. It defines a true consultant.
- Ramesh

Blog of Simple Simon
Tags: Tai chi, progress update

We are a third of the way into the long form of Yang style tai chi chuan. In his innovative way, Pritam introduces the underlying martial techniques one by one. While nowhere near our teacher's grace and fluidity while performing the long sequence, I am probably feeling the benefits of the exercise system. The perennial cough and cold that dogged me for the last few years after shifting to Amsterdam have disappeared. I have also noted that a session of *tai chi* in the early morning generally takes care of all the digestive disorders.

The *chin na*, on the other hand, is a different story altogether. We are struggling with the sophisticated holds, locks, strikes and pins. Amrita and I have at least managed to remember the classification of the techniques into the categories of *Fen Jin, Cuo Gu, Bi Qi, Dian Mai* and *Dian Xue.* I am secretly quite excited about *Bi Qi* – or sealing the breath. While Madhu struggles with the names and manages to remember some of the techniques, Trisha continues to start afresh every class. As Pritam has pointed out, regularity does count. Amrita and I have not missed a single class yet. Madhu continues to miss classes due to *Sur Soiree* and other ventures. Trisha too has been a frequent absentee. She often tells me that married women from India have particular responsibilities at home and she cannot get away if her in laws are in town, which happens quite often.

But, as my buddy-sifu puts it, the path to perfection is a lonely trek. Arduous and probably rewarding.

~ ~ ~

Mail from Simon to his mailing group
Sub: Angst of an Author and Confusing Culture

The morning started with Madhu Deb's congratulatory mail and soon it opened the floodgates. The passing hours saw little work done by our team. Mails and calls were exchanged in group and one on one. (For those who missed the one liner I had sent in the morning, Pritam Mitra the consultant has turned out a novel under the pseudonym Sandeep Gupta and Madhu has hailed it as the next big thing in the world of Literature)

Madhu Deb was effusive in her praise of the writing style – and I got away before long winded parallels could be drawn with the many stalwart authors who had graced her eventful life. Trisha was once again fascinated by the multiple facets of the remarkable man. As usual, she again rediscovered her insignificant limitations. Amrita just looked reverent. Ajay Yadav made his customary faux pas while sending a congratulatory mail. And Gunjan called me up with his characteristic remark that with the blessings of senior management one could afford to devote time to many things other than work.

In the wake of this gamut of laudatory communication, I was waiting with anticipation for my limelight shunning buddy to come bounding to my cubicle, full of candid reactions, colourful expressions and peculiar philosophising.

However, he disappointed me. After a couple of hours, I peeped over my cubicle to find him seated in a pensive manner, hunched over his keyboard.

I came back to my seat and resumed working for a while, but simple human curiosity got better of me and I soon found myself walking over to his cubicle.

"Hey buddy, I have often noticed your reaction to publicity. How come you are so placid today? You are neither jumping with joy, nor scurrying for cover."

In response he smiled and asked me to take a seat.

"It is strange," he confided. "For several reasons, I can't afford publicity."

I did not know what he meant by that, but seeing him in a reflective mood, I did not interrupt.

"For several very good reasons," he repeated almost to himself. "And yet, knowing fully well that the eventual result would be like breaking a dam, I gifted a copy to Madhu Deb, the very day after I had received the copies from the publishers."

I reminded him that people were going around asking for copies.

"True, people love getting things for free. But, I was over eager to be read. An author craves recognition. And adulation. I guess that's what made me do it."

Throughout our interactions, he had never come across as someone who wanted to be under the glare of the spotlight. I reminded him that he had been reluctant to disclose his identity as a martial artist.

"It was for a different reason that I did not want to teach. For another subsequent reason I wanted to give it a go. But, here it is an author's ego that needs massaging."

I have seldom seen him in such a state, where his usual way of overcoming challenges with macabre humour was conspicuous by its absence.

"And you know what Simon?" he continued. "The moment I saw Madhu Deb's mail, I knew I was done for. I mean, I knew that my intention of keeping a low profile was defeated. But, the strangest part is that I liked it ... Some part of me liked the acclaim for my writing... I seem to be such a different person when it comes to my identity as an author."

He murmured something about losing focus of the circumstances.

I was about to ask him what the circumstances were, but was interrupted because at that juncture Amrita walked in brandishing a USB Drive. It seemed that her own USB port was disabled and she needed to use Pritam's.

However, Pritam was back to his normal self during the *tai chi* class of the evening. Talks about the book and the reviews in papers were quickly brushed into the background and we had yet another excellent session.

At the end of the class, nowadays Pritam puts on his jogging shoes and runs home. Today, we saw Amrita follow his example and do the same. After they left, while turning out the lights, I observed something about sincerity and dedication towards the art that made one follow the illustrious footsteps of the master. I thought it was a pretty neat word play on 'footsteps' but Madhu sounded serious.

"Running after him is more like it," she observed.

I looked at her and saw a meaningful expression. Trisha was watching her with one raised eyebrow and half a smile.

As they saw me looking at them with some confusion, Madhu became her jocular self again.

"I bet he runs too fast for her to keep up," she remarked.

I shrugged. I have always found sniffing into another's kitchen to be one universal trait which has found a welcome home in the Indian psyche. But, then, it is a different culture – takes some getting used to.

Cheers
Simon

~ ~ ~

Amsterdamse Bos

"Do you think it's wrong?" Amrita asked, her breathing still hampered by unpractised exercise of the lungs.

Sandeep had slowed down and eventually stopped after noticing Amrita trying to keep up with him on his run home.

"Eh?" he asked. "Of course. I have been running for nearly twenty five years now. And the distance home is more than eight kilometres. I also wanted to run longer today through the Amsterdamse Bos area ... You been there?"

"No."

"Don't you guys even bike? The *bos* is a great place. A huge expanse of land full of trees, greens, nice little canals and pools. But, as I was saying, you have never run long distances in your life. How did you think you could keep up with me?"

The dark girl looked away apologetically.

"I know I can't. I spoiled your run, didn't I?"

Sandeep looked around him. They were standing on the outskirts of the Bos, at the entry point from Uilenstede. He wondered which path to take.

"I guess I have had enough exercise."

"I saw you running in the morning."

"Did you? I went out at half past five today."

"I woke up before that. In fact I did not even sleep."

Sandeep decided to walk along Rentmeesterlaan towards the Binnenhof. They could take a bus from the Amstelveen Busstation.

"I have run earlier. I am used to running on the treadmill."

Sandeep, who was thinking about the new set of synopses he had sent earlier during the day, looked at her in some confusion.

"Treadmill?"

"Yes."

"What about the treadmill?"

"I have run on the treadmill. I am not new to running."

"Ah ..." mystery cleared, Sandeep went back to his thoughts. George Bernard Shaw had been rejected by sixty publishers before being published. Was he on course to better that illustrious record?

"I did not mean whether you think *that* is wrong."

The convoluted sentence made no sense. Sandeep turned towards the girl whose breathing had returned to somewhere in the regions of normal again.

"Look, I don't know what you mean."

"I asked you whether it was wrong. And I did not mean running with you."

It was a struggle. Sandeep gave it up.

"Will it be better if we switched to Bengali?"

The girl turned her face away. And even as he relapsed back into thoughts about his rejection slip collection, he sensed something was wrong. A close scrutiny of Amrita's half turned face revealed two tiny rivulets rolling down her cheeks.

"Christ. I'm sorry. I mean, I shouldn't have said that."

She shook her head and her voice reached him in sniffles.

"You're angry."

"What?"

"You're angry because I sent you that poem in Bengali."

This again proved to be quite a poser.

"I'm sorry I am not sure what you mean. Did you mean that I am angry because you wrote the poem in Bengali? Or is it that I am angry because you sent me the Bengali poem? Either way, I am not angry. Why should I be angry?"

The girl looked at him with a strange expression – anxiety mingled with hope.

"What did you feel when you got the poem?"

Without any suggestion that could be misinterpreted as belittling, Sandeep started speaking in Bengali.

"I got so many mails today, I didn't really read all of them."

Once again the eyes looked pained.

"I understand. There are a lot of mails that you get...."

Sandeep thought hard. There had been a lot of congratulatory mails triggered by Madhu Deb sending across her evaluation of his book. The gamut had included one from Amrita. As usual it had been something fruity and poetic. He had not really read it.

"I remember you asked me for a copy."

Amrita smiled sadly. Sandeep frowned. He was being burdened with too many cryptic, sad smiles in recent times.

"Yes, I did."

"Well, of course I will give you a copy ..."

There was a brighter smile this time.

"But, could you please tell me why the poetry you sent should make me angry? Or do you suggest I take another look?"

Amrita looked at him, her eyes searching.

"You mean you didn't find it offensive?"

Sandeep wondered how to answer it.

"I think it was poignant."

"What?"

Return of the language barrier.

"I said it was moving. I am not sure why I should find it offensive. Don't worry about what people think. It is your own work, right?"

Amrita closed her eyes.

"Yes. It is my own. Can I help it if my thoughts are those?"

"No ... right, you can't really help it."

She turned towards him.

"I just hope you will speak to me tomorrow."

"Of course. Why not?"

She closed her eyes yet again.

"You are married after all ..."

"Eh ? Oh yes, I keep forgetting that myself... right, but ..."

Suddenly it dawned on him. He was an idiot. The girl had given him enough hints with her fruity poetry about the rain, the soul and the languishing pains of life. Her sms, emails and regular calls for help involving flash drives and ports should have been indication enough. He had indeed detected traces of crush. He had not really read the poetic piece in question, but no doubt it was a culmination of all the pent up feelings – a passionate appeal for his affections. That explained the trickling rivers of languor on her cheeks as well. And he had been talking about it as a piece of literature.

Now that the mystery had been cracked, his next problem was what to do about it. There was no doubt that the girl was smitten.

"Er ... Let's not make a big deal of it, shall we?"

He realised his mistake. English expressions, if they deviated from literal meanings, resulted in communication gaps.

"I mean, it will pass ..."

The girl laughed. A mirthless note signifying discord.

"You think so? You think it is madness of a young girl?"

This was serious. Sandeep looked at her. She was not that young for an adolescent crush. He put her somewhere around twenty six. But, Pritam was thirty two and he had swapped identities to go on a European trip with a girl he had hardly met. So, one never knew.

Had he encouraged her in any way. Of course he had. All those smart assed answers to her poetic lines on rain. His uncontrolled penchant for repartees – bright and entertaining. Stepping into the shoes of the future characters of his novels. Controlled experiments in the test bed of life. Aided by the virtual world of electronic mails and short message service. The words of Dr. Suprakash Roy suddenly raised their collective head from a corner of his mind. Internet promotes lack of inhibition.

However, he had not been flirtatious with this girl. To him flirting came naturally and was always limited to witty wordplays, clever compliments and the occasional date. Something he had been working on Cynthia. But somehow, with his successful image and carefree lines, he had unmindfully swept Amrita off her feet. In spite of his official marital status. He groped for an answer to the girl's question.

"Of course not ... but, you see, time is a great healer."

The girl sniffed again, tear laden laughter.

"Time? He has never been on my side."

"Nonsense. Time is on your side. You are young. And look, I am married, am I not? I respect your sentiments, but being married ... I have never really thought of you in that way."

A pair of troubled eyes were cast in his direction now.

"And what if you were not married? What would have happened then?" the words were a challenge, thrown in simple rustic expression. With his encyclopaedic knowledge of a myriad books, Sandeep struggled with it.

"I ... well ... you see that is a hypothetical situation."

He checked himself, wondering if the word would fox her. The earnest emotions that he was faced with made him feel guilty. He should have seen through this and taken steps, big ones and in the other direction. He could not tell the girl that the first step for a relationship was communication. And that is where there lay a huge gap.

"Let us consider the hypothetical situation," Amrita replied. "The question is simple. If you had not been married, would you have been interested in ... me?"

She waited for the answer with bated breath. They had stopped walking and people on bikes flitted by. A black Labrador, released from her leash, bounded into view and sniffed up Sandeep's tracksuit. He patted her on the head and searched for inspiration.

"The question may be simple, but there is no simple answer to it."

Her face was crestfallen.

"I understand. I am not good enough for you in any way. Even if you were not married."

She turned away and sniffed.

Sandeep left the Labrador and scratched his own head. This would be tragic. A rejection with a blow to her image of self. A double whammy.

"For god's sake, Amrita, I never said that. Being good for someone or not is a load of crap. We are not comparing here," he said. "Relationships are exactly that. Relationships. Compatibility ...Which means whether two people can get along together or not. I have not really made an analysis about you to know whether we would be compatible or not. Because I am married, you see ... If I was not, maybe something ... well, maybe we could have got to know each other and then something may have worked out. Right now, I can't answer the question. I don't know you well enough and you don't know me either."

Amrita put her small hand through her long straight hair. Sandeep wondered if she was trying to untangle her emotions.

"I do know you. I have studied you closely."

Sandeep laughed.

"You think so?"

The girl nodded earnestly. "And I do love you. I wouldn't have said that unless I knew you."

Sandeep did not know how to react other than mumble "It will pass."

He wondered if he should have taken the road back to Beneluxbaan. A quick ride on 51 and this conversation would have been much shorter.

"We will see whether it passes. I know I can't expect anything in return. But, could I ask you for some help?"

"Would you mind if we walked towards Zonnestein? We can get a bus from there. I actually have to take a bus into Amsterdam. There is something I need to do ..."

The face had become gloomy, relenting but at the price of happiness.

"I understand," she said. "Please go ahead. Don't worry about me. I will find my way home."

Again Sandeep felt uneasy. He ended up putting his hand on her shoulder. The girl looked up with quivering eyes.

"First tell me about your request. What sort of help do you want?"

She had stopped walking again, and Sandeep pressed her shoulder lightly with his palm to ease her forward.

"Only if it is not a demand to you."

"Let me hear it."

There was a gradual intake of breath.

"I understand my English is bad. I can somehow communicate with people, but cannot follow you or Simon or even Madhu-di when you talk about topics other than work. My education is incomplete ... I mean it is very one dimensional. Could you suggest some ways in which I can improve?"

Sandeep, who had not known what to expect, heaved a pleasant sigh of relief.

"I can tell you you'll be okay," he said jovially. "You know, the key is to enjoy life, and there is no better way than to sharpen your own edges in absolute terms and also enjoy the process."

Amrita nodded. "You say the same thing when teaching *tai chi.*"

Sandeep stopped at Laan Walcheren to wait for the 199.

"And it is the same with English. Once you start enjoying the goldmine of the English Language, you will need little else in a life time. Let me see. What do you read? Apart from technical books, what have you read in recent times?"

The red Connexxion bus emerged from the corner.

XXVI

Blog of Simple Simon
Tags: Indian infiltration in the corporate world

A lot of the readers of my blog have asked me for an insider's view into the changing world. For the ones not aware of this request, it can be surmised as an analysis of why and how the Indians are taking over the world by someone who works with these guys.

There a lot of Indian haters and baiters in the Western world. That is understandable given the way a strange culture has gradually crept in and infiltrated into most of the corporate systems, steadily chipping away at the employed mass of local population. They crop up everywhere across the length and breadth of the hierarchy – from the corporate boardrooms of fortune five hundred companies to the helpdesks who answer my call from Bangalore when my Windows suffers routine crashes.

It is strange, really. I have worked with several people in the PMO of the Operations and IT wing of the Bank and have not yet come across exceptional talent. But then, who needs talent for running a Project Management Office? The question is, why go to the Indians? Is it only cheap labour? Or is there something more?

I won't really go into the nitty-gritty of the complicated topic, Thomas Friedman explains it adequately in *The World is Flat.* A million other blogs speak of it. I will try to construct some deductions based on my daily journey from Utrecht to Amsterdam Zuid and back.

The Inter City, crowded with the daily office going passengers, is a defining snapshot of the Indian infiltration. More than half of the professionals on their way to the daily grind are Indians. Headphones plugged to their ears as they converse with colleagues and family at home, with surprisingly equal distribution, or as they tap their feet imperceptibly to Bollywood music – their gadgets are more yuppie than the normal Dutch guy. iPhones and Blackberries seem like fancy toys that a nation deprived of a privileged childhood has suddenly discovered in late youth. Much of their conversations are centred around electronic wonders, the features and the value adds.

I am able to follow most of the dialogue, since a large percentage of them take place in English. Strange it may see, but as Madhu Deb explained to me during another three hour conversation, there are nearly twenty major languages in India and innumerable dialects and English is the common denominator of the urban classes. Sometimes the odd dialogue does take place in other languages, but then too it sounds familiar, being liberally sprinkled with corporate jargon. If two Indians sit near you and bits of the tête-à-tête drift into your ears, it is often difficult to make out whether it is a casual conversation or an interview. They talk shop like people possessed and that underlines the hypothesis in one of my earlier blogs that there is little line of demarcation between their business and personal lives.

I hardly see anyone with a book, and if I do, more often than not, it is either a technical manual or a guide for making quick bucks. The other topics that I sometimes find them discussing are mutual funds, cricket and weekend plans, the last of which boil down to supermarkets, Indian shops and Bollywood movies.

It is perhaps dangerous to draw conclusions with my limited knowledge, but my train journey does point out several factors regarding the Indian infiltration – I resist calling it domination.

English language is definitely a very important facet and the years of suffered exploitation as a British colony is now paying off in major proportions. That people from different parts of the country choose to converse with each other in English is something unique in the non-English speaking world.

The other facet is this absolute lack of distinction between work and life. Whereas a common Dutch person stops thinking about work after his weekly thirty six hours, and a non-workaholic American employee does so after four more, for these people work is their life. While one would find a Dutch employee arriving and leaving office almost in the same timebound meticulousness as the GVB Transport Service, the Indians are flexible to stretch office time into a canopy over their lives. And to some extent it is understandable. Maslow all the way.

This being the major differentiator, the work force of the average Indian thrive by putting in their readiness, availability and this round the clock commitment to work to their advantage. Maybe out of Darwinian adaptation, the dimensions of hobby, passion and entertainment have been limited to less time consuming gadgets, Bollywood and shopping malls whereas the endeavours demanding time like outdoor sports, enchantment with Literature and gardening are left to the temporarily more secure Western population. The grand scheme is probably to work on the ulterior motive of the evil corporation to get as much work out of the employees as cheaply as possible, and thus usurp the livelihood of the unsuspecting children of affluent nations who have been brought up to believe that the concept of work life balance is axiomatic.

I read that India is a country of extremes – the mysterious land full of diversity in the spheres of geography, economics, social conventions as well as individuals. That too is apparent from my co-passengers, who range from the well oiled hair with the smear of sandalwood on the forehead to the spiked shock and chic standalone beards.

Similarly, there are extremes in terms of outlook and culture as well.

I was reflecting on these when my cell phone rang three times and stopped. A protocol established between me and my buddy. It was an SOS, and as the system demanded, I picked up my phone and gave him a call. I could hear his phone ringing a few cubicles away and soon he came into my view, carrying on an animated discussion with himself.

"Thanks mate," he said on joining me. "The kid has just returned from a field trip and you better be on your guard. Have you accrued some leave? I think this is the best time to go on a vacation." (This will make sense to members of my mailing list.)

I wondered whether I should speak to him about my reflections on the Indian infiltration of the world. He is Indian after all, and if I deviated from the razor's edge of political correctness, one could not rule out the chance of coming across as offensive. The current day white man's burden comprises of history of assumed superiority that one now has to play down with an overdose of acceptance and humility.

However, once I had decided in favour of him of his opinion, he threw some characteristically unorthodox light on the discussion.

"You take a look at the bank around you. It is a complicated organisation. It started as a small venture a century back and grew and grew. And soon things got complicated. In most of the big giant corporations across the world, little deltas of change have added up to assume mammoth proportions. Systems have got complicated. Organisations and industries have become too complex for management."

I agreed. The banks had grown and the systems had become more and more complicated with added services, requirements, changes in business. Hardly anyone had the full picture of any product or line of business.

"It is chaotic. The magic that the Indian brings into the equation is the ability to function in a chaotic world. The institutions back home grooms one for it. The government offices, the traffic, the education system, the hospitals, the parliament – everything is in a strange chaotic equilibrium. People who have been through the experiences back home have been baptised by fire."

As I considered this profound thought, I asked him whether the knowledge of English played a part as well.

He became even more reflective.

"You know we had been colonised for over two hundred years. That works in multiple ways now for our benefit," he smiled. I am never able to decipher between seriousness and mockery of this peculiar guy outside the *tai chi* class. "Colonisation helped us learn English. And along with it, it left a peculiar relationship dynamics with the white man. Most of the Indians are gratified when a white guy from any level of the hierarchy accepts him in his fold. And this is something that has led to levels of motivation that is impossible for a normal workforce to achieve. And it does not stop with the white boss, it peters down to any supervisor. However, at the same time, there is a pent up desire to topple the white – and by induction any – supervisor from the position of power. This can be linked to strategic motivation. It's not uncommon to find both ends of the spectrum in one psyche."

I was more than a little confused.

"But, Pritam, these are two opposite things ..."

He smiled one of those maddening smiles of his which pave the way for cryptic wisdom.

"As a learned man preaches, everything comes with its in built opposite."

We were interrupted at this juncture by the smiling Lahari who had come to invite us for the *rice eating ceremony* of her son.

~ ~ ~

Paris

In the confines of Louvre, Mona Lisa was visible like a small postage stamp over the heads of a thousand visitors.

Pritam looked through the beer induced fog and tried to edge ahead.

"There it is," he announced to his friends. "There's Mona Lisa."

Sagar seemed confused.

"Are all these paintings by Mona Lisa?"

Pritam turned towards him and smiled. He even went to the extent of patting him on the shoulder.

"Mona Lisa is a painting. Not a painter."

"One painting?"

"Yes. One painting."

"One painting that's so famous?"

"Yes, one painting that's so famous. It's so crowded because all these people want a glimpse. You see there?" he pointed.

Sagar and the other two followed Pritam's finger and looked at the da Vinci masterpiece.

"That's Mona Lisa?"

"Uh huh," Pritam reassured him.

"But, I've seen that so many times."

Pritam smiled broadly and enfolded Sagar in a hug.

Amsterdam

Ajay Yadav spoke into the phone with infinite caution. At the other end of the line was the esteemed ear of K. Ramesh. One un-weighed word and his head was on the proverbial chopping block.

"I fully appreciate his deciding to postpone his vacation for these talks," he reasoned.

The sagacious words of K. Ramesh reached him clearly.

"He is also collaborating with me for a specific purpose."

The account manager took a deep breath.

"I understand that. My only concern is that he is not being billed and this may raise some questions. I mean with his seniority, the profitability is taking a big hit ..."

The voice from Budapest was once again serene.

"Whoever asks questions, refer him to me."

Ajay Yadav looked around him, and noticing no peering or eavesdropping associate, allowed himself a frown.

"Ramesh, I agree that it builds goodwill, and the ones who are asking questions will stop if I mention your name, but after the quarter, if people ask questions about the bottomline ..."

"The problem with any corporation is that entire business strategies hinge on fifteen minutes of fame," Ramesh responded. "We are accustomed to look for immediate benefits. What we need to remember is that we are in the BeNeLux. It is a potential goldmine without low hanging fruits. To build relationships here, one has to sow seeds, do favours and wait for years. I have sown a seed – an expensive one, but one that I think will bear the best fruits. So, to answer your question, yes he will continue and yes he will be billed to your account."

Ajay hung up, but the frown remained etched on his brow. With the cost of this resource, who knew when fingers would be raised in his direction? What if the prevailing winds of recession hit the mast of *Axiom* and K. Ramesh was sent packing with his far sighted philosophising? Who would be there to justify an unbilled consultant on his team? How long would it take for him to capitulate in the cascading effect?

He was still thinking of deep seated negative thoughts when Lahari came into his cubicle to invite him for her son's rice eating ceremony.

As Sandeep walked towards the dental clinic in the Herengracht, a strange feeling of unease pierced through his fabric of thought. Something was not quite right about the place. When he walked into the chamber and noticed the plump form of Madhu Deb seated in the waiting room he saw through the train of complex cognition. His subconscious had scanned the parking lot and had noted the presence of Madhu Deb's Peugeot parked parallel to the kerb. The logical conclusion dawned now.

As the cheerful lady greeted him with a loud hello, he wondered if premonition was nothing but subconscious pattern recognition. He would need to have a discussion with Suprakash Roy.

"Hello," he responded. "What on earth are you doing here?"

"Well, I remembered you had your appointment today. I had come in for a check up myself. Thought I would pick you up and we could go together to Lahari's place."

"Lahari's place?"

"Yes, she invited us for the *annaprasana*. Or has the writer's mind already forgotten that?"

Sandeep, who had indeed conveniently blotted the invitation out of his immediate memory, looked at her with a painful expression.

"Awfully kind of you, but – I don't think I can go ..."

"Why not?"

"I have this dental check up. I ..."

Madhu Deb dismissed his misgivings with a managerial laugh.

"I will drive you, don't worry."

"Jesus ..." Sandeep's exclamation stopped halfway as his eyes fell on Cynthia who emerged from behind the curtains of the chamber. "Hi."

The Chinese girl flashed another of those smiles.

"Hi, the doctor is waiting for you."

"Aren't you?"

The girl looked at him with mock reproach and Sandeep heard an exasperated sigh escape Madhu Deb.

"My camera is ready. I guess I'll shoot first and ask questions later."

Cynthia laughed.

"I wonder if this is the best day for a photograph."

"Why not?"

"I don't think I look my best."

Sandeep rolled his eyes.

"On your worst day you are a sight for sore camera lenses. On your best one needs solar filters."

He started fishing his Olympus out of the sachel.

"I think you should go in first. The doctor doesn't like waiting. And you don't want to be in the bad books of your dentist."

Sandeep smiled and went in. When he walked out after the brief check up, Cynthia was working on the computer. Seeing him, Madhu Deb took her considerable bulk off the waiting room sofa.

"Done? Shall we?"

"You in a hurry?" Sandeep was a wee bit annoyed. With the insides of his mouth under careful scrutiny of the elaborate dental apparatus, he had been thinking of possible developments of a plot. The chance meeting of a regular office goer and a model in a dental clinic. Two souls wanting to blossom out of their current occupations. The dialogue with Cynthia had held considerable promise for interesting development along fictional and real lines. He wanted to proceed along the real path to a threshold from where imagination could flow freely. In this scenario, an overweight boss was an overwhelming blot on the landscape. "You can go ahead, Madhu-di ... I really have some business to finish."

He looked at Cynthia as he finished the sentence and noticed the mischievous gleam in her eyes.

"Would your wife like it?" Cynthia asked playfully.

Sandeep looked peeved. It was that predominant inclination of his curious marital status to creep from behind and bite him on an unsuspecting heel. He glanced at Madhu Deb with a look of reproach.

"The cat is out of the bag," she remarked.

"So is the camera," Sandeep turned and faced Cynthia. "I am capturing a feeble digitised version of the real you. It takes serious restraint in any man of flesh and blood to stop at this with you around."

Cynthia stooped down to retrieve a fallen sheet of paper. "With the rush of blood you spawn through specific regions of flesh." He added, out of audible range. He caught the eye of an exasperated Madhu Deb. "My wife would be fascinated by my loyalty. So how did my marital status become a topic of wide interest?"

Cynthia laughed.

"We were talking about you."

Sandeep bowed. "I am honoured. No doubt you were interested in knowing whether this dashing youth from your neighbouring motherland was available?"

Cynthia slapped him playfully on the arm.

"I don't know about your wife, but I get terribly annoyed when my boyfriend takes pictures of other girls."

Madhu Deb smiled wisely.

"Aha ... So, he does go about running after photogenic females, does he?"

"He is a photographer."

"That explains it. Relationship of convenience, you don't have to aim too far to shoot," Sandeep clicked several times. "There are so many things one wishes one had been ..."

"Photographer?"

Sandeep shrugged.

"Either that, or your boyfriend."

Cynthia laughed. "Too bad."

"Give my regards to your boyfriend."

In the car, Madhu Deb looked at him with a cryptic smile.

"I don't quite understand your motives."

Sandeep was browsing the pictures just taken with his Olympus.

"Why are you so bent on understanding them?"

"I could have sworn that it was more than casual flirtation. Was it?"

Sandeep switched off his camera and shrugged.

"I don't know."

She started the Peugeot and shook her head.

"Dashing knight in shining armour, aren't you? I guess you haven't got used to your not being a bachelor anymore."

Sandeep laughed. "You can bet on that."

XXVII

Blog of Simple Simon
Tags: Indian Hospitality, Cuisine, Festival

I have used up a lot of server space of my blogspot account discussing the Indians, their lives, habits and idiosyncrasies. During narcissistic perusals of my posts, I do realise that while being ostensibly neutral, I have often been critical about characteristics strange to my culture. After all, I have picked up some of the condescension that is the national trait of the great land of opportunities.

However, today I was introduced to another facet of the Indian culture for which I have nothing but fascination and respect. The virtue of hospitality.

Lahari's son is six months old and according to the custom of the Bengali community, it is time for the little one to be introduced to grown up food – also known as rice. Accordingly the ceremony is called the rice eating ceremony. All the colleagues were invited to her apartment in Zonnestein. I was doubly obliged to be there, since Lahari was my official mentor.

Reaching the apartment – a spacious one with a big field in the rear – I was greeted by Lahari and her smiling husband, baby in lap, but was soon handed over to Lahari's mother. This elderly lady, in a traditional saree, took it upon herself to purge me of my years of unenlightened western feeding habits. Like a culinary conjurer she kept producing one edible item after another for me to sample, items of different shapes, sizes, density and taste – all uniformly delectable. In her pidgin English, she made me realise that she could not bear the realisation that I had grown up to full manhood largely on bread, cheese and meat, without having access to the delights of the Bengali kitchen. The round flour *luchi,* the baked potato *dum,* followed by an uncanny wizardry concocted with the prawns to produce something that stuck to the ribs, fish filets coated with grounded biscuit crumbs and fried in deep oil, the specifically made for me spice free mutton curry which melted in the mouth and spread a feeling of goodwill all over as it made its way to the stomach. By the time Madhu Deb and my buddy arrived in tandem, I was being treated to the sinful delights of the most wonderful sweets of the world, rich in sugar syrup and spongy to sink one's teeth in. The elderly lady all but wept when she heard that this was my first taste of authentic Bengali sweetmeats.

Indian food cannot be eaten with cutlery. According to Lahari's mother, to do proper justice one had to use one's hands. And unpractised as I was in this acquired skill, I used both of mine, gently encouraged by the group of Indian colleagues.

Simon had taken refuge in the sweetness and calories provided by Indian hospitality as an oasis to cleanse his mind through the taste buds. He had reached the festivities after a mentally arduous journey, Gunjan accompanying him all the way and cluttering the conversation with his whines, pouring sob stories into reluctant ears. Working harder than the rest without rewards, deprived of timely promotion. There were people who left office early, put in half as much effort as he did and got double the salary. With Madhu Deb, it was Hidori. With Gunjan it was his royal cribs.

He tucked into the syrupy delicacies, much as a tapir escapes predators by jumping into water. And as he showed his appreciation with signs and sighs, his dish kept being replenished in the inimitable Indian way.

He was biting into his fourth exotic sample of the eastern world of sweetness when he remarked that with such a storehouse of delicacies, it was no wonder that India had been attacked again and again. As he finished his remark, he noticed his offical buddy look at him reproachfully. It took him a minute, but he understood why when Madhu Deb took off on the topic like a verbal gazelle. Soon he was being instructed on the historical influence on culinary expertise associated with each of India's geographical parts. The platter was further flavoured with digressions about her friends from each of these fragments of the nation and mind numbing accounts of several mounth watering feasts in those realms. Finally, with a practised connecting anecdote, she was on to Hidori and stories about his reaction to each of the eight hundred plus nectarous delights of the Indian subcontinent.

The centre of hospitable fuss, Simon noticed through the sweetness of palette and the light of thrusted knolwdge that a stealthy hand was creeping towards his cell phone that lay unattended on the table, both his hands occupied in gourmet endeavours.

With a fast practised martial swipe, the consultant had taken possession of the handset and was keying in numbers like crazy. A couple of seconds later, his own cell phone started to ring and with a hastily mumbled excuse, he sprinted out of audible range, his art of animated conversation with himself perfected with practice.

His buddy's engineered getaway set Simon hankering for the wide open outside. After his fifth sweet, the Dutch-Irish-American excused himself to hasten to the rest room. He was crossing the passage on his way back when he noticed a spacious balcony overlooking the field behind the house. Not a soul was in there. No Gunjan, no Madhu Deb, not even the blessed mother in law of Lahari with her plate of sweets. In short, the attractions were enormous. He made his way there and looked at the vast field behind the house.

The solitary figure of Pritam stood in the middle, no doubt inhaling lungfuls of rare Hidori free air. It was after a while that he noticed two more forms on the ground. Behind his friend had emerged the small dark frame of Amrita, who stood at a distance, looking at him. And from the side of the house entered a happy fawn coloured Labrador retriever, wagging his tail, bounding across the open space.

Pritam got down on his knees to pet the dog, and soon he was lying on his back, blissfully allowing his stomach to be tickled.

Simon could see Amrita smile and walk towards the man and dog when the latter, struck by some sudden thought, bolted towards the apartments and in no time had emerged again with a ball throwing stick in his mouth. Bored by loneliness, he no doubt had discovered in the consultant a potential partner for playing catch.

Pritam extended his hand, took the thrower and threw the ball that was stuck to the end. The dog bounded after the orange ball and soon dropped it at his feet.

Pritam picked the ball up with the thrower. He stood in a graceful stance, feet wide apart, arms spread across the torso. His arm moved in one smooth martial motion diagonally upwards, the thrower having been transformed into a makeshift sword. To Simon, the flourish was awe inspiring, and the follow through saw him taking a step towards the strike. The ball flew out in a parabolic curve and disappeared from sight. This was followed by the loudest of crashes. Somewhere in the higher stories of the apartment, a typical Dutch glass door had received the Labrador's ball and was not the better for it. The dog looked confused as it tried to follow the sound. The consultant looked upwards, dropped the thrower and whirled around. This was when he noticed Amrita behind him and started. And after a moment's thought, he picked her up in one motion, his arm encircling her waist, and with a couple of strides and a dive had disappeared collectively in the trimmed hedges around the ground.

There followed internal and external cries of alarm, incensed exclamations of disbelief and running feet. A confused Labrador retriever greeted the angry horde with wagging tail and heartfelt invitation to join the fun.

Sandeep crawled inside the foliage, Amrita next to him in precarious contact. Through the bushy openings, he could see the bewildered feet running into the ground, welcomed with an excited play-bow by an equally baffled Labrador.

"What on earth were you doing there?" he asked in a whisper.

Amrita crept on the ground – knees and elbows buried in the untended soil.

"I was watching."

Sandeep scowled. This was not the first time that he had suddenly discovered Amrita watching him go through unusual actions.

"Could you let me know the next time you want to creep up on me?"

Amrita looked at him as they lay hunched in the bushes. As his darting glances swept the ground and returned to focus on her, he noticed a strange bewitched expression.

"I'm sorry. I was just watching you play with the dog."

Sandeep peered through the bushes.

"I hope the dog doesn't give us away." Confused feet still walked this way and that, trying to gauge the kinematic problem of the unwanted projectile, feverishly calculating the source and trajectory ... discussing conjectures in Dutch.

Sandeep felt Amrita's fingers grip his shoulder tightly, her face brush against his arm.

"Sorry, but I had to take off with you. Else you would be in a spot."

He felt the girl nod and creep closer to him.

"Hang on, I think it will be okay ... unless the dog suddenly thinks of us."

As if on cue, the Labrador turned and pointed his nose at the bushes. The arrival of the crowd had, for a moment, raised his hopes for a game. But, as the people seemed preoccupied with some mundane problem, he remembered the decent young man who had been so enthusiastic a playmate. The smells and sounds guided him towards the bushes.

"Shit ... move," Sandeep rolled over, carrying Amrita with him and tried crawling faster through the undergrowth. The Labrador was close now, sniffing for them, some eager footsteps following him. He almost sensed the first beefy hand reach out towards the bushes when another loud voice made itself heard. There was something familiar about the voice, although it was speaking in the unfamiliar Dutch tongue.

"Simon," whispered Amrita.

There were a couple of exchanges with the people in the ground.

"De andere manier, de andere manier," the voices seemed to concur. The multitude of hands and feet retreated and hastened towards the other end of the field and beyond.

"What did he say?" Sandeep asked.

"I don't know. I don't know Dutch."

"Why don't you? You've been here long enough," he said irritably. "I guess our friend diverted them in the other direction. Should we try to get out?"

The girl clutched on to his shoulders as they half sat, half lay in the hunched position.

"Let's wait for a while. Let all of them go away."

Sandeep crouched, trying to peer through the other end of the bushes.

"What's on that side?"

"It's a bicycle path."

"Let's get out that way."

Amrita clung on to his shoulders.

"Shouldn't we wait for some time?"

"Why? This is the time... they have all gone the other way."

The girl looked away. There was a peculiar expression on her face, and that strange air of acceptance.

"What is it?"

She shook her head.

"Nothing. In some ways it's like a dream."

"Dream? It's a bloody nightmare. Getting struck in a bush like this."

"What's nightmare to you is the most pleasant dream come true for me."

This was said in Bengali. And the fruity soulfulness of the voice hit home yet again.

"Christ, is this your idea of a romantic getaway? Pardon me, madame, the bushes may be lovely, dark and deep, but I do have promises to keep. And miles further we have got to creep."

There was a sniffle. For a moment Sandeep agreed with O'Henry ... sniffles were indeed the predominating expressions of life.

"Sorry, I was not being mean ..."

"I don't understand you ... You must think that I'm a fool."

The sniffle became stronger now, tending towards a sob. The situational proximity made Sandeep reach out and stroke her head, the latter nestling on his chest. The girl looked up at him, a curious gleam in her eyes.

"No, I don't think you are a fool. In my younger and more vulnerable days, my father gave me some advice which I have been turning in my mind ever since. 'Whenever you feel like criticising anyone,' he told me, 'just remember that all the people in this world haven't had the advantages you've had.'"

He felt strange. Was he being sympathetic or a smart ass? He had just spontaneously quoted from *The Great Gatsby* in the guise of comforting the girl. Had his job as a ghost blogger left indelible marks?

The person in question was however somewhat mollified. She looked at him, entreaty etched in her eyes.

"I am making an effort. I have got hold of the books you mentioned. I got *Daddy Long Legs* from Torrent. Roald Dahl from Truly Free."

"Torrent? Truly free?"

"They are web sites."

"You downloaded the books for free?"

"Yes." The eyes searched Sandeep's face, trying to detect hints of reproach.

"Most interesting. A friend of mine would have been intrigued by your learning methods. But, I personally believe that if you get something for free, you don't really appreciate its value."

"You mean I should buy them from Waterstone?"

Sandeep sighed.

"Either that ... or as a cheaper option go down to the second hand book shops of Amsterdam. There are many. One in NieuwMaarkt, just off the ... well ... canal. There is a book market every Friday on Spui. Else, you can always become a member of the Openbare Bibliotheek or get the AdamNet pass and become a member of the University Libraries as well. But, could I suggest something? Environment is absolutely essential for learning."

The girl's head bobbed up and down near Sandeep's chest.

"A thorny bush is not exactly the place of enlightenment, unless we are trying tantric meditation. We have come a long way from the day Moses was accosted by the burning bush. Nowadays bushes are nothing but trouble for the world. If you don't believe me, ask Michael Moore."

There was confusion with the essence of laughter in the girl's expression.

"What I mean is that we need to crawl out now."

As he prepared to move to the other end of the bush, Amrita left his shoulder and almost in the same motion put her hands round his neck and kissed him on the cheek.

For a moment or two, he could not react. He did not know what to do. In front of him Amrita was crouched with her eyes tightly shut.

"I am not sure that's the best idea," he said hesitantly.

The girl turned her face away with a pained expression, eyes still shut.

"I'm sorry. Pardon me if I offended you."

Sandeep crawled through the outgrowth and emerged on the *fietspad*. A couple of cycles were retreating in either way. The solitary figure of a tall, stocky Dutch youth in formal clothing hovered around. On seeing Sandeep, he smiled.

"Coast is clear. I was wondering if you had already run away."

The puzzled face of Amrita peered from underneath the bush and then she came out, squeezing herself through rough branches.

"Thanks, Simon," Sandeep remarked. "I did not quite get it, but I heard your voice. Did you convince them that the miscreant had gone the other way?"

Simon laughed.

"Yes. In full throated Dutch. So, I think they will be on a wild goose chase."

"I wish your Dutch could also make the dog bark up the wrong tree. By the way, did you see the entire thing?"

Simon nodded.

"I saw you playing with the dog and then your flourishing sword technique."

Amrita giggled.

"And no doubt you saw our synchronised dive into the bushes?"

Even as Simon nodded in assent, Sandeep could see the girl turning her face in abashment. The archetypical Indian girl, demure and coy at being discovered with the beloved. How could this same archetypical Indian girl not only cross the social barricades by making her feelings known to a supposedly married man, but also fling herself onto that same man uninvited and kiss him passionately?

"Did you employ any specific martial technique for the lift?" Simon asked.

"Desperation. When you suddenly discover a partner in crime ... well, shall we go into the festivities? Our pursuers might return banking on the well known criminal psychology trait that culprits return to the scene of crime."

Simon pointed at their clothes.

"The hosts are also starting to worry about you, but I suggest you freshen up."

Sandeep looked at his suit, by now crumpled in several places and splattered with vegetation. Amrita looked even more dishevelled.

"Quite true. Ours is a classic example of one professional on land being cleaner than two in the bush. Simon, could I impose on you to go in with a dusted version of our mademoiselle here while I follow after a while, freshened up and engaged in some world changing phone call from abroad?"

"What do you mean?" Amrita asked, puzzled yet wary.

"Dust yourself and go in with Simon. I will follow after some time. I am a senior consultant, so I won't face too many questions."

Amrita's smile was replaced by a flustered frown. She switched to Bengali.

"You don't want to go in with me?"

Sandeep shook his head.

"I am more worried about the conclusions that the fertile Bengali brains in there can jump to. Simon, is the great Gunjan still in the premises?"

"Unfortunately yes."

"There you go."

~ ~ ~

Half an hour later, Sandeep was discovered absorbed in Lahari's collection of foreign DVDs.

Madhu Deb sang out the declaration of detection.

"There is the man we are looking for. Pritam, people have been looking for you for the last hour or so."

Sandeep turned and smiled at the group.

"I was browsing through this excellent collection. I actually lost track of time. Lahari, I must say you have great taste in films."

The good natured Lahari came in and glanced at the fifty or so DVDs of French, Italian and Iranian movies.

"I know ... unfortunately, the moment you have a kid life changes. I've had most of them for over a year, but haven't watched half."

"Actually this is a phenomenal collection. I have watched only one Majid Majiedi, but it seems you have four of his ..."

"Children of Heaven, Baran, Father and Colour of Paradise."

Simon crept up to him when he stepped out into the living room.

"How on earth did you manage to sneak in?"

Sandeep smiled.

"Training."

"Are you from the Mossad?"

"Do you expect me to tell you if I am?"

"Maybe you are a communist agent, here to ensure that the Capitalist countries never recover from the Financial Crisis. Armed with hidden cameras and camouflage."

"And maybe I go about spreading the manifesto in the guise of corporate lectures."

"Maybe you broke the window on the top floor to create a diversion, so that your lethal partner could enter the other side of the building unnoticed."

"And the whole thing was witnessed by an unsuspecting half Irish half Dutch guy who actually helped the espionage unknowingly. And thereby became a suspected terrorist."

"We are doing good, aren't we? Can this become your next novel?"

Sandeep shrugged.

"I doubt it. I am not the one for this cloak and dagger stuff. That's too real life for me."

"So what's fiction for you?"

"Maybe a literary agent who reads."

∾ ∾ ∾

Mail from Paramita Verma to Sandeep Gupta

Dear Sandeep,

I am a friend of Shruti. I guess that Shruti has told you that I was asked to purchase a copy of your book for her.

Well, to cut a long story short, I wanted to browse through your book, started reading a few pages and then got hooked. I stayed up till 3 AM last night to finish it. It is one of the most honest and fresh books I have read in recent times. My compliments to you and am looking forward to reading more of your works in future.

If you are on Orkut, please visit my account – vermapara. My nick now reads –' Doppelganger Days – a must read'.

Thanks for writing such a book

Paramita

Email dictated to Shuktara Lal by her grandfather Professor Lal

Sandeep, dear boy,

Thank you from the bottom of the heart for sending across the book.

I spent most of the Sunday after my return from the Mahabharata reading poring over your novel, Doppelganger Days. It is a wonderful work. I find your style distinctive. The content, the exhilarating humour, the exceptional use of the mot juste – it reads like a dream.

Having said that, the book as a product leaves much to be desired. The pages have been glued together rather than bound. The print has also been centred in the pages, which may be mathematically perfect, but somehow the human eyes prefer the asymmetry that we find in more traditional publications.

I found another couple of mentions of your novel in the Tribune and the Biblio. Not quite reviews, but publicity helps all the same.

What about your search for the strange breed called literary agents in the far away land? Did you manage to hunt down a sample of the species?

During your quest, please remember that a flower never forgets to produce the fragrance while its petals are busy welcoming people to sniff.

Best Wishes,
The Professor.

Late night text message from Amrita at 12:03 AM

I haven't taken off my clothes, because they still smell of your perfume.
How did you feel when I kissed you? I hope you will still talk to me tomorrow.

Reply from Sandeep

Your sms just woke me up. It's deo and not perfume. Change your clothes, you rolled about in the bushes ... you might end up with toxoplasmosis. Then go to sleep. It is already tomorrow.

Part VI:

Magic of International Diversifications

XXVIII

Amsterdam

"This is the heaven that makes me return to Amsterdam over and over again," the sun shone through the tall green trees of Het Amsterdamse Bos and K. Ramesh's head glistened. Was it in *Man and Superman* that Shaw had described a man who could heliograph instructions to army camps on a sunny day?

"And all of it is man made," the visionary continued. "Each and every shrub of these thousands of hectares have been painstakingly planted, nurtured and maintained. On land reclaimed from the sea. Makes you think. Thanks for joining me here on a Saturday morning, anyway."

They had met in front of the Manege at half past seven. Cyclists, joggers, riders on horses, and running dogs passed them as they walked under the shady trees.

"No problem at all," Sandeep replied. "I spend a large part of the weekend mornings in the Bos anyway."

"I have just this day in Amsterdam and will fly to London in the evening," the Vice President informed. "I love weekends in the Bos. You see ..." he turned out his pockets. " No blackberry, no cell phone. It is detox. But, the point I was making. India is full of trees, forests, vast lands ... and look at what we have done to our treasures. And these people have actually allowed nature to come to them, to grow. Could we draw the same parallel in our world?"

Sandeep wondered.

"You mean in the industry? In the business world?"

The great man nodded.

"I am sorry I have not been able to spend much time with you on our proposed methodology. However, what I am looking at is just like natural treasures. India is full of knowledge, thought, systems, processes. It is not something to be kept unused, forgotten, in tatters. These people have planted trees and made them grow. They have also applied thought, written procedures and policies and made them work. For us, half the work has already been done. There are resources of knowledge that remain unused – we just have to utilise it. Package it, dress it, convert it to meet the modern requirements and propagate it."

He paused as Sandeep kicked a fallen branch.

"The key here is the time. This recession. People are looking for solutions. Now is the time to pitch in with processes, thoughts. And, my dear writer, if I was slightly apprehensive after your paper presentation, I am fully confident now after knowing about your literary ability. You are the man for the job."

Sandeep looked at the huge expanse of greenery.

"My literary ability is restricted to the world of Literature. Or should I say writing ability. Only time will tell whether it is Literature or not."

The older man smiled wisely.

"Accepted. Writing is definitely a vocation much higher than the pursuit of money, isn't it?"

"People may differ in their views on that one. The current trend is to think the other way. Even the quality of writing is judged by the amount of money it rakes in with the rough edges. But, then, I ..."

"I understand how you feel. You are gifted with the talent of a writer. However, if we go back to prehistoric times, to the times when written records were introduced for the first time, do you know what it was used for?"

Sandeep waited for the answer to the rhetorical question.

"It was not for jotting down poetry or philosophical thought. It was used to keep records of business transactions. Man shall not live by bread alone, but then whatever he lives by is in addition to the bread – the bread that he earns by the sweat of his brow."

Sandeep smiled as he walked.

"One can't really argue with that."

"No one can argue with the role of money in the fabric of our lives. To this day, wars are fought, people are killed, nations are devastated because of money. You can write only of life, and life is linked to money – you can't prise them apart."

Sandeep laughed.

"Life and money in rigor mortis?"

"I will have to reflect on that one though. However, the gist is that you can't get away from money – be it the root of all evil."

"For someone wanting to propagate Indian thoughts, you are too full of Biblical quotes today."

"Am I? Are not all these concepts well rooted in Indian philosophy as well? And much more? Doesn't Buddhism talk of desire as the cause of all suffering?

That is my prime grievance. Ideas and opinions out of India are used by western success stories, but we seldom get the credit as pioneers."

He paused.

"You know of Fibonacci numbers?"

"Why, of course. I have a post graduate in Mathematics."

"That doesn't necessarily answer my question. Every idiot knows about Fibonacci numbers because of *Da Vinci Code*. And who do you think came up with this idea of Fibonacci numbers?"

"Leonardo of Pisa?"

"Well read, but wrong. Leonardo of Pisa revolutionalised finance by changing the way people counted. And he did so by borrowing from Indian mathematics. Fibonacci numbers actually originated from India. There is a reference of it to be found in the work of Pingala, the Sanskrit scholar, under the name *matrameru*."

"Wow."

"That is my point. Indian ideas have been used – plundered as its riches have been – and whatever still remains, lies unused."

The man was definitely learned.

"If you are looking at a synthesis of hidden knowledge of ancient India, it is the task of a lifetime."

K. Ramesh looked towards the skies and laughed.

"And no one has a lifetime to focus on one goal, right? Even three months of relationship building without revenue has to be justified. We are all running after fifteen minutes of fame."

"I was thinking about your focus on the current recession being the key ..."

They crossed a canal and made for an open air restaurant in the Geitenboerderij.

"I intend to use this crisis as the watershed. The immediate success will pave the way for bigger and better things. Your series of talks for the HMH is turning out to be something real special. I am working on every segment that I receive. Topping them up with insights, having a special task force draw parallels with the financial nitty-gritty of stocks, bonds, securities and banking. I am sure I am on to something special here. I have a plan, but you see I am not asking you to tailor your progress based on it. I don't want to stifle your creativity. You have the full liberty to experiment with your thoughts. With the kind of people I know in Gartner, in the Ivy Leagues and upper crust business schools, good stuff will be easy to push for acceptance and even awards ..."

"Awards?"

Ramesh took a seat in the restaurant overlooking a vast field full of content cows and happy horses.

"Awards, appreciation – on the global scale. Do you find it far-fetched?"

Sandeep shook his head.

"Not at all. I know something about how awards are won."

"Uh huh?"

"I follow the Bookers closely, I watch the Oscars."

Ramesh sighed.

"Cynical, are we? Do you think it stops there? What do you think of the Nobel prize? Especially in Economics. Do you know how many economists have won the big prize for un-validated theories that never worked?"

Sandeep shrugged.

"I don't find it hard to believe. If Pritam Mitra has the erudition to write papers that are accepted for phenomenally important financial conferences at the height of the financial crisis, anything is possible."

Ramesh laughed loudly.

"There is self effacing sarcasm in you which I find absolutely hilarious."

"It is hilarious in more ways than one," Sandeep observed.

They dug into the ham and eggs. The crisp morning air had whetted their appetite.

"What further innovation do you have in your mind for the series? I do understand that change is the only constant and all that, but do you have anything sufficiently out of the box in your immediate plans?"

Sandeep looked at the visionary reflectively.

"Now that you mention it, I have been thinking of something for quite a while. Change in an organisation is essentially dependent on group psychology ..."

∾ ∾ ∾

Paris

Three priests descended the giant steps of Sacre Couer, dressed in their white robes.

A young Indian tourist looked at them and pulled the sleeve of another.

"Pritam, look," he whispered. "Three popes."

Pritam looked at his young friend indulgently and smiled from ear to ear. This was heaven.

∾ ∾ ∾

Amsterdam

Ajay Yadav looked apprehensive. To be precise, he looked even more apprehensive than usual. His eyes, never trendsetters of steadfast calm, darted to and fro as if witnessing a three way tennis match. So did his mental machinery.

"It's unusual," he muttered.

In front of him, Lahari stood undecided. Coming over to the account manager's cubicle to ask about his availability that afternoon she had encountered a curiously tense man nervously pressing keys on his laptop. He was not yet aware of her presence.

"I know it's unusual," he repeated to himself and Lahari felt concerned about his well being.

He picked up his phone with a shaky hand and punched a four digit number. "Hello, Pritam? Could you come over please?" His perennially fretful eyes, more fretful now than ever, roamed around his table and finally shot uneasily towards the entrance. On noticing Lahari he blinked and started.

"Oh, Lahari ... have you been standing there for a while?"

"Are you busy?" Lahari smiled in her friendly way. "Madhu-di was wondering if you would be able to attend a meeting on the next *Sur-Soiree* this afternoon."

The account manager looked with fidgety eyes at his Outlook calendar.

"I think I can manage it. But, wouldn't it be better if we could meet after office hours? You know what I mean ... the client shouldn't think that we are too caught up in fun events ..."

Lahari's smile disappeared. She did not mind the musical events and other varieties of packaged nonsense under the versatile guise of team building, but she was zealously protective of the time she spent with her kid.

Sandeep walked in as she was weighing her reply.

There were three distinct furrows from a severe frown. He had been in the process of finalising another version of the synopsis, catering this time to a 'champion of new experimental writing', when the unwelcome call from the account manager had torn him away from his cubicle. He did not like being with this man. There was always something around him suggesting imminent catastrophe.

"Yes?" he asked. The sharp edge to this straightforward query startled Lahari and cut through the fragile nervous system of the account manager. Ajay was never at ease with this unconventional young upstart, never too sure about lurking surprises. What made him even more apprehensive were the blessings of K.Ramesh cast over him with conspicuous invisibility.

"Hello Pritam," he offered a hesitant smile.

Sandeep scowled at him and smiled at Lahari.

"This session with the external consultant that you have scheduled," Ajay Yadav began. "I … I mean … this is somewhat unconventional."

Sandeep raised his eyebrow.

"We are talking Change Management here, and it is never a conventional process. All through my approach has bordered on the unusual and it has paid dividends …"

The account manager nodded and tried to smile.

"Yes, I know … but, since things are going on pretty well, do we need …?"

"I think we do. I have talked to Ramesh."

A choked groan escaped Ajay .

"I … er … that was not necessary. I mean, we don't need to disturb him for every small thing. Did he okay it?"

"Yes, he did. We had met for an early morning constitutional followed by breakfast at the Amsterdamse Bos on Saturday morning."

In the mind of the manager, fuddled with fear, there were multiple interpretations of each word before the meaning became apparent.

"You ... you had breakfast ... Well, but you informed me only after you sent the meeting request ...You did not speak to me …"

Sandeep shrugged. "I don't have that much time."

Ajay Yadav was struck dumb for a while. This bordered so heavily on insubordination. However, challenging someone who spent early weekend mornings picnicking with the Vice President could be dangerous as far as his own status and job were concerned.

"You see Pritam, this type of guest speakers is ... is ... unusual. The person you have invited is not even from *Axiom* …"

Sandeep kicked a trash can under the table.

"*Axiom* does not have in-house psychiatrists ."

"Well … er … is a psychiatrist really necessary?"

"Change in the organisation is primarily a psychological challenge."

"Well …"

"Haven't you heard of the Stanley Kubrick theory of personal loss – the five stages of dealing with it? It is a psychoanalytical theory common in cutting edge change management as well …There is very strong coupling."

"I understand your point. What you say is definitely true … But, again, this psychiatrist you want to invite is …"

"He is from the Leiden Medisch Centrum, with the soundest credentials."

" … that makes him something like a third party vendor. And any decision regarding using the services of a third party vendor involves approval …"

"He is doing us a favour because I have asked him to. He is not going to charge anything …"

Ajay Yadav was feverishly figuring out cosequences.

"Well, there is the NDA to think of. Non-Disclosure Agreement …."

"He will be under the Hippocratic Oath."

The account manager sweated.

"Well, you could have let me run this through some members …"

Sandeep sighed.

"What on earth are you afraid of? Are you on the run from some mental establishment?"

Ajay started. No one had ever asked him such questions. He looked at Sandeep's face, searching for hints of mockery or inside knowledge of forthcoming doom. He followed this up with a weak smile.

"It's not really a question of fear. But, you see, we are working at the client's location and there are certain protocols we need to adhere to … You could wait for a couple of days, and I would have got back to you."

Sandeep smiled back.

"It's okay. Ramesh thinks that this is a good idea … it will be a differentiator as far as our method of consultancy is concerned … getting a professional psychiatrist to speak about getting ready for change. The Dutch are always interested in the workings of the mind. Go to any Boekenmarkt and there will be shelves full of psychology books. Well, what do you think?"

He had turned and directed his question at Lahari.

"Er … I don't know. I guess it's a good idea ," she said hesitantly, with an amused look. "But, of course, I am not the one to take decisions."

"In other words, it's not your head that's on the chopping block."

Ajay Yadav's startled eyes darted across Sandeep's face.

"Settled," Sandeep smiled. "I don't think we have a choice now. Even if we wanted to back out, we could not. Our delivery credibility would come under scanner." He laughed. "And relax. A psychiatrist on the premises will be pretty handy if the bank does collapse."

"Eh? …"

He reached across and patted the account manager on the shoulder.

This was getting too hilarious for Lahari. A guffaw was rising up from within her with the unstoppable effervescence of aereated water, her torso ready for the shimmy that reminded Simon so much of a mouseover event.

"Okay, Ajay-da," she said, suppressing her smile. "I'll send you a meeting invite after talking to Madhu-di."

"And I've already sent you my meeting invite for the session, so I will follow her excellent example and get back to my cubicle," Sandeep declared.

As they walked out and away from the audio-visual range of the mesmerised account manager, Lahari bent double and released the pent up laughter in tumultuous bursts.

"I can't recall when I've had more fun," she said, surfacing for breath before submerging in mirth again. "What a character."

Sandeep snorted.

"What is he afraid of? I mean, he trembles at every flutter of a butterfly's wing across the face of the earth. Somehow connects it to fire under his ass. Chaos theoretic way of management. It's a blessing that it doesn't thunder in this land, or he would have recurrent heart attacks. Is that why he has relocated to Netherlands?"

Lahari, exhausted by the recent jovial callisthenics of her bulk, held on to the cupboard of office stationery to steady herself before another go.

"He's afraid of losing his job. As far as I know he was sacked from his previous company. Once he came perilously close to being fired here too … when he copied and pasted appraisals of two underlings. I guess he is ultra cautious since then."

Sandeep helped himself to half a dozen large envelopes. More query letters and synopses were on their way to the slush pile.

"Well, he should have a one on one with the psychiatrist who is coming," he remarked. "Severe anxiety disorder."

"True. Interesting idea, a professional psychiatrist for a guest session. But, Pritam, tell me something. What was that Stanley Kubrick stuff? Did he really have a psychiatric theory?"

"Stanley Kubrick?"

"That's what you said."

"Did I?" he laughed. "Must have been a slip of tongue. It is Kulber something or the other. Yes, I remember. Kubler Ross. Anyway, it's all the same to Ajay Yadav. It's strange that I should have said Stanley Kubrick. Interesting cognitive process, I guess. Are you familiar with his works, too?"

Lahari nodded.

"I've watched a couple of his movies. Although the films I like best are more in line with the stuff Truffaut used to make …"

"Francois Truffaut?"

"Right. Films like *400 Blows*."

They walked along discussing films before Madhu Deb came romping in, gate-crashing her way into the conversation, gearing up for a panoramic retrospective of the myriads of films she had seen and not seen. A quick missed call from Sandeep ensured rescue in the Gupta Van der Wiel method.

ᔕ ᔕ ᔕ

Leiden

"It is great that you are enjoying yourself."

"You bet. Away from the German Unification and the Single Market Program"

Dr. Roy enjoyed walking over the quiet, cobblestoned paths of Leiden.

"Having fun?"

"Yes. I am hopping from bar to bar across the great European cities."

"How are your new friends?"

"They are a delight. We start for Rome tomorrow. One of them has the firm conviction that it is in Romania."

The doctor walked up the steps of the Medisch Centrum.

"Yes, it is a great leveller, isn't it? The mysterious modern education."

"Does the knowledge of Rome's geographical location help him in any way? Does it increase the hourly rate that he is billed against?"

"Of course not. That's what Sherlock Holmes stood for."

"What?"

"Sherlock Holmes. He did not care whether the earth revolved around the sun or the moon."

"That's greatness. The best thing a doctor can do is hitching on to people like him, like that Watson fellow did. Leave curing the human mind to beer."

"It may interest you to know that I am speaking as a guest lecturer for *Axiom* tomorrow."

There was a pause.

"I thought you said you were speaking as a guest lecturer for *Axiom.*"

"I did."

"What the ...? Where?"

"In the premises of HMH."

"Who the hell invited you as a guest speaker?"

"You did."

"What?"

"Pritam Mitra."

After a most eloquent sound of silence, Pritam's buoyant voice came back with a refreshing crispness.

"Go ahead. Join hands with the snake."

"Snakes don't have hands, Pritam."

"Destroy my career. I don't give a damn. I am joining Accenture in three months."

∾ ∾ ∾

Amsterdam

Chat between Sandeep Gupta and Amrita De

(A lot of editing has been carried out on the script to correct spellings and grammar and enhance readability)

Amrita: Hi. Good evening.
Sandeep: Hi. Amrita of Axiom?
Amrita: Yes
Sandeep: How did u get my email id?
Amrita: From ur book
Sandeep: U have my book? Am flattered.
Amrita: I borrowed it from Madhu-di
Sandeep: Ah, my PRO
Amrita: Pardon?
Sandeep: Great to see u online, but I am kind of busy ...
Amrita: oh ... okay
Amrita: Could I say something?
Sandeep: If it can be fit into one and a half minutes
Amrita: I have ordered your book from Amazon
Sandeep: Really? That's great. Let me know how long it takes to reach you and the condition of the book when it does
Amrita: okay
Amrita: Another thing
Sandeep: y?
Amrita : When you were in the bush with me, I shouldn't have done what I did
Amrita: But, I was so relieved to see your sms
Amrita: In which you said that it was already the next day.
Amrita: Are you there?
Amrita: hello
Amrita: Are u there?
Amrita: Won't u talk to me?
Amrita: Hello ... please tell me, are u there?
Amrita: I am sorry if I am disturbing u ...
Amrita: Hello !!!
Amrita: If u don't want to talk u can just say so

Sandeep: Hey, cool down. Had just got busy with something.

Amrita: Sorry

Amrita: Actually have been having lot of problems

Amrita: U have been helping me with English ... could u give me some advice?

Amrita: Could u please?

Amrita : Are u there?

Sandeep: Y

Amrita: I want to leave my job.

Sandeep: Atta girl

Amrita: ?

Amrita: I don't understand

Sandeep: Just an expression of encouragement

Amrita: u think that's a good idea?

Sandeep: I don't know. I have done it. With mixed results.

Amrita: I don't like this boring job

Sandeep: Join the club

Amrita: Which club?

Sandeep: Forget it ... so what'd you do once you quit?

Amrita: I want to get into actuaries

Sandeep: You think that's less boring?

Amrita: I know u have a math background. U think this is a good idea?

Sandeep: Believe me mademoiselle, I'm the last person u shd ask

Amrita: u don't want to tell me?

Sandeep: I am not qualified enough to tell you. But, if u think Actuaries is your thing, why don't you go for it?

Amrita: I need to clear a tough exam

Sandeep: Everything comes with its inbuilt opposite.

Amrita: Meaning?

Sandeep: Never mind. So, what's the problem?

Amrita: Neha, the girl who stays with me, does not cooperate

Amrita: She's always putting on the TV loudly, or listening to music ... Or, having friends around. Staying awake long hours.

Sandeep: Complain to the warden.

Amrita: Who?

Sandeep: Don't get me wrong. I am sorry, but these are common problems of adjustment. I can't possibly go and ask your roommate to behave herself.

Amrita: Yes, I know. You can't.

Sandeep: I can almost see the gloom reflected on ur screen

Amrita: What?

Sandeep: U must find solutions urself. Why don't u find a better place to study?

Amrita: What place? I have never been able to study at home. At first my parents were insensitive, then my sister ... I have come all this way from India to get away from my family.

Amrita: Now I don't even have the peace at home to study. If I say anything she quarrels, like my sister had done back home.

Sandeep: Why don't u treat her to a little dose of White Swan bends for a drink? Small joint manipulation works wonders in settling petty disputes.

Amrita: lol. Tai chi won't help here. She'll scream

Sandeep: Sealing breath may be a bit too extreme

Amrita: I am so greatfull (sic) to u for teaching me Tai Chi. At least I can concentrate.

Sandeep: Why don't you make off to the Openbare Bibliotheek after office? U can carry ur books and study there.

Amrita: That's a good idea.

Sandeep: The main branch near Centraal Station is open from 10 to 10. U can easily study three hours a day.

Amrita: Yes, I can ... thank u so much.

Amrita: I am so greatfull(sic) to u

Sandeep: Thanks, but it's spelt grateful

Amrita: Thank u.

Amrita: I would like to send u a summary of Daddy Long Legs ... could u check it and let me know what mistakes I made?

Amrita: I really want to improve my English

Amrita: Hello

Amrita: u there?

Amrita: I know u won't be there forever.

Sandeep: True, that's why I want to leave my mark on the generations to come ... and consequently require one of these blasted literary agents to actually read what I send them.

Amrita: I don't understand

Sandeep: I can't translate that now, dear, I am woefully short of time. Could we pick this up sometime later?

Amrita: Pick what up?

Sandeep: Could we discuss this again some other time? I am about to log off. I have work to do ...

Amrita: Ok, bye ... thanks ... and I do love u

XXIX

What could she say about her feelings? They were like the water of a wild stream, which manages to find its own unrestrained way past rocks and boulders of logic.

One of her colleagues from her previous company often used a complicated English word whenever someone claimed that she was in love. "Infatuation." She knew if she were crazy enough to take that colleague into confidence now, she would repeat the expression with a nasty wave of the hand. But, she would perhaps never speak of it to anyone. It was her own to treasure. And did it matter by what name one called it? His smile would still playfully brush the foolish strings of her heart. His clear open eyes would still hold hers with the invisible thread of magic. And when, once in a while, in the *tai chi* classes or while discussing lessons, his hand would touch hers, her skin would tingle with the same fascinated ecstasy.

Crazy, crazy girl. He would never be hers. He was married. He belonged to someone else. And even if he were not, he was a writer, of books in English. He used words that she hadn't heard. Would he ever...?

She didn't know. She didn't care. She loved him. Was it wrong to fall in love? Was it within one's control? Could any specialist undo the complicated knot the strings of her heart had wound around him? After all she didn't want anything in return.

Why had she told him? She didn't know. Maybe she was crazy? She stood to lose the minimum contact that she had with him. She could not help it. And he did not cut her off with the cruel sword of aloofness. He was too compassionate. He tried his best to make her realise her mistake – mistake as the world saw it. He tried hard not to hurt her. How could he succeed when fate had already made up its mind to convert her love story into a painful strife? She could make out that he thought she was being childish, that she would grow out of it. Only she knew that she would love once and that once was the present.

And how did he feel about her now? He was patient, helpful and kind. She knew that he did not think of loving her. Yet, when she asked for his help, he was there with suggestions, with solutions. He treated her as one would treat a child – a naughty but loved child.

She bothered him much with her troubles, she did realise that. But, he wanted to know what her problems were. And listened with patience.

Was there any chance of his loving her?She dared not think about it. The day they lay in the bush behind Lahari's house, she experienced closeness with him. She was more than sure it was not too disagreeable to him as well.

Whenever she was near him, she felt a desperate urge to rush to him and bury her head in his chest – where he would love and protect her forever. Did he feel even a small percentage of her stirrings?

During the *tai chi* classes, she saw him take pains to be normal, but when he touched her, she did sense a tenderness that peeped out from behind the mask of gravity.

And sometimes, when she discussed books with him, he playfully struck her on the head or called her dear. She understood that he thought of her as a kid ... but she was growing into a kid whom he liked. And kid girls didn't take long to grow into women. So, who knew?

That raised another question. He suggested *Daddy Long Legs* to improve her English. Was it simply because of the English? Or was it something more than that? It was the story of a child growing into a woman and ending up marrying the man who had cared for her when she was young. Did he want to say something to her through this book? Oh, that was crazy. How could she even think about that? But, then, why not? Was she the only one who could be crazy? Could he not?

XXX

My fair friend,

I long to feel the facile fingers that keyed in two hundred and twenty six poignant pages. Profligate that I am in the eulogy of feminine charms, I turn into a churlish miser while paying homage to present day scribblers. Yet your genre transcending prose does not scrounge grudging appreciation as a polite product of early days of friendship. It snatches warmest applause from the delighted cockles of my heart.

The pieces that you present are disconnected yet subtly synchronous for the insightful. They delightfully paint a vast canvas of geography and society, yet remain focussed unwaveringly on the vagaries of the human mind. They held my attention throughout. The departures into multiple paths of structure and style were linked by the common beauty of language, the masterly balance maintained between humour and pathos.

A gorgeous lady with a well endowed funny bone is for me a wish-fulfilling dream.

I think of all those blurbs that frequent the mass market publications today – where every book is touted to be touching and funny – even the Booker Winning efforts. No work upholds those two enticing qualities more. Yet you are shooting for a miniscule population of readers. Is it not depriving the world from potential delight? At the same time, I wonder how many of the busy publishers and agents would have managed to spare the required fraction of a minute to read a page, and if they did, how many would understand and appreciate – and in the miracle of miracles of this landing up in the hands of an enlightened decision maker, how many would actually risk their money on an unknown name with a bizarre style, without the benediction of an industrialist hubby, a Nobel prize winning buddy or other such indispensible literary props.

Your unique prose and sometimes poetic renditions give the manuscript a Borges like aura – but that is as far as I will go in parallels. Let the uniqueness of your work stay untarnished by the age-old human failing of casting meaningless shadows of historic luminaries.

May your thoughts keep turning into such magnificent manuscripts.

Sandeep (who once thought he was the unique author of his generation)

∾ ∾ ∾

Excerpts of the final minutes of Dr. Suprakash Roy's guest lecture at HMH Bank – arranged as an Axiom initiative of Beyond Expectations – compiled from the mpeg file provided by Simon van der Wiel

"Let us summarise what we have covered today.

"The first phase. 'No it's not true. It cannot be me.' These thoughts are not only common to people who are informed that they have been let go, but also to those who arrive at such anxious conclusions on their own. Denial is a temporary defence that is soon replaced by partial acceptance.

"Next we get angry. There is a sense of injustice. This anger is projected onto the immediate environment at random. A phase which is the toughest on family and friends.

"The following stage is of bargaining with the powers that be and fate. A temporary stage, almost always transient, but which perhaps plays in the back of the minds the longest after the tragedy passes, a blow to one's esteem – which makes one bitter and vengeful.

"After this is the stage of depression, when the world seems to go on as usual even as financial burdens are added to the plight. Little luxuries and later even necessities cannot be afforded any more. There is the added guilt of failing as a provider.

"However, if the afflicted receives enough help during all theses stages –emotional support more than anything else, he can reach the final stage – that of acceptance. And that is when the wheel of fortune turns, and positive steps can be taken to make a fresh start.

"The understanding of all these phases helps you in being prepared in the best possible way to face the gossip in the grapevine, and the eventuality of its coming true. You see, present day gossip has an unprecedented snowball effect with blogs, chain emails, facebook, twitter and text messages. The virtual shadow of doom makes it loom larger than ever. Additionally, with this knowledge you can also help the colleague who has suffered a loss of job."

The neutral, sympathetic tone of Suprakash Roy had a soothing effect. The initial scepticism shown by many was mollified. A lot of the employees still had reservations about the rationale of this series of talks by *Axiom,* but most of them had accepted the events as an hour of intellectual entertainment. They enjoyed it.

∾ ∾ ∾

"That was a neat little trick of yours, getting me here to talk of the psychological aspects of recession."

They were sitting in the *Magic Pot* – one of the more sophisticated Coffee-shops of De Wallen. Simon knew the proprietor of the establishment, which meant easy access to some of the harder drugs that did not quite qualify as legal even in the grassy green pastures of Amsterdam. They had taken the 51 to NieuwMaarkt immediately after the evening's *Tai chi* classes. Now, as the doctor and the impostor sat in the plush leather chairs, the Dutch-Irish young man had gone behind the counters to make clandestine arrangements for something called Frozen Lightening.

"You were more than eager, weren't you? In fact this Kubric method was your idea."

"Kubler Ross."

"Whatever."

"Yes, it did give me the opportunity to take an insider's view into the cubicle bound organism."

"The Dutch aren't the real representative samples. You should visit a technical firm in Bangalore. They enjoyed the session, though. Something new."

"Ever eager for novelty."

"I was also not getting enough time to compile *Gita* based intellectual horses-hit. I have to keep them interested."

"*Gita* does have universal appeal," the doctor nodded sagely. "That's the key. Appeal to their fundamental senses. That's why it has been successful."

A reflective smile expanded across Sandeep's face.

"That gives me a couple of ideas."

"So you are teaching martial arts as well," Dr. Roy's tone turned grave. A look of admonition flickered in his practised passive eyes.

"Circumstantial necessity," Sandeep replied. "Largely harmless."

The good doctor nodded as he scanned the wide variety of characters who sat in the stools and chairs, in various states of euphoria.

"Let us look at it objectively. Circumstance had first of all necessitated the swap of identities ..."

"With mutual consent."

"Ah," the older man smiled. "Consent has so many connotations. I believe manufactured consent is a common term nowadays."

"Thanks to Noam Chomsky."

"Slowly circumstances demanded that you keep adding fascinating dimensions to Pritam's character. It started with knowledge of the *Gita* , something Pritam will probably never read even if he lives to be two hundred."

"I needed to present something in place of his paper. I cannot bring myself to read his pathetic stuff even if *I* live to be two thousand."

"Creative juxtaposition of Hindu philosophy into the topic of financial crisis. I believe the accepted term for this sort of nonsense is Out of Box Thinking."

Sandeep nodded. "Or innovation."

"Right. Circumstances forced you to join hands with the top boss of European Operations to create an esoteric model ..."

"Yes, a learned man caught in an industry propelled by knee jerk reactions ... I get the feeling that he is struggling to make an impact with his ideas, in a quest for delegated self actualisation."

The doctor followed a young American couple with curiosity as they inhaled a carefully laid out line of white powder.

"The fifth layer of Maslow, having nothing left to achieve in the four below. You know the problem with creative artists? They tend to reach out for the fifth level without giving a damn about the other four."

"That's profound."

"I would take a bow if I was standing. Next was your circumstantial necessity of being married ..."

"Ah ...," the guilty smile that had been drawn on Sandeep's lips by the doctor's allegations spread into a wider satisfied version. "That was indeed a faux pas that has stood by me in times of crisis. Without that act of god, I would have struggled to fight off amorous advances."

Suprakash Roy paused.

"Amorous advances. Do you mean that? Or is it your weakness for the literary – figures of speech, aren't they?"

"Well, you saw Amrita."

"The dark girl. The one who was none too pleased because you were not homeward bound today?"

"Was it that apparent?"

"You forget that I can see more into the mind than an amateur."

"Well, she has confessed infatuation ... in fact, she has gone further and proclaimed love. She demands a lot of my attention almost as if it was her birthright. And think of my plight if I had not had the protective shield of a manufactured marital status."

"Is this the same girl who sent you electronic updates on rain?"

"The same."

"As I discovered from some messages forwarded by Pritam, you had added fuel to fire with your poetic responses."

Sandeep shrugged.

"Compulsions of an author. I realise my mistake now, but I did not expect her to fall for me like a pancake."

Dr. Roy looked at him keenly.

"Pritam says you are a flirt."

"He is biased. A verbal flirt maybe, when there is the promise of word play in the air... but no more. Certainly not with a specimen of the female kind whose vocabulary hardly runs into double figures."

Dr. Roy's eyes twinkled.

"That should make you a force to reckon with in the world of virtual relationships."

"I am. My services were hired by friends and foes alike, trying to set up blind dates by ensnaring damsels with words."

"You have been employed in most curious professions."

"These were strictly pro-bono stuff. Non profit. For literally challenged virtual playboys. My success rate was stunning."

"I believe you. After all you are an author."

"But, we are digressing. All I am saying is that I am not a flirt in the real life Casanovasque sense of the word."

"You are handsome."

Sandeep waved dismissively.

"Not overly. I really don't consider myself a Don Juan. In college, yes, I did have a couple of affairs. But, nothing since then. I honestly did not expect this girl to jump at me."

The doctor sighed.

"What did you expect? This is an industry filled to the brim with pot bellied stereotypical Indian professionals. And in you come in the guise of a successful consultant, who is also a talented writer, an unconventional wit, who is also a martial arts instructor. Do you think it is surprising that people grown up on a steady diet of Bollywood heroes will fall for you?"

"But, I have told you ... I am not usually hit upon by girls like this."

"The aura of success does wonders."

Sandeep sat silent as he played this back over his mind.

"What made you display your multiple facets? Don't you think you are making it almost impossible for Pritam to get back his old life if he has to work among these people?"

"It was a domino effect. Caused primarily by Madhu Deb getting hold of the cover illustration of my book. Then one thing led to another."

The doctor shuddered.

"The fat lady?"

"Yes."

"The one who talks about her son?"

"Interminably."

"I guess there were too many strange factors in this situation for you. Things spiralled out of control."

Sandeep nodded. "The same reason why we can't predict financial slumps. Too many parameters. Chaos theory. But, things have not really gone out of control."

The doctor raised his eyebrows.

"The girl remains infatuated ... or smitten, whatever. But, she's understood she cannot expect reciprocation."

"Uh-huh?"

"She is studying for an examination. She wants to get into Actuaries. Away from this mundane job. That should keep her busy."

"She has discussed her plans with you?"

"She has her problems. The girl she shares her apartment with is not really sensitive to her preparations, putting on music too loudly and all that. I asked her to take a membership in the Openbare Bibliotheek and study in the library premises."

"So you are solving her problems?"

Sandeep looked confused.

"I really don't see what you are driving at. I was just trying to help her."

"Why?"

Sandeep shrugged.

"That's the decent thing to do. Anyway, she has her hands full. She has never got too much attention of her parents, has almost rebelled and come away from home on this assignment. And now she wants to escape from the industry ..."

He paused.

"Wow. It does seem ridiculous, doesn't it? I am kind of telling you her biography."

The doctor kept the quizzical gaze and the hint of a smile trained on him.

"She ... well, now that I think of it, she has poured all her troubles into me."

"Have you poured something into her as well?"

"What? No, not at all ..."

"Yet you are trying your level best to get her out of the rut she claims to be in. While you struggle with the challenges of taking on the role of Pritam, teaching tai chi, collaborating on peculiar papers and trying to build on your literary life," the doctor paused." And keeping admirers at bay."

"Just one admirer."

"You think so now," Dr. Roy chuckled as Simon walked towards their table, smiling brightly.

"The very best stuff," he said as he produced an etched and ornamental cannabis bong. "Mild, yet deep. According to Joost there, it will take you up into the clouds in the smoothest elevator."

The three of them stooped over and took long pulls.

"Simon here has an excellent blog," Sandeep observed.

Dr. Roy looked interested.

"Are you on twitter?"

"Yes I am."

"How do you find it?"

"It's great. Information was never this accessible."

The doctor nodded in a trance.

"Never was a truer word spoken."

Sandeep opened his eyes.

"The information highway is clogged. Information spills over. Overload. Beep like crazy."

"There in a laptop or a cell phone we are bombarded with thoughts that we would never come across twenty years back. Who would hunt down obscure volumes from dingy libraries now? Everything is available at the click of a mouse. We don't crave for knowledge any more ... we filter it."

"Is that wrong, doctor?"

"There is no right, no wrong, buddy. The only truth is here and now. And the elevator to the babel tower of knowledge is beeping because of information overload. It will creak, give, dangle and plummet."

"Never mind our friend Sandeep. He is not used to cannabis."

"Pritam, you mean? Sandeep is his pen name."

"Pen name. Should it be keyboard alias? The words of the prophet are written on the wall to wall."

"To answer your question, I am not talking of right and wrong. All I am saying is that the concept of environment has changed. Earlier the physical environment was all important. The place where you grew up, the people you associated with. Now with blog, web cam, chat, sms, one can be in real time touch with people across the world. One needs a cell phone or a computer. Thought process is not restricted to physical habitats or surroundings. It is now a function of the accessed websites, the facebooks, the twitters, the blogs, the orkuts . The fundamentals of consciousness have changed."

"People want to know your thoughts or not, you push them onto their devices. That's twitter. The mating calls of a bird-brained populace."

"Pritam, that's unkind."

"And the thoughts get forwarded. Not messages, but immediate thoughts. So people can contribute without thinking by buying into other thought processes."

"People have always done that. Think of Brand propaganda."

"Simon's pet topic."

"New paradigm of thought. How many people will continue having individual opinion if thoughts are filtering into their intelligent devices? "

"The electronic herd. Or is it the ultimate consciousness? Cosmic consciousness of primordial philosophy? Where consciousness is manipulated and manufactured. One human being is not an entity – he is part of a future mankind linked together with conglomerate thought flowing across fibre optic cables."

"Is someone taking notes?"

"Push it to the world with twitter. Doctor Suprakash Roy. With cosmic consciousness, will it be treating one patient or the entire humanity? What is the cognitive theory of cosmic consciousness?"

"I am currently entering the super-consciousness layer."

"Who needs reason when you have heroin?"

"This is not heroin."

"Another literary allusion down the drain."

∾ ∾ ∾

Raving Reviewer,

Most heartfelt thanks for the truckloads of praise that you heaped on me. This casual brush with the pen, does it really merit such applaud? Or is the lightness of the brush accentuating the deep impressions in contrast. The commonplace delights expected in professional prose cropping up as serendipitous surprises in the amateurish effort.

I am blushing at the parallels drawn with Borges – aptly called parallels because never can I hope to touch him no matter how long I try. However, it is curious. Your story, as I heard in Amsterdam that evening, did often remind me of that Chinese hero of Borges. I guess you know the one I am referring to –who chose all the paths available to him instead of just one.

I agree with your sentiments on the agents and publishers faced with my work. I would have never managed a half page synopsis of my work.

Let me have a go at a query letter.

I am writing to enquire whether you would be interested in representing my work as literary agent. It is a drama about a young prince who learns that his father has been killed by his uncle and moves through five acts finding ways to delay the act of revenge, in the process talking to himself at length and, directly and indirectly, causing the death of his girlfriend and her family. Self Addressed Stamped Envelope directed to Stratford on Avon.

Does it sound like the most famous play of all time? - Shruti

XXXI

Blog of Simple Simon at blogspot.com
Tags: Dutch decisions, Indian decisions

The ways of Dutch and the Indian approach to business in a corporate organisation are diametrically opposite.

If a senior manager in an Indian firm expresses his views, he expects his underlings to nod their heads in collective agreement, submissively jotting down the words hot off the lips. And if his Dutch counterpart notices similar accord, he will wonder what on earth is wrong with his team.

To the Dutch, discussion and argument are infinitely important. Agreement is the last possible measure, to be considered only in remote emergency. Everyone has his own opinion and is eager to put it on the table to be weighed, dissected and discussed. Concensus is all important and therefore rare. It is not true as often denoted that the Dutch are not respectful of the superiors. No one really challenges the authority of the decision maker. However, everyone gets a chance to provide opinions, fiercely concentrating on the issue at hand, with various points of view. In the end it is the discussion and argument which is more important, nothing is directed at the people involved and no weight is attached to theatrics or rhetoric. At the end of it all, the organiser asks if everyone agrees, and there is always at least one who does not. Analysis, counter analysis and debate is not a show of disrespect, and reaching a solution is often a painstaking process of several discussions, involving several meetings which involve an almost graph theoretic problem of synchronising the calendars of all the mandatory attendees. And with the Dutch calendars being overly cluttered with appointments from schooldays, it is a tedious process.

The Indians on the other hand give me the impression of looking for superior light to show the way. Heads nod devoutly when important lips pronounce directions and decisions in words that often strive for the sensational effect. The most mundane and straightforwardly simple strategies are presented as landmark innovations. People agree wholeheartedly in the meetingroom, while in the bossless canteen, in the discussions that follow, a hundred smarter ways of doing things are uncovered and remain unimplemented. Decisions are therefore a lot quicker, largely halfbaked and universally unpopular.

I think this is the result of a combination of the lack of a despotic sovereign in the past and job security linked to works council at present for the Dutch and a history of colonial rule and sudden new hits you on the face globalisation for the Indians.

My buddy is, however, the exception proving the rule. Not only is there monumental mockery in his speeches, he is also rampantly irreverent of the sacrosanct hierarchy.

Mail from Simon to Mailing List
Subject: Packaged Solution

Today was a glittering example of my friend's absolute irreverence for authority. I had just rescued him from the clutches of Madhu Deb with our established routine of on demand phone calls. He was walking with me towards the mail room, debating whether or not to patent the Gupta-van der Wiel escape technique. When I raised my eyebrows about the Gupta element, he explained that he preferred his pen name to go with anything he put down on paper. We were about to enter the mail room, my buddy's second favourite haunt after the supplies cupboard, when we noticed a gesticulating Ajay, unusually excited about something.

We peeped inside and saw him talking animatedly to Amrita. The dark girl was sitting on the table with a large package in her hands.

"This is the office – more importantly it is the office of the client. If we make any use of the office facilities, it should be strictly for official purposes," Ajay was preaching.

I looked at the package in the girl's hands. It was a delivery carton from Amazon.co.uk.

"The bigger packages are generally left at the Rental Office. I thought it would be safer if this was delivered here," Amrita's voice had a degree of defiance that surprised me. However, it was not sufficient to take the wind off Ajay's sail.

"Nevertheless, the things are personal. Have you thought what would happen if the CEO of the IT department got wind of our employees using the facilities ..."

I was feeling sorry for the girl. With no Works Council lurking around the corner, Ajay apparently had no qualms about shouting at her in front of us. This is when my buddy broke in.

"It was a delivery. Which in no way adds to the expense of the Bank," he observed.

Ajay turned to face Pritam with an expression of semi-terrified soreness. He wanted to contradict, but at the back of his mind there was the obvious interplay of cause effect computation inevitable when challenged by the blue eyed boy of the big boss.

"It's – er – not ethical…"

"Let's see," Pritam counted on his fingers. "To date I have used fourteen envelopes, one hundred and fifty A4 size sheets and regular service of the Hewlett Placard printer for blatant personal use. There are ominous signs that I have just scratched the surface. And you know something else? When I asked the CEO of the Operations and IT department about the nearest post office to send some of the material to literary agents, he asked me to make use of the mail room facilities."

"But …"

"He has excellent reasons, mind you. Just think about it mathematically, being plain logical just this once. I post about ten packages each week. All on weekdays. If I walked to the post kantoor and back during office hours ten times a week, I would kiss ten solid work hours good bye. That is precisely why offices have mail rooms and don't discourage personal use."

I knew perfectly well that Ajay would never make the list of five favourite persons of my buddy. Nevertheless, this sort of a barrage was surprising, although – I must admit – of the more pleasant sort.

"If she had tracked the FedEx delivery on the internet at fifteen minute intervals, and had gone down to the Rental Office to retrieve the package during office hours, just think how many hours that would flush down the drain … In new fangled jargon – you do the math."

Ajay searched for something to say in response. Unequal to the uphill task, he murmured something about there being policies and rules to follow at the client site. He scurried away after that, and I could almost make out the coiled outline of a tail between his retreating legs.

Pritam chuckled.

"You see my friend, I am riding on the crest of recent successes. Right now I have the blessings of the high and mighty. This pathetic creature will keep thinking about what to do about this without bringing his own ass under fire. The moment will pass and he will swallow his peevishness like an unavoidable pill."

I laughed, and as I expected, most of the speech was lost on Amrita.

"Thanks for the help," she managed to say, somewhat overwhelmed. Her eyes, as she looked at her rescuer, were very much like those of a medieval damsel in distress, blinded by a flash from the shining armour of her knight.

"Such a huge package from Amazon? What's in it anyway?" I asked.

"DVDs."

"DVDs? That's interesting," Pritam said. "May we take a look? If it's not too personal."

Amrita said something in Bengali which made Pritam raise his eyebrows. She proceeded to tear open the package and there emerged a collection of excellent movies – movies I had only heard of, and that too from knowledgeable movie buffs like Lahari.

Children of Heaven
Colours of Paradise
Baran
Two English Girls
400 Blows
Day for Night

For some reason, there was bewilderment on Pritam's face. I must have looked quite surprised myself. Amrita is not exactly someone whom I would have expected to go beyond the easier entertainment of Hollywood when it came to international films. I guess I have not yet looked beyond the surface of these folks. Why, even Gunjan may have redeeming characteristics.

Cheers
Simon

∾ ∾ ∾

Chat on office communicator between Trisha Paul and Madhu Deb

Trisha: Sagar from HMH is confirmed for Sur-Soiree. He sings Carnatic
Madhu: That's great ☺
Trisha: But, we will need him to practice rigorously for the next few days
Madhu: Don't worry, I'll keep a tab on that. I will attend all the rehearsals
Trisha: They coincide with the Tai chi classes
Madhu: Yes. That's a problem. I'll have to skip the Tai chi classes in that case . . . too bad. Pritam doesn't like people missing classes
Trisha: Yes, he always frowns at me when I do that.

Madhu: Yes, he wants people to be as dedicated as he is
Trisha: Yes, but I cannot afford that sort of dedication.
Madhu: I understand. You are married . . . and not even for a year ☺
Trisha: Simon and Amrita are the dedicated ones. They don't miss a class.
Trisha: In fact, Amrita is more than dedicated. She emulates the teacher
Madhu: ??
Trisha: Yesterday I saw her coming out of the Bibliotheek. With a lot of books.
Madhu: What sort of books?
Trisha: All sorts. Didn't really check. She said that Pritam had recommended them.
Madhu: lol. Good for her.

Mail from Madhu Deb to 'Pritam Gupta'

Sub: Thought of telling you

I know you are a kind hearted type who goes out of his way to help others at the drop of a hat. I would just like to caution you about a couple of things.

Be careful about helping or getting close to some people.

As a well-wisher, which you know I am, let me tell you that people don't take friendship or help in the right spirit. Especially the Indian middle class.

Regards,
Madhu

P.S. Lahari is competitive and different from us. Please keep that in mind when you interact.

Text Message from Sandeep to Shruti

Basking in limelight
Suffocating well wishers
Confusions galore

Reply from Shruti to Sandeep, via email

Spotlight always sweet
Side effects hazardous. Yet
Yeh dil mange more. . .
OR
The heart yearns for more. (if you are a purist)

I don't quite know what the suffocation is all about, but certainly wish for a fast return to normal.

Professor Lal says that your book is one of the best he has read in recent times. He is always generous in praise, but I can make out that he is genuinely moved. I can't wait to read it.

What's the current scenario in your quest for literary agents?

- Cheers,
Shruti

Mooi mate of mine,

A recent encounter with a mender of minds has set me thinking. A characteristic phrase dropped in one of the rare yet rarefied exchanges with Professor Lal has resurfaced onto my consciousness. The past couple of months have been fraught with fervent communications to literary agents and publishers, and at the other end of the spectrum following up on various establishments for cataloguing and storing my published book. If I count the number of pages I have written in the form of entreaties, implorations and appeals, it must number beyond thousand. However, in contrast, I find myself hard pressed to account for more than a thousand words of creative composition, if I ignore the corporate speeches made with Gita in the subconscious pockets of my mind.

Is this how I want to spend the rest of my life, running after agents and writing half a page over a period of two months? Our elderly friend sketched the artistic allegory of a flower producing fragrance without trying to beckon the sniffing populace. Adding on, I wonder why the flowers that are conspicuous with colour seldom possess the whiff to attract the sniffing savant. A rose is a rarity, with the best of both. Maybe that is why it is endowed with thorns.

The agents remain professionally prompt at the generation of rejection slips. But, even as I prepare elaborate traps to ensnare them into my web of storytelling, I have to ensure that the web does not peter out into a puny network of half baked pseudo-connections , the substance filtered by dragnets.

I am now at the height of my creative powers, and it makes sense to ride the crest even if does not lead on to shores of success.

As far as your query letter is concerned, should we not have a hook to catch the attention of the agent at the outset? Something taught by the hundreds of experts in the art and science of getting a new author published?

"There is something rotten in the State of Denmark"

A father murdered. A family betrayed. A fall into madness.

When young Prince Hamlet returns to his Father's funeral, into the sea-swept Scandinavian landscape and the sensuous charms of oomph oozing Ophelia, he finds all is not well. Murder most foul has left its treacherous mark in the clandestine corridors of the royal palace. Exploring the darkest corners of the human mind, the tale unfolds as a riveting mix of lust, power, intrigue and retribution. Terrifying yet funny, chilling yet deep, Hamlet is an erotic psychological thriller etched with mind games and sword fights in equal measure.

This, methinks, has the ingredients to enable the slings and arrows of outrageous fortune to smile on it.

~Sandeep

ᘓ ᘓ ᘓ

"What on earth are you doing here?" Sandeep asked.

Returning late in the evening, he had found Amrita sitting in front of the door of his apartment. When he approached, she looked up at him with ardent eyes that seemed to burn holes on his face.

"I am sorry if I *hurted* you ...," Amrita began.

"*Hurt* you," Sandeep corrected compulsively.

Amrita flung her head back in a display of pain-mingled irritation. She switched to Bengali.

"You see, that's what I mean. I don't know English ... while you are a writer. I have come from a very mediocre background, conservative education in the suburbs ..."

"How does that matter?"

"I ... I want to become more worthy ..."

"Worthy of what?"

Amrita closed her eyes.

"I am sorry. I know you are married and ... I cannot hope for *that.* But, if measuring up to you makes me a more worthy person, is there anything wrong in that? I heard Lahari-di speaking about all those films that I had not even heard of. I jotted down some of the names and ordered them. I just wanted to become a better person."

Sandeep looked around. From the adjacent balcony, he could make out the fecund-like profile of Gunjan watching them.

"Do you honestly think watching these movies will make you a better person? There are excellent people across the world who have never heard of them. And there are intellectual scumbags who have watched each and every one of them."

Amrita looked down, a picture of desolation.

"Maybe I should have said a more complete person."

"Jesus Christ. I am not a template for completeness. No way. And why on earth have you come up here to explain yourself?"

The girl looked at him with a slight frown touching her forehead.

"I am sorry if you are offended because I bought all those movies you and Lahari-di talked about."

"Offended … no, I'm not offended … freaked out perhaps, but not offended."

"I just want to be better ..."

"I was purely putting forward an objective point of view. I mean, just scraps of movies here and there won't educate you …"

"I know. I want your help. I want you to suggest more books that I can read … to improve my English, to make fewer mistakes … also to get to know some of the good works of Literature."

Sandeep threw his arms in the air.

"Well, I can certainly help you, but I can't solve your problems. Certainly not here, in the common passage. At nine in the evening, with a dinner to cook and loads of work to finish. "

There was the by now familiar sorrowful nod of acquiescence.

"I understand. I am leaving. You won't want people talking about us. You are married."

Sandeep cursed.

"It's not only that. Gunjan out there hardly has any credibility, I don't really care about what he says. But, I've got work to do."

"I did not want to go into my apartment. There will always be a row with Neha."

"How am I supposed to help?"

There was the sad nod again.

"I know you can't."

"You ... you are preparing for your exams, aren't you? The one with the Institute of Actuaries. How are you going to manage the time to read classics and watch these movies?"

"I will manage."

Sandeep shrugged. "Up to you. But please keep your objective in the proper perspective."

"I beg your pardon?"

Sandeep struggled to repeat the phrase in Bengali.

"Be clear of your objective. I mean, you want to speak, write better English … you want to read good books, watch good movies. Perfectly understandable. And appreciated. But, the objective is as you said – to make yourself a more complete person. It is not a question of measuring up to me."

Amrita smiled, a tinge of pain in her eyes.

"Is there a better way to achieve completeness?"

"Amrita, you are freaking me out. I am not God."

"I know you think that this is a crush, an infatuation that I have for you. You think that with time I will mature and it will pass. But inside me, it is a feeling more deep than any infatuation. Yes, I know that it won't lead anywhere . . . but, I don't ask for anything . . ."

Sandeep looked around him. For a moment he wondered if a blow on the head with a flower pot would bring her back to senses.

"But, you don't even know me."

Amrita smiled sadly.

"I know you with my heart. That is enough for me."

Sandeep stamped his feet.

"You have no earthly idea who I am. Believe me. You are young, with a full life ahead, Amrita. Give it time. . ."

The morose smile flitted by again.

"You think time will cure this? I won't argue. And anyway, you will be gone in a few months. Why bother about me? Now, could you please let me know the names of some books? I have finished *Daddy Long Legs.*"

"Could you please have this conversation sometime later? In office? I ... I have to get to work."

The girl seemed to stoop under the burden of disappointment.

"Okay. I will leave if you want me to."

Sandeep looked at the pitiable form and the balance tilted more towards irritation from sympathy.

"Don't make it sound like that. If you feel that the whole world is just a machinery of injustice ..."

The blank stare stopped him and he started rephrasing.

"I understand that there are several reasons why you feel deprived, but if you continue to wallow in self pity it just won't help you."

She stood there, her eyes resilient in the light of the allegation.

"You think I am always sorry for myself?"

Sandeep let out an exasperated sigh.

"Amrita, you have told me each and every problem you have... You give me the impression of being immersed in troubles, from childhood till now ... But come on. No one is really coasting through life in a luxury yacht."

"In what?"

"Yacht ... one of the big sail boats the very rich have ... Christ..."

"You are impatient with me. I understand. I am troubling you with my problems ..."

"The problem is that you understand everything, but are not prepared to take a positive step ..."

"I have taken steps ... I got all these books, these DVDs ... I want to be positive."

"I meant a step towards home. I have to do quite a bit of work before I can afford to call it a day. You have said at least five times that you understand that you should not have come here now with your colossal truckload of problems, and yet you haven't budged from my doorstep."

Amrita closed her eyes and winced. The aggression in the voice left her vulnerable. Her small hand flew in front of her face, almost in a defensive gesture.

"I ... I am sorry... I am leaving at once. I ... I wanted too much."

She shuffled a couple of steps and turned around.

"I ... I detected a tenderness in your eyes and your touch when we lay in the bush ... I may be wrong ..."

"You are."

"I am sorry ..."

She shuffled away, neck hunched under the weight of dejection.

Sandeep stood for a while, trying to reconstruct the ideas that had germinated in the corners of his mind throughout the day, the intricate fabric of thoughts that he had been waiting to lay out in his laptop ever since his last email to Shruti. On entering the apartment, he irritably discovered that the frozen tortillas had gone bad. He would have to cook rice for dinner.

It was when he was waiting for the beep of the microwave that he received a text message.

Don't you have any feeling for me? Not even pity?

He cursed. His reply was short and terse.

I had respect. Don't make me lose that.

When he had mixed the rice with the chicken curry cooked three days back, he received the next sms.

Now you have insulted me. You have helped me a lot. Could you please do the final favour of giving away my books and DVDs to deserving people – people who unlike me are educated – once I am no more?

XXXII

Email from Professor Lal, typed by Shuktara Lal

Sandeep dear boy,

Only an author knows the travails of creation. Hence, only the author requires the necessary fortitude to withstand the reaction to the work or the lack thereof.

For several days you have been plagued with apologies passing as reviews penned by semi-literate scribes associated with the dailies – who limited themselves to reproducing the blurb available on the back cover of your book in part or shameless whole.

Ultimately, today, my web literate granddaughter found a well written, comprehensive review in the Chandigarh Tribune. The electronic avatar of the newspaper – a contradiction if there ever was any! Someone at last has really gone through your offering.

It is the rule of the world. Only a small percentage of the public will appreciate brilliance. It is precisely this low percentage which makes it worthwhile.

News on the internet. Soon the tactile delight of the turning the daily front page will be a thing as old as me. The anticipation of the thud of the vendor's throw announcing the summary of the day before will no longer be a part of our mornings. But, then, the fascinating maya-jaal of the Internet is changing the pleasures of the old and opening multiple windows for the new.

At the click of a button I am sending you some contraption which my young grand-daughter says is called a link and supposedly allows you to see the same news article I referred to. How this takes place, at the speed of thought, is something I will probably never learn – I leave you to read the full text using the wonder of the modern times.

The Professor

∾ ∾ ∾

"Good morning," Madhu Deb's greeting was sung out with characteristic verve and gusto. "I hear *chin na* has resulted in a few sore joints."

Sandeep tried to conjure a smile.

"It's part of the game."

Madhu Deb laughed.

"Too bad I miss classes. Yesterday I had to conduct a rehearsal of the next *sur-soiree.* You can't believe how immature and emotional some of the performers can be. When I reached home, Hidori immediately said, 'Mama, you look tired.'"

Sandeep's weary fingers moved towards his cell phone. Help at hand, just one missed call away.

"He got the idea that I was tired from the *tai chi* class. He often wonders what goes on in these classes. However, I was really sorry to miss the class yesterday. One feels so good after the hour ... and it takes your mind off the troubles. I came across Amrita while returning, and she was almost glowing ..."

Even as he was about to press the call button, Sandeep paused. His fingers froze and he looked at the loquacious leader.

"You don't look too good," the good lady exclaimed. "Are you all right?"

"I am fine."

"Is Ramesh making you work too hard?"

"Madhu-di, do you have some time?"

The lady beamed.

"Of course. You want to talk?"

Sandeep hesitated. He could almost sense the confusion raging in him cloud his eyes.

"Come on," the Senior Manager approached him and pulled him by the elbow. "Let's have some coffee."

"Where?"

She laughed.

"In the Netherlands you don't have to look too hard."

"Tell me all," Madhu Deb beamed at him as they sat in the Cafe Belmode.

"Did you have anyone specific in mind when you sent me the mail about the reaction of middle class people?"

Coffee with milk was known as *Koffie Verkeerd* in Dutch, which literally translated to Wrong Coffee. It was blasphemous to adulterate the pure brew with anything, be it as pristine as milk. Madhu Deb took a long pull at her drink and looked at Sandeep with a knowing smile.

"I understand you are decent ... want the best for everyone."

"Do I? I'm not that sure. What makes you say that?"

There was a twinkle in the lady's eyes.

"You have taken a lot of trouble to help Amrita, haven't you?"

Sandeep raised his eyebrow.

"And what makes you say that?"

Madhu Deb laughed.

"Come on. She is obviously making a big effort to walk in your footsteps. It is obvious she asks you for advice, she has started reading books that only you could have recommended, she has started running after *tai chi* classes, her dedication to *tai* chi is transparent, she is also going over to your place and waiting for you. People do notice things."

Sandeep sipped his cappuccino and found it bitter.

"In other words people like Gunjan notice things."

There was a patient smile on Madhu Deb's face.

"There will always be people of all sorts."

"They can migrate to any part of the world, but cannot forget their roots, can they? The roots defined by slander and bigotry?"

"You cannot change everyone, Pritam. I understand that you are genuinely trying to help her, but I wanted to tell you that she may not take it in the best possible way."

Sandeep twirled the liquid around and for a moment remained absorbed by the vortex in the glass.

"And it is very easy for her to fall for you, Pritam, I hope you realise that ... You are dashing and impressive."

Sandeep looked at her with reddish eyes.

"She has a crush on me," he said.

Madhu Deb's wise eyes twinkled knowingly.

"She has said so in as many words ... only she claims that it is love."

"It may be," the lady beamed. "Love is a wonderful thing and can hit you anytime, anyplace. It can be painful as well."

She paused.

"Only, it's odd that she has gone ahead and proclaimed it. I mean, she knows you are married."

"Yes."

"What about you?"

"What about me?"

"Do you reciprocate her feelings?"

Sandeep looked at the probing eyes in the round, bloated face.

"I am married."

The good lady laughed.

"Married? Is that enough to control the strings of the heart? I think I mentioned to you once ... human beings are not meant to be monogamous."

Sandeep looked at his watch. The lady was in no hurry. The ideal manager. She had all the time in the world for an underling.

"Samit and I are married. He doted on me. However, I have hardly ever looked at him as more than a very good friend," she paused and smiled, lips parting in the sorrowful manner as on the day at the dentist's. "I don't mind telling you that I have had an extra marital affair. I well and truly fell in love two years after my wedding."

Sandeep shifted uncomfortably. The tension of the previous night had scythed through his thoughts, leaving them scattered in fragments. He had clutched on to Madhu Deb's concerned fellow feeling as a possible route towards solution. Now, he had ended up in the unaccustomed to role of a confidant.

"It was only after the birth of Hidori that a gradual acceptance of my marital life established itself."

Sandeep found his finger moving towards the call button on the mention of the kid's name. Interesting cognitive phenomenon.

"I have come through ... the affair is no more ... It's just that my sex life is in a mess."

Sandeep winced. This guided tour of the dark side of the good lady's life was uncomfortable. He struggled to form what seemed to be the most appropriate expression on his face.

"So, if you tell me that you are in love with her, I won't be judgemental ..."

Sandeep held his hands up almost in a gesture of self defence.

"It's not that ... I'm in a different sort of a problem."

The lady beckoned the waiter and asked for one more koffie verkeerd.

"I was indeed somewhat sympathetic... and did not want to hurt her in any way. She wanted to improve herself. Improve her English, to appear for some sort of Actuarial exams. She wanted guidance from me. I tried to help ..."

"And you did not fall in love?"

"No, not by the most elastic stretch of imagination. She sent me essays in most terrible English, and I corrected the grammar, spelling, syntax as much as possible. I suggested books to read, how to find ways to study and all that ..."

"Increasing her infatuation ..."

"Maybe I encouraged her in certain ways, but she was insistent. And suddenly, it seemed as if I was practically living her life. I was solving her problems, becoming upset at her troubles ... She somehow began to expect that I would take care of her problems for her, I would guide her endlessly. Every time I tried to hint that she had to deal with her own problems, she went into this dark brooding mode that made me uneasy ... it was like feeling pity for a most helpless creature."

Madhu Deb was not the best listener in the world, but she was silent for once. Her face was sympathetic, her fingers touched Sandeep's across the table.

"There were occasions when she freaked me out. She wrote a review of *The Reader* – the movie based on Bernard Schlink's book. From the review it was obvious that she had no clue about the second world war or the holocaust. When I mentioned as much, the next day I found her carrying a volume of *The Rise and Fall of the Third Reich.* I discussed movies with Lahari – she has an excellent collection of foreign films. I did not even know that Amrita was eavesdropping. One fine day she got a package from Amazon with the very films that we had mentioned."

Madhu Deb rounded her eyes.

"That must have been scary."

"It was. And yesterday, I told her in as many words that I could not continue to solve her problems, could not afford to spend such a lot of time on her life ... she has to take ownership ..."

"That's exactly what you should have done," the lady interjected. "I know this sort of people very well. They project themselves as helpless and manipulate your sympathy ..."

"Hang on ... I haven't finished. She went into that brooding mode again. I decided to be firm. Did not give an inch. And she went home ... and threatened me with suicide."

Madhu Deb's mouth had already opened to state her opinion and it remained that way, an astounded cavern in a chubby landscape. For once words failed her.

Sandeep retrieved the fateful sms and handed her his phone. Madhu Deb read it with goggling eyes.

"When was this?"

"Around eleven yesterday night."

"And what happened after that?"

Sandeep sighed. The fatigue of the sleepless night ran through his joints.

"I called her. Asked her what exactly she meant. She kept sobbing, weeping ... Hardly trying to communicate. All along I realised she knew I would call and wanted to cling on to the conversation ... And it went nowhere. I tried ramming some sense into her ... it was painstaking conversation lasting nearly two hours. A monumental struggle. God ... I can't afford this."

A successful suicide or an attempt – with text messages from the victim's cell phone pointing to Pritam Mitra ... and Sandeep Gupta ... complications of colossal proportions. Besides, he could not spend nights like this. He had a novel to publish. His writing – new writing – had come to a standstill. Madhu Deb reached out and patted his hand.

"Don't beat yourself."

"What's that supposed to mean?"

"I know you are taking much of the blame for the girl's reaction. You are decent ... you actually feel for her in your own way ... "

"I ..."

"People connect in multiple dimensions, Pritam. Just like you and me. We are somewhat more than just colleagues, don't you think so? There are all sorts of relationships ..."

"I don't know what you mean, Madhu-di ..."

Madhu Deb smiled.

"I can understand that sub-consciously you are taking the blame for encouraging her. Please don't beat yourself. You meant no harm. You just wanted to help her."

"It's not a question of whether I encouraged her or not that's bugging me ... It is just that I am scared. This suicide threat has broken through my defences. Can you imagine the repercussions if she goes ahead and ends up carrying that out?"

Madhu Deb gulped down the last of her coffee.

"She's bluffing."

The words were reassuring – exactly what Sandeep wanted to hear. He looked at the lady for affirmation.

"Are you sure about that?"

Madhu Deb patted him on the palm and nodded.

"Believe me. If she was intent on suicide she would have just gone ahead and done it. She wants to use the threat."

Sandeep rubbed his tired eyes.

"It's just that this can't be left to chance."

"Pritam, relax. I understand you've had a tough night, but trust me on this. I know what I am talking about."

She paused.

"If I am not too mistaken, she has Borderline Personality Disorder."

Sandeep's frown dissolved into confusion.

"Borderline Personality Disorder?"

"BPD," Madhu Deb nodded. "It's a psychiatric condition. I have had some inkling about her, but the suicide threat has convinced me."

"But, what is this BPD all about?"

"Borderline Personality Disorder is very difficult to cure. Probably cannot be cured. These are people who are impulsive and have a very unstable self image. They also have unstable relationships. Some of the most difficult people to interact with.

Pritam, what you have got involved in is unfortunate, but what you need is a clean surgical break. There is no other way. Otherwise, your life will be sucked out of you. Believe me. She meets all the requirements for someone to be diagnosed with BPD according to the DSM IV criteria."

"DSM 4?"

"Diagnostic and Statistical Manual for Mental Disorders."

Sandeep massaged his temples slowly. Madhu Deb had always been an honorary expert on every topic. But, this was a highly specialised domain.

"Excuse me, but how are you so well informed on this?"

There was a tinge of sadness in her sympathetic eyes.

"I have done a lot of reading into DSM IV. Samit is a chronic case of NPD. Narcissistic Personality Disorder."

"Another kind of personality disorder?"

"Yes," the lady smiled sadly. "A grandiose sense of self importance ... and a sense of undeserved entitlement. They are difficult to live with ... and I have had to prepare myself painstakingly to deal with the situation – for me and Hidori to get through family life with the minimum number of marks."

She waited for the underlying gravity of the situation to add to the weight of her words.

"I have dealt with Personality Disorders, Pritam, so believe me. Surgical break. That's what you need."

~ ~ ~

I understand the crossroad you find yourself at. If the number of pages you will write are prenumbered, should you focus on novels and stories or query letters and synopsis. And as our learned friend tells us, the choice is ours.

The world of literary agents and publishers is like an impregnable wall against which you keep beating your head. Maddeningly, this wall does have cracks and crevices, unknown to us, through which some slip through, not often the deserving ones. However, as the professor has often said to me in our exchanges, convert the negative experiences of life into literary creativity.

Coming to our query letter for Hamlet, shouldn't we get a reference letter from a stalwart of the literary firmament?

"Dear Godwin, Please find enclosed a proposal for possible publication by my protégé Bill Shakespeare. Needs a lot of editing – especially the parts where the hero talks to himself – but overall has some neat action scenes. Thanks – James Hadley Chase."

- Shruti

~ ~ ~

Blog of Simple Simon
Tags : Ad lines

I play the recreational mental game of creating advertising punch lines – often with branding undertones. Whenever I see a product, a brand or an institution, I start attaching an appropriate marketing catchphrase to it.

Today, in front of an Amsterdam Cafe near my offce, I conjured up the neat little jingle - "Brewing through differences." It was spontaneous, concocted immediately when I saw a colleague sitting with another whom in normal circumstances he takes pains to avoid.

I have come up with some neat lines in my time. Here are some of them. They are available for use, provided there is a small cut for me.

Sports Shoe – Designed to keep your heart in your boots.
Butter – The joyous side of Cut and Paste

Mail from Simon to his mailing list
Sub: Doubt, Dilemma and Double-Meanings

The punch line that I have come up with in the recent blog was a result of seeing Pritam engrossed in a most serious contemplative conversation with Madhu Deb. One of those rarest of rare sights that people tend to wait for years – almost at par with double rainbows, Halley's Comets or Dutch world cup football triumphs.

When, later during the day, tired from the preparation of red amber green dashboards, I popped into his cubicle and asked his views on the byword, I found him couple of notches lower than his stratospheric level of humour.

"I understand you found the coffee table combination as sinister as the last supper. However, there were insinuating circumstances."

I waited for him to continue. He was silent for a full minute before turning towards me.

"Simon, do you feel the urge to proclaim to the world that you are considered desirable?"

It was a deep, complicated question and I obviously had no immediate answer.

"Is something bothering you?" was the best I could offer.

"I spilled beans – proprietary personal beans at that. Ostensibly because of the insinuating circumstances. However, I can't get over the unsettling pangs at the back of my mind that it was also the desire of being projected as desirable."

I told him in strictest terms to keep his conundrums limited to his series of talks. He chuckled.

"I appreciate your attempts at levity, Simon. I may give the impression of passing through a humorously challenged phase, but there are very valid reasons."

I observed that there seemed to be reasons for a lot of bizarre stuff.

"I agree Simon. My sitting with bottomless coffee mugs at Cafe Belmonde with a tested, proven and agreed upon conversational calamity. Then my apologetic attempts at laughter resulting in near mimicry of a Dutch man saying *Van Gogh*. All this may give you the impression that the sun has chosen the route of Singapore Airlines. In an Achebean way, things have fallen apart. The more I think about it the more I seem to be convinced that it is the infinite interplay of *Karma*. You know, a wise man once told me that everything comes with its inbuilt opposite."

He paused for a while in a thoughtful silence.

"Isn't it the dream of every man to be rich, charismatic, a guy girls die for, with the luxury of doing anything one wants?"

"Dreams of every honest man. And undeclared ones of the dishonest ones."

He nodded.

"I know exactly what it means to achieve these hyped dreams, Simon. It's probably the worst nightmare of all."

Interesting though the dialogue was tending to become, we had to discontinue. I was called away by some infuriating report wanted ASAP. I left my strange buddy in the same brooding mood, a poignant picture of obscure philosophising.

The mood remained strange even as we went through the motions of *tai chi* in the evening. My friend looked tired – the infectious joviality and love for the art were lukewarm. I have neither ability nor audacity to judge the quality of his techniques, but will take the liberty of saying that they retained the masterly touch, but lacked the spiritual *joie de vivre*.

Madhu had returned after a long soiree-induced break, but even she seemed subdued. Amrita had a darkish pall over her face. Only Trisha managed to lighten the mood with her trademark yawns and obvious bloomers.

The day ended with another strange cryptic message from the teacher. Trisha had been partnering me during a complicated *chin na* manoeuvre. As usual we had muddled the confusing sequence of grips to the extent of being almost locked to each other.

Sifu came up to us and asked, "Who is applying the pin?"

There was cause for great hilarity when both of us pointed at the other. Unusually, the joviality of my friend failed to be tickled. The look bordered on disappointment.

"Come on, guys," he said. "At least the two of you are shooting at the target."

He walked away before we could respond.

After the class, I asked him what he had meant.

"When an archer sees his mark, he is focussed. As soon as he also sees the medal that he will wear around his neck, he shoots at two targets," he explained. "It's one of those much popularised Zen proverbs."

I asked him whether I was meant to understand the relevance.

"It's as simple as Simon," he said before taking off for his daily run.

XXXIII

Excerpt from the third of the series of talks given by 'Pritam Mitra' for HMH

Under the supervision of the mighty corporations of the world, the industry produces transactions of trade. This is the cause of all that goes on in the material world, from profit to loss, from employment to retrenchment.

The ignorant fail to recognise the power of the financial world. They are not aware of the corporation as the supreme master of all beings. They are deluded. Their hopes in ventures are in vain, their knowledge is vain, they are utterly bewildered.

The ones who meditate on the might of the corporation with unwavering focus, no matter how unscrupulous they are, they are the chosen ones. They attain the eternal entrepreneurship that frees them from the constant cycle of being born again and again in different roles.

~ ~ ~

"I read the transcripts of all your speeches," K.Ramesh's voice reached him a couple of seconds after his image had already spoken. In the quiet video conference room of HMH, Sandeep sat wondering about the new avatar of the organisational god – a creature built up on blogs, email circulars and fleeting image on the plasma screen.

The video conference had been arranged at the expense of the client. After Ramesh had loaned a superstar resource like Pritam Mitra to HMH, the bank could not say no even in the worst period of crisis.

"I liked the things that you said about the consultant arriving on the scene every time there is crisis," he laughed and his chuckle followed after the two second delay. "Innovative use of the Gita."

Sandeep winced.

"I would much rather use a different word."

"Innovation is not the exhilarating buzz word anymore, is it?" the big man laughed. "True, each new wave is raped and re-raped by this industry till it loses all its bloom through ritualisation. But, one philosopher is good enough between us. I will tell you what I think about divine incarnation in times of trouble. That will give you an idea why I want this collaboration now. It is my belief that every time there is some strife in the world, god does not come down to set things right ..."

"He doesn't?"

"No, nothing is set right for the masses ... but that is what they like to believe."

Sandeep thought about it.

"You mean it is hallucination? In lines of Opium of the masses?"

"It is wishful thinking. Every time some calamity takes place which makes mankind open their eyes and wonder at the meaning of it all, they want to believe in some higher truth. They question the rigmarole of their day to day life and all of a sudden want reassurance in some eternal truth that lies above everything. Something that lends sense into a senseless world."

"Wow."

"You remember the Tsunami? Sudden devastation. Hundreds and thousands dead? And if you remember the period, there had been quite a few catastrophes at that point of time."

"Sensuously named Hurricanes causing mayhem along coasts of United States?"

"Yes. TheTsunami made people wonder if there was any meaning. They wanted to believe in something esoteric. There were all these fables of animals that had escaped unhurt from the disaster ..."

"Hadn't animals indeed escaped?"

"Some had ... maybe ... but as usual there was a lot of media hype based on what people wanted to believe. People wanted to be convinced that it was the fault of men. They had lost their connection with nature..."

"Hadn't they?"

"I don't know. All I know is that the mass wanted to believe that there was a meaning of life that people had forgotten because of their preoccupation with the mundane. This credit crisis has been a similar earth shattering episode. Hordes of people have been affected in a way they had never imagined earlier. Their faith has been shaken ... they are bound to want a core belief which convinces them that there is a world beyond financial loss ..."

"You want to trade on that ...?"

Ramesh smiled.

"As a consultant, I guess you should not sound scandalised. To answer your question, no. I want them to find peace and that too by providing them a solution. And here is where I want to do my bit for Indian thought ... If you remember, people were looking everywhere, clutching on to symbols of truth just after the Tsunami. For a large percentage, it was a new look at religion. CNN organised a David Letterman show to talk of the probable cause and effect of Tsunami with four religious leaders across the world – or, to be precise, four leaders of diverse faiths who were close at hand in the United States. A Christian priest, a Buddhist monk, a Muslim cleric and a Hindu representative. You know who this Hindu representative was?"

"Deepak Chopra?"

"Great guess."

"Actually I saw the program ... And so, now you want to be the Deepak Chopra of the financial crisis?"

Ramesh laughed again.

"No ... I want to promote the treasury of Indian knowledge – capitalising on this situation. I have told you of Fibonacci numbers, haven't I?"

"Yes ... developed by Pingala, propagated by Fibonacci."

"Leonardo of Pisa. Similarly, Indians have made contributions in every field of science which have never been recognised. People even acknowledge probability theory being referred to by ancient Indians but Pascal and Fermat get the credit. Similarly, even to this day, there are some phenomenal thoughts in India – which are usurped by the West. The Radio, for instance. Also, I know instances of Ayurveds actually discovering drugs which were patented and marketed for millions by European drug companies. We have always been dealt the wrong end of the stick ... The way we are taking over the world now is through a model of large numbers – not really the cerebral path. But, I intend to do my bit to change the world. India needs to be given the credit that it deserves ... in the world as pioneering thought leaders."

Sandeep nodded.

"One great achievement of Indian thought which settles the scores."

"True."

"However, there is one pioneering achievement that the entire world acknowledges as an Indian coup de force. The one around which all other thought revolves."

"And what is that?"

"The *KamaSutra*."

This time the lack of synchronisation between the surprised gasp, the laughter and the expressions that went with them was almost comical.

"You know, Pritam. This is the unpredictable strain in you that I love. What is the subject of the next talk? Do you have another surprise up your sleeve?"

Sandeep nodded.

"Yes. I do. The Dutch are already way advanced in the spiritual world. Scavenging for the last drop is not their way of life. I can see pop wisdom dipped in the knowledge of Gita makes sense to them, but isn't as eye popping as it would have been to Americans. I need to appeal where they are sensitive."

Ramesh smiled and his remark reached Sandeep before his lips had started to move.

"You have the license, Pritam. And my full faith."

Sandeep looked at the man across the video conference link.

"May I ask you a question?"

"You need not ask for permission."

"With your depth of knowledge – philosophical and cultural knowledge at that – how did you manage to land up at the pinnacle of one of the worst read industries in the history of civilisation?"

Ramesh looked with amusement at the young man, probably trying to read into the sarcasm behind the query from the image on the video screen.

"Worst read industry? Well, is there a correlation between erudition and rank?"

"That's what I want to know."

"Believe me, I was equally surprised when I found an educated writer under the guise of a consultant. Progress through the rungs of the corporate ladder is not powered by intellect or education. To me it is nothing but a chancy thing of being at the right place at the right time."

"Is that modesty?"

"No, it is truth. Take the example of a trip to say ... anywhere in Netherlands ..."

"Maastricht?"

"What? Well, why not? You need to go to Maastricht. And you live in Amstelveen. You start at half past one. You reach the metro station at one forty. And there is a sneltram at one forty one which takes you to the Centraal Station at ten past two. There is a train to Utrecht at a quarter past two. You take it and find yourself on the train to Maastricht at a quarter to three, reaching there by half past four. Now you have a friend who reaches the Metro station at one forty one. His train reaches the Centraal Station at twenty past two. He misses the connection and reaches Maastricht half an hour later. Even though he is a wonderful runner and a master of jumping into trains."

"A wonderful metaphor."

"Thanks. There are other points to consider. Suppose someone had been on the same train as me to Centraal and decides to wait for a direct train to Maastricht which gets cancelled. And the one who reaches earlier is presented with a lot of choices ... The one who gets there earlier has more chances of making the right connections."

"Snowball effect of chance. No wonder one finds so many perfect idiots sitting on top of departments ..."

"This is the dose of irreverence that will make our ideas even more sellable to the audience. The world loves the offbeat during a crisis."

"True. Whether shades of duality fall from their psyche or not, people love the story of priests flinging Buddha statues into the fire to keep themselves warm."

"Yes, people love pop philosophy. They make their way to the corporate world. Have you ever seen the Upanishads making their way out into the corporate battle grounds? They are too difficult. In the age of Wikipedia and instant coffee, popularity has taken another ..."

The jerky interjection of cost cutting regulations forced the videoconference to end at the stroke of the half hour. The accomplished shine radiating from the dignified bald pate of K. Ramesh merged with the dissolving blip of nothingness as the mechanical female voice informed that the call was over. Sandeep stretched out on the sofa and started dozing.

~ ~ ~

Late night sms exchange between Amrita and Sandeep. (Amrita's grammar corrected for convenience)

Amrita: *I have mailed another piece. Will you please check it?*
Amrita: Please, will you not check it and tell me my mistakes?
Amrita: I am sorry. I won't ever threaten you again.
Amrita: Please ... how will I improve if you don't help me?
Sandeep: *Goddamn it. I am trying to work. I can't help you twenty four seven.*
Amrita: I am sorry. I should get used to being unwanted.
Sandeep: Stop feeling sorry for yourself and do something constructive.
Amrita: I am trying to do things that are constructive. You are just not helping me.
Amrita: I attend every tai chi class ... I read whatever you tell me to. Is that not constructive?
Amrita: Do you want me to go away? To leave you in peace?
Amrita: Why don't you answer me?
Sandeep: I am switching off my cell phone.

~ ~ ~

Email from Sandeep to Shruti

James Hadley Chase. If such a shining star of the literary firmament focuses his beam on the budding dramatist, can his work be ignored?

I can see the blurb on the back page.

Jonathan Kellerman meets Stephen King.
Hamlet is an erotic psychological thriller set in the phantasmagorical world.
A father murdered. A family betrayed. A fall into madness. ...
New York Times Bestseller.
The winner of the Rendell Award ...
A sensational new author.
"Rip Roaring Action – James Hadley Chase"

So there you go ... we have scripted a success story for Hamlet. The great play will no longer be pushed into slush piles by literary agents.

However, we can say goodbye to the comedies. The market has accepted this new Shakespeare kid as a writer of devious mysteries.

He could have written a sequel of Hamlet set in Amsterdam, but the Dutch would never get to decide between to be and not to be. The whole play will be an existential drama around conference tables. And our new author is not a Camus. So, what can be his forthcoming releases?

Othello will go through, but it is Desdemona who needs to be black and beautiful. Julius Caeser can still get past the editor, provided Act III Scene I is shifted to the end. Macbeth falls in line – with a couple of adjustments and comments on the witches by Dean Koontz. Of course the beards have to go, and the witches more in the siren mode.

But, Merchant of Venice? It is politically abominable. Besides, legal thrillers are more in the line of Grisham. Comedy of Errors? Ridiculous. Next you will have Ludlum writing Blandings capers.

Mailbox being clogged with rejection mails and thoughts equally clogged with peculiar problems, I desperately needed some diversion. I have more than a simple writer's block. My prolific output of query letters, synopses and self addressed stamped envelopes is on the verge of being reduced to a trickle. I keep wondering about the meaning of it all. My first novel has already reached the shelves in India, albeit not in spiral heaps and conspicuous corners. There have been reviews of it, around twenty of them plagiarised from my blurb, and a couple of actual analyses, well written and laudatory. But, even if I manage to trap a big publisher with the masterly crafted query letters polished with practice, what is the guarantee I will get a better deal than what my friend Sunil Pillay of Amphibian Books has been able to provide? There are so many 'promising' Walrus and Perennial publications which disappear after a couple of months in limelight.

With all these quasi-existential questions in my mind, I took the easy way out – surfing the internet for cricket bulletins. In one of the most respectable cricket sites I found an article by Laxmanchand Raha. I have had some recent interactions with this great man.

Indian penmanship has had its share of luminaries in recent times, but none of them brighter than this Walter Scott in the reverse, a trendsetter in his new genre of 'fictional history'. Since he claims not to understand fiction too well, he keeps practising it diligently in his opinions about cricket.

Cricket being a game of universal appeal, the lovably misguided views of confirmed amateurs have their own charm. However, preferring the Benaud like expert or robust journalists of the John Arlott variety, with occasional sprinkling of the unpretentious and lyrical musings of Cardus, I tend to avoid this redoubtable man's offerings, somewhat assiduously. But this piece suddenly caught my eye, not because of the contents, but more due to the way this pseudo scribe had been hailed. "Mr. Raha is a polymath who happens to write wonderfully on cricket."

He now stands shoulder to shoulder with Plato, Decartes, Leonardo Da Vinci , Tagore, Russel ... certified by the most popular cricket website as a polymath. And this comes within a few days of Mayank Manhas being put astride Dostoyevsky and Steinbeck by a people's paper. We share the planet and era with remarkable men and mania.

When does your Occidental Express finally break in Maastricht? I believe that there are more reasons than one that the place merits a visit, including the most beautiful bookshop in the world.

~Sandeep

Email from Shruti to Sandeep

So Shakespeare's career takes off. He has to concentrate on Murder Mysteries, preferably with a fantastic twist. That's unavoidable. The histories, if written, have to have the blessings of Dan Brown. The Indian editions of Richard III, with the fine-print stipulating sales in the Indian subcontinent only, may even need a foreword by Mr. Laxmanchand Raha.

Sandeep, Sandeep, Sandeep ... Why does your last email read like something written by an aged Celine – Castle to Castle or thereabouts, without the ellipsis? For someone so delightfully talented, as my limited understanding and the professor's learned approval leads me to conclude, you complain too much. So what if Mayank Manhas is painted in the same canvas as Dostoyevsky and Laxmanchand Raha touted as a polymath. Can you even begin to imagine the amount of time and energy they have to spend to create this illusion around themselves? Can you project that into their lifespan and find the ratio of hollow drumbeats that reverberate against their stipulated number of heartbeats? Ask yourself if you are prepared to spend that many hours trying to create an idol of yourself to be worshipped as a false god. Or would you rather create something that is eternal, that stands through the trials of time and, most importantly, manages to wring out every drop of the author in you?

What is even more disturbing in your mail is this guarded reference to irritants other than the demi-literary which seem to have an unacceptably strong effect on you. What is bothering you? Is it something related to your day job – I find it hard to believe since you seem to be blessed with a comic strip hero kind of ability to take it or leave it. So is it some other extraneous factor?

I reach Maastricht on Saturday. Why not meet under the arches of Selexyz Dominicanen?

Shruti

XXXIV

Blog of Simple Simon
Tags: Crisis, Babel Tower, Outrageous wages, Indian story

I have often provided in these blogs essays on the market, the financial situation, the soul of corporations and such meaningful mundane matters (my buddy-sifu will appreciate the alliteration). However, in his half philosophical sessions, my buddy takes it to a level that flickers in the fuzzy boundaries of enlightenment and mockery. Inspired thus by this electric mate, I will try to crystallise some of my recent reminisces into these unrestrained pages.

If I am to view the recent financial collapse in the analytical light, let me offer some statistics. In 2007, Lloyd Blankfein, the Chief Executive Officer of Goldman Sachs got a whopping salary of $73.7 million. Richard S. Fuld at Lehman Brothers earned $71.9 million. Compare this to the average American salary of $34,000 per annum paid the same year. These earnings were nothing compared to the gross earnings of Angelo Mozilo of Countrywide Financials who earned $102.8 million. And all these high and mighty figures pale to insignificance when we find that the new prophet of modern economy, a guy named George Soros, lapped up $2.9 billion. And meanwhile, nearly a billion people worldwide struggled to get by on a dollar a day.

The lopsided economy is set in perspective when one pauses to consider that the net revenues of Goldman Sachs during that year was over $46 billion, exceeding the GDP of more than a hundred countries, some of whom, like Slovenia, are now in the EU. Isn't a financial situation this unbalanced, bound to topple?

In the illustrious footsteps of my new friend, I have also thought of a parallel, which – because of my protestant background – does reach religious realms, if not the philosophical peaks of the Gita.

The Bible tells us the story of the Tower of Babel. When humans, for personal glory, reached for the skies, to build a massive tower which would traverse the heavens, God came down and confused them with multiple languages. They could no longer understand each other.

Can we map similar parallels in the human quest for wealth? The speculators and Wall Street CEOs earning massive stacks of lucre, trespassing the natural boundaries of balance and harmony. And this endless pile up of riches has ended with the crash of economy, that has brought in its wake, confusion galore. As masses are struggling to understand the different economic jargon they had blissfully ignored and trusted in the heydays of the boom, the financial language is indeed proving to be a discovered obstacle for many who cannot even make out how interest builds on their credit card loans. And the monolithic financial institutions that had towered over the financial world with their mergers and linked economic models are fast retreating to the old banking ways – back to basics.

...

When I asked my buddy what he thought of the writing (the part I have provided above) he had his own insights.

"I would have added that the financial systems got complicated as they started being built one on top of the other with mergers and acquisitions. This led to a point where the banks were huge organisations that rolled with financial power without anyone understanding the whole – systems and sub-systems that were – Hebrew to everyone to keep with the Biblical theme. This is when people stopped understanding each other. Everything became chaotic and in walked the Indians, celebrated survivors of chaos and masters of the vocation of being middle men."

New angles of looking at the Indian story indeed.

Mail from Simon to his mailing list
Sub: A Midsummer Afternoon's Sex Comedy surrounding Crimes and Misdemeanours

I had written the first half of my blog when I stepped out of my cubicle – desperate to find someone to pat my back. Trisha near the coffee machine listened to me with interest, but at the same time looked with the innocent ignorance that characterises her when I mentioned the Tower of Babel. Gunjan, scenting conversation and a potential fertile breeding ground of gossip, sauntered up to us, the perpetual cup of corporate coffee glued to his hand. He opened his remarks with a query about the *tai chi* classes and I hastened off, leaving my chubby cheeked friend to supply the martial details.

To ensure unadulterated scholarly discussion on the topic without being sidetracked by gossipmongers, I made for the cubicle of my trusted buddy. I found him staring bleary eyed at his laptop, and when I entered, he gave a start associated more to a hapless dear at the waterhole, who looks up to find himself looking at the jowls of a lioness.

"Simon, just the man I wanted to see ... if I indeed wanted to see anyone," he greeted.

I asked him if he would be interested in the article I had saved and not yet posted on blogspot. He nodded and we started going through it together in silence interjected by a couple of colourful remarks on coming across the figures associated with the financial luminaries.

He had just enriched me with his celebrated insight (see my blog) when our scholarly perusals were interrupted by the sound of furtive footsteps and a tension mingled tap on the panel.

"A word with you if you don't mind, Pritam," said a more than usually pensive Ajay Yadav, fretfully fidgeting on his feet.

My friend frowned. I could almost sense the radiating irritation and hear his hair bristling as he turned to confront the nervous account manager.

"Yes?" he said, the clipped monosyllable doing nothing for the taut nerves of the other man. I have hardly ever heard the English affirmative sound more ominous.

"Er ... It's about this session that you held today ..." I could see the shifty eyes glancing off me meaningfully and had half started to move in an attempt to make myself scarce when the practised hand of Pritam stopped me with a grip on my wrist exerting subtle martial persuasion.

"Well, Simon is my partner and advisor when it comes to these sessions, so you can speak freely in front of him," he replied. "And if you don't mind, can this be quick? I am fighting to meet a deadline for K. Ramesh and a headache which just got worse."

At the mention of the hallowed name, the account manager visibly swallowed. He looked at me with reproach, almost willing me to go away. Pritam's hand under the table, with the persuading pressure applied on my radial nerve, had the deciding say in the matter.

"I ... I was wondering if Ramesh knows about your presentations in advance."

My friend straightened up and the account manager seemed to shrink.

"Ramesh has given his okay – he has verbally signed the license for me to conduct these sessions any way I want to. He says as much in the last video conference with me. You want the tape?"

The man wilted, but some deep-seated grievance would not allow him to go away.

"What exactly was the matter you presented today?"

I had not attended the session because of a report which I had to submit by the proverbial EOD. I looked at my buddy with anticipation for what seemed to hold a lot of promise.

"Why do you want to know? I think the attendees never enjoyed themselves more."

Ajay Yadav winced.

"I know they looked ... er ... happy. I ... I heard them discussing the session among themselves near the coffee machine. They spoke in Dutch but I could make out some of the words ... and the ... actions. Pritam, could you please let me know what went on in that session?"

My friend shrugged.

"I just showed them a film on how to work as a team for the overall benefit of the organisation. That's pretty much the bull shit that is used as the fertiliser to reap profit in such companies. Interchanging livelihood and a game of basketball wherever necessary. What's your problem?"

The supervisor fingered his moustache.

"Pritam ... what sort of film was this?"

The consultant now got up and walked around his desk towards the harried manager.

"Relax, Mr. Yadav. The more I see you the more I wonder how you can survive a nervous breakdown. You know I am seriously thinking of engaging the services of Dr. Suprakash Roy for you. There are supposedly wonders that Cognitive Therapy can do for anxiety disorders."

He patted the diminutive manager on the shoulders. I could see the older man struggling with his fears and emotions, and the former winning through as always.

"Pritam, I just saw the people who attended your session make gestures that are to some extent unnatural ..."

"Unnatural? You say unnatural? That too in Amsterdam?"

Ajay Yadav coughed.

"Unnatural ... er... in the professional world."

"Do you know what the second oldest profession is?"

"Pritam ..."

"Relax, my dear account manager. The film that I showed is a minor classic. It is made by one of the most respected filmmakers in the world today."

The next question was mouthed rather than voiced.

"What was it?"

"It was a Woody Allen classic. Everything you wanted to know ..."

I dropped the mouse I was fiddling with and it clattered against the panels of the desk.

"I'm sure you have heard of it. Simon has, if the clatter of the mouse is anything to go by."

The puzzled face of the manager turned towards me. As I straightened, I found his shifty eyes goggling for an explanation.

"What movie is that?" he asked, staring at me. Somehow I had become an integral part of the discussion.

"I guess Pritam showed an excerpt of *Everything you wanted to know about ... er ... Sex and was afraid to ask.*"

I could make out a streak of fear pass through the entire frame.

"Sex?"

"Er ... yes ... that's correct."

"What is it about?"

His eyes still looked at me for the answers. I shrugged.

"If I remember correctly, it was a compilation of a number of disjoint episodes ... all about some sexual topic or the other."

The account manager's lower jaw hung near his tie.

"Well, it has this episode about a doctor who makes love to a ...er ... sheep in panties ..."

There was an inaudible shriek.

"Also a part in which a couple are chased down a mountain by a scientifically engineered giant ... er ... boob."

The poor man sat down and Pritam peered at him keenly.

"I may add that there is also a game show called *What's your perversion* which ends with a rabbi being tied to a chair and whipped by a sexy babe in a bikini," he offered. "But, great as these episodes sound, I did not show any of them because – obviously – they did not really seem appropriate in a corporate world. Do you agree? Or do you think it makes sense to have follow up sessions ..."

"I ... I agree ...," a cocktail of all possible human emotions bubbled across the hapless man's face. Other than titillation and mirth that the filmmaker had originally intended. "What was it that you showed them?"

"Working as a team. How each one has a role to play, to make a semi-defunct organisation stay on course and carry on business as usual even in trying situations."

Ajay Yadav looked at Pritam with flinching, untrusting eyes.

"That sort of thing is also included in this ... film?"

Pritam nodded.

"Of course. In a neatly packaged snippet about what goes on in the body during an orgasm."

There were multiple noises as the manager simultaneously lost his physical and mental equilibrium.

"You see, the various body parts play different roles ... it is arranged as a science fiction set where different people work towards a goal – that of a successful orgasm. There are scientists shouting orders for the thigh to be scratched, for the hand to be placed on the breast ... There is the eye focussing on the different assets, a group of people raising the erection and holding it in place ... There are the multitude of sperms, trained to go out into the unknown for the sake of the project, disregarding the risks of masturbation where one can end up on the ceiling or the rumours of crashing against rubber walls. In fact Woody himself plays a sperm. With horn rimmed glasses and a mouthorgan."

"Pritam ...," I asked him to stop. I was having serious doubts about the older man's health. He was breathing heavily and blood had rushed to his face – not out of arousal. When he spoke, his words came out in a hoarse whisper.

"Can you imagine the after effects of this?"

Pritam patted him on the back.

"Let me tell you something. We need not imagine anything. That will give rise to anxiety disorder and again we have to consider cognitive therapy. Dissociate yourself from the field of action and think of what has taken place. This is Amsterdam, not one of the ivory towers run by traditional South Indian Brahmins. Sex is not kept under surreptitious wraps of a thriving pornography industry out here. It is unwrapped and displayed in the windows. Sex is the only mode of interaction that is common across the world, across communities and cultures. We have targeted the one place where it is bound to hit home. And you know how big Ramesh is on proprietary Indian thought. It is in this field that we are the pioneers. No one challenges the kama sutra. This was all decided in collaboration with him. What we have brought to the table is Innovation with a Big O. That's redefining the rules of the alphabet and business. Ajay Yadav, even if your fears come true and you are sacked because of this incident on top of your other blatant inefficiencies, rest assured that when the semenal – er – seminal work co-authored by Ramesh and Mitra is published, your contribution as the impotent bystander will be fully recognised. Simon, coffee?"

So saying, he used another semi-martial grip on my arm to pull me away from the cubicle. The man left inside quivered and shook and I could smell the fear that seemed to reek off him.

Once out of hearing range, I asked my buddy whether he had really shown the film to the attendees.

"I have indeed, my friend. In fact, the recent times have been quite taxing. I have scarcely had the opportunity of settling down to think about the Gita and to link it with the financial situation. I went for an off the shelf solution. In fact, if I had known you were on your way to writing this wonderful Biblical treatise on the financial crisis, I could have spared the Woody Allen retrospective. However, I think the men enjoyed it."

I smiled. I could yield to a greater talent. I have always been a big fan of Woody Allen.

Cheers
Simon

~ ~ ~

The two men lay stretched out on the sofa and closed their eyes. Their legs spread across a stool, trousers rolled up to the knees. At the feet of each was a middle aged Chinese woman, expertly anointing the feet with fragrant gel, working on the sensitive sole with fingers, knuckles and fists.

"You think this is the best place to talk?" Sandeep asked. His voice increased in pitch halfway into the question, in reaction to a dextrous prod of the oriental knuckle into the hollow of the arch.

Dr. Suprakash Roy opened his eyes.

"If you can control your inflexions, yes. This is perhaps the most luxurious replacement of a psychiatric couch. So, what's the problem?"

The meeting place had been the choice of the doctor. The China Massage Centre immediately next to the Nieuwmaarkt Metro station. Sandeep looked at the two Chinese ladies engrossed in conversation as they worked on the two pairs of feet.

"Do you think it's okay to talk?"

"Absolutely. Their English is as good as our Chinese. And we can talk in Bengali or Hindi if required."

Sandeep closed his eyes again as his toes were pushed back and a thumb caressed his meta tarsals.

"Borderline Personality Disorder," remarked Dr. Roy. "Do you know how the term originated?"

Sandeep shook his head.

"I guess I ought to brush up on my psychology. In fact, there has been a strong relationship between psychoanalysis and literature ..."

The doctor laughed.

"Strong and not necessarily healthy. You see, a writer also deals with the mind. And sometimes, the amateurish probes lead him to believe that he, and more predominantly she, knows all there is to know. You have no doubt heard of Fay Weldon ..."

"Yes."

"She had declared war on the psychoanalysts in the nineties. We don't go ahead and teach you how to write novels, do we? So, why not reciprocate our excellent example and shut up about things you don't understand?"

Sandeep almost moaned at the pressure on his heel.

"Have you read Svevo? *Confessions of Zeno?*"

"Not really. I know that it is supposed to be a psychoanalytic novel."

"Right. You can try. Takes time, but it is excellent. I was wondering if Cognitive Psychology could be used to write stream of consciousness novels."

"You mean like the stuff of James Joyce?"

"Among others. After all, stream of consciousness is actually what the Cognitive Psychologist explores."

"Have you heard the wise words on little knowledge? Or do you want me to collaborate with you and this entire story of BPD is just a ruse?"

Sandeep winced.

"It most definitely isn't. To answer your question, no ... I don't know how the term originated."

The good doctor fingered his cigar case as he closed his eyes to maximise the delights under his feet.

"There are different Personality Disorders, the odd or eccentric ones include paranoid, schizoid and schizotypical, the anxious or fearful ones being avoidant, obsessive compulsive and dependant, and the emotional ones consist of narcissistic, antisocial, histrionic and borderline."

"I got that much from Wikipedia."

The Doctor smiled.

"Bravo. Open source psychiatry. However, there are still areas where expertise overrides information availability. Of all these disorders, the borderline was the one with the greatest overlap with the others. It was hard to classify some patients because they showed symptoms of multiple personality disorders. They thus fell in the so called borderline zone. The borderline was literal. Hard to understand and classify before DSM. I gather you know what DSM is?"

"Yes, I do. Madhu Deb talked about it and I checked Wikipedia again."

"It makes it all the more surprising. This lady you speak of, not the young lady you charmed to the brink of death, but the other one who has given you this psychiatric advice. How was she able to diagnose this case as a BPD? Is she a social service volunteer?"

Sandeep opened his eyes and looked at Suprakash Roy with admiration.

"You are good, doctor Holmes. How did you figure that out?"

The doctor did not look pleased.

"We have some serious problems with social service volunteers who receive training in psychology. In seven days, they become experts."

Sandeep shook his head.

"I don't think so. She is definitely a big one for social service, arranging soirees and all that, with proceeds going to NGOs for deprived children of the third world. But, I doubt she ever did any course on psychology for the social cause."

"What makes you so sure?"

"She doesn't look someone capable of spending quiet hours on self study. She is a manager – a senior one. She delegates."

The psychiatrist took his time to nod as he savoured an upward stroke across the medial plantar nerve.

"I understand what you mean. Attention Deficit Hyperactive Disorder. A kid's disease most middle managers of the corporate world are afflicted with today. She takes *tai chi* lessons from you, but that goes with her personality of being involved. Is she regular?"

Sandeep thought about it.

"She skips classes when there are other events taking place – which require her expert meddling. The only two regular students I have are Simon – our Cannabis friend – and this girl."

The doctor nodded thoughtfully.

"And what is her story?"

"Story?"

"She cannot just say that this girl is a case of Borderline Personality Disorder. She must have furnished reasons. Not only symptoms, but reasons that make her an expert in these matters."

Sandeep hesitated.

"Well, she has reasons of a personal nature."

The good doctor reached across and patted him on the shoulder.

"She has played the doctor, but there is no Hippocratic Oath binding the two of you. And, anyway, the oath does not run the other way. On the other hand, I do acknowledge that you are seeking my professional advice – in a far more acceptable way than my first cousin. So, you can trust my confidence."

Sandeep cleared his throat.

"Her husband suffers from Narcissistic Personality Disorder."

"Aha."

"So, she has read up most of the available literature on Personality Disorders. The DSM IV. She can identify personality problems."

Dr. Roy closed his eyes and concentrated.

"And it matches," Sandeep reasoned.

"Matches? What matches?"

"The diagnostic criteria. This girl has this idealisation of relationships, the imagined abandonment syndrome, suicidal threats, uncontrolled anger, feeling of emptiness ..."

"Aha ... so I find another budding expert. But, then, you are quite adept at taking on roles which are not always your forte..."

Sandeep smiled sheepishly.

"I'm sorry, but I was desperate to check the symptoms. I am not claiming to be an expert in any way. I can impersonate a consultant, not a qualified doctor."

"Even as a consultant, you have bitten more than you can chew."

Sandeep detected a hint of reproach under the professional detachment.

"It's this irritant in the scheme of things. I did not budget for a silly girl to fall in love with me and turn out to be BPD in the bargain."

The doctor turned to face him.

"Sir, please ... Lig."

"Of course. Sorry madam. My friend here is suffering from delusional disorder. Sandeep, please listen to me. Don't make the mistake of trying to cure cancer patients based on a hastily attended first aid course. That's one of the biggest threats of the internet as I see it. Get BPD off your mind. You don't know for sure. Faced with a suicide threat, you wanted to clutch on to a logical explanation. You wanted support, in your peculiar situation of facing a death threat while impersonating. You wanted to believe this makeshift analyst. Take my professional advice. Leave diagnosis to specialists."

"But the threat ..."

"How was it made? Was it verbal? Was it face to face? Was it on telephone?"

"No ... sort of ... it was sms ..."

The doctor tilted his hands, palm upwards, universal gesture of a winning argument.

"That's the change in the world view. The world is not what it was twenty years back. The DSM IV you speak of was written in 1994. Since then we have had the internet, the sms, the chat, the blog, the facebook , the orkut, the twitter. Diagnosis based on interpersonal interaction is not what it was back then."

"Sup-da, are you serious? A threat is after all a threat."

"No. It is not."

"You sound like a Zen monk."

"It's based on solid science. In 1994, if one wanted to threat another with suicide, it would have to be done either face to face, or a call, or a letter written in long hand. All these were interactions involving active participation of both – actual interactions. Except for the letter, but that required preparation, commitment, a constant purpose. Now one can threat by text message, by email, by chat pop ups, by scraps, wall to wall, blogs, tweets. Things are way different. The patient is not actually interacting with another individual. She is behind a web, a network, a machine. And this leads to a lack of inhibition. In normal life, the threat may have never taken place. Now, in an electronic world, inhibition is at an all time low. Starting from promiscuity, people indulge in all sorts of communication that they would never even associate themselves with in normal social life. So, a threat sent through sms does not qualify as a threat in the traditional sense. We cannot decide on the brand of personality disorder based on that. Take your mind off this."

Sandeep put his head on the back rest and relaxed.

"So, if I tell her to buzz off, there is no chance that she will actually go and kill herself?"

The doctor looked at him patiently.

"I have not said that. We don't know enough about it. There is no evidence to suggest that she will not, but neither is there any evidence to the contrary."

"What if she does kill herself? And all these messages are retrieved from her cell phone. That implicates me and then Pritam ... what do I do in this situation?"

"That's what's bugging you, isn't it?"

"Of course. She keeps disturbing. Sending messages at odd hours, sending emails that are sometimes pleading, sometimes angry, sometimes accusing, sometimes with a half-veiled threat. This is taking too much of my time and energy. And when I strike back with an unkind word, she goes into this enormous self pity ... almost hinting at consequences."

"Feeling manipulated?"

The question threw Sandeep into a silent period of soul searching.

"You have no doubt read up on BPD – how to get rid of them, how to come out of a relationship without unpleasantness. Right?"

Sandeep nodded gingerly.

"You are already under the pressure of leading a borrowed life, finishing this ridiculous series of talks and then this paper with the big boss. Then there is this tai chi class and your literary ambitions. And if you add the web based research on BPD – how do you think you ought to fare in terms of stress?"

Sandeep sunk further into the couch.

"Forget BPD. There is no end to articles on the web. You can never end your research and take a decision. If you want to tell her to stop bugging you, just go ahead and do that. Stop thinking endlessly."

"There are other problems too," Sandeep confessed. "I was riding on the high-points of the delightful Dutch tradition of vacations. The day after agreeing with K. Ramesh that I was to be loaned for this series of talks, Dave de Boer, the CEO of the Operations and IT division, went on a long holiday. No one else knew what I was here for. Now, this man is back, with a vengeance. He gives ominous signs of wanting to pick my brain."

Dr. Roy considered this.

"That would have been an anatomical impossibility if you had not replaced Pritam. How are you going about it?"

Sandeep sighed.

"Yesterday, he asked me about manpower optimisation schemes in the market offered by McKinsey ... if I subscribed to the methods applied."

"Did you have any idea what he was talking about?"

"Absolutely none. I told him that my opinion did not really matter. McKinsey was the Harper Collins of consulting. Even if they published mediocre yet arrogant theories, customers would hasten to the shelves to load their shopping carts. I managed to divert the topic to Dan Brown and Khaled Hosseini and ultimately to William Hermans and Harry Mulisch. Disaster was avoided temporarily."

"Done sir. Was good?"

"Goedso. Prima. Heel goed."

The two men stretched and bent down to put on their shoes.

"Should I throw her out of my *tai chi* classes?" Sandeep asked.

"That's your decision. You preach the Gita, don't you? The options are there. The choice is yours."

"Madhu Deb recommends it. She says that Amrita knows *tai chi* is my soft corner. She wants to attend the classes for my company. She knows I will dissociate the student from the person and allow her to continue."

"You said she is one of the two sincere students."

"She is."

"35 Euros sir."

"I will pay it ... consultation fees."

"I will pay for dinner in that case. If she is one of the sincere students and you don't allow your personal life to get in the way of the classes, there is no reason to throw her out."

Sandeep opened the door and walked out into the chill of the evening air and the brightness of De Wallen.

"I need the classes to go on, Sup-da. Otherwise I will go crazy."

XXXV

Email from Kailash Nayak to Sandeep Gupta

Sandeep,

I took it upon myself to circulate copies of the excellent reviews of your book in the Chandigarh Tribune and The Dawn to some supposedly influential people in the world of Indian Literature and Academia. This is a response from one of them. Please try to overlook the audacious linguistic blunders and remember that he is the General Secretary of Shakespeare Society Press, with extremely strong liaison with the Rabindra Bharati University. Please bear with being a 'new born author' of 'Doppelgang Days'. I always told you titles should have populist appeal. A tongue twister is a deterrent to acceptance.

Also, I advise you to adjust cultural deviants like 'curry-culum' to the more traditional English vocabulary.

If you ignore the ridiculousness, this guy is influential. Recently, he had his picture with Günter Grass in the front page of The Telegraph's Metro Supplement. I know the girl who ghosted his final year papers and dissertation, and she vouches for his networking skills.

Enjoy,
K

Dear Sir,

Received your mail of introduction of your friend the author Mr.Sandeep Gupta. The reviews are good.

I am the general secretary of the Shakespeare Society Press. We are active in university education. Since your friend is a new born author, I can help him in a lot of ways – as we have helped a number of similar new born authors including Mrinal Guha (author of Tobacco Worker).

I can arrange a soiree for the reading of the book (Doppelgang Days). The author (Mr. Sandeep Gupta) can read out sections of his book to an audience including students and teachers of the University Literature Department with sufficient press coverage. I can arrange for an article on the reading along with the photograph of the author to appear in leading Indian dailies. (I have arranged the same in the past for Mrinal Guha). He will have to bear the nominal cost of the arrangements of the evening, which comes to around Rs. 20000.

For an additional fee I can reach out to some of my colleagues to include a selection from the novel as compulsory reading in the University Curryculum. That will ensure purchase of the copies of the book by the teachers , students and university library.

Every new born author needs publicity and I will be glad to arrange for it for my esteemed friend.

Yours faithfully,
Partho Ghose,
General Secretary, Shakespeare Society Press,
M.A.(Eng Lit) First Class First,
Author of Waiting for Beckett – An Analysis of the Modernism in Goddot and Malone, Shakespeare Society Press.

Email from Professor P.Lal, typed by his grand daughter Shuktara Lal

Dear Sandeep,

I understand your frustrations with semi-literate middle men who influence the so called Indian intelligentsia. With the advent of the strange avatar called the literary agent, the racket of the book market is now nothing but a nexus of intermediaries.

But, what is to be done? In the age of the great maya-jal of the Internet, connections have taken on a new connotation.

As I often say, alternative publishing is desperately needed wherever commercial publication rules. Most English book publishing today in boom-time India and outside is book-dumping. There is a nexus between high-profile PR-conscious book publishers, semi-literate booksellers, moribund public and state libraries, poorly informed and nepotistic underlings in charge of book review pages and supplements of most national newspapers and magazines, and biased bulk purchases of near worthless books by bureaucratic institutions set up—believe it or not!—to inform, educate and elevate the reading public.

Best of luck in your endeavours – just make sure that you choose correctly.

The Professor.

∾ ∾ ∾

A knock on the panel of his cubicle made Sandeep raise his eyes and start. In front of him, dressed in his impeccable banker's suit, Dave de Boer stood smiling at him.

"Busy, mister consultant?"

Sandeep looked at the man standing at the entrance of the cubicle. Some cognitive quirk in his consciousness idly computed the probability of a quick getaway eluding the great man's lunge for his waist and time. He forced a smile on his face.

"Somewhat."

"Ramesh is a hard task master, is he?" the Dutch man stepped into his cubicle. "I was just wondering if I could ask your opinion about the McKinsey 7S Model. Do you think we should go for it?"

Sandeep looked at the man and his screen and wondered why this godforsaken buzzword kept following him.

"There is no simple yes or no answer to that," he replied.

The CEO laughed.

"Ah, yes, I quite understand. And without a proper work contract I can't really ask you for a detailed analysis, right?" he winked at Sandeep. "But, can you offer me some insights on the banks that have used it for restructuring? What is the feedback? What does van Eyck think about it?"

Sandeep eyed him apprehensively.

"Mr.van Eyck is known to keep his cards close to his chest," he said, hoping he had managed to repeat the name correctly.

De Boer laughed again.

"That's true, but he is an intelligent one, eh? He knows how to get the best off the vendors and to manage the Anglo Saxon board members."

Sandeep nodded cautiously.

"He is a hard nut to crack," he grudgingly agreed. He would have to look van Eyck on Google, stepping around the difficulty of approximating the correct spelling.

"I wonder if you can say the same about Jos de Vries. How did you find him in van Bosch?".

"How did I find Jos de Vries, eh? In van Bosch? I guess you don't have to look too hard..."

"Ramesh did tell me you did a project for them in Utrecht."

"I see ... well as far as Meneer de Vries is concerned ... there were not too many one on one interactions with ..."

"The company did involve Accenture, didn't they? What was your role in the transformation?"

Sandeep shifted uneasily in his seat.

"Well, Accenture gave them the options. I helped them ... er ... transform."

"So, you played the change agent."

"Quite so ... you know, the ideas of a paper on being a change agent popped up from that experience more than anything else. Choices are clear ... the company has to choose and all that. I helped them see the choices and choose ..."

The top boss was in a mood to go deeper. "Didn't Accenture prepare a cost benefit analysis for them?"

"Er ... that will infringe on the non-disclosure agreement, you know, the NDA," he offered, a wary eye on the super-client. "We at ...er... *Axiom,* are very strong about these policies ..."

The CEO smiled.

"I understand. I wouldn't like you to go and talk about our policies and procedures to Chase Manhattan ..."

"Certainly not ... you know, as Thomson and Thompson used to put it – mum's the word, that's our motto ..."

"Thomson and Thompson?"

"Yes, the twin detectives of Tintin. There may be a Dutch variant, though. I know Tintin is Kuifje. Ah ... do you know the Dutch variant for Thomson and Thompson?"

The last question was directed at Madhu Deb who had come bounding in to the cubicle propelled by the firepower of enthusiasm. Sandeep idly wondered about the absurdity of his position. Madhu Deb, the story toting psycho-mom, welcome like the US Marines. US Marine? Maybe that was a dated expression in the wake of the twenty first century atrocities.

Madhu Deb blended into the discussion like seasoned Douwe Egbert coffee beans. She was soon asking about Dave de Boer's recent holidays, which included a motorcycle ride across what sounded like a sizeable chunk of Western Europe. It logically followed that Madhu Deb had been on a comparable Che Guevera-sque motor cycle tour with a friend in the other America, across the wild west. During her university days. Yes, she did study in the United States. Metallurgical Engineering ... How was she into this industry? Well ...

The phone rang seconds after Sandeep's desperate thumb had pressed the panic button. Simon's welcome name blinked on his small getaway screen. Leaving the tormentor to battle with more than his match, he stepped outside, where away from the voices in the cubicle, there was peace.

Mail from Simon to his mailing list
Sub: Post Colonial Slave Drivers

This is going to be a short mail. It is very seldom that I compromise with my work ethics to key in a personal mail while in office. It is not that my ethics are unduly robust, but since I don't hang around after six, I try to work as much as possible during the eight hours. My colleagues, on the other hand, habitually stretching the hours to breaking point, naturally intersperse work with breaks for coffee, cigarettes, gossip, luxurious lunches, and weather permitting – long loquacious walks. *Swa-dharma* or way of the self, as my favourite buddy put it.

However, I just overheard a segment of loud communication which I need to share, if only to pour some coolant over fuming rage.

I was on my way back from a rescue mission of the Gupta-van-der- Wiel system, this time delivering Pritam from the clutches of double edged danger in the forms of Dave de Boer and our own Madhu Deb. I happened to cross the cubicle in which Amrita works and heard her engaged in conversation on the desk phone – kept in the speaker mode to facilitate something she was doing on her machine.

I could make out the disembodied voice of Govindrajan, her immediate superior, who works out of Chennai. It was apparent that the man from India was peeved. He was demanding an explanation for delay, of several deliverables. I could hear the poor girl protesting that there had been too many exacting demands in recent times.

It was during this exchange that a particular sentence from Govindrajan caught my ears and set them ringing with indignation.

"If you think you will go home at six, things will not get done. Remember that you are not one of those lazy Dutch guys. You can't afford their life style."

I walked on – even though I would have liked to hear the girl's retort. I was still bristling as I started to write this mail ... but then it struck me. This type of remarks had been an integral part of the emotional send off given me by my American friends.

"You gonna work with a bunch of number crunchers? Don't tell me man, you gotta be kidding."

"Don't become one of those Indian wierdos pal."

Well, even as the world gets smaller with globalisation, we, in our innermost psyche, remain as narrow minded xenophobes as ever.

It was, in fact, the great Indian poet – Tagore – who wrote ...

"Where knowledge is free ...

Where the world has not been broken up into fragments by narrow domestic walls....

....

Into that heaven of freedom
My father, let my country awake."
(Thanks to Lahari for sharing these lines)

Simon

~ ~ ~

When Amrita walked into the office gym, seeking solitude for the suffocated soul, she found her heroic tormentor inside, practicing *tobi yoko geri.* As ever, the chance meeting lifted her to delighted throes and plunged her in melancholy depths. She stood near the doorway, in stealthy silence, willing herself into invisibility – fearing the retreat of the man she had grown to love, as had so often happened in recent times whenever they had met.

Sandeep had come in to the gym in a state of confusion. The multiple building blocks of his long list of troubles had been enhanced by the sudden return of Dave de Boer. He wanted a break. Stepping into the gym to get the malaise out of his system, he had started performing a series of shotokan katas. When he had made a mistake in the *Kanku Dai,* there had risen in his mind a sinister feeling that life was not going anywhere. The vigorous kicks were an expression of frustration.

The tobi yoko geri is a flying side kick. When someone as tall – by Indian standards – as Sandeep performed them, each of them covered quite some distance. As a result, the entire stretch of the gym was good enough for just five of the kicks with the right leg. So, at the end of the fifth, Sandeep turned to restart the routine with his left leg. And it was then that he saw the silent, dark figure of the brooding girl near the doorway. He stopped halfway through his spring, staggered and let out an oath.

"God almighty!" he said.

To Amrita, the doubly divine expression was cruel. They were symbolic of the multiple forces of the world that had teamed up against her. Someone she had trusted with her innermost thoughts was now bitterly against her in the moment of dire need. Was this the price one paid for love?

Two rivulets trickled from her eyes, the topography of her rounded cheeks made them converge towards her nose and the end result was a sniffle. It undid the last restraining thread of Sandeep's thin tapestry of patience.

"Stop that for heaven's sake. Woman, cease your detestable boo-hooing instantly or seek the shelter of some other place of worship."

Amrita turned her face even as Sandeep wondered at his stupid compulsion of quoting Bernard Shaw to someone uninitiated to the world of Enid Blyton.

"You find me too intolerable, don't you?" the girl sobbed.

Sandeep groaned.

"Nothing special about you. I find the whole situation intolerable."

Amrita sobbed some more.

"It's okay. I won't stay if you don't want me to."

Sandeep executed a mae geri, mawashi geri, ushiro geri combination and as expected, saw the girl hanging around in the doorway. Several long unending dialogues had taught him that the initial words of farewell were but prologue to an unfinished magnum opus of further negotiations.

"I don't see you going anywhere," he remarked. Cruel, but forced.

Much in the time honoured O'Henrian model, there was a sob, sniffle and a sigh.

"I ... I did not come here because you were here. I ... I was just looking for a quiet place."

"Don't you have work to do?"

There was another sigh.

"Yes, I do."

"What's that excruciatingly slow answer supposed to mean?"

Amrita's tearful eyes looked at him, uncomprehending.

"Did you mean anything specific when you replied that there was work to do?"

"Govind is loading me with work."

"Who the hell is Govind?"

Amrita winced.

"My offshore manager. He knows that the work he expects me to do is more than humanly possible. He expects me to put in long hours."

Sandeep put one foot on the hand rails and stretched.

"I can't help you there. You must manage your own manager."

Amrita lowered her head.

"I know you can't help me. It is fate. I ... I want to get out of this place, but I can't. It's my luck. Even when I feel like studying, I cannot concentrate and then there is this additional load of work."

Sandeep cursed.

"You want to cut through this problematic period with the sword of self pity, do you?"

There was incomprehension in the eyes, followed by the recognition of two key words

"It is not self pity ..."

"The whole world has nothing to do but load you with problems. It's your bloody fate, isn't it? Look at yourself, in the mirror. You see these mirrors in the gym? They are there for a reason ... look at yourself."

Amrita looked at her image uncertainly and closed her eyes, fresh tears trickling down.

"I know I am not good looking. You need not point it out. I ... I have given you the right and the privilege to insult me, but must you?"

Sandeep groaned.

"Goddammit. Can't you think beyond your protracted universe? I will tell you what I see in the mirror for you. I am not talking about looks. I see a semi-emaciated, sickly girl who stoops from lack of self confidence. Doesn't that make you sick? Don't you learn anything from the Dutch girls you see around you?"

There was a confused look as Amrita tried to come out of her shell to throw light on the question.

"They ... they are more sportive... We Indians don't think girls should be that ..."

"Why the hell not?" Sandeep was surprised by the conviction in his own voice. "Look at them on their cycles with hockey sticks ... Do you see anyone pining away for unrewarded love like the mission of your life?"

"They are Western girls – love is not the same for ..."

"Where do you pick up such hackneyed lessons of life? From Karan Johar movies? Do you see these people with their families? Don't they look genuinely concerned about their wives, husbands and kids? Not the society shamming office goer of the Indian middle class for whom the wife is an extension of the furniture and a kid he would not recognise awake and standing."

There was a distinct bafflement in the girl's eyes. "I am sorry ...."

"Forget it. You know why they can live an uncomplicated life? Because they are healthy. Physically healthy. You know what girls like you need? A rigorous introduction into the world of physical fitness. And I don't mean walking daintily on the treadmill to have a narrow waist until wedding day while your underarms sag to the ground in the way of the traditional Indian beauty."

"But, I am doing *tai chi.* I also wanted to run ..."

"Run for yourself. Not after someone. Listen up ... I am going to show you something. Do this. Keep doing this every morning ... Join a gym if necessary, one near your place. AllSports for instance."

As Amrita oscillated between elation and confusion, Sandeep proceeded to show her the basic isometric exercises followed by stretching, the basic punches, blocks and the front kick.

"Five sets of each. I will show you some basic exercises with weights as well ... get a gym instructor to show you in more detail."

"Should I work with weights?"

"Why not?"

"Is it good for girls?"

"Damn ... you are a relic from the Ice Age? Don't you watch the Olympics? Don't you watch tennis? Where do you think Serena Williams gets all those muscles? Or Madonna for God's sake? Do you follow the workout of any supermodel, even the Indian ones? Try googling them."

"Can I come and check with you time to time whether I am doing the exercises properly?"

"Absolutely not. I can show you after the *tai chi* sessions. That's all."

"I love you."

"Do these exercises regularly ... every day .... and you stand a decent chance of getting cured."

By the time Sandeep walked out, he was sweating profusely. Amrita was still inside, running on the treadmill.

XXXVI

Dear Mr. Gupta,

The worldwide recession has had its effect on all the industries. Publishing is no exception. Due to the major reduction in the book sales in all genres in the market, we are not taking on any new projects.

Wish you success in your literary journey.

Kathy Mason
Napier Publishers

∾ ∾ ∾

Set in an old Dominican Church, the Selxyz bookshop of Maastricht is widely regarded as the most beautiful bookstore in the world. Under the classical arches of the erstwhile place of worship, the altar has made way for a coffee corner and *The Lost Symbol* has replaced the Bible. The glorious painted ceilings with the interplay of reflection and transparency of mellow lighting and stained glass windows lent an aura of enlightenment for the devoted reader.

Deeply absorbed in *A Gentleman of Leisure* by P.G. Wodehouse, with an eye on the arched doorway, Sandeep looked up expectantly as a female form approached him.

However, it was not the friend he was waiting for. A tall young Dutch attendant stood over him, casting her long shadow across the pages of lyrical humour. Sandeep looked up questioningly.

"Gaat u dat kopen?" she asked.

"Excuse me."

"Are you going to buy that?" she pointed at the volume in his hand.

"I am not too sure. I might."

"You have been reading it for a long time ... That's not allowed."

Sandeep was puzzled. Arriving at the unique bookshop set in the magnificent Southern Dutch town, he had set about trying to celebrate reading in this atmosphere by picking up a novel by the master of glittering humour. In the past few months he had hardly found time to read anything at all, with the crazy borrowed life, the rehashing of submission letters and query notes and synopses. He had settled down to soak in the masterly concoction, rediscovering the joys of reading a simple, well told story, when the shadow had been cast across the pages.

"I would have expected this sort of a thing in College Street or thereabouts ..." he began, almost talking to himself – turning the puzzle over in his mind – when there was an interruption. A sunburnt, earthy version of the image which had so often flitted by in his mind during the last couple of months, suddenly materialised in their midst. The apparition cut across the conversation and enfolded the bemused protagonist in a friendly embrace.

Sandeep, who had jumped up on the emergence of Shruti, returned the hug with relief and the lady attendant, who was a trainee after all, looked at them for a moment before deciding to withdraw.

Sandeep looked at Shruti with a wide smile. As so often happens, when you meet someone once and follow it up with regular intimate communication, and then come across the person once more in real life, you have to adjust the image in your mind's eye – a brush here and a dab there – for the outlined mental sketch to merge with the real version. Sandeep modified the approximations of the adorable tilt of the nose, the couple of highlights in the hair and a birthmark on the right cheek. Shruti was perhaps making minor modifications to her corresponding image as well as they stood for a while smiling at each other.

"Well ..." Sandeep started the conversation tentatively.

"I guess we got rid of the warden," Shruti observed.

"So we have," Sandeep agreed. "She said I was not allowed to read too long in the bookshop. Something I would have not dreamed of hearing in the Western Hemisphere."

Shruti took a seat in front of him.

"Western Hemisphere? That's interesting."

"Even in India, after the big chains like Starmark and Crossword came into being ... but, then, you have scared her away."

Shruti bowed.

"In a manner of speaking, yes, I believe I have. For some reason, I guess I happen to look more blended into the society. That was the trick."

Sandeep looked at the girl thoughtfully. Hands crossed in front of her, her jacket tied around her waist, she could be easily deduced to be an Indian. Pritam, for instance, would never have had hyper romantic dreams about her if that were not so. At the same time, he did agree that there was something very local about her. Difficult to define, but some tiny elements of characteristic, from the confidence in her eyes, the slight deviation in the manner of dressing, the bag held in the crook of her elbow, openness of her attitude and the sporty vigour of her carriage. All these summed up into a very local flavour.

"I understand what you mean," Sandeep concurred. "Although I will be at a loss to put my finger on it."

"An undefined problem has infinite solutions. However, I think it is because of living here for the better part of the last decade. Your characteristics tend to get woven into the texture of the society."

Sandeep kept his eyes on her.

"I would say you combine the best of both worlds."

Shruti made a face.

"There goes our compulsive Don Juan."

"I am being an unbiased academic judge. You kind of strike a balance between the charms of the Indian good looks and the whiff of Dutch outdoors. You would look equally at home in a ghagra choli or a tracksuit and a hockey stick."

"Last time you spoke about the mevrouws of this nation, you were circumspect about their looks unless armed with a telescope. Was it a tall tale told by an idiot?"

"The idiot now wants to carry on the conversation along the same lines, having clutched on to an excuse to gape at you."

"You think unbiased academic judges are people celebrated for gaping?"

"I wish I could gape into your mind as well. It would be a treat."

"Thank you. It was strange though – picking on you for browsing."

Sandeep nodded ruefully.

"Do you think it had racial undertones?"

Shruti thought for a while.

"That's what I am wondering. The Netherlands is not a racially biased country at all. They don't have the condescending pseudo-tolerance of the immigrants like the Americans. They respect fellow men in the truest sense. They have traded with others too long and have interacted with all sorts of people."

"Would you say it is an effect of the recession? Do they see us Indians coming over and taking their jobs away? Is that cognitive map making them antagonistic?"

Shruti frowned.

"That's an interesting suggestion, but I wonder if our friend there had any such mental undercurrent. It is surprising. Normally, the Dutch can be very direct, but always when they are on the right side of the considerable volume of rules and regulations."

"If I put myself in her large shoes, this is what I see. An Indian guy reading a book for quite some time. Back in New York, I had some colleagues who used Barnes and Nobel like a library, returning technical books within fourteen days for free, photocopying them using the copiers at office. If that is the tendency people see in ..."

"Are all Indians like that?"

"No, but unfortunately a susbtantial percentage of them are. However, now that we have looked at the sociological problem from both points of view, shall we go Dutch again in the coffee shop?"

Shruti got up.

"Your finances have improved?"

"Yes, they have. Due largely to the magnanimity of our mutual friend whom you plagued and tortured till he had to tear himself away from your travel plans."

Shruti nodded with sympathy.

"What's he doing now?"

"Last heard, he was leading a life of orgy and debauchery in the more sinister streets of Hamburg. He is indeed having a whale of a time. He has travelling companions who pose in front of coke machines for photographs when they reach a historic European town."

"I am so happy for him. How much have you progressed in your literary quest?"

"The quest turns into conquest by the day ... and the only prominent writing making rounds seems to be on the wall. It was as it is difficult to get query letters read by the agents and publishers. Now that the crisis has spread across the canvas of life, the excuses are dipped in the flavour of the season."

Shruti ordered coffee for the two of them.

"And what are you working on right now?"

"Query letters and synopses."

"I would have thought this was the ideal time to get some real writing off your chest ... with publishers and agents looking the other way."

"Stimulating thought. Wonder how many share your optimism for life. However, let's not talk about the sorrows of my literary trials. Does Maastricht end your Odyssey?"

Shruti sipped her coffee and smiled.

"Yes. It is fitting that I end retracing the history of twentieth century Europe at the birthplace of the Euro. Although I do want to walk about in Amsterdam for a while."

"Haven't you done quite a lot of that in the past few years?"

"Not with the Europe on a Shoestring guides."

Sandeep looked up from his cup.

"Europe on a Shoestring? It is a pretty small world, isn't it?"

"Going by the Shoestring?"

"Not exactly. There is this visionary vice president of the European Operations, who has recommended this group as a fascinating business model..."

"They do have a great business model. They don't charge anything at all."

"That sounds original, but I am not too convinced if that is the ideal way to bring home the bacon..."

"Most of the tour operators are young backpackers with a passion for travel, and a gift for story telling. They entertain the tourists with anecdotes, history and stories, and at the end of the day, a large percentage part with decent tips."

"Wow. So crisis can never hit them."

"Not in terms of customers, no."

"Sounds interesting. Great way to live through backpacking."

"Very much so."

"Wasn't it a member of this excellent group of guides who tried to tickle Pritam with a feather somewhere in Eastern Europe?"

Shruti chuckled.

"Yes. They almost came to blows."

"Lending a new dimension to featherweight bout."

"And then there was the banner."

"What banner would that be?"

"An advertising banner created as a collage of two pictures. Both of which featured a grumpy faced Pritam ..."

"It's hilarious."

"More so because without specifically pointing to him, the caption said something about coming back to them irrespective of mood."

Sandeep's lips parted in a beatific smile.

"Turning risks into opportunities, as our corporate gurus would say. They are indeed masters. Would you mind if I join you for the Amsterdam excursion?"

"I was almost going to ask you to."

"They can very well be the wampeter."

"The what?"

"Wampeter of our karass. Somehow I do feel we belong to a karass. You know what a karass is?"

"Vaguely familiar."

"Disappointing after bugging Pritam no end about Billy Pilgrim."

"Ah ... how could I forget? *Cat's Cradle*. A group of people joined together for a purpose in life. Vonnegut could be so irreverently deep sometimes. But what is a *wampeter?*"

"The hub around which the *karass* revolves. You see, I have an idea that you and I are part of a *karass*."

Shruti looked at him quizzically.

"Your friend thought so too."

Sandeep waved his hand dismissively.

"He has been too busy earning money to have his thinking in working order. Unused, out of condition, flabby muscles of the brain misinterpreted a *granfalloon*."

"And what is that?"

"A false karass. People who imagine themselves to be a part of a karass – where there is actually no connection. Much like Amrita and me."

"And who is the bearer of this interesting new name?'

Sandeep shuddered.

"A dementor demented enough to mistake herself for a veela."

"I am slightly tired of pottering around knee deep in literary allusions. But, is this in any way related to the mind-clogging peculiar problems?"

"You amaze me. You are way beyond just a pretty face."

"She sucks out happiness, does she? Much like your travelling companion to Prague?"

"Madhu Deb? No ... not at all like the chubby cheerleader. Madhu Deb is someone who has made endless enthusiasm her watchword – who goes ahead and bludgeons any gathering with accounts of her colourful experiences in life, especially partial to the ones about her four year old son. She does not suck out happiness, she drowns it in her overflowing milk of human kindness, some of the milk being flavoured a wee bit too much with the joys of motherhood."

"You seem to be in colourful company."

"That I am. None so stimulating as the present."

He chuckled.

"Something funny?"

"Kind of. In all probability, going by the time tested traditions of wooing associated with the successful Indian male, my dear old friend may have thought his journeys with you would end with a walk down the altar."

"Was it? He will certainly have to alter his design."

"I believe he has. He will never again look at a member of the female species who thinks Nice is a treaty rather than the biscuits her husband loves with bed tea. She will be blocked from his mailbox, blackberry, facebook, linked in, orkut and twitter. But, in a convoluted way, I am having coffee with you at the end of your European travels in what had once been the altar."

Shruti looked around herself.

"Can one get married in this church?"

"I doubt it, but if you are willing I can make enquiries."

Two pairs of mischievous eyes met each other.

"Unbiased academic judges should not be strangers to hypothetical questions."

"True, but being academic I find the book filled surroundings a bit too tempting."

They paid the bill – in the accepted way of going Dutch – and walked out into the town with great Churches and river banks, and strangely for the Netherlands, some hilly roads.

The milk of human kindness meanwhile sloshed about in an Indian restaurant in Leidseplein. The quarterly lunch of the *Sur-Soiree* volunteers was in full swing. Madhu Deb was in her element. Along with the half a dozen employees of *Axiom* and *HMH,* there was seated next to her someone whose fame had preceded him to the dining room. Though he needed a high chair to reach the table, the tall tales of his exploits were household legends in this gathering. Hidori, an apprehensive kid with cropped hair, followed the proceedings with guarded unease. He would much rather be at home, watching the Jetix channel.

"Whenever Samit and I have coffee, he wants chocomel. He is crazy about it. And after going to the British School where they are fed Dutch lunches, he wants three breakfasts a day. The moment I told him there is dinner today, he asked me whether we were going to a Dutch restaurant ..."

Gunjan, Trisha, Amrita all nodded their heads and laughed. The three others at the table, Indians working for HMH, either as direct employees or contracted through companies such as Wipro and TCS, smiled synchronised appreciation.

There was a pause as Hidori passed on the important decision of whether or not to have the rest of the chicken *do piaza* to his doting mother. Since he was more comfortable talking in whispers, the rest of the company fell into a contemplative silence that engulfs the immigrant populace when faced with the nostalgic sight, smell and taste of homeland.

As the jovial round face of Madhu Deb returned to face the admirers, Gunjan cleared his throat.

"So, Amrita, those high kicks and punches that I see you doing in the mornings ... and sometime in the evenings, are they part of *tai chi*?"

At the question, Madhu Deb turned sharply to look at the dark girl, who had been in refreshingly high spirits throughout the meal. The answer sounded a bit embarrassed.

"Er ... no ... they are more to do with karate. At least I think so."

"Karate?" Madhu Deb asked, interested, full of good humour. "You are doing karate too?"

Amrita wanted the subject to change.

"It is more for fitness. Nothing serious. I do some punches, kicks, and exercises."

Gunjan nodded.

"Yes. I have seen them. She does push ups as well."

Amrita turned towards him.

"I think you can do some exercises as well, instead of watching others. Your paunch needs it."

Taken by nasty surprise, Gunjan did not lose his charm.

"If you inspire me some more, I might take it up. Are you taking instructions?"

"Sort of," the answer was evasive, she fiddled with her spoon.

Madhu Deb looked at her closely

"Did Pritam share some tips with you? I believe he is a black belt in Karate as well."

Gunjan looked impressed.

"He is a man of many talents, isn't he? I wonder how he finds the time. I often want to take up a hobby really seriously, but cannot get around to it. I can hardly get away from work before half past eight."

"That's surprising," Amrita remarked. "If you have seen me exercising in the evening, you must have been home and in your balcony by half past six."

Madhu Deb looked with curious and smiling eyes at both of them.

"Well, Gunjan, if you are interested, I can pass you one of the time management tricks of Pritam," she volunteered. "He never talks about the loads of work that he is doing. That probably frees up half his day."

Gunjan did not look amused, but maintained a smiling front.

∾ ∾ ∾

Text messages

Madhu Deb to Sandeep: At the risk of repeating myself, I must urge you towards a clean surgical break from Amrita. You don't know what you are dealing with. Helping her will backfire again, as it has done in the past.

Sandeep: If by helping her you mean suggesting exercises, it seems to be working. She has less time to pine away in languor.

The cell phone rang as Sandeep sat in a bar opposite the Athenaeum Bookstore in Spui. Over the rim of his cup of Irish Coffee with whipped cream, he looked at the gorgeous Dutch waitress who smiled back at him.

"Hi Madhu-di."

"Where are you? There seems to be a lot of noise in the background."

Sandeep smiled.

"I am in one of those balmy bars of central Amsterdam. One of those with a warm glow and homely atmosphere, where old friends meet and genteel waitresses ask you what you want with bewitching smiles."

"Have you had a lot to drink?"

"Enough to get drunk and madly in love with an exquisite waitress ... while being in full control of my faculties to realise that she is gorgeous. In fact I know her name. Marijn ... works in this bar and studies in the University of Amsterdam ... She is fascinating. I wonder whether she will agree to have dinner with me if I ask her to be a template for one of my characters ...In the net age, a muse becomes a template."

Madhu Deb smiled even as she spoke firmly.

"Well, keep your flirtations under check."

"You speak like a Dutch aunt."

"And what is that?"

"A female equivalent of the Dutch Uncle."

"I would have thought you would be home writing ..."

"Well, I need the experience as well ..."

"I will leave you to your philandering ..."

"You pain me ... I am doing hardly anything of that sort ... But, the poet has to be the observer of things of beauty to document them as joys forever."

"Just make sure that you take my warnings about Amrita seriously."

"Dear lady ... I am in the company of a room full of friendly, if somewhat morose Dutchmen ... and a fascinatingly sweet waitress ... whose charms are like the moon herself, if you take the luminous beauty and the vertical distance into account. Why do you want to spoil my evening with references to gloom?"

"Because I fear you are helping her out with fitness programs and karate routines. I can see a new hope in her."

"What's wrong with that? Surely you don't want her to be plunged in hopelessness."

"I don't, but the danger remains if that hope involves you. What will she do when you go away? As you will eventually do? I tried my best to distract her ..."

"Huh?"

"I made Govindrajan load her with assignments ..."

"It was you?"

"But, she doesn't care. She just ignores him. She has developed an audacity ..."

"Confidence?"

"Over confidence. I think she has the conviction that you are there to stand by her. And your exercise regimens are just helping things along."

Sandeep scratched his head. Looking towards the counter he saw the lovely Marijn smiling at him. He smiled back.

"Madhu-di, you are spinning a web of confusion. Physical training has been a time tested model for healthy living. I wonder if there are so many strings attached."

There was an experienced and knowledgeable pause.

"Your relation with the girl is not one of physical trainer and student, Pritam, you know it as well as I do. There is a web of confusion there already. Don't lose perspective. Sometimes it helps to look at it from a distance."

"Wow ... thanks. You are looking from a distance so admirably for me ... I will give it some serious thought, Madhu-di. Thanks awfully. But, right now I am looking at something else from a distance. May I proceed along the more delicious lines?"

Madhu Deb laughed.

"Go ahead, dashing young knight. Do you have protection?"

"What a nauseating question! It takes the shine off my armour."

"I speak words of wisdom, dear."

Sandeep rang off and shook the confusion off his head before looking up and beckoning Marijn.

XXXVII

Dear Mr. Spokeshave,

The worldwide recession has had its effect on all the industries. Publishing is no exception. Due to the major reduction in the book sales at all levels in the market, we are not taking on any new projects.

Wish you success in your literary journey.

Kathy Mason
Napier Publishers

Dear Mr. Mitra,

The worldwide recession has had its effect on all the industries. Publishing is no exception. Due to the major reduction in the book sales at all levels in the market, we are not taking on any new projects.

Wish you success in your literary journey.

Kathy Mason
Napier Publishers

~ ~ ~

They met in front of the national monument. And the hug was spontaneous – without the erstwhile stirrings of hesitation. Beside them, a small group of young people in red shirts milled around. Tourists in small numbers gathered around them. This was the *Europe on a Shoestring* tour.

"Three notes. Same text. Three different names. What is this all about?"

"Having been at the receiving end of the auto-responder clones passing as agents, I decided to enjoy myself. I sent three sets of query letters, synopses and first three chapters to this acclaimed publisher. And got the same answer on all three occasions."

"Something tells me you did not send the same three sets."

Sandeep laughed.

"Therein lies the rub. When I sent the set for my novel and got this response, I got an idea. For a literary experiment. Under the name of Spokeshave, I sent the synopsis of our own ... Hamlet. Something's rotten in the state of Denmark. I changed the names of the characters. Hamlet became Jaap and Ophelia Saskia. Denmark transformed itself to dear old Holland. I have the full text of most of Shakespeare's plays on my machine and used the original script of the first three scenes. And Shakespeare was rejected because of recession. There was no detection of plagiarism."

Dam Square echoed with the loud laughter Sandeep found so endearing.

"And then I sent a third set under the name you recognise so well, Pritam Mitra. The synopsis – a cordial invitation to join me for an evening meal starting with Seafood Tom Yum Soup, followed by Pad Thai and Chicken in green curry. The three sample chapters contained the three recipes, downloaded from the most authentic website of Thai cuisine. However, the result was the same."

Shruti had to sit down on the steps of the national monument to prevent toppling over with mirth. In her case, life was a sum total of glee, giggles and guffaws with glee predominating. Sandeep was tickled, touched by her full throated merriment.

"I intend to branch into the world of Booker, Pulitzer ... I am itching to send one under the pseudonym Aveek."

"Why Aveek?"

"He follows naturally after Pritam and me. The three of us were inseparable in school and college days. He sort of petered out into thin air, with the vacant uncomprehending looks that accompanied him. I often wonder what happened to our dear friend. I owe him at least one synopsis. *Herzog*, maybe ... "

"Welcome to Amsterdam, ladies and gentlemen. I am Ben. In other words Ik ben Ben," the guide with spiked hair started the tour.

∾ ∾ ∾

Amrita received Madhu Deb's call while running on the treadmill in the gym.

"Hello Madhu-di," she panted.

"What's wrong? Why are you panting?"

"I was working out."

On the other end of the line, there was a pause as the older woman sighed and shook her sagacious head.

"I was just calling to find out whether you have any idea of where I can get hold of Pritam."

At this end of the line there was a pause as the younger woman started and allowed coyness creep into her voice.

"I ... I don't know ... This is the weekend, he may be anywhere."

"Don't you have any idea?"

"No ..."

"He's not answering his phone."

"Oh ..." Amrita gasped.

"He is like a child, dear... he doesn't even know what he wants. If it's a weekend it's as if school's ended, so he has to go out and enjoy ... Seniority and age aside, he has not really grown up."

Amrita's brows were both raised with curiosity and knitted with confusion. The motherly concern in the voice was endearing. But, why was the question being asked to her?

"He is childish, yes," she agreed, forlorn.

"Yes, and hence prone to hurt and get hurt," the mature voice observed with a sigh. "Anyway, Ramesh can't reach him either and asked me to chase him. If you get any news please let me know."

∾ ∾ ∾

Mail from Simon to his mailing group

Sub: Strange Summons from a Friend in Need

It is a common and confusing signal that I get from my colleagues that even though I have been recruited to work for an Indian firm, I am given special privileges.

Gunjan, in fact, points them out to me on a regular basis approaching official obligation. For example, although it is an unwritten rule for the Indians to stretch their working hours beyond what qualifies as normal by any stretch of imagination even in this peace screwing world post-globalisation, I am exempt from such demands purely because of my occidental origins. The same applies to receiving office and work related calls during weekends.

In fact, in the guise of the equivocating well wisher, the slimy colleague mentioned above has often made it clear to me that this infringement on the fundamental rights of the employee is a result of clear instructions of Madhu Deb herself, who keeps everyone instructed that one has to be sensitive to the Dutch culture and way of life. And as sad as it makes Gunjan, it gladdens my heart.

Today, therefore, was quite a surprise when – just back from the Saturday exertions of the squash court, I was sitting with a relaxed glass of non-alcoholic beer and leafing through – guess what, *Doppelganger Days* by my buddy, when I got a call from the great lady herself. She apologised profusely for disturbing me during a weekend and asked me whether I knew the whereabouts of the author of the book that I held in my hand.

When I replied in the negative, wondering to myself whether the curious consultant would have been very keen on my revealing his whereabouts on a week-end afternoon even if I was aware of it, it did nothing to elevate her spirits. For a couple of minutes she kept me entertained with a monologue on the sense of responsibility or the lack of it in some very senior and very brilliant professionals. A trait which she advised – almost beseeched – me to avoid.

Having extracted my grudging promise that I would pick responsibility and maturity over brilliance whenever faced with the horns of dilemma, she rang off with the intimation that Ramesh was looking for Pritam and if I happened to come across him in person or over phone, email, sms or any connecting medium, I would have to inform him to call either the great man himself or to get in touch with his emissary.

After silence had mercifully been restored to the Saturday calm, I debated whether there was cause for action. Several chauvinists of old would have no doubt frowned on me at not jumping on my steed and riding off in all directions at the entreaty of a lady, but there were several factors to consider.

It was a debatable question whether the Sir Lochinvars and the Sir Galahads of old would have troubled their gallant selves by getting too close to the fire breathing dragons if asked by a woman whose waist had gone significantly past the mending magic of the best available corset. My primary doubt, however, concerned the willingness of the hunted man to being tracked down. However, ten minutes later, I decided that a call could not do any harm and used the emergency Gupta-van der Wiel one touch method to dial his number.

He answered on the twelfth ring.

"Simon, my friend," came his cheery greeting in the foreground of the colourful cacophony associated with the livelier parts of Amsterdam during a Saturday summer evening. "Has my apartment burnt down? Yours is probably the twenty fifth call I have received in the last couple of hours, the first one I have answered."

On hearing my exclamation of surprise, he elaborated.

"I've had calls from Madhu Deb, which I obviously didn't pick up on this very special of days. I am walking around Amsterdam with a most interesting girl who is a part of my *karass* ..."

I asked him to repeat that ...

"Well, look it up in Wikipedia. However, with such excitement in my life, I am not in the right mood for the latest Hidori anecdote. However, it followed with phone-calls from ... er – well – the entire *tai chi* class in short."

I told him that I was honoured to be the one whom he graced with a reply and informed him that the matronly lady in question did not really want to talk about Hidori. In fact, the phone call I had recently concluded with her had been the first one in my immediate memory in which she had spent more than five minutes without springing her son into the scheme of things.

"You intrigue me. There must be something rotten in the state of Noord-Holland in that case. Murder most foul? I do know, however, that certain probable suicides have not taken place. Dead people don't generally call your cell phone. So, what's new?"

I informed him that the Big Boss had been trying to establish connection with him and the venture had reached me through the system of delegation that has become a part and parcel of the organisational value system.

"Ah, Simon, Simon ... please stop before you get knee deep into your curious corporate consciousness canon. Did you hear that, Shruti? The alliterative affliction spreads with intimate infection. But, then, Simon, it clears the mystery of calls going down the steps of the organisational ladder. As also it clears the mysterious ring from a peculiar number before this concatenation of calls. Is our great man on the other side of the Atlantic? European cells cease to work in the land of opportunities. I guess he has turned multi-cellular to face the challenges of the New World."

I told him that Madhu Deb had not been very impressed with his unavailability.

"Don't worry about it Simon, it is a frailty of the fairer sex ... something I would have shouted out to you were I not in the company of an intellectually formidable specimen of that very species."

My friends seemed to be in very high spirits and he was about to return to his world of delight after thanking me for the news when a sudden thought occurred to me.

"Buddy, half a sec. The name that you just took ... Shruti ... is this the same one who is your wife? I mean, is she here?"

The smooth flow of rhetoric that was so characteristic of my friend when in the best of moods was suddenly interrupted. There dawned on the cellular connection what seemed to be a pensive pause.

"A web of confusion, Simon. A dream concocted on a midsummer night. The answer is yes and no."

I confessed that I was being hurtled into darkness.

"That is a good thing, Simon, for what has enlightenment brought us but lives rushed through at breakneck pace?"

He did not elaborate any further and rang off.

I spent some time wondering about the peculiar message. There was no doubt that my friend was enjoying his day with an interesting lady. What surprised me was his elusiveness in answering my question. I had not really given it much thought, but in the long hours that I have spent discussing everything under the sun with this curious friend of mine, not once had he mentioned his wife. I picked up *Doppleganger Days* again and looked at the short author bio. It spoke of his association with martial arts, with the software industry, with investigative journalism. It said nothing of his family.

I went back to reading what was an engrossing story written in excellent style. It was after quite a while that I got up to prepare dinner and my cellular phone jumped to life with the distinctive ring tone that was used in the Gupta-van der Wiel method.

When I answered, the voice was sombre and the erudite effervescence, although present as ever, was focussed on a mission.

"Now is the time for all good men to come to the aid of their buddy. Are you there to offer your ready help?"

I asked him what the matter was.

"Unforecasted trouble brews darkness around the western corners of the sky, but out of this nettle we must pluck this flower. Forgive me if I am in the quotation mode, for the eternal women beckon us upwards. To cut a long story short, can you arrange a table for four in the excellent establishment called the *Magic Pot* on Thursday evening? We shall go directly after *tai chi*."

I wondered aloud at the collective pronoun ...

"Ah, buddy ... what did I say about now being the time to separate the men from the boys? Thursday seems excellent. I have looped in the good doctor ..."

"The psychiatrist?"

"The same. I know very well that you want to meet him again. You will be there too. And so will Shruti ..."

I must have cleared my throat at the mention of the name, because his voice became grim.

"Strange are the ways of the world. What seems and what is and the plenty that is in between may fill up pages and pages of exciting story telling. However, Simon, I believe that we should never try to explain. A friend won't need explanations and others won't be convinced anyway. So, when I tell you Shruti is going to be a member of our select gathering, please note that she is a friend for the time being."

I said that I really did not need explanations and his personal life was no business of my own.

"That's what I like about you, buddy," he effused. "You may be wondering about the sudden emergency nature of the meeting. I am suddenly beckoned overseas, nay, over oceans, hastily summoned by our Big Boss. There seems to be lined a serious conference in Pasadena, Los Angeles, where he wants our monumental work to be showcased. This journey of a thousand leagues must of necessity begin with this single indispensible step."

Groping about in the maze of oratory, I could make out that K.Ramesh had summoned him to the good old west coast with a compendium of ideas to present at a seminar in California.

"It is a combined venture of Washington Mutual, Union Bank of California, IndyMac Bank and Chase Manhattan. They are in some sort of collaboration with Berkeley and some other godforsaken universities. It is supposedly the epoch making moment when our names will be engraved in the gold that's disappearing from the world. Goddammit, Simon. I believe Banking Institutions are more dangerous to our liberties than standing armies. You know buddy, I did not say that. In fact, no one of the modern times said that ... you know who did?"

I did not.

"Thomas Jefferson. One of the founding fathers of your adopted country which will be graced with my footsteps shortly. In fact, in a strange coincidence, Jefferson also smoked hemp. And never in the history of mankind have those words rung truer than now, when the world is reeling under the financial turmoil caused by banks."

I agreed wholeheartedly, but could not help wondering what our motley group of a psychiatrist, a writer-martial artist- consultant, and a Dutch-Irish-American hybrid working for an Indian firm could do to help him, even if this mysterious Shruti joined forces.

"The need of the hour is ideas, my friend, helped along by the Magic Pot. Please ensure a ready supply of the Bong and its contents ... the strength limited to ensure a long lasting meeting."

With this curious communication, he rang off once again.

And as so often happens after conversations with my buddy that are so intriguingly on the borderline of professionalism and absurdity, I was filled with exhilarating anticipation. A delicious streak of the unpredictable had popped up in the otherwise metronomic life.

Cheers
Simon

Part VII:

Volatility Risk Lover and Amor-tisation

XXXVIII

The day had started on wings of expectation and had progressed to the heavenly Amsterdam City Tour. The hour long bumpy ride through the cloudy summons of K. Ramesh had been an aberration, but seat belts had been tightened with the curious meeting set up for Thursday, with the promise of happy landing.

The end rolled in with a prolonged dinner, varying pressures conveying complicated meanings through brushes of hands, a brace of hugs lingering that wee bit longer and promise of future tête-à-tête. Sandeep could feel the lips of his soul part in a smile, and creative juices rush through the opening.

He was filled with an ardent desire to write. No, not about Shruti or the sights of Amsterdam or the subjects of philosophy, society and literature dissected through the day. The dormant piles of stacked up ideas inside him seemed to have been sparked with a philosopher's stone. The long day had left him tired. But, even then, there had to be a couple of keys pressed before bed ... a passage, as short as a couple of paragraphs, needed to be written. It was an irrevocable command of his innermost being that could not be postponed.

However, his day had far from ended. As he ran up the stairs of his Maarten Lutherweg apartment building, tired legs being lent the lightness of inspiration, he was brought up short in front of his flat by the vigilant figure of Amrita.

"Wh ... wow ... you ... you scared me."

Amrita looked at him with what seemed like reproach. She was close to tears.

"Where were you? I've been calling you all day... why weren't you taking calls?"

The voice was demanding, even accusing. Sandeep stopped in his tracks. He looked at the pathetic figure of the girl in front of him and raised his eyebrows.

"I was busy. I rejected your calls. When you kept calling I had no option but to add your number to the screened list."

Amrita looked at him, brows knitted together and a pair of rheumy eye displaying pained reproach.

"Does it ever occur to you that I worry?"

Sandeep shrugged.

"Sorry, it didn't. It slipped my mind. I don't want this at this time of the night. I am tired and have work to do. And I seem to remember asking you not to come up here."

The girl looked away and sobbed.

"Please. Please don't start that same old story of tears and self pity. I thought with you exercising and all that, you had become positive."

He walked past the dejected figure and approached his door.

"But, I am following whatever you have told me to do. I am exercising twice a day."

"I can't keep coming up here with the threat of finding you lurking in the corner. Can't you just stay at home and read a good book?"

Amrita held on to the rails and sobbed again.

"You think I am here to create a scene. To throw a tantrum. Whatever I say sounds like self pity to you."

Sandeep put the key in the lock. The peaceful inspiration within him had been wiped clean by dark fumes of misguided emotion. He felt tired.

"I don't want to argue. I have plenty of things to do. Please leave right now."

Amrita turned towards him with disbelieving eyes.

"I'll go. But I came for another reason."

"And what's that?"

The girl closed her eyes.

"Today was *Karwa Chauth*."

"What?"

"I haven't eaten or even had a drop of water all day."

"What?"

"I cannot ... I could not ... Until I saw you."

"At the risk of repeating myself, what?"

Amrita opened her eyes, confusion written large in them.

"*Karwa Chauth* ... you surely know about that?"

Sandeep squeezed his temples.

"I know it from those formula films of Bollywood. It's a fast, right? One of those sickening rituals, a relic of the middle ages? In which the anaemic heroine ends up fainting?"

Amrita's eyes grew wide.

"You perform that sort of a thing sitting in the hub of modern Europe? Whole day without food or water? Are you crazy?"

Amrita closed her eyes again.

"Yes, I am," she said softly.

"And for God's sake, why did you have to see me before ..."

"Girls have to see their husbands before they can eat ..."

"Oh Christ... Jesus ... what kind of balderdash is this?"

There was fearful incomprehension in Amrita's eyes.

"What kind of *what* is this?

"Balderdash. Nonsense. Height of ... please leave. I will go crazy."

The pitiable vulnerability had disappeared from Amrita's eyes, replaced by something close to disappointed anger.

"You think my fast is nonsense ... Can I help it if my heart has accepted you as a husband? I did not drink a drop of water even though I trained as you said ..."

"What?"

" ... to you it is nothing but nonsense and big words for nonsense, isn't it?"

Sandeep looked at her again.

"Just a minute. You ... you trained today."

"Twice."

"What did you do?"

There was a haughty look in her eyes now.

"How does it matter to you?"

Sandeep closed his eyes now.

"It does not matter to me, but it does to common sense. If you have run as much as I have asked you to and have done every routine, and have had nothing to eat or drink, it is a miracle that you are still walking about without fainting like Lucie Manette."

"Like whom?"

But Sandeep had opened his door and rushed in. He rummaged his fridge and came out with a carton of orange juice.

"Please. Do me the favour of drinking this. Bottoms up ..."

The hand was shaking when it received the carton. She looked at Sandeep with eyes that had changed again to something nearing worship as she lifted it to her lips.

Sandeep looked about. It was too dark to see what was going on in the balcony of Gunjan's apartment, but something told him that the whining wimp was taking in each and every detail.

"You know, Karva Chauth is supposed to end with a drink from the hand of the husband..."

Sandeep uttered something monosyllabic and guttural. He was as shocked as the sensibilities of the crazy Indian girl who stood in front of him. A girl who broke into a supposed relationship between a husband and a wife and managed to consider herself righteous enough to observe rituals, a girl who worked in one of the most modern cities of the world for a multinational bank and still swore by age old traditions of the past, a girl who clung on with an illusion of love and became more of a burden by the minute.

"Get out of here, I beg you," Sandeep shouted. "And please don't come to my class for a few days. Till by some miracle you develop a semblance of sense."

He shut the door on her face and switched off his cell phone. He tried to sit in front of his laptop, but could not write any more.

Morning after.
Cellphone restarted.
Eleven messages received.

22:25 Amrita: You have made my way very clear. Thank you. Keep well

22:31 Amrita: If you wanted me out of your life, you could have told me so at the very outset. You need not have killed me with such cruelty.

22:39 I have taken a bunch of sleeping tablets. I am feeling drowsy.

22:43 You must be enjoying yourself – watching me die this way

23:04 My very last question to you. Do you have a heart or is it stone?

23:11 I beg of you, let me hear your voice once. Please.

23:14 You never wanted me, did you?

23:21 You are a teacher. Why do you want me off your class?

00:12 You are heartless, goodbye

00:27 Hope you have a nice life once I am gone. With novels and big words. What can an illiterate girl who does not know English, who is superstitious, offer you?

00:51 You won't answer. I know you won't.

∾ ∾ ∾

Sandeep looked at the round-faced young kid sitting across the table. To say that he had heard a lot about him would be the greatest understatement since 1949 when Popular Mechanics had prophesised that computers of the future might weigh no more than 1.5 tonnes. He had grown to dread the name. But, now, as the innocent face behind the name stared, sizing him up silently, he smiled in response.

"Can't decide whether or not to trust me, eh?" he asked, as Hidori looked with a lot of apprehension at the offered Sultana biscuit. "I am sorry I don't have any sweets. I am not a big fan of sweets, and I live alone, you know. That's why I guess some people say that I am bitter in my writing. Funny but bitter."

Hidori looked at him without lifting his face and joined his hands together.

"I don't like sweets," he said in a refined British accent.

Sandeep smiled.

"Ah, that makes us share something common," he liked the chubby cheeks and the short prickly hair. "Although that contradicts with some of the stories concerning brownies ..."

"I like brownies," the kid remarked, his eyes sparkling for a moment, perhaps wondering if there were any on offer.

"Ah, so you do. I'm afraid I don't have brownies either. I don't often admit it but I am over thirty and this is not the time of life to indulge in sweets. But, then, have you decided whether you want the biscuit? Your mom will be back soon ..."

Picking up the biscuit gingerly, Hidori started nibbling.

"Ah, there you go. Incidentally, I have heard so much about you that meeting you was almost like déjà vu. You understand? No? Well, I guess I will never be much of a writer for kids. Avoid my stuff till you turn fifteen or so, when you start getting the inkling that all those moral stories about respecting elders and authorities, being honest and all that rot actually amounts to snowballed conspiracy. But, then, tell me ... how did you come here?"

At a sudden question that made sense to him, Hidori became more communicative ... stretching his input to two sentences.

"In a car. Mama drove."

Sandeep looked anxiously at his watch. It was twenty minutes since Madhu Deb had dropped Hidori and gone off on her mission.

"That's a shame. Your Mama must be tired after working the full week. You should have driven."

Hidori looked at him with round eyes, trying to figure out whether he was kidding. Sandeep looked deadpan, even agitated. The child concluded that it was a genuine question.

"I can't drive," he conceded.

"You can't? Haven't you turned eighteen yet?"

"No. I am four."

Sandeep went to the window and looked out into the lazy Sunday morning.

"You could have biked here, with Mama on the passenger seat."

Hidori turned glum.

"I can't cycle," he confessed.

Sandeep turned towards him with rounded eyes.

"You can't cycle? How can you say that? You are in the Netherlands."

"Mama says she will teach me next year. No one in my class can cycle, except for the Dutch children."

Sandeep nodded.

"Dutch children are different, I agree with you on that. They are born on a *fietsen*."

The kid looked at him with puzzled eyes.

"Didn't you know? Dutch kids come out of their Mamas' tummies riding a bike. They actually cycle around a lot when they are in there. That's why you see so many of these kids cycling before they can actually walk without a waddle."

The small eyebrows knit themselves in an effort to detect some mischief in the words of the strange grown-up. He was still thinking when there was the unmistakable sound of energetic bounding and his mother came rushing into the apartment.

Madhu Deb was clad in a track suit, her cheeks red from the climb and her short hair in disarray.

"Talk of Sunday morning excursions."

She flopped herself down on a sofa.

Sandeep looked embarrassed.

"I'm sorry ... you must have rushed over. But, eleven sinister text messages can make even the steadiest man reel. I switched off the cell at night, and switched it on again at seven in the morning. Got all at one go ... I did not really read them in sequence ... It was a shock."

The good lady nodded.

"I can understand. I myself could not stand the tension after you called me. I got in the car, went back to the toilet ... and a lot of ...," she broke off. "Actually I had blood in my urine."

"Oh my God."

"That's okay. I have it sometimes in times of extreme tension. And thanks to living with a NPD, problems haven't been too rare."

Sandeep opened the fridge and retrieved a carton of orange juice.

"Thanks. While driving down here I received your last text message. That was scary in itself. What did you mean?" she fumbled for her Nokia and retrieved the annoying piece of communication. "*Went for a run around the apartment clusters. No excitement.* Now what was that supposed to mean?"

Sandeep smiled uneasily.

"I ... I didn't know what to expect. If she had really done something, I guess there should have been some ..."

Madhu Deb waved her hand.

"She didn't do anything. These are tricks of manipulation. It's good you didn't read the messages at night. You wouldn't have been able to sleep. The biggest problem for me was to find an excuse to ring the bell this early in the morning. That too on a Sunday. I made up a cock and bull story of wanting a couple of girls to help me out with the next edition of Sur-Soiree ... with some trips to Brussels. I could see she was depressed, with chronic weeping..."

"She wept?"

"I saw this show on TV last week," Hirdori piped in from the table, with solemn gravity. "They showed the baby being born in Groningen. But there was no cycle."

Madhu Deb, who had opened her mouth to speak, lost her thread.

"Cycle?"

Sandeep shushed him.

"Come on, why do you think they showed it on television? Because it was special. The first time a Dutch baby born without a cycle."

Hidori went back to nibbling his biscuit thoughtfully.

"What was that all about?" his mother asked.

"I was just giving him some metaphorical fable about Dutch cycling skills. But, was she weeping in public?"

"Yes, sir. I noticed a remarkable difference. All these days, whenever anyone with authority – from Ajay Yadav to Govind – has tried to get her to do anything, she has fought back like a tigress. She has seemed answerable to no one. She has been living in some dream in which nothing can happen to her. And now she is shattered. You should have done it days back, Pritam, when I had asked you to. She has to come out of her imaginary paradise. It will be more painful now that you have encouraged ..."

"Madhu-di, I have not encouraged her. I was her teacher as far as *tai chi* is concerned and slowly eliminated encroachments into my life. I withdrew from all the ridiculous problems of English and Mathematics she came up with. And then she threatened me for the first time. I withdrew further and then tried to snap her out of the negativity with physical exercise. It seemed to be working ... Then she was back yesterday with all her drama about *karwa chauth.*"

There was a knowing smile on Madhu Deb's lips and a twinkle in her eye.

"Ah ... who are you trying to kid, Pritam? Couldn't you make out that she was falling more and more for you when you started helping her out with something that can be intimate like physical training? Anyway, today she was almost defenceless. She started sobbing and then weeping uncontrollably when I started talking to her. I asked her what the matter was and she became stubbornly silent. After three or four attempts, I asked her whether she had fallen in love and she started out on another fit of sobs."

"What did she ultimately say?"

"She did not say anything. I spent all this while counselling her ... telling her that life has to go on and whatever her problem, she is not the first in history faced with it. But, all that's past. All you should do now is to stick to the decision of not letting her attend classes. She has to grow out of it, and you have to help her. By being detached."

Sandeep looked towards Hidori who sat fingering a volume by Karel Capek from the pile of books on the dining table, still nibbling his biscuit.

"Don't worry about him. The moment he understands that the conversation is out of his familiar territory, he goes into a world of his own. He's probably still thinking of the bike. You have some weird imagination. But, it is this mechanism of a self sufficient little world of his own which will probably help him survive the relationship between his parents."

She looked dreamily at her son.

"I know it's difficult, Pritam, but I hope you have learnt your lesson yesterday. Personality Disorder patients actually delight in sucking life out of you. And you have been through a lot of trouble through no fault of yours. Surgical break. That's what is needed."

She paused and drank her juice.

"I don't say it's easy, mind you. I spoke to you about the affair that I had – after I got married. I was mad about him. I wanted to turn my back to the society and live with him. I wanted to move out of my house. He did not agree. I felt jilted. I screamed at him. I thought he was heartless. But, now I realise. He knew what he was doing. There would never have been the stability in my life as there is now, especially after Hidori. Sometimes you have to do that for mutual benefit ..."

"Madhu-di, I did not have an affair with her."

The lady smiled.

"Look, it is up to you to name it whatever you want. Relationship, affair, tiff ... But, there is a connection between the two of you ..."

"I would not say connection. I would much prefer interactions."

She lay her hand on his.

"Whatever. People connect at different levels. This is not the first time you have worried about her and not all the worry has been caused by death threats. You have been decent, but there are different sorts of relationships. You got trapped into one that is not a very pleasant one. And now, you need to put it behind you. When are you going to the United States?"

"Huh? Two weeks to put the finishing touches to our paper. And then off I go."

She put her arm around him.

"Use this opportunity. Just get cut off from her. Time will heal her, don't you worry. And now, there is an excellent place I know in Binnenhof. Can we go out together and have a bite of breakfast?"

XXXIX

Mail from Kailash Nayak to Sandeep

Hi Sandeep,

The Shakespeare Society guy has added the promise of a photograph on the first page of the City Supplement of The Telegraph *into the bargain. For an all time low price of 20000. He cannot understand your hesitation. As a matter of fact, neither can I. 'New born author' that you are, you should be gurgling in delight at his benevolence. Can we have a better man in place to decide what should go into the University 'Curryculum'?*

I don't know whether you can access the Indian television channels in the Netherlands. I guess you can, with so many websites streaming to the 'tastes' of the NRI. Next week is full of literary entertainment. The damned booker winner is on prime time to talk about the geometry of unbridled liberty, whatever that may be, on India TV. And with What seems to be the Problem? *premiering shortly in theatres, with a dance number by Shadab Khan in the fare, our friend Pran Mehra will be one of the guest judges of Indian Idol. He is also scheduled to take part in the Dance Program – Jhalak Dikhla Ja.*

It is a synthesis of media. Literature, please pardon my use of the word in the same page as Pran Mehra, has stepped out of books and is merrily swinging hips on television. When I heard about it, I could not sleep a wink at night, fearing the possibility of turning on my television set one day and finding Mayank Manhas shaking his legs with some nubile professional danseuse.

I also spoke to Ms Deshpande of Walrus. However, she said she can recommend you, but in addition to her recommendation, you have to send periodic reminders to make sure that your manuscripts are actually read. The readers employed in major publishing houses are woefully short of time to read.

I hope as a writer you still manage some time to write. But, I will advise you to groom yourself with proper dancing lessons and award receiving deportment for your future growth.

The only other idea I have to set you off in the writing industry is to hire someone like Mallika Sherawat to model for your books. Picture her standing there, with only the cover of your book running diagonally across her wonderful bosom, leaving the audience eager to turn the pages ...

I leave you with this delightful thought.
K

∾ ∾ ∾

"Hello dear," Madhu Deb sang out in her characteristic vim and vigour.
Amrita looked up from her machine.
"Hi Madhu-di."
"Are you hungry?"
"Not really. It is not even half past eleven."
The lady laughed and put her arm around her team member.
"You will be in a moment. Come, let's step out, I need some protein."

They sat in the nearby *Food Court.*
"I really don't have an appetite," Amrita remarked. She was sitting with the menu thrust under her nose.
Madhu Deb ordered for both of them.
"Trust me, you will like it." Her voice was calm, knowing, comforting.
The waiter withdrew and the senior manager looked closely at Amrita's face.
"What's bothering you?"
"Nothing."
She tried to smile, but it did not come through.
The older lady nodded sagaciously.
"People notice you. They notice things. And some of them care."
Amrita's expression changed. A frown hesitantly formed on her forehead.
"Who notices things? And who are the people who care?"
Her scowl was met by a smile.
"I do for one. I have seen you depressed for quite a while now. The way you wept yesterday was quite revealing."
Amrita fiddled with her spoon.
"It's nothing."
"Come on girl, you can tell me. Is something wrong?"
"No."
"Everyone okay at home? Back in India?"
"Yes."
"Are you missing your parents?"
This produced a shrug.
"They don't miss me."
"Do you miss them?"

"No."

The chubby face went up and down in small movements signifying comprehension.

"Do you keep in touch with folks back home?"

"I talk to them once a week," Amrita answered. "Why are you asking all these questions?"

The good lady took a deep breath.

"Have you fallen in love?"

Amrita looked up sharply. The manager was watching her closely. She met her gaze with puzzled eyes and then looked away.

There was a long period of silence. The waiter brought the bowls of Caeser salad. Amrita nibbled it for a while.

"I don't like this stuff," she said all of a sudden. "Would you mind if I do not eat?"

Madhu Deb laughed. These people knew so little about things.

"That's just the salad, silly. The main dish is on its way."

Amrita winced. That probably meant another hour of grilling questions.

"I am not hungry."

"Have you given up eating? What for? Love?"

Again Amrita looked away without answering.

"You don't want to answer. But remember something that I say. Not as a boss. I know you do not report to me directly and even if you did, it would not be appropriate for me to say all this. Even then, as an older and wiser friend, I will give you some advice. Always be careful about the object of love. If it is beyond reach, it is better not to extend your arm."

Amrita excused herself and went to the washroom. She did not return to office after lunch.

~ ~ ~

Blog of Simple Simon
Tags: Taichi, Shanzi, Philosophy

It was a hectic day which ended with a display of immense brilliance almost fragrant with love for an art, strangely augmented with sadness.

Flitting from one demanding task to another, I was looking forward to our *tai chi* class. Apart from the Project Management Office reports due every Monday morning, there was the additional responsibility of contacting Alex at the Magic Pot to book a nice spacious table and arrange for smooth psychoactive substances – another deliciously insane demand of the crazy consultant who is my buddy sifu.

I was held up in the most annoying manner on the verge of closing shop, by the perpetually worried senior person in the organisation whose life seemed to depend on the modification of certain figures in a report.

I reached the gym ten minutes after the scheduled start and was surprised to find my buddy sitting alone on the top of an exercise ball, deep in thought.

"Hi Simon," he offered in not too cheery a tone. "I am afraid it's just you and me today."

I asked where the others were.

"Caught up in life," he responded with a sigh. "The key, Simon, is to weave your passion into the fabric of your life. If it has not become as natural and necessary as breathing, it does not make any sense to go through the motions."

He looked and sounded dejected. Justifiably so. Here was a guy into multiple activities, balancing his profession as a consultant, persona as a writer, passion as a martial artist and plight as a collaborator in some fuzzy, world changing work with the top boss. He took the trouble of sneaking off for an hour each evening to share his expertise in *tai chi* and *chin na*. And now people who had demanded the time were turning their collective backs and he sat there alone, wondering whether anyone would have the decency to show up and tell him whether the class was on or not.

"Simon, I will not be here for too many days," my buddy continued. "And if you have grown to love the art, find a school before I leave so that you can continue to train without inertia of rest creeping in."

I told him that I wanted to do so anyway.

"There is something I want to show you," Pritam said and walked to the corner of the dojo. On the top of his bags lay a small wooden box – with decorative oriental characters embossed on it. Pritam opened it and revealed a set of exquisitely carved Chinese fans.

He took hold of one of them and following a graceful flick of his wrist, the decorated object unravelled itself into a flourishing semicircle etched with far eastern calligraphy. I exclaimed in wonder.

"This is called a *shanzi*," he said. "An ancient weapon. One of the most beautiful instruments to aid warfare, with the probable exception of Mata Hari. I was fortunate enough to learn some of the *shanzi* forms from Sifu Schmidt in a recent camp here in Amsterdam. I was fascinated by the flowing grace of the movements. I ordered one to be made after sometime, when my monetary ... well , when I settled down in HMH anyway. And after a few days, I modified the order to make it a set of five."

He arranged four of them in a semi circle and asked me to choose one.

"I wanted to gift one to each of you, the ones who have stuck through the few months ... and I wanted to pass on some of the fan forms and techniques as well ...," he paused and I could see him carefully feeling his way before continuing. "But, these are things of beauty ... things that need to be handled with love, care and respect. I would hate to see them fall into the careless undeserving hands ... forgotten in the corner of a table loaded with banalities. Anyway, now that you are here, should we spend an hour practising some forms with these?"

Each of the words seemed to nurse some deep injury. I looked at him with concern, but by then he had already adopted his posture of beginning class. The hour that followed with the *shanzi* was one of the most stirring of my life and this leans more towards an understatement than an exaggeration. I have seen Pritam perform *tai chi* routines before, but with the folding fans, it was elegance of a different strata. There were moments when he seemed to be spiritually merged with the weapon. In some of the popular snippets of online Zen literature, I have often read about the artist becoming merged with his art. The true meaning of the imagery now dawned on me. I observed as much, to his considerable embarrassment. In a selfish way I was thankful that the others had not turned up. It was the best training I could hope to get.

After the hour, I started asking questions about some of the more complicated *chin na* techniques. My instructor was in a state of trance. He went into detailed explanation of each stretch of the joints, the removal of the muscle from the tendon, the pressure on the extended tissue. The science behind the manoeuvres was explained with a degree of depth to which he had never taken us before. While I am amused by his social commentary and unorthodox corporate behaviour, his understanding of the martial art and its innermost secrets left me fascinated. As I read over this blog again, I realise that it reads like a prolonged eulogy, but then, I unabashedly confirm that I am an admirer.

We did not look at the time. It was long past the normal closing hours of the class when pangs of hunger hit both of us almost simultaneously. At half past nine, neither of us wanted to go home and cook. We made for the nearest Chinese restaurant. There were other eateries nearby, ranging from Indonesian delicacies to the atrocities of burger and french-fries, but somehow, after a prolonged session of tai chi, we both wanted Chinese food.

While eating I remarked about the absence of other students, at least one notably being the very first instance in all these months.

Pritam's answer was esoteric.

"I was flattered when you talked of the artist being one with the art. That is the target that any student should aspire for. However, when the art tends to become one with the teacher, you only delude yourself, drag the art to lower depths."

I wondered what he meant, and went on eating the noodles and Peking duck expecting elucidation. However, my friend fell silent.

After a while I asked him whether everything was okay with all the students.

"Did you as a kid read the *Charge of the Light Brigade,* Simon?" he asked in response.

I was surprised and answered that I had indeed learnt it by heart in junior school.

"In it you will recall two excellent phrases. Ours not to wonder why, ours not to make reply."

I laughed and said that I got his point and was sorry for snooping around.

"I don't think you were snooping around. You were concerned. That's commendable. And as a friend you can ask me any question. You know why I quoted those two lines?"

He paused while enjoying a fleshy portion of the duck's wing.

"It is because of the dojo that we share, the art that we pursue. The mind of the martial artist needs to be still, peaceful. It is like the water in a tranquil lake. As long as the water is still, the trees and birds and the passing clouds are reflected in it with absolute accuracy. However, the moment the water is disturbed, the images get distorted. As long as it remotely concerns our dojo, keep yourself away from the disturbances. Only absorb the lessons. Not my words. From Munenori to Bruce Lee, everyone agrees on these."

It was another of the multiple faces of this peculiar person, the clandestine consultant, the closet writer, the passionate philosopher and the martial arts maestro.

⁂

Simon was still thinking of what he had said when his cell phone rang. He looked at the name flashing on the display and said, "Talk of the Devil."

"Munenori or Bruce Lee?" Sandeep asked.

"Amrita," Simon winked.

Sandeep frowned. It was ten in the night. His mind worked quickly.

"Hello ... Ah, yes, hi ...No, it's okay, I am not in bed ... In fact, I am not even home ... Still in Amsterdam... You okay? I mean you didn't turn up for the class ... Ah yes, the class did take place, though it's only me and Pritam ... No, Trisha was not there and neither was Madhu ... Ah, we were in class quite late, till ..."

Simon looked on with a strange expression on his face as his cell phone was whisked away from his hand. With his hand on the speaker, Sandeep mouthed "Emergency" and put the phone to his ear.

"Till when? Simon? .... Simon? Hello?"

The voice was edgy, frenzied. The answers demanded rather than asked. Sandeep listened for a while. In the background he could make out the noise of a passing car and the voices of a couple of pedestrians.

Text messages:
Amrita to Sandeep

It was a good way to cut me out of your life.

I was the most regular student you had. Do you think it was just for you that I went to the class? Do you think I don't care for tai chi?

If you wanted to punish me, you succeeded.

Madhu Deb to Sandeep
It was the correct decision. Don't worry.

Madhu Deb to Amrita
Are you okay?

Madhu Deb to Trisha
Quite an eventful day!

Trisha to Madhu Deb
You can say that.

Madhu Deb to Trisha
I believe Pritam has asked Amrita to discontinue classes for a while.

Trisha to Madhu Deb
?? I am surprised. Is that why Amrita reacted like that, going home after lunch!! Gosh. Drop it.

Amrita to Madhu Deb
Please stop worrying about me. You have already done enough.

Madhu Deb to Amrita
I can't help it. I feel responsible for you. So, I tend to worry.

Amrita to Madhu Deb
The actual problem is that you think you are God.

Sandeep looked at the messages received after switching on his cell phone. He felt tired. Standing in Station Zuid, he knew that Amrita was still out of doors, either in front of his apartment or near the main entrance. She was waiting for him, eager to fight her losing battle – a battle that had no end. Conversations with no conclusion. It was the conflict that seemed to sustain her. She thrived on it, hung on to it.

She must have called him dozens of times, grown restless and turned to Simon to try and find his whereabouts.

His cell phone rang. He saw Amrita's name come up on the screen and rejected the call. She called again, and again ... with an interim message – "*Please answer the phone. I just want to talk to you.*"

Sandeep put the cell phone on mute, wondering what to do. This was probably a good time to get out of this borrowed life. A pity. He had all but settled down. He was really looking forward to the trip to California. He had never been to the West Coast. Why not try peddling his literary stuff physically in the land of opportunities? Or soak the experience, to be squeezed out into the concoctions of his future works.

But, this night, he was at a loss. There would be the dark forlorn figure, lurking in the doorway, for another verbal joust, the unreasonable demands, the irrational fear of being abandoned and the tear-filled manipulation. He looked at his cell phone, it showed 12 missed calls. The gadget started blinking again, with Amrita's name appearing hauntingly on the screen. He wondered whether there was a chance to sleep in the studio at Jordaan.

A 51 going towards Westwijk approached. Half a dozen people got off. Sandeep toyed with the idea of getting on. He looked at his cell-phone. It was blinking again. The girl was persistent, he had to give that to her.

He looked again. The name on the screen was not the one that he had come to dread. It was, in fact, completely unexpected, a discovered delight.

"Hello," he gasped.

From the other end, the warm, friendly voice seemed to work miraculously against the chill.

"I hear the ding-dong of a closing metro door. Is the author braving the cold to research his novel late in the night? I was afraid that I would be disturbing you just as you had curled up inside the warm blanket."

Sandeep smiled.

"No such luck, mevrouw. I know you are the damsel, but it is I who am in distress."

"Indeed? I was wondering if you could provide me with an idea, but I guess your problem is greater than mine. What is it? Have you been locked out?"

"Looking at it from some angles, yes."

"Oh dear, are you out in the cold?"

"Not now, with your warm voice pouring through my ear."

"I don't think my cell phone service provider will allow me to provide heating for long."

"I will keep the heat stored in the hump of my memory, a psychological camel walking through the desert of barren human emotions."

"Ingenious metaphor. But, coming back to practicalities, what are you up to or up against? Are these the peculiar problems that you mentioned in your mails? Have they materialised in real life, standing between your door and yourself?"

Sandeep smiled.

"You have hit bullseye. Or is it the bovine eye in these days of sexual equality?"

"Do you have a plan B?"

"A what? Oh, I see. As a matter of fact I was thinking of checking into one of the hotels for the night ..."

"My God. Is it that bad?"

"Worse. I don't know how to get back home unscathed by fury worse than hell. I am really tired ..."

"You spurned a woman?"

Sandeep was amazed.

"What makes you say that?"

"Tracing the literary strain in your words."

"Am I that predictable?"

"When you stick to quotations."

There was a brief pause.

"Would you allow a damsel save you from distress?"

"What did the damsel have in mind? Do you intend to appear before my tormentor, armed to the teeth to fight for my honour?"

" Where are you now?"

"Battling the icy precursors of the North Wind on the platform of Station Zuid."

XL

It was a dark and stormy night. The rain started in droplets and increased to torrents. Sandeep, changing trams at Rudolf Haartplein, got drenched in his jumper. In Amstelveen, standing in the shade outside Sandeep's apartment building, looking intermittently at her watch, Amrita got soaked. The sweeping eddies of rain blew around the city carried by the wind.

When Sandeep ran from the Wiltzanglaan tram stop to the apartment, he was caught in a deluge, but when he entered the small one bedroom kitchen and hall unit, he walked into a towel, a mug of steaming hot chocolate and warmth.

Watching from the rain-swept balcony, even Gunjan was moved to an approximation of pity as he saw the shivering, shrunk form of Amrita under the inadequate shade of the opposite building.

Sandeep, dried and fortified, enclosed Shruti in a grateful hug. It was returned with restorative warmth. He could do with the warmth. So could she.

She stayed alone, the apartment partly financed by her parents. Where were her parents? They had ceased to be a unit. They were not meant to be a *duprass.* Sandeep laughed. That's the beauty of Literature. One can laugh at the shortcomings of life, allude to them in light brushstrokes which cut deep but tickled the funny bone as well. But, where were her parents?

Shruti's father was in Paris, working for a television channel as a news editor. Her mother was in New York. She was with a few artist friends who ran their own gallery. Poor folks. They had been passionate about each other, but had got too caught up in the ways and means to sustain the love that they promised. Passion had slipped through. By the time they got around to creating a secure abode for their affections, there was nothing left to put in it but the teenage girl who remained the only souvenir of the feelings they had once shared. They were still searching all day, but away from each other, for something that they were not at all sure of.

Amrita wiped her soaked forehead and redialled Sandeep's number till her battery ran out. She looked unbelievingly at the temporarily useless device in her hand and flung it into the wet pavement. Water streamed down her face, not all of it was rain. Dialling her number out of something that can perhaps pass for concern, Gunjan was informed that the cell phone was not available.

How long had Shruti been alone? Last four years. Of course, her parents visited her whenever they were able to. The facade and the falsity had been lived together by them till she had reached an age and maturity to pull along on her own. After which the imprisoned butterflies of two creative souls had flown away to flit around for sweetness. Elsewhere. She was largely on her own.

How was she so full of humour? She had nothing to be sad about. Her parents were at last liberated from the rigmarole of social etiquette. She was happy for them. She was happy at having grown up. She did not lack anything. She had received all the love and excellent education. She had her own circle of friends. There were lessons to be learnt from the lives of her parents. Now, could she be party to Sandeep's deep dark secrets that made him a creature of the night, a renegade writer braving the cold and rain on the streets of Amsterdam?

Amrita noticed the approach of a man with an umbrella, but he was too short and fat to be *him.* She sobbed silently. Without her cell phone, she was cut off from the world, alone as she had always been.

The man with the umbrella, in the meantime, came nearer. There was a distinct turn towards her. She looked on with tired eyes as the newcomer approached her. The umbrella was removed to reveal the scraggy features of Gunjan. The bristly moustache, the effeminate build, the round glasses.

"Are you waiting for someone?" the query sounded ridiculous to Amrita. It was true that she enjoyed the rain. However, one did not stand outside on a wet, freezing night in Amstelveen enjoying the downpour just for fun.

"Yes, I am waiting for a friend," she said and looked away.

Gunjan smiled to himself.

"Not too good a friend if she makes you stand in the rain. Or ... is it a he?"

There was mischief in the voice, a pseudo avuncular strain that made Gunjan smile and Amrita squirm.

" Would you like to squeeze in under the umbrella?"

"Aren't your wife and kid at home, Gunjan-da?" Amrita asked, thankful that the rain, that faithful friend of hers, had swept across her face, sharing her sorrows and merging with her tears, hiding her embarrassment.

Gunjan feigned surprise.

"No, they are at a cousin's place in Antwerp. It's strange how your relations sprout up across the globe. I came down when I saw you standing here. Come on, it's late. I will escort you home. Else ...," he paused. "You can come in, dry yourself and get something hot to drink at my place."

Amrita looked sharply at the miserable little man. Her eyes spoke for her. Gunjan took a step back.

"If you are sure your friend will turn up, I will leave you to wait for her ... or him ... whatever ...," he ventured.

Even as he spoke about Amrita and her vigil near his apartment, Sandeep wondered if it was necessary. The girl was crazy, probably an advanced case of mental disorder. But, in her own way, she was faithful in her demented devotion. She had been cornered by some of the big honchos of the company and had refused to be cowered. She had refused to divulge her innermost secrets to Madhu Deb's intrusive benevolence. And here he was, speaking of her feelings and messages to someone who was a complete stranger to her. Was it because he wanted to demonstrate his irresistible charm?

He shook his head. What was he thinking about? He was in the house of a friend being unable to get home past a stalker, someone who was lurking in his doorway, calling him incessantly on his phone, sending him suicide threats.

Shruti smiled at him.

"I can see an inner struggle. Relax, Sandeep. You can stay the night without explanations."

Amrita saw Gunjan's retreating form. The flash in her eyes died down. She was alone in the world as usual. For a fleeting month in her twenty seven years had she felt someone was there to share her burden of life, but again she had been wrong. A third child, unwanted by her parents, she had been going through the struggles of life – always the last on the preference list. She was destined to remain that way. When she had loved it had been with all her heart, with trust that was frightening in its absolute immensity. And she had turned out to be unwanted in the life of her beloved.

True, she knew he was married, but she did not want anything from him ... was this the just return of her trust, her devotion, her sacrifices? She hated this life. She looked at her dead cell phone and cursed. She needed to be connected. It was past eleven. She could not stand here any longer. It was raining and cold. "You have to choose between running home and a running nose ..." She wept. Why did he have to flash in her life and disappear? Why? Why did he try to repair her life with the experimental exercise routines, the English drills? Was she a guinea pig? She needed to ask him. Why did he start working on her and leave just as she was improving? A half finished work of art ... He had to explain. She had to talk to him. Damn the cell phone. She could not be thrown out whenever people took fancy. How could she run home and put the cell phone on charge while waiting here? What to do if he returned and went in while she was away? Should she have given Gunjan the cell phone and asked him to get it charged? What was she thinking about? That creep. That ridiculous letch. In fact Pritam had said something funny about him. "It is my firm belief that he is a closet cross dresser," he had said and Simon had burst out laughing. She had come back to her desk and looked up closet cross dresser on the internet. He was so witty... and she could not understand half of what he said. She had to get down to study ... but how could she do that if he tormented her by moving away? Why? Did he set up Madhu-di, or had she come to her independently? And now Gunjan, the ridiculous closet cross dresser had come over and wanted her to go to his house to dry herself and get something hot to drink. How dare he? Did people get the impression that she was available for anyone? She had to tell him about Gunjan ... and she had to ask him about Madhu-di. And why on earth was she not allowed to attend *tai chi* classes? It was not only for him that she went there. He ...he could be so cruel. How? And where was he? How could he be so late when ...? She was worried. She had to call him. Maybe he had sent her a text message. No, he wouldn't. She was not wanted in his life, or in any one else's.

She started to run towards home.

He was running away from a crazy female who stood waiting for his return, who worshipped him and fantasised of him as her husband, who could be tenderly passionate about him and also send him suicide threats if he did not respond.

"My God," Shruti exclaimed.

And she could not understand half the words he said. Her English vocabulary did not run into triple figures. It was difficult to communicate with her.

"So this was what you meant when you said your mind was full of peculiar problems?"

Sandeep nodded.

"Dementor who thinks she is a veela?"

"I was uncharitable. She knows she is not a veela. And that sustains her. She wallows and thrives on self pity."

"So your literary perusals have taken a back seat?"

Sandeep weighed the question in the vibrating balance of his mind.

"I wonder. In fact, I have done more soul searching in the last few days than ever before. May I be honest?"

"I hope you were not anything but ..."

"I mean honest to the extent of ruthlessness?"

"Ah, that's interesting. Sounds like Dostoyevsky. Or Woody Allen."

Sandeep looked around him. He was wrapped in a quilt on the sofa. Shruti sat near him on her computer chair. They had their palms pressed against warm mugs of hot chocolate.

"I have done very little on the literary front these last few months apart from following up and rework. I have not written a decent sentence."

"Except in mails and sms ..."

"A psychiatrist you will meet on Thursday will have something pretty interesting to say about that. Anyway, when all this was going on ... unable to write, subconsciously, I had thoughts of ploughing the field of life out here, to look at the way the yield grew and later use this germination to fullest extent ... in future writings."

"And that included this stalker?"

Sandeep paused.

"Not exactly. It included her when she was infatuated, it included her when she became smitten and declared her love ... It was merged with my experiences in a foreign land ... but, once she became her present self, with the death threats ... she ..."

"Became too hot to handle."

"Right. I ... should I be ashamed?"

"For not really pulling the plug when the infatuation was revving up?"

"I did try pulling the plug, but not to the extent that high school girls do. I did not stop seeing her, or forbid her to meet me. What I mean is that I was not totally unhappy about the whole thing. It was more than just a kick to my brash, irresistible image. It was a thrill of getting to see unusual human traits at close range. Lots of material for future masterpieces."

Shruti did not respond.

"I was like an observer of human character. Researching for my future magnum opus. You know, there is this sweet little fat lady. Another student of my *tai chi* class. The very same about whom we exchanged the poetic text messages. She considers herself to be an amateur psychiatrist and spoke of all sorts of personality disorders. According to her, this girl has Borderline Personality Disorder. She may or may not be correct. My psychiatric friend requested me to leave such conclusions to qualified doctors. But, it actually got me started on some of the DSM IV characteristics. And there are moments I can swear that I have this Narcissistic thing. I do definitely feel a grandiose sense of importance for my works ..."

He paused.

"Why don't you leave that diagnosis to experts as well?" Shruti asked. "Do you know any author who does not think that his works are important? Any artist for that matter?"

"I guess not. But, was I manipulating the emotions of the girl, by playing the sympathetic good guy?"

Shruti looked straight into his eyes.

"Can you be brutally and ruthlessly honest about the extent of your relationship with her?"

Sandeep smiled.

"I see what you mean. No, I've not poured my creative juices into her. And neither has there been promise of any. But, I have helped her ... I found her offloading more and more of her troubles on me till my mind got cluttered with peculiar problems. And somehow, in the course of time, it had become my responsibility to solve her problems. Almost at gun-point."

"I understand your problems right now, but isn't it even more material for writing?"

"For Jonathan Kellerman, yes. Or for Thomas Harris. I am not the author of spine chilling psychological thrillers."

She was at her door. Neha would be there, probably still awake. She would ask her what she had been doing all this time. She was so nosy. She did not care for her, though. She would have expected a call from her by now if she was really concerned. It was all superficial. But, the cell phone had run out of battery. What was she to do? Should she go in and plug it in ignoring Neha's questions? Or should she prepare some good excuse? Should she ask him what a good excuse could be? How could she? Anyway her phone was dead. And he would not answer his call. Where was he anyway? Was he in the Red Light District? Could he be there? If he was there it would be as a writer ... researching. He would never sleep with one of those women. He had never even tried to make love to her. Did he not like her physically? He liked the fair, tall, sporty Dutch girls. He had said as much when asking her to exercise. Was he making her desirable for him? Just like Daddy Long Legs. Why had he asked her to read it? It was not just because of the English. There were so many books in the world ... She would ask him directly when she could speak to him. Damn her cellphone. She remembered slamming it on the ground once it went dead. What if it didn't work? She had to check it. Else, she would borrow Neha's cellphone for the night. She had to go in ... She put her key in the door.

"There you are ... she is calling again," Sandeep put his phone on mute.

Wasn't it a bit too late? Yes, it was, but the girl was neurotic.

So, why not use the experience to write some psychological novel? After all *Crime and Punishment* was of that genre. Right, Sandeep had read it when he was fourteen and his spine still tingled at the recollection. He needed to read it again. A truly great book should be read in youth, maturity and old age.

Was a real life psychoanalyst going to be there on Thursday? Yes, but not exactly an analyst. A psychiatrist. It would be interesting. Sure. And more than that. The analyst dealt in the world of cognition of modern digital times. By the way, had Shruti read *Confessions of Zeno*? No? It was definitely recommended.

Sandeep decided to switch off his cell phone. Seven calls and three text messages in the last few minutes.

So, what are you reading right now? Not too interesting. *The Economics of European Integration.* Something to scare off Pritam for sure.

Emily Dickinson. Did he like her? Actually he was not well versed in poetry. Well versed? Ha ha.

"Simon and Gurfunkel trivialised her ... note our page with bookmarkers, the moments that we have lost."

"I think the world would be richer if dangling conversations were interspersed with sighs of depth."

"Where did you get hold of a bilingual version of *Ficciones*?"

There, beside the table and the book case, along with the stimulation that possessed him whenever he was with her, he discovered the tension of the last few hours slipping away and a tenderness spreading through him in gently lapping waves.

"Are you okay?" the sleepy voice of Neha reached her as she waited yet again for the call to be answered.

"I am fine."

"I dropped off when you did not get back by half past ..."

"I said I am fine."

"You want some dinner?"

"Please leave me alone."

"The rain has stopped. The moon is out yet again. Amsterdam weather in a nutshell."

Shruti looked out of the window.

"How sweet the moonlight sleeps upon this bank that the rain has made the apartment."

"In such a night as this when the sweet wind did gently kiss the trees, Sandeep methinks mounted the GVB Tram and hurried towards Haarlemmerweg, where Shruti lay that night."

"Becoming poetic are we?"

"By proxy. However, life has been much too graphic for me to turn to poetry at the moment."

They lowered the mugs on the window sill at the same moment and the hands touched, and the fingers tentatively felt their way forward, ultimately becoming intertwined.

"In such a night, did the gallant Shruti rescue the dude in distress from demons and downpour, and warm him up with hot chocolate and compassion."

Their eyes met.

"In such a night did the dude in distress come in desperate for shelter and then attempt to get friendly with his rescuer weaving wizardry of words."

Sandeep turned towards her and drew her close.

"In such a night were the limitations of prose and poetry revealed to the egoistic writer. Nothing that he could pen would hold water to the maiden in moonlight."

"In such a night did the maiden in moonlight detect obnoxious innuendo in the egoistic author's proclamation."

Sandeep held her close to him.

"In such a night did the author bare his soul to the maiden in moonlight, with disclaimers that said no pun intended."

They kissed.

"In such a night did ..."

"Shh ... Jon Donne said it and Tagore repeated. For God's sake, hold your tongue and let me love."

Following the excellent example of the fingers, their bodies entwined. The verbal exchanges made way for gentle physical interactions. The mental stimulation of togetherness changed to delicious physical tingling. The moonlight, in allegiance to the Amsterdam weather, was soon shrouded by clouds. But the magic remained. The age old magic, blossoming love breaking through the dams of restraint.

XLI

Leiden

"Are you sure you won't be missed at office?"

Books sprawled across table and floor, the small apartment was cluttered to the extent of untidiness. In the erudition that cried out from the un-dusted volumes across the space, it was not unlike the flat of Shruti now sweetly ensconced in a very special chamber of Sandeep's memory. The subjects covered were more specialised, though, and completely absent in comparison was any visible effort to put the rest of the apartment in any sort of order.

"No. Right now I am like the love child of the big boss," Sandeep answered. "He wants me to focus on the virtual impossibility of creating a paper on undecided subject matter within two weeks and then to rush across to California to present it. I have said that I have to do some serious research in all the University Libraries of Amsterdam and beyond. I am practically a free spirit for the time being. And I want to keep it that way. I am not venturing near the office or the apartment for the next few days."

Dr. Suprakash Roy nodded with the practised poker face. At eleven in the morning, he was still in his night clothes, the quintessentially Bengali dress of loose pyjamas and wrinkled kurta. He had been in bed when Sandeep had announced himself at his doorstep, dishevelled, tense, yet with a beatific expression on his face.

"A most curious problem. In fact, looking at you and Pritam and then this unfortunate girl ..."

Sandeep objected.

"Excuse me, Sup-da. It is me who is unfortunate ..."

The psychiatrist lifted a finger.

"Ah, yes. As a victim. But I must look at it from the point of view of the patient. This particular case gives me a lot of insights into areas that are linked to my sphere of interest. These threats that you tell me of ... were there any verbal ones?"

Sandeep looked at the researcher who was dissecting his haunted peril with the casual detachment of a scientist. Behind him were bookracks crammed with volumes of psychiatry and vinyl records of Viennese concerts. Was the doctor sane?

"No. No verbal threat. Ever since the first threat, there has been the underlying hint of sorrow, dejection, something not quite all right. It may have been contrived, to keep me on the tenterhooks. However, there has been no occasion when she has gone on record saying that she will commit suicide in as many words. It has always been on sms, on instant messages ..."

"Ah, glory be to the networked world. This phenomena of hounding you with messages, with calls and emails ..."

"What about it?"

"There is a new term in our subject. Legislation systems are waking up to it. Cyberstalking."

Sandeep shook his head irritably.

"I understand you are intrigued at how this new cognitive world is baring its facets in the present case, but please ... I am sitting here facing the crisis. Since last evening I have not been home. I can't switch on my cell phone without being assaulted by text messages and phone calls. And she has gone beyond the cyber world. She has been physically haunting my flat ..."

The doctor agreed sagely.

"I am afraid the physical intrusion took place only when you blocked yourself out of the networked world. That made her desperate."

Sandeep shook his head.

"I couldn't help it ..."

"I don't think that she will do anything more desperate. However, I am much too away from the scene to make a proper diagnosis."

"Madhu-di recommends a surgical break."

"Ah. The amateur psychiatrist. You brought her into the scheme of things didn't you?"

"I ... I had no choice. There I was in the morning, switching my cell phone on and looking at eleven suicide threats."

"Life is complex, Sandeep. One just cannot switch identities and expect to keep up the facade for months. There are too many parameters. Things we cannot predict. We fool ourselves into believing that we are in control. And then it spirals into disaster ..."

"Are you going to tell me that you told me so?"

"Shouldn't I enjoy that smug satisfaction? Imagine if Pritam had access to his mails and chat and ..."

Sandeep winced.

"Please. There is one neurotic case on my hand. I shudder to think what might have been if that hypochondriac had got wind of all these problems ..."

The doctor gazed out of the window. The studious hustle of the scholars filled the quaint streets. He wondered if there were problems beyond the peaceful cobblestoned paths. He pursed his lips. There were problems in every nook and cranny if one bothered to scratch the surface. And now, problems existed in the strange realm of the virtual world as well. The subject matter was intricate and immense.

"You know, Pritam is back in the United States."

Sandeep nodded.

"I know as much. He is waiting for me to be done with what he calls my fooling around ... well, that's a close enough approximation..."

"You don't have to explain that in words of one syllable to a disciple of Freud."

"Ah ... right. Especially someone who smokes cigars and listens to LPs of Viennese concerts."

The doctor laughed.

"One should be permitted his idiosyncrasies."

"True. However, returning to Pritam, at first, he was haranguing ... adamant that I get out of his life. And now, I tend to hear from him less and less. Twice a week, standard reminders to stop fucking around ..."

The doctor, reminded of his cigars, produced one and proceeded to light it.

"I followed his case from a distance, but with a lot of interest. You remember the day I asked you to modify the password of his company email account?"

"Yes ... it was only the physical distance that saved me from getting murdered ..."

"Right. I followed him since then, keeping a tab on him with phone calls ... He went around with the girl for a while, then broke off when she kept putting him through the hoops in that heartless fashion ..."

Sandeep looked reproachfully.

"I would say it served him right. It was he who rushed halfway across Europe, running after her."

The doctor smiled.

"No doubt about that, but he was helped by a Machiavellian author. But, to come back to the point, when he was cut off from his trusted Blackberry, unable to get minute by minute updates of his professional world, I detected a strange reaction. It was like going back to days of the jungle. In fact, to use a better medical metaphor, he went through almost classic withdrawal symptoms of a drug or alcohol addict."

Sandeep looked at the older man in surprise.

"Are you serious?"

The doctor nodded.

"There are classic withdrawal symptoms – both physical and psychological. Obviously, in this case, the reactions are limited to mental. At least I haven't heard of chronic physical reactions. There may have been weight loss, but I cannot vouch for that. However, I noticed stages of paranoia, helplessness at losing control and the preoccupation at finding ways and means to get connected again. Ultimately, it got down to having a good time with beer and a couple of imbeciles – by which I mean Software Engineers."

"That's not necessarily a synonym the world will agree with."

The doctor laughed.

"True. The sunshine boys of modern India, earning unimaginable amounts and putting the name of the nation on the map of the world. But, to come back to what I was saying, I had detected advanced symptoms of Attention Deficit Hyperactive Disorder in Pritam before this episode of identity swap. He came to see me, to talk about this idiotic plan the two of you had hatched. All the while he kept checking his mails and reviewing presentations on his fancy toy. He had to be dragged out of the mode of constant flitting from subject to subject ... I was most interested to find out how such a modern day addict of the gadgets would react when detached from the network."

"And he reacted as a drug addict would when undergoing rehabilitation?"

The two students of society looked at each other in silence.

"If not an exact map, at least an approximation. It was definitely painful. Withdrawal symptoms vary from drug to drug, depending on the potency, the extent of use and so on. I guess we will find that it's the same with dependence on the internet and its various avatars – the blackberry, the i-phone. After a few days of painful paranoia, helplessness, preoccupation ... he resigned himself to his fate. When he ended up with the other job, he did not care any longer. He was out to have a good time, purge himself of all the intellectual overdose that he had been subjected to."

Sandeep shrugged.

"You make it sound Orwellian."

"Orwellian?"

"Well, somewhat unbelievable really ... Is it really that bad? Like drug addiction?"

The doctor chuckled.

"I know. It is somewhat counter-intuitive. And there are defenders of the net age who argue that people in the past have been similarly sceptical of Graham Bell and the Wright Brothers. I am just an observer pointing out the parallels. Now that Pritam has accepted the situation and is biding his time for you to call it a day, he is, I suspect, beginning to enjoy himself. To enjoy the break."

Sandeep got up.

"I am almost happy for him."

"Don't you think you should take this incident with Amrita as a warning signal and get back to your normal life?"

Sandeep picked up the yellow pages and leafed through it.

"I really don't know. I want to utilise this opportunity, visit the West Coast ..."

"Use this borrowed life to see the world, enhance your experiences, earn some more money , try to find some publisher ..."

"Right on all counts. But I also want to see where this ends. What comes of this peculiar collaboration with the Big Boss. He is too high in the echelons of the industry to speak sense, but he has a grand vision which somehow manages to fit my Gita flavoured extempore ideas."

"We are meeting for an idea generation session on Thursday, are we not?"

Sandeep smiled.

"Yes. With mild hallucinogens, we can work wonders."

The doctor walked up and started to change.

"Well, I have to go to the Medisch Centrum. Stay on as long as you like. And my last advice. You have run away once. If she was watching your place, she has realised that her desperation has driven you away. I predict a distinct reduction in her stalking."

Sandeep's face broke into a winning smile.

"There is a silver lining, my dear doctor."

~ ~ ~

Blog of Simple Simon

Tags: Taichi, Boom, Crash

It is funny how strength and vulnerability seem to saunter hand in hand. It is funny how the greatest of pleasures can make you prone to the deepest of pains.

And if the quotes above are startling fits for the economic stability and volatility of the great Western banks in recent times, they are equally poignant in the more artistic and spiritual world of the martial arts.

"Everything comes with its in-built opposite as a learned man once told me," my friend had said.

Yesterday, during the three hours of training and the discourses during dinner, Pritam had demonstrated his excellence as a martial artist and his depth as a thinker. And today, in the same world of *tai chi,* his vulnerable side was bared to all, when a dedicated teacher found that his painstakingly shared knowledge, garnered and blossomed through years of diligence, was casually ignored and flung aside by a group not suited to rigours more than that required for ridiculous corporate certifications.

It is just like the buoyant banks, too big to fail, riding on the crest of optimism, tripping at the same time on diminishing credit ratings, mortgage linked loans and toppling in the great crash.

In fact, the progress of the financial world is almost onomatopoeic. Boom crash, boom crash, boom crash.

In tai chi? Grasping bird's tail to find it has flown? Do the birds realise what they have refused?

Am I homing in towards an eternal truth? The meaning of it all?

Mail from Simple Simon to his mailing list
Sub: Perils of passion

(A modified version of this mail was posted on a tai chi forum)

I am worried about my buddy. He takes his art too passionately, plunging in with commitment bordering on dedication to share the learnings that he treasures. And when these treasures are not recognised, he can get hurt – in a way that can hardly be understood by those to whom it was never more than a temporary diversion.

He had not shown up during the day. It was towards the afternoon that I received a text message from him saying that class would take place as usual, and he would arrive directly at the gym.

When I reached the *dojo,* my friend was not there, but Trisha and Amrita were both present, still in their formals, a tense silence throbbing through the hall.

I greeted them cheerfully, mentioning that after a long while we were going to have a near full house. Both the girls smiled hesitantly, fleeting apologetic shadows of varying kinds flitting across their faces. However, neither of them provided any explanation. I started warming up, and the girls declined to join me.

When my friend did come in, he was openly aghast. There was a pause after which both the girls wanted to meet him alone for a while. Hardly ever, faced with corporate bigwigs, hostile audience or clandestine recording devices, had I seen him at a loss and he always dazzled audience and students with his *tai chi* expertise. However, now, faced with two slight girls on his favoured turf of tai chi, he stood wondering how to react.

At last, asking me to start warming up and to follow it up with the long form, he asked the girls to accompany him out of the gym. It was after quite a while – after having gone through the long form half a dozen times – that I saw him walking in, alone and, if body language was anything to go by, crestfallen.

In answer to my query, he smiled another of those sad smiles which I had seen him put on since yesterday.

"Lawrence Gallente, Subramanium with an S no one quite knows what for, Thomas Wong of New York, Schmidt of Germany, Yang Jwing Ming of Boston, add to that instructors from Prague, Honkong, Taiwan – whoever I have managed to visit and whoever visited India. From New Delhi to Bangalore, from Mumbai to Chennai. I have travelled to learn. Long and short forms of *tai chi,* broad sword and staff, *chin na* tehniques and *shanzi* katas. Simon ..."

He sat down on one of the exercise balls. I waited for him to continue.

"Things have not always been easy, buddy. You look at me and you see a successful consultant, preaching nothingness in elaborate style and making a pile out of it. Believe me it was not so always, and it will not be so forever. There have been trials and tribulations ... challenges, physical, financial and of livelihood. I have learned through all that."

He paused. For a moment he looked vulnerable to the brink of embarrassment.

"These are lessons that have been acquired with sweat and not a little blood thrown in from time to time. And that's why they stick to my very being. These are not lessons that I can throw into the realms of dim, distant, once learned now hazy bits of memory. That's because of the rigours I have been through to pick up each technique from the masters. Not for shameless pandering of an exotic art to a patronising western world. But for my own selfish sake, for learning as much as I can. Because of a simple reason. If I don't write, I am faced with the physical pain of being burdened with something in my soul which yearns to be put forth on paper, to be compiled in doc files of my laptop. Similarly, if I stop learning the martial arts, if I stop training, there is restlessness within me, a physical pain combined with mental unrest. I have travelled across the world and have always had my mind and body open to the masters of the great schools. And you know something? Somehow, within my limitations, I have managed to accumulate quite a collection of pearls of knowledge. A treasure that makes fellow martial artists envious. People are not often this fortunate or desperate to travel far and wide for martial arts."

I remarked that we were fortunate to have him here to share his experiences. He responded with another of those disheartening smiles.

"I made a mistake, Simon. I shouldn't have allowed Madhu Deb to talk me into this. You see, if a group of middle class Bengalis find something free for the taking, they take a few bites for the sake of it while the fad lasts, to go back to comfortable ways of life as soon as things get complicated. It is an art, Simon, not as easy as one of the professional certification courses ... one has to be dedicated."

I was taken aback at the allusion to the particular community to which he belonged along with the others in our small *tai chi* group.

"It's true with people everywhere and not limited to any particular group or society."

However, he was not really interested in what I was saying. He needed an outlet.

"I expected people to drop out one after the other at the beginning. However, the last four of you stuck around for a while. And bit by bit I opened the entire treasure for all of you, without making it hard to get. Without letting the students sweat a lot or spill blood. And there it was on a platter for you to take it or leave it. Do me a favour Simon ..."

I waited for him to vent his obvious bitterness.

"Join a club as soon as possible. And if you have begun to love this art, as I suspect you have, never give it away to the undeserving. Make them earn it from you."

I solemnly told him that I had an inkling of what he meant. Anyway, it would be years before I would be in his position, skilled and passionate enough to open the treasure trove of knowledge to others. Having said this, I asked him about the two girls.

"It's gonna be you and me, buddy," he replied. "I don't expect Madhu-di to give up her fan following of *sur-soiree.* She has chosen her vocation. She may grace us with an appearance once in a while, but that will be all that we will see of her in this room. The girls unfortunately will no longer train."

"Neither of them?"

"Yes. Trisha seems to have developed some problem in her family, however, there is a whiff of middle class pseudo Puritanism that I suspect."

I wondered what to make of that. I dared not ask anything about Amrita.

We started to train, but he called it a day soon.

"I know that popular sentiment is that the show must go on, but unfortunately, this is not really a show."

He declined my offer to grab a drink and went off as briskly as he had arrived, assuring that it would be business as usual from the following day. I was not sure what had gone on between him and the two girls.

Once outside I called Trisha. She informed me that she had to give up the martial art training because of some problems in her family. I asked her to elaborate and wondered aloud if it was not up to her to decide what to do. I was cut off with a brisk and almost curt explanation that things were not so simple in a traditional Indian household.

I hung up and wondered if it was any of my business. I wanted the classes to continue as usual because I had fallen in love with the art. I had asked around and the traditional tai chi schools around Amsterdam and Utrecht offered lessons in the short and long form of various styles, but practically none of them included *chin na* in their curriculum. Few had even heard of *shanzi.* In Pritam I knew I had a special store of knowledge which could be filtered with masterly care for the consumption of newbies like me, with the erudite history and philosophy of the arts also available from the vast recesses of the gifted mind. I was not sure that there could be a one stop replacement for my friend.

However, more than that, I was pained. I was pained at the stoop of his posture, at the irked dejection of his voice, of the obvious helplessness that he felt as people he had poured his hard earned knowledge into managed to casually walk away with disinterest.

Simon (Not the right day to sign off by saying Cheers)

~ ~ ~

Late night chat.

Madhu Deb to Trisha: *I heard you have opted out of tai chi*

Trisha to Madhu Deb: *Yes. There are problems in the home front. In Laws not keeping well. My Mom-in-law doesn't want me to be involved in 'fights'.*

Madhu Deb: That leaves Simon and me

Trisha: :-(Yes. True

Madhu Deb: Can't you convince Mangal?

Trisha: He doesn't want to take sides. And anyway, I want peace. I've hardly been married for more than a year. Mom in law is great in the rest of the things, but then, why should a wife be in fights?

Madhu Deb: It's difficult when you are newly married.

Trisha: True

Madhu Deb: How did Pritam take it?

Trisha: Not very well. He was already agitated when I began speaking ... He had been speaking to Amrita ...

Madhu Deb: Amrita turned up????

Trisha: Yes. But she left after a few words. Pritam was not happy at what I said. He asked me if there was no way out.

Madhu Deb: Poor guy.

Trisha: I feel sorry for him. But, family comes first. Hobbies can wait.

Madhu Deb: Right. He has to grow up too. I have missed a lot of classes and he does not like that.

Trisha: He is passionate. He expects others to be like him.

Madhu Deb: Yes, but I have these kids to train, the projects to manage and the Sur Soiree.

Trisha: When's the next?

Madhu Deb: Week after next.

Madhu Deb: What did Amrita say? Did you manage to be in earshot?

Trisha: No. I was not interested either. She did not tell me anything.

Madhu Deb: Crazy girl

Trisha: :-)

∾ ∾ ∾

How could someone who had been the softest human being Amrita had ever encountered change into a man of stone? She could not forget the tender moments when he had rolled about with her in the bushes, the infinite care with which he had helped her with her English and the delicate touch of his hand with which he had guided her in the classes. What made him so rigid now that he could not forgive one wrongdoing of a girl who had been driven crazy with love for him?

Where had he been yesterday? Did he not know that she would be waiting for him, her thoughts restless, fluctuating between the worst nightmares and the deadliest apprehensions? She had kept sending him the very same text messages that she knew drew him away from her. But, there seemed to be an invisible hand that guided her. She was not herself.

She had come to know that he had sent a text message that there would be a class. At least he had been okay. He had not been answering her calls or her messages, but he was safe. She went down to the dojo to see him. Trisha had also been waiting for him when she arrived. She had not slept a wink the night, had caught a cold and was in a most pitiable state. She was certain that one look at her and he would be concerned and tender again, caring and thoughtful as she knew only he could be. For a moment, when he arrived, she thought he looked surprised, no doubt by the sickly look on her face that greeted him. However, she was mistaken.

When Trisha and she both wanted to see him alone, he insisted on seeing Amrita first.

"Please, I would like to talk to you for a while. Please finish with Trisha first," she implored him.

He sat there, rigid and grim in the locker room.

"I don't enjoy impending doom hovering in the horizon," he said curtly. "I want to deal with normal people later. I have nothing to do with you. Go."

She begged him not to dismiss her and started weeping and he snapped at her asking her not to make a scene.

"I told you not to come to my classes, didn't I?"

She nodded between sobs, agreeing that it had been a mistake. She had been worried about him. He had not been home ...

"It is precisely why I have not been home. You have been stalking me, do you get it? If one knows that he can't step into his rooms without being dragged into a never ending fight with a neurotic woman who sends death threats as a hobby, one doesn't want to get back home."

She begged him to stop speaking to her in that manner.

"Please. I will never threat you again ..."

"Threaten," he corrected.

"I can't get better if you don't help me. You see, I keep making mistakes. In English and in life. Please help me."

He dismissed her again with angry waves of his hand, saying that it was not his job and he had to see Trisha.

"Please allow me to attend your classes. It's not for you. It's for *tai chi*."

He seemed to be annoyed, but did not answer for some time. She could make out that his soft inner self was striving to come out of the austere shell he had put on for the meeting.

"No, sorry. I don't want to have anything to do with you. You may leave."

He threw her a gym towel to wipe her tears and got up.

"Please dear," she begged. "I have realised my mistake. It will never happen again. If you hadn't reacted this way, I would never have realised what I was doing. Thank you dear, but please, allow me to continue classes ...."

She implored, almost on her knees. She could not raise her voice or make gestures of sorrow with Trisha watching through the transparent glass from the room outside. But, she was quivering to keep my sobs in check.

"I won't allow you to attend classes now," he said. He was adamant. "*Tai chi* is a healthy art. I can do without mental patients."

He waved at Trisha and asked her to come in. She could see that he did not want her in there any more, preferring the sophisticated, English speaking, fair, cheerful Trisha instead of the rustic, uneducated, tearful, dark girl who had given herself to him. This in fact has been her lot ever since she was born, who could argue with fate?

"And another thing. If I receive one more phone call or text message from you I will change my number and file a harassment case."

As she withdrew, she waited in vain for a flicker of a smile, a twinkle in the eye which would reassure her that he spoke in jest. But, all she got was the stark, grim set face that had remained unchanged since the beginning of the discussion.

O fateless? What had she done? God had given her someone who cared for her and went out of his way to help her. With proper nurture, who knows, maybe even love would have burgeoned on his pliable heart. And with the impatience of the deprived, with insatiable hunger of someone who has been fed on unloved morsels since childhood, she had managed to drive him away by clinging on too hard. Never would she be able to love anyone else, and never would she be able to offer her love to him.

Part VIII:

Speculations of an Odd Lot

XLII

"Madhu, I have been wondering ... Pritam is not around for a while," Ajay Yadav's eyes were characteristically shifty, tottering on the fringe of stealthy.

"I know," the lady smiled. "Ramesh called me up recently, he wanted him to prepare for the paper at all costs. They are presenting their ideas in California in two or three weeks."

At the mention of the hallowed name, the wind predictably whooshed out of the sails of disgruntlement, but the account manager persevered.

"I know, but since Dave de Boer is back in office and we have sold our man ..."

Madhu Deb's eyes twinkled.

"Not exactly sold him, have we? He is not paying for an expensive consultant. So, all he will be getting out of him are the series of presentations that have become so popular ..."

Ajay Yadav swallowed.

"Ah, yes. The presentations. Well, the last few have not really adhered to ... well, you know ... the accepted standards ..."

The good lady beamed.

"Yes, I know, but that has been the whole point of Ramesh's scheme, hasn't it? A new school of thought, proprietary and original, from our own body of knowledge ..."

"Yes, I know ... but when Dave asks me about the consultant and his empty cubicle, it is ..."

"We will present him a free sample of our proprietary work," Madhu Deb suggested. "In fact I was wondering if we could invite him for the next *Sur Soiree* session ..."

Fifteen minutes later Ajay Yadav walked away from the Senior Manager's cubicle with throbbing temples.

"Religion as a means to financial nirvana?" sitting in the now familiar coffee shop, Suprakash Roy's voice sounded incredulous. "Isn't that one of ... well, the word escapes me now ..."

The bong was ready, mild, intoxicating and almost heady. Simon had been exacting in his instructions.

"Oxymoron?" Shruti asked. The doctor had looked at her with special interest. So, this was the damsel who had started his cousin off on a European odyssey fraught with academic peril. Now, looking with his clinical, experienced eyes at her and Sandeep, he almost smiled. Not only had Sandeep been living Pritam's professional life, he had quite obviously taken over his desires as well.

"Exactly."

Sandeep was making the final adjustments to the camera phone. No one would remember a thing the following day.

"Again I tell you, it is easier for a camel to go through the eye of a needle than for a rich man to enter the kingdom of God," Simon interjected. "Jesus Christ. And your boss seems to think that you will use religion to provide breakthrough strategy to put the money making world in order."

"Well, he is more concerned about epoch making ideas coming out of India. And the Indian thought is slightly more charitable to everyone, rich or poor."

"Believe me, it won't stick," the doctor was inhaling the intoxicant a bit too frequently for Sandeep's liking. "Jung was very much into mysticism, the way of India. He was one of the main proponents of there being a mind body whole rather than the dissociation of the two so common to the Western psychologists. And although he made major breakthroughs in many areas, including being one of the spearheads of Cognitive psychology, he is not given due importance. It is difficult, my friend. Eastern ideas may work excellently in yoga classes, art of living – those fancy, feel good, packaged spirituality for the mindless moneyed westerners. But to be accepted at a so called scientific level – I am sure everyone considers economics to be a so called science – it is a long shot."

Shruti took a hesitant pull at the bong.

"Aren't we mixing up religion and philosophy? After all the core of Indian knowledge – ancient Indian knowledge – is nothing but philosophy. And don't we see valuable lessons in the Art of Wealth, Arthashastra, in the Japanese way of business ..."

"Kereitsu," Sandeep had at last managed to get the recording device to the exact square centimetre to his liking.

"Hinduism is an adaptive philosophy," he continued. "We can absorb sinners like rich men and live with it. We have the concept of the *Rajarshi,* the philosopher king. I guess K. Ramesh sees himself as one."

"Even then, is religion and economy that far apart?" Shruti asked.

The doctor kept pulling at the bong. "Easy Sup-da, we have a long evening ahead of us," Sandeep's voice was calm and coaxing.

"My private mental experiments. Disintegration in a way Steve Waugh would have been proud of. Religion has always fed on economy. Look at the popes and their equivalents all over the world."

"No wonder the dollar bill says 'In God we Trust'," Simon observed.

Shruti cleared her throat.

"More than that. Judas Iscariot supposedly gave Christ away. And thus historically the Jews earned a bad name for themselves. The holocaust is seen to be a culmination of hatred against the community. After effects still rocking the world's secular boat from time to time. But, is that the only reason? Was economy in no way related to it?"

"The Jews controlled the economy."

"Yes, they did. Baron Rothschild. He pulled the strings of his purse and decided the fate of nations. His wealth gave rise to fables of the philosopher's stone..."

"Great idea," Sandeep's absorbed head rose from the fumes. "Philospher's stone. What a poignant name for the discourse. With Shakespeare joining the fray. Not on thy sole Jew but on thy soul. There were no courts of law upholding the rights of the minority group of money lenders."

"Don't mind this temporary insanity. Pray continue," the doctor egged Shruti on.

"With Jews controlling the purse in Europe, it was quite natural for the dictators to turn against them. It was economic motivation cloaked in the garb of religious cleansing. And history is full of such atrocities ostensibly for religion where economic interests actually drove the show."

"The crusades?" Simon asked.

"Crusades – for God and glory. The granddaddy of all oxymorons," Sandeep laughed. "Holy war."

Shruti nodded.

"The crusades were for the riches of the east. In the name of God. And even in the modern age, we have the Afghan wars, the Iraq wars, the Palestine-Arab issue, modern religious warfare with Jews, Christians and Muslims battling out age old hatred. And that all consuming modern religion. The dollar."

"Profound."

"Tell me, doctor," Shruti turned towards Suprakash Roy. "Why is it so easy to cover up atrocities? Why is it so easy to put the shroud of religion or media over the mangled bodies and severed heads left as litter in the wake of ages of financial empire building?"

"The successful write the history," Simon remarked. "That way we read books on the holocaust and conveniently relegate Dresden, Hiroshima and Nagasaki to footnotes."

"It does not matter what the truth is. Intelligent people soon forget logic, facts and beliefs. Religion is the opium of the masses," Sandeep pitched in. "Even in Gita we see such paramount brainwash. In the guise of the philosopher and guide, one coaxes another to fight his brothers and friends. Unless you are speaking of the Buddha or the Christ, there are few examples of momentous individual realisation in the immensity of the world. And the populace in general is very easy to sway. Two newspaper articles and it is manufactured consent. America is actually liberating Iraqis. Hollywood is supposedly producing meaningful movies. Booker prize winners are actually writing important, readable stuff. Nobel prize winners are actually working for peace, making stable economic models. People believe everything, provided they can lap it up in marketable print and electronic media."

The doctor looked on dreamily.

"Control of media is passé. The powers need to control the internet. I guess they are already into it."

"Documented grapevine," Sandeep mused. "You know why Gita makes such a lot of sense even today. In these days of economic slowdown, corporate organisations are faced with the dilemma of downsizing. Get rid of those very people whose labour made you thrive. And in the end, people forget to ask what is this animal called corporate. Is it just a bunch of people who sit at the board making decisions and a lot of money?"

The yellow lighting spread a sense of warmth around everyone. Simon looked at the group with a content charm.

"So, for the last few minutes we have essentially concluded that money is bad – the root of all evil. It is money that makes people mass murderers. There is no limit. It is more and more that one wants. Is it a good idea to propose the end of money?"

"You won't find financial backers for that idea," the doctor quipped.

Shruti shook her head, the movement turning out to be slower than she thought. The stimulating seeds smoothly slackening her senses.

"No nation – not even states of dictatorial communism like North Korea – has managed to get rid of money from the equation. It will take a major mutation of the species to find an alternative. Trade and commerce is not all that bad..."

"It was a good idea to have her on the team, Pritam," Simon said.

"Sandeep," Shruti corrected.

"Right. Sandeep. Sorry. She seems to have the floor."

"And she has us floored too," Sandeep agreed.

"In spite of the wars it has caused from the earliest recorded history, you claim money is not all that bad?" Simon asked.

"It is the nature of man to wage wars. For expansion, for profit. Either openly as of old, or surreptitiously using economic hit men as in Iran and Nicaragua. However, trade, commerce and money can be used to stop wars too. It was essentially by linking the Coal and Steel industries of France and Germany that visionary politicians actually managed to stop two nations who had been at each other's throats during two world wars ... and for centuries before that. That's what led to EU. A conglomeration of finance and industry, preventing war since no one could afford to cut one's own arm. We need thinking politicians. Konrad Adeneur, Jean Monnet, Gaspari, Schuner ..."

The doctor's lips parted in a wondrous smile.

"My heart goes out to my cousin. Pritam, what must you have suffered."

"Excuse me, dear doctor. The hardened consultant, he refused to admit that he was out of depth. The great pretence."

Simon frowned. "Cousin?"

"Forget it Simon. It's complicated. Let's get back to the discussion," Sandeep huddled the topic back on track.

Simon nodded. "I take it that combining fortunes by linking industries has worked so well for the EU nations ... we haven't had a war in the EU for more than half a century. Why then is the financial collapse attributed to the merging of the greedy big banks who tried to monopolise the financial world? Why didn't the same principle work there as well?"

"We are talking of different domains, Simon," Sandeep reasoned, eyes closed.

"If I may venture an opinion," Shruti began. "Although I am no economist ..."

"I doubt if there is anything of that sort," Sandeep laughed long and loud, a bit too long and way too loud. "Fitting into models that don't work and then retrofitting. The world is too complex. It is not deterministic. Just like the good doctor was telling me the other day. We fool ourselves into believing that we are in control. There are too many parameters and too many different chaotic trends. We cannot predict everything ..."

"Well, the problems started with prediction to a certain extent. With creative banking, first risks related to corporate loans were bundled into derivatives and sold off, and later mortgages of people," Simon reflected dreamily. "In the end what resulted was a lot of default and bad credit. Corporate loan defaults can be predicted to a certain extent, but individual mortgages? Credits? A lot of dust was thrown into the eyes to get away with it."

"Making everything available to the world, and at the click of a mouse," the doctor chimed in.

"That's most true," Shruti nodded and felt queer at the movement of her head. "However, if we get back to the question of the merger of banks, what are these organisations that we are joining. These are essentially money making institutions, whose only goal is to increase the bottom line. As Sandeep pointed out, the employees who make the profit happen are expendable. What matters is that money keeps trickling in – nay, flooding in. The organisation is bigger than the individual at all times."

"Fascist," Simon suggested.

"Interesting parallel. Think of making an oligopoly of fascist nations. What would happen?"

"A procession of clowns like Mussolini," Simon smiled. "All we will be left with are ruins and laughter."

"And cut off vital organs. Profound. We have opened the doors of perception." Sandeep agreed. "What's your take on this doctor? A filmmaker went about making a film on the character of a normal corporation, considered not as a group of people but an individual – someone who is interested in the bottom line and nothing else. And the end result was the psychological profile of a psychopath."

The doctor closed his eyes and smiled.

"Pop psychology. Good for raising mass eyebrows. That's what bothers me. If you want to use philosophy for your epoch making paper, go for simple stuff. Art of War packaged as a series of bulleted quotations. Zen Buddhism quips of emptying your cup. Don't go too deep into Hinduism. It's difficult. People won't understand. Your boss wants to be a hero in his lifetime, a pseudo philosopher whose serene picture sticks out of the cover of Forbes. He doesn't want the truth."

Sandeep stretched his hands and slipped down in his chair.

"Indian body of knowledge is difficult. In fact India itself is difficult to understand. The occidental mind is happy with quaint approximations, the glamorous oriental jewellery, saffron robes, the shaved heads and the crazy dance of Hare Krishna. It is a nation of contrasts. With the erudition of ages led by a parliament full of halfwits. However, it is peculiar that the poorest of nations ends up infiltrating the world in every corporate wing from the helpdesk to the boardroom. Things Simon and I have discussed quite often. Nation of contradictions. It is the classical traditions of adaptability of our philosophy that allow us to accept Jesus as one of the avatars that has also enabled us to accept English as one of our languages. That seed of colonial past that is reaping its karmic harvest. Historically we love rubbing shoulders with the *firangis,* as a symbol of social achievement, and also get a kick out of plotting their downfall. We fuel all these on the engine of English, and later html and the rest which have seamlessly got woven into our repertoire of languages. With the information systems of the world merging and forming conglomerations, we are left with huge systems, organisational stubs which are supposed to talk to each other, a virtual tower of babel where no one really understands anyone else. And culturally, Indians are wonderful as middle men. And we love cutting chunks out of life to perform this job of tedium. To our previous generation, to the awestruck neighbours of our small towns – computers, foreign lands and internet are fairy tales. We live in the world of middle class dream. When you update an excel sheet it seems wizardry on laptop for a culture that was busy tilling the soil one generation back..."

The doctor broke in.

"But that's the story of the Indian infiltration into the world's systems. How is that to give you a solution? How can the Gita or the Upanishads provide us answers? "

"The Gita raises more questions than answers," Sandeep remarked. "It points ways for us to choose."

"Tower of Babel in the financial world. That resulted in chaos," Simon had his eyes closed like the rest of the participants. Shruti pulled long and hard into the bong. "If in this chaos the new avatar of the Indian middle man comes to the rescue, using principles of ancient philosophy ... will it lead anywhere? Or am I spiralling into the realms of the CEO, looking at things from the stratospheric heavens above from where reality and imagination become merged and fuzzy?"

There was a smile that played on the good doctor's lips.

"All of you have had economists preach you different versions of the cause and effect of the crisis, haven't you? Bad credit being circulated, the monolithic banks being merged and all that. Will you allow the excellent cannabis and the fanciful suggestions of an experimental psychiatrist give you another perspective?"

Sandeep gestured with a favourable wave of hand.

"That's what this meeting is all about, dear doctor. Ideas and opinion nurtured by erudition and elixir, combining to shake the foundations of the intelligent world. Let's hear it."

The doctor bowed, taking a considerable amount of time to resurface in their midst.

"As I have maintained for quite some time, it is a new world view. The old rules have ceased to exist. The world connected with Internet, i-phone, blackberry and the phenomena of blogging, twitter, facebook, linked in and all the rest. To summarise, people lack the inhibition that was once the restraining factor in interactions. Face to face, a lot of words would remain unsaid, a lot of opinions unexpressed that one ends up sharing from behind a chat window or an sms screen. It is my humble opinion that this has played its role in the crisis as well."

Shruti looked at the psychiatrist with a curious frown.

"And how do you mean?"

The doctor filled his lungs.

"The concept of money. Let us look at it from the cognitive point of view. We tend to think of avarice as the eyes of greedy merchants, shining with desire at the sight of gold. Is it the same today? With plastic money, does anyone actually picture gold when one thinks of bank balance? Money has undergone metamorphosis, from the pots of gold and treasure chests, to the bank notes and dollar bills, bank statements or updated pass books , gold plated credit cards ... and now just an electronic line in a website informing us our bank balance. Credit cards made us slightly more adventurous. A swipe and no pain of having to part with a wad of notes. Forget the whole thing till the bill in the post box comes along a month later. And then there came along this trend of online purchasing, online trading. A click of button to pay a thousand dollars for the latest gadget. Another click to buy the shares or bonds or mutual funds. The same lack of inhibition that plays its role in online promiscuity showed another face. Paying a broker and asking him physically to invest for us is one thing. And my contention is that it is a completely different matter when the entire thing is online. If someone comes up with the statistics, one will definitely uncover deals and purchases that defeat wisdom through the media of internet, egged on by user friendly websites, the mass herd psychology promoted by the use of twitter and facebook and orkut."

Suprakash Roy paused either for breath or for savouring the wavelets of dreamy hallucination in the chambers of his mind.

"Wow, doc," Simon was impressed. "You mean to say that a lot of the bad credit and financial transactions gone wrong were caused because of online transactions? Clicking a button to take a mortgage loan? Corporations buying up CDOs with their combined computers?"

The doctor nodded.

"The human mind asks questions at every step, which cannot really be replicated with a simple 'Are you sure you want to continue Yes No Cancel'. Lack of inhibition is one of the major differences between the real world and the bizarre virtual world of the modern man with all his technology in tow. My friend here knows the best and the worst of it. And here is an area where this lack of inhibition has played a decisive role, almost imperceptibly."

"Do you mean internet should not be used for transactions?"

"I am the observer, Simon. Not someone to make a judgement call. However, technology has its uses and abuses."

"However," Simon nodded. "Let us look at the triggering of the collapse of the huge financial tower created with CDOs, SIVs and Mortgage Linked Super Senior Loans – they themselves are fiendishly difficult to compute or understand without resorting to computers. It all started with banks being bailed out by the government, delay in offering plausible explanations, and finally panic spreading across the world, through emails, blogs, sms, social networks, blackberries... People stopped buying mortgage and risk derivatives all of a sudden."

"We come back to the electronic herd. The modern phenomena of cosmic consciousness, the universal unity of thought. Publish your thoughts, inundate others with posts and twitters... No individual ideas ... but a confused collective sum total. Information overload .... Is this the lack of duality between self and other that the sages hinted at? Universal knowledge sharing?" Sandeep paused.

"Stream of Consciousness to the fore," Shruti laughed. "So, you mean that one is looking at the end of free will."

"There is no free will," Sandeep declared. "Only fragmented thought ..."

"Attention Deficit Hyperactive Disorder ... A condition of child psychology, but with the new fangled toys in the hands of grown men, it is an affliction of the populace. At least the professional," the doctor leaned back, closing his eyes.

"Robert Musil did hint at fragmentation of thought," Sandeep observed.

"Calling for help?" Simon was looking at Shruti. She was dialling into her cell phone with careful, slow fingers, fighting the encroaching fogginess.

"I am calling for a great mind," she answered. "Sandeep, I am ringing the Professor. I hope it is not too late..."

"It is almost half past five. It will be ten in the night. Why on earth ...?"

"Hello," a heavy, distinguished voice sounded in slightly confused enquiry. The phone was on speaker.

"Professor, this is Shruti ..."

"Shruti? And where are you calling from? You young people go around the world on the wings of thought these days, Phileas Fogg could never keep up with you with his nineteenth century methods."

"In Amsterdam. And quite fogged ourselves."

"I could have sworn you were in the next room. Glory be to the technology of mahakala."

" I have Sandeep with me."

"Ah two bright young authors scribbling the city red. However in Amsterdam, I guess it is redundant."

Sandeep bowed and touched his head on the wooden table beside the bong.

"Greetings Professor. There are two more with us. A Psychiatrist and a financial philosopher."

Simon and Suprakash uttered their greetings.

Sandeep continued, "If we sound somewhat stoned, it is because we are under the influence of mild gaseous intoxicants ... what with trying to find a remedy for the financial crisis being such a handful ..."

A firm feminine hand on his mouth stopped what promised to be a long confessional.

"Young people in the prime of life and cradle of liberty," the erudite voice sounded amused. "Trying to solve the financial mysteries by unlocking the doors of perception. Why then is an old man from the other side of the world invited to join the party? Can the modern technological marvels of the internet channel intoxicants through the web of wonder into the living room of Lake Gardens?"

"I am afraid not professor. We were having a brain clouding discussion, based on the assumption that clouds generally produce storms. We were discussing the madness of the world with money and can't seem to decide whether it is good or bad," Sandeep had managed to take his head off the table and resume his erect position. "It is the craze for money, and according to our psychiatrist the abuse of technology that has led to the financial crisis. What do you say, Professor? Do the ancient texts point a way towards the solution?"

There was a pause. Shruti put her cell phone on mute.

"I wonder if this was a good idea after all," she wondered.

"O young people, I am not quite used to long distance discussions, so you must excuse me for taking a while," the Professor was back on line. "I know all about the modern world becoming a global village, but my ancient eyes are still used to the concepts of township and city and country and other old fashioned ideas. But then, I cannot give you an answer. The Indian texts, as you put it, are a complex source of enlightenment. It is there for you ... to interpret and use, but what is the way out? It is different for each one of us. At twenty five, your way to salvation will definitely be different from mine at eighty."

Shruti looked apologetic.

"Professor, I sure hope we did not disturb your sleep."

There was a laugh from the other end.

"Don't worry. I am sleeping only in the metaphorical sense. In the physical sense, an old man does not need much slumber. But, to look at it in another way, I have made the Upanishads and the Mahabharata available to you. It is up to you to interpret and use. One has to go through the phases. *Brahmacharya, Grihastha, Vanaprastha* and *Sanyas*. The meaning of the Upanishad vary from age to age. And at every age it is true. At a subsequent age the truth can become false. One has to pass through the phases, not the paraphrase. And the way is different for every individual. That is the brilliance of Upanishads. I quote. *In the whole world there has been no study so beneficial as the Upanishads. It has been the solace of my life. It will be the solace of my death.* Whose words are these? Can you make a guess?"

The four of them looked at each another.

"Schopenhauer. Now, coming to your other question. Money. Is it good or bad? In the eyes of Christianity, it is a deterrent to heaven. Jesus denounced riches, advising the rich man to get rid of his wealth."

"That was the start of our discussions," Simon said smiling.

" Unfortunately, my friends, the Hindu texts do not provide such convenient answers in black and white. It is the brilliance of etymology. *Artha* is one of the four pillars of character in Mahabharata. Along with *Dharma, Kama* and *Moksha*. And while *artha* can mean riches, money, it can also mean *meaning* of it all. It is your choice. You want money or the meaning. Or is it the meaning of money? *Dharma*. Is it the *way*? The *religion*? It is up to you to decide whether it should be ritual or spiritual. *Kama*. Should it be love or lust? *Moksha*. Escape or liberation? The sages have given the answers. It's all there and confusing. It is for you to choose."

"Opens up angles of thought," Sandeep nodded. "Professor, I don't know how to thank you."

A brief self effacing chuckle reverberated off the phone.

"It's quite all right. It is not every day that I have the honour of being called by a group of young people from the other side of the world."

Sandeep inhaled deep and long, this time without the necessity of heady fumes.

"There is one who does not need hallucinogens. Great mind. Self sufficient."

Simon stretched himself.

"You said it, buddy."

"I guess we need to get going now if we want to reach home at all."

"Sandeep, do you want to switch that thing off?"

Sandeep pocketed his camera phone.

"I have got all that I needed. The brilliant backdrop of religion and economics, the coalition of fascists , the Indian in the milieu, the fascinating insights of internet caused crisis and ultimately the multiple choices and the four pillars. I can fill a couple of books with this stuff. Here I come, California. Mr. K. Ramesh, no one can stop our paper."

XLIII

As Sandeep stepped out of the Wilzanglaan apartment, the old gentleman next door greeted him cheerfully.

"Goede Morgen."

"Goede Morgen Meneer van der Kooij."

The buurman was over seventy, and in the lovable Dutch style, active and independent – powered by healthy living and pension policies. Geert, his middle aged golden retriever wagged his tail in appreciation. When van der Kooij visited his daughter, Geert often stayed with Shruti.

As the old man passed Sandeep, he brought his wrinkled eyelid down on his twinkling eye in an endearing wink. Sandeep could not help but break into a smile.

He walked down the steps and felt quite content. Identification as an integral part of Shruti's life filled him with content. He had spent three of the last four nights with her, not always driven by necessity and not always making love. Intertwining of thoughts was as titillating as the embrace of bodies. A natural feeling of comfort flowed through their senses in togetherness. There had been a mutual weaving into the worlds of each other with seamless continuity.

However, the fabric of the relationship was held together by the accepted Velcro of impermanence. The haziness of the future asked uncomfortable questions and gave frightening answers. Neither of them was prepared to talk about it. They agreed about it wordlessly.

~ ~ ~

Blog of Simple Simon

Tags: Taichi, Art, Bliss, Constraints

The enigma of an oriental art is revealed to me with precise, practised hands that guide, point and remove the confusing layers. Yet, the intricacies of the complex Indian society continue to keep me out with its impregnable, intimidating wall.

Hard and soft mingle into each other. The rigid oak breaks in a storm while the yielding bamboo survives. The stiff is the dead whereas inside a soft bundle of a wrapped up baby is a strongly beating heart. In everything masculine there is something feminine, in everything positive something negative. Concepts of yin and yang as my buddy-sifu explained during a more verbally active class. As has been for a while, I was the lone student.

After class, I asked him whether the yin-yang concept was another way of putting across his favourite aphorism – everything comes with its in built opposite.

My friend shrugged. "Eternal truth, buddy, as they converge, it becomes one truth. Why ponder about the different schools of thought?"

The last few days have marked exponential revelations in my martial arts lessons. The more I look into the depths the more fascinating the treasure store seems to be.

Happy as I am to cash in on this remarkable opportunity to receive closed door instructions from an obvious expert, sometimes we miss a third member. There are partner exercises and techniques that I can do with Pritam, but it is very difficult to master unless the instructor observes the manoeuvres from a neutral position. This demands another student.

However, in his inimitable style of contradictions, my instructor shrugs this off as necessary."Constraints are as necessary as opportunities, Simon. Else, the body picks up the lessons, but the soul remains detached."

Mail from Simon to his mailing list
Subject: Culture Conundrums

I was having lunch with Trisha and Amrita when I broached the topic of tai chi .

"I would be glad if one of you returned to train with me. I enjoy the one on one sessions, but partner practice is a bit difficult. And Madhu is always involved in the Sur Soiree."

There was an uncomfortable silence and I had the distinct impression of stumbling around in the intricacies of a strange and convoluted culture. Trisha's face informed me of sacrosanct boundaries clumsily crossed by colossally ignorant western feet. Amrita, the recluse she had turned into in recent times, looked away and did not answer.

"I can't help it," Trisha declared after the pause had become too uncomfortable. "A married girl in the Indian society has to abide by certain norms ..."

"I respect your norms, rules and traditions, but find it a little difficult to digest that you are not free to do what you want," I remarked, not a little impatiently.

I was annoyed at this refuge behind the impenetrable wall of cultural differences and marital status. On retrospection, however, I was more mad at her for failing to realise the opportunities that had been given her, which I was reaping like a madman. It was perhaps unjust on my part to expect her to feel for the art with the same passion.

"I don't expect you to digest everything, Simon," she answered firmly. "As of now, this bread based lunch should be a handful."

She did have her humorous moments, especially when astutely avoiding discussions.

At this juncture, Amrita excused herself with an inaudible whisper. Trisha watched her retreating form with concerned eyes.

"Is she okay?" I asked.

"Silly girl," Trisha remarked, almost to herself. Turning, she looked at me with mild reproach.

"You had to bring up *tai chi* while we were eating, did you?"

I answered that I did not think *tai chi* was unpalatable.

"Well, as I said, there are lots of things I don't expect you to digest," she repeated before skilfully steering the conversation towards some involuntary clowning by Ajay Yadav.

As I listened to her, I wondered what all the complication was about. And there was one truth that reverberated in my mind – something shared by my buddy in his moments of wisdom.

"As long as it remotely concerns our dojo, keep yourself away from the disturbances. Absorb the lessons with an unfettered and uncluttered mind."

Well, I am doing that and will continue. To hell with whatever is wrong with the rest of them.

Cheers
Simon

~ ~ ~

"I'm working. I've a paper to present in a week's time."

"I just wanted to know whether I can come to class today."

"I've told you. The answer is no."

"I want to learn."

"No."

"I know Simon is finding it difficult to learn alone."

"No."

"He is ... he told me so ..."
"The answer is no."
"I will never threaten you again."
"No."
"Can't you forgive?"
"No."
"Are you made of stone?"
"Yes."

Extracts from the working paper of Sandeep

The industry is the field of action. The perishable field which can be devastated by a crisis or made fertile by the blessings of time, the bubbles and booms, electronic advances and credit crisis.

The people involved in the industry, the ones disillusioned by the seeming omnipotence of business and their bondage to the same are perishable.

However, the one who combines knowledge of the field and the values of professionalism does not perish. He participates in creation of livelihood and can outlive the devastation of the industry.

"Do you realise what you are making a mockery of? Kshetra and Khsetrajna. One of the most profound concept of the Gita..." Shruti was glancing at the work in progress.

"I don't know. The pent up creative process, bogged down under the weight of synopses and query letters, and honed in by rejection slips, seems to have found a vent. A ridiculous outlet, where imagination knows no restraint. The irresistible urge to make a mockery of everything."

He sat on the sofa, typing his fantastic fabrication. Shruti sat on the computer chair, her dextrous fingers digitising the results of her recent travels for her dissertation, pausing from time to time to read and laugh through the progress of Sandeep. Geert, left in Shurti's apartment for the night, took turns in curling up on the rugs placed near the feet of each.

She burst out into another of her endearing guffaws. Infectiously, the ridiculousness hit home and Sandeep joined in.

"This puts things in perspective, doesn't it?" Shruti stretched herself and broke into a contagious smile. "I am writing an honest, thoroughly researched paper based on stark reality. And it is just a paper for my individual doctorate. You are jotting down the illogical extension of the ramblings of a group of people under the influence of cannabis. And there is more than a negligible probability that your work will be an appreciated model, even followed by organisations to become success stories. Powered by corporate funding. And my efforts are to be buried in a remote shelf in a library, lucky if ever noted in the bibliography of other papers, miraculous if ever read."

Sandeep shifted on the sofa and moved closer to the computer table.

"That's the wonder of the modern world. Substance does not matter. Now is that a contradiction? Antithesis revealed during our mutual thesis."

"The wordsmith gets caught in the web of words again."

"I am not Rimbaud to tell you great words, I am not Verlaine to tell you poems, I am just myself to tell you I love you ..."

"And quotations."

"That's one way to tell you that I love you."

"It gets complicated."

"But ..."

"Remember Diane Wiest in *Bullets Over* Broadway? Hush ... Don't speak. Instinct has taken over and caution has stepped out of the room. Let's keep it out ... let that be one thing that we don't discuss."

"Uncertainty and commitment?"

"Hush ... and hush."

"Kshetrajna – the knower of the body. Knowing in Biblical ..."

"Stop the sacrilege. I have another chapter to write."

"I was just analysing words ..."

"For you, who likes to play with words, foreword is synonymous with foreplay."

"Can I quickly browse through the contents?"

The tinkling of the cell phone cut through the sweet and spicy nothings. Sandeep noted the Indian number flashing on the screen and looked at his watch.

"It's past eleven back home," he sighed. "Most glorious night, thou were sent my number. Hello."

The voice of Subramanium was unexpected and welcome.

"You change your address so often, I wondered if you were still in Netherlands."

"Sensei?"

"I got your mail about your planned trip to Los Angeles."

"Yes ... the circle of weird karma."

"Are you on assignment or on one of those book signing trips?"

Sandeep laughed.

"Book signing trips? I've not won a Booker yet, Sensei."

"I read an excellent review of your book. Sethu of the Shotokan Dojo had brought a paper along."

"Wow. That's great."

"So, to keep it short, George Salinas teaches in the Venice Beach, which is a couple of hours from LA. So, if possible, visit the *kwoon* and convey my greetings."

The name struck a chord.

"George Salinas? Ah ... the writer."

"Yes. And an excellent teacher."

Sandeep tried to remember.

"The one who tricked you ... and you want me to visit him and convey your regards?"

Subramanium sighed.

"Sandeep, if there is one lesson that sticks to you let it be this – no one is greater than the art. One weekend at the Venice Beach, a couple of classes under George and you won't come back poorer."

He did not answer her calls. He did not reply to her messages. When she spoke to him, expecting the warmth that touched her for a brief period of dream in an otherwise nightmarish life, she shuddered at the icy coldness of his response. His heart, which was soft as a new born baby, had transformed into the most rigid of stones. Why? Was it because of her madness? Had she become too demanding? Had she become too dependent? She never demanded anything from him. All she wanted was the permission to love him.

She knew she had been scared. Extremely scared of losing him, of the chance of his going away from her ... of the guiding hand that she had grasped slipping away from her fingers, of finding herself back in the abyss that she had grown up in, lived in ...

What could she do to convince him that she wouldn't do anything that would cause problems for him, never threaten him again ... why had she been stupid enough to do that?

Or is this how it would remain forever? Would she remain the unwanted girl everyone wanted to get rid of?

XLIV

Madhu Deb loved her food. While rushing headlong into the bacon, eggs and mashed potatoes early in the morning, she maintained that the first meal of the day was the most important. On most days, she ploughed through the evening spread with all the gusto of a dinner devotee. Now, as she sat in front of Sandeep, her chubby hands almost disappearing to the wrists as they excavated the buried delights of the potted roast, she seemed to be a lunch lover as well. Julius Caesar would have appreciated it, for she showed no weak inclination towards growing lean and even less for being hungry.

"The problem is that the next level is not prepared," she managed to say between gnaws and chews. "I am trying to build up the leaders of the next generation who will be able to take this forward without my involvement, but they have to mature further."

Sandeep nodded absently. He knew the lady's commitment to *Sur-Soiree.* He could live with that without her trying to project it as a breeding ground for future leaders. It somehow did not tally with her earlier story of teaching people about there being a life away from work. What troubled Sandeep was that the good lady had started on the topic to make him understand why she could not make it to the *tai chi* classes regularly.

"But, don't give up on me," she beamed. "I will be back. It has really helped me a lot, and I mean it. The tension at home does not affect me that much anymore. I seem to have a life of my own ..."

"Don't you get that from *Sur Soiree*?" Sandeep asked.

Madhu Deb's eyes twinkled and she smiled.

"You are annoyed aren't you?"

"No ... not really ..."

"Come on, Pritam. I can see through you. In a lot of ways you are very like Samit ... not the worse parts of course. I am your friend and it's your demand that I attend your classes, giving it proper importance. When I miss classes for the Soiree, you are annoyed..."

"Not really ... it was just a question out of curiosity," Sandeep frowned, wondering if there was any annoyance in his voice.

"Come off it. I can understand. I hardly enjoy the *Soiree.* Obviously it can never give me the same sense of satisfaction and well being as *tai chi.* After a while it becomes a headache. But, I have the responsibility. Don't worry, I'll be back."

Sandeep wiped his lips.

"The only problem that I am facing right now is that Simon is alone in class. When there is partner-work involved ..."

Madhu Deb nodded sadly.

"I know. With Trisha having left and Amrita ... well ... Has there been any more problem?"

"Not major ones."

"Any more threats?"

"No. There have been promises that there won't be any more threats."

"It's just been a few weeks. BPDs can lull you into a sense of security before reverting again."

Sandeep frowned and finished his salad.

"For Simon to train properly, it's necessary that ..."

"Surely you are not going to allow her back in your life."

Sandeep shrugged as he got onto his feet.

"She was never in my life in the first place. And anyway, there are too many things on my mind right now, starting with the presentation in Pasadena."

Madhu Deb smiled, a hint of unexplained sadness in her eyes.

~ ~ ~

Dear Mr. Gupta,

Thanks for your query, but we think we are not the ideal vehicle for your literary journeys. Wishing you all the success for your book – The Dutch Gambit.

Thanks,
Angie Fraser
FST Literary Agency

The self addressed stamped envelope had served its purpose and had borne back the synopsis and first three chapters on disappointed wings. Sandeep tore the SASE open carefully and extracted the contents. His mathematical background and growing consternation had made him perform a detailed analysis. The numbers stared revealingly back at him. Statistics is proverbially like the bikini – showing the obvious and hiding the essentials. However, much like the long legs of the Dutch damsels, the visible obvious was staggering in itself. The number of rewrites of the synopses based on the profile of the agent and publisher amounted approximately to the size of Ulysses and Finnegan's Wake put together, and almost as widely unread. It was an awakening. He decided to reuse the same synopses from now on. The thoughtful authors of the helpful guides for success in the publishing industry could go and indulge in self assisted fornication as far as he was concerned.

∾ ∾ ∾

Mail from Simon to his mailing list
Sub: About a Girl and The Mind of the Author

Manouk Kruif is a stunner. My buddy agrees with me. In his slightly obnoxious words, Continental Europe's one member managerial secretary division has a profound effect on one's member.

I had often heard about this looker, most often in the confiding confines of the men's room, but this was the first time that I saw her. She was in the HMH office to organise a video conference connecting all the senior managers of Continental Europe, in the capacity of what Pritam termed *stunning steno.* The enterprising consultant, probably driven by our mutual admiration for her considerable charms, managed to grab a table for the three of us during lunch. He had come across her during his trip to Prague, and used this delicate foothold dextrously, steering her away from the compulsive cordiality of Madhu Deb that threatened to keep this local attraction under domineering wraps.

I felt that Manouk herself preferred our obvious attentions to the good lady's company. She was livid about the pomp and splendour of such video conferences. A lot of expense but resulting in a massive load of crap. However, my adept friend charmed her by pointing out that while she was burdened with flickering pictures of the drab old farts for company, the others had a splash of brightness sprinkled on their pitiable crisis harangued days in the form of her inviting image on their screens.

Having started in this vein, Pritam indulged in the performing art of poetic flirtation to an extent which would have become quite embarrassing had it not been for the obvious relish with which Manouk seemed to enjoy it. When the lady in limelight quickly computed the euro value for each such session which could very easily be carried out through a compilation of mails or a conference on msn messenger, my friend observed that she was not just a phenomenally pretty face, but excelled at figures too – and after a pause he added that it could be taken literally or *figuratively.* He was thoroughly enjoying himself and was probably contemplating a longish afternoon in her company, when Madhu Deb crashed through his scheme by hijacking her for some official purpose. She was probably lurking in wait for a logical interlude for the ambush, because her chubby form rolled into the frame as soon as we were done with our longish lunch.

As my buddy looked at the disappearing duo with eyes that seemed to reflect on what might have been and a brief uncharitable remark that the two together looked like a perfect ten, I winked at him.

"I find you like female company, mate," I observed.

He nodded. "Given the right kind."

I made a casual remark that he was probably having dark thoughts about the congeniality of the senior manager, when he shook his head.

"I can take it or leave it, Simon. For me, unless we are talking of someone special ..."

"Like Shruti?"

"Yes, like Shruti ... Unless it is someone that special, I don't really care whether she spends a lot of time with me or not ..."

"Good while it lasts?"

"Not exactly. I wonder if you'll be able to understand. Whenever there is a discussion with an interesting lady, and by interesting, I mean from the point of view of trimming her into the right size and dressing her up as a character in one of my masterpieces, I start experimenting. All the while I was paying her compliments, I was in the shoes of a fuzzy idea of a character whom I may or may not romantically link to her fictional counterpart in one of my novels."

I was slightly surprised, but it was quite an insight into the mind of the author in him. However, I did have some questions.

"But, then, don't you think that is misleading for the lady in question?"

He looked at me thoughtfully. There was a lengthy pause before he answered and I was half worried that I had offended him.

"I hope not. I am generally able to make a distinction between my experimental and real self. And it is always for casual encounters."

He had become distracted, and for a moment failed to respond to my next question. I had to ask him a second time.

"Has there been an occasion when you started off on an experimental mode and then it was no longer casual and you switched back to your real self?"

He threw his head back and looked at the ceiling for a while before responding.

"Yes, perhaps there have been occasions. Shruti for instance."

"Pritam, about Shruti ... she is the one you have officially married ..."

He smiled at me. "Simple Simon asking difficult questions."

I laughed.

"For future reference. I would like to have something handy to write about you once you become acknowledged as a great author."

He shrugged.

"I don't think that's possible today, Simon. The only authority that stamps greatness is time. And true greatness surpasses lifetimes. Since you and I are contemporary, I daresay you won't be offered the chance ..."

He broke off at this moment as an extraordinarily timid form of Amrita walked towards us. She was looking at Pritam with a pair of eyes that was an odd cocktail of sentiments. I am no expert, especially in the curiously closed and mysterious interactions of the Indian social life, but as far as I could make out, she managed to portray misgiving, reproach, guilt and a flicker of hope all at once. I had to wonder what had become of the cheerful girl of a few months back, the only problem with whom was a limited vocabulary.

Again, I stuck to the sound advice of my friend, to stick to the art and ignore any controversy as far as matters related to *tai chi* were concerned. I excused myself and walked out of the canteen.

I managed to peek into the workings of the artist in my friend who performs experiments in the cauldron of life to remodel the resulting outcome into works of imagination. There is a richness in his different dimensions that continues to reward casual excursions, while there remains a mystery and something eerily askew about his entirety. Is it enigma of his persona or some unrevealed secret that refuses to tally with the rest?

Cheers
Simon

∾ ∾ ∾

The mind works in mysterious ways. It can be simultaneously callous in its forgetfulness and also photographic in its memory. When Govind asked her in the morning about the risk projection report that was due today, it was a while before she managed to remember what he was talking about. It must have infuriated him, because he had spoken about it two days back and it had slipped her mind.

However, she could not ever forget any of the words, the motions, the touches, the pleasure and the pain associated with *him*. It was probably a week back that, browsing in the library, in a desperate attempt to read through the languishing pain of separation, she had come upon a book on Taoism. He had mentioned Taoism in his first demonstration class on *tai chi* and she had remembered. She had read it and had come across the lesson that one can learn from the flowing water. The gentle lapping water, rolling over the hardest of rocks for years and years can change their shapes.

Probably she had managed to do the same. She had managed to make the slightest of chinks in the rigid stone that had taken the place of his heart. And her mind, which had somehow made the mistake of expecting the soothing shade of his protective hand for eternity, had found the clause ridden permission to resume *tai chi* classes cause enough to celebrate.

She approached him today, ready to be refused, bracing herself for beating her head against an impenetrable wall, literally begging to be back in his class which she enjoyed so much. Simon was with him, but the gentleman that he was, politely withdrew when she walked up to them. Would any of the others have done the same? She was sure Madhu-di would not have. She would have taken up her position as the outer wall for the sake of the precious jewel in her collection. With all her *sur-soiree* and other tall tales that she recounts about associations with artists, Amrita found her thinking of the lady as a collector of gifted talents, who took more than a personal interest in her acquisitions. Obviously, the good lady also enjoyed people going around her putting her on a pedestal to worship as a god. She enjoyed being the divine mother of all her wards, and *he* was a prize item in her collection. All the same, Amrita could not get rid of the niggling suspicion that while she had taken pains to keep her feelings for *him* between *him* and her, largely bottled up in herself, *he* had actually gone and discussed it with the divine mother.

However, such was her lot and she had to stay content with the small blessings of life. And when she asked him, probably for the hundredth time, whether she could resume classes, he frowned, looked at her in that tired, irritated way that wrenched intolerably her my heart and said, "You don't give up, do you?"

She bit back tears that rushed up to her eyes from the depths of her soul, since he had made it abundantly clear that he was not too impressed by what he called her 'self pity'.

She answered that she would keep asking him again and again even if he never reopened the door for her. She tried to say that in English and must have made a mistake, because she could see him wince as he often did on such occasions.

He became silent for a while, without his spontaneous negative reply that she had by now grown used to and in spite of all that she had borne, her hopes rose within her.

"Why do you want to come back?" he asked. "Do you honestly want to learn *tai chi*?"

She choked a sob and told him that she wanted to learn the art. It was dreadful for her to break off from something that she had started to love. He winced again. May be she had made another grammatical mistake.

"I won't be here for three weeks or so, I will be going to Pasadena," he said.

"I know that."

"During that time, Simon needs a partner to keep training."

She waited with bated breath as he paused to think.

"You will need to come in after both of us have reached the dojo and will be the first one to leave," he said.

She wondered whether he had really said that. She could hardly believe her ears, so long subjected to the echo of rejection.

"I agree. I will do whatever you ask me to ..."

She did not think she made a grammatical or usage error but he winced anyway. Was she so repulsive? Whatever she said seemed to make him irritable.

"And there will be no communication – verbal, written, emailed, sms-ed, physical or even optical – during the classes or otherwise, any time during the day or night, which has to do with anything other than *tai chi*."

She had some problems in grasping what he meant, but managed to understand. She smiled sadly.

"I will not bother you in any way. I will try hard not to. I cannot promise about the look in my eyes and the reaction to your touch. There are some things mind and body cannot control. But, I will ensure that there is no more trouble for you."

He looked at her with eyes hardly concealing irritation.

"Don't sound so helpless and self sacrificing, please. You are an individual and if martial arts has any purpose, it is to make one confident. You are not living to be a shadow of someone's whims. Get a life."

The softness of his face that had drawn her towards him during the initial days of their relationship had been wiped away, perhaps never to return. Was she to blame? Why did he take the death threats literally? Did all that had bothered him about the threats amount to the complications that could arise if the implicating text messages were found in her cell phone? Did her living or dying at all matter to him?

"I am trying to improve myself ... Please help me a little more. And please don't worry, there will never be any more threats from me."

He walked past her, without bothering to answer. She hastily added that she loved him, but she was not sure whether he heard her whisper over the noise of the lunch room.

However, the door of the classes had been reopened. She spent the rest of the day trying to remember the forms and techniques. More than the break, the anxiety and conflict she had been through in the recent past had ensured that she was back to being a beginner.

During the class, to which she took care to arrive after Simon and he had started warming up, she struggled with the basic movements. He corrected her wherever necessary, but it was with a deliberate aloofness that he observed her actions, always on the guard, placing an invisible barrier between her and his softer self.

She departed quickly as soon as he ended the class. Simon barely got the time to thank her for coming back. As she walked to the station, alone as she had always been, all life long, she could smile through the tears. After all people like her needed to count the small blessings of life.

∾ ∾ ∾

Text Message from Madhu Deb to Sandeep

Confused. I heard that Amrita has rejoined classes.

Text Message from Sandeep to Madhu Deb

That's right. It's a martial arts class, I think whoever wants to learn should be welcome. No one is bigger than the art.

Madhu: So she is back in your life. If she has manipulated this decision out of you, I must say she is smart.

Sandeep: Relax. She is not in my life, has never been. This is a tai chi class. She is under strict rules and regulations and won't violate them to risk getting thrown out again.

Madhu: Don't say that I didn't warn you.

Sandeep: Relax Madhu-di. I am not helping her in any other way. But, I don't consider myself privileged enough to stop someone from learning the art.

Madhu : It's your decision.

Sandeep: It is :) When are you going to come back from your self inflicted break?

Madhu: I will :)

XLV

Email from Ms Shikha Bhatkhande to Sandeep

Dear Sandeep,

Thanks for your mail. Professor Lal is of course, as you stated, the common thread binding us. He continues to do yeoman's service to aspiring authors for generations. As you may have heard, I had published four of my first books through his Writers Workshop establishment before, after long struggle, rejections and self-doubt, I was finally able to become an author under the Walrus India banner.

Professor did indeed send me your book. I have skimmed through it, and it seemed extremely interesting. I have not really read it yet because I am working on a novel. During periods of extensive writing I read nothing but crime fiction. However, a niece of mine did borrow your book and while returning it sung the most effusive praises.

I have never had an agent, but I was represented by a lady called Margaret Craig in the United States. She has not managed to sell me in the States (probably people don't like my writing there), but managed to pull off a French translation deal. I will send her an email so that you can get in touch with her, but don't expect too much.

As far as Walrus and the other big publishers in India are concerned, you are quite right, they don't read what you send. However, Shanthi Ranganathan of Walrus did ask me to keep an eye open for young writers and I can recommend you to her. Once you get back to India, in case nothing fruitful takes place in USA or Europe, you can contact her. Then, of course, there is the process of regular follow ups and reminders to ensure that they don't forget your manuscript in their pile. If you are lucky, you may ultimately manage to get read.

For now, explore opportunities in the West.

Best Regards,
Shikha Bhatkhande

Sandeep read through the mail with Shruti.

"I often envy Aveek. Do you know about him?"

"The third dimension of your youthful triumvirate?"

"Right. The three of us used to paint the farmhouse owned by Suprakash Roy's parents red in our distant days of exuberant youth. He seems cut out to be the happiest of us."

The skies were darkening and the moon was on its silvery way up. Without premeditation, the two of them in the Wiltzanglaan apartment realised that they would be together for the night. Sandeep's noble intention of returning to Amstelveen had not been totally absent, but togetherness had shackled the reluctant limbs, making them oblivious of the gentle flow of time. Now there was no point of a lonely journey on chilly Amsterdam autumn night leaving the alternative of mutual warmth.

"He carried what Mr. P.G. Wodehouse would call a cheap substitute for the mind. I was going around, laying my hands on anything that I could read, training in the martial arts like a man possessed. Pritam was steadily working his way to a position of educational accomplishments with superbly sculpted cultural ignorance on the way to amassing sinful wealth. This guy had nothing specific to do. To my knowledge he never read a book after the Nick Carters we all masturbated with in school. He was bothered about nothing except having a good time with liquor and Bollywood movies."

Sandeep paused in reflection.

"We lost touch after college days, but I often wonder what he is doing. He joined an event management firm. I guess he is the one who is the happiest. No screechy scamper up the corporate ladder in strange rat races ..."

"Screechy scamper ... I guess you are back in mid-season form."

"No consuming angst borne out of the unwritten magnum opus and unpublished masterpieces."

"I wonder if this pair of u-m combination qualifies as hashed-alliteration. So you think a limited mental capacity is the key to happiness. Is that why a dog is so delighted with a simple tennis ball? Makes you think."

"In the modern world, is that the secret of happiness? Like the banks, should the civilisation go back to basics in terms of intelligence?"

Shruti raised an eyebrow.

"Are you recording this too? Is this going to go into the phony paper of yours?"

Sandeep shrugged. "I don't know. The paper is taking a life of its own. But, let's forget the monumental lies to concentrate on the moment of light..."

"Monumental lies and moment of light. Another hashed alliteration."

"Aveek is somewhere in India, perhaps earning a decent amount of money in a tension free job. Probably he has risen up the chain of event management organisations and now takes important decisions regarding the budget allocation for a housie tournament for the Marwari wives or the marked price of a pressure cooker in a *tol mol ke bol* contest. And after an honest day's work, he probably unwinds by watching some David Dhawan classic and betting on the outcome of one day internationals. He possibly goes on trips to Thailand and comes back with imported ipods and silk shirts from King Power Duty Free. Woody Allen's worries with existential puzzles don't tie him in knots, Dostoyevsky's dilemmas of crime and punishment will be known to him only if there is a ghastly pseudo-intellectual Bollywood remake by Sanjay Leela Banshali. He lives, breeds and is happy in ..."

"Would you like to be in his hypothetical place?"

"That's the point. I can't. And because of some useless development in the cranial quarters compared to the happy fellow, I am doomed to a life of continuous misery ..."

"Everything comes with its in-built opposite."

"Do you mean that far away, in his secure life as a strategic event management partner or whatever it is, Aveek is seething within and telling himself that a struggling author has a better life?"

Shruti removed the laptop from Sandeep's knee and took its place.

"Perhaps he knows that you are in the Netherlands. He may find himself thinking of all the good old days of school when he could have applied himself better and could work his way around the world instead of being stuck in the rut of Calcutta."

Sandeep peered into her eyes.

"Maybe you are right. Maybe he has his own list of miseries. And ... if he somehow manages to see me in this position, with the brain-blended-beauty on my knee, he may turn green with envy."

"But, let us consider the other third of your triumvirate. What if Pritam saw me sitting on your knee?"

"He would start off with a pang of jealousy of proportions that would give Othello a new dimension ... Othello could not turn green, but that is venturing into politically incorrect domain."

"Let us moor the diversion here. But after the initial shock, he would perhaps call the Marines to come to the aid of a childhood buddy."

"One man's meat is another man's poison."

"It is the perspective that matters."

"There is a Kashmiri saying. One man's beard is on fire, another man warms his hands in it. Now if Moses comes across the divine in a burning bush..."

"For God's sake hold your tongue ..."

ᔕ ᔕ ᔕ

Excerpt from the work in progress paper

Ethical, Knowledgeable, Alert or Neutral, Speculative, Powerful or Unscrupulous, Ignorant, Stagnant ... these are the groups of qualities based on which organisations operate or individuals interact. The groups of qualities at various times nourish the limitless opportunities that are forever available in the world held together by the machinery of finance as pearls on a string, interconnected across space and time through the inhibition stripping phenomena of electronic finance.

For individuals and organisations to achieve the imperishable state, to be unaffected by similar crisis in the future, one needs to cut through this source of limitless opportunity with detachment.

Decisions in that state are not influenced by the low hanging fruits, immediate benefits, possible lucrative operations in the inhibition free world of electronic transfers, credit derivatives. Ultimately, in unpredictable ways, the network of cause and effect binds every transaction across time and domains, industries across the world and the underworld, where an advantage of the moment is compensated by a crisis that creeps up unnoticed.

The need of the hour is hence robust control systems for the individuals and institutions which will test the detachment in decision making, analyse the motivation involved, and put embargos in place whenever the balance seems to shift to the second or third group of qualities.

K. Ramesh did something he had never done before. He touched Sandeep's excerpt that lay open on his laptop screen and devoutly brought his hand up to his forehead.

ᔕ ᔕ ᔕ

Simon's Post in Tai Chi forum
Subject: Parting Advice from Sifu

My sifu is going away for a month or so on work in another continent. And if I know him well enough, his work will not be limited to board rooms and conferences, but there will be a fair amount of training in the kwoons on the other side of the Atlantic.

These days I have discovered that my otherwise blasphemous teacher turning on his vicarious self during the classes.

He took us through the routines and made us write down several workout schemas to follow during the weeks of his absence. There were step by step methods for us to remember the various complicated *chin na* techniques. Since my partner was not yet introduced to shanza techniques, he took me through the drill alone and with painstaking perfectionism.

After that he was full of parting advice, some practical, some philosophical. I am reproducing most of it. We attend classes as a sport in a hierarchical organisation where some senior members sometimes grace the classes with their presence treating it as no more than casual pastime. So his words of wisdom were tailored to the corporate environment.

Make sure you get together for an hour each weekday. The phenomenon of inertia of rest is one of the most detrimental in martial arts. And even while I am not here, please abide by the rule of having no conversation in the dojo which does not directly relate to *tai chi*. Make the rule clear to any incidental visitor putting in a cameo appearance with no exceptions, even at the risk of sounding rude or insubordinate.

A martial art can very seldom be learnt alone. Especially an art like *chin na* is not possible to master without a training partner. So, both of you are important to each other. Insincerity on the part of each one will affect the development of the other. You are not only training for yourself, but also your partner. And the faster your partner develops the faster do you. It is a collaborative process. So, take responsibility for mutual growth. Be sincere in your training for each other.

When I am not here, you will probably find it more difficult to remember the movements and techniques. It is natural. It is an art which is not easy, and the difficulties will show you how much you have conquered. It is something to be encouraged and not otherwise.

He paused and finally a faint hint of a smile touched his uncharacteristically serious face.

"In certain circles, Pritam Mitra is known to be a Polonius when it comes to parting advice, so I think I will stop."

Mail from Simon to his mailing list
Sub: Diverse disciples

Two days remain before Pritam makes the trip across the Atlantic to sow our cannabis induced ideas in the fertile new world. I have been promised a completed version of the paper as soon as it is finalised.

I must confess I wish I could be over there, in the most important country of my complicated inheritance, surreptitiously holding a camera-phone to record the proceedings of the epoch-making event.

However, even as he leaves, his binding advice about sticking to taichi and no more has been instrumental in letting me survive the strange Indian dynamics surrounding the classes.

In fact, this microcosm of the tai chi class is giving me a crash course in the peculiarities that surround interpersonal relationships in an Indian group of any kind.

Today, no doubt busy connecting our figments of fancy, Pritam scheduled a two hour *tai chi* session at two in the afternoon. He had to leave early to put the finishing touches to the paper. However, the important deadline notwithstanding, he was his same devoted self in class.

Amrita did not have a clue about the allusion to Hamlet with which he ended the class (see my Tai chi forum post), but she did not wait for explanations once Pritam dismissed class. She has developed this habit of sprinting away as soon as the class is over.

I went back to work, with an energy that can come only from a full fledged *tai chi* class. It was nearing closing time when Madhu peeped in for a quick word.

"Are you done for the day?" she asked.

I told her that I was almost on the verge of closing shop.

"Should I get my bag? We can move together."

For a moment I did not know what she was talking about. She had attended about half a dozen classes in the last couple of months, so it was obviously difficult to correlate.

"Ah ... you mean the *tai chi* class? We already had it this afternoon."

I could see that she was taken aback.

"You had it this afternoon?"

I informed her that Pritam had to leave early to work on the paper and so we had had an early class.

Madhu did not seem amused.

"I see. Somehow I was not informed."

I was not very sure why she expected to be intimated about changes to the class schedules, going by her 'cameo' appearances, as my buddy put it. I asked her whether she wanted to join us on the following day, the last before Pritam went on his tour. I also wondered whether she would like to join us for training during the period he would be away and Amrita and I would be training without supervision.

She looked thoughtfully and said that she would let me know. She withdrew after that, which was a relief given that Pritam was busy with his paper and it would not have been okay to contact him in case a volley of Hidori anecdotes necessitated the Gupta-van der Wiel manoeuvre.

Even as she withdrew I could make out strong undercurrents at play, gushing out of corporate hierarchy and personal equations of the traditional Indian workplace. Great for my education on the culture. However, as buddy-sifu had pointed the way, I decided to relax and bother myself only with *tai chi.*

Cheers
Simon

Email from Professor P. Lal to Sandeep

Sandeep,

So you are on your way to the Bush-land, and you declare that the words of Janardana Krishna will go with you, to be presented in a new avatar.

Even as I wish you god speed, and marvel at the resourcefulness that has made all these assignments possible in the kala of recession ridded kali, I would ask you to spread the confusing concoction of words with care in the new world. War mongers that they have been, destruction is but a touch of the fanciful button for them. Do they need the lessons that resulted in the annihilating Kurukshetra?

Keep Well,
The Professor

XLVI

Email from 'Pritam Mitra' to Madhu Deb, Simon van der Wiel and Amrita Saha

Hi All,

It was good to see all of you in class today. I will hope you will continue in the same vein while I am away. I have already harped often enough on the necessity of collaboration in martial arts. Whenever some important issue in the busy world of ours seems to rise up the chain of priorities, please remember that your presence in the class is not only for your own development but also the progress of your fellow students. The quicker each one of you learn, the better it is for your entire group.

I would like to leave you with a single thought.

Have any of you wondered why we call the place where we train the 'dojo'? It is not a Chinese term – they would have said kwoon *or* dao chang*.*

Dojo is a Japanese term I use because I had started out on the martial path with karate do, the Japanese way of the Empty Hand (or Chinese hand as some experts say).

It may sound serendipitous, but dojo is a fragmentation of a Sanskrit word – Bodhimanda. The word denotes the place under the Bodhi tree where Buddha attained enlightenment. It can also be translated as a place where we try to strip ourselves of our ego and strive for truth.

Please bear this in mind.

See you in a month,
Pritam

ᘓ ᘓ ᘓ

Sandeep looked at his completed paper and grinned. He had always been aware of the difficulties of writing for children. Over dependence on imagination, with reality relegated to the background – while he generally applied faint fictional strokes to the fascinating foundation of facts. Looking at his paper from some angles, it contained unrestrained creativity, stretched away from truth with elastic license. He had probably evolved as an author. He chuckled.

There was a knock on the panel of his cubicle and he looked up to find the round form of Madhu Deb beaming at him.

"Oh hi," he said, shutting his laptop down and starting to wind up.

"All set?" the cheery voice of Madhu Deb was mingled with the minutest of melancholy.

"Yes, I am ... Westward ho."

The good lady nodded.

"It brings back fond memories. I used to ..."

"Quite so ... right... the Americas always have a certain nostalgic lure ... ha ha," Sandeep put his latop in the bag and rose.

Her anecdotes grounded before gathering sufficient momentum to take flight, the lady looked confused and was silent for a while.

"I'll miss you," she said.

Sandeep laughed.

"It's just for a few weeks. I'll be back here before you start to realise what a good thing not having me around actually is ..."

Madhu Deb sighed.

"I am trying hard, Pritam, to get used to living with an NPD ..."

"A what?"

"Samit, Pritam. Narcissistic Personality Disorder ..."

"Ah yes," he shuffled uncomfortably.

"It is difficult, with all the emotional tension. However, I am trying to get used to it. I really felt very relieved whenever I discussed my problems with you ..."

Sandeep nodded. He sat down on the edge of the table.

"That's good to know, Madhu-di. I doubt whether I have done anything worthwhile to help. On the contrary, I am grateful for all your help."

Madhu Deb smiled with eyes shiny not merely from joviality.

"I tried to help. I doubt whether I succeeded. Anyway, I think Ramesh wanted you to be here for the period to help him write the paper ..."

"Help?"

"Well, to write your co-authored paper for him. You don't expect a VP to actually do anything but provide ideas, do you?"

Sandeep laughed.

"He has ideas. I will give him that."

"He is intelligent, a visionary perhaps."

"With proper marketing he can be get himself included in the list of avatars of Narayana."

Madhu Deb laughed.

"You and your sarcasm. I will miss you once you are gone. Once the paper is done, Ramesh won't require you here anymore. And our friend Ajay Yadav has been quite busy counting the account euros that are being spent on you. I will miss you. Make sure you keep in touch."

She took a step closer to the desk on which he sat and enfolded him in a parting embrace. As Sandeep hesitatingly brought his hands lightly down on her back, she kissed him on his cheek.

"Bon voyage," she said. Sandeep resurfaced from the chain of command that had bound him, wondering if the supervisor took *pecking order* in a transposed literal sense. "And wish you all the best in your American journey."

Sandeep unmindfully lifted his shoulder to wipe his cheek.

"Keep training. And if you can, find a school while I am away."

He walked out of his cubicle. Manouk Kruif, in the office again for some urgent administrative issue, approached him with an outstretched hand and a blinding smile.

"All the best," she said. Sandeep grasped her hand and shook it for a few lingering moments longer than necessary.

"Thanks. That's the most charming parting gift I could wish for. How come you are in office today? It's too early for the next video conference of the high and mighty."

Madhu Deb joined in their laughter.

"He gets sarcastic at times," she observed.

"Ajay had some issues with profitability figures."

"He did, did he? Anyway, that brought you here. Goes to show that everyone contributes to the society in some way. But, how can one concentrate on offending figures with you around?"

Madhu Deb sighed and shook her head as Manouk laughed.

"Manouk, let's step in to look at the resourcing sheet," the good lady offered. "Pritam will drive you nuts."

The two ladies walked towards Madhu Deb's cubicle, waving their mutual farewells, while Sandeep stood there musing absentmindedly on the resemblance to a disappearing figure 10.

This was when Simon ultimately found his buddy, the latter looking forlornly at the delicious but departing derriere of Manouk Kruif. Well, there was the accompanying expanse of Madhu Deb's behind as well, but knowing the male mind in general and his buddy's sensuous speculations in particular, Simon had no doubt that the considerable horizontal spread crept into the purvey of his senses only for the sake of comparison, if at all.

"The figure ten is reputed to be perfect," Sandeep observed wistfully as Simon walked up to him. "But a receding version leaves something to be desired. I would prefer a binary dissociation of digits, in which the one and only approaches and the round zero merges with the nothingness it symbolises."

"I must say that is mathematical, poetic and also uncharitable," Simon winked.

"Is it?" Sandeep debated. "Let us stick to the field of interesting recreational numerology. There is a well known school of thought that breaks up the phenomenon of chancy concurrence. This particular hypothesis states that when it happens once it is accident, twice points to coincidence and the third accounts for conspiracy."

"Flowery with figures, but not making too much sense."

Sandeep nodded.

"The problem, Simon, is that you are not aware of the facts and hence the figures seem abstract. So, let me dip my brush in the palette of truth and make the imagery clear with a few broad strokes. Do you remember my trip to Prague?"

"I do have a documented, rhyming memoir of the predicaments of the high flying consultant when he flies high with Madhu Deb."

"True. I wonder if I have told you that in the course of my Prague visit, I attended some *tai chi* classes as well."

"I am aware of your inclination to attend classes worldwide. I am not surprised."

"To cut a long story short, I got injured during a *chi sao* routine, when a gorilla of a man planted his elbow on my cheek with a lot of will to win. It took off some enamel from my molars, something that I painfully realised while sipping a cup of coffee in Sare Mesto. The sun was painting the cobblestones rust and Madhu Deb just starting to get vocal on the subject of Hidori and his weakness for Brownies. I see you wincing my friend, and I appreciate it. It was prior to the discovery of the celebrated Gupta-van der Wiel manoeuvre, so you could not come to my rescue. But, the outcome was that the helpful lady managed to fix an appointment with a dentist once we returned to Amsterdam."

"That was very kind of her."

Sandeep looked thoughtful.

"It was indeed. She went about extending her helping hand so much that I could not walk around it. She volunteered to drive me all the way to the clinic. There is an enthusiastic drive in her altruism that steamrolls over your hapless self. So, once I was there, she sat in the waiting room. The assistant of this dentist was a Chinese version of Manouk. Do you know what I mean?"

Simon's lips parted in a knowing smile. "I can well imagine. Asian girls, in my book, score perhaps the highest in many of the categories of sex appeal."

"I agree wholeheartedly. So my experimental self took over and soon I was having a conversation with her that could be approximated as frivolous flirtation. Within the course of the appointment, I extracted her promise to pose for the benefit of my camera."

Simon patted him on the back. "Well, I guess I should congratulate you. Had he transference from experimental to real taken place with the Chinese corker in question?"

"No, and that is not germane to the discussion, as my old English teacher would have put it. However, what did happen was that I armed myself with the digital camera and reached the place on the date of appointment, ready to shoot at sight and ask questions later. And who did I see waiting patiently in the clinic ..."

"You're kidding."

"I assure you, she was there in person. She had remembered my date of appointment and had got an appointment for her own, some cavity to be filled – her story was full of holes. While my experimental self was toying with the idea of filling that one all important cavity, in the rehashed version of the flirtation in my next masterpiece."

Simon asked him to pause in his convoluted rhetoric and thought about it.

"So, she was there. She remembered the date of the appointment."

"Yes she did. It also happened to be the day when we had that ceremony at Lahari's place. We went there together in her car."

Simon remembered that day and smiled. "It must have been an extremely eventful evening."

Sandeep shuddered.

"Yes, in more ways than I care to remember. But, the crux of the matter, as my English teacher would again have put it again, she was there as an insurmountable barrier in my experiments with the Chinese girl. And later, on two occasions, she has successfully managed to snatch Manouk out of my grasp, walking away with her, a disappointingly disappearing figure of ten. So, it makes three counts ... and according to several authorities, from the witches of Macbeth to the current school of thought on coincidences, three is a significant figure."

Simon patted his buddy on the shoulder.

"Don't read too much into the thing. " He added something to the effect that there were bound to be girls aplenty, each more attractive than the other, in the land of opportunities and Madhu Deb, substantial as she is in girth, could not stretch across the ocean and plant her forbidding self between him and the feminine fascinations on the other side of Atlantic.

"I assume so," Sandeep nodded, not too perked. "I have been most intrigued by the bevy of female beauties who bare themselves during the summer months in the Central Park. On the other side of the great country, I am sure there will be a gaggle of girls lying in wait to brighten up the life of a burdened man."

"Definitely. West Coast is full of sunny beaches."

"We can always hope for the best, Simon, and I sincerely hope that was not a pun," Sandeep sighed. "However, don't let this compulsive altruistic disorder, or the meddling mother syndrome, come between you and *tai chi.* Stick to the rules of the dojo like the accomplished adhesive, grandest of glues. And do the *shanzi* routines on your own. Remember, the other two have not yet done enough to join my *fan* following."

He walked away with this piece of advice. Simon was left with the feeling that his buddy was back to his irreverent best, but, in his inimitable way, he had ended up imparting essential wisdom.

∾ ∾ ∾

He was going away. And already she felt like a wife whose husband had been placed abroad. While there was the pain of separation, there was the anticipation of the weeks passing in preparation and the passionate reunion.

Indeed. Crazy girl, whom was she trying to deceive? While she shed unseen tears, and suppressed unheard sobs in the solitude of her cubicle, did he even think of her once as he stepped out on his journey?

He had given instructions for the classes, mailed them repeating more or less the same thoughts. But, they had been addressed to all – Simon and well, Madhu-di too, since she put in an appearance that day. Nothing specific was said to her, not one word, not one look, not one gesture to convey that she meant something to him other than a face in the class.

In the last few minutes in office she had heard him exchanging words with Madhu-di, Simon and Manouk Kruif. Manouk. She had always noticed he enjoyed the company of beautiful ladies. And fate-less that she was, she could not even lay claims to being jealous.

She also saw Trisha come out and bid him good bye, and since she was someone who spoke fluent English, he exchanged a couple of clever jokes with her. Did she like her because she was fair, smart, reasonably good looking? She did not know, but knowing him as she did, it could very well be the reason.

She walked quickly down to the lobby where the lift emptied the passengers in the ground floor. She stood there pretending to wait for the elevator. She had been asked not to speak to him about anything but *tai chi.* So, she had to engineer this coincidence.

He must have got involved in some more discussions, possibly with the Dutch ladies of HMH, since it was another fifteen minutes before he stepped out of an elevator. Her heart, which had skipped a beat every time a chime announced a descending shuttle, leaped up and throbbed so hard as her eyes fell on him, that she was afraid that he would hear it.

He looked at her, seemed puzzled, unsure how to react. He stepped one way, and for a moment she thought he would be walking away without speaking to her. However, he seemed to have second thoughts and paused.

"Bye," he said.

She thanked providence again and again for the one syllable that he had uttered.

"Bye, please take care."

He nodded and almost smiled.

"Keep training. And remember, you are going to the dojo for *tai chi* and nothing else."

She nodded and as planned, dropped her pen. As she stooped to pick it up, she managed to touch his shoe and as she came up touched her forehead and breast.

She thought it would go unnoticed, but knew she had failed when she looked at his face and met with that scowl which chilled her heart.

"Damn it all, why the hell do you have to go through all this drama?" he asked.

He spoke loudly and the security guard at the reception briefly raised his head to look at them before turning away.

"What is drama for you is belief for me," she replied, waiting for him to shout his way out of the situation. She was already expecting him to ask her to discontinue classes again.

"Just shut up," he said irritably. "I have asked you not to get into that mode, haven't I?"

She felt herself cowering. The anxiety of being torn apart again for this innocent action was eating away at her nerves.

"I am sorry, it won't happen again."

"Jesus Christ," he said. "What's the point in learning martial arts if you stick to the age old convictions that the place of women is at the men's feet? I don't fucking understand how you manage it. Never try that again."

With a couple of sentences he managed to upturn all the values that she held dear and sacred. He had that power. She had given him that authority. With a snap of his finger he could alter the flow of her life.

"Please take care," she whispered as he passed her. "And I am sorry if I offended you."

He clutched the curly locks that hung over his forehead and reverted to the same impatient mood that had always accompanied her interactions with him in recent times.

"If there is any damn lesson that you learn from all this training, please grow to respect yourself as an individual. Why do you need to grovel?"

She did not know what grovel meant, so waited for him to explain, but he did not.

"Keep training, and focus on training alone," he said as he walked away, disappearing for the next few weeks.

She managed to whisper again that she loved him, but would never know whether he heard it or not.

But, then, she had managed to wish him and had got what she wanted. And she was back in his class. With her fate, could she afford to complain?

∾ ∾ ∾

"Don't you think the political scenario in EU, especially the negative effects, is to some extent influenced by the great United States of America?"

Shruti looked up from the packet of Chinese takeaway. Neither of them wanted to spend time cooking tonight.

"Name one negative phenomenon in the world of International relations which has not been influenced by the great land."

"The attack of the Bush-men?"

"The erstwhile Bush-men. They are busy liberating the world from various problems. With specific focus on countries blessed with exceptional natural resources or strategic geographical position."

"Bolivia, Nicaragua, Iran, Iraq, Afghanistan?"

"The secret list is well known."

"Don't you think your treatise on the negative effects of the EU will remain incomplete without a three week visit to the United States? To place the empire under microscope?"

Shruti laughed.

"Tempting, but I have promises to keep ..."

"And one not made?"

“Let us not work towards manufactured consent.”

Sandeep’ s cell phone tinkled to life.

“Our psychiatric friend. Hello Dr. Roy.”

The practised voice from the other end was as impassive as ever.

“So you are on your way to Los Angeles?”

Sandeep laughed.

“Yes, sir.”

“May I ask a question which has been disturbing me for a while?”

“Of course, as many as you like. Do you want me to lie on the couch?”

Suprakash Roy winced.

“I think I mentioned the difference between the psychiatrist and the analyst, Sandeep.”

“I guess the Freudian cigar is misleading.”

“You are impersonating Pritam on this visit as well, aren’t you?”

“I confess, I am. How is he, by the way? Haven’t heard from him for a while.”

The good doctor pursed his lips.

“He is somewhere in United States, biding his time till you keep your end of the promise to get out of his life once this paper episode is over. He will resume his life in the new company.”

“That’s what he said in his last mail as well, not exactly in language suitable for the whole family.”

“There has been a sense of acceptance. However, did you guys exchange passports?”

“Eh? No ... we haven’t gone to that extent.”

“How did you manage to obtain a US visa?”

Sandeep got up from the dinner table and moved towards the window.

“A tourist visa. From the embassy here in Den Haag. Took some convincing.”

“That’s a relief.”

“I detect in your voice, my dear Doctor, the returning strain of reproach.”

“Pritam is my cousin, Sandeep. Unfortunately maybe, but that’s how it is. A prolonged period of uncertainty may have adverse effects on him, and I have a sense of responsibility. I was just wondering if this should not be the last adventure under swapped identity.”

“My sentiments exactly. I want to take this excellent opportunity to hand over my resignation to the great Ramesh.”

“I was wondering whether you were finding the borrowed life too lucrative.”

“Good heavens, no. I can’t carry on forever. Already there have been too many complications. This is a logical moment to end the madness.”

"That's a relief. I wish you success, but not too much of it. Don't be too famous or Pritam won't be able to get back into his shoes."

"Let me reassure you that I am not going to the land of opportunities in order to make a splash with my paper. I have more serious writing to promote."

"Agents and publishers?"

"Right."

"I had an inkling that something hatched in a smoking joint is not on the top of your list of priorities."

Sandeep shook his head.

"You can be mistaken there, doctor. This particular paper is all about Indian wisdom. And if you look at Maheshwar of the holy trinity ..."

"Hallucinogens come in handy. I agree. Analysts and psychiatrists have been known to experiment with that sort of stuff. Let me warn you about something. Don't be surprised if you land there to find Pritam lurking in wait."

"Does your analysis tell you that it is a possibility?"

"It does."

"I'll welcome him with open arms. He is a dear friend, after all."

Sandeep returned to the table. Shruti had put his packet back in the microwave.

"Quite a discussion with the doctor."

"Interesting exchange of ideas."

"Freudian enough to move away from audible range."

Sandeep looked at the upturned tip of the nose, thrust at him at the familiar challenging slant.

"It was strictly man to man."

"Is it manly to hide behind the cloak of chauvinism?"

"There is a sense of propriety in your chagrin I find most inviting."

The upturned tip of the nose quivered.

"Wordplay won't get you off this hook, charming chicaner."

"That's alliteration at its best."

"Neither will false flattery."

"What about foreplay? To add to the brace of effable alliterative?"

"Temporarily tabooed."

"You cast a net of helplessness around mind and manhood. What do you want to know?"

The nose quivered again.

"How many of your cronies are party to your secret?"

Sandeep tried to look beyond the distracting nose, the quivers dangerously indicating the whiff of a rat.

"There you take me into deep waters, Shruti. What secret?"

"I remember you telling me that I looked at home with a hockey stick."

The path of the conversation was turning particularly bumpy.

"Shruti, I have a flight to catch tomorrow ..."

"You can fly, but you can't hide. You are grounded. I think I will fetch my stick after all."

"I am eager to offer you mine."

Sandeep's collar was grabbed by a quick hand with a firm grip.

"Enough of your infamous innuendos. Who else, apart from the two of you and the surreptitious shrink, knows about your identity swap?"

For a moment Sandeep's eyes flashed in alarm and looked past the fist and the curling nose. And then, as their eyes met, he relaxed. The flame of annoyance that burnt holes into him was obviously fanned by the wind of hilarity.

"How did you find out?"

The shake of the collar almost choked him.

"All the lofty adulations of the cerebral component of my charms – were they fickle flattery? Now you insult my intelligence? Whenever you guys spoke Pritam whispered in hushed tones and resembled an agitated octopus. He had a near cerebral attack when you brought *Bhagavat Gita* into the scheme of things. And later, in the drug den, Simon openly called you Pritam ..."

One of the assets of being a trained martial artist is in the expertise of bodily manoeuvre. With a slight twist of his torso, Sandeep clasped her to his bosom, planted her on his lap.

"A temporary arrangement, to try and give my literary career a kick start as he romped about Europe."

"In an attempt to woo me, if I may add."

"When the plan was hatched, I did not know that you were *you*."

"It had to be someone."

"Pritam is good enough for someone, isn't he?"

"Well, ... I guess he is."

"I had to present a paper for him ..."

"This one?"

"No, another one. Here, in Amsterdam. The plan was to present it and get out of sight. But, I couldn't really prepare for the event, the paper was drab, boring and made no sense. I ended up presenting extempore, some derivation from the *Gita* ... one thing led to another..."

"Including ideas hatched in smoking dens, *tai chi* classes, Prague trips and stalking females."

Sandeep shrugged.

"I guess there were lots of things I could not control."

There was a pause during which, holding Shruti close to himself, Sandeep felt as if exposed to the after effects of a seismic wave. A concerned check found her convulsed with laughter. He joined in.

"It makes sense. The look on Pritam's face as if the world had crashed through the floor. The anxiety of turning the page of his appointment book and finding doomsday writ large. Sandeep, should I be annoyed and make a serious attempt to find my hockey stick?"

"Why do you think I am holding you so tight?"

"You are the biggest liar I have met on the face of the earth..."

"What about George Bush and ..."

"I have not met them personally. And even in the face of this grand deceit I find myself chuckling, and more ... You are crazy, and ... by induction, so am I."

They kissed in the echoes of fun, in mutual realisation of the absurdity, and kissed again, the vibrations of laughter leading to resonance of souls, union of bodies. It does credit to the alarm system built in the Nokia handset which shook Sandeep awake in time to catch his flight.

Part IX:

Dollar Rolls

XLVII

Pretty Partner in Crime,

I have reached the sun-kissed land, stepped out into the glorious weather of the West Coast. It is a far cry from the misty, damp Amsterdam that I left.

Even then, sustaining warmth seems to have been shut out of my life with a twist of the knob of fate. The Taoist priests were right in pointing out that without the nasty negatives one cannot really appreciate the pleasant positives. Where can I, in this sunny heaven of a land, experience the comfort of rushing through bone chilling rain laden gusts to snuggle under the blanket on your sofa, hot chocolate in hand, with you restoring warmth with your eyes, voice and touch?

Hush, hush ... says Diane Lane. But as my learned psychiatric friend puts it, the medium of Ethernet takes inhibition out of the equation.

Ramesh says he understands that I will be under the weather – well, here that does not sound too bad – after my long flight and will give me time to recover before our meeting tomorrow. I feel sorry for the man, but will be immovable as a rock, without a sympathetic nerve in my soul and declare that this will be the last time I work with him.

All the best as you paint the stark image of the European situation in your thoughtful thesis. Wish you were here with me to sketch the American perspective as well.

Absence Makes the Heart Grow Fonder,
Sandeep

∾ ∾ ∾

"The project promises to make a stir," Ramesh observed. There was a mellow beam in his bearing, the satiated sagaciousness that comes with a profound job well done. In front of them, vehicles bustled along the sun swept Colorado Boulevard. Tall ficus trees smiled down on the main thoroughfare of Pasadena. Sandeep sipped his cafe latte, battling the jet lag.

"So do I, Ramesh," Sandeep paused with the hesitation of the executioner about to flick the switch of life.

"Of course, Pritam. It was a great job," Ramesh continued. "The more I read, the more I feel that you have not only captured the essence of my ideas, but have gone way beyond."

A young man with an obsolete laptop sat in the far corner of the Starbucks outlet, typing furiously. Sandeep wondered whether he was an upcoming author.

"Before I heard your presentation in Amsterdam, I did not know what to do about my ideas. I had asked the senior management of Business Consulting to come up with a treatise based on an independent Indian model," he shuddered. "It turned out to be ... well ... a collage of everything available in the market. No one thinks out solutions any more. Thoughts are an overhead. The internet is there for the taking, so jump in with copy and paste... In fact, after I saw the presentation they prepared, I am kind of glad that they don't think."

Sandeep sipped his coffee and nodded.

"I know what you mean."

Ramesh beamed some more.

"I wonder how you have managed to hang on to the faculty of thoughts, when you are supposed to sell bull-shit by the bushel. "

"I sometimes find ways to stimulate thought."

Ramesh looked interested.

"Could you let me in on some of your secrets?"

"I wonder if it is legal. LA is not as legally liberal as Amsterdam."

"In that case I am probably too old for such stimulants," Ramesh laughed. However, he soon became the visionary again. "Once we make a hit here, there's no stopping us, Pritam. The ideas are too good. I am glad you are a creative writer. We must collaborate."

Sandeep looked at the older man with a cautious eye.

"Isn't that what we have done?"

"I mean take it along its logical continuation, Pritam. I can almost see how things will turn out."

"And how does it look in the crystal ball?" Sandeep braced himself to withstand and thwart another burst of innovation from the shiny bald head.

"I see a book, Pritam."

"I beg your pardon?"

"I am thinking of making this into a book. And if the attendees are sufficiently impressed, I may even get the book idea sold and funded here. I think I can woo McGraw Hill ..."

Sandeep stood up.

"Now, please ... let's not rush ..."

Ramesh nodded, looking at him with his eyes still focussed far in the future.

"Of course not. The first step is to present this, make it a big hit ..."

"This is not a Broadway musical."

"Ha ha ... but works on the same principles. My instincts say that it will be big. After that, we will wave our success in front of Dave de Boer's supercilious nose ..."

Sandeep held up his arms like an airfield attendant, waving airborne fantasies into a quick descent back down to earth.

"I don't know what your plans are, but I get the impression that you have it all chalked out in precise detail. But, please, I am not a non-fiction guy."

Ramesh looked puzzled. He noticed unexplained fear streaking through his eyes, much in the same vein as during his first discussion with him. When the seeds of this excellent idea were planted in a hotel room. It made him stop, but his thoughts had not returned sufficiently close to reality to make sense of his exclamation.

"You're not what?"

"I am into fiction, Ramesh. For what you propose to do, you must get a solid non-fiction stalwart, who won't be swayed into story telling even if tempted with knobs on."

Ramesh frowned. Why classify needlessly and add to confusion? He slipped into his role of the motivational leader.

"Nonsense, Pritam. You are the best writer I have come across. And even if you think you are only into fiction, it's simply because you are yet to discover the full range of your talents. This paper proves your versatility."

"Ramesh, believe me, this paper is the purest piece of fiction I have written in my life."

The great man saw the funny side.

"This is what makes you priceless. One cannot come up with ideas without the gift of humour."

"What you need is a Thomas Friedman, or a Nicholas Taleb. If you want the Indian angle badly, you have to go for Shiv Khera or some clown like Laxmanchand Raha, perhaps..."

Ramesh laughed.

"I want you, Pritam. And I am going to have you."

Sandeep's desire to protest was humbled by the decisive voice of the Vice President. For all his humane side, Ramesh knew when to put employees in place.

"We can negotiate on the requirements. We will make the format suit storytelling if required. We are speaking of entirely new approaches, aren't we?

What is the way of teaching in the Upanishads? Dialogue, anecdotes, similes, metaphors, allegories and stories. I think you are just tailor made for this," Ramesh paused and patted Sandeep on his shoulder. "And I know you won't disappoint me. It was really nice to see you, Pritam. It's been quite a while hasn't it?"

Sandeep found himself nodding.

"I will leave you to settle down. Get ready for the big day."

With the well emulated trick learnt from Dave de Boer, Ramesh left a ten dollar bill on the table, got up and walked to the door. Seated on his chair, Sandeep wondered absently about the perils and predicaments of Abhimanyu.

∾ ∾ ∾

Blog of Simple Simon

Tags: Taichi, Training, Without Master

With the teacher, the path seems easy. And without, every step becomes a question. In more ways than one.

Every evening, when following Pritam's motions, or performing under his watchful eyes, corrected at the slightest deviation from perfection, the movements of our art had been manageable. Now, without him to guide us, we end every step wondering whether the weight was supposed to be on the back foot or front, the hip to be rotated after the step or with, the arm was unfurled with too much speed or just right? It does not help when two students have conflicting opinions, and the third disappears after a brief appearance during the first trainer-less lesson.

Amrita and I most often end up in bouts of laughter, wondering if there is any hope to ever achieve some proficiency. So, sometimes, we take confidence building breaks. I do a routine with the *shanzi,* where at least no one can argue with me over the correct feet positions. Amrita resorts to some vigorous kick and punch drills which she informs me are the basics of Karate.

I did send a mail to my buddy informing him of the confusion, and his answer was characteristically cryptic, "*If the confusion clears, you will stop learning.*" When I mentioned it to Amrita, she said that people who had become experts could afford quips like that.

It is good to see her training with the single minded dedication of old. While Madhu is too busy with her next edition of *Sur Soiree,* the girl is in time for every class, working hard till her forehead gleams with sweat.

Mail from Simon to his Mailing List
Subject: Confusing Confidences

The departure of my buddy has left me without the trusted Gupta-van-der-Wiel manoeuvre, which makes me susceptible to the anecdotes of Madhu Deb. She has been bounding into my cubicle more often than I would have budgeted for or preferred. She is never short of topics of conversations, and it is but one easy step for her to proceed to the saga of Hidori. She came to me yesterday, all perturbed about some incident of police brutality that had taken place in Kolkata. I resigned myself to a long and graphic account of the atrocities that police descended to in her home country, her own personal interactions with the men of law and so on, ending with her hesitation in returning to India and letting Hidori grow up in a state where law implied lawlessness.

I had braced myself for a sequence of Hidori stories, putting on my best interested smile, when her cell phone rang. Thanking my stars for the divine network signals, I got up from my seat to engineer a getaway beyond the tales from far and wide. However, the call was short and she was done even as I was on the way around my desk.

"Are you leaving? Okay ...," she said in a disappointed voice which almost made me feel sorry for her. "I won't keep you any longer ..." she paused, "Have you heard from Pritam?"

I told her that we had exchanged a couple of emails. He seemed to have reached the United States safely and full of vim and vigour as usual.

Madhu Deb smiled at the news, adding that for all his accomplishments, the man in question was still a kid. "I wonder when he's going to develop some maturity to survive without mothering." I did not know what to make of it, so laughed. My buddy's warning to beware of the meddling mother syndrome sounded prophetic.

"One expects a formal mail informing arrival," she complained. "Anyway, he lives in a peculiar world of his own."

I agreed with her on that count, pointing out that he was an author after all.

"He is, but he is also supposed to be a professional. He is brilliant and I admire him for all his qualities, even without his martial arts or writing skills. But, as a professional a lot is expected from someone with his seniority. He had been placed so close to Dave de Boer, but Ajay complains that he has seen no endeavour on his part to win business. I agree. One expects a consultant to at least make some visible effort. Of course he went around charming the HMH people with his series of lectures, but even if you are brilliant, you are expected to do something for the company. I can't always protect him saying Ramesh expects him to work on their paper. There are explicit and implicit expectations and sometimes, with all his brilliance, he drives me nuts ..."

She was speaking with animation. Being a self confessed fan of my weird buddy, a lot of disquieting thoughts criss-crossed across my mind. I could only half suppress a smile when I heard of her reference to the brilliant series of talks – which included extempore rehash of philosophical texts, guest psychiatric speakers and an episode from Woody Allen's *Everything You Wanted to Know About Sex and were Afraid to Ask.* I also wondered how anyone could magically win business from a bureaucratic Dutch Bank in the nadir of recession.

While I agreed to some of the immaturity alluded to by the lady, I could not make out why she had singled me out for her analysis of Pritam. I could understand she was perturbed, perhaps even frustrated, but I was too insignificant in the hierarchical rungs of the organisation to be a party to such confidences. I put it down to one of those inexplicable Indian traits incomprehensible this side of the Suez.

"I know he is very impressive, but he has a lot of shortcomings which is better not to emulate," she concluded. I could make out she was upset. She also wanted to drive home a point. And having done her driving, she reversed and wheeled away, I guess with the intention of making me mull over her message.

I was moved enough to think about it. And even as I thought of the words *motherly menace,* I wondered about the choice of her phrases.

Did Madhu think I was emulating Pritam in walks of life other than *tai chi* and wanted to warn me? Am I in fact influenced by him? He is definitely my teacher and I respect him as far as *tai chi* is concerned, but what about other aspects of life? Even you guys have mentioned that I have been writing a lot about him.

The philosophical lessons of *tai chi* do have their uses in real life too, and I am still trying to find out the positive applications. But, that is an effect of the art and not the man himself.

There are other influences. I can make out the change in my writing style, the satires becoming more farcical and the figures of speech making more conscious inroads into my prose. I thoroughly enjoy his warped view of the world, his all encompassing irreverence, ripping apart of the society with ridicule. Even though I do not fully subscribe to it, it may have influenced my corporate philosophising, which was never built on stable ground to start with.

We fend for each other in the face of ... well, the other face of motherly menace. I definitely share a bond and to an extent I am a fan. Who can resist admiring someone who rubs Ajay Yadav in the way that he does, indulges in hidden cameras and organises brain storming after clouding them with cannabis?

The longer I thought, the more I felt that the motherly warning was unwarranted and interfering. I could do without maternal meddling in what was strictly my personal business. Perhaps it was a trespassing of personal boundaries caused by difference of culture, something that I myself had probably been guilty of on numerous occasions.

Although my official buddy seems to be at his helpful best, uploading instructive clips of video on youtube from the wonderland of Los Angeles, Madhu has shown no inclination to try out the techniques. In fact, after an initial class which she left halfway to attend some tennis match, she has declined our invitations to join us for training. There is something that has upset her about the whole thing involving my buddy, tai chi classes and the visit to the good old new world. I have an inkling that the venom in her tongue was concocted by these strange dynamics, the exact nature of which continues to fox me.

So, I resorted to that single piece of advice given to me by my buddy. If it concerns the dojo, stick to *tai chi* and nothing else. That proved to be the end of dilemma and the gateway to peace.

Cheers
Simon

~ ~ ~

"Kinley Literary Agency, good afternoon."

"Hi, I am calling with a query regarding possible representation."

"Are you calling on your own behalf?"

"Yes, I am."

"Have you sent your synopsis and query letter by post?"

"No, ma'am, I am in Pasadena, and so I ..."

"Sir, you have to send your query letter by post."

"Isn't it possible to arrange a face to face interview?"

"I'm sorry, the rules are ..."

"Yes, but the rules are man-made. They can be changed. Or at least bent."

"Not in our agency. You can try another."

"Isn't it easier if I talk about the synopsis and read out a few lines rather than sending it by post?"

"No, we don't arrange face to face interviews."

"In that case do you want me to open the package and post the SASE back to myself instead of going through you? It will be easier and less taxing on your slush pile."

"I think you are wasting my time ..."

"Do you even realise the amount of time the authors waste trying to hunt down agents? Time that could have been spent writing ...?"

"Sir, you are not the first one to face rejection ..."

"No, Bernard Shaw was rejected sixty one times. We could have had another couple of Pygmalion or Man and Superman had it not been for this endless process of searching for one agent who can actually read."

"Good bye."

"At least I know that you can hear ... so don't you think reading to you is an option?"

The line went dead.

Email from Kailash Nayak

Hi Sandeep,

Great to know you are in LA. Must be a change in weather. I have not responded to the Shakespeare guy yet, but I take it that you don't want to go through with his scheme.

As for your book in the stores, the news is not too good. Except for the couple of shops in Delhi where bought copies are replaced with new ones in the fiction shelves, the stores in the other cities have a propensity to declare they are out of stock the moment the one solitary copy is sold. It takes anywhere between a month and three to get it on order. Amphibian as publishers have produced a very professional copy and have managed to get your book to stores, but the distribution leaves a lot to be desired.

My instincts of an investigative journalist, even after the discouraging battering in the hands of Uproar, seem to be active enough to pick up a trend here. The distributor seems to refill the stocks in the stores based on the location of the authors. So, your book is replaced in Delhi whereas Sunder Rajan Swamy gets his stuff in ready supply in Chennai. But, buy one of your books in Chennai and you face the same ephemeral fate as Swamy's book in Delhi. I wonder how one can expect such a puerile trick to fool the connected world of today.

Send some pictures from good old west coast.

Regards,
K

XLVIII

Mail from Sandeep to Simon, Madhu and Amrita

Comrades in arms,

I hope you are spending your daily hour together, moving slowly in those weird forms. Hope you are also inflicting enough pain on each other as you separate the tissues, stretch the bones and try the brutal manoeuvres of chin na. *Have you ever wondered at the convoluted mental makeup of the masters who dedicated their lives to the refinement of ways and means to inflict pain and then claimed to practice meditation in action?*

George Salinas is one such master, who has been undergoing such sadistic pursuits for the last four decades and currently passes on lessons in pain and proficiency on the Venice Beach of California.

Sifu Salinas is an old friend of my own master and since Venice Beach is famed as a most colourful attraction of the west coast and just around half an hour's drive from Pasadena, I took advantage of the sunny weekend to zoom down in my rented Ford Explorer.

With yellow sand, blue seas, green palm trees and brown mountains afar, with the promenade full of some of the most kaleidoscopic crowd of tourists, it is a congested heaven. Surfers, skateboarders, street dancers , stand up comedians, shops selling peculiar curiosities – in all this commotion, Master Salinas has one quiet corner of the beach to himself. There, in step to the rhythm of the waves, he moves through the long form, as alive an embodiment of poetry as one can witness.

When I referred to my master, he greeted me like a long lost son, which surprised me somewhat because the two have not really been in the best of terms over the last couple of decades. But, then, it is another lesson for the taking – no one is greater than the art.

He taught me with the minute care of a parent eager to correct the smallest blemish in the upbringing of a child raised elsewhere. When I spoke about my interest in the grappling art of chin na, he conducted one of the most esoteric sessions I have ever attended.

I have captured some of the techniques he demonstrated with my Olympus on the video mode. He broke the techniques down into several steps, and I managed to do quite a decent job with the camera. If you have followed my instruction and remember the base techniques, in many you will find a subtle variation which makes it even more effective and excruciating. Here is a genius who has dedicated his life in the pursuit of perfection in pain.

I have uploaded the mpeg clips on youtube and the link is at the bottom of the mail. I will expect you to take a look at them with the possibility of adapting the variations into your technique.

Happy Training,
Pritam

~ ~ ~

Night was spreading its shroud across the streets of Pasadena. Along the Colorado Boulevard traffic flowed along, oblivious of the time of the day. The restaurants filled up with the glass windows displaying droves of diners tucking into lavish spreads of versatile flavours the city had on offer. Sandeep chose two of the dozen or so short-listed books and went up to the attendant. The man behind the counter of *Book Alley*, the second hand book shop, was a thickset, bearded youth in his late twenties.

"You found something after all? You seemed so quiet down there ..."

Sandeep placed his books on the counter. The stocky man looked at his them, as if weighing the choices in his scales of approval.

"Hamsun? He is good, real good. Not heard of the other guy though."

"Lu Xun? He is Chinese. *The Diary of a Madman* and his other stories together are supposed to be one of the hundred best books ever written – according to *The Guardian*."

The bookseller scratched his beard.

"Is that what you are doing? Reading through a list?"

"Sometimes."

He turned the cover page to look at the marked price.

"I often find these lists biased. And it of course depends on the region of publication ..."

"You mean the region from where the list was published?"

"Yeah, if it is British it will include Dickens and Hardy ..."

"I guess all lists should include those two, with Dostoyevsky and Tolstoy ..."

"Yes, but in a British list you will find the Amises and Waugh as well, and perhaps Lessing and Woolf and Maughm. Whereas in a list generated in this country, you will have Hemingway, Steinbeck, Tennessee Williams, a couple of Millers and Bellow. The French will clog it with Stendhal, Balzac, Zola, Flaubert, Proust, Gide ..."

"And Celine."

"Of course. And then there has to be an international flavour. You start alphabetically and there will be a number of A's catching your attention before it wavers ... Achebe, Andersen, Austen ..."

"That's interesting. So, if someone has a couple of A's to kick-start his last name, he is at an advantage?"

"Definitely. Lot of lexicographic manipulations do take place. The idea is to catch the eye. That counts for everything."

"That shines a complete new light on the feng shui experts who change the spellings of names."

"Believe me, there are a lot of things that influence such lists. The quality of writing is ..."

"Secondary?"

"I would say even lower. The book business is dirty. Does your list contain some of the booker prize winners as well?"

"Well, I guess Salman Rushdie is there. And Kingsley Amis too – although for *Lucky Jim* and not *Old Devils.*"

The man behind the counter thought for a while.

"Why only Bookers? Even some of the Nobel Prizes are ridiculous. The Swedish bias. And this lady –," he picked up a slim volume. "Jelinek. She is a Nobel winner and yet has to get published through some kind of a boutique press. You know where you can find some of the best writing of modern times?"

A part of Sandeep's mind was engaged in contrasting the man with some of the second hand book selling counterparts of Free School Street in Kolkata. He thought about it.

"The slush pile?"

The man looked up.

"I see you are acquainted with the technical terms. Are you an author?"

Sandeep extended his lower lip.

"Writer, yes. Author? Who knows?"

The man nodded, knowingly.

"I know what you mean. A group of us have been trying to put up enough money for a couple of our friends to publish their works. Great talents. And they cannot make it past this safety net of literary agents, who won't recognise art if presented in a platter."

He reached beneath his counter and took out a slim volume with black and white cover art and very basic print.

"I will throw this in free for you," he said. "It's a compilation of some of the writers of the West Coast, mainly the Los Angeles area. None of them have been published by Harper Collins or Random House. Few of them will ever be. But, if you want to look at talent ... and compare with the junk you get on the shelves today..."

A strange feeling of solidarity eddied through Sandeep. At the other end of the world, there were people trying to make it – going through the same struggle as he was, and from these thousands of talents, may be one would be able to break through the ignorant walls, displace some of the super-models, MBAs and WWF wrestlers hogging shelf space.

"So, this is what you meant when you asked me about where to find the best writing?"

The man smiled.

"Not exactly. The best writing, according to my humble opinion – which as you can quite clearly make out is not that humble, but extremely opinionated – is in the blogs."

Sandeep had not been expecting this. In the distraction, he lost his grip on the books and the work of the aspiring authors symbolically thudded on the floor.

"I'm sorry ... It's just that I had once been employed as a ghost blogger ..."

"Excuse me, a what?"

"A ghost blogger. Someone who writes the blogs for a big shot who is incapable of turning out anything worth reading."

A smile appeared through the bushy expanses of the man's face.

"I guess it takes all kinds. The reason I mentioned blogs is that out there, in a few among the painfully many, you find sincerity, honesty, telling tales because it is something that one has to do, and something that is not written for selling one's wares ..."

"Do you think this is a new kind of publishing?"

Another late browser had come up to the counter and the bookseller had to hurry.

"Why don't you do something? There is a rendezvous on Thursday night. It's in a place called The Coffee Gallery in Altadena. Just a ten minute drive from here. Authors will gather at around eight. Why don't you join us if you feel like it?"

"Visitors welcome?"

"Mention my name. That's Jason. And I'll be there. Will see you."

"Sandeep."

"Indian?"

"Yes."

"Bookers come easy to you guys these days."

Sandeep laughed.

"Not to all."

A pudgy hand squeezed his shoulder.

"I know what you mean. It will be eleven dollars. For these books I mean. And as for the meet up on Thursday, I'll buy you a drink. Everyone pays for his own dinner."

"Wow. I'll come over. I can pick you up from the shop if you want. I have a Ford Explorer. A huge dinosaur of a car, but that's the only one in Hertz that had a GPS."

"You'll stick out. I'll take my beat up 1989 Volks. I'll blend in. But, thanks for the offer."

~ ~ ~

Blog of Simple Simon
Tags: People, prediction, chance

There are pundits aplenty who, in retrospect, fill pages of the finance columns of newspapers and magazines to describe how the crisis came about. And they take it to the logical conclusion of formulating step by step instructions to make the future of the world economy robust and immune to similar capitulation.

All this leads me to wonder why none of these wise men, a lot of them drawing sinful salaries and with numerous awards and recognitions under their bursting belts, managed to predict the coming of the slump. A renegade Nicholas Taleb perhaps, and that too will be strongly contested by economists hungry for the spotlight. They have their models, their sacrosanct predictors. It is sacrilege for others to be correct and prove them wrong.

Sceptical though I remain of Dr. Suprakash Roy's explanation of the crisis as a result of the inhibition-less internet, it does raise several questions in my mind. Have we overused technology to our own destruction? Much in the way people had predicted that the world will degenerate into a mushroom cloud resulting from advances in nuclear physics. We came close, but the extinction of the human race was once avoided by the presence of mind of one of the most unsung heroes of humanity, a seldom remembered Soviet general whose name I will Google up later.

Perhaps we have avoided the nuclear disaster with the fall of the Soviet Union, which leaves the United States with little excuse to press the panic button. There remains the threat of Chernobyl like accidents in US, UK, India, Pakistan, Israel, North Korea and all the other countries who are the proud owners of weapons of mass destruction. But, in an inconspicuous way, the innocuous technology of fibre optic cables and hyper text transfer protocol may have reformatted the spherical world into a flat one and may have been ignorantly and irresponsibly responsible in accelerating one of the biggest non-violent disasters in history.

To return to the question of the failure of predictors, I wonder if I have managed to obtain a humble insight into it. And at the risk of being branded pop-economist or pretentious, let me forward the theory in the comforting solitude of my blog.

A couple of days back, a senior person of our company had come popping into my cubicle and indulging in an impassioned and incensed tirade against my buddy. I have related feeling not a little strange about the entire episode. In the corridors of Axiom, the relationship between the two is rumoured to be hand in glove – a situation not very favourable in the insecure eyes of some senior people and also the reasonably insignificant point of view of a few grumpy ones.

All these lead me to believe that for whatever cryptic reason, the manager has developed a temporary pointy edge in the soft corner reserved for my buddy.

I guess you must be wondering what this relational dynamics have with respect to the financial world. The lateral approach to the way of looking at things, introduced by my buddy, and taken to a transcendental (please, please notice the pun on trance) with the session in the *Magic Pot,* has helped me to draw a curious solution.

Could any economic model predict this change of relationship? I hear some of you scoffing at me and pointing out that it is not the job of economic models or financial analysts to work out sentiments of complicated individuals.

But, on second thoughts, is this absolutely true?

When light shines through an aperture in a physics experiment, there is no emotional conflict between the photons, and that makes the result predictable. However, with two tiny apertures, we get an interference pattern due to the uncertainty in the world at the level of quantum physics. All this confusion and a proprietary uncertainty principle exist in the physical world even without the involvement of emotions.

What about the economic or business world? It is a world predominantly governed by human beings, who are not projected photons of light through apertures, but a complicated conglomerate of emotions, sentiments, values and thought. Is it possible to predict the complicated turbulences caused by interpersonal or intrapersonal relationship with any degree of accuracy?

Let us deviate a while and consider a game between Mets and Yankees. The detailed records of all the Murphys, Wrights, Castillos and the Jeters, Swishers and Canos are documented with precision in numerous sports databases and can be found in the pockets of any self respecting junior school collector of baseball cards. However, with all these facts and figures at our fingertips, can we predict the result of the match with any degree of certainty? With the help of the form-book, maybe we can make a decent effort, but when it comes to the individual performances, we cannot even dream of approaching certainty.

What if Sabathia pulls a muscle and can't pitch? Can a predictor based on the statistics database foretell it?

Similarly, in the more heated battlefield of business, can we predict whether a sudden terrorist attack on the Empire State Building will make speculators behave erratically? Can we say for certain whether the best financial adviser of HMH will suddenly decide to spend the rest of his days locked up in a monastery in Bhutan after coming close to choking on his liquorice stroopwaffels? What if Dave de Boer, after a satisfying spree in de Wallen, decides to go against the board of advisors and sell off a section of HMH to Rabo?

When it comes to people, it is very difficult to predict. And therein lie the problems of prediction where we compute the trends, drifts and direction of numbers and charts without accounting for people. We have on our hands a human race that is being exposed to a new plaything every day, with e-commerce, Swift, identifier, secure socket layer and the orkut, facebook, twitter, linked in, blogs ... I guess I have ultimately identified with the good doctor after all.

Shruti :
Gifted impostor
Wizard weaving wand of words
Web of confusion

Sandeep:
Confused is the world
Emotions blur as lives rush
Yearnings yet yield you

XLIX

Pasadena, California

From: Shankaran Balaji (Axiom)
To: Pritam Mitra (Axiom)
CC: K. Ramesh(Axiom); Ashwin Palit(Axiom); Abhijeet Singh (Axiom)
Sub: Conference Paper – Review Session

Dear Mitra,

I have been asked by Ramesh to attend the review session prior to your presentation of the paper in the conference. Ramesh talks about the Upanishad method of discourse, ***doing away with visual aids for the event and relying on verbal interactions****. It sounds most interesting.*

Could you send the presentation up front so that we can take a look at the slides up front to come prepared with review comments if we have any?

Thanks
Shankaran Balaji
Account Manager – Axiom
Washington Mutual and IndyMac Bank
(PMP Certified)

From: Ashwin Palit(Axiom)
To: Shankaran Balaji (Axiom); Pritam Mitra (Axiom)
CC: K. Ramesh(Axiom); Abhijeet Singh (Axiom)
Sub: Conference Paper – Review Session

Hi Pritam,

I agree with Balaji. It would be great if you could send the slides to us before the session.

Thanks,
Ashwin
Assistant Vice President
Axiom North America Operations – West

Even as Ramesh's voice came flowing into his ears, Sandeep could not help but sense the sagaciousness that seemed to accompany the man in every endeavour.

"Hello, Ramesh here."

Sandeep cleared his throat.

"Hi, Pritam here."

"Hi, how are you?"

"*Good* here, *fine* in England."

"Is it about the mails?"

"Inanities."

"I thought it would be a good idea to run through the presentation with some very senior people ... as a kind of mock up."

"The key word being mock."

"I hear a hint of sarcasm in your voice ..."

"Just a hint?"

The great man paused to think.

"You don't think this is a good idea, do you?"

"To have this reviewed by a bunch of people who want the slides of a *verbal* presentation sent upfront? While appreciating the Upanishadic approach?"

There was a pause, a faint chuckle and then proclamation of judgement.

"Forget the clowns."

"I second that. I am not uncontrollably addicted to comfort feel."

"I guess the old habit of meaningless corporate reviews crept up on me."

"Addiction to corporate crap."

"I beg your pardon?"

"Corporate crap. It's a concise alliteration."

"Alliteration? You are addicted to them, aren't you?"

"Yes. It makes you immune to spoonerism."

"What's spoonerism?"

"Hissing the kind-side may be a good corporate example."

"I don't quite get what you mean, but I'm counting on you."

The receiver replaced on the bedside phone of Hotel Mariott, the Vice President cleared his throat.

"Ladies and gentlemen," he began, a throaty quality added to his sagacious voice, talking to his seated image on the full length mirror opposite him. "From time immemorial India has been an exotic country full of unknown mystery and untold wealth. Over centuries it has beckoned adventurers, explorers as well as plunderers and colonisers.

"The material riches of the country have been looted and plundered, and later milked and harvested, so much so that the Indians have had to start the reverse journey of exploring and adventuring, sneaking into the different available workplaces in the quest for fortune. And in a lot of ways, this reverse infiltration is linked to the immense riches in philosophy and erudition that the plunderers could not take away. There have of course been the imposition of thought and culture of the conquerors, but the wise assimilating thought leaders of India, absorbed the different influences to add and enrich their own wisdom. As a result, the Indian whom you meet in all the rank and file of the organisations today, from the operational floors to the strategic boardroom meetings, speak in the international language with proficiency, and preach the business secrets of the west back to you.

"Now, with the Indian becoming such an accepted piece of the picture, the time is ripe for harvesting the underlying wealth of Indian wisdom, to combat the financial crisis which has floored the west. The Indian has arrived, the wisdom of his nation that he brings with him is waiting to be offloaded from the conveyor belt. With Western Capitalism, riding on the crest of the flat world and the global village, breaking on the recessional rocks in the alarming way – a colossal crash that is frightening because of the lack of forewarning and the fumbling for explanation in retrospection, the Indian philosophy and erudition can derive the cause, make the seemingly mysterious karmic connection to the effect, and ultimately show the way ahead – the types of regulations and controls recommended by the logical analysis through ancient wisdom that can help secure us against such phenomenon in the future.

"I now hand over the session to my fellow presenter, young Pritam Mitra, to show exactly how the lessons of the Upanishad and the Gita, considered by Schopenhauer and Max Muller to be the absolute and rewarding wisdom, can be used to explain and combat the situation.

"In the traditions of the learnings passed across from the Upanishads, we will speak without trivialising what we say with pictures, slides and visuals. It is not a simplified concept and we would like it to remain that way."

He paused and looked at himself as he bowed deeply to the mirror and introduced the imaginary analyst to the invisible audience in the room.

∾ ∾ ∾

Blog of Simple Simon
Tags: Stand Up Comedy, Activists, Attitudes

There are not too many things that I miss about America. Except for the Niagara and the Grand Canyon, substitutes of all possible entertainment is available in Europe, in more subdued shades, at a more relaxed rhythm, in a tempered tone.

From the point of view of variation and novelty, there can be few places as diverse as the continent. Every two hour drive brings you face to face with a new culture, another language, different geography, history, cuisine and architecture. Madhu claims that India is the same, though, with marked deviations in race and religion as well, but having never been there, I find Europe a fascinating enough concoction.

The Netherlands itself is commonplace as far as terrain is concerned, but it more than makes up with the curious human and natural landscape that make up the various facets of city and suburban life. What I miss in terms of the madness of the baseball season is compensated by the brimful sports bars whenever clubs clash or nations negotiate with their soccer skills. What I miss in terms of the parlour perfected and the gym generated varieties of female forms is filled in by the natural and robust type of beauty that is all the more ravishing because of the rough edges, with the moisture of the soil still glistening on the earthy roots.

However, what I definitely miss in this country are the hilarious, sparkling stand up comedy shows so much in abundance from New York to San Francisco. I had been an addict of the talents who so often ignite the spark of life into souls dead with drudgery.

The only way I can have the missing amount of passive fun in my life replenished, other than by reflecting on the peculiarity of the corporate life, is by attending the shows of Boom Chicago in Leidseplein. These are skit shows, with a fairly decent dinner thrown in for a few extra euros, most of them are side-splitting, and I have grown into a major fan.

I generally turn up at their shows once or twice a month, more or less in proportion to the amount of inanity I am subjected to in office. I had gone down to Amsterdam today to catch them in another of their crazy comical acts. I reached the Centraal Station at five, and since it was some time before my date for the evening, a distant friend of my sister called Annelis, was supposed to meet me at the Theatre, I decided to walk all the way.

I never get tired of the way across Damrak to Spui, with colourful crowds and interesting sideshows all the way. I paused in front of the Royal Palace where an American youth was busy entertaining the audience with his glib wit while simultaneously juggling a sword, a lighted torch and eating an apple. It was quite a spectacular show and I was absorbed in it when a tap on my shoulder made me turn and I saw myself looking at the well remembered face of our mutual friend from the *Magic Pot,* Shruti.

She greeted me warmly and I hello-ed back, slightly uncomfortable at the back of my mind mainly because of the uncertain picture of her relationship with my buddy that the latter had refused to elaborate on.

I said that I had come to catch a show of Boom Chicago.

"Ah Boom Chicago, they are fantastic," she said. "Hope you enjoy."

I thanked her and asked whether she was there on some particular purpose.

"Well, I wonder whether I should tell you, because guys I know tend to take off like a jackrabbit when I tell them anything of this sort."

I told her that I was quite broadminded, and if I did take off like a jackrabbit, it would suit my purpose in getting to Leidseplein quickly.

"Ah," she said. "Funny and a wordplay on broad that can border on the explicit. No wonder you have hit it off with Sandeep."

For a very brief moment I was lost, but then I remembered and said, "Pritam ... well, we do have things in common. But, no pun intended, I assure you."

"Pritam, indeed," she agreed. "Well, there is some sort of a demonstration out here, with a group of Indians gathering under the National Monument with placards to collect signatures ... It is a petition for the punishment of some rogue cops in Kolkata ..."

I looked across the street and saw an Indian contingent – with a placard full of pictures and write ups in English and Hindi. There were people of all ages, dressed mainly in jeans, jackets and caps – but, I managed to detect some in traditional attire – kurtas, salwars, even a few sarees. There were a couple of enormous chart papers some of the younger men held, filled with scribbled signatures.

" ... I have come to show my solidarity and also to sign the petition," she continued.

"And what's there in all this to make guys run away?"

She laughed. "I am someone passionate about the wrongs in the world. Vocal about government policies and international politics. So, when I say that I support some cause, guys generally think I am an incurable activist, with feminism thrown in for good measure."

"Feminism? Where did that come from?"

"Well, Dr. Roy will probably put it down to cognitive categorisation. Female activists and feminists are mapped together ..."

I thought this was strange and said so. "Does Pritam also take off like a jackrabbit?"

She thought for a moment and smiled mischievously. "Well, yes and no ..."

I could not really make out what she meant by that and decided to keep smiling. It was then I made the connection.

"Shruti, is it about those cops who got involved in the life of a young married couple and threatened the guy to leave the girl ...?"

She raised her eyebrows, clearly surprised.

"You know about it?"

"Yes ... they drove the guy to suicide, didn't they? Because the girl's rich dad did not want the marriage?"

"That's right. It may have been murder too. But, how did you get to know?"

I said that I had been given the details by my senior manager.

"Wow. There is a demonstration here as well? Say what? I think I will go and sign the thing."

Shruti was plainly delighted. She spoke, fast and passionate, about the problems with corruption and power in a society like India, with its rich divide between the rich and the poor.

I went up to the people holding the placard and signed. In fact, I was not the only Western guy. Some American youngsters had even joined the organisers of the demonstration.

A thought struck me. I took out my cell phone and called Madhu.

It was on the fifth ring that she answered.

"Simon. What a surprise," her jovial voice bounded energetically through the network. "What makes you call on a weekend? You are lucky, I was just about to take a bath. Just got back from Hidori's singing class."

I hastily apologised for calling her on a Saturday, and added that she would probably want to hear of this.

"The police brutality case," I explained. "The one you talked about. There seems to be big demonstrations all over the world. In India, it is already a major story with the public baying for the blood of the police officers. Demonstrations are taking place worldwide and signatures are being collected everywhere for their punishment. I just signed the petition under the National Monument..."

"There's one in Amsterdam too?"

"Yes, and a very passionate one," I said. "I tell you I just signed the petition."

She appreciated it. "Great. Are you still there?"

"Yes, I just signed it. However, I won't be here for long ... I have a show to attend."

She laughed. "Of course. It's great that you signed it. Could you do me the favour of signing it for me as well?"

I looked at the people who stood braving the chilly Amsterdam wind, gustily holding the placard even as the sun went down, leaving them to battle the cold alone.

"Of course, Madhu," I answered. "Good bye ... Madhu-di."

Shruti was still flushed with her spirited opinions, her cheeks red with the sincerest of words bottled up inside, waiting for me to hang up so that she could pour forth her passionate plea. As her excited eyes met mine, I noticed a change come over them. There was a poignant change in her way of communication, something that I guess is called empathy.

"Something wrong, Simon? You seem a bit ... dazed."

I shook my head. "Could I add a couple of signatures for my friends?"

"Of course. If your friends feel the same way ..."

I smiled and added two signatures to the placard. *Sandeep Gupta* and *Pritam Mitra.*

Chat between Amrita and Sandeep

Amrita: Hi
Amrita: How are you?
Amrita: Won't you talk to me?
Sandeep: I think I told you to limit your conversation to tai chi
Amrita: I have an injury ... I hurt my right shoulder during training
Sandeep: I'm not a doctor, especially across an ocean
Amrita: I don't want you to help me.
Amrita: I don't want to disturb you
Amrita: I just wanted to wish you all the best for the presentation
Amrita: If I'm not allowed to do that, please forgive me
Sandeep: You insist on being a doormat, do you?
Amrita: A what?
Sandeep: Forget it. Thanks anyway. Bye.
Amrita: We have been training. Simon and I tried to do the techniques that you have sent
Sandeep: Good. What about Madhu-di?
Amrita: She's not coming.

Amrita: She's been busy
Sandeep: And the two of you? Are you regular?
Amrita: We haven't missed a class.
Sandeep: Good. Keep it up.
Amrita: :) Love you
Sandeep: Bye
Amrita: Bye

L

Mail from Sandeep to Professor Lal and Shruti

Subject: California journeys

As I lie in the depressing dingy room of the Vagabond Inn, Pasadena, I have in my hand a key which opens the door to a world incredible in untold wealth, and the key word here is 'untold'.

The Vagabond Inn is shabby and totters on the brink of the ramshackle. I have had to be put up in this ghastly hotel ostensibly because the Axiom lady who arranges the accommodation of short term visitors is sealed in wedlock with the manager of this establishment. The only members of the company who escape this painful marital arrangement seem to be K. Ramesh and his kind, lodging as the great man is in the creature comforts of Pasadena Hilton.

However, I don't mind. It gives me a sense of belonging, turning back and touching my roots and as I turn the pages of this fascinating collection of writing of the unknown writers of the West Coast, I almost blend in with the authors.

There are eight short stories – some not quite stories, but quaint deviants – three one act plays and twelve poetic pieces in this unofficial publication. I won't go as far as saying that all these are works of genius – I could not make out anything of some of the poetry and at least a couple of stories – but the quality shines through most of the others and makes you wonder why one has to struggle to find readable material on the shelves of the better known bookshops, to plough through the pages that pass for fiction today. Why read plot-less politically correct tripe about an autistic kid, or a historical and geographical mutilation of Afghanistan dressed up as fiction by someone who has evidently not been there, when such gems are lying around unread?

I will take you through two particular journeys along the green state of California that you may find delightful even in retelling.

Susan Frobisher presents an understated allegory in 'Dissonance' in which she chills the soul without hinting at violence or fright. She tells us the story of a hesitant woman in her thirties, driving up the San Gabriel Mountains towards the Mount Wilson observatory. The bends are sharp and the climb is steep, and she is not the most confident of drivers. There are expert and fast motorists who appear behind her and react with brusque impatience, some even resorting to honk, till she pulls up each time in the designated places for slow drivers. One such stop is near an Indian preservation area, where she gets off the car and takes a few photographs before being struck by the primitive tune of Cherokee flute which plays from the store of the campus. Alone amidst the green mountains around her, the haunting music touches the most primordial chord of her soul. She rushes inside the stall, where the Indian woman behind the counter tells her that the CD is not for sale.

She is given the name of the artist and she stays there, with no one around her, listening to the ancient music, to which the mountains and trees seem to perform in exotic accompaniment.

She resumes her journey and then we are taken forward in time when she is back in Los Angeles, hunting down the CD of the artist at the Amoeba Records. She is excited at having found it, and cuts a dinner party short to rush home and play it on her hi fi. And then she finds that the same CD with the same notes fails to stir her in her home. She wants to like it, she wants it to rule over her senses, and she is disappointed again and again.

There are unstated parallels drawn to the slaughter of Indians for the 'progress' of the West, and the 'progress' in turn cutting us from our innermost nature. As the lady in the story kept on playing the CD again and again, in the futile bid to regain the magic that she felt in the San Gabriel Mountians, it was a claustrophobic chill that I felt within myself.

If Ms Frobisher looks at the world with starkest pessimism, the optimistic view is supplied on yet another journey authored by Joshua Ahmed. Writing in the first person, he speaks of a drive from Los Angeles to San Diego, a large stretch along the picturesque Route 1, with the Pacific on the right.

He writes of pulling into a rest area, having his burger, fries and coke, and stepping on to the viewing hills, trying hard to capture the expanse of the blue sea with his camera, digital, but slightly primitive going by the standards of modern age. He is struggling to fit the ocean into his frame when an old gentleman comes up and congratulates him on his excellent choice of photographic matter.

Slightly confused, since, as he puts it, man's yearning for the sea is as old as mankind, and certainly captured in the frame ever since camera obscura, he asks the genial old man to explain what he was doing so well. He is told that he has managed to position himself perfectly to shoot the magnificent tree that sprawled across, in the backdrop of the ocean. And here, the author for the first time looks at the tree, a soothing green spread close enough for him to touch and climb, which had eluded him in his quest for the elusive ocean.

Poignant in the point it makes, it is also subtly satirical in the description of the American clichés of freeways, weekend getaways, people and roadside joints.

I will be meeting some of these people for a drink on Thursday. If I come across Ms Frobisher or Mr. Ahmed, I will definitely pass my compliments and tell them of the absolute delight they have given me. They have passed my benchmark test of a good read. They can be read in a train and can be remembered during the next journey.

Regards,
Sandeep

ᘓ ᘓ ᘓ

Twitter posts of Kevin Havens

Justine Ballroom & Piazza, Sheraton - 5134 sq ft. 4 more rooms. 300+ attendants at 9, speakers,delegates, attendees. Conference on crisis!!

Bankers, economists, media, academics - speak for 3 days, network, pander selves & wares - wine and dine to bursting pt. Crisis conference!

Conference Topic 1 – Financial Regulations in the wake of the Crisis. Debates, panel discussions and even entertainment will deviate quite a bit from the noble point.

Conference Topic 2 – Role of media in foretelling, spreading or stalling the crisis, the art of storytelling derived from the crisis,

Conference Topic 2 Continued – Merit of the several instant best sellers that emerged capitalising on the mass phobia.

Chief Conference Attraction –Exhibition of the works of Economist cartoonist Kal Kallaugher.

Expense, expense, expense ... does one ever learn from the crisis?

ᘓ ᘓ ᘓ

Amsterdam

Amrita was engrossed in thought, keying in considered thoughts on her desktop, when a flickering shadow on the screen made her turn.

"Oh, when did you turn up?"

Behind her, Trisha was standing with a smile, looking at the screen.

"What are you writing?" she asked.

"Nothing related to work," Amrita pressed the alt-tab keys and the outlook window shot up, the madness of daily mails pushing her creative snippets to the background. "Was just thinking of a story."

Trisha was amused. And also impressed.

"You write stories? I read a lot, but can never really get around to writing anything. I often wonder how people actually write."

"I am not much of a writer. I was just putting my thoughts ..."

Trisha laughed.

"Were you writing a story or your diary?"

Amrita's fleeting misgiving was hastily shrouded by a smile.

"Every story is written from experience," she answered.

"You must know," Trisha said, smiling. "Can I read what you have written?"

"No. It's not completed and not worth it."

Trisha slapped her playfully on the shoulder.

"Neither are you a great writer nor am I a great critic. Can't you allow your friend to read what you have written?"

Amrita smiled quietly.

"If it ever becomes worth reading I will share it."

Extracts from report on Financial Crisis Seminar in Pasadena on freakishfinance.com
Seth Robertson

Kevin Havens, with his twitter posts, came close to being a documenter of the times.

What can be said about a million dollar seminar to underline that we are going through a financial crisis?

The keynote speech by Berkeley professor Keith Hughes, mercifully stripped of the academic jargon for a wide audience, was delivered with eloquence and rhetoric to justify the importance of the event. The underlying message was that there was a financial crisis on our hands and we needed some strict regulations to combat this in future. That, unfortunately, comes up short in the category of news, Dr. Hughes ...

....

The debate on the role of the media in the crisis got so heated that for a moment I overheard the Sheraton staff debating whether to switch the air conditioning to full. The veteran investor Sergei Petersen managed to stir the hornet's nest by implying that the crisis had been helped along by the print and electronic media, converting minor bumps into major snowballing terror. Melisande Middleton, founder of the International Media Ethics, had to be at her charming best to keep Petersen and Wolfgang Dennis, the financial editor of Economic World, from coming to blows. I wonder if her charm can make the bigger crisis blow over as easily.

....

The West/Central room, with its display of the best works of Kal Kallaugher, the celebrated editorial cartoonist of the Economist, was actually the most popular attraction. His cartoons on the crisis re-underlined the age old wisdom that Laughter, indeed, is the best medicine, even for major economic upheavals.

...

There was an interesting talk on how Lean processes of Toyota are a must for organisations to clamp down on unnecessary expenditure by Stuart Takahashi, the director of the LeanSigma Institute. Lots of figures were presented as evidence, pointing at the every day activities that we take for granted, which added to non-value added waste – or muda. *There were roadmaps for eliminating them. However, Professor Takahashi did not really see the funny side when someone from the audience asked him whether the very conference was the mother of all* muda. *Or had the funny bone been removed from the great man to ensure a lean distribution of calcium?*

...

It was the second day of the seminar when, while making notes during a presentation on *The Story not Reported,* by the Jason Snecher, the Risk Management Advisor of Wachovia Bank, that Seth Robertson found a tweet from Kevin Havens pop up on his blackberry.

Come down to The Colorado. I have a feeling something special is taking place.

When Seth reached the comparatively smaller room, there was standing room only. A young Indian man had the floor with a learned looking bald headed man sitting beside him, nodding sagaciously to the pronouncements. People were listening in rapt attention while the man talked. Seth could see no slides other than one solitary picture on the screen which had the euro on one side, the dollar on the other with the Sanskrit symbol for *om* in the middle.

He squinted and made his way to the third row where Kevin sat, engrossed in the talk.

"Hey, man. Has it started?"

"Hi ... yes, we are well into it."

"Where are the visuals?"

Kevin shook his head. "I will fill you in, pal. There ain't no visuals. It's Upanistic ... something or the other."

Seth squeezed in to share the chair with Keith. Sandeep carried on.

"Even as we fumble with words to explain what this crisis is all about, we have at least one universally acknowledged term that can be associated with it. Credit. Somehow or other, individuals and institutions accumulated a lot of bad credit. As we heard in the debate which took on the proportions of a minor crisis yesterday, it snowballed into what we have now. A credit crisis.

"Let us map this problem in terms of ancient Indian knowledge.

"The *Upanishad* gives us the magnificent metaphor of the wish fulfilling tree. The cosmic fig tree that can fulfil the wishes of everyone. *Gita* points out that each goodie in life comes with its inbuilt opposite.

"In the modern world, what is the wish fulfilling tree that spreads its tentacles to touch – literally touch – everyone? What has suddenly propelled the common man of today to live and experience whatever life he wants? What has made small corporate bodies take giant steps in huge ventures? And what dangles in front of everyone as a wish fulfilling mechanism, ready to respond like one of those genies of the Arabian Nights, to grant your heart's desire?

"If there is one phenomenon that has made the world flat, one technology which we have used and abused without thinking of the consequences, it has been the internet. The online communities, the electronic means of buying and selling, have changed the way we deal with finance. We have everything available to us at the click of a button, paid for by credit cards whose malicious workings can be temporarily thrust to the back of the mind. Industries have grown around this. And we have internet money transfer, e-identifier, SWIFT and all sorts of possibilities for transactions over the net. In this life and the second. The currency of Second Life is richer than that of some of the economically stable nations. Doesn't it make us pause and think?

"The internet is the wish fulfilling tree of modern times. And along with it comes the lack of inhibition. As cognitive psychologists explain, we are more prone to losing our social inhibitions on the internet than in real life. We can flirt, woo, abuse and exchange opinions, under the cover of the world wide web, under pseudo and aliases, living multiple lives and taking on different identities. It is easier to say I love you online than in real life. It is easier to say I hate you too. It is a phenomenon of stretching to extremes all of you are familiar with.

"And it is easier to spend a hundred dollars online than it is to part with a single dime in real life. We don't feel the tactile touch of a dollar bill crinkling in our hands, we don't feel the moment of doubt when the credit card is swiped in front of our eyes. At the industry level, it is also true as transactions and deals are easier to make with the electronic signatures and emailed approvals, without face to face interactions.

"Is one message box asking us to confirm the transaction enough to replace the doubts, the niggles, the second thoughts of actual transactions in real life? Far from it.

"According to Indian philosophy, all the decisions are taken based on groups of qualities. We can be ethical, knowledgeable, alert or we can be neutral, speculative and use power, or we can also be unscrupulous, ignorant and stagnant. The groups of qualities influence our choices, and at various times nourish the limitless opportunities of interaction of individuals, organisations or both. The world is held together by the machinery of the internet and finance, as pearls on a string, interconnected across space and time through numerous channels of e-commerce, emails, blogs, twitter, social networking ... where personal ebbs and flows are automatically multiplied manifold by today's cosmic consciousness of a connected world, where a butterfly flapping its wings in Shanghai will actually be surprised if there is no rain in San Francisco. The world is today susceptible to the tipping of the cauldron of optimistic speculation, to be snowballed into panic by the rampaging electronic herd. Ultimately, in unpredictable ways, the network of cause and effect binds every transaction across time and domains, industries across the world and the underworld, where an advantage today is compensated by a crisis that creeps up unnoticed.

"Greed fuelled corporations, watering this cosmic fig tree with the hoses of their short-sight – making the crude world available to the individuals and groups at the click of an uncomprehending and delighted mouse played their part without the wisdom of connected karma. In the uncontrolled snowball effect of multiple credit linked derivatives, CDOs, SIVs, ABCPs, Mortgage Linked derivatives, a host of bankers tried to do away with the basic karmic principles of what is sown will be harvested, nothing can escape the cycle of cause and effect. The system was injected with loans, the liability of which was sold off to make more profit, to clear up liquid funds. Risks of transactions were sold off with a swagger of invincibility. Mortgages, loans and immediate, unthinkable returns of investment blinded more and more people with greed. Everything one wished for was available, at the click of a mouse. And when the good days ended, it was through the manifestation of the in-built opposite of the connected world, the global panic that was spread through mails, blogs, blackberries and twitter worldwide.

"With disconnected segmented profit seekers struggling to make an impression till the next quarter for a pat on the half turned back and filthy annual bonuses, without the global vision necessary to pause and think about the possible disasters of the immediate future, they managed to shoot the entire merged financial super octopus in each of the multiple feet.

"For individuals and organisations to achieve the imperishable state, to be unaffected by similar crisis in the future, one needs to follow the ancient wisdom of cutting through this source of limitless opportunity , the cosmic fig tree, with detachment. Decisions in that state are not influenced by the low hanging fruits, immediate benefits, possible lucrative operations in the inhibition free world of electronic transfers, credit based operations, mortgage linked derivatives. The need of the hour is hence robust control systems for the individuals and institutions which will test the detachment in decision making, analyse the motivation involved, and put embargos in place whenever the balance seems to shift to the second or third group of qualities.

"We are not talking of an embargo on free will, of removing the roots of capitalism or turning the economies into states of financial policing. No. The controls we speak of will enumerate the decisions and make the decision making principles known to the individual or the organisation in question. It will make everything known. In the eternal way of the ancient teachings, this will enable the decision maker to make a conscious choice. In the Bhagavat Gita, reflected in a large way in the Jungian psychology, the alternatives are always available and the key is to choose correctly. In a world with blatant materialistic choices, these metaphysical controls, built into the corporate consciousness, implemented by rigorous psychometric tests checking for the decision making group of qualities, to determine if the right set of values have been used to promote honest business –this can result in a dynamic equilibrium that keeps the world from crashing through its now flat virtual surface."

Sandeep stopped speaking and after a moment of silence, the hall erupted in applause.

Questions and Answers after the seminar compiled for freakishfinance.com – Caleb Johnson

Q: Metaphysical controls sound complicated as a concept. What exactly do we mean?

Ramesh: We are faced with a crisis which no one could predict. Do we expect to get by with simple solutions?

Q: A lot of problems have been created by building complex instruments which no one understands, everyone thinks is innovation and ultimately comes back to bite itself in the tail. Several regulators failed in the process of identifying all the madness of the world for what it actually was. How can we say that the new regulatory model that you are suggesting will work?

Ramesh: We are not talking of creating a new Gaussian cupola or any other model for financial prediction or accounting. We are not talking of regulatory models like Sarbanes Oxley or Basel. Neither are we talking of those numerous indices that hold the world at tipping point. We are talking of a way of evaluating whether the choices we are on the verge of making are built on the correct motivation, the qualities that have gone ahead to make the choices are advisable or not. It is a new paradigm, a new way of looking at things – simply because the deterministic dreams of the west simply did not work .It is a way of evaluating personal choices while making business decisions.

The crisis has shown us that unrestrained greed for profit making can bring short term glory, but can plunge the whole world into a soup of meltdown. The remedy should come from a relook at the values of the industry. As the Institute of International Finance think tank pointed out in the spring of 2008, it is time for simpler, transparent and more honest style of banking. Our proposed regulations will allow an individual banker, investor, venture capitalist or a firm to evaluate their decisions to scrutinise whether the decision making steps have been driven by the right set of core values. As the chairman of the Fed, Jerry Corrigan, said in August last year, the industry needs a renewed commitment to collective discipline. Our methods are to instil discipline and values into the system.

Q: You have spoken of the Indian way of infiltrating into the world, and now of the Indian way of wisdom. Why is it that Indians were not considered a dynamic bunch till a couple of decades back? Why were they branded as plain lazy? And now, why are they indefatigable number crunchers while the west in comparison can be termed lethargic?

Ramesh: I wonder if that is quite relevant ...

Mitra: I can take that. In my humble opinion, it is nothing but the role of the climate. (reactions ... loud debate) Writers of the colonial ages have often remarked about the Indian weather and how difficult it is to work hard in the tropics. Till the eighties, the Indians suffered from the heat and dust epitomised by Ruth Pavar Jabhvala. And then came the great leveller – air conditioning ...

(laughter and discussion)

Mitra: After the air conditioning came into the offices in a big way in India, more or less corresponding in time with the policies of Open Economy of Dr. Manmohan Singh, the Indian worker could stand shoulder to shoulder with his counterpart in the west. In fact, the heat and dust outside actually makes the Indians loiter about in the office, late at night, enjoying the cool air on his brown skin, and this habit stands him in good stead. (laughter)

The Mitra-Ramesh presentation, without a doubt, was the high point of the three day conference. In addition to the revolutionary old ideas, so old that they can actually be considered new, they did a remarkable job in making the world sit up and take notice of the toy they had become in the hands of the technical advancements of the internet. The metaphysical controls spoken about seem fascinating and according to the grapevine, there is a book on it to be written by Ramesh and Mitra in collaboration with the Berkeley University Press.

LI

Mail from Madhu Deb to Sandeep

Congratulations. I heard from Ramesh that the speech was a grand success. He was also very impressed with the way you handled questions.

Madhu

Mail from Ajay Yadav to Sandeep

Congratulations. It is indeed a wonderful achievement. I am happy that the HMH account was where you did your final research. Looking forward to many such collaborations in future.

Ajay Yadav

Mail from Amrita to Sandeep

I want to talk to you about something important. Is it possible? - Amrita

Mail from Sandeep to Amrita

Only if it is tai chi *related.*

Mail from Amrita to Sandeep

Please come online

Chat between Amrita and Sandeep

Amrita: How was the conference?

Sandeep: What do you expect? It was so loaded with monumental bull, it had to be a success.

Amrita: If you are involved it will definitely be a success.

Sandeep: Ha ha ha. So by associativity, I am the bull... why don't you tell the agents, publishers and Uproar?

Amrita: ?

Sandeep: Forget it.

Amrita: Is the conference over?

Sandeep: Not yet. Tomorrow there is a networking session, dinner and prize distribution

Sandeep: What did you want to talk about?

Amrita: Madhu-di .

Sandeep: That's not exactly something I am dying to talk about. What about her?

Amrita: She started chatting with me.

Sandeep: I pity you. Online?

Amrita: Yes. After I returned home

Sandeep: What did she say?

Amrita: She asked me whether you had been talking to me.

Sandeep: ?

Amrita: She said a lot of things

Sandeep: What things?

Amrita: About your being immature and how she is always worried about you.

Sandeep: ?! Hell's bells

Amrita: ?

Sandeep: An expression.

Amrita: I told her you sent everyone some video clips.

Amrita: She said how does he find time to train every weekend and film videos when he is on an important assignment?

Sandeep: She asked you?

Amrita: Yes

Sandeep: Why on earth?

Amrita: On msn messenger

Sandeep: Yet another expression. How long did she chat?

Amrita: For a while ... then she started talking of the trip to Italy they are planning

Sandeep: Who is planning?

Amrita: Her Soiree team

Sandeep: They want to go to Italy together?

Amrita: Yes

Sandeep: Good riddance.

Amrita: Sorry, I did not understand

Sandeep: From the next time I will type (e) to denote expressions. Mathematically, you can think of them as transcendental phrases

Sandeep: Sorry, that was unkind

Amrita: It's okay. I always make you impatient

Sandeep: Did the good lady mention Hidori?

Amrita: She always does

Sandeep: I mean in that chat you are referring to

Amrita: No, she didn't

Sandeep: Wow. This is worth thinking about.

Sandeep: By the way, have you by any chance saved the conversation?

Amrita: Yes.

Sandeep: Can you send it across to me?

Amrita: Mail it?

Sandeep: Yes

Amrita: Will it be okay? I mean it was between her and me. Between two people.

Sandeep: I'm sure it was. But so was the Gita. It's just that I can't figure out why she discussed me with you. It just doesn't make sense.

Amrita: She seemed worried about you.

Sandeep: Why the heck does she have to worry about me? I just want to know what's happening here. So, if you don't mind could you send it across to me? If it's too much of a problem you can keep it one of those secrets that you will take to the grave.

Sandeep: (e)

Amrita: I will send you the part where she discussed you

Sandeep: Great. Thanks.

Amrita: You don't need to thank me for anything

Sandeep: Well, thanks for that as well

Amrita: You seem to be in a playful mood

Sandeep: I am riding high on my latest success ... which just goes to show that the world would actually make sense upside down.

Sandeep: But, please excuse me. I have some work to do

Mail from Amrita to Sandeep

(Corrected for grammar and syntax)

Even if I feel that I am doing something wrong, I can rejoice that I am doing it for you. Not that it is wrong – since she talked about you behind your back, but it was in confidence. I suppose she knows about my feelings for you. She wants to find out if there is still some communication between you and me.

General opinion may be that an Indian girl should be scandalised when her name is linked to a married man. But, as Radha said, even if she is called the Krishna-kalankini, the Krishna-scandaliser, she rejoices because in some way she becomes linked with Krishna.

I am attaching the chat script, only the portions that involves you.

Love you,
Amrita

Sandeep clicked on the attachment to open the saved chat script wondering about the self effacing romanticism. Crazy girl, a considerable measure of sense needed to be rammed into her stubborn slab of a head. Even so, in her rustic way she had referred to Krishna to proclaim her love – and in a completely different forum, Sandeep had rehashed the teachings of the same Krishna to enthral a mixed audience consisting of academics, journalists, investors and financiers. The mystical magic of Indian mythology worked in mysterious ways.

The rich text file opened in front of him, and his philosophical contemplations were stalled by the unexpected reality of the content.

"A couple of mentions in the Financial World, a significant quote in the Economic Times and all over the websites. I'd think that we have a winner."

Ramesh closed his eyes and enjoyed the moment.

"I knew I was backing the right horse."

The voice of the *Axiom* supremo was mellow across the transcontinental telephone line.

"Congratulations again. If I am not mistaken, this signals a new era of thought leadership in the industry."

"Yes. I have a personal score to settle with Dave de Boer of HMH," Ramesh laughed. "But as we ourselves have proclaimed, everything comes with its inbuilt opposite. If he had not pushed my buttons, this may not have been possible. But, after the brief interlude in Amsterdam, I want Pritam all to myself. He will work with me on this book. He is an author ..."

"Oh is it?"

"Yes. He wrote a novel."

"Novel, huh?" the CEO chuckled. "I guess it takes all kinds."

"Once I seal a quick-fire deal with HMH, I will need him to work solely with me. His being an author will definitely help, the book will open all sorts of business for us."

There was a slight pause.

"It will be authored by you."

"Co-authored. By me and Pritam Mitra."

"It will of course be mentioned that you are both employees of *Axiom?*"

"Of course."

There was yet another pause, as the man in New York seemed to delay the hand on its way to sanctification.

"I am just wondering whether there will be any ... any sort of criticism that the company is sponsoring what is essentially the self actualisation of an individual..."

Ramesh smiled at the attempted veil of negotiation.

"It will have the IPR."

"That, I think, is true."

"What if we have a subtitle – *The Axiomatic Way?* Remember *The Toyota Way* and *Straight from the Gut.* I don't think I'll be far from the truth if I say that the book is going to do the same for *Axiom* and the Indian industry ..."

The CEO was deep in thought.

"All the same, Jack Welch was someone the public could immediately relate to as GE. He was synonymous."

Ramesh's smile widened.

"How does the mention of a foreword by Thomas Armugam, CEO of *Axiom,* sound? People picking it up on the bookshelves of Borders and Barnes and Noble will definitely find that impressive."

The voice of the CEO, when it filtered through, was mellow once again.

"Now you want me to write the foreword for you, Ramesh?"

"If it won't be too much of a bother."

"Tell this writer fellow to send me the material you want me to insert, after your review of course. I will take it up from there. Do you have a timeline for this book?"

"A year."

"A year?"

"It's a book, Thomas. It has to be researched thoroughly. I'd want a team, but first, I have to have this guy working for me, no strings attached."

The silence that followed echoed with the affirmation.

"Done, Ramesh. Copy me on your mails with the instructions, I will take it up from there."

Ramesh replaced the receiver and caressed his hairless pate with a sensitive palm. He recited in Sanskrit:

"Those who worship me and surrender all their karma to me, who regard me as Supreme God, and devote themselves to me with single minded yoga, because their minds are set on me I speedily become their saviour from the ocean of birth and death named as samsara."

∾ ∾ ∾

Chatscript

Madhu: Did Pritam contact you?
Amrita: Pritam? No
Amrita: He only sent the videos of tai chi. *I think you also got them*
Madhu: Yes I did
Madhu: He is so immature.
Madhu: Given his seniority and the role ... he is way too childish
Amrita: I think he is good too, else his paper wouldn't be selected
Madhu: I know he is capable of great things. It is the lack of maturity that scares me
Madhu: He flits from flower to flower.
Amrita: I did not understand
Madhu: Didn't you?
Amrita: No

Madhu: He moves from tai chi, to consultancy, to writing. He dreams of being perfect and successful in everything and also to get his due ...

Madhu: That's why he is so immature. He is there in USA because of an important presentation with Ramesh, for God's sake. How can he afford to make videos of tai chi movements?

Amrita: I think he trains wherever he goes

Madhu: The day he will get frustrated from lack of success... that day he will make life hell for everyone

Amrita: Success means different things to different people ...

Madhu: That's hogwash, dear. Everyone wants recognition

Madhu: He hasn't even mailed to say how he's getting on. Ramesh specifically asked me to arrange for their collaboration. He has no professional sense

Amrita: He has his shortcomings. Like all of us, I guess

Madhu: Anyway, it will be his problem if something goes wrong. Tell me, did Trisha mention the Italy trip?

Mail from Professor Lal to Sandeep and Shruti

Sandeep, my boy,

I had started the workshop with a few wonderful writers who along with me spent futile days looking for sympathetic publishers. The strange animal called agent had not yet evolved, at least in India. Things seem to be the same across the world even in these modern times.

Fifty years ago when the workshop started, there were writings almost as brilliant in literary quality as you have described in your insightful summaries, and yet they ended up in manuscripts waiting to see the light of the day. So, we decided that we could spend our time more fruitfully if we just wrote.

Follow your creative passion and write, Sandeep. You never come across an ugly tree – because it always grows towards the light. So follow the light in your soul and write on. And pass on my message to Susan Frobisher and Joshua Ahmed and the rest of them. Carry the torch and follow the light.

The Professor

Mail from Shruti to Sandeep

The two stories, summarised by you, and then Professor's advice. There is nothing more for me to add that won't pale into absolute insignificance amidst such crème de la crème.

So I will only add that we writers are a self important lot. And we are at our best when we pamper ourselves and ensure our writings make us feel good. Else we lose the individual essence of the art that we create. Synopsis and SASE are not what you want to write for the rest of your life.

The only other thing that I would like to add is that – I miss you, and it scares me.

Love
Shruti

Part X:

Reverse Swap and Interest only Strip

LII

Twitter posts by Kevin Havens

Party again at the Justines Ballroom/Piazza. Involving over 250 overfed delegates who fattened themselves while the world battled crisis.

Liberators of tomorrow now being entertained by Latin Jazz suited to establishments like Paseo Colorado. Dinner after winners are named.

If all this does not lead you to reflect on the inanity, what will?

Indian duo knew what they were talking about. The answer lies in the change of outlook and philosophy. Hare Krishna may be the way to go.

"Hi, I'm Ramachandran," a dapper, thickset man approached Sandeep. "It was a great presentation."

"Thank you," Ramesh beamed and Sandeep managed a smile.

"Can you let me know of projects or organisations where you have actually implemented the model? Some case studies?"

Ramesh continued to ride the crest of the successful wave and beam some more.

"It is a model which goes back in time, Mr. Ramachandran ... we have suggested this because this is a kind of truth that is universal. Something like gravity does not need to be proved with a case study, it is always there in front of you ..."

Sandeep intervened. "May I suggest the Mahabharata? Kurukshetra? You find case studies there ..."

The start of the networking session had jarred him with people walking up to him, dropping jargons and business cards.

By the end of the first hour he was reeling from the emphasis of Cobit and Coso on the Enterprise Risk Management paradigms and possible collaborations with numerous delegates who thought they had good ideas for implementing the *Axiom* way. In between there had been periodic queries precariously pointing at excellent resumes on the way to his mailbox. His initial idea of collaring Ramesh in a corner and informing him that he would be quitting had been blown away by the plans for the future. Ramesh had already approached Thomas, and had received his full go ahead on the book idea. Pritam did not have to bother about the issues of salary, growth path or anything else that may have been sowing doubts in his mind... And then the great man had periodically rushed across to tilt his shiny head and beam at another admirer of the excellent ideas.

A face now flashed a smile in the distance and the body attached to it showed inclinations of jostling through the crowd in his direction. Sandeep's head swam. He resorted to something he knew he was good at. A pillar in the corner stood inviting and stout. With a quick skip, he was behind it, shielded from the perils of admiration.

"Life of a high flying consultant getting to you?"

Sandeep turned towards the voice, the underlying sarcasm a welcome break from the adulation of absurdity.

The man who had spoken was looking at him with piercing eyes. Under the sprouting of a sudden growth of semi-attended beard and the accelerated increase of jowls, the face could have resembled his to a large extent.

Following an initial hesitation, Sandeep broke into a smile and enveloped his friend in a warm embrace. His hands, in a subconscious manoeuvre, went over Pritam's body, unmindfully looking for potential weapons of destruction.

The new chord struck up by the band was full of lively frolic. Sipping his scotch, Ramesh watched the crowd of liberators of the financial world as most of them swung their hips and started stepping on the dance floor. Kevin Havens slid into the chair beside him.

"So what does Indian philosophy say about drunken dancing in the times of destruction?" the pioneering satirist of the financial world asked, sardonic, salivating in search of a new quip for his twitter.

"The dance of Shiva," Ramesh beamed. "Before we once again repeat the cycle of the creation of Brahma, maintenance by Vishnu and the destruction by Shiva."

"I see," Havens laughed. "It's cyclic."

"Of course it is."

At the Sheraton Club Lounge, the reunited friends sat as far as possible from the forty two inch plasma HDTV.

"I see in front of me a more mature, a more philosophical, a sort of happier Pritam Mitra," Sandeep said, sipping his Mojito.

"And I see before me the selfsame snake."

Sandeep smiled. "What is this obsession with snakes? Why not Machiavelli? Why not Mephistopheles? Why not Macavity?"

"Shut up."

The command was sharp, but it lacked the desperation that Sandeep had grown to expect in the days of telephonic communication across Europe.

"That was a great speech ... I did not understand anything that you talked about, but it was extraordinary. I could make out from the reactions."

Sandeep was touched.

"Thanks man. You came down all the way for my presentation. That's really touching."

"Shut up."

"Quite so."

"I have always followed my own career."

Sandeep's eyes twinkled as he peered over his glass.

"I have been looking forward to handing your career back to you."

Pritam frowned.

"Have you?"

"Of course, old man. You don't suppose I want to stick around in this pathetic play-station full of cartoons."

Pritam seemed pained.

"Would you really call it that?"

Sandeep looked up at his friend with concern. The question had been asked in a tone that was almost pitiable in its haplessness.

"What's wrong, my friend? What happened to you? I half expected you to jump on my head with hob-nailed boots the moment you met me, but apart from a couple of ridiculous comparisons to the reptilian, your attitude has been exemplary ... people have been awarded the Nobel Peace Prize for less ..."

Pritam nodded, looking into his drink. The lounge was filling up, but it was softly silent compared to the celebrations at the crisis conference.

"For the first few days, I was really scared shitless. I had been stupid to go through with what you – manipulated ..."

"That was the unkindest cut of all ..."

"Shut up. When you said that you would work on this ... this ... *thing* ... with Ramesh, I was almost at the end of sanity..."

"Even when you had the fascinating lady for company?"

Pritam shuddered. "Please. I beg of you. Let those days be buried in my past. After you blocked access to my mailbox, for a few days I struggled ... struggled with the feeling of not being connected with my work ... not being able to know what's going on. Each day I would wake up with the anxiety that you had made a colossal fool of yourself ..."

"You underestimate me, Pritam," Sandeep nodded wisely.

"No. It was the other way round. I overestimated myself. After a few days, once I left Shruti and joined this gang of excellent young boys, who cannot tell Berlin from Bermuda, it suddenly hit me. If you hadn't been found out in the first few days, you would probably manage. And that's nothing to do with your expertise at taking on roles. It was because ... well ..."

He paused. Sandeep peered into his eyes.

"It was because of what, Pritam?"

"It was the art of promoting oneself. And you had actually promoted yourself using your talents –writing and martial arts. At least you had some talent. I had promoted myself based on nothing. The first presentation actually gave you a niche. The secret was to stick to the image that you had created. And I developed the faith that you could do it. Besides ... there was nothing to do if you could not carry it off, other than prepare myself for the worst. And that is what I did. I got this job and started enjoying myself. I told them I would take a break and roam about a bit and that went down so well with these recruiters. In India it would have been unthinkable..."

Sandeep smiled.

"It was indeed like therapy for you, just as Sup-da ..."

Pritam shuddered again.

"Keep Sup-da out of the discussion, will you? But, yes, I kind of realised I could enjoy myself for all these days. What your impersonation did was it knocked the idea of doing great important stuff out of my head. I romped around Europe, Paris, Rome, Hamburg, the Nordics, grew a beard without thinking of possible reactions of the client– and came down to America. I spent time in New York and then read in a journal that I subscribe to about *my* presentation in California..."

Pritam spoke with a hint of mellow humour that Sandeep found endearing. A change had come over his friend, something that was reputed to take place after near death experiences. Had his colossal joke changed the life of his friend forever?

"Don't worry, Sandeep. All that happened was I started taking myself less seriously. All these years of getting all sorts of intra company awards – the Young Achiever, the Rising Star, the Superhero, Consultant of the Year. I thought that you would put my job in jeopardy, and I would have to quit. Now you have left me with no choice, because there is no way of living up to the peculiar standard you have set. Ridiculous as it sounds, it happens to be true. So, to continue, I was enjoying myself till then, waiting for you to complete this great assignment with Ramesh and hand my life back to me, while I came back refreshed from my holiday. With this conference underway, I thought of getting around to doing another of those things I have always dreamed of ..."

"And what was that?"

"Driving across the entire stretch of America, from coast to coast."

"You mean you have driven all the way?" Sandeep was impressed. Whatever changes had come over Pritam seemed to have done him a world of good.

"All the way. In my Toyota Camri. "

"Doesn't it feel like driving in a video game? All roads of America are so similar ..."

"Not in the least. I drove all the way, stopping in motels, eating at the rest areas... sometimes stretching a bit. Planning my way from one stop to the next. Without a care in the world, without the delusion that the industry will collapse if I did not intervene at the correct moment. Without wondering what Single European Act was all about. Without the dings and peeps and chirrups of the blasted Blackberry ..."

"My word, an alliteration ... What has come over you?"

"A what? Anyway, for the first time in maybe a decade or so I have started enjoying myself. So, although I maintain that you are a snake, I must thank you for this opportunity."

Sandeep sighed.

"Karmic connection. All the while, I played your role, I did not actually make any progress in my literary life ..."

Pritam frowned.

"You didn't?"

"No. And the only serious offer for a book I got was from K. Ramesh. He now wants me to co-author a book on the Ancient Indian regulations to combat crisis."

Pritam looked at his friend sharply, and then the intensity in his eyes seemed to be turned off as a glassy expression took over.

"I think anything is possible. It is weird."

Sandeep nodded knowingly.

"I need to get out of this mess, Pritam. I wanted to start a literary journey – not a romp in the world of the ridiculous."

Pritam shrugged.

"The world is ridiculous."

Sandeep looked at his watch.

"Let's go. We'll be late for the awards."

Extract from the report on Crisis Conference from freakishfinance.com
Seth Robertson

The song and dance – as is evident from the twitter post of Kevin Havens – followed by the elaborate nominations make us wonder whether we are at a conference for combating crisis or in an award function of Hollywood. Well, I think these can be put together if I call this the Poor Man's Oscar Night'. Rings true.

Marion Blanchett's oft repeated, oft used and novelty challenged paper on Risk Mitigation Strategies was a surprise inclusion, and not a very pleasant one at that. However, no one had any such problems with the nomination of the Axiom duo of Ramesh and Mitra. A roar of applause made it abundantly clear that the Indian pair had full control of the popularity charts.

In the absence of Governor Arnold Schwarzenegger, who could not make it to the ceremony, the award for the winning paper was given away by David Samford, President of the West Coast Banking Association.

Sandeep joined Ramesh at the table where the wise old man sat, a beatific smile on his experienced face.

"We have been nominated for the award!" Sandeep gushed. "To speak of all the insanities of the financial world ..."

"Why be modest? We did a great job, Sandeep. I expect more."

The smile on the face of the syndication seer was all pervading. With a wince Sandeep realised that the colossal fabrication that he had indulged in, letting his imagination free over the lively landscapes of lucre, had been transformed into truth in the great mind. He now believed in his collaborated calumny.

"It has been a fascinating conference, in which a lot of breakthrough strategies were discussed, deliberated and unearthed. I firmly believe that the thought leadership of this conference will create ripples across the country and across the globe in bringing sanity back into the craziness that we have seen in the world of finance. The time has come to decide on the best paper of the entire conference, a gathering of some of the pioneering minds in the industry as well as in the academia. Choosing one among the many fascinating ideas was a challenging task, and there were quite a few papers which deserved to win. But, there can be only one place for the winner, and our eminent panel of judges have scientifically judged the merits of each one and unanimously agreed upon – *The Ancient Indian Method of Imposing Regulations to Combat Crisis by Ramesh and Mitra of Axiom Consulting.*"

The bald head shone under the spotlight as Ramesh stood up. After a full minute, Sandeep was on his shaky feet as well.

"Can you make any sense of this scientific judgement?" he muttered under his breath.

Ramesh looked at him and continued to beam. "It'd be more fitting if you accepted the prize," he said with characteristic magnanimity.

A man in his thirties with an ill-kept beard stretched himself on the seats reserved for the audience, and exclaimed, "Would you believe it? I am a fucking legend."

"We are not mercenaries. Neither are we missionaries," Ramesh was flowery in his speech as he answered the newsmen. "I'd say we walk on the razor's edge between the two. It is the middle path."

No one could stop him now. Dave de Boer had wanted Indian wisdom. He would get Indian wisdom.

Sandeep crept near him, coming dangerously close to brushing the halo around his stratospheric head.

"Ramesh, could I have a word with you?"

The great man turned.

"Of course, my dear collaborator."

"A quick word in private."

"Now? We have a full year to have all sorts of chit chats. The book, Pritam ..."

"About *that,* we need to talk ...and the sooner the better."

LIII

"Is it your chronic urge to vanish from the scene immediately after a conference?" Ramesh stepped out of the Piazza Ballroom into the lobby. "We will be the most wanted men in the conference, Pritam ... we need to go back."

Sandeep nodded. The big boss was enjoying himself on the highest crest of triumph, something he believed that he had envisioned, engineered and earned. In his success intoxicated imagination, plans were being hatched, dreams were being designed and the future was being laid out. Books were already being conceptualised, crafted, printed and bound – reviewed and handled in the shelves. Perhaps a visiting lecturer to Ivy League universities, shaping future economists and MBAs who would be part of a similar circus in the years to come. Sandeep looked at the man's dreamy expression and pursed his lips. As another man before him, who had brutally stalled his benevolent patron, he thought "If it were done when 'tis done then 'twere well it were done quickly."

"Ramesh," he said, apologetic, yet firm. "About the book ..."

Ramesh smiled.

"I have left no stones unturned, Pritam. Your time will be freed up after a brief assignment with Dave de Boer of HMH. After that, you will be doing what you like to do ... write ..."

Sandeep cleared his throat.

"Ramesh, it's true that I want to write. But, not this. Fiction is a whole different ball game. It's at least based on reality."

Ramesh waved the objection away with his magnanimous hand. "We have been through this before, Pritam. The book is taking off."

"I hate to say this, but you'll have to write it yourself. I quit."

Sandeep looked at the expression of the great man and was disappointed. The beaming expression lost some of the shine, the halo flickered for a millisecond, but Sandeep was almost forced to admit that even so great men great losses should endure.

A tiny furrow made its way past the smile.

"Is this your idea of using the situation to bargain, Pritam? I wouldn't have thought you capable of that. Or are you sore at my having disrupted your holiday plans? Don't you see what we have achieved and what we are going to achieve? Pritam, I will get your wife here, or wherever you want to have a vacation. Australia? Tahiti? Cayman Islands? Name it. We will discuss it later, let's go in now."

Sandeep got in the way even as Ramesh tried to move towards the glitz and glitter of glory.

"The problem lies elsewhere."

"Problem? Pritam, how can you be so naive? Do you see something here? We start with this award, followed by this book. With proper development this model can actually take us beyond our wildest dreams. I was just telling myself. This is in the line of Economics. Even the Nobel Prize may ..."

"The model is balderdash. You know that as well as I do ... just fancy rehash of philosophy ..."

"What do we care? Public accepted it. Academia accepted it. The Industry accepted it ... And that's what matters. Even for the Nobel Prize. Don't you want to take a shot at winning the Nobel?"

"Not in economics."

"Pritam ..."

"Dash it, you have managed to deceive yourself."

Ramesh sighed.

"Pritam, it is not me. The world has managed to deceive itself. Nobel Prize may be too farfetched now, but I don't rule out the possibility. This thing has a real potential. Why are you even contemplating giving it up?"

Sandeep raised his palm and asked the great man to stop speaking.

"Ramesh, I will speak to you tomorrow, after you have slept off the success and are in a more sober state."

"Say, that's an excellent idea. Let's go back to the room."

Sandeep shook his head.

"I have a different meeting to attend, maestro. Please go forth and enjoy the undivided attention."

Ramesh was genuinely surprised.

"What is this with you and disappearing after a seminar?"

"Tell them that your partner has gone to carry on the ancient Indian tradition of offering human sacrifices after victory."

Ramesh patted him on his shoulder.

"Don't let sarcasm spoil the taste of success, young man. Go if you have to, and I am starting to wonder if the consultants have a wife at every port of call ..."

He winked.

Sandeep smiled. The man, deluded by success, had after all been good to him. He saluted.

"Enjoy the moment for both of us."

"Do you have to go?"

"Yes, I promised some writer friends."

"See you tomorrow then. Can you come around noon? We can have lunch at the Hilton."

"Sure."

"And forget all the ideas about quitting and not writing non-fiction. I have it all set up. We are on a roll, Pritam. I've asked Kannan to come over during the week. We can have a talk together."

With this reassuring proclamation, Ramesh left the quiet lobby to rejoin the festivities. As he opened the door, a snatch of lively music splashed across the lobby. From behind a nearby pillar an incensed form of Pritam emerged as if in tune, almost hazy with frenzied gesticulation.

"If Kannan comes, we are done for. And this dreamer won't let you leave without a fight."

Sandeep looked at him vaguely.

"Who is Kannan?"

"My boss in New York."

∾ ∾ ∾

Mails

Madhu Deb: Congratulations! We are in for a great treat. This is a great honour for Axiom and a feather in the cap for Ramesh and Pritam.

Ajay Yadav: Congratulations. It is an honour indeed for the entire organisation. I feel privileged just to have played a part in this.

Trisha : Congratulations. It's great news. When's the treat?

Amrita: I now feel like the wife of a general receiving the news that her husband had been victorious in a war. Congratulations my love.

Simon: Congratulations buddy, three cheers for Magic Pot. You have successfully made me lose faith in the world. I'll never be able to invest confidently again. The atmosphere here is electric. Amrita is glowing like a freshly purchased bulb, Madhu Deb goes on the loudspeaker mode proclaiming the brilliance of her protégé while Ajay Yadav's hair almost stand on their ends in apprehension of what this entails for his sensitive behind. Dave de Boer, who supposedly received the news from Ramesh himself, has personally come over and congratulated the duo of Ajay and Madhu.

Suprakash: On the top of a Virtual World. Beware. Nothing to hold on to.
Shruti: Champion chameleon ... now it's time to change colours
Professor P.Lal : Brihannala won it for Virata

∾ ∾ ∾

Pasadena

The table was already full when Sandeep made his way across the Coffee Gallery to join the motley group of people. He had not expected anything typical except dishevelled shabbiness with which authors all over the world are depicted. He noticed no weird idiosyncrasies. The people gathered around the three joined tables with mugs of beer in front of them mostly wore glasses and looked scholarly. In general they were not well groomed, but there were exceptions. The characteristic that surprised Sandeep the most was the age. He had expected a group of young talents, long haired, under thirty five. The age in the group ranged from early twenties to late sixties, ranging from flowing tresses to complete baldness.

Jason stood up and greeted him with a wide smile.

"Allow me to introduce to you our visiting author, Sandeep. He's from India."

Hands were shaken around the table.

"India? Wow," the speaker was a young lad with a trimmed, well kept beard. "You are quite some way from home, aren't you? Are you here to read at Barnes and Noble? From your Booker winning novel?"

"Ah, Chris. That's rude," a girl named Samantha interrupted.

"What's rude about calling someone a Booker winner?"

"Try reading some of the stuff."

There was a roar of laughter.

"If he was a booker winner he'd not have been here with us, Chris," Jason put in.

Sandeep laughed.

"If I was a Booker winner, I wouldn't be writing. I would be appearing in TV shows, leading protest marches and accepting awards."

This warmed them up. Sandeep held up his copy of *Doppelganger Days.*

"I have a copy of the Literary Magazine with your writings, my friends. I thought of giving you a copy of my only – and going by the look of things, maybe only ever – published novel."

The book was passed around.

"Only one copy, friends. I can't afford more."

There was laughter. Chris took the book in his hands.

"How much does this cost? Two hundred and twenty five rupees? That's in India. And it says twelve dollars elsewhere."

"It's the price on Amazon.com. My publisher won't manage to find shelf space in any bookstore in United States."

"We'll pay you twelve dollars. Fifty cents each around the table. Agreed?"

Wallets and purses were drawn out. Jingling coins passed from hand to hand, converted into dollar bills along the way.

"It's a gift," Sandeep protested.

"It's the author's sweat and blood. We as a group hate free copies people take for granted. We insist on paying you," Chris declared.

The money was collected and handed over.

"So this is on Amazon?"

"Yes."

"Amazon.com or the country sites as well?"

"Amazon.com only."

An elderly man named Pete shook his head.

"That's no good. In a year your book will disappear from the stores. And if it is only Amazon.com, it is like local distribution. The POD gives a better deal."

"POD?"

"Print on Demand."

"iUniverse, Lulu, Create Space, Xlibris, Trafford ... you name it," Chris explained.

Sandeep looked uncertain.

"Are you okay with POD?"

"Why not?"

"I am not okay with it. POD is vanity," Samantha made it clear.

"Self publishing. Mark Twain has done it. Balzac has done it. Why not? Why beat your head against the agents and die unpublished?"

"What is a writer's life if not the struggle?

"Take us. In every American town there is a club of this sort, with unpublished writers comparing rejection slips. Some of them phenomenally talented," Chris held court. "In big towns like New York and Los Angeles, there may be hundreds of such clubs. And that is probably just the tip of the iceberg. There are probably many writers who don't even bother with the clubs. They sit and write... just write."

"Write for themselves. The ultimate art."

"Is art for the artist alone? What is art if it dies the death with the artist, if no one knows, it's as good as not being there."

"A violet in the hills where no one treads, does it exist?"

"An author in the cafe where no one cares, does he exist?"

"A book pulped after a few days of shelf life. An author vaunted as the New York Times Bestselling author, but his work is doomed for the unfathomed depths of the remote shelves of libraries. Did he exist? What then is existence? Is it the fifteen minutes of fame, or is it the moment of creation?"

"Gentlemen, and ladies ...."

"Chris, always a chauvinist. Ladies almost an afterthought."

"Sorry, ladies. But we are deviating. I wanted to point out that there are thousands of such writers clubs, tens of thousands of writers, in America itself. Add to that the UK, the English speaking and writing world – India, the Booker land. Of all these maybe one in a thousand will ever get anything in print, on shelves. It is a game of chance."

"A good book is always published."

"Says who? Who has checked the locked trunks of dead writers to see how many Pessoas they can uncover. The answer is no, my friend. If mathematical probability is any indicator, there are thousands of unread masterpieces to every published inanity."

"Don't you think agents and publishers have a role. They control the quality, even though at times at the expense of good material ignored."

"Hush, Sullivan. You are new. Don't indulge in sacrilege, you may be lynched."

"The selection is unscientific."

"Hence biased," continued Chris. He had the floor again. "Joshua Bell experiment of Washington Post. The public cannot identify genius when handed to them on a platter. No one paused to listen to him play Bach in the subway. The same is true for Literature. If Opal Mehta is touted to be the next big thing after Doris Lessing, people will go for it. And agents are nothing but a section of the public. So, my question is why leave it to chance? Especially today, when reading is a disappearing art."

"Ipod, Playstations, DVDs... people read more blogs than books."

"As I was telling our new friend the other day, the best writing these days are on the blogs."

"Makes sense. Only time tells the quality of a book. The author may pass away, but make the material available. Don't leave it to be made into recyclable paper bags for groceries."

"What are you driving at Chris? We were supposed to hear Sullivan's poetry."

"I am telling you the secret of immortality. People read blogs. So publish there."

"In blogs? On internet?"

"Yes. And have the print edition on the POD. Even major publishers go out of print on past bestsellers. With POD, it will always be available."

"While the POD company lasts."

"They will. Back the right horse. They are the ones who make self publishing cheap. They are the ones who take the agents and other middle men out of the equation."

"But, what about sales?"

"Promote the blog. Sales are in no way proportional to quality. And look at the future. Brick and mortar shops are limited. The public wants bookstores, but unlimited stock. Soon, shelf will be electronic with all the Literature of the world virtually searchable, browse-able from the bookshop, with the technology to print and bind and sell a copy at the click of a button. Works will be available to the public, stored for posterity. POD is the way to go, for a clean world of publishing."

"Cool man. I had this same discussion with Chris some days back and was like – wow. The time we spend to hunt down agents will be saved ... we can just write and write."

"And starve."

"That's destiny. We cannot choose to be famous. Fame and success are thrust upon us. The short cut is Book Packaging and author speeches. And success makes you flabby. Angst goes out of the equation, nothing compels you to put your innermost struggles down on the paper, because there is no struggle – except with your values which you have sold to Harper Collins. If there is more success, you become an industry with shareholders – with employees whose livelihood depends on your works and their by products. Rings a bell? Harry Potter. And soon you are writing for the industry, not what you want to, but that is ratified by the shareholders... for the film ..."

"Is there a whiff of sour grapes?"

"Art is the human effort to imitate, supplement, alter or counteract the work of nature. The moment the focus shifts from it to the awards, it is a compromise."

"But art is ever changing, so cannot be pinned down. So, focus cannot change since focus itself is not possible."

"Absolute at one level, changing at another... but the intent of art is to reproduce the image of nature that is cast in the innermost honest being of the artist. And pandering it to the illiterate tastes of publishers and agents is the prostitution of the noble characteristic which elevates men to the realms above beasts."

"Wow."

"POD and blogs allow you to bypass the passages of pandering. You can create and make it available, and keep the mathematical probability alive of being discovered at some point in the everlasting stream of time."

"Internet has made us probabilistically immortal? Cool, man."

"Storytelling was verbal at the beginning, Pete. It has evolved from myth, to fables, to tales, poetry, drama ... the novel is a comparatively new development, more or less developed with the advent of the printing press. Now, guys ... and the beauties ... the internet is the next big thing. Like electricity and telephone in their infancy, people are still struggling to find its uses. But, it is reshaping the art of storytelling. With attention spans being infinitesimal, why not go in for the web page novel in html? Or the powerpoint novel? Think ahead ... and for the traditionalists, the good news is that POD will make your work as readily available as *Da Vinci Code* in the virtual reality bookshelves of the future bookshops which will combine brick mortar and technology ..."

"Let's drink to the future. Mankind made of mind, body and modem."

Glittering falsehood
Truth pales insignificant
Words of confusion

LIV

Blog of Simple Simon
Tags: Success, Truth, Falsehood

A cauldron named *Magic Pot,* with cannabis as our principal ingredient. The resulting concoction cooked up with gifted fabrication skills. The dish is good enough for the collaborated mental faculties of Ivy League academia and coveted industrial economists to be touted as the next big thing in the financial revolution.

The good doctor, who had played such a crucial role in the entire production process of this commercial crap (I am the next in line for *alliterationist* of the year, buddy), informed me that he was not surprised. Psychedelic art and rock music are nothing new. In fact, according to him, the British psychologist, Humphrey Osmond, coined the term psychedelic to mean 'mind manifesting'. So, we may have come close to collaborating in the first major work of psychedelic economics.

Shruti, who sounded a little dazed, said that she had been surprised at first, but then, she hardly expects anything rational in a world where George Bush gets a second term. She also referred to Huxley's *Doors of Perception* as drug induced greatness.

For my own self, I don't quite know how to react.

I have not really read Huxley, but I am second to no one in my admiration for Jim Morrison and the *Doors* and was at one point of time fascinated by the *Yaga Letters.* I know companies like General Electric promoted psychedelic advertising at one point of time, but psychedelic economics is a different kettle of fish altogether. To me science can investigate psychedelic phenomenon as in psychology, can produce it through modern day fractal art, but cannot *be the result of* drug induced thinking.

I did write that I would never be able to invest in anything with trust, but when one thinks of it, why not? Commercial brands have always got away with enticing emptiness. We have often fallen for Mountain Grown Coffee without pausing to think of the impossibility of beans growing in lowlands. Hair raising excitement has touched our consumerist nerve centres on hearing Pro Vitamin V 5 without even knowing what it is. And fuzzy logic in washing machines. That really washed us clean.

So, with the brilliant storytelling of Pritam, and the experienced laundering of knowledge by the visionary vice president, was it not quite probable that our flights of farcical fancy would be touted as the saviour of the financial world?

For the last few days I have been quite at a loss to decipher the fine boundary between the true and the false in the modern world. It is confusing and contradictory. Was it always so, or is it a modern manifestation of progress?

Pasadena

Ramesh sat in the lounge of Pasadena Hilton, his dignified hairless head pleasantly perched in stratospheric clouds.

"The journal was sent for a proof review. Here it is – *Aayyappan , Ramesh K, and Mitra, Pritam – The Ancient Indian Method of Instituting Financial Controls.* Pritam, the more I read this, the more I am certain that this has real potential..."

"Er ...," Sandeep sipped his strong coffee and flung his voice to cut the daydreams short. "I am ... well, where did this Aayyappan come from? I did not know you had something like that shoved behind the enigmatic K."

Ramesh smiled with the beam that had become permanently etched in his visage.

"For all practical, portable purposes I am K. Ramesh. Ramesh is simple, even for these Americans. Or they can shorten it down to Ram. However, one of the benefits of coming from the part of India I do is that we always have a couple of names to fall back on. My full name is Karthikeyan Aayyappan Ganeshan Ramesh. However, for the purpose of the paper, we will stick to Aayyappan."

Sandeep frowned.

"Any particular reason?"

Ramesh smiled.

"The world is linked by indecipherable karma, Sandeep. As you put it succinctly, especially in these days of the internet connected world. There is no reason why karma cannot be kick-started with a bit of manipulation. The fate of a paper lies in the number of times it is referred to by other papers, the number of times it is cited in bibliographies. And most of the bibliographies are lifted from the past bibliographies or paper repositories, because in these days of rush, no one can really find the time to actually refer to papers. So, when the papers are cited at random, it won't harm us to head the alphabetical list with the name of the principal author starting with two A's. We will top the list everywhere ... It will be common recall."

Sandeep had forgotten to swallow his drink, and now it almost scalded his tongue.

"And we will follow the same principle for the book as well, my boy. Aayyappan Ramesh K and Pritam Mitra ... "

"About the book," Sandeep raised his arm and beckoned. "We have to discuss it in some detail. The time has come for desperate measures, Ramesh. Will you please step into the lounge?"

An edgy, apprehensive man with a beard and the beginnings of a paunch stepped into the lounge and took the seat next to the two of them.

"Excuse me, we are having a private discussion ..."

"Here, Ramesh, let me introduce you. This man you see before you is Pritam Mitra. Pritam, this is K. Ramesh. Alias K. Ayyappan Ramesh."

Pritam Mitra, anxious and uncertain, nodded his overwrought head and offered his shaky hand. For the first time, Ramesh lost his equanimity to an extent. The smile on his lips became uncertain. The hand that shook Pritam's was dubious.

"Hi," Pritam piped.

Ramesh cancelled an incoming call and looked at the stranger.

"Your name is Pritam Mitra?" he asked.

"Well ..."

"He can't deny it," Sandeep replied for his friend. "His passport will verify."

"What are you? Homonyms?"

"Eh?"

"He's never been too good at Literary quizzes. Nor geographical or political ones. Homonyms are words spelt and pronounced the same way, but with different meanings," Sandeep explained for Pritam who was clearly out of depth. "Though, I doubt whether it would cover individuals with the same name."

Ramesh sat in the corner of the lounge and mused.

"I thought I would look up Spoonerism when you mentioned it the other day. I came across homonyms too. After all there is a book to write ..."

"Yes," Sandeep said brightly. "Way to go. After all I won't be there to help ..."

Ramesh lost some of his legendary cool.

"Why do you keep saying that? Can't you see we are on to something enormous here?"

"Don't you get it, Ramesh? He is Pritam Mitra. I am Sandeep Gupta, the writer. To be precise, the struggling writer. We had swapped roles for a reason."

Pritam could not do much more than nod in agreement. Whether it was a sudden change in lightening or a wave of mental turbulence interfering with the shine on his bald pate, there was a distinct quiver around Ramesh.

"What?"

"For the last few months, I have collaborated with you. But I was never a consultant. I was helping out my friend here, who is the real Pritam Mitra ..."

At the mention of the altruistic motive, Pritam cast a reproachful glance at his friend. Ramesh could not quite decide which of them to focus his eyes on.

"But, that's the wildest thing I've ever heard ..."

"Ah, you see ...," Sandeep shook his head sadly. "It varies from person to person. For Pritam, it was the idea of Bhagavat Gita in a financial speech. That was the wildest thing that he had ever heard. For me it was the announcement that our stupid paper had won the first prize. And for you it is a mere identity swap ..."

"Mere? And how is it possible? What about identity proofs?"

Sandeep pursed his lips. "Well, that requires some explanation. I actually used his passport to get my identity card at HMH generated. I really did not face any further issue with ..."

"But how?"

"Well, if you look beyond the fungus that disfigures his face, you will detect in him the slightest of similarities with me. In fact, in days long buried in the pages of history, we once won the second prize at a separated at birth contest ... and we deserved it far more than what we did here. A few months back, I was struggling in life to make ends meet, and he was struggling to maintain the successful career that he had made for himself. I guess we had the same hangdog looks. So, with a few small manipulations to my face, I was able to pass for a suitable likeness to his passport photo."

"But, that's fraudulent ..."

"Isn't it? Almost as fraudulent as this paper which ..."

"Why are you telling me all this?"

"Because I have to get back to my life. He has to get back to his. He has already got a job with a premier consulting firm. And I haven't written a word worth mentioning in the last few months. We have to swap back. It would help if you don't insist on collaborating on this book. It makes things complicated."

"But ..."

"The number of creations of an author, I believe, is limited. I would rather stick to realistic fiction rather than this nonsense prose of academic papers. And my friend here, with all his experience in the corporate life, cannot tell the difference between the Gita and Foucault's Pendulum."

The smile of the magnanimous victor, the confidence of the modern day visionary, the insightful look of the man who was to amalgamate the past and the present into the future, were all but vanished. A strange sense of disbelief glassed his eyes.

"You are kidding, right? Pulling my leg. Another of your priceless jokes."

Sandeep sighed again. "No Ramesh, we wouldn't do that. Your leg hasn't been pulled for the last twenty years. They remain un-pulled. Here, take a look at our passports."

Two documents were waved under his dignified nose, making disturbing patterns in the racing mind of Ramesh. The Vice President grappled with his thoughts.

"What about your amazing insights?"

"Ah ... that drives home the point. Ever met a consultant with insight?"

Aayyappan Karthikeyan Ganeshan Ramesh seemed to see the point, and that did not make him any happier.

"I can have you arrested," he remarked.

Pritam, who had never thought highly of the idea to whisper secrets past the halo into highly positioned ears, visibly started, but Sandeep was more than equal to the occasion.

"Ah. I see from your choice of words that you hint at a theoretical possibility rather than a resolution. Yes, theoretically you can have us arrested. The entire success story that was so painstakingly created will be covered by the murky underbelly of deception. The applause will turn to scandalous whispers before your ears have become used to it. Golden opinions from all sorts of people, should be worn now in their newest gloss, not cast aside so soon. Aayaappan K. Ramesh, the visionary who changed the world of finance by going back to the roots of Indian philosophy will be forgotten and replaced by the controversial Aayappan Karthikeyan Ganeshan Ramesh who used the services of a struggling author to ghost what he claimed to be his own. People love scandals and the underdog. It will soon be an uncomfortable secret much rather pushed under the corporate carpet ... *Axiom* will lose its reputation, clients will be sceptical when dealing with such people ... wide negative publicity ... and the CEO who had been promised the world at his feet will suddenly ..."

Ramesh looked up.

"I see. You seem to think that I will be susceptible to the lure of fame and ..."

Sandeep shook his head.

"I am not assuming anything. I am outlining the implications. I will also point out the positives of forgetting the whole thing. You won't be doing the uncharitable thing to the one who actually slogged night and day to bring your thoughts to maturity. Believe me, if the swap had not taken place, you would never have found an ally to create this work. Everything in life is linked with karmic cause and effect. If Pritam Mitra had not fallen in love and had run halfway across Europe after the girl he wanted, leaving me to take his place in Amsterdam none of this would have materialised."

"Love?" the visionary was not immune to the all conquering word.

"Yes, he fell in love. The idea was for me to say his piece and get out of there, but it was so rotten, I could not bring myself to go through it. I performed an extempore act. And it charmed you so much that you insisted on this collaboration even as I wanted to escape."

Pritam's fervent eyes studied the face of the Vice President. He wondered whether the slight softening of the features was for real or a figment of his wishful thinking.

"Look at the bright side, sir," he continued from where Sandeep had left off. "You won't have to share the book with a collaborator. The ideas will be attributed to you and only you when the book comes out ..."

Now the wise hand rose and brought their passionate speeches to a standstill. The noble head bowed down and the great mind dived into deep thought. Possibilities and permutations were evaluated ... When the visage resurfaced, it was with a hint of a smile on his face.

"And what happened to the girl?"

"Girl?" Pritam fought with incomprehension.

"Ah ... the girl. You mean whether the love story came to a conclusion or not? Unfortunately, Ramesh, as Whittier put it, *for of all sad words of tongue or pen, the saddest are these: 'It might have been.* Our hero ... well, we may say character actor here, pursued the light of his life, or so she had seemed, across the Schengen zone. Berlin, Dresden, Bratislava, Prague, Budapest ... but then they discovered that it was not a match made in heaven. She spoke of European treaties even as the Biergartens beckoned. Sarkozy was more of a topic to her than Romeo ... and ..."

"He came back with tail between his legs, did he?"

"Er ..."

"Looking at it from some angles, yes, that is an adequate way to sum it up."

A curious reflective look turned Ramesh's eyes glassy.

"Our company is full of morons like you."

"Er ...I am one of your most successful consultants."

Sandeep patted his arm.

"What he means to say is that he was ... He is handing over his resignation."

Ramesh glanced at the two of them with keen eyes.

"Karma. The amazing chain of cause and effect links our lives," he observed.

"Precisely, sir."

Ramesh looked at Pritam and sighed.

"Precisely, is it? Do you know what I am talking about? I think not. Consultants are not meant to ... Dave de Boer's mockery, your wild goose chase, Sandeep's speech ... now this award. It is amazing," Ramesh nodded. "The cosmic world moves in strange ways, but I believe it does for a reason. You guys want your lives back, do you?"

He was not beaming, but the look was composed, the moment of uncharacteristic choler had passed.

"Yes, sir," Pritam linked his fingers together and waited for the next words of the new corporate guru. "If Kannan comes into the picture now, we will be in a terrible soup. Sandeep, me and ... you ... and *Axiom.* They may revoke the award because of using the services of someone without a proper contract ..."

"Ah. So, you are also good in your own moronic way," Ramesh observed. "Consultant to the core ... Mr. Mitra, I am aware of the implications of a lie of this magnitude. However, with this intermingling karma, what is there in it for me? How does it help me if I let the two of you go scot-free?"

Sandeep cleared his throat.

"Single authorship, undivided royalties, sole claim to fame ... even if a Nobel Prize awaits you at the end of this farcical journey, it will be for you and you alone, not to be shared. It will be Aayyappan Ramesh K all the way. No Mitra or Gupta for lexicographic dilution. The first choice for future papers, the first reference book. You will head lists as Chinua Achebe does."

Ramesh put his hands behind his hairless head.

"And who will write the book for me?"

Pritam and Sandeep looked at each other.

"Well, since you don't have a co-author, it seems to follow that the onus will fall on you," Sandeep began. "But, obviously you have already been through that process of thinking and have reached a dead end. If we think about our collaboration in detail, we will soon deduce what the problem is. You always wanted something along these lines, something original, Indian, dipped in philosophy, and ostensibly relevant. However, when it came to putting all this in concrete terms, you were always pathetic. You are too far advanced in age and rank to actually write or even outline what is required. So, the question is, this creative grunt work, who will do this for you?"

Ramesh closed his eyes.

"Information is power, Sandeep," he observed wisely. "And knowledge and talent is nice to have, as you put it."

Sandeep tried to see through the now relaxed eyelids, to read into the man's mind. It was obvious that he was far from helpless in the situation. However, it was Pritam who spoke and with a rapidness that was surprising.

"Sir, think about it this way ... If I, or Sandeep for that matter, posing for me, had been on your payroll, think of the amount you would have to spend on the entire project of bringing the book out. Now, with no one around, you not only have full IPR on the ideas, but also avoid paying the salary ..."

"Which is huge, unnecessarily huge," Ramesh conceded.

"And the bit about writing ... I am sure we can come to an understanding. You see, Sandeep was drawing forty percent of my pay for posing as me ..."

"Only forty percent? You consultants have it real easy."

"And now, when he goes back to India, he will have his old job, which does not pay much. Or he will try to start a newspaper or sit at home writing his book. If you take him on as a part time consultant ..."

Sandeep started.

"What on earth are you talking about?"

"I know what I am talking about Sandeep. If it is agreed that he will work eight hours a day ..."

"I can't afford to. I have to write."

"Okay. Four hours a day ..."

"Forget it."

"Or even ten hours a week on that book, at something around twenty five euro an hour ... he can have a steady source of income while – I believe the term is ghosting – your book. And you can definitely hire a contractor for such a noble endeavour."

Sandeep put his foot down.

"I refuse. I have my own works to ..."

"Sandeep, face it. You are unknown. You cannot live on what you write as yet. And this is a fixed source of income. We have no choice ..."

Ramesh smiled again and this time there was a definite return of the beam.

"Mr. Consultant. You are not bad. You see Sandeep, with these circumstances, he has made both of us winners, whereas he has managed to save his own ass. However, I want to make you pay as well, Pritam Mitra. It's odd using that name for you, but you are not going scot free. Or free in any case."

He paused to pour himself some more coffee.

"Sir, I have your best interests ..."

"Oh, yes, young man. I have no doubt that you do. Sandeep Gupta, the author, has followed his swa dharma, his path of the author. And his way is fraught with impediments to his writing. Karma has brought him weird success, but not satisfaction. However, you have been guilty of gross negligence of duty, fraud and impersonation while being an active employee of *Axiom*. Your actions should not go unpunished. However, there is another major player. Namely, me. I have used the services of Sandeep Gupta without knowing ... and am standing on the crossroads. I can choose to ruin your career, Pritam, and act out the role of the exemplary leader who does not care about fame. I can also let you go scot free and make Sandeep compromise on his swa dharma by writing for me as well, for the undeniable material necessities. And with the choices in front of me, I choose – the middle path."

Ramesh sipped his coffee.

"Here is my offer. I don't report you. I tell Kannan to cancel his flight and stay put in New York. You hand me a resignation letter which I accept and brow beat Kannan into accepting as well. Sandeep flies back to Amsterdam and finishes his tenure with a few more speeches for Dave de Boer and his team. We will speak of the specifics of that later. After that, from wherever you are, you start writing the book. I agree to ten hours a week, twenty five euro an hour. It is negotiable within certain constraints. However, I fully respect your writer's dilemma, and can agree for a lesser number of hours. I will also acknowledge you as a co-author, may be *by Aayyappan Ramesh K* with *and Sandeep Gupta* in lower font. The string I attach to this is that I don't pay a single penny for this, other than a nominal retainer of fifteen thousand rupees a month to be paid by my company. The remaining charges will be paid by our consultant friend here ..."

A choked squeal escaped Pritam, but the great man continued.

"... It will be paid to my account. On the completion of the book, the entire amount will be transferred to Sandeep's account. This is to ensure that the consultant does not get away from his penance with the help of his friend. Failing this, I am afraid, the proverbial cat will be out of the bag. Sandeep's pictures during the conference and during other recent *Axiom* occasions will be sent to the future company of Pritam Mitra ..."

"I ... I ..."

"I doubt whether Sandeep will resent the publicity. Anything that brings one to the public eye helps in sales of books. But, it will be the end of your career, Pritam."

Pritam sat there, his mind absorbed in the uphill struggle of coming to terms with the conditions of the visionary.

Sandeep lifted his cup to his lip, and finding it empty, put it down again.

"Ramesh," he said. "I have perhaps been a little irreverent in outlining the shortcomings that creep into the being of a senior corporate entity ..."

"No my boy, you were quite accurate."

"I must tell you this. Strangely, you have not lost your ability to think. We will get back to you with our detailed offer, Ramesh. Let me see how I can make it least taxing on our friend here."

With his arm around a pensive Pritam, Sandeep walked out of the Pasadena Hilton. Ramesh looked after them and shook his head in wonder.

LV

Pasadena

"Not too many have your insight," Susan's studio apartment was a chaos across time and space. She still used a typewriter. Sheaves, reams and rolls of paper lay around the tables, floors and also hung in strips along the walls. Curious glass etchings were lined along the shelves.

"Thanks," Sandeep replied. Invited to afternoon tea and chat after his effusive praise of the story of the Cherokee flute, he stood in the confusion and followed the mousy woman in her thirties with curious eyes.

"I am flattered by the term you used – Kafkaesque claustrophobia," she continued. She was in a white blouse and blue jeans, not a dab of makeup. "That's what I feel too ... in the everyday strangulating obstructions on the path to our real selves, dressed as the symbols of progress. It is suffocating. Incidentally, I had already started reading your novel before Clare took it home. It is too early to comment, but you definitely mix humour and pathos in the right cocktail."

"Thanks," Sandeep repeated. "By the way, are those glass etchings also your creations?" he pointed towards the walls.

Susan laughed.

"A curious way to utilise periods of writer's block. Each of us does something different. Samantha cooks her way out, Jason becomes a gardener, Chris says he never has writer's block. He is the whiz kid. He uses some software called mind-maps, which supposedly makes him immune to it. What do you do?"

Sandeep looked at the etchings.

"I visit charming and talented women," he replied.

Susan laughed again. "That's a very sweet thing to say. As far as I am concerned, I don't just etch, I blow too."

Sandeep looked up sharply as a smile flickered across the face of the serious author at her own unexpected innuendo. She held up a striking piece of glasswork, made out of numerous small pieces, at various distorted angles to the small mirroring central piece.

"This is the best I have done in a while. It depicts the distortions that result from worldly distractions in the quest for our own naked soul."

Sandeep took it in his hands with care, looking at the central mirror with the haphazard collection of random shapes beside it.

"You can find the central distortion-less mirror quite easily in this."

Susan looked at the glasswork and laughed.

"I was right about your insight. Your perceptions are exciting. That is the essence of this creation. If one wants, one can look into the heart of his soul, but the gaze must be away from the sensual cacophony that surrounds it. Just like this," she stood in front of the object and her image appeared in the centre. "Do you like it?"

" Now that your image is in it, I can't help liking it."

"Charming and naughty. Just like you write. What about now?" she turned the piece so that it faced him.

"I guess I am too distracted by the surroundings to find my soul."

"Flattering," she turned the artwork towards her again. "If you want it, you can have it. As a gift to a fellow artist, a fellow author, who has been charming."

Sandeep thought for a while, a smile touching his lips.

"I do like it, Susan, the work is excellent."

Sandeep returned to the Vagabond Inn with the glasswork in a package under his arm.

∾ ∾ ∾

Chat between Amrita and Sandeep

Amrita: Hello

Amrita: Congratulations

Sandeep: Thanks. Isn't it late in Amsterdam?

Amrita: It is past three

Sandeep: I am feeling sleepy myself. Why are you still awake at three in the morning?

Amrita: It is night

Sandeep: Oh, well ... but, why are you still up?

Amrita: I was reading the different websites which have reported the conference

Sandeep: Ouch. Please, go to sleep

Amrita: I was also hoping that you would come on line

Sandeep: Neither is a good enough reason

Amrita: They are, for me

Amrita: Sorry if you are offended
Amrita: Please, I will not mention it again if you don't want me to
Amrita: Madhu di was asking about you again
Sandeep: Christ. What did she want this time around?
Amrita: She wanted to know if you had contacted me
Amrita: After the conference and the award
Sandeep: Why is she obsessed?
Amrita: She is very fond of you
Amrita: Did you go through the chat I forwarded?
Sandeep: Yes, I did.
Amrita: How did you feel?
Sandeep: I felt like buying some glass
Amrita: What?
Sandeep: 'What?' is considered rude. A better expression is 'Pardon?'
Amrita: Thanks, I will try to remember
Sandeep: And thanks for the chat script. I really appreciate it.
Amrita: :) Would you mind if I showed you something?
Sandeep: Well ...
Amrita: Can you request my web cam?
Sandeep: What do you want to show?
Amrita: I have practised the kata. Could I show you?

Amrita was in her long nightgown. Sandeep wondered how she was going to perform the kata in that dress. But, the girl had done him a great favour by sharing her communication with Madhu Deb, an eye-opener if ever there was one. If she wanted to be indulged, he was ready to play along for a while.

The girl got up, and in one unexpected movement, tugged at the strings of her night gown. The next instant she was in her sports bra and panties. She went through the motions of *Heian Shodan*, the very first time Sandeep had ever witnessed such a performance of a karate routine. His eyes had popped out first in surprise, and then in intrigue. It was unexpected and not lacking in the fascinating quality. If the intention had been to titillate, the results were not satisfactory, but the very fact that the girl could think of this bold manoeuvre was impressive. The kata was quite well performed, the movements jerky but thorough. The number of hours put into training was evident.

"How was it?" Amrita's voice piped in through the machine.

"Well, quite different from what I expected."

The girl picked up her night gown and put it on again.

"Am I doing it correctly?"

"Well, I wouldn't say old Funakoshi would quite approve, but yes, I ... I was impressed."

A smile touched the girl's lips and it made its presence felt an ocean and a continent away. Sandeep felt eerie.

She was a middle class Bengali girl. She had performed kata routines with him in the gym. But for the magic of web cam, would she have ...

"Is there anything else you would like me to do? For you?"

Sandeep sleepily wondered about the internet, inhibitions stripped off the socially conscious individuals. Suprakash Roy's words.

"Shouldn't you go to sleep now?"

"I'll wait for you."

"Don't."

"I can perform the tai chi form if you want me to."

"In bra and panties?"

"If you want me to."

"Heavens."

The girl got up again, with a soft, knowing smile and dropped her gown again. With her attire down to the bare essentials again, she went through the slow movements of the ancient form, pausing from time to time to check the camera angle. Sandeep watched her and wondered why she was doing it. Was she still clinging on to the hope that her love would be returned? Would she relapse to her sobbing spree and threats? Or was she over it?

Lots of other thoughts. Madhu Deb. Why was she haranguing her with enquiries? Someone she herself had dubbed as BPD? What was she playing at? Where exactly between truth and lies was she? Was there a distinction between truth and lies or was it just points of view? Ramesh. For him was the paper true or false? Everyone's soul was distorted with the noise of everyday life. What was he himself doing, playing the role of a married consultant, pretending to be an author to himself? The girl was phenomenally deranged, with dreams merged with reality. It was true virtual reality for her.

He awoke with a jerk.

"Do you want me to do that again?" Amrita was asking, face close to her web cam.

"No, please go to sleep. And keep training, with clothes on."

"You are ..." the girl giggled.

"I am dozing off."

"Good night. Love you."

൬ ൬ ൬

Mail from Sandeep to Shruti

Maugham wrote that after reading Tess of D'Urbervilles, he was ready to marry a milkmaid. I know the story of an American gentleman, eagerly awaiting the next instalment of Old Curiosity Shop at the shores of Atlantic. When he was informed by a sailor of the ship carrying the papers that Little Nell was dead, he had burst out crying. I know that after reading Crime and Punishment, there were moments when I roamed around the campus of the hostel I stayed in, my mind in convoluted confusion instigated by Raskolnikov.

Greatness of literature is no way indicated by the number of weeks on the best seller charts – that way Harold Robbins and Da Vinci Code would have been immortal. Neither is the number of Google hits or count of reviews or the rating in Amazon any indicator. The electronic herd of cosmic consciousness plays a major role in the virtual reality, which is virtual reality in more ways than one.

However, if the writing does induce one to react and explore in novel ways, in my opinion it succeeds in making an impact, and can be considered important. When I speak of reaction and exploration, I refer to individual reaction and not the group trips around the Louvre following the trail of Dan Brown.

Susan Frobisher did make me get into my Ford Explorer and drive up the San Gabriel Mountains, eager to hear the haunting Chreokee flute while surrounded by the primordial greenery. I did manage to find the Cherokee reservation centre but they were not playing music. I continued to the top of the Green Hills to the Mount Wilson Observatory. As I looked down the mountains, with trekking routes reaching down in virgin appeal to the Southern Californian plains, I wondered whether it would be a good idea to go all the way into serious exploring down the slopes, taking my foray into the lap of nature to its logical conclusion. I had started on my way, looking at the signboards for directions and tips. The first sign told me in some minute detail about what to do if in the course of the enticing expedition one happened to find a group of bears making their way into the entertainment programme. This particular piece of writing, although no great shakes as far as Literature goes, did induce me to react more than any classic has ever done. A millisecond later I found myself in my sturdy SUV, locking doors and rolling up windows. Yet another reminder that everything did come with its inbuilt opposite and sometimes the opposite does dominate the scheme of things.

Joshua Ahmed was also eloquent enough in his writings to spur me into driving my trusted GPS enabled Ford Explorer along the scenic Route 1. I did look for the tree, and cannot really say that I found it. After all, as the Professor says, all trees are beautiful, growing as they all do towards the light. But, with my eyes open for all sorts of vegetation, the Pacific, the mountains and the greenery opened up to me in ways that I am seldom perceptive enough to acknowledge.

So did the travel bug bite me in the west coast. I journeyed to San Diego, spent time beside the ocean and also experienced some excellent tai chi and chi kung instruction at the Healthways Centre.

I drove all the way down to the Mexico border, with my voice enabled GPS warning me that it was the last exit in United States. I went as far as the turnstiles, dipping my toes into the soil of Mexico's Baja California. The shopping mall at the border and the difference in the intensity of the border control of the neighbouring nations defines the premier nation of the world in broad strokes. However, with La Jolla Cove and the white beaches on the way back, petty politics did get pushed into the recesses of the backseat.

During the past few days, I have driven to the beaches of California, to the dingy streets of Hollywood, to the desert casino land of Palm Springs, trekked in the Indian Canyon. I have loaded a lot of pictures on Picasa Web Albums. As you click on the arrows to navigate through the images, you will notice one major aberration, a mistake of destiny that stand out of the frames. The equivalent error of what pursued you through your European journeys. There is no sudden snap capturing the exact moment when I am in the raptures of laughter at one of your witty remarks. There is no picture where you trod on the stars along the Walk of Fame, outshining them like the moon. And there is no picture of the two of us, in front of the hundreds of windmills that one encounters on the way to the Palm Springs, with my arm around you ... our elbows and a substantial part of my forehead missing from the frame as the camera clicks on auto.

Love,
Sandeep

Comments on Sandeep's Picasa Web Album – West Coast Wonders

Madhu Deb: Shuttling across the world giving you a major kick, is it?

Simon: Did Hiuen Tsang know tai chi? Just curious. Incidentally, Madhu Deb came down to discuss her own experiences in California and beyond. She stayed close to three hours.

Suprakash Roy: Are the real places as beautiful?

Trisha: Lovely pics.

Amrita: I am seeing a new world through your eyes

Shruti to Sandeep

Wordsworth revisited, meets Wordsmith.

Don't stir dream into wakefulness, lest the image perish.
Unvisited O Yarrow of yore I do so faithfully cherish.

Sandeep to Shruti

O that my lady's lips were near,
To utter notes of gladness,
And kiss this silence from the air,
That fills my heart with sadness.

LVI

Amsterdam

They snuggled on the sofa of Shruti's apartment, the fingers around the brown cups of hot chocolate.

Sandeep spoke:

"For busy thoughts the brew flowed on
    In creamy agitation;
And slept in many a plastic cup
    For quiet contemplation"

Shruti smiled and brushed a lock of hair off her forehead.

"Wordsworth revisited, teaming up with the Wordsmith. What can the poor weak woman do now?"

"Isn't it the same poor, weak woman who had threatened to wield a hockey stick on the eve of my departure across the oceans?"

"On your victorious voyage of versatile vilification."

"Did you feel like the beloved of a glorious knight who had donned his shining armour to battle unknown dragons across the ocean?"

"The knight with the sorcerer's sword. Who crossed the ocean to utter meaningless incantations to ensnare the eagle into being the decoy for the dragon. Not too difficult since the dragon is currently the banker of the eagle."

Sandeep rolled his eyes and blew a whistle.

"I submit to your superior wordplay ... never can I dream to merge two alliterations into a statement of modern economics. I recommend the golden silence to deliver me from the crisis. In fact, let me ensure it."

He kissed her on the lips and they embraced. Chocolate and *slagroom* flowed into breezy thoughts before merging into quiet contemplation in little pools on the table.

Madhu Deb was bounding back to her cubicle, the auditions for the forthcoming *Soiree* and the logistics for the trip to Italy foremost on her mind. When she found the curly haired smiling face in the doorway, she emitted a reverberating whoop of welcome.

"So good to see you again," she bounced along, and having ensured that she had cut off all angles of escape, locked Sandeep in an embrace. "Congratulations again. It was really a great show."

Sandeep wondered what to do with his hands, and softly placed them on her pudgy back.

"You look good. The West Coast with all the sun must have done wonders for you. How does it feel to be back?"

Sandeep shrugged. The dark, wet Amsterdam autumn was about as gloomy as things could get. Yet he loved the city with its crooked buildings and canals.

"In sun and under the cloud," Madhu Deb remarked wisely. "When I had come to Amsterdam for the first time ..."

"Right ...er ... there is a little something for you, if you go in ...," Sandeep had his cell phone in ready mode, for the tried and tested Gupta-van-der-Wiel manoeuvre and more.

"Oh, is there?" Madhu Deb sounded elated. A flash of delight brightened her face. On the shelf behind her seat was a curious looking glass object, with multiple shreds of glass arranged in a haphazard way towards the centre. "Wow. What is it?"

"That depicts the search for man's soul amidst all the distractions of the world. It's by one of the rising West Coast artists ... who is also a writer," Sandeep paused. Madhu Deb was contemplating the piece, looking at it from different angles. "She is one of the major young women in the talent pool of California. Susan Frobisher."

The senior manager beamed.

"It does look quite a work," she agreed as she sat down. Sandeep sat in front of her. "When I was in San Francisco, I ..."

"Yeah ... I also sent a mail to the people here announcing I am back and there are sweets in my cubicle. But you know how it is. An unchecked mailbox for three weeks. Mails pile up, calendar items keep popping up, the send receive action never ends. I don't know whether the mail went through. Can you please check?"

Madhu Deb beamed again, unlocked her machine and logged on to her mailbox.

"Well, I haven't received the mail. Do you want me to send the mail?"

"Sure. Please say that the sweets are in my cubicle."

"The only problem is that my machine is misbehaving too. Some of the stalwarts of our Network and Support Services will be coming soon to help me out ... well, there they are."

A couple of young Dutch engineers came into the cubicle.

"I have a problem with setting up the Centra system. I guess I will step out for some coffee, are you willing? I can send the sweet mail after that," she got up as the Network Engineers took charge of the machine. "As I was saying, in San Francisco, I was running this program for the ..."

Sandeep's cell phone rang following the trusted GvDWmanoeuvre. Talking animatedly into the handset, he excused himself and walked back to his own cubicle.

Once there, he lowered his phone and played back the video recording. The image was small, but he knew he had got what he wanted. As he looked at the downloaded mpeg file in the full screen mode in his laptop, he could make out the exact keys that the lady had typed. The strategically placed glasswork had captured the image of the keyboard to perfection, and his camera had been focussed on the natural core of being, without being distracted by the aberrant reflections of the shreds that led up to it. He now knew Madhu Deb's log in password, the password to her outlook mail id and as an unexpected bonus, the secret password of the master-user used by the network team.

The chat script forwarded by Amrita had alarmed him. It was more than concern that had been displayed, and in the conversation, the manager had come across more unbalanced than the infatuated girl. There seemed to be a bottled up resentment that he did not like. The glasswork was supposed to be striking, yet disturbing, but to the uninitiated eyes of Sandeep, it looked hideous. The idea of using it had germinated in the mind of the investigative journalist at once, but the final decision had been made when, shortly after his return, Simon had hinted at some uncomfortable encounters with her. Access to the workings of the mind was handy, especially now that he was about to switch back into his normal life.

Simon had been eagerly waiting for discussions on the surprise award for their drug induced concoction. When he mentioned the possibility of having invented psychedelic economics, however, his buddy was less than impressed.

"It is actually psychedelic consent," Sandeep exclaimed. "The human herd coaxed into acceptance of ideas by the drugs injected by media. Internet has been a giant shot in the arm as far as general drugging by the media is concerned."

"But how does it feel to be a pioneering thinker in the Financial world?" This flattering question was rewarded by a blank stare.

"I feel like a character out of a Blandings novel manufacturing the Emperor's New Clothes."

"Could you please refrain from talking through your hat? Specifically because of the multiple numbers of headwear you habitually don?"

"It is a mystery buddy," Sandeep observed gloomily, "The more I look at the visible crust of the world, the more I wonder what's baking within. You know, Ramesh, who will very soon call himself Aayyappan Ramesh, is dreaming of winning the Nobel prize for this."

"That's not stretching it too much, because Obama has won it purely based on his intentions." This made Sandeep lighten up and chuckle.

If the socio-economic discussions had suddenly turned a trifle too philosophical, Simon was nonetheless delighted at the resumption of the Madhu Deb avoidance technique. They used it three times during the course of the first day.

Simon had been forced to use it when the lady, Trisha in tow, had come in just after lunch, wondering whether he would be interested in joining them and some dedicated members of the *Soiree* team for a trip to Italy.

"Thanks, but I have things lined up," he had replied. He was not too keen on missing out the remaining days of his buddy's tenure in Amsterdam, with the *tai chi* classes going full steam. Besides, there was always the Gunjan factor to consider.

When Madhu Deb asked him to think it over and settled down in his cubicle, SImon proceeded with the Gupta-van-der-Wiel manoeuvre.

Trisha had been back in his cubicle after a short while.

"You really can't spare a day or two for the tour?"

Simon had felt irritated. He knew from Amrita that she too had been asked to participate in the tour and there had been subtle and not too subtle pressure on her as well. He had the decided to treat Trisha to a taste of Dutch directness. "You see chubby cheeks, I am not really salivating for the opportunity to spend a few days cooped up with Gunjan."

"But this will be a good opportunity of cultural exchange and getting to know each other."

" I can see you have been sent with the definite instructions to pass on management bull shit by proxy. I don't really enjoy being told what to do during a holiday and that's the first thing one needs to learn about the Dutch."

For a moment Simon had wondered if he had been a bit too blunt and had offended her, but the girl had given the impression of not having quite grasped what he had said and had gone away with a friendly expression.

The second time he had to use the GVDW technique was perhaps more of a preventive measure. Just as he was about to set out for the *tai chi* session, he had detected Madhu coming towards him with an expression of urgency on her face. He could almost predict some urgent report to be developed, delivered and documented ASAP from the little wrinkles on her lips and forehead. He had been in no mood to miss or be late for his buddy's class the day it was supposed to resume, and had taken no chances. The phone had started to ring even as Madhu had been about to blurt her instructions and he had walked off, talking and nodding into the device.

Blog of Simple Simon

Tags: Taichi, Master, Return, Privacy, Cultural Differences, Dutch, Indians, Veronica

The return of my buddy was welcome in multiple dimensions, each more delightful than the other.

Our *tai chi* classes were obviously resumed with the guidance and expertise it had lacked these three weeks. The excitement in us, as we went through the practised steps and started on new ones, was palpable. Amrita's eyes shone in the buzz that seemed to come from within. I was almost too eager, something which often has an adverse effect on tai chi forms. As for Pritam, he was positively delighted at the amount of training the two of us had put in. He made minor corrections to the techniques we had picked up from his you tube videos and proceeded quickly to new ones. We had trained ourselves, but after today's class, the glow and feeling of well being that I had come to associate with the sessions was back.

My buddy's return, as had been with his arrival, has again brightened things up. There is excitement of the clandestine cell phone tactics, the serio-comic discussions, and of course, sublime training.

Onto something else.

Since the last couple of posts, it must now be apparent to the followers of the blog that I am no longer making a real effort to keep this blog politically correct as far as office peculiarities are concerned. This is due in no uncertain measure to certain established people in the senior management trying to pull their weights to win friends and influence people in murky territories.

Is it cultural difference? Or is it something more than that?

I have been asked to join the cultural sub-group *Sur Soiree* in a romp in the sunny land of Italy. While there is nothing unduly alarming about this invitation, apart from the somewhat sinister company that it would necessitate, what got on my slightly agitated nerves was the subtle and not too subtle manipulation that seemed to take place across a pecking order of the organising group in an effort to force me into accepting the invitation.

Particularly infuriating about this manoeuvre was the ostensibe effort of the senior management to brand this trip as an opportunity to promote cultural exchange and a sense of togetherness.

Well, I expressed myself in no uncertain terms. I told the girl entrusted with the instructions to convince me that the first thing to understand about the Dutch was that they were not very keen on being told what to do during their holidays.

The Dutch take their privacy very seriously. Behind their large glass windows, they have the right to be whatever they want to be. Even in places known to promote camaraderie in most societies, like the bar and the crowded public transport, the Dutch can be observed to be aloof, not really interested in talking to people who are not really close friends. This might seem strange for an Indian, who more often than not merge into the life of the colleagues. But, while doing business in the Netherlands, is it not expected of these people, at least the senior management, to learn about this feature of the Dutch character?

I had the misfortune of being accompanied on a car ride by one of my co-workers on the way to a immensely hospitable and ultimately hilarious social occasion in the home of a female colleague (refer to an earlier blog where I have documented in some detail the delicacies of the Indian cuisine). This guy, possibly the most eminently avoidable whiner in Amsterdam, probably in the whole of Flanders, had one pet peeve. Indians had to struggle to earn their livelihoods, working close to twelve hours a day while the Dutch people could afford a work life balance and afford to be occupied with gardening and expensive concerns like the environment. When one did not have to think about ways to fill one's stomach, according to this human equivalent of a yawn, one could afford to indulge in social consciousness. He called the Dutch people lazy in no uncertain terms. No one was prepared to do anything more than what his job description decreed. There was no concept of going the extra yard. Comes from a culture which thinks splashing about merrily in water is schoolwork.

If I had not dreaded a prolonged argument with this abhorred adhesive of a man there were a lot of reasons I could provide.

The Dutch have reclaimed most of the land from the sea, which is perhaps the hardest a people have worked to set up a nation, with the probable exception of the Israleis. To them, flooding of the lands and being at the receiving end of the fury of the sea is neither a past easily forgotten nor a threat completely ceased. They know the importance of holding the sand together with carefully planted vegetation, the dangers of the melting of the polar ice caps. They are conscious of the environment because they are directly affected by it, addicted to gardening precisely because of this consciousness. The reason that the Dutch children have to learn swimming in school is to be prepared for the eventuality of another flooding of the land. And fighting off the sea as a community meant years and years of organisation, with the entire population making a coordinated effort, where each and every task was planned to perfection, little left to chance and individual heroics. So, if the Dutch seem inflexible when asked to deviate from their job description, there is a very good reason behind it.

However, do the Indian workforce make any attempt to understand the complex history of the people? At least the account managers and senior folks of the company? Do they try and negotiate with the clients by utilising the knowledge of their past? Nada.

They are too occupied at beating the Hollanders at the whining game. They love to come across as a misunderstood community, who are at the receiving end of insensitivity of other cultures – the Americans being the leaders in this respect.

But when it comes to understanding other cultures, they are too eager for quick fix solutions. Cultural barriers are supposedly bridged with a human resource presentation showing powerpoint slides with pictures of windmills and clogs and Ruud Gullit.

Perhaps the one solitary exception is K. Ramesh. His way of infiltrating the organisation of Dave de Boer was to place Pritam Mitra as a free resource virtually outside the organisation who reaches the people of the department through his series of talks. This does have uncanny similarities with the history of the popular channel Veronica. With the Dutch radio channels dominated by the pillarised structure of Protestants, Catholics and Social Democrats, and with new channels unable to get through the complex consensus process of approvals, Veronica was started through the broadcast of a series of programmes from a station located on a ship outside the territorial waters of the country. It reached people without being obstructed by formal barriers of bereaucracy.

Did K. Ramesh really reuse the learning from history? I would not put it beyond the great man. There are brilliant exceptions which make the Indians such a fascinating people.

Unfortunately, the same can hardly be said about the hordes that we see around us.

∾ ∾ ∾

Theatre Cassa Rosso

"Unlike the others, this theatre is well lit," Dr. Suprakash Roy leaned back in his comfortable chair and took a long pull at the *mai tai*.

The two of them had met at the Centraal Station and had walked down to the famed establishment at Oudezijds Achterburgwal. To his surprise, Sandeep noticed that a good percentage of the thoroughly respectable audience were women.

The entertainers were attractive too. A supremely athletic girl, clad in the thinnest of straps, performed splits and high kicks, moving sensuously to the rhythm of popular music, while putting innovative apparatus inside herself. This was followed by a couple of good looking individuals swaying to the rhythm of the romantic numbers as they stroked and sucked each other into a state of arousal.

"Quite a surprise that you have never visited this place," the doctor observed quietly as they followed the mechanical gyrations. "Squeamish, aren't we?"

Sandeep shrugged.

"I never quite understand it. Sex without passion, for the public."

The psychiatrist fondled his unlit cigar.

"True, but even then, I guess if one is an author one has to research the place in detail ..."

"I am an author of fiction dealing with human interactions, where emotions do come into play. I will leave writing about this sort of thing to the travel magazines."

"I guess you will soon be a ghost writer of an economic best seller."

Sandeep made a face.

"Yes, I guess so."

"So, what was the final arrangement? Is Pritam getting cut to the quick?"

Sandeep nodded.

"The great mind has seen to that. He will have to cough up six hundred euro a month."

"And what do you get paid?"

"A sub-contracted fifteen thousand rupees a month."

"And the amount Pritam pays will be made available after the book is completed?"

Sandeep nodded.

"Up to a maximum of ten thousand euro. If it takes more time to complete, Pritam keeps paying, but the money on top of the ten thousand remains with Aayappan Ramesh."

"That's a master plan. The pressure remains on you, as a friend, to finish it within a year and a half."

"Right."

"I did not know he was called Aayappan."

"A recent discovery. A lexicographic requirement. Kick-starting karma."

"I guess our entertainers are kick-starting their act as well."

A hush descended on the spectators as the young man in the spotlight, with three quarters of an erection, entered the blonde woman.

"I don't understand it," Sandeep complained. "The audience knows it's fake. And still this is a ..."

The psychiatrist focused on the act.

"Reminds you of your paper?"

Sandeep nodded slowly.

"It could have been Ramesh and me on the stage, in a metaphorical sense of course."

Suprakash Roy nodded.

"Man has always been moved by flights of fancy. That's what your Dutch friend called it. Is there anything real about pornographic magazines? Or websites?"

"But finance?"

"Sex and money ... they can be equated, can they not?"

"If Freudian associativity is valid, sex is the wildcard. It can equate to everything."

The bodies became sweaty and the gyrations increased in tempo.

"He surely would have loved Cassa Rosso."

"Who?"

"Freud."

"And as a psychiatrist, why are you here?"

Suprakash Roy paused as the act reached its climax.

"It is a melting pot of human emotions, Sandeep ... or the lack of it. I like to observe the people."

"You have kept your unwavering focus on the performing artists throughout the show."

The good doctor bowed.

"Ah, that. How can I analyse unless I have gone through the same experience myself?"

Sandeep retrieved his long coat.

"Pardon me for saying so, but it does sound like a load of crap to me."

Suprakash Roy patted him on the back.

"Then accept it, my friend. The doctor is as human as the next person. I was curious and you were an author ..."

"What does that mean?"

"It means that as an author, you seemed to be someone who would not be squeamish about these places. So I asked you."

Sandeep stepped into the wet night air and sighed.

"An author is cut out to be miserable. So much for being the engineer of souls."

They walked through the lanes with the lit up windows. Inside, the women stood looking bored and texting on their cell phones.

"The digital world in action amidst the oldest profession," Suprakash Roy remarked.

"I believe one of the first uses of the internet was to promote pornography and prostitution."

The doctor nodded as he looked appraisingly at a girl who knocked on the glass window to attract his attention.

"Mankind evolves slowly. It is the world view that changes."

"The *Weltanschauung?*"

"Exactly. The basic nature of man remains approximately what it was."

"Why then does he fail to hear the Cherokee flute?"

"Is that an allusion to a song? I am a bit prehistoric in that area."

"Even here, surrounded by all these lovely and not so lovely ladies, I find it difficult to digest. Fifty euros, wham bam ... One position, zero foreplay ...Suck and fuck."

"People don't come here looking for romance, Sandeep."

"Sex without romance, how good can it be?"

"What if life is unkind? What if a person is romantically challenged?"

"I guess it takes all kinds."

"No, that's the major kind."

They crossed the Damrak and entered *Teasers.* A girl in revealing bras and the shortest of shorts received them with the friendliest of smiles.

"It will soon get too loud to talk. What do you make of Madhu Deb's conversation with my students? Especially the lady in question?"

The doctor pointed at the television set where Ajax locked horns with Eindhoven in a recorded match.

"When you are a goal ahead and there are two minutes to go, you know what to do?"

"We did take a walk through the Red Light District, but neither of us scored."

The good doctor smiled.

"I meant play for time. Finish your assignment and get out of here."

"Just a few weeks. I have to transfer knowledge to Dave de Boer. I will outline the mumbo jumbo. Pritam will fill in the technical details."

"Another masterstroke from our friend Ramesh, I guess."

"Aayyappan Ramesh."

"Go away. Get out of here. Scram. The equilibrium will soon collapse."

The music suddenly became blaring and a couple of Teasers girls started dancing with abandon. It got too loud to talk.

Part XI:

Information Content Effect, Identity Theft and Original Face Value

LVII

Very soon we will look at an important conversation, which would be of no meagre academic interest to our psychiatrist. It took place in the medium of instant messages, where the eye does not meet the eye, voices do not quiver, fingers do not cross in consternation. Irrespective of mood, degree of decency or truth, the messages pop up in front of the participants in unvarying electronic text, making one immune to the telltale flickers of falsehood. Expertise required for mutilation of truth in face to face conversations is unnecessary.

If the participants of the conversation had met in real life, would the discussion have been different? Tempered, yes. But, different? I don't know. Even as the two went ahead with a discussion where truth was dispensed with after an initial apology of attempt, both the ladies involved had convinced themselves that they were acting for the general good, following the instincts of their noble souls.

Some of us may find the two to be pretentious, superficial, pathetic – but this is what we do all the time. How often do we modify the truth to the slightest of degrees to suit our convenience, and convince ourselves that it was necessary, and even admirable?

Trisha was made up of strong middle class values – hush, please don't say narrow-minded morality. She led her life straight according to her solid principles. Almost always, except for a couple of occasions of a blissfully forgotten early youth, when she had transferred her affections from one soul mate to other with an abruptness and lack of ostensible reason that had snapped the tender strings of the sundered hearts, hustling the young romantics into a world of cynicism. But those days were long past and she had been purified by the holy fire of matrimony. And the day she had sniffed out a certain degree of association between the instructor and one of the students, drastically amoral in her spotless one dimensional book of ethics, she had compounded it into her reasons for leaving the *tai chi* classes. The recall of Amrita as a student had been a surprise. Purpose defeating too, since she had made it a guarded secret duty – visible to the likes of Madhu Deb through semi permeable cover up – to help her friend get over it. Because she had been taught that nine times out of ten, the girl needed help, and she knew there was a senior manager who appreciated altruistic action, and took a personal interest in all that happened in the *tai chi* classes. She was supposed to be an innocent, well meaning girl and from her formative days, superiors were meant to know it. It was natural for her to be scandalised at such stirring relationships. So, if she made her 'fears' apparent to the good lady in the conversation by conjuring up a cock and bull story, it cannot really be attributed to her failings. She was convinced that she was doing good and wanted the senior manager to know it. So, a brutal tug on the carpet of reality to rearrange facts was within her license.

As far as Madhu Deb was concerned, she had always been concerned about Amrita. Well, she wanted the good of everyone. She was the champion of her employees and that was all there was to it.

The common thread that bound them now was the proposed trip to Italy. They had planned it with a lot of effort, and now it was falling apart. Lahari had withdrawn because of her son's fever. There had been a couple of drop outs from the established Soiree team. And now both Simon and Amrita had refused to go. Well, to put it in another way, Simon had adamantly refused and Amrita had dared to say no.

So, when Madhu Deb looked at her communicator window and saw that Trisha was available, she sent out a feeler.

Madhu: Did Amrita ultimately confirm?
Trisha: No. She won't go.
Trisha: I asked her again yesterday and she said no. She was in a hurry to go to the tai chi class.
Madhu: Silly girl. When will she come to her senses?
Trisha: :)
Till this minute she had been unsure where Madhu stood when it came to Pritam.

Madhu: I have some news.
Madhu: I have dropped out of Tai Chi
Trisha: :O I am surprised
Madhu: I was liking it, but then suddenly it seemed that all was not okay.
Madhu: There are other tai chi institutes in the town, but P ends up visiting them
Trisha: Madhu-di. There was something which I have often thought of telling you.
Trisha: Some of the folks here are actually laughing about it
Madhu: What is it?

Trisha: Amrita spoke of her roommate objecting because someone came to meet her in her apartment. When the others asked who this someone was, she became shy and said 'Your consultant'
Madhu: :O
Madhu: Trisha, in that case you know quite a lot.
Madhu: The two had an affair
Madhu: I have often tried to counsel them, individually and together
Madhu: But, they were not to be corrected
Madhu: Everything was going along fine for them, with Shruti being back in India. And then Amrita became too demanding. And as happens so often, Pritam found it too difficult.
Madhu: And then he called me for help. He wanted to save his skin and told me he wants to end everything with Amrita.
Madhu: I rushed along and helped him. Counselled Amrita. Made P promise to stop her from coming to class. But I did not realise then that P always wanted a group of admirers around him who would keep boosting his ego.
Madhu: I saw him taking Amrita back in class. Restarting the relationship. Promptly I sent him to USA. But now that he is back for a few more days, I guess he wants to have his bit of fun.
Trisha: It's terrible
Trisha: When P was not here during his conference, I spoke to Amrita. She was crying a lot and I comforted her. Later, I saw one of the stories she was writing on her PC. It was a touching description of the life of the other woman in a person's life.
Trisha: But, she is incorrigible.
Trisha: Now that P is back, she doesn't mind playing the other woman in his life.
Trisha: She is a fool.
Madhu: I am concerned about Simon. P will ruin his life now.
Trisha: To tell you the truth, Madhu-di, I discontinued tai chi for this very reason
Trisha: Something did not seem right
Madhu: I know. That's why I did not try to talk you back into the class.
Trisha: Tell me Madhu di. How much does Amrita or Simon know Gunjan-da. Why do they hate him so much? It is because of P. He has them mesmerised
Madhu: I had once taken Simon aside and told him that P was not that great. He seemed surprised. I am working on changing his seat location. If he can be relocated to the Bijlmer Arena, he will be relatively free from P's influence. Oh, the things I have had to do to contain the damage caused by P!
Trisha: And he is happy playing games. He does not stop with tai chi. He even gives A gym lessons.
Madhu: Gym lessons? If they go to the gym together everyone is going to talk about it!!
Trisha: I don't know when they go, but I know A is committed about gym now
Madhu: Now he will be leaving all this behind, and he won't even think about where this leaves A
Trisha: Nothing will happen to P. He manages things well. I wonder if he enjoys talking about it.

Madhu: Talking? Who else does he talk to?
Trisha: I don't know. Manouk may be. I see them together quite often.
Madhu: Manouk?
Trisha: Axiom's PMO
Madhu: Should I give him a final blasting?
Trisha: Forget it Madhu-di, you will become the villain
Madhu: No, I have got to blast his head off
Madhu: And if he or A spreads rumours about me, no one is going to believe
Trisha: I know.
Madhu: Sometimes I think I am a stupid boss
Trisha: No Madhu-di, you are a wonderful boss
Madhu: Thanks for the chat, Trisha
Trisha: Take care
Madhu: I feel somewhat lighter

∾ ∾ ∾

Dave de Boer's eyes shone. The concept of three *gunas* had attracted him with its ancient allure. He looked like a child who, tired of the mass produced expensive electronic toys, turns to the charms of primitive African masks and handmade alpaca cloth dolls.

"So, you say this system of testing the driving motivation for financial choices can be applied both at personal and organisational level?"

Sandeep nodded.

"It is a concept that can be used for one's personal way or the way of the organisation. Individual or collective dharma."

"And the results cannot be tampered with."

"The metaphysical controls have to be installed through psychometric tests to be taken after the decision has been made and the transaction is on the verge of taking place. The psychometric tests cannot be doctored. However, we are still in the process of finalising these tests. So, you have to wait for them to become available. It is a highly confidential process right now."

The CEO smiled.

"Ramesh has won our bet," he conceded.

∾ ∾ ∾

Communicator Message from Madhu Deb to Sandeep

Pritam, you are an adult and a damn smart one at that. I say it for your own good, for the good of Amrita – I am not even thinking about Shruti. Leave the girl alone.

Sandeep saw this instant message on his screen when he returned from the long afternoon meeting with Dave de Boer. With the corner of his eye, he noticed Madhu Deb leaving, with the bouncy steps of the organiser she carried specifically on hallowed occasions of Sur Soiree rehearsals. The communicator message had been sent a quarter of an hour back. He walked up to her cubicle, and unlocked her machine. The chat was still open, in an unsaved window. Sandeep took a cursory glance at it, pasted it into an outlook body and mailed it to himself.

"Did you ever talk to the employees of Axiom or HMH about me visiting your apartment?"

The eyes that had looked up with unexpected delight at his arrival in her cubicle now shot him a glance of hauteur. A spark kindled in the soft languorous look.

"Do you expect I will ever do that?"

"Did you weep and cry when I was not here?"

Her face softened. She did not answer.

"Did you?"

"Isn't it natural?"

"In public? Did Trisha have to comfort you?"

The hauteur returned to her eyes. It was mixed with confusion.

"What? ... I am sorry, you told me to say pardon."

"If you are shocked, 'what' is good enough. Are you positive?"

She looked angry now.

"I know you have spoken about our relationship to Madhu-di, but to me it is personal, for me and only me ..."

Her look was of pained dignity. He had a lot of arguments against it – the death threats, the never-ending stalking, vigils near his apartment door. But, this was not the time to go into them. She was telling the truth.

"Did you write a story where you played the role of the 'other woman'?"

She started.

"Yes. And Trisha was looking at it. She was behind me when I was writing it. But, why? What has happened?"

Sandeep shrugged.

"I will mail you a discussion. Read it and find out."

Instant Messages from Amrita to Sandeep

Lies. Lies. Such a lot of lies.
Madhu-di needs to be punished.

I have never ever caused them any harm
This is disgusting

Mail from Professor P. Lal to Shruti and Sandeep

O you young hearts,

This old man too has a heart that is young, but it is untutored as far as the modern mayajal of the wonderful world wide web is concerned. My granddaughter informs me that the same mail can be sent to the two of you simultaneously without copying or cloning, even if you happen to be literally a world apart – which makes me wonder whether this is the real Krishna-leela.

However, I have even more remarkable news. The Rabindrabharati University has decided that I deserve to be conferred a doctorate because of the transcreation of the Mahabharata. Isn't it fascinating? To be honoured for something that started as a fun thing?

Having said that, it is the fun element that leads us to the best of our abilities.

So have fun – o young one
You've begun –I'm almost done

The Professor

Sandeep looked up from his laptop and found himself looking at the bloated peering face of Madhu Deb. Her visage, stripped off the constant jovial expression and without the occasional proprietary wise look of a confidant, had taken on the unused pallor of guilt. In her hand was a printed sheet of paper, broadly marked with red permanent ink. Her eyes lacked the confidence of yore. To Sandeep they portrayed the fluster associated with senators caught in embarrassing acts with interns.

"How did you find this?" she took a seat more out of necessity than willingness or invitation. The printout was dropped in front of Sandeep on his desk. Snippets of the recent conversation on communicator was circled by big red letters alleging – GOD PLAYER.

"Could you remove that piece of trash from the table?" Sandeep asked, his voice lacking the desired degree of nonchalance. The last few syllables had come tantalisingly close to being shouted. Madhu Deb groped for the sheet of paper. "My reading habits never included third grade gossip magazine stuff. And incidentally, I was just reading something sublime by someone who can be your absolute antithesis."

Madhu Deb blinked. A small bead of tear rolled down her chubby cheek. Sandeep noted the glistening display of emotion, but remained unmoved. At the back of his mind he wondered at the ability to come up with alliterations even when anger grated his sensibilities.

"I understand your anger ..."

"I don't understand your vulgarity. And I am sick of women – of all kinds – weeping their hearts out in front of me and plotting my destruction in sickening ways behind my back."

The good lady bit her lip. Her habitually energetic eyes were lifeless, looking at her feet. Sandeep, who had rehearsed a reserved, dispassionate, clinical censure found himself sounding uncontrollably bitter.

"I wonder if you are even capable of looking inward after all these years of three hundred and sixty degree ego massage, but have you ever imagined the consequences if I went ahead and disclosed the story of your extra marital affair to someone living in a world of one dimensional middle class morality like our so called innocent friend Trisha?"

Madhu Deb still looked at her feet.

"Could we step outside office? To the cafe?"

"Why? Is my voice too loud? Will it taint the glossy picture of your glorious, fellow feeling managerial genius if it is heard and ..."

"I am not bothered about myself, Pritam."

"I see."

"I know I have broken your trust. I know you won't believe me now. But ..."

She paused. Sandeep glanced at her face and looked back at the screen displaying the Professor's mail. He frowned.

"I am worried about what people might think of you ... if this gossip becomes public."

Sandeep leaned back in his chair and laughed.

"I wouldn't recommend going out, lady. With such declarations you stand more than a fair chance of being struck down by lightning."

"I am sorry, Sandeep ... I ... there were too many windows, too many mails, too many communicator messages ... I know I should have discontinued the conversation, but ..."

"Is technology to blame? Attention Deficit Hyperactive Disorder of middle managers? But, then, you happen to be a senior manager."

The lady tried to smile.

"I know you are bitter, Pritam. I understand. I can promise you that I will control the damage. If you can still believe me."

"That's indeed a tough ask. It just happens that I have unearthed this particular conversation. But, I have no idea how many of the same sort have taken place in the past with your altruistic facade smiling at me all the while."

"I know it's difficult for you to believe me at this moment, but I've always had your best interests in mind. I ... I have never discussed anything with anyone ... This was a mistake, my only one."

"The single flaw in a great personality, was it? Like the Shakespearean heroes. Tell me something. When you discussed my immaturity with Amrita, was it also with my best interests in mind? And what about making my negative aspects visible to Simon?"

The senior manager looked at him uneasily.

"Right now you are biased against me, Pritam. But, if you think with proper perspective you will realise that it was for all of you ..."

"Universal Mother, aren't you?"

A sad smile touched her lips.

"You want to be nasty with me right now, Pritam. I understand."

"Stepped back into your godly shoes after splashing mud all over with the middle class narrow minded slippers you actually wear. You know, every gesture now stinks of superficial pretence with that piece of snowballed fabrication ..."

Sandeep pointed at the piece of paper. Madhu Deb looked at it, a thought creasing her forehead.

"Did I accidentally print it out, Pritam? With so many windows ..."

Sandeep allowed himself a smile. A satisfied one.

"It may be news to you, but some people are somewhat smarter than you. Now, if it is not too much of an imposition, could you excuse me? I have some important work to finish."

The lady got up, a frown etched on her face.

"I can only ask to give it some time, Pritam. I am not saying what I have done is right – in fact it is wrong, very wrong. But, I hope with time you will understand me. I also have to think about it. Why I did such a thing ..."

Sandeep looked at his laptop. He scrolled up and down, scanning the mail of the professor as the manager waited for one look of reassurance. He did not indulge.

"Another thing," he called back as Madhu Deb was halfway out of the cubicle. "*Tai chi* is holy to me. Please bear that in mind. The *dojo* is not a brothel where Simon will ruin his life. If that is all that you have learnt in the few minutes you could spare from your *Sur Soiree,* it's your business. But there are people for whom this is a way of dedication."

~ ~ ~

Mail from K.Ramesh to Sandeep

Pritam / Sandeep,

It is confusing... I have called you Pritam so often that your new name comes slow off my keys, but it clarifies a lot of stuff as I look back and wonder at the unconventional approach that stood out in your work.

Congratulations yet again for this path-breaking idea. I have received an email from Dave de Boer in which he states that you have explained the theory in meticulous detail. I attach his mail below. I think it is time for you to shed the garb of the consultant and go back to your life of the author. I will handle the formalities.

Looking forward to working with you on our book,
Please look at the mail below, it just about made my day ...

Ramesh

<Attached mail from Dave de Boer of HMH to K. Ramesh>

Ramesh,

Mitra took me and a few of my senior colleagues through the details of your paper. I am impressed. The complex philosophical aspects were very well explained by your consultant. He broke it down into simple tangible terms.

The idea of putting metaphysical controls based on psychometric tests is fascinating. I know I have to wait for the actual tests to be fine tuned, and as Mitra told me, it is highly confidential and proprietary. But, please consider this email as a yes to any piloting that you would like to do in HMH. We can go further and try financial arrangements with a proper work order if the piloting is successful.

You proved it, Ramesh. Indians, as you point out in your mail, are set for historic transformation. 2010 being the year when manufacturing will finally outweigh agriculture in the country, I believe it when you said that your country is going to make rapid steps to lead the world with ideas as well.

I am convinced and as always, in the spirit of partnership, offer my humble assistance to take steps with you.

Thanks / Met Vriendlijke Groet
Dave

Mail from Sandeep to Shruti

Mark Twain did remark that a lie travels halfway across the world while truth is still putting on his shoes. It took Professor more than three decades to start getting recognised for what to him is the one truth of his noble life. And here is a lie that emerged out of a coffee shop in Amsterdam which has already been heralded as a winner even as it is in its crap-loaded diapers.

In the corporate corridors are the waves of another gossip, spread by the demigoddess of philanthropy, which makes me wonder what greatness and grandeur is all about.

Too bad that your aunt visits now. My days here are numbered, and I would have loved to lie with my truth.

Love,
Sandeep

LVIII

Snippets of conversation between Sandeep and Amrita at the Waterlooplein Station (mostly in Bengali)

"I need to talk to you," the girl was adamant. She did not want to get on the Metro 51 to Sportlaan, preferring to cling on to his company, even if the medium was to discuss the slander.

"I told you I will be busy."

It was a battle of expressions in Amrita's eyes, as indignation fought and won against the imploring look.

"You want me to take care of this alone?"

Sandeep frowned.

"There were some conditions when I allowed you back in the class, remember? Nothing but *tai chi.*"

There was anger surfacing from the whirlpool of emotions.

"So, when you want ... when Trisha and this Mother Superior chats about you, when it affects you so badly, you can take your liberty and talk to me about it. When I send you messages with Mother Superior's opinions about you, you have no problem in accepting them. In fact you ask me to. But, when I need something in return, I am not allowed to breach the conditions. Is it an equal relationship?"

Sandeep looked at the swarm of people going in and coming out of the entrance of the Metro Station. He felt tired.

"Sorry, but this is not an equal relationship."

"That's your wish, is it?"

Sandeep rubbed his eyes.

"I have spent a lot of emotional energy pretty needlessly today, Amrita. What is it that's bugging you?"

"Will you take the Metro with me? I need to talk."

Sandeep shook his head.

"No. Tell me. What is it?"

"The discussion. Do you think it is right?"

Sandeep almost laughed.

"After the conference I doubt whether there is a definition of right and wrong. But, I have already blasted Madhu Deb. She will feel it sting before she goes home and rationalises the situation in her favour."

"What about Trisha?"

"What about her?"

"All those lies about me. Do you think she was right?"

Sandeep looked at her. Her lips were quivering with emotion.

"I know you don't care. In another few days you will be gone from here. I will have to carry on living with all these horrible people. I've got to work with them. And bandying a girl's name is so easy. The slander will not even affect you, as you will move on with your success and enjoy life in a different location. I will become entertainment. Gunjan, Ajay Yadav everyone will get to know ... have their vulgar fun at my embarrassment."

"It is up to you to give it importance ..."

"That's easy for you to say. I'll have to work with these same people for days, months – maybe years to come. And why do I have to face all this gossip? Is this the price I have to pay for falling in love?"

"Jesus."

"I know you don't want to hear it, but it was you who brought these people into the picture. It was you who discussed me with Madhu-di."

Sandeep looked around. Across the street, Simon stood beside his car. He wanted to cross the road and get away.

"We need not go into that, Amrita. I wouldn't say I had a choice ..."

"We always have a choice. That's what you always say, don't you? You chose the easy way out. You trusted people who talk behind your back, and now you are angry because you know they have been spreading rumours about you. And you chose not to trust someone who is yours..."

The girl paused, her slight bosom heaving from emotion.

"I can't bear to think of all the mails that will pass between these people, between offshore staff and our onsite team, where excerpts of Madhu-di's analysis of our relationship will do rounds as the tastiest bits of gossip. Your wonderful work in California won't be remembered, only your relationship with me will."

Sandeep frowned. He could well imagine – the dozens of team members in the group headed by Madhu Deb, each one cooped up in a crammed cubicle, the high point of life being an appreciating mail by the manager, lives sucked dry by the hours spent in office, the man-hours worn round their necks as medallions, sensibilities roughened to coarseness by corporate consciousness, souls parched from lack of meaning – the gossip to them would be like spicy manna from heaven.

"I want to know what Trisha has been going around spreading about me. I want to destroy all the rumours she has spread about me," her small hands clenched and unclenched.

Sandeep looked at her, wondering why discussions with her never seemed to end.

"I can help you with that if you want," he replied.

Blog of Simple Simon
Tags: Tai chi, Wisdom

We had class at an external school today. It was not premeditated, and my buddy-sifu decided all of a sudden that we needed exposure elsewhere.

The studio at Kirkstraat was not far from the office, but as with so many locations in central Amsterdam, getting there was a motorist's nightmare. Pritam did suggest the Metro, but that would mean coming back for my car. So, at the wheel, I dodged the trams, buses, construction sites, cyclists and pedestrians like a contortionist.

The ride was tense, and not only because of the traffic – which even by crazy Amsterdam standards, was bizarre. My sifu sat with a grim face, allowing a glimpse of his strong and silent side. Amrita on the back seat had a frown that seemed to have been etched on to her brow permanently. Neither spoke much.

When a vehicle from the Gemeente all but razed us to the ground as I swerved in to Utrechtstraat, it was followed by some animated exchange with the chauffeur employed by the city fathers. Pritam's sole contribution to the exchange was an expressive solitary inverted middle finger pointed towards the mutual adversary.

"You can do well to study the art of war, Simon," he remarked after the incident. "It is more applicable in office and city roads today."

I laughed. "Fist shaking and angry exchanges have become a part of daily driving – and a somewhat dangerous one at that. To prevent accidents, Toyota had taken innovation to another level by manufacturing a car which can show emotion by glaring, slitting headlights and also smiling. Keeps drivers from getting distracted in bodily display of emotions."

All the response I got to this learned remark was a noncommittal grunt.

The class, on the other hand, was excellent. The instructor guided each one with personal attention. It was, however, limited to traditional *tai chi*, very much along the lines of the form Pritam had been teaching, with minor modifications.

During the class, Pritam, participating as a normal student, was of course excellent, and even my movements were appreciated. Amrita, however, kept making mistakes and, alarmingly, still had the same frown etched on her brow.

By the end of the session, after the necessary payments for the hour's training, we walked out together. By this time Pritam had distinctly perked up.

"How did you guys feel?" he asked.

"The class was excellent, but there were none of the *chin na* techniques," I remarked.

"That's true. Chin na training is not easily available. But, if you manage to maintain your love for tai chi through study and keep training after I leave, someday surely you will find opportunity to learn *chin na* somewhere. At some point of time, the seeker of martial arts has to travel. All the arts are not available everywhere ... If one is dedicated, the path of life needs to be paved along the temples of learning."

We were interrupted in this impromptu sermon by a gasp of pain from Amrita who had somehow missed a step and had landed painfully on the instep. Pritam caught her arm firmly to steady her and continued.

"There will be problems in life, which will distract us from our goal. The lesson I wanted you to learn today is that *tai chi* is not limited to our small dojo and our few individual members and ex-members with their protracted universe. There is a whole big world out there, which is far more lively, colourful and full of riches for you to discover. Please pick and choose the school you are most comfortable with and ensure that you continue to train after I leave. Otherwise, all these classes will mean nothing."

I had the irresistible urge to retort with something on the lines of, "Confucius say train thyself." However, this sudden preachy side in my buddy did leave me with lots of thoughts to ponder.

~ ~ ~

Amrita, who had walked a couple of steps, now limped with a grimace. Simon asked her whether she was okay.

"It's not the foot," she said under her breath. "It's not the foot."

Sandeep and Simon had dinner in a Thai restaurant nearby after they had seen Amrita off at the Waterlooplein Metro Station, after an unnaturally long conversation.

Once they were alone again, Simon asked whether everything was okay. Sandeep shrugged.

"The atmosphere was heavy enough to be cut with a knife, was it?"

"Both Amrita and you seemed very disturbed – at least till the class had got underway."

"I have it from reputed sources that your life is being ruined, Simon," Sandee friend replied with a serious wink. "And I have been identified as the principal perpetrator."

"I am not sure what you mean."

"Simon, I wonder whether I will be stepping beyond some personal lines with this question, but I will ask you nonetheless. Unlike our celebrated Indian colleagues, I know the rules of privacy in this country. Please feel absolutely free not to answer."

"Please go ahead and ask by all means."

"The person who has been instrumental for the birth of the GVDW manoeuvre, the great lady behind the musical menace that threatens us every month, the not so winsome woman behind the never-ending narration of Hidori histories ... you have an inkling who I am referring to?"

"I do have quite a concrete idea."

"Did this lady attach herself to the button of your coat and start pouring into your ears poison toxic enough to make even Claudius of Denmark envious? Mind you, I am speaking of verbal viciousness of vitriolic proportions. "

"You mean spreading malice?"

"I do ... with the target of the malice being yours truly. Answering this is totally up to your sense of discretion."

Simon thought for a while.

" On some occasions she has said some quite strange things about you, a part of which could be indeed interpreted as malice to a reasonable degree."

"I surmised as much from some of your blogs – especially the interesting one which you wrote about predictions in the world of people. What was the lady harping at specifically?"

"At your remarkable lack of maturity."

"Many a times and oft?"

"That seems a neat description of the frequency of her complaints. She did also mention that your glamorous footsteps are interspersed with some booby traps and pit-falls."

"She might be trying to throw her considerable weight around to ensure that you are re-located to the office at Bijlmer Arena. To prevent me from spreading my evil tentacles into the realms of your vulnerable sensibilities."

Simon laughed. "You must be kidding."

"I have her written confession."

"What?"

Simon was quite aghast, as he believed anyone in his senses would be. He had grown used to the unauthorised interference into other people's lives by the so called mentors of the Indian corporate world in the name of grooming. However, till now he had thought of himself as someone immune to this phenomenon due to the politically incorrect advantages of race, creed and colour. But, this devious interest in safeguarding his mental health streaked beneath his skin and struck one of the most sensitive nerves of his very being.

"As I said, I have been guilty of ruining your life," his buddy continued.

"Has it ever occurred to this sick woman to find out whether or not I want to be ruined?"

This succeeded in making his old friend laugh at last. There was a healthy guffaw that escaped from beneath the gloomy shell of the evening.

"No, and she is never too keen on hearing the other side of the story. She was up in arms to convince people that I was the incarnation of the devil."

"You have indeed fallen from grace. She being the compulsive god-player, you were quite close to being Gabriel itself. Till a month back you were her blue eyed boy, a prodigious protégé ... I wonder if blue eyed boy is politically correct. One can never be sure these days. They are even thinking of banning Zwarte Piet. But, coming back to the weighty matters, what's the secret of your rapid descent? "

The sage in his friend surfaced once again.

"Gravity of the circumstances. Probably because she thinks I like my arts ancient and my women young."

Mail from Shruti to Sandeep

I dread to think what lies ahead. However, your atrocious wordplay will perhaps bear fruit, in the strictest idiomatic terms, with my aunt deciding to go to Athens a day earlier than planned. Pretty strong statement about the Amsterdam weather. No one stays.

Love
Shruti

Mail from Madhu Deb to Sandeep late at night

I have thought a lot and analysed. There is so much that has happened. There was a lot of anger against you that had somehow been bottled up in me. I am not saying what I did was right, but I think I managed to find an explanation. Could we discuss tomorrow?

LIX

(Snail) Mail from New American Literary Agency to Sandeep

Dear Author,

We received your submission. We believe there is potential in your material and with proper nurture it can be successful.

We strongly believe that a writer should spend his creative efforts writing while it is the agent's job to finish his product by refining it to perfection.

We therefore recommend you to submit your full manuscript to our editing team for smoothing out the rough edges that exist in every masterpiece. The tariff for the editing services can be found in the enclosed leaflet.

Once the editing is complete, we will proceed with submitting your work to the publishers who we think are a perfect match for your kind of writing.

We are smaller than the biggest agents in the market, but we are bigger than the smaller agents. We have sold our fourth manuscript this year to a mainstream publisher in New York.

Hope to hear from you soon,

David Cavell,
Consulting Agent.

Sandeep held the letter in both hands and stepped into the position poetically known in *tai chi* as White Crane Spreads its Wings. The piece of paper was ripped into two asymmetric shreds. He brought his hands together again and repeated the process, the number of pieces doubling. He seemed to like this routine and when an elderly woman walked into the apartment building, putting a stop to his calisthenics, there were thirty two fine pieces.

∾ ∾ ∾

It was a compromise. Madhu Deb wanted to speak outside the office. The last thing Sandeep wanted was another coffee with the good lady at Cafe Belmondo. It was characteristically wet and chilly, and walking with her was not an option. The only alternative was to go for a drive. Madhu Deb had not brought a car. She claimed she was unstable and was not comfortable driving on the skidding roads. Sandeep borrowed Simon's Camri.

"It started when you stopped communicating with me altogether," she confided as Sandeep turned into Beneluxbaan. "Just before you left for California. All of a sudden, I felt so isolated. In you, I had not only found a colleague I respected, but also a friend I was fond of. I discussed things with you. We shared secrets ..."

"Well, the leaking has been one way. As also the fabrication ..."

"Please listen to me."

It was a shout and Sandeep had to jerk the car to a stop at a red light.

"I know what I have done is wrong, but ..."

"You have also rationalised and found a way to wriggle out of the muck of embarrassment."

"No." She shouted again. "I am embarrassed at what has happened. I have asked Trisha not to go around discussing all this because it will be bad for Amrita and our image as a company."

Sandeep laughed.

"Probably it did not occur to you to let her know that you lied – about counselling us together and promptly packing me off to USA, ruining Simon's life. It's too much naked truth to be shared with someone who thinks you are a wonderful boss."

Madhu Deb looked with eyes that were red, tear smudged and hurt.

"I may be guilty, but it is not that you were not responsible. After all that I had done to help you, after ensuring that Amrita does not give you more death threats, after taking personal interest in the matter, driving all the way to your apartment on a Sunday, I suddenly found that I was out of the classes and she was in..."

Sandeep pulled into A.J. Ernstraat.

"It was nothing to do with you or her. I had to ask myself what the martial art demanded of me. I'm not bigger than *tai chi.* And in all your pomp and grandeur, neither are you. Amrita and Simon are sincere students, and learning *tai chi* is on top of their priorities. I can't help it if you spend your time in *Sur Soiree* and expect me to throw students out because you want it that way."

"I have a sense of responsibility, Pritam. I don't like being involved with *Sur Soiree,* but there are people there who look up to me as mentor. I can't wash my hands of it"

Sandeep took a left from Gelderlandplein towards Zuid again.

"The truth is you could never adjust to being just a student in the *tai chi* class. You had to call the shots. It has become so integral a part of your life. And when it did not go your way, you decided to malign the minds of everyone who was involved in the class. Simon, Amrita – the very girl whom you wanted me to kick out. Could you please clarify what you meant by ruining Simon's life?"

Madhu Deb shook her head.

"It was perhaps too much of me to expect you to treat me as a special friend. You changed timings of the class and never bothered to inform me – I always came to know of it from Simon. Was it not obvious that you did not want me in class? I am human too. I can get hurt. Maybe I expressed myself too much because of that. But, about Simon I didn't mean what it sounds like. All I meant was that he has to prove himself in his work first before becoming like someone he admired, that is you... I was more concerned about his career."

Sandeep brought the car to a halt beside De Boelalaan.

"I think I have heard enough. I understand now why you think you were provoked into malicious slander. I'm sorry, but I'm not impressed. It doesn't seem reason enough for a so called mature mother figure to go around discussing manufactured private lives of others with juniors."

Madhu Deb cradled her forehead in her palm.

"I know. With the mention of your name I should have diverted the conversation. But, with so many windows, so many mails, so many chat sessions ..."

There was a pause.

"My exercise bag is still packed. I haven't been able to unpack even though I know I'll not do *tai chi* again."

Sandeep sighed.

"Forgive me for not being carried away by onrushing sentiments. Would you mind walking back from here? I feel like going for a ride to clear my head. I could do without a self proclaimed demi goddess on the passenger seat."

As she stepped out of the car, the jauntiness of her characteristic movements was distant memory. The unusual position of guilt had brought with it a sense of helplessness and lethargy that she had not experienced in all these years of positional power.

∾ ∾ ∾

Boekenmarkt at Spui

The rain was a drizzle now and under the two umbrellas, wrapped in their long coats, Suprakash Roy and Sandeep browsed through the stalls of second hand books. The market convened every Friday.

"Extremely interesting," the doctor observed. "Every Dutch book sale has a decent collection of psychology volumes. And our old Freud is still such a big draw. You know why? It is the privacy culture. They do not talk of their own problems to anyone other than very, very close friends. So, specialists are an outlet."

Sandeep, who had pounced on a rare English translation of Heinrich Boll, pocketed the book after paying the four euro.

"And what do you think about the quaint Indian middle class community residing in the very heart of Amsterdam? How interesting is that?"

The psychiatrist returned a thick volume on Freud's notebooks on Dora to the shelf.

"My Dutch lessons are not going anywhere. The language is ridiculously difficult. I often wonder whether Cognitive learning patterns vary from language to language. I do know Mathematics is easier for Asians because of the language. Ah, about this new development – you see, the world view changes, the world opens up, becomes smaller ... but the psyche manages to remain the same. It is a classic example of the mixture of old fashioned gossiping girls in the new medium of instant chat. Commonplace ... if you go to most of the forums of teenage gossip, things are not too different...One can almost have the same conversation back in time, in the forties or fifties among semi-literate house wives of Calcutta. But, the degree of malice is a lot more instant – this is the jet age after all."

The stalls selling English books were few, the selection was littered with obscure volumes of varied interest. Sandeep brushed his fingers over a collection of translations from foreign languages.

"Behind the web, even the biggest amateur can lie as smoothly as a tried and tested confidence trickster," the good doctor continued. "So, snowballing gossip is something to be expected. I hope you have realised what the lady's wrath is all about."

Sandeep nodded.

"Hell hath no fury like a woman scorned."

"Quite so. When you took her into confidence after those suicide threats, the lady here thought of herself as someone very close to you. Later, when you decided to follow the principles of martial art and accept Amrita, it was disparaging. If what I infer is correct, she took it right to heart."

The two moved towards a nearby cafe.

"And what do you infer?"

"Narcissistic rage. Have you ever met her husband?"

"Her husband? The narcissist? No. Why do you ask?"

"I wonder whether he is a real narcissist. It is this lady who goes around looking for adulation, doesn't she?"

"She does."

"With hints about her special qualities?"

Sandeep thought about it.

"She does claim to be sophisticated and intelligent, even beautiful. She is also a patron of talent. All sorts of talent. That's what *Sur Soiree* is all about."

They ordered coffee, something really hot.

"And of course, she liked you a lot. She was almost a mother to you ... and when you preferred this rustic girl with a limited English vocabulary to her, she lost it ..."

The doctor caressed the books he had picked up and put them in his bag.

"There was no preference. This lady never turned up in class due to her constant fixation with *Sur Soiree.* And the other girl was a sincere student."

"In her book, you preferred her – the dark village girl – to her educated, articulate, sophisticated charms. She probably wondered if this was because of age ... You no doubt note the particular point in the chat conversation where she erupts and wants to blast you."

"When Manouk is mentioned."

"Right. I take it that this lady – Manouk – is young and good looking."

"She is wow. A stunner."

"So, she is livid. Narcissistic rage all over, knowing no boundaries. She does not care for truth. She can manipulate it because she thinks she is privileged."

Sandeep looked into the warmth of the cafe, at the pretty waitresses moving around with the laden trays.

"I have wondered about this. She kept getting in the way every time I came across someone I openly showed interest in. Cynthia. The assistant of the dentist. She was there, intercepting my visit when she had no business to be there. She always called Manouk away on different excuses whenever I tried to step out with her. And Lahari. When I exchanged a few notes about world movies with Lahari, she was prompt to warn me that she was competitive. And the farewell kiss. Eeks. It falls into place like a jigsaw. But, why?"

The doctor waved his hand.

"Don't be so naive."

"One Amrita was enough. Why did two women with particular disenchanting qualities have to fall for me at the same time?"

Suprakash smiled.

"I think you know the answer, Sandeep. I remember having discussed it earlier. You with your unconventional ideas, writing skills and martial arts prowess, your borrowed aura of success ... it all combined to give you powers of seduction. You came across as someone who was a hero in the drab world of the bank."

"But ..."

"And you kept succeeding. Had uncanny wit for all times. Engineered these peculiar sessions. Went against authority. The stuff that heroes are made of – especially in Bollywood. And in the process, you had this mature lady and the other young woman locked in a tussle of jealousy over you."

Sandeep sipped his beverage slowly.

"I've never really been this desirable in my life."

The doctor nodded.

"I understand. It's probably Darwinian. Attraction of the female to the successful. It is the aura of success that made it different for you in HMH. These is a price one has to pay for success, my friend."

Sandeep tried to swallow this with his coffee.

"Success, intellectual stimulation, anti establishmentarian, sportsman, martial skills. A hero across space, time and preferences."

"And I objected to people branded polymath. What about this strange allegation that she makes? Of requiring a group of admirers around me."

The doctor called for the check.

"That is what I was hinting at when I asked about her husband. It is a theory... probably her husband has nothing remotely close to NPD. It is she who is afflicted and knows it. She is intelligent and has read it up. A transference of guilt took place. Whether she believed it or not is an academic question, but her husband was projected as the patient. And now, with her assumed bonding with you, with her opening up to you, her guilt has found a new transference target. She has casually shifted her characteristics to you. As I have said, in cases of Narcissistic rage, being devalued, passed over, neglected ... truth hardly enters the picture."

Sandeep sighed.

"I am struggling to find where truth matters in the whole big picture."

They laughed.

"One word of professional advice. Get the hell out of here before anything else takes place."

"I will doctor. Pritam and I have submitted our combined resignation."

"Will I be acknowledged in your book? The one you are writing for Ramesh Aayyappan?"

"You bet."

They walked out into the rain.

The shock of brown hair was familiar and so was the voice as the attendant walked towards him in the American Book Centre.

"Jeroen?"

"Been a while, hasn't it?" the cheerful young man smiled back at him. "Did you like *Beyond Sleep*?"

Sandeep was pleasantly surprised.

"Oh yes. I would like the other one. *Darkroom of Damocles*."

"I'll get it for you."

∾ ∾ ∾

"Aunts aren't gentlemen," Sandeep observed as he sat on the sofa, Shruti wrapped around his frame in various knots, the muzzle of Geert, the golden retriever, eagerly trying to squeeze in between the two.

"This one was. Would you have wanted her to overstay her welcome?"

"No, but I have an irresistible inclination of overstaying mine."

The hold around the neck became firmer, the bosoms pressed closer. With one free hand Sandeep patted Geert's head and gently pushed him away.

"And what about your stay in this small country?"

There were some questions that could not be answered. Even by two wizards of words.

"Want me to make our typical hot chocolate? You can spread your latest booty on the bed. I see from the assortment of bags that you have plundered Spui Boekenmaarkt as well as the ABC."

Sandeep held her close.

"What's the matter? I'm getting hot chocolate for you, not my hockey stick."

Sandeep kissed her lightly.

"It was a dreary day that ended with delight. I walked into the American Book Center. ..."

"Such tales generally start with it being a dark and stormy night."

"There was this fellow. Jeroen. A brown haired man who works in the book shop. When I had visited the shop way back before I even had thoughts of swapping identity, he had recommended *Beyond Sleep* and *The Assault*. Today, seeing me after all these days, he remembered the exact books I had bought. It was a connection. Between book lovers – a connection between two human beings, that I found delightful. I had a sort of satori."

"Sort of Satori," Shruti reflected. "Not the best, but ingenious."

"*Lessons*, love, *Lessons*. Professor Lal's *Lessons*. A most fascinating autobiography. I had found it a magnificent piece of writing, but somehow the essence was lost to me in the brilliance of language. Alliteration? Try *maelstrom of kinky kama* to describe pornography. That's Professor for you. But if you read it, it seems to be a collection of brief life stories of people who have been associated with the great man over the years. Some famous, some not so famous. The message was lost on me. Today, suddenly, when this man popped up from behind the shelves and asked me about books I had purchased months back, it was a delight. The message became clear. Our life is nothing but a sum total of interactions with others, an intricate network of inter-related *karma*. The connection with this man, a book shop attendant in Amsterdam, was more satisfying than any of my associations with the Ivy League academics who had flocked to the California conference. Again, the interaction with Susan and Jason and all the other authors in that coffee bar of Los Angeles, the discussions with Simon and ..."

Tears were suddenly streaming out of his eyes, water-bodies of uncertain origin. He did not know whether he was happy or sad. He clung on to Shruti and she enfolded his wet cheeks into the secure softness of her breasts. This was an interaction that required no further words – words that confused and confounded. The most sublime moments of truth were silent.

Near their feet, Geert contentedly chewed a piece of buffalo bone.

LX

The phone rang early, even as darkness of dawn refused to let light through and sweetness lingered in the bed of togetherness.

"Hello," Sandeep blinked at the unrecognised number.

"It is me," the feminine voice from the other end yanked at the slumber chains and made him sit up.

"The correct grammar book response would be *it is I*. Jesus Christ. Where are you calling from?"

"Office. I am into her system. What do I do now?"

For a moment nothing made sense. Shruti lay beside him, asleep, glowing, beckoning and beautiful in the faint blue light of the Nokia handset. The time according to the bedside clock was six forty nine.

"Whose system?"

"Trisha."

"What on earth do you mean?"

"I want to delete all the chats and mails that she may have in her machine. I got in with the administrator password you gave me. What do I do now?"

Sandeep yawned. The administrator password. His mind was sleepy, sluggish, but it registered. The girl was in office early, looking for means to strike back.

"What do you want to do?"

"I want to remove every message she has saved. Tell me, what do I do?"

"Are you using her desk phone?"

"Yes."

Sandeep thought hard.

"The Dutch start work early. Don't you think you may be seen?"

"None of our team is here."

Sandeep tried to squeeze sleep from his eyes.

"You can't access her mails with that id. What you can do is delete her outlook file. I don't know where it is in her machine. You can look for dot p-s-t files and delete them. But, heavens, is it that big a deal?"

The voice from the other end was unwavering.

"To me it is."

"May I go back to bed now?"

"Bye."

Sandeep dropped the cell phone on the floor and collapsed on the bed again, snuggling into the peaceful frame of Shruti. In her sleep she stirred and lowered her knees. Her arm reached across and held him close.

The movie that Sandeep and Shruti had watched the previous night had been *Match Point.* One of the best Woody Allen films of his later days. The opening lines ran – *"The man who said 'I'd rather be lucky than good' saw deeply into life. People are afraid to face how great a part of life is dependent on luck. It's scary to think so much is out of one's control. There are moments in a match when the ball hits the top of the net, and for a split second, it can either go forward or fall back. With a little luck, it goes forward, and you win. Or maybe it doesn't, and you lose."*

Even as Sandeep went back to sleep, the warmth of Shruti engulfing him, his thoughts wandered briefly on the strange errand of the disturbed girl early in the morning. Trisha hardly ever appeared in office before half past nine, and this thought was enough to lull whatever little misgiving he had felt for Amrita.

That was the norm. Starting work at ten and leaving at eight, the normal working hours of the Indian knowledge migrant. No one expected her to arrive at twenty minutes past seven. It was a conference call with offshore, the rarest of events scheduled at the crack of dawn. Some peculiar problems with Lycamobile, the cell phone service provider, had ensured that the call could not be taken from home. Of course, her hubby's phone was at her service, but the man of the house had to leave by seven.

Besides, the file had been hard to find. Never a stickler for attention to detail, she had struggled to find files with the extension .bst. It had taken her a while to realise her mistake and use Google to find the actual file type. She had just clicked on the shift and delete keys when Trisha walked in, her face red from early morning exertions.

The two young ladies stared at each other for a while.

"What ... what are you doing with my machine?" Trisha demanded, her eyes confused.

Amrita, taken aback by the sudden appearance of her colleague, struggled for a plausible explanation. None were forthcoming.

"Did you discuss about me with Madhu-di?" she asked.

"What?" Trisha placed her bag on the table and frowned. "What's the meaning of all this?"

"Did you discuss me and my writing and my affairs with Madhu-di?"

At the unfortunate choice of words, Trisha's eyes registered a flicker of guilt. To cover up, she raised her voice to a shout.

"What are you doing here early in the morning? Why are you tampering with my machine?"

A couple of heads rose from other cubicles. Light haired, towering heads of early morning Dutchmen. Amrita got up and moved towards the exit. Trisha, demanding an explanation, got in her way.

"Explain. What have you been doing?"

Amrita glanced at her face, at the incensed eyes demanding explanation. The details of the lies came back to her. Her eyes flashed.

"I owe you no explanation," she muttered. "You can make up your own story, you are quite good at that. And with all your phony innocence, everyone will believe you."

She tried to walk past her, but Trisha shifted her position at the same time. They collided lightly, but as Amrita stepped hurriedly into the aisle, Trisha lost her balance, slid on the desk and finally ended up on the floor.

A concerned HMH employee from a nearby cubicle peeped in.

"Are you okay?"

Trisha looked at him with confused eyes and stood up slowly.

"Eh? Yes ... I'm sorry about all this, my colleague has gone nuts."

The Dutchman smiled.

"It happens if you work too hard. Can I get you something?"

Trisha sat at her desk and looked at her machine.

"Er ... no thanks. I've to get into a call."

Ajay Yadav looked as if the sky, after having threatened for all these years, had finally fallen through. His eyes fidgeted at the rate of knots, straining to divine danger from all possible angles. Two of his team members raising a fracas, pushing and jostling each other and then tampering with files ... this was not the way to start a day. Girls too, both of them. He shuddered to think what might have taken place if they had been men.

Fights, identity theft, security incident all at the client location. He shuddered again.

Mail from Simon to his mailing list
Sub: Crime Wave?

I was more than surprised when my buddy asked me if I had come across our furtive eyed account manager. As a rule, the man – for the want of a better expression which will not be blocked for profanity – ranks somewhere in the late twenty thousands in the list of people Pritam wants to meet. At the mention of this, my friend turned to me with sad eyes and said that it was the curse of the times.

In fact, the 'man' in question had been cooped up in a meeting room with some of the high ranking managers of *Axiom* Amsterdam. I did not really know the reason for the assembly of glitterati in the HMH premises, but obviously something was going on.

"Is Madhu Deb also in the meeting?"

I answered that to my knowledge she was not and my buddy went away preoccupied.

As I was returning to my cubicle, I came across a HMH associate from England I had worked with a few months back. He greeted me with a nod.

"What's the story, man?" he asked.

I was not too sure what he was talking about.

"You mean you don't know? You still work for *Axiom,* don't you?"

I replied that I did, if what I did could be classified as work.

"It seems *Axiom* is also doing some rough work these days. Seems to have been a proper cat fight this morning."

"Cat fight?"

"Two chicks from your company, man. It seems they got into a punch-up. Early in the morning."

"You're kidding."

"That's what I heard from some folks who were eyewitnesses. Don't have the details. But, please do me a favour. The moment you know what exactly happened, come back and let me know. Nothing like a bit of excitement to brighten up the workplace."

I went away perplexed, trying to fit the arrival of the bigwigs of the company with this peculiar piece of information. It did not make much sense, however. I could not picture any of the *Axiom* women in the team swinging at each other. Indian women just did not do that. To put a little uncharitable touch to my thought process, I could not imagine Madhu Deb or Lahari indulge in a physical fight without the official launch of unfit women's sumo wrestling. Trisha was too much of the archetypical Indian good girl, with a lot of things on her list of taboos with fights in the realms of the unimaginable. Amrita, though, was unpredictable – but even then a fight was stretching the imagination a bit too far. However, if she had taken a swing at any of the others, with the training regimen behind her, I had reasons to be very worried about her opponent.

I peeped into Madhu Deb's cubicle and found it empty, with a hideous glass-made supposed art work perched on her shelf. Trisha and Amrita were not in their cubicles either. Lahari was, and she did not seem to have a scratch on her. I wondered how I could find out what had taken place and from deep inside me there was one resounding answer. Gunjan.

It was turning out to be a strange day with my buddy seeking Ajay Yadav and I finding myself in a bizarre search for the most eminently avoidable person in my contact list, probably in all of EU.

I found the – well, let me use the word 'man' here as well, though it is questionable in too many senses – near the coffee machine, which judging by the perpetual cup of beverage in his hands, seemed the most likely place.

"Hey Gunjan," I greeted him, and he grinned back , gratified at the honour. Here was someone in whose capable hands the lamp of colonial heritage burnt with borrowed pride.

I did not have to frame a question. He was already halfway into the story.

"What do you make of all this? What ... you haven't heard? Come on. You are close to the people concerned – with all the *tai chi* stuff. Well, Amrita came in early this morning to hack into Trisha's machine and delete some mails... You're surprised. I see you didn't know anything of this. And Trisha came in early and caught her in the act. And our Amrita – well, she pushed her and walked away. Poor Trisha fell down. I am not too sure what she wanted to delete, but probably it is some mail that Trisha received ... with a lot of details about ... well, I don't know whether I should be telling you all this or not ... but, surely you know there is something between the student of *tai chi* and the instructor. I think everything was because of that ... You see I have seen her often from my balcony, waiting for Pritam. And I have often noticed that Pritam does not return to his apartment at night. Something had been going on ..."

I had heard enough. With each syllable Gunjan uttered, with a leer on his face and a knowing surreptitious droop of his eyelids, the urge to slug him in the eye was growing stronger. Two fights in a day would become the proverbial last nail in the coffin for Ajay Yadav and our clinging account at HMH. Even as he talked on, enjoying each and every second of filthy gossip mongering, I turned and walked away.

I called my buddy immediately on reaching the cubicle.

"Yes, Simon," he responded. "There has been some sort of pandemonium in the premises. Something the good Dr. Suprakash Roy warned me about."

I asked him about the seriousness of the issue.

"Seriousness? It is an issue and there are scavengers who will try to take as much advantage of it as possible. I don't really know of the seriousness."

I rephrased the question and asked if anyone had been physically hurt in the scuffle. He seemed surprised.

"Scuffle? Oh well, there was nothing of that sort. The ladies in question collided and one of them fell to the ground. No question of hip bone injury due to the excellent padding in the area. The figure of the archetypical Indian woman after wedded bliss does have its utility."

I heaved a sigh of relief. But other questions remained. I asked him what Amrita was doing in Trisha's machine.

"Well, you do remember my telling you about our self proclaimed personification of maternity voicing her concerns about my evil tentacles reaching out and vilifying your pristine internal ..."

I told him that I very well remembered the exchange (I guess I will have to fill you guys in on this later) but failed to see what it had to do with the strange incident of security violation.

"Well, her concern about you was just the tip of the malicious iceberg. The rest of it was the product of quite colourful imagination about the degree of penetration that I have in the life of Amrita. As you may realise that penetration here has a strong physical angle to it. And the angle is just about right, geometrically speaking. Amrita was trying to remove all traces of the communication."

I grappled with the complications of the matter and my buddy's choice of rhetoric. I had been with him all the while, having first hand visibility into the guerrilla tactics he indulged in to be away from Amrita. And here people were accusing him of an affair with the same lady. From Madhu Deb to Gunjan. Two questions perplexed me. One, how did everyone reach the conclusion that there was an affair. The more important was how it happened to be any of their business?

My buddy laughed in his sage-like manner.

"The human mind chooses to believe whatever is convenient to him.Especially the middle class Indian. Irrefutable proof is a nice to have. A girl showing uncanny interest in a martial art is not something in tune with the Indian psyche. Much better to look for other explanations. A young girl having an affair with a married instructor is much more believable and spicy. Extramarital affair and slander is the fuel on which the unproductive intellects chug along. Just look around at the gossip magazines. The Dutch, zealous of their privacy, have to turn to the Hollywood showbiz to feed the page 3 of the tabloids, but for Indians, each and every creature on earth is in the line of fire. The common Dutch response to a juicy story about the royalty is that the Queen is not there to defend herself. But, for the Indian middle class morality police ..."

I said that I knew all about it. I had just been talking to Gunjan.

"Ah, the torch bearer of the community. No one better to take you on a guided tour of the underbelly of the slander loving Indian psyche. Pretty soon I will be leaving. And it will lead to a very delicious conclusion that I scooted because of all this rumour. And in six months it will go down as an incontrovertible truth. Truth, you see Simon, is a very uncertain commodity and very, very malleable. As for how it is any of their business, well, welcome to the Indian workplace. Or any Indian community. But, you will have to excuse me. I have just caught sight of the great Indian worthless manager. I need a couple of minutes of his time."

My buddy rang off. I was left grappling with the peculiar problems.

All the people involved in this turn of events were my colleagues and some of them had developed special relationships with me. Now, all of a sudden, I am finding out all over again that things operate in a way that I can perhaps never fathom. India with its mysteries will remain the enigma it has always been. At once enticing, beautiful and repellent, full of muck.

Cheers
Simon

LXI

Ajay Yadav closed the door with care and spent a good ten seconds ensuring that there were no cracks and crevices through which a discrete whisper might trickle out.

When he turned back to face Sandeep it was with a half smile.

"Congratulations again for all the success in Chicago."

"It was Los Angeles."

"Oh yes, Los Angeles. I hear you were treated like superstars ..."

"And it continues," Sandeep snapped. "Even here, superstar status follows me and all that accompanies it. Namely public curiosity in one's personal life. I guess you already know what I am talking about?"

Ajay Yadav paused and looked with controlled furtiveness.

"I do have an idea. But why don't you tell me about it?"

Sandeep shrugged.

"After all the grilling you have subjected Amrita to, I guess you know all there is to know about it."

Ajay Yadav's expression of hesitant cordiality underwent hurried change. He shot a glance at the door.

"I wouldn't say we grilled her. Some of the people from Human Resources had come to enquire about what had taken place. We needed to ask her some questions."

"And you obviously heard the reasons she gave."

" I am not going into ball by ball details ..."

"I don't expect ball by ball details. It is an anatomical absurdity when it involves you."

Ajay Yadav looked shocked and then straightened himself after a quick look at the door.

"Am I right in supposing that she did say that a senior manager of your hallowed company indulged in some brutal character assassination with a junior employee, amounting to malicious gossip and slander, using the company's chat utility? The software, according to the policy mailers, should be used only for official purposes?"

Ajay Yadav hesitated. The attitude of the upstart – well, much experienced and renowned, but he looked like an upstart to him all the same – was aggressive. Obviously, he considered his own athletic ass immune to this incident. If the grapevine was to be believed, he was involved in some way. However, if his current position of strength was taken into consideration after the success of the conference in Chicago –er, Los Angeles – he was actually impregnable. He racked his brains for a proper risk free approach.

"She did mention some gossip, but then, there was no concrete evidence. We just have her word for it. And if you look at the crime ..."

"That's too strong a word."

"Well, identity theft is a crime. She deleted the outlook file of Trisha ... and whenever it is the legal issue, one looks at the crime, isn't it?"

Sandeep looked into the account manager's eyes and the latter seemed to shrink back.

"You know all about legal procedures, do you? Sitting as you are in the seat of judgement? Have you ever heard about something called extenuating circumstances? Do you know how in Northern Africa sentence for murder is varied based on whether there is a sirocco or not?"

"Sirocco?"

"Yes, it is a warm wind which rushes about coastal regions of North Africa. There is a play by Noel Coward by the same name and a film noir starring Humphrey Bogart, but I was not referring to them. The heat makes people crazy and punishment for crime is toned down if the perpetrator was driven crazy by the wind. News to you, is it?"

Ajay Yadav nodded.

"What if I give you documented evidence that the circumstances were extreme? What if I hand over a script of the chat that took place between our beloved senior manager and a junior resource? What if it points out that the circumstances were indeed extreme?"

Ajay Yadav's laryngeal prominence went up and down. Sandeep viewed the movement with disgust.

"Do you have it with you?"

Sandeep fished out a bunch of print outs.

"Here you go. The complete and unabridged chat script. Along with it there are a couple of mails that I can share, where she is salivating all over me. Read them for yourself – *what it is about you? Why do I say all the things to you ...* and all that rot. Our senior manager was infatuated by me, and went out of her way to slander me when it did not work out. If you want, you can have the electronic versions of all these. Isn't it better if the whole thing is pushed under the carpet rather than reaching the grapevine? Which will hurt the account more?"

Ajay Yadav fingered the sheaf of printouts and swallowed again.

"What are you implying?"

"I am not implying. I am telling you. The documents you see in front of you outline the reasons for this girl to go and tamper with Trisha's machine."

The account manager stole another involuntary glance towards the door.

"This chat is between Madhu and Trisha."

"That's what it says."

"How did you get hold of it? My god ... how many have access to the administration password?"

Sandeep got up in exasperation.

"Heavens. You are sitting on judgement on a security breach issue, and you don't even know the technical details. With an administration password, one can get into another's machine and hack his stored files. But one cannot access the mailbox or the chat utility. These are protected by the login password of the outlook and messenger programs. What Amrita did was to log in to the machine and delete the .pst file, disabling outlook for good. She could not access individual files."

Ajay Yadav struggled with the flow of information.

"So, how did you get this script?"

"Why is that important?"

"Because if this is another security issue, the focus will be totally different. My priority will be to find out how the chat script reached you. The content of the script will have little ..."

"Your priority will be to barricade your backside. But, it was mailed to me."

"By whom?"

"From Madhu Deb's mailbox."

The account manager sat confused, fingering the pages.

"Why did Madhu mail it to you?"

Sandeep shrugged.

"There you take me into areas of the female mind that I cannot fathom. Probably you will have to equate it with why she barged into my cubicle and planted a kiss on my cheek. Ah, yes, that's one shiver down the non-existent spine that I share with you. However, I do have the email in case you need electronic evidence."

Ajay Yadav nodded slowly.

"Could you send it to me? This does lend a new dimension to the issue."

Sandeep took a step towards the chair in which the account manager sat.

"Well ... I will definitely send it if the entire matter is forgotten."

There was another furtive glance towards the door.

"Er ... the best solution is to resolve it within the team."

"Thank you."

Sandeep got up and walked towards the door. He had known all along that he could scare the supervisor into submission. There was a triumphant follow through as he shut the door behind him.

The equaliser in the 83rd minute dampened the frequency and amplitude of the supporting sound waves. The raucous Ajax fans, expecting the ball to storm into the net of the lowly rated NEC at least half a dozen times, sat in disoriented daze, hands frozen in midst of continuous clapping, lips changing from the perpetual whistling purse to wide parting of surprise.

"That must have made your day," Shruti poured some of the boiling anger of the ardent Ajax admirer on to the placid Sandeep.

"But I am merely a neutral onlooker, out to enjoy a good game of football." On field, Bjorn Vleminckx was being mobbed by the nine other NEC players.

"You have been all but rooting for NEC. You were not very good at hiding your glee at the goal. Any moment the camera will show you on the giant screen - against the crowd. A Brutus among the Romans."

"Hold on ... I was wondering how he managed to score, carrying the weight of a vowel-challenged name all along. However, I do like the underdog."

"Don't you?"

"To decide against your convictions is to be an unqualified and inexcusable traitor. They are playing with ten men, for heaven's sake."

"Not counting you that is."

Sandeep laughed and put his arm around her as the desperate attempts at NEC's goal were foiled by the towering Gabor Babos. The disbelief seemed to hover around in the atmosphere even as the players regrouped for extra time. The relative silence in the crowd made it possible for him to hear the ring of his cell phone.

"It is I," the voice was tense, edgy, the breathing heavy. Sandeep's first irritated reaction was stifled by the anxiety apparent in the tone. Somehow, at the back of his mind the grammatical correctness of the phrase registered with considerable surprise.

"I am in the middle – or rather in the extra time of the match between Ajax and NEC. Could you please ..."

"I have been asked to meet Ramamurthy tomorrow."

Sandeep looked at the giant screen, the camera panning different sections of the crowd. Absorbed in the festive football atmosphere, the obscure name did not ring a bell. He almost expected Ramamurthy's name and photograph with jersey number to be displayed.

"Who on earth is Ramamurthy?"

The voice at the other end became impatient.

"Please be serious."

"In all seriousness I cannot recall who Ramamurthy is, could you please call me back tomorrow ...?"

Amrita sobbed.

"Ramamurthy. The HR Head of Continental Europe."

The enormity hit Sandeep hard.

"Is this regarding the incident?"

"What else can it be? Ajay Yadav just rang me up and asked me to meet him in the *Axiom* office tomorrow. You said everything was under control."

Sandeep frowned. Two days had passed since his meeting with the Account Manager. The interim hours had more or less convinced him that he had scared the spineless supervisor into submission. The matter would be handled in the usual way that such people are prone to deal with controversy – look the other way and wait for the problem to disappear on its own.

"I ... I had assumed that you'd not hear of it again ... but ... maybe .... maybe Ramamurthy will just let you off with a warning."

Amrita sobbed again.

"I don't know what to do. I don't want to go back to India ... I don't want to go back to my family."

There was a roar as an attempt was made on the NEC goal at the very outset of extra time.

"Please relax. No one has told you anything about going back to India ..."

"Can I meet you?"

"No. I am at the Ajax Arena."

"I am scared."

Sandeep hastily uttered a few consoling words and rang off as incredibly NEC went up by two goals to one.

The crowd flocked out in the rain – in throes of jubilation known only to fans whose heroes have turned the game on its head and snatched victory in the last few minutes. The 3-2 score line was hardly flattering against NEC, but did nothing to curb the celebrations of surviving a scare.

As they entered Burger King, Shruti was still hanging on to the fluffy edges of cloud nine.

"How does it feel to be an author in the crowd and witness your team losing the plot towards the last minutes?" she ribbed.

Sandeep smiled.

"It's hardly my team ... and the plot I witnessed was one that was hatched against the visiting side. Think about it – playing the mighty Ajax with nine men."

Shruti received the ordered Double Whopper menu and peered into Sandeep's eyes as they sat down to eat.

"Why's the humour coming out of the well oiled funny bone, but not touching the eyes?"

"I beg your pardon?"

"The last few minutes of the game, when the proverbial pendulum swung from side to side, your mind was not on the supposed plot against NEC or the plot of green on which the game was being played. Why did the obsessed girl's call affect you so much?"

Sandeep pursed his lips. Around him, the famished fans were reliving the last moments of the game over burgers and fries. The words in ardent Dutch made no sense to him, but the atmosphere did. Things were the same in the Eden Gardens or the Wankhade or any other stadium.

"She has been asked to meet the Human Resources chief."

"You told me that much. I would say that was expected given that she was caught red handed hacking into the system of this other girl."

Sandeep shook his head sadly.

"She's obsessed. You're right there."

Shruti swallowed a large portion of whopper with cola lite.

"I don't know whether our somewhat strange relationship makes it any of my business, but why are you so worried about what happens to her?"

"Double edged question if there ever was one."

Shruti shrugged.

"I think it was pretty plain as far as questions go. Of course, you are welcome not to answer it."

"That's what I mean by a double edged question, sweet. The first is one we are both scared to answer. Is this any of your business? I suppose it is. As far as the second question is concerned, it is complicated."

"Why on earth should you get so involved? I mean, from what you have told me this girl has been the cause of nothing but trouble. She has made matters complicated with her habit of playing dead ... I know, with your perilously unsteady platform of impersonation, you had been driven right to the edge by her suicide threats. Now she has overreacted and hacked into another girl's account. Why are you trying to protect her?"

"Er ..."

During the football game, Shruti's shell of hardened maturity had fallen off revealing the young fan rooting for her heroes. Now, in front of Sandeep, the animated appeals to his reason revealed a warmth and possessiveness that swept him with equal amounts of comfort and chill.

"Think of what you have been doing, Sandeep. You have bullied that account manager, something you had no reason to do. And now, even as Ajax was tottering on the verge of an upset, you ..."

"Got upset myself?" Sandeep smiled.

"Exactly. On receiving the phone call. Didn't the girl bring it upon herself? Or is it solidarity for a *tai chi* student? That rings pretty thin if you ask me."

Sandeep dabbed his lips with the tissues.

"The girl did hack into the machine of a colleague. But, she did not have the knowhow. Guess who supplied the expertise."

Shruti stopped on her way to a big bite into the whopper.

"Don't tell me it was you ..."

"And how do you suppose she got hold of a private chat shared between two ..."

"You hacked into ...?"

"I would not say that I hacked. I didn't write complicated scripts in esoteric languages to break into the systems. Neither did the girl. However, my on the job training as an investigative journalist gave me the expertise to get into the system of Madhu Deb. I needed to, since I had a lot of information to suspect that she was stabbing me behind my back. Well, I also got lucky and came to know the system administrator password. When Amrita came to me fuming and wanting to delete the last trace of the chat records, I did make the mistake of telling her that there was a way it could be done. I honestly had no idea that she would go ahead and carry it out."

Shruti whistled.

"No wonder hack is a word associated with writers."

"Well, I am not one of those authors. I suggested the idea of getting into Trisha's machine and deleting the pst file."

Shruti sat transfixed.

"And you dare accuse Ajax of plotting?"

"Well – I was not on level playing field. The rules of the game are slightly different."

"Any other criminal activity you have been associated with?"

"The only others that come to my mind are impersonation in two continents and pre-marital sex in a Wiltzanglaan apartment."

Shruti chewed her fries thoughtfully.

"So, are you implicated in this ...?"

"Security breach incident? That's the official term. It is always referred to as an *incident*. However, to answer your question – and several of your questions at one go – no. And that's what prods me to take all these steps."

"What do you mean?"

Sandeep sipped his cola and leaned back.

"The girl has been grilled by the account manager and the human resources. She has been subjected to all sorts of bullying, browbeating and barraging that a corporate organisation is capable of. You see, in companies such as this, the people in positions of power seldom have either the qualification or the human values to handle such situations. So abuse of authority and kicking an employee who is down is rampant, especially when there is any semblance of heat near their protected asses. And this weird girl, with her obsession, ensured that my role in the password security breach remained secret. In the face of the severest interrogation."

LXII

The world did not want her and neither did God.

Who was really at fault in this case? A supposedly respected lady high up in the organisation discussed me and *him* with a supposedly innocent girl, about a dozen years her junior. The chat was retrieved by *him* with methods that are known only to *his* genius. *He* told her how to erase the chat and the mails of slander that have gathered dirt by being passed around in vulgar hands. Nothing happened to anyone who was really at fault. She was the one who would be made to leave the organisation. She was sure of it.

However, whatever happened, she had made *him* realise that her feelings for *him* were not just obsession. She had protected *him* to the best of her ability. *He* would get away from it all unscathed. She could see that *he* understood that *he* was indebted to her, but why? Was she not supposed to do what was best for *him?* She could see *him* trying *his* level best to help her in this situation, to repay her for the favour of withholding information. *He* still did not consider her to be *his* and *his* alone. Yet, if this entire episode made *him* think about her with something approaching affection she would be grateful, grateful to that very God who had forsaken her every time.

Mail of Simon to his mailing list
Sub: Curious Rules in the Corporate Ring

The events of the recent days have been extraordinary to say the least. And today, with first hand experience of how corporate games are played out, my beliefs and convictions are somewhat jarred, jolted and jaded.

I wondered whether to get this out of my chest in a blog or through a private mail. Lots of names will be bandied, but I was actually beyond caring and wanted the world to know all this. However, some of the crucial information has been obtained from a source who needs to be protected, and hence I opted for the email.

I had gone into my buddy's cubicle to enquire whether the *tai chi* class would be held as usual or not. I found him hunched over a pile of books and papers.

He welcomed me with a tired smile.

"Not really busy, Simon, just trying to figure the truth from all these exhibits."

I looked at the books he had with him. A beautifully bound gold embossed volume named *Lessons* lay on top. There were other books underneath whose names were hidden from sight.

"Autobiographies. Professor Lal, the one who joined our global cannabis conference on phone. Another couple from which I have learnt the most. Neville Cardus, ever heard of him?"

I said that I had not.

"No wonder, coming from a genetic pool which has never really embraced cricket. One of the most erudite autobiographies. Norbert Wiener – *Ex Prodigy*. And on the other side you have some of the highly avoidable life stories of supposedly successful people, some of them straight from different parts of their anatomy. And in the middle you have a bunch of responses from literary agents and publishers. There is also a chat script shared by innocent and pathologically altruistic individuals. And finally you have an award winning paper on economic crisis and its ancient Indian solution. I am just trying to figure out what makes sense and what doesn't."

He paused and I wondered if he was approaching levels of philosophical contemplation too abstract and rarefied for my challenged spiritual development.

"Intelligent design has been refuted again and again, although there are advocates of an unseen God. But, design still has some meaning to it. Execution of the world is ridiculous."

He may have expounded on this mighty line of thought for a while, but a knock on the cubicle panel stopped him and made us both look up with our proverbial tongues lolling out. For there stood behind me the Dutch apparition called Manouk Kruif.

"Hi guys," she called. "Should I come back later?"

"Not at all," my buddy exclaimed. "Everything else can wait."

Manouk stepped in and looked at me.

"Goede Morgen meneer."

I greeted her and asked whether I was in the way.

"I guess you are also concerned about the fate of your one and only *tai chi* partner. So please stay by all means. Manouk, I don't think you are going to share information that is highly classified and unfit for other ears."

The beauty shrugged.

"I don't give a damn."

"Well, I'd believe that. You do have a waist like Scarlett O'Hara."

Manouk looked lost and I politely pointed out that it was a compliment which unfortunately had *gone with the wind.*

"Nevertheless, it should not leave the room," Manouk pointed out and we agreed.

She put her hands on the table and exhaled. A gesture most commonplace yet effortlessly stirring the deepest chord of any man of flesh and blood. Yet, I was more than surprised to see that Pritam was actually hanging on to what she was about to say, with just passable attention to the physical.

"For starters, there were several meetings during the last few days, not all of which I could or was allowed to attend. There are several discussions which are still in progress, but no final decision has yet been taken."

I asked her whether she was heavily involved in HR activities as well and she laughed.

"We cannot afford too many non-billable people to manage internal systems like HR, PMO and Admin. There are around half a dozen people who are all odd job men and women. Two of them are Continental Europe Heads. So, the remaining four have to do the grunt work. I happen to be one of them."

Pritam walked to the entrance of his cubicle and looked out.

"It is billable bodies that one needs. Augmented by a couple of beautiful ones. Tell me something, has Madhu Deb been implicated in any way?"

Manouk smiled.

"People that high up? Even if they are implicated you won't hear anything about it, will you?"

"I was assuming *you* would."

The pretty head seemed to weigh the pros and cons of unravelling the deepest organisational secrets.

"I should not be telling you this, but as I said, I don't care. I understand that you intend to help the victim here. Yes, Madhu Deb's name has been implicated. I don't know the fullest details, but for a few days there will be some discomfort."

"Less bounce in her step?"

"Precisely."

"Less lilt to her sung out hellos?"

"I guess so."

"Less ..."

"Shut up."

"So what you mean is that she will suffer from some embarrassment, but is any official action going to be taken against her?"

Manouk smiled the all knowing smile associated with human resource personnel privy to important information.

"The official answer is that I don't know. However, a more honest answer is a plain and simple no. I have seen reports being written about the incident by various stakeholders and none of them mention the role played by our friend."

"Our fat friend?"

"At the risk of sounding uncharitable, yes."

I looked at Pritam who seemed to be computing even greater problems in his mind than the ones that plagued him when I had come into the cubicle.

"And yet, reports are being written about the incident?"

"That's true. According to Ramamurthy, a chat utility is like the telephones provided by the company. The maximum one can do is to request the employees not to use it for personal purpose."

I got the feeling that with higher auditory capacity I would be able to hear my buddy bristling.

"I can't understand it. I would have expected the entire episode to be swept under the carpet. At least after I provided Ajay Yadav with the documents."

Manouk smiled again, and this time the superior smile of a Human Resource executive dealing with a talented but immature resource.

"Pritam, you are new to the Netherlands. You don't have that amount of clout to influence a decision of Ajay Yadav. Even in the wake of your success in California."

My buddy looked at a loss.

"Manouk, I all but threatened Ajay Yadav. He quivers in his shoes if someone sneezes. He looks back to check whether his job is safe every time it starts to rain. And you mean to say he went ahead pursuing the matter even when an implicating scandal of giant proportions faced him?"

The girl from the head office continued to smile.

"You have underestimated him, Pritam."

"You mean to say he is not a spineless creep crawling around in his hole diving for cover every time a leaf drops to the ground?"

"Well, that seems a fairly accurate description, but you have to admit that he has survived in the industry and risen to a position of authority all the same."

"That's not too difficult in this industry, is it? With mediocrity all around?"

"Thank you."

"For Christ's sake, you know what I mean Manouk. Look at the people who come onsite from India ... are they really the cream of the Indian talent pool?"

"We always refer to them as talented resources, Pritam, and I will stick to that. The point that I am trying to make is there is a reason for Ajay Yadav being where he is and also, there is a reason for his being scared shitless every time a leaf falls."

Both of us looked at her expectantly. Her tone indicated secret information.

"Ajay is very, very senior. He supposedly joined *Axiom* at a grade far inferior to the one he deserved with his experience because he had been forced to resign from his previous company. And as far as I know the Indian system, you don't have the kind of social security that we Dutch enjoy. I don't have any idea what happened in the previous company, but once he joined here, Ajay moved around as if on eggshells, trying hard to hold on to his job while making a bid to fast track his growth. You know, the ratings in appraisals, promotions ..."

"The holy grail of the Indian executive."

"Right. In the process he made a great error. He had joined the Amsterdam office four years back, and if you have heard as many Hidori stories as I have, you will know the period I am talking about."

We winced together at the mention of the name before it registered. Four years back would have been the period when Madhu Deb had been on maternity leave. A long leave full of prenatal and post natal complications we have all heard over and over again. I observed as much.

"Dead right again. The account was small and starting when Madhu Deb went on maternity leave. And suddenly it started to grow. Ajay was placed here to take charge of the bigger account, and when Madhu returned, she had to play the role of a senior manager. Ostensibly under Ajay. She never really liked the idea, but there are very few accounts in this BeNeLux region, with vacancies filled to the brim. Ajay was under constant threat of the popular, well connected ..."

"And well rounded ..."

"... well, yes, well rounded Madhu climbing over him back to her position."

"Tussle for power under the ostentatious guise of teamwork. Is it a life worth living?"

"That is for philosophers to decide. However, it was while our lady was still on leave, Ajay made this serious error. There was this girl called Annie. It was an Indian name, but shortened for our benefit. I can't quite recall it now."

"Ananya? Annapurna? Aninidita?"

"May have been any of those. And there was Lahari. During the appraisal cycle they realised that their appraisal forms had been filled up by this new manager. The ratings and comments had been copied and pasted."

I let out a chuckle and said that I had heard this referred to by Lahari. However, my buddy was still unable to connect.

"So, what was the big deal? Most of the people do exactly the same job and there is nothing to write home about. Copy paste does seem a good idea."

Manouk frowned.

"Pritam, I am still the HR of *Axiom.* Not all people look at it in the way you do. And believe me, the two girls involved were furious. All the hard work, the appreciations and ...."

"Right. I get it. Appraisals, after all. You know Simon, in all our discussions about the Indian workplace, we have omitted to discuss this phenomenon. "

I assured him that we could go into it someday and requested Manouk to continue.

"The two girls called their mentor ..."

"Who was basking in the glory of motherhood and pregnancy piles, washed down by placental bleeding..."

Having been subjected to detailed description of her post pregnancy ailments – to use Pritam's words, the boil by boil details – I could not help but smile.

"Very true. And I am delighted to find someone else who has had to make that journey down memory lane with her," Manouk continued. "However, the good lady was not so blissful with childbirth to ask them to forgive and forget ..."

"I understand, with most of her milk of human kindness devoured by a voracious young Hidori. I guess you have heard about the legend of the newborn's appetite. I guess everyone in *Axiom* BeNeLux and maybe beyond, encompassing the entire EU zone, has made the journey down the cervix and has followed the life and times of the blasted baby in minute detail."

Manouk laughed. "So, what the new mother advised them was to make the whole faux pas known to the ..."

"HR?"

"Not only the HR. The bigwigs of *Axiom* CE, all the high, mighty powerful people the lady hobnobbed with. The results were terrible for poor Ajay. To use your words, never predominantly erect, he started crawling from that day."

"He invested his spine in his pension plan."

"Exactly. He even went to the extent of telling the two girls that they were like his sisters."

I winced and so did my buddy.

"What a revolting thought."

"Well, not to the girls. Off the record, as the whole conversation has been, the two girls used it to the full. After that, they never got any rating lower than the highest. They were sent to trainings at the expense of other, more deserving candidates, got appreciation at the drop of a hat ..."

"The whole industry runs on appreciation and escalations. Ego and fear factor. Simon, something else to earmark for future discussions."

"Our new mother tried to manipulate the situation and claw her way back to the position of absolute power, but somehow it did not happen. She remained a popular, successful, valuable senior manager whom everyone acknowledged. At every opportunity Ajay was ingratiated to her, to Lahari, to Annie till she got pregnant herself and quit the job. As you put it, he looked back every time someone sneezed to make sure that his job was still there. But, he managed to hang on. And that was not only by creeping and crawling, it was by doing so along the right corridors."

"You have a wonderful storytelling style, Manouk, which goes to prove ...," Pritam hesitated.

"Goes to prove what?"

"You have talent Manouk. You should try your hand at collecting rejection slips. What I really meant to say is that you are not just a pretty face."

"I guessed as much. However, what *I* mean to say is that this guy is perpetually scared, but he is also shrewd and knows how to utilise situations. He has been under constant threat because he always felt Madhu breathing down his neck. That was because of her contacts, her popularity, her image. The explosive material you handed him believing that it would help to push everything under the carpet was actually the ammunition he required to blast that image to ... what's the expression?"

"Smithereens?"

"Absolutely. Did he promise you that he would hush things up?"

Pritam looked dazed. "Not in as many words. He said that the best solution would be to resolve it within the group."

"Airy and vague. He just allowed the entire process of incident reporting and HR involvement run its course, while he added the chat script as exhibits. He knows no one will take any action against Madhu, but her image will be tarnished at least for a while. He can relax and worm his way up the corporate ladder."

"Worm his way is right."

"He knows that it is a difficult decision for the HR. To terminate the girl's employment without raking up the muck associated with a senior manager. So, he has left it to the HR. In the meantime, his purpose has been served. Madhu's show of immaturity and lack of professional etiquette has reached the ears of every important player in *Axiom.*"

Pritam let this sink in slowly.

"So all the time I was thinking that I was bullying him into submission, he had actually been using me with cool calculation?"

Manouk looked at Pritam with a half smile and a half raised eyebrow. I am certain that had my buddy not been reeling under the weight of the information, he would have written a haiku on the expression.

"I don't think his mind works that fast. He was definitely not sure how to use the information when you supplied it. But, he gave it a lot of thought and things fell into place. Not the brightest, not the most debonair, but he knows how to use the right issue the right way."

"The great Indian Manager in short. His equaliser against Madhu's manipulation of his faux pas years earlier."

"Precisely. He is ahead by some distance now."

My buddy's eyes and fingers hovered for a while on the volume of *Lessons.*

"Tell you what, we will leave the two clowns to play against each other in their peculiar game. They can score creepy points and get high on them. They can crawl along the corridors of power or bounce up and down the podium of the ridiculous *Sur Soiree* shows in relentless pursuit of positional supremacy. Tell me, what happens to the girl in question. Is she just an expendable pawn?"

Manouk stopped smiling.

"It definitely seems to look that way. The fact is that she is not important, but a lot of people perceive a non-negligible amount of dirt that can hit them if she is sacked. So, no one is prepared to take any decision. Madhu's involvement has made the entire situation delicate. Everyone is hoping that someone else will make the decision."

"Meanwhile the girl can rest on tenterhooks?"

"Pritam, the three of us are probably the only ones who care about what happens to the girl."

"What if I manage to influence Ramesh to step into the matter in his giant shoes?"

"K. Ramesh?"

"Right. He goes by the name K. Ayyappan Ramesh from the time the paper became a success. What if I use my significant influence as a collaborator and ask him to interfere?"

Manouk expelled another of those knowing, patronising laughs.

"Pritam, Ramesh is known all over the industry as a clean guy. There has never been any controversy around him. And at this stage of his career when he has taken up the role of a seer, he will never get involved in this pile of shit."

I cleared my throat and asked her about the rights of the employees, the portals of the company which promised psychological and physical well being and all that rot. Manouk smiled defensively.

"This is an extraordinary situation, Simon."

My buddy was somewhat less evasive in summing up.

"The ladies in De Wallen, standing in their stringy bras and panties behind glass windows, are protected from danger by panic buttons. Unfortunately, this company – or this industry – lacks that sort of facility for their so called talents. If someone powerful wants to abuse you, there is nothing to do but to take it lying down. Quite expected. Behind the windows you are just selling your body. Here you sell souls. To a complex organism called the corporation which is interested only in the bottom line."

He paused for a moment, eyeing the beautiful volume of *Lessons* once again and chuckled.

"I wonder what would happen if Professor was forced to make a cost benefit analysis and ROI presentation before embarking on his mission to translate the *Mahabharata.* Anyway, Manouk, thanks a lot for your time, your information and your lovely, lovely presence."

"You are most welcome. I have done this only because I was assured that you want to help the girl."

"I do. I know Simon does too. We really appreciate this Manouk, and I am sure you will allow us to show our gratitude by joining us for dinner later this week?"

Manouk flashed one of the signature smiles which make the knees go weak and the throat go dry.

"Next week maybe?"

After we showed her out, I went back to Pritam's cubicle and sank into the chair. The revelations had taken their toll on me. I feebly asked my buddy-sifu how he had got Manouk to share this degree of organisational confidences.

"My irrepressible charms? Not really. I was lucky. It is one of those girl things, although in a very Dutch way."

On my somewhat churlish request to spell it out in words of countable and understandable syllables, he relented.

"Manouk used to play field hockey with Shruti." He paused and added. "That must have been a sight for the gods."

I asked him whether he was referring to the Shruti I had met and collaborated with in the Cannabis conference.

"Buddy, I know nerves are somewhat strained right now, but could you please emulate my excellent example and speak hereinafter in words of countable and understandable syllables? Which other Shruti do you think I would be referring to?"

I patiently reminded him that several thousands of miles away there was a legal life partner who awaited him and also answered to the name of Shruti. Light dawned on his face.

"Ah ... there you make sense yet again. I see Simon that you are still confused with the metaphorical allusions of the Indian culture which often people tend to misinterpret with their literary meaning. Well, before you ask me to follow your excellent example and revert back again to simple and countable syllables, let us end the discussion on the marital affairs. We have more probing problems to deal with."

I agreed, although his peculiar stance on the Shrutis of the world was becoming more intolerable a mystery with time.

"We will meet in the *tai chi* class as usual, but before that I have an important phone call to make. I think dawn will be breaking in Chicago by now."

I asked him whether the *tai chi* class was indeed taking place. He nodded vigorously.

"Why, of course. At least that is one thing which I can claim to reasonably understand. I would do well to stick to it."

Simon

~ ~ ~

Pritam responded after the fifth ring, it seemed to Sandeep that the ocean between them had washed away the worries from the habitually agitated voice.

"I need a favour," said the voice from Amsterdam.

"Favour? Certainly, old man, what is it?"

"Your new company ... is it recruiting?"

"Yes ... I mean, that's how I was recruited, wasn't I?"

"Could you place a girl there?"

"Uh-huh? A girl?"

The taunt in the voice was friendly and genuine, and Sandeep laughed.

"Yes, a girl. But, it's ultra urgent and ultra non-sexual."

"Skill set?"

"Come off it, Pritam. After the Pasadena circus, do you think skill set matters?"

Part XII:

Deutsch Marks and Exercising Options

LXIII

Ludwigsburg, Germany

They sat in the bar outside the dojo of the Ludwigsburg training centre. In front of Sandeep, Sifu Wolfgang Schmidt slowly sipped from his post training tumbler of beer. Through the glass windows, he could see a steady drizzle of snowflakes. The day had been long – a six hour train journey through Frankfurt and Stuttgart, followed by three hours of training, and finally a surprise examination.

Wolfgang closed his eyes and let the amber work its rejuvenating wonder inside him.

"This part of Germany is beautiful all the year round," the revered instructor spoke in admirably fluent English. "It is close to the Southern end of the Black Forest. Right now, the Black Forest will be white, covered in snow. You must come back in June, when we have a camp in the Herzogenhorn mountains, near Titisee. It will be wonderful if the weather is good. It is generally a camp only for instructors, but now you are officially eligible to attend it."

Sandeep smiled hesitantly. In his hand was a glass of diet coke. Sifu Wolfgang had asked him to celebrate his official grade of the instructor of European Tai Chi Association with a drink, but he had declined. Alcohol and martial arts somehow did not gel for him. Wolfgang could afford it, though, after forty years of *tai chi.*

"I must admit this grading came as a surprise. I have never stuck around at the same place for too long to continue to advance through grades in *tai chi.* I had resigned myself to being a student all life."

Wolfgang smiled through his beard. He was touching sixty, but with the long dark hair and the brownish bush around his face, he looked barely forty two.

"All dedicated martial artists want to keep growing, keep learning. But, after a particular stage, you can grow only by teaching as well as training. It is important to teach, because it clarifies so many of your own doubts. You will realise."

Sandeep nodded. His brief experience in teaching had already taught him a lot. It went beyond the fine tuning of techniques and probing into the secrets of the art. A few of the other students sat around them in small groups, sipping their drinks and talking about *tai chi* and more. The atmosphere was warm, jovial, buoyant. Sandeep slowly allowed the convivial spirit cleanse his psyche, washing away the petty politics of the recent past. Sifu Schmidt went on speaking.

"Subramanium and I discussed you during the camp in Amsterdam. We had decided that you were ready to become an instructor. I am glad that you decided to come for this weekend session. Something on your mind?"

Sandeep hesitated. The trip to Ludwigsburg had been decided on the spur of the moment, with a hastily put together backpack. *Tai chi* was therapy.

"Wolfgang, I know I have trained for quite a while, and you have found me capable enough to become an instructor – but I personally have my doubts."

Sifu Schmidt raised an eyebrow.

"A very positive approach. If you think you know, then you stop learning."

Sandeep shook his head.

"It's not that. I have my share of the big martial artist's ego. I think I know a lot, with my karate background and having learnt *tai chi* for all these years with a fair sprinkling of *chin na* techniques."

Sifu smiled and his eyes panned across the bar, at the students and instructors gathered there for drinks and banter.

"Join the club, Sandeep. Everyone you see around you, apart from the newbies, think they know a lot ..."

"Wolfgang, it is about my ability as an instructor that I have my doubts. I would prefer to be a student all my life. Let me make a confession. I have trained a few people..."

"Really?"

"Recently. In Amsterdam. I wanted training and moreover, the *chin na* techniques that I had picked up were getting rusty ... I started teaching a group of interested students – well, they seemed interested."

Wolfgang smiled. "They left? *Tai chi* is a soft martial art. In this age of instant coffee and podcasts, a very few will stick around to learn something with their body, mind and soul over decades. They would much rather look it up in Google or Wikipedia and be done with it. It is to be expected, Sandeep."

Sandeep laughed. "I understand that. People did not even stick to the karate classes some fifteen years back, so it is definitely to be expected. What happened was far worse. One of the girls fell for me."

"Interesting," Wolfgang chuckled. "But not unusual. Especially with Martial Art instructors, with all the Bruce Lee, Jackie Chan and Van Damme culture making us heroic in common eyes."

"It did not end there. There was scandal – with a lot of people, irregular students, students who left the class, everyone indulging themselves. You see, interfering in other people's relationships and affairs is a typical Indian trait ..."

"I wouldn't say that. Look at all the Brangelina tabloids around you ..."

"There were influential people who wanted me to throw the girl out of the class. I did not do it. The girl along with a Dutch guy were the only ones who continued to train sincerely. And then all hell broke loose. Scandal of gigantic proportions. I was in the middle of everything. I had tried to synthesise the teachings of the many *tai chi* masters around the world I had trained with, to make the resulting knowledge available to these people. And they could not even appreciate the lessons. On the contrary, they were more interested in petty positional power play, minor career advancement or ego massage using the scandal around me. Which makes me wonder. Am I capable of instructing? Was there something wrong with my classes? Or did I make an error in judgement, and manage to waste my energy in trying to teach the undeserving? And are you making the same mistake by making me an instructor?"

A loud cheer from a neighbouring table made him stop. He looked around to see hilarious, amused faces of Günter, Carmen, Birgit, Manuel – all high ranking *tai chi* students, tickled to death about some philosophical argument.

"This is when the beer hits them and the party gains second wind," Wolfgang laughed. Carmen and Manuel were playing *mah jong*, while Günter tried to draw some Taoist parallels to the game. Did Confucius really develop this game or was it an apocryphal myth? How was it comparable to the Japanese *Go?*

"Are the classes continuing?" Wolfgang turned back towards him.

"Well, I have been urging the girl and the Dutch guy to join some local *tai chi* class, so that they can continue after I have gone back to India. I have even accompanied them to the local classes. Meanwhile, they insist on training with me. A big class of threesome."

Wolfgang finished his beer and called for another tumbler.

"The secret of alcohol is to take a very small amount in your mouth and enjoy it for long. If you can rush through the drink, it is not worth drinking," Sifu Schmidt smiled. "You can try some wine along these principles."

"Thanks. I will stick to Diet Coke."

"Sandeep, from whatever you have told me, you are a very successful teacher. No, I'm not kidding at all, I am dead serious. People who join your class will come because of a lot of reasons, and very few due to the right ones. Tell me, after you leave, will the two students continue to train?"

Sandeep thought for a while.

"I am certain one of them will. Simon. About the girl I am not too sure. She is unpredictable to say the least."

Wolfgang nodded.

"That means you have managed to introduce at least one individual to the world of *tai chi*, who has grown to love the art. I would say that's success. Any class has its share of scumbags, but just because people are blind to the treasures around them we can't say we will lock our gold and keep it under our bed. True learning takes place with sharing. And if someone is interested more in scandal than the secrets of a great martial art, it is strictly his problem. He will lose out on the physical, mental and spiritual benefits of the art."

Another wave of noisy enjoyment rushed across. Sandeep wondered how a nation full of merry people had been pivotal in two world wars.

"Your success will depend on your own development and the number of people you can bring into the world of *tai chi*. With you withdrawing from teaching because of a few petty people, there will be future Simons who will miss out on something that can be life changing."

Sandeep washed the thought down with the remainder of his Coke.

"Sandeep," Wolfgang continued. "A martial arts instructor of modern times very seldom teaches people something that will help them earn their living. But he teaches them something that makes life worth living. We deal with passion – something which the individual holds dear. We have a great responsibility."

Sandeep lowered his empty glass and smiled.

"I think I will have the wine after all."

∾ ∾ ∾

Mail from Professor P. Lal to Sandeep (typed by Shuktara Lal)

Sandeep my boy,

It is part and parcel of the experiences of an educator, the inbuilt opposite of the fulfilment that comes from moulding minds. Many a times as I expounded the most stellar topics in the firmament of English Literature, I could see students with cherubic smiles indicating an enjoyable journey through the paradise of the written word, concentrating frowns of some who struggled painfully through the purgatory of the complex concepts to come out purified and beatific, as well as the unregistering faces of others who clung on to the last benches raising inferno. It is the divine comedy of life and inferno is inescapable.

The great teacher of martial skills – Dronacharya – had students like Arjuna who was his favourite, who absorbed whatever was imparted and beyond; like Jayadratha who remained satisfied with just the amount that was taught; and also like Yudhishtira, who equivocatingly lied to bring about his demise. The answers are all there in the Mahabharata.

The Professor

Mail from Pritam Mitra (Sandeep) to undisclosed recipients

Returned from Ludwigsburg today sitting beside a window in a Deutsch Bahn Inter City Express. From Southern Germany to Amsterdam, through Stuttgart, Frankfurt and Cologne is quite a journey, a lot of it stretching along the magnificent banks of the Rhine, from Karlsruhe to Cologne. The river winds through the heart of the country, snow laden banks scattered with medieval castles, some of them perched on imposing hills.

I sat reading Billiards at Half Past Nine, *which for the uninitiated, is a novel by Nobel Prize winning German author Heinrich Boll. The Rhine meandered alongside me, with its quaint documentation of history on the shores, the fascinating geography of its valleys, the many bridges of Mathematical precision, with Boll's masterly use of the multiple first persons and a painful back from three days of rigorous martial arts training to keep me company.*

Travel, Literature, History, Geography, Mathematics, Sports –my favourite subjects. Helps to keep the mind broad and the waist narrow. When one's subject of preference changes to Current Affairs, the characteristics of the mind and waist tend to change positions. There are treasures in every corner in this world, and there is muck. The choice is for us to make.

~ Sandeep/Pritam
I disagree with you o Caesar, let me not have men around me who are fat.

Mail from Simon to Sandeep

Wow! And once again wow!

The way you have made your point necessitates a third 'wow'.

The signature, though, is somewhat below the belt ... but then again, the paunch is mostly above the belt.

I hope you had wonderful training. Expecting new techniques from today.

Mail from Sandeep to Simon

To be very honest, it sucks. The mail did give me the cheap thrill of some sort of retribution, but the targets of the acerbic comments are so negligible if you consider the brighter side of life, I could as well have brushed the ill feelings away as one wipes his shoe after having stepped on shit. Taking out the rifle and going after the creature who was responsible for the excrement is literally overkill.

The training was excellent. Plenty to share.

Madhu Deb bounded into Lahari's cubicle. Her steps were propelled less by the characteristic spring of enthusiasm and more by the negative energy of outraged vanity.

"Hi Madhu-di," Lahari looked up with her ready smile.

"Did you just receive a nasty mail from Pritam?" the good lady demanded.

Lahari refreshed her mailbox.

"Yes, there seems to be a mail. I haven't read it though, was too busy this morning. Why? Is it nasty?"

Madhu Deb flung herself into the spare chair.

"You do know the kind of guy he is, right? Very, very shrewd. If you read the mail, you will find no hint of anything particularly mean. But if you read between the lines, you will find a direct nasty, demeaning insult blatantly targeted at me," her face was red and her eyes glassy, tempering the spark of offended dignity. Lahari, who had retrieved the mail and had been trying to go through a rather irrelevant description of a train ride through Germany, became slightly concerned.

"Madhu-di, are you all right?"

The senior manager raised her dumpy hands to rub her temples, a sad smile forming on her face.

"He probably thought I would not be able to deduce the insult. People who think they are too intelligent sometime make that mistake, of assuming that others are stupid. But I understood. Have you seen the mail?"

Lahari nodded. "I am glancing at it now, but ..."

"He calls me narrow minded and fat, can you see that?"

Lahari was alarmed. People did not say that sort of a thing about Madhu Deb. Definitely not to her face. Why, she was supposed to be the exception to the rule that bosses sucked.

"But, he does not mention anyone in particular. He says something vague about current affairs ..."

Madhu Deb nodded. "I see the problem, Lahari. Someone like you who gives more than hundred percent to the job will find it difficult to relate. You are not really tuned in to all the whispers in the grapevine ..."

Mail from Simon to his mailing list

Sub: Day of Awakening with a giant jolt

Day of being woken up with a gun shot? Day of multiple masks slipping off the faces of people?

While there has been light shed on hidden facets of many, hitherto unknown corners of horrifying internal mechanisms of the psyche, my biggest surprise has come from the unravelling of some of the dark mysteries surrounding my buddy-sifu.

As a mentor, Lahari has often told me to detach myself from the interpersonal dynamics and concentrate on my job. Which actually amounts to following her admirable example. I have never seen her being invoved in anything other than her professional duties. To the archetypical Indian professional in our team, this amounts to a meagre percentage of commitment.

On the other hand, my *tai chi* master has often repeated his parallel advice to ignore rumours and concentrate on the art. A philosophy I have taken to heart.

So, the joint teachings of the two respected members of *Axiom* was doing fine for me till I stepped into Lahari's cubicle today for a short discussion about the carpet planning of monthly deliverables and realised only after it was too late that she was not alone. In fact, that is an understatement, because she was in the company of a very vocal and serious Madhu Deb.

In the light of the incidents of the last few days, I was not really keen on proximity with this lady, whose society, as followers of the mailing list know, I don't really look forward to even in periods of peace.

I politely excused myself and had been about to step back out of the cubicle, when she looked at me with commandingly compassionate eyes and asked me to join them. What she was in the process of saying would benefit me as well, and actually could go on to have a serious contribution in saving my soul. Well, she did not really say that in as many words, but from her voice, expression and gestures, that was the idea I got, and perched unwillingly on the desk.

"So, as I was saying," the lady continued from where she had left off, "These last few days I have attended several meetings with the Human Resources and have had several calls with Ajay to decide the fate of the girl. It is a sad decision, but I have recommended that if she has actually gone ahead and tampered with another colleague's machine, moreover at the client location, she should be dealt with severely. I know that it is unfortunate, because our friend –," here she paused and turned to me, " – Simon, I am talking of Pritam here and this is something you ought to know. We know that the girl is not in her senses, being emotionally controlled by Pritam ..."

I interrupted, asking her if I really needed to hear all this.

"Simon, it's time to face the truth. The person you are dealing with controls Amrita with his charms, and he also controls you ... let me tell you this."

I interrupted again, saying that perhaps she was going a bit too far. I knew it for a fact that I was a straight guy with normal preferences, and as far as I could gauge, my buddy had never shown any inclination towards such *gaiety*.

The lady shook her head sagely.

"I am more experienced, Simon, and I know the type of person he is. He likes power and control. Whether the person he is controlling is male or female makes little difference to him. He uses people and destroys them, just as he has destroyed Amrita. Last week I had gone to his cubicle and asked him to leave you alone ..."

"Me?" I did not really know what to say.

"Yes. I could see how he was controlling your life, with the relationship you have with him as your *tai chi* instructor. I told him to leave you alone, and he flew into a rage ... these people also have a temper ... a common trait in narcissists. I asked him to talk to me in the office, but he insisted on going out to Cafe Belmondo. I was not keen on making a scene there and I wanted to take my car for a drive, but he insisted on driving – and took your car, Simon. And I was scared for my life, with him driving along at more than a hundred an hour, fuming in anger."

Lahari, who was sitting with a shocked expression on her face, turned towards me.

"Did he borrow your car?"

I said that he had, and added that he often did.

"A word of advice Simon. Don't lend him your car. He has an infamous temper and is a very rash driver. In fact, Amrita is not the only girl I feel sorry for."

"Who else is there?" Lahari was more than a little out of depth with the accusations piling up.

Madhu Deb lowered her voice.

"I know some people in Kolkata who are close to Shruti, his wife. And they tell me horror stories about what the girl has to put up with. There is a very good reason why she is not here with him, the girl, in fact, is a nervous wreck. That's what happens when he sucks life out of people."

If ever the situation demanded a quick application of the Gupta van der Wiel Manouevre, this was it. All my beliefs, senses and convictions cried for me to get out of there. My fingers moved nimbly to the magic button, but at the last minute I pulled away to ask something which was bothering me.

It was tricky. In a Dutch organisation, questions would have been blunt, aggressive and straightforward. However, in a traditional Indian company with hierarchy cast in stone and the complicated protocols surrounding god players and god fathers, I had to weigh my words very carefully. Yet I made the effort.

"I don't really want to go into the accusations and slurs against the character of someone who cannot defend himself at the moment. I will not go into how the marital or extra marital affairs of an independent adult happen to be any of our combined business. However, I am definitely within my rights to know how someone else can decide for me whom to associate with and whose influence to allow in my life."

The partial Dutch contribution to my complicated genetic soup must have leaped to the fore, because the question came out in a very direct manner in spite of my efforts of censoring words and modulating my tone. For a moment, Lahari's jaw dropped under the weight of surprise. Madhu Deb also seemed more than a little taken aback. However, she quickly recovered herself.

"As a supervisor I have a moral responsibility, Simon. All these young people are far away from their home, and I am responsible for their well being. I tried to counsel Amrita and also Pritam, to stop them from spoiling the environment ... but with the way things turned out, I spent days questioning myself. I stopped advising people. But it has dawned on me that innocent people are being deprived of the help that I can render them with my experience and position. So, I opened up the facts to you, Simon ..."

Her cellphone rang at this moment and she excused herself. For a moment Lahari and I were left alone, silence reigning between us, apologetic smiles touching our lips, the combined embarrassment at a situation neither of us had any way of predicting.

After a few uncomfortable moments, I started excusing myself, hastily uttering that I had better be getting back to the predictable normality of my work station. The carpet planning of monthly deliverables were forgotten. Lahari nodded, blowing a dazed whistle. However, as I moved away, she called me back.

"Simon ... not all Indians are like that. I mean not everyone interferes in other people's business."

I laughed and said that she need not worry, since I had plenty of Indian acquaintances now to know that they were a varied lot.

" And," she lowered her voice conspiratorially and I braced myself for what was coming. "You are aware now that there is some difference of opinion between Madhu and Pritam. I understand Pritam is a close friend of yours, but you must remember that we will have to keep working with Madhu. So, I would advise you to take a neutral stance on this ..."

I laughed and said that I would rather live my own life than get involved in altercations between two supposedly mature adults.

Although character assassination and slander are despicable vices and the rational mind tries hard to ignore the malicious rumours, a few seeds of doubt are always sown. There were some irritating saplings of disquiet that kept bothering me as the winds of thought made them sway about. I stayed back after the *tai chi* class, a fascinating one with a lot of new techniques fresh from Germany.

Amrita was in the class too, subdued but sincere and perhaps not very happy that I stayed back. After she had left, I sat down on one of the gym balls and informed my buddy that I had been through a discussion with the great lady and Lahari.

"So while I was attending the *tai chi* seminar in Ludwigsburg, you were busy with the proceedings of the fat Indian ladies convention in Amsterdam?" he remarked.

By now, I was quite accustomed to his way of describing the most commonplace occurrences, and chuckled. I added that not all the fat ladies had been flattered by the analysis of the relative width of minds and waists that had been so eloquently expressed in his last mail.

"I know fat people are historically attributed as the merry ones, but even then one cannot please everyone," he responded. "Especially in circumstances when pleasing almost corresponds to pleasuring."

I said that a lot of the minutes of the fat ladies convention had been devoted to the discussion of the effects of allowing a *tai chi* teacher influence one's life. In fact, it had been insinuated that the martial arts master took pleasure in controlling the students not only through the *chin na* joint locks and pinning techniques, but also through esoteric mind manipulation methods.

"I have just been officially ordained as a certified *tai chi* master," my buddy exclaimed. "And already legends are developing around my powers. It is of considerable curiosity that the convention of massive matrons was so interested in mind over matter. And how do I supposedly manipulate minds?"

I informed him that our ex *tai chi* partner had hinted at his hypnotic effect on individuals, male and female. This apparently came from his desire to control people.

"I am at a loss to draw a mental image of myself as depicted by the weighty wench. Is it a bisexual psychic monster or is it an embodiment of Vishnu? But, tell me my friend, was this homage paid in your presence?"

I said that the lady in question was in the throes of righteous indignation, which, according to Lahari, had been caused by the mail sent by him. And it was done in my presence with the noble intention of warning me of the evil effects of associating with a narcissist.

"Ah, that explains it ... in fact, our psychiatric collaborator of the Cannabis conference has already spoken to me in some detail about this tendency of transferring guilt. Anyway, you need not worry about my tainted tentacles following you for life. I will be clearing out of here in another week or so."

I said that I did not really care as he very well knew. Character assassination was not one of my favourite pastimes, and the only reason I was repeating all the malicious slanders was that I wanted to hear his side of the story as well. However, there was an accusation which was pretty serious in my view and I would like him to put me at rest.

"I will definitely endeavour to do so, as much at rest as you can be with my tentacles hovering about you."

I asked him point blank whether he had driven my Camri at a hundred miles an hour in the throes of murderous anger. He looked stunned.

"Simon, Simon, Simon. Do you think it was my idea to take the lady on a joy ride? Forget the innuendo, this for once was involuntary. There has been a small change in the version that you have heard with the lady and me exchanging positions as far as wanting to stay in the office is concerned. She said she had not brought her car and did not feel stable enough to drive. Do you think it is physically possible to drive at hundred in Amsterdam? With peculiar streets by the canals, right of the way given to *fietsen* and *eigen weg* signs popping up in the most innocuous looking corners? In fact, driving in Amsterdam on a date has been set as a challenge to prove your imperturbability in times of stress."

I remarked that it was an extraordinarily innovative idea, but was not sure that it was a common practice since I had not heard of it before.

" Well it takes a great mind to set such great challenges. The idea came out of one of the brightest and prettiest heads in Amsterdam – that of our other Cannabis Conference Collaborator, Shruti."

The mention of the name made another of the annoying saplings of doubt brush abrasively against the growing semblance of calmness. I cleared my throat and hesitatingly told him about some acquaintances of Madhu Deb who knew the other Shruti, his wife, in India. This seemed to touch a raw nerve. He looked up with a start, an incredulous expression on his face.

"My friend, in light of all that we have been through together, could you please repeat what you said just now?"

I repeated Madhu Deb's claim. There was a touch of growing pallor on his face, and I wondered if I had stepped into the realms of a deep, dark secret of his life.

"What did these people tell her about my wife?" he asked.

I wondered how to tell him. It was definitely none of my business, and there was a kind of confidence in which the information had been shared with me. However, at the same time, this was a serious allegation and I wanted to know the truth, simply because I had grown to respect and like this guy. I decided to be brutally frank.

The curious attention with which he was listening to me gave way to amazed silence and ultimately a quiet smile traced out on his face.

"Narcissistic rage does not care for truth," he mused, almost speaking to himself. "That's what the good doctor told me. Well, Simon, the moment has come to brace yourself. I have often told myself that you deserve to know the truth, and have been at a loss to figure out what would be the proper occasion. But, as Zen masters say, the only moment that matters is now. Truth, let me warn you, can be stranger than fiction – and in this case, my truth and Madhu Deb's fiction will run neck and neck to prove or refute the claim. Are you ready for it?"

I said that I was and if he wanted to say something important he would better hurry and get back to words of understandable and countable syllables.

"Quite so. An admirable idea that has been growing in you. So, here it is, Simon. The truth is that Shruti is an extremely complex character. I am speaking with Mathematical certainty now, leaving nothing for future ambiguity. Like everything complex in Mathematics, she has a real part and an imaginary identity. The reality is what you see here, the friendly frame of fun, the infectious tilt of the nose, the electric wit and the delicious depths of the erudite mind – all of which light up the bright city of Amsterdam. Whereas the imaginary part lies in India, linked to me with the necessary bond of matrimony..."

I repeated my request of sticking to certain types of syllables, underlining my entreaty with a couple of semi-guttural invectives. My buddy smiled.

"All I am trying to say, Simon, is that the wife in India was a figment of imagination born out of necessity. I am not married. The person whom people know well enough to report to Madhu Deb does not exist. Oh, I see that truth can be very powerful. Are you okay?"

He was concerned because I had not been fully prepared for the revelation. Sitting as I was on the unstable surface of the gym ball, my agitated reaction at this stunning piece of information was at loggerheads with the forces of rotational dynamics, equilibrium and gravity. My exclamation of surprise, which bore little similarity to any word in any classical language, started with me moving violently from the sitting position and ended with me on the ground, the gym ball mockingly rolling over me, starting on a brief journey to the nearest treadmill.

"The diameter of a gym ball is less than a metre, so I guess the fall isn't a fatal one. Please don't get up, I have something more to say which may be even more unsettling, so that is probably the best position to hear it. I am not Pritam Mitra, the consultant. I am Sandeep Gupta, the struggling writer, the martial artist, the ghost blogger, the investigative journalist and soon to become the ghost writer of a book on esoteric economics."

Cheers
Simon

LXIV

Mail from Amrita to Sandeep

I tried calling all through the weekend, but I guess you were in the camp. When I tried to be alone with you for a few minutes after the tai chi class, you deliberately insisted on staying on with Simon.

The critical circumstances may have driven you to take a few steps for me, but I never expected it to last. After all, pity and kindness can only go this far.

The authorities have not yet decided what to do with me. I think everyone wants me to disappear without having to take some decision that may have some implication on Madhu Deb. You hinted the same when you last took interest in the matter.

Please don't think I am demanding anything. I know that I am not in a position to. I am just expressing some stark truths.

However, with the tension killing me (that's not a death threat, please) I do think I will be able to offer the spineless management a way out. By some miracle, God did hear my cries for help. On Friday, an American company I had never heard of suddenly expressed their desire to take me on board. I had an interview with them on the same day, and it went off well. They seemed to like a rustic village girl who does not know adequate English. They have a small set up in Netherlands (they explained that opening branches in Netherlands is really easy) and they can recruit me here. Later they will work on my Work Permit for USA, Dubai or Singapore, wherever they want to place me.

They haven't given me an offer letter yet, but will be sending it by the end of this week.

Hope you had an absorbing and stimulating discussion with Simon.

I have said it often, but let me say it one more time in spite of your attitude,
Love you

Mail from Sandeep to the private mailbox of K. Ayyappan Ramesh

Dear Ramesh,

I have received information that you pulled the right strings. The girl will probably be getting the job by next week.

I am grateful for your help.

Sandeep

Mail from Ramesh to Sandeep

Sandeep,

I am happy that things have come to a favourable end. I understand this girl will also get a substantially increased pay. I hope this reaffirms your faith, if not in Axiom, *at least in me.*

I maintain my stand. I cannot get actively involved in such a scandal which will anyway blow over in a couple of months. My association with this will only raise eyebrows and lead to speculation. The best thing to do is to detach ourselves from these petty matters and concentrate on being productive. No one has come out the loser – a most acceptable situation.

Let us get on with our book and forget this unsavoury thing.

Thanks,
Ramesh

Mail from Sandeep to Pritam

Hey Pritam,

I thought you were an empty vessel, decibels and jargons summing to zilch. The archetype of the successful consultant. In fact you had just about edged past Aveek in the race for my regard.

But now I realise that you are an astute player in the corporate world. Your idea of threatening Ramesh with the chances of my pulling out on moral grounds worked wonderfully. He managed to retain his squeaky clean image by not getting involved, while finding the girl a job. His book is his Achilles heel, and you hit the nail on the shiny head.

People instrumental in starting this entire circus are going scot free, with temporary distortion of their images, but there is hardly anything that can be done about it.

Mail from Pritam to Sandeep

Sandeep

The secret of a successful consultant is to know exactly what the stakeholders want. In this case, I led Ramesh to believe that your faith in Axiom was tottering. Your dedication to the martial arts might force you to decide not to publish anything bearing the name of the company if the girl was victimised. On moral grounds.

I had the great leader in dilemma. It dealt with morals and your art, not money or grade. Unusual domains for a vice president. Additionally you are not a regular professional, with hardly anything to lose.

You should have heard him venting his wrath about that Madhu female. The newly appointed seer had some pretty strong adjectives to describe her way of management, her compulsive popularity syndrome. At the same time, he told me that it was impossible for him to get involved. The situation was clearly at a stage where reversing decisions would mean getting knee deep into the muck.

So, he managed the alternative. I hope it will make everyone happy.

As for this Madhu woman, the stinker of a mail that you sent will do enough damage to her vanity to last a year. Why not make the girl fire another such stinker when she resigns? Hit her where it hurts. These people are like armadillos, they can't tolerate their snow-white image splashed with mud.

I bet you a month's salary (mine being considerably more, I am the one who stands to lose a lot) that Aveek has no idea what an armadillo is. We consultants are a lot of empty words, but most often the right ones.

Finally, this should be a lesson to you. Maybe it's too difficult for you, but try to keep your hands off young girls.

Pritam

Mail from Professor Lal to Sandeep (typed by Shuktara Lal)

Sandeep,

Man is mortal and revenge is therefore sweet. It is in our nature to rejoice and savour in the blood of one who wrongs us. So, being moved to strike back, even at people whom you on hindsight think are not worth it, is extremely normal, as old as man himself.

Forgiveness, on the contrary, is not natural. There is no Indian word for forgiveness. Kshama? *It means fortitude, forbearance. Only after the Roman Catholic influence was forgiveness added as the seventeenth meaning of the word. So, if you have reacted with meanness, there is no reason to be apologetic. The best course is to absorb the sufferings and transform it into creative energy through writing. An author is blessed that he has that choice.*

~The Professor

Mail from Sunder Rajan Swamy to Sandeep

Dear Sandeep,

I am an author myself, under the dubious banner of Amphibian Books. Recently I had a telephonic conversation with your friend Kailash Nayak, who informed me that your book is available in certain cities and not in others. He also pointed it out to me that my books have similar distribution issues.

My trying to contact Sunil Pillay has not really helped because it seems that all of a sudden he has gone underground.

There have also been a number of other authors who have come out saying that they have been waiting for their royalty payment for the last couple of years.

We are thinking of joining hands and suing the publishers. Would you like to join us?

A fellow author,
Sunder Rajan Swamy

Mail from Sandeep to Sunder Rajan Swamy

Dear Mr. Swamy,

(Forgive me for the formal tone. I was not sure which of the three names to use)

I can always join your group as long as all that is needed is a signature on a petition. However, apart from that, I would rather sit at home and write.

Not getting paid for the written word is getting to be a kind of a hobby for me. However, what is more alarming is the growing addiction to indulging in peripheral nitty-gritty – from chasing publishers for representation and then royalty – at the expense of producing what an author is meant to produce, namely creative work.

I have decided to put everything behind me and go ahead with writing again.

Thanks,
Sandeep

Mails deleted by Sandeep without so much as a glance

From Aphrodite Literary Agency Sub: Re: Query about Possible Representation
From Saya Publishing House Sub: Manuscript
From Sunil Pillay (Amphibean Books) Sub: Howdy?

Chat message pops up on Sandeep's laptop screen as he writes and Shruti sits opposite him

Peace spreads on visage
Joyful path woven with words
Flying time creases brow

Sandeep's reply

Fingers weave to soothe
Future inevitable –
Words to recall now

Mail from Ajay Yadav to Ramamurthy

Ram,

A decision need not be taken. I think the crisis has been averted. Amrita has uploaded her resignation on Peoplesoft. I think that makes things easy. We can just wait for her to disappear.

Ajay Yadav
Account Manager – Axiom HMH

Mail from Ramamurthy to Ajay Yadav

Ajay,
That's a real relief. It really lets us off the hook. We don't have to decide anything.
Please ensure that there is no farewell given to her.

Thanks
Ram
Head of Human Resources
Axiom Continental Europe

∾ ∾ ∾

He had avoided her deliberately since *his* return from Germany. She wondered if it was because of the terse language of her mails. She had tried to ask *him* often, with gestures of her eyes, since *he* has taken pains to avoid being alone with her. *He* had been using Simon as a shield, to block her from the few moments that she could have shared with *him*, that would have filled life with meaning.

For a brief while, after the incident of Trisha's machine, *he* had gone out of *his* way to help her. *He* had spoken to the spineless account manager, had even taken pains to find out information from the HR. However, as soon as *he* came to know that she had been approached by another company, *he* had withdrawn into a shell. She met *him* only during the tai chi class, and Simon was always there, sticking to *him* like a bodyguard.

Was this because *he* wanted her to be prepared for the inevitable separation with *him*? Does it make any sense to pour boiling water on one's foot drop by drop to prevent the whole cup falling at once?

Or is it because *he himself* could not face the separation and it was *his* way of becoming immune to the pain? Stupid girl. How could she even dream of having that sort of an effect on *him*?

The most logical solution seemed to be that *he* had felt partly responsible for the events that unfolded. It was guilt that had driven *him* to try and help her and she – the fool that she was– had welcomed all the injustice because of the bliss of the little attention that *he* had sprinkled her with. And the moment *he* had come to know that the problem had been solved, *he* had withdrawn.

Everyone had withdrawn. Ramamurthy had never taken any decision, and had shown that *Axiom* cared for the employees by guiding her to some psychological helpline. She could see the relief on the faces of both Ajay Yadav and Ramamurthy when she submitted her resignation. Why was she surprised? Was it not absolutely certain that everyone would forever withdraw from her? When would she wake up to the fact. She had to fight it out alone, and get back on her feet alone. No one had helped her to get the new job. She had fought for it and got it. Things would remain the same. The brief moments of sweetness that she had dared to dream of were over.

Today *he* had come to her cubicle, deliberately within visual range of the two Dutch guys beside her, and asked her to expect a mail from *him*. It would be a farewell mail that she could send to everyone involved in this nasty business, her way of getting back at them. A brief moment of delicious togetherness again fizzled out when she noticed that *he* did not want to stay on or discuss any further. It was something that *he* wanted her to do with the understanding that she would do it. Probably because it was *he* who wanted to get back at the people who had rubbed *him* the wrong way.

But, she would do it. *He* might use her, but *he* had the right to do so. She had given *him* that right... In hindsight, she had grown to look back at the scandal with fulfilment. There was at least some way that she would remain connected with *him* in the pages of the past.

∾ ∾ ∾

Sandeep wrote. The thoughts and feelings germinated for long, tottering perilously on the brink of miscarriage, cascaded forth as he forced the self imposed dam out of the way. He felt the keyboard under his fingers, listened to the keys as they clicked the typed words onto the small plasma screen. It was not just the chapters produced, but the exhilaration of keying in each character.

"Professor Lal writes with Schaeffer calligraphic pens," he observed. "He rejoices the flourish of the windings his nib scrawls out on paper. He creates not only poetry, but also a visual art. Each stroke for him a way of self expression."

"One of my friends fixed his computer for him," Shruti replied. "Professor paid him with a cheque signed with his calligraphic pen. My friend photocopied it before cashing it."

"The modern marvel of the feather-touch keyboard, it makes writing effortless ... but can we create visual art as a by-product of Literature?"

"Embargoes of progress. Soon hand writing will be an ancient art, much in the lines of swordplay in the age of AK-47."

"Maybe it will take somewhat longer."

"The pen is after all mightier than the sword," it was said together in chorus.

Sandeep resumed writing in long hand, his fingers scribbling tender lines across the ardent face, tracing paths eloquent with unstated endearments, hesitant at the hint of the ephemeral.

The world grew smaller, distances larger. Paradox of the times.

LXV

Mail from Amrita to undisclosed recipients, sent late at night

Time has come for me to move on.

An eventful association comes to an end with a farewell reserved for celebrities.

I always felt special here – especially during the last few days. My heart goes out to the ones who cared for me with selfless steadfastness spending every available hour discussing matters about me that were nowhere remotely close to their business. They even took the trouble of taking up the cudgel against redoubtable foes like decency and truth.

The extent of my popularity is evident from the two hour chat show sponsored by the company resources, with the well rounded show host joining forces with Miss Innocence Amsterdam. They went out of their portfolio, job description, boundaries of company policy and even decorum expected of civility in their appreciable zeal to step into my private matters. A privilege thus far reserved only for matinee idols and rock stars.

After the bestowed superstar status, I feel a tinge of disappointment in leaving my ardent well wishers. However, having experienced fame, let me now dabble at being rich. A 55% increase in salary is difficult to refuse, especially in the current economic crisis. Further, in spite of repeated disappointment, I cling on to the hope of someday stumbling across a vertebral column in the upper echelons of organisational hierarchy.

Among my takeaways from the association, the premier is the ability to fight, something that I have managed to continue and will continue – more so due to the efforts of the well rounded show host and Miss Innocence Amsterdam.

As a parting gift, there is a senior management tip that I would like to share.

Practice pavanamuktasana to get rid of all the airs that you fill yourself with.

Adieu

Two minutes after the her arrival in office, a round form bounded across the carpeted corridors, propelled by fumes of burning *amour-propre,* before grinding to a halt in front of Lahari's cubicle.

"Amrita sent a nasty mail, did you receive it?"

Lahari bit down her smile.

"Yes, she seemed rather caustic."

"But, why? She could have just walked across and had a word with the people she had problems with. Why tell everyone? Did she send it to the clients as well?"

Lahari looked at the reddened face of the senior manager, the heavy breathing suggesting fast approaching boundaries of apoplexy.

"Calm down Madhu-di. I don't know who she sent the mail to. It was bcc'ed."

"She definitely did not write it ... She cannot write even one proper English sentence... It is obvious who wrote it ..."

Lahari got up and offered Madhu Deb her chair.

"Take a seat Madhu-di, we cannot help it. The mail is already in circulation."

Madhu Deb pushed the chair away.

"I have to find the group of people the mail was sent to ..."

She bounded off and Lahari could almost feel the radiating steam that she left in her wake.

Mai from Simon to his mailing list
Sub: Sweetness and Light of Revenge

Your overwhelming response to the previous mail makes me post the follow up regarding the interesting events that continue to take place in my corporate zone.

Amrita left today and as a legacy left a parting mail which I have attached herewith.

The mail was so striking in irony and mockery that it hit you with every phrase. My first thought was to nominate it as an exhibit for the Amsterdam torture museum. Given the type of person Madhu is, I dreaded to contemplate the effect on her.

In fact, I did not have to use my imagination for long. I had just recovered from a great bout of laughter after looking up *pavanamuktasana* on Google (it is a yoga exercise for wind relieving, which supposedly results in a lot of farts) , when she bounded in, her face red, and lips quivering.

"Did you receive Amrita's nasty mail?" she demanded without introduction or preface.

I said that I had indeed received a well written and colourful mail. "I would not really qualify it as nasty unless I was the object of the vented vitriol. Why are you worked up? Do you somehow think that you are being referred to in any way?"

I could see her struggling with emotions. As my buddy had observed a few days back, glossy paint was peeling off her painstakingly polished halo.

"Do you know if this has been sent to the clients?" she demanded.

I replied that I did not, and judging by the mail, the meaning of it all would be clear to only a few – the ones who were aficionados of the currently popular indoor sport of mudslinging. Dutch clients would anyhow struggle with the double meanings and idiomatic expressions. English as a language thrived in irony and the masterly mail was full of it to the brim. The straightforward Nederlanders would struggle to reach behind the surface and extract the hidden meanings.

This reassured her to an extent, but the anxious chagrin soon found a new channel of fury.

"You trained with her, Simon. You knew her. You know the extent of her English vocabulary. Do you honestly believe that she wrote this?"

In response I wondered what difference my opinion made. "If somebody has indeed written it for her, he or she has done a mighty good job."

"You know who has written it, don't you? We both have read enough of his works to recognise the style."

"I really cannot not be so sure. I have recently realised that there are hidden talents in everyone that sometimes come to the fore in situations of crisis."

"This is not a professional thing to do," she fumed. "There are ways and means of addressing employee concerns ..."

I wondered aloud if she was referring to the professional senior management approach of engaging in chat sessions to wash dirty linen. Her transformation from the altruistic, responsible corporate mother figure to the domineering boss wielding her positional power was a fascinating study in unmasking. It made my day.

"Simon ... before you rattle off those smart comments to defend your dear *tai chi* partners, you have to try and understand the culture of our country. An unmarried girl being violated ..."

I wondered if by violation she implied being stabbed in the back by her senior manager in chat sessions. When she hesitated, probably in the process of choosing the most acerbic of the several responses that rushed to her, I continued my somewhat rehearsed speech.

"I have absolutely no time for muck rakers. Besides, your particular brand of slander and sick distortion of the truth is the worst advertisement of an ancient and respected culture, which I am actually proud to be associated with. I thank you for your concern about my car. My Camri is in fact in excellent shape. I know it for a fact that it has never been driven over fifty in the city. In fact, tonight I intend to take some people out on it."

She was still groping for a response, so to fill up the time I continued, "The alluded group includes Shruti – an excellent woman I know and consider to be a friend. She is as far from a nervous wreck as you, although cloaked in your false senior management regalia, are from God."

I added that the only horror story I had heard about Shruti were the shameless lies that had been spread the previous day.

I got up and moved towards the entrance of my cubicle. Madhu Deb stood there in a trance, her face expressionless to the point of being eerie. During the past few minutes of my somewhat brutal barrage, colour and animation had fast disappeared from her visage reminding me of those blisfully forgotten chemical experiments with litmus papers. I had one last observation as I made a move to depart from the cubicle.

"I know I am still struggling with the understanding of the complex Indian culture and psyche, but if you are under the impression that you can bully a Dutchman with your air of pomp and grandeur, like you are used to bullying vertebrally challenged group of corporate climbers, you lack the basic idea about the culture of the Netherlands."

I half expected her to pull me up for insubordination and partly to storm out of the cubicle in a grandiose managerial huff. I also did not entirely ignore the possibility of her jumping up at me and trying to claw my eyes out. But, she just sank into the visitor's chair and sat with her elbows on the table, temples cradled in her palms.

In all honesty I had absolutely no idea what to do. After an unsure minute I tentatively asked whether she was all right.

"Please leave me alone. I don't think I am stable."

Axiom has been a lesson to me as a microcosm of the corporate world, more or less symbolising the interplay of bullshit that makes up the whole community. The transformation of Madhu Deb seemed to be a symbolic representation of a hallowed brand being stripped of the logo and cruelly revealed to be the pretentious and paltry product that it actually was. I waited for a couple of more minutes and then, observing no change in her position, moved away to my buddy's cubicle.

"Simon, my friend. Just the person I wanted to see," he greeted me. "I was just clearing my mailbox and the hard drive. Time for me to depart to my real life, although I will constantly wonder about the exact coordinates of reality."

I told him that I had read the farewell mail from Amrita and he had really outdone himself.

"Well ghosting mails and blogs has been a profession for me, one that will soon extend to the realm of books courtesy K. Ayyappan Ramesh. However, speaking of ghosts, did you happen to see one in the very recent past? You certainly look as if you did."

I informed him that the grand lady of *Axiom* had come to my cubicle immediately on reading the mail. He shuddered.

"That explains parts of it. Not really a ghost, being corporeal to the extent of corpulence, but dimensionally equivalent along the terror axis."

I said that I had been pretty nasty in the interaction, making it pretty clear that I had seen through all her lies, and knew she was nothing but a narrow minded gossip-monger.

"You shouldn't have done that, my friend. Megalomania sustains itself on half-truths, and in times of crisis becomes terribly photosensitive to the light of truth, shielding oneself with shades of deception. This sort of beacon of reality directed at the face must have been terrifying."

I gave him a graphic description of her reaction, with her final posture of self reprisal, her claims of instability.

"Ah, like a wild horse, she is so often far from stable. Don't worry. Remorse will soon give way to self justification, rationalisation and finally flip reality on its head to project her as the magnanimous victim. Her brief period of self loathing is, I assure you, not remorse. She will soon transfer the regret to not getting what she deserves. Simon, the good doctor has pointed the way and I can understand her fully."

Indeed, as I was returning to my cubicle I ran into Gunjan who informed me that he had found the good lady in tears because *she could not save the girl's job even though she had begged the management.*

I pointed out that the girl in question was in fact getting a 55% raise in her salary. In response Gunjan laughed.

"Come on Simon, do you really believe that it is possible in such market situation? Haven't you heard of sour grapes? I think you'd better consider finding a new place to practice your Chinese kung fu, because I have it from trusted sources that the other person in the affair has also been asked to leave."

For a moment or two I debated with the idea of letting this despicable character know what I really thought of him. But then it was just better to wipe the shit off the shoe and walk on rather than getting the rifle and going after the creature responsible for the excrement. The prophecies of my buddy had come true.

Madhu Deb had gone back to polishing her halo, and people had chosen to believe whatever they wanted to.

"Go, enjoy your roll in the muck," I observed with a laugh and moved on.

Cheers
Simon

∾ ∾ ∾

"I want to speak to you ... alone," the smile that had genuinely lighted up her face on discovering the surprise farewell party in the *tai chi* class had disappeared. The voice had a certain edge that seemed to cut the frills of festivity into pieces. Simon took a hasty step back.

"Hang on, Simon," Sandeep called. "It's late and Simon and I have to be at a gettogether ..."

"It will take just five minutes," her voice was firm. "Simon, can you please excuse us?"

"Sure," Simon looked hesitantly at Sandeep and walked out of the gym with his exercise bag.

Left alone, Sandeep looked at the dark girl in front of him with a certain degree of apprehension.

"Have you asked yourself whether whatever you are doing to me is right?" the question was asked in a firm, controlled voice. The tone demanded an answer. The eyes were burning, desperate.

"I have no idea what I am doing to you," Sandeep replied. "I have not done anything."

"Exactly," the girl cried. "The last few weeks you have been avoiding me. You have forbidden me to call. You don't return home, I don't know where you spend your nights. The moment you came to know that I had got a job offer you stepped away from my life ..."

Sandeep packed his workout clothes.

"Amrita, we are anyway going different ways. I am going to India – I mean US – and you are ..."

"I will relocate, wherever you are ... I have got a job in this situation, I will get another. I will do whatever it takes to ..."

Sandeep raised his hand.

"Why on earth? I am married, I am going away. Begin a new life."

The girl kept looking at him, the pained eyes trying to burn holes.

"After what we have been through, do you still think it is something that I can just switch off, like an electric light?"

Sandeep exhaled a tired sigh.

"Amrita, we have had several such discussions and they have never gone anywhere. They have never been resolved in five minutes. I am sorry if you think I am being a jerk ..."

"I'll never think you are a jerk ... I don't even know what it means. Please, don't cut me off from your life like this."

Sandeep hoisted his bag onto his shoulder. Outside Simon was waiting for the reunion of the Cannabis Conference members. The final dissection of the world with scalpels of unusual and lateral insights – the last of its kind during this Amsterdam trip. This strange girl from a world of her own, with mismatching parameters, asynchronous rhythm of life – trying to link their lives with non-existent strings. For a moment a gentle wave of compassion stole into him.

"Please, let me have some contact with you ..."

"You have my email ..."

"I need to see you, I need to spend some time with you. I cannot live without ..."

Wrong choice of words. The ripple of pity ebbed in hasty retreat, a flicker of fear shone through and the eyes became stony.

"I really have to go," he said and turned back.

"I really can't live without you," Amrita called back. Sandeep walked on towards the door. "Better believe me."

Sandeep felt two burning eyes on his back. The last phrase spitted as the last roll of a desperate dice rushed through his tranquillity, sowing doubts of unrest. But he walked on.

∾ ∾ ∾

"The world is getting flatter," Dr. Suprakash Roy mused. "And smaller. And people are hurtling across the globe, constant state of flux." The music played loudly and two voluptuous yet athletic girls clung to the steel pole as they gyrated their ample bosoms for the benefit of the clientele.

La Vie en Proost was surprisingly the only topless bar of Amsterdam. The good doctor had requested Sandeep to come along to the peculiarly located joint in the Red Light District.

"Not only is the world view changing, especially as we have seen in our practical experiences with the over dependence on online communication. The role of the analyst also needs some rethink."

They paused as one of the dancing blondes came close enough to the doctor for him to exhale on to her nipples. It was half a minute before he could speak again.

"With people changing positions – I mean locations – to the extent of almost reflecting the uncertainty that exists in the domain of nuclear physics, it is time to think seriously of distance psychoanalysis."

Sandeep looked at the dancing blondes and the motley group of assembled people.

"I guess there are already doctors opening online clinics."

"True," the psychiatrist mused. "But I have always been sceptical of playing around with age old doctor patient interaction. But now, with two successful cases under my belt, I can actually look at ..."

He broke off. The person sitting immediately to their left had placed the request for a lap dance.

"Interesting. The psychology of people who buy various services by women in this part of the town is really interesting. What possible satisfaction can one get from a lap dance?"

Sandeep snorted.

"I wonder what possible benefit can a psychiatrist get from choosing these particular joints for his discussions?"

The good doctor smiled.

"As I said, Sandeep, I am a student of the human mind, who has his organ in the right place. Amsterdam with all its attractions is a terribly interesting place for a psychiatrist. In fact, there is a eatery on psychiatric theme called the *Freud Restaurant* ... Run by people with psychiatric background ... "

"Wow," Sandeep was impressed. "Must be enthralling, but I guess you informed me a bit too late in the day. By the way, what about the two successful cases?"

The doctor paused as the danseuse at the adjacent table arched backward to a physically demanding and stimulating angle.

"Right," he responded after the passage of half a minute and a hundred and fifty odd degrees. "You did come out of the situation relatively unscathed, didn't you?"

"Well, just about. Yes, your tips about the narcissists did help."

The doctor chuckled.

"You can expect a few more wild stories. Narcissistic rage is fiery, and stems from a feeling of degraded self worth. You have done an amazing job of provoking her. And our friend, Simon, also played his part. The natural reaction of the narcissist is to pull down the image of the others by any possible means, to repair their own self image, apply balm over the hurt. That's what worries me now. You are taking off, but Simon will be here."

Sandeep waved his hand.

"He will be able to take care of himself. Social security plays a big part in dealing with superiors."

The doctor nodded.

"There is that. And also, narcissistic rage is short lived. It lasts as long as the patient takes to rationalise the humiliation. Normally it is a quick process."

"She has already rationalised it. We don't need to worry on that front."

"What about the girl?"

Sandeep tapped the empty glass of rum on his teeth and put it down again.

"She has got another job. I at least managed to set things rolling in that direction. I don't really care what happens after this. She is weird and I will leave her with her peculiarities. Pritam played the cards really well in this matter."

A beatific smile played across the older man's face.

"Pritam. He is my other success story. So calm and composed these days. The way the anxiety was kept in check ..."

"You think that was due to long distance counselling?"

Suprakash Roy shrugged.

"I am not too sure, but it is definitely a case for detailed analysis. But yes, I do consider it a positive sign that long distance counselling works."

"You can also patent your choice of consulting locations."

The doctor laughed. " I will think about it. But, this girl, you said she had cornered you today?"

The dancing girls and the loud music were little more than distraction to Sandeep. He looked at the doctor's face.

"Well, I sort of moved away deliberately after I became certain that she would get a job. I was pretty sure that this particular incident – her steadfast refusal to divulge my name in the matter would be a definite card she would play to make a connection with me. Place me under her obligation. I definitely did not want that."

The doctor was concentrating on the curves and angles demonstrated by the pole dancers.

"You can expect another desperate death threat from her, over email or sms. But, my advice will be to ignore it. The human mind. I have looked professionally into every available nook and corner, but it never ceases to fascinate me with its variations."

Sandeep chuckled.

"What about the human body? Aren't you equally fascinated by it? Especially the female form?"

"I would be doing my vocation a great injustice if I ceased to be fascinated by female forms. Which brings us to the most important question. What about Shruti? What happens to the two of you?"

For an instant, Sandeep's face became vulnerable. He focussed on his glass.

"Are you planning a test tube view of modern day relationships across the flat world?"

Suprakash Roy shook his head.

"I am stepping out of the professional shoes. You are here as a replacement of Pritam, aren't you? And I was Pritam's local guardian. As the concerned elder, someone who knows the triumvirate of Pritam, Sandeep and Aveek from way, way back."

Sandeep shrugged.

"I have no idea. Maybe absence will make the heart grow fonder. Or maybe we will realise with distance between us that we are quite mutually expendable. It is a very uncertain world, doc, and we, with our constraints and limitations, cannot afford to plan."

The good doctor considered this.

"Just out of plain and simple curiosity, Sandeep, will it be easy for you to move back and forget whatever it is you have with her right now?"

He did not need to hear the answer. The look on his face said all. The music rang hollow in the doctor's ears and the dancing girls were nothing but meaningless shapes.

He called for the bill.

Part XIII:

Cross Border Risks and Partnership

LXVI

Mail from Professor P. Lal to Shruti Rattan

Dear girl,

Can anything come to the aid of the author more faithfully than words?

Antara *means distance. Yet* antara *is interval. The same word can be interpreted as opportunity, difference, balance and that what is within.*

The distance that is imminent between the two of you can be an interval in time, a silent interlude in the harmonious duet produced by the resonance of two souls. After all it is the silence between the notes that supposedly lends beauty to music.

Or is it an opportunity? According to a learned Frenchman, absence diminishes lesser passions and increases greater ones, as the wind extinguishes candles and fans a fire. Maybe it is an opportunity to find out the difference, evaluate differences or make a difference. To decide on the choices of life and find the right balance for what is within you?

If the hearts are in harmony, it is better not to adjust the tune. There are too many strings attached.

~ The Professor

Mail from Simon to his mailing list
Sub: Leave Taking

I am congenitally ill equipped for leave taking. To use a much hated and baited Americanism, I suck at it.

I volunteered to drive Pritam – well, Sandeep – to Schiphol. And by the time I had picked up the fourth member of our Cannabis Conference colleagues – who incidentally insisted on sitting beside me, propelling my buddy beside Shruti – and was about to hit the expressway, I was already feeling morose. In fact, I had serious apprehension that soon I would be tainting the Dutch, Irish and American manhood of my complicated genetic pool by producing a few substantial teardrops.

I am not overly emotional. Most often I can underplay my emotions in solid Irish traditions. But, when I looked at the rearview mirror and saw the fingers of Sandeep and Shruti intertwine, the two of them look at each other with visible effort at freezing time, I encountered a rapidly rising lump somewhere in the regions of my throat.

As I drove, I kept thinking of the past few months of my association with this peculiar guy, who never failed to surprise me, and kept the biggest surprise for the fag end of his stay. He had introduced me to the amazing portal of *tai chi chuan*, thus opening a fascinating new world for me. It promises to be a major part of my life from now on, may be as influential as the lodestar. I fully believe it when he says that you know that you are a martial artist when you don't have to give yourself a reason for your dedication.

However, the world that he has opened up does not end with *tai chi* – not by a long way. I have been introduced to the world of hidden cameras, the art of consulting by referring philosophical texts and if that fails using some of the sexually explicit episodes of Woody Allen movies. In retrospect, given his real identity, the bizarre modus operandi did make sense, and made it all the more hilarious.

All of this culminated with the famed Cannabis Conference leaving me to wonder how much of what we perceive as unequivocal truth is actually shaky at the very foundations.

The unfortunate affair revolving around Madhu Deb, Trisha and Amrita did nothing to sour the taste of our camaraderie, and if anything brought us closer, revealing the true face of many.

And how can I forget our own joint invention – the one footprint that our collaboration will leave across time and space, a technique for every employee duo blessed with an overbearing, welcome overstaying supervisor – our Gupta-van der Wiel manoeuvre.

I chuckled even as the car neared the airport. I was going to miss him.

Simon

Dr. Suprakash Roy led Simon away for a cup of coffee.

"It's the quintessentially Dutch way to let them be alone," he observed, smiling.

"Only if the koffie is zwarte," Simon looked back to see the two of them merging into a single close knit form.

"Going into your core research area, doctor, in the digitised world that we live in," Simon paused to select his brand of coffee from the Starbucks counter in front of the famous Meeting Point. He hated American coffee, but was interested in the way Starbucks worked. The employees were supposed to be the most satisfied and the satisfaction was poured into the coffee. Or was it eliminating competition by opening as many stores as possible, even taking hits at the bottom line? "What is in store for them? The two of them have no idea what's to happen to their relationship, but do they have a chance?"

The doctor looked at Simon with a twinkle in his eye.

"Off the record, I am going to follow them closely. Strictly as observer, although I will be personally concerned for them as well. You probably know that I am a cousin of the ..."

"Real Pritam?" Simon laughed.

"Right. The real Pritam. There were three of them. Pritam, Sandeep and Aveek. Close friends who often visited our farmhouse during vacations. If any social scientist had observed the three of them, Sandeep was the best bet for success – if you go by the theory of survival of the fittest. The most intelligent, the one with the zest of living, in the best physical shape. Pritam was the mediocre in all respects. The other one was one of those slow nitwits who would never get anywhere. And now, it is Pritam who is the most successful ..."

Simon stirred his drink.

"Of course, it depends on what you define as success."

Suprakash smiled.

"Yes, very true. I was latching on to the Indian definition. A third world country where it is money that makes the difference between a decent life and one of continuous struggle."

Simon looked at him quizzically.

"Is there no middle path in India? That seems to be strange in a country which gave us Buddhism."

"You can afford the middle path only when you have enough money."

Simon laughed again.

"That now seems to be a paradox."

"India is the land of paradoxes, my friend. The secret is that there are the affluent, very rich and the filthy rich. And then there is an impoverished middle class and the poor. The statistical middle path in this distribution tends to shoot through the floor."

Simon struggled with this analysis.

"Complicated stuff, but I seem to get your point."

"India is complicated."

"I am aware of that. Are you online often?"

"I have to be, for my professional studies. Observation of the online community."

"I was wondering if we can have a web based Cannabis Conference on a regular basis. You know, so that we can keep discussing ... It's actually going to be pretty boring now that Sandeep is leaving."

The doctor nodded. "Not a bad idea. A sort of secret society – in lines of the Illuminati, Masonic Lodge or the Bourbakis..."

"Nothing that sinister ..."

"However, I know what you mean, Simon. I am going to miss this guy as well. Especially the trips we used to make to .... well, to get back to your question ... whether or not I think they will make it? There is one thing that will definitely work for them."

Simon raised his eyebrow. "And what's that?"

"They are more at home in the world of words. It is almost as important to them as physical touch. Why, for all you know, they are rattling off quotes at this moment."

"Only in the agony of parting do we look into the depths of love," Sandeep quoted.

"Will it be an interlude? What form will *antar* take?"

They were silent for a while. Around them travellers rushed by. Schiphol a stationary focal point in the infinite continuum, the dymanic and complex plane people hurtled along, disappearing around bends of time and corners of space, tracing complicated paths of life that made the cosmic probability of intersection frighteningly low.

"Email me your touch."

Shruti smiled through a tear.

LXVII

The mercurial writer of chronicles
With predisposed bias to ironical
Most moving of his art
He inscribed on my heart
Forging his memory into manacles

The feisty dissector of conditions
Dissertation in silk bound renditions
She stuck to Netherlands
Why no one understands
India imploring for expeditions

Blog of Simple Simon
Tags: Internet, India, West, promotions, celebrations

Just before leaving for his distant homeland, my buddy –sifu had gone into his philosophical mode and related the story of a falconer and his protégé. The student of one of the most difficult of arts in the world had complained of demands placed on his life by his post marital life leaving less opportunity for pursuing falconry. The master's suggestion was to get a new wife.

I have not followed the suggested path to perfection, probably aided by the helpful marital status which still renders it inapplicable. However, I have increasingly noticed that I have started to live a new life. *Tai chi* has become a kind of epicentre of my activities. The other facets of life have been readjusted to revolve around my passion.

My buddy has also whetted my appetite to know more about the mysterious splendours of the distant country, with his curious multi faceted personality and his ingenious analysis of the Indian culture, epics and workforce. After his return to his homeland, my fascination with Indians and India have been kept in mid season form with the new friends whom I discovered through him.

The remaining three of the Cannabis Conference team make sure to meet often, in pairs or threesome. The psychiatrist is one of the most interesting guys I have come across, with his queer yet disturbing ideas and opinions about things online. And the charming Shruti never fails to surprise me with her insights.

There is of course the first virtual cannabis conference on the cards, with the meeting scheduled next Thursday.

Association with my new found friends makes me more eager to visit their land, as a seeker above all else. I no longer wish to see the Indian workplace, how the off-shored and outsourced products are developed and delivered to await the stamp of various brands before being marketed to consumers caught in idol worship of the logo. However, I do want to see how so many contradictions reside in mutual harmony. How the techno savvy engineers writing esoteric programs that virtually run corporate and banking products end up sifting through the resumes of prospective brides and claim huge dowries in nuptial bonds. How is it that the society that has overtaken the world in the use of high tech mobile phones still flock to a southern temple once a year to shave their heads and offer their hair to Gods?

According to Shruti, India is too vast and too complex to know in its entirety and confesses her own ignorance about parts of the nation.

My buddy managed to send across his knowing smile across the fibre optic cables. His opinion over the VOIP lines was that India is a culture of absorption.

"We assimilate all philosophies, my friend. The essence of Hinduism is in compilation. We accept thoughts of Buddha, Christ, and with a little struggle to overcome the unfriendly neighbourhood, even the Prophet Mohammed. From Zoroastrianism, Sufism, existentialism, nepotism, communism to net-ism, consumerism and capitalism, from democracy to meritocracy to bureaucracy to plutocracy. We welcome every fad with open arms. So we embrace modernism with one foot firmly in the middle ages."

We have had some nostalgic discussions about the corporate world and India, the fateful intersections between the two, talks sparked off by the annual performance appraisal process and the associated workplace flux.

In interesting announcements, our account manager got promoted, a reward perhaps for his *admirable* handling of the crisis at *Axiom-HMH.* It can also be something to do with a complicated wrap on the knuckles for a senior manager, making the shifty eyed leader well and truly her superior. The vertebrally challenged man had obviously played his cards well ... a lesson to us all that there was potential in even the creepiest of creatures.

However, the high echelon corporate games have an esoteric enigma which I can do happily without unravelling. Far more bothersome was the frenzy in the workplace among people at lower grades who for all intents and purposes sat fawning at the seats next to client managers and coaxed appreciation mails out of them. Well, with most of the workforce performing glorified clerical tasks, it is quite difficult for me to conceptualise appreciation for extraordinary exploits. Yet, the results of this hustling did translate into high ratings and increments, followed by celebrations galore in the form of unrestrained drinking.

My buddy however was quite dispassionate about the phenomenon.

"You see my friend, in India things work differently. It is probably one of the few countries where government workers have to be bribed – not to break or bend the law, but to do what they are supposed to do. In the sophisticated corporate world, the bribes change to appreciation – leading to incentives, and here too the results are demanded for doing what they are paid to do."

I told him about the aftermath of the promotion cycle, frenzied merry making washed down with alcohol. He came up with a curious parallel.

"The Indian work culture is somewhat a direct offshoot of primitive farming background where toil was the watchword, backbreaking labour taken for granted and celebration came in the ritual form after successful harvesting. The current IT work style of the Indians mimics these rustic agricultural origins. Work hard party harder and all those brainwashing buzzwords. It is the same ritual of celebrations you see today, the *vilaiti daru* having replaced the toddy."

The doctor from Leiden may have his semi sardonic views on the Internet, but it keeps the magic flowing – in the form of these incredible interactions.

Shruti, however, has opinions diametrically opposite to both of them.

"I understand his problems in identifying with the Indian workforce and their lack of what our friend would term sophistication and spark. However, if you come from a country where crossing the road without getting run over is a fifty fifty affair and ten thousand hands stretch out for every position promising a better life, can one really be too critical?"

As far as the doctor's diagnosis is considered, Shruti definitely offers a second opinion.

"Aristotle was critical of writing, since it supposedly messed up memory. Every new technology requires time for acceptance. Could we have found out about the atrocities in Iran had they not been posted in the social networking sites?"

Well, I guess there in both the cases, the truth lies in varying stretches of the middle.

Mail from Amrita to Sandeep

I have received no response from you, except for a much thought out and laboured composition – 'Hi. Best of luck in your new job.'

You have been a teacher to me. I don't deny that I have learned more from you in the past few months than from everyone put together during the rest of my life, the biggest lessons being the most painful ones.

I have learned that I am unwanted. I have learned not to have any expectation.

Can you tell me what such a person can look forward to in life?

Please don't be under the obligation of having to reply to repay a debt – an obligation created by my obstinate refusal to mention the part played by you in the so called data security breach. I free you of any such imagined bondage. Whatever the situation, I would not have mentioned your name.

The new job has taken off slowly but steadily. There is not too much to do, but the salary is good and the people are nice.

However, I wonder what all this is for anyway? Does it make any sense for an unwanted girl to keep struggling against the flow?

Gupta Sandeep
When he does sleep
Dream walks across time zone
Next to one he thinks his own

Shrutti Rattan
Pressed a button
To hear the dreaded thought
The one you seek's here not.

Part XIV:

Bullish Buyback Offer and Path Dependent Option

LXVIII

The boy was not particularly handsome. Stylish and smart in the adolescent way that either provokes censure or begets an indulgent smile.

The effort that went into his carefully gelled hair, stopping just short of raising the principal's eyebrows, was at once audacious and endearing. The quality that frequently got him off the hook was the unflappable earnestness in his attitude that went into all his endeavours.

He now looked at Sandeep with all the limited patience of a fifteen year old. The older man sat making the final entries into his register. The sweet sound of the willow stroking the leather drifted into the games room.

"Something on your mind?" Sandeep smiled. The erratic star of the sports field had been hanging around him fifteen minutes after the end of the practice session. He had relinquished post game banter with fellow studs that was such a high point in the day of sporty kids. Something was bothering him.

"Sir, I ..."

There was a blush, hesitation, uncomfortable shuffling of the feet. He was sitting on the victory podium which served as a makeshift stool on all but the sports day, resting his training tired feet on a semi-deflated basketball. Sandeep's mind wound back one and a half decades.

"Shiv, is this about a girl?"

The boy started. His ears had so far been touched with a mental brush dipped in faint pink. Now, the whole red palette of embarrassment was emptied onto them.

"Sir ... how did you know?"

Sandeep laughed. He knew his youthful looks and ill-disguised anti-establishment views charmed the older boys into sharing confidences.

"I have been a kid myself, Shiv. And more than that, when a soccer star starts to blush, there is only one reason. But, let me be very frank with you, my friend ..."

"That's why I am here, Sir," Shiv looked around the games room to ensure that they were not being overheard, although he did not mind people watching. "You are very frank and free with us. I don't know where to turn for advice ... I mean ..."

"That's what I wanted to say, Shiv. When it comes to advice about matters of the heart, I may not be the best person to turn to."

He thought about himself – a sum total of nearly half a dozen half baked and ephemeral relationships. Pathologically confused about the current concoction of feelings for someone half a hemisphere away.

"Why Sir, haven't you been in love?"

Archetypical question. A teacher's personal life was eternally one of the most fascinating areas of interest.

"I don't really know. I have had a few relationships ... but never quite settled down in life with roots firmly in place ... but, then, what seems to be the problem?" He had not been able to master the art of distancing himself from the students.

"When you say relationships Sir, were they ... er ..."

"Pure and platonic or the more spicy kind? Let me respond to that with one of the most dangerous answers for a teacher. No comments."

He paused. Shiv was recording the talk as treasured confidences of his teacher, to be shared with only the best of his friends. Multiple relationships and never amounting to marriage was too good to pass up as a secret that he would keep to himself, but he was prepared to swear his friends to secrecy.

"I will leave that to your combined imaginations when you get together with your cronies. Let us discuss your life. That's what you wanted, didn't you?"

Shiv was disconcerted. How did this guy almost read his mind?

"Go on Shiv, I understand. It is easy for me, because I never took enough responsibilities to really grow beyond my teens."

"Sir, I met this girl over the internet. Have you ever picked up someone in the chatroom?"

Sandeep cleared his throat and checked the flow of expressions before they made to his face.

"Well, when I was your age, we had not heard of the Internet. Let alone chat-rooms. And picking up girls at fifteen was something that came with globalisation. Just after my schooldays.

There was a brief pause.

"Later perhaps? When you were older?"

"Maybe."

Shiv was not satisfied with the elusive answer, and Sandeep was forced to smile.

"Kid, I was an investigative journalist at one stage of my life. So, I can evade questions. Let's come back to you."

Shiv nodded.

"This girl I met ... I cannot make out whether I like her ..."

"Many wise men have struggled on that front."

"The point is, she seems a completely different person when she is online. Outgoing, cheerful, cracking jokes – even some of the more ... er ...."

"I understand."

"Thank you Sir. Whereas when I have met her IRL, she ..."

"Pardon me for interrupting, but what is IRL? I have heard of Uniform Resource Locator."

"In Real Life," the boy explained. "I have met her about six times. And she seems so different when she sits in front of me. She ... well ... she is quiet, has no sense of humour, hardly smiles. Well ..."

"You know, there is a psychiatrist I know who would have really loved this problem."

"I am sorry Sir, who would love this problem?"

Sandeep smiled.

"Never mind. It happens, Shiv. When you cannot be seen and you know no one is watching you, you tend to be a lot more uninhibited. In the present world, we have to accept the real and the virtual faces of the person."

Shiv was not impressed.

"But, Sir, I cannot decide whether I like her or not. She is so great when she is on Gtalk. And then ... well, Sir, is there any guarantee that she is the same person? I don't know. This is driving me nuts."

Sandeep raised his eyebrows.

"Don't you guys chat over video and all that?"

"No Sir, that's not allowed at home."

"Small mercies. Or will we sit here twenty years from now and laugh at the parental folly? Well, an intriguing problem, but one that has a simple enough solution."

"Sir?" Shiv looked at him with expectant eyes, full of puppy faith. The teacher had divine powers.

"The next time you have a date, set it up in a cybercafé. Let her sit in front of you and look at each other as you chat online. That will phase out the inhibition. A transition from the virtual reality to the realistic virtuality. And if by chance your misgivings about her having a ghost chatter chatting for her are true, you will easily find out."

Shiv's young eyes looked at him with devotion so overflowing that it splashed at Sandeep's persona, making him uneasy.

"It may be a bit farfetched..."

"Sir, you are wonderful."

"I'm not too sure of that. However, I would love to have updates on your progress ..."

"Would you really, Sir?"

"I will await the news of your dilemma with duality with eager anticipation. You see, your secret is safe with me. You are an unnamed source from now on. But, your case will definitely be of interest to ..."

"Are you going to discuss with the faculty Sir?" Shiv's voice grew alarmed.

"Faculty? Not even if there is a gun at my temple. But I do have a bunch of buddies who meet every once in a while to discuss the world. We call it the Cannabis Conference. If you give me your permission, I will take up your case with them. Without naming you of course."

Shiv smiled.

"Okay Sir. I will keep you posted."

"I wonder if the expression needs to be modified to I will keep you emailed. But, Shiv, excellent as your company has been we must part now. I have a meeting with a man who is far more confused than you about the reality and illusion."

He picked up the register and made his way out of the games room. The light was still good enough for the few conscientious cricketers who trained at the nets. Sandeep shook his head a little sadly. One boy in ten wanted to do fielding drills, a sizeable proportion itched to have a bowl and almost all hankered to bat.

Towards his left, in the assembly hall, were groups dancing to beats of the portable cd-players, a phenomenon augmented to the sights and sounds of school life after his days. He walked across the badminton courts, where a group played a fast game of tennis ball soccer – in the reassuringly same way Pritam, Aveek and he had played years ago. He wished back as the after school revellers stopped their sweaty pursuits to bellow genuine greetings.

The greeting he received from the man seated in the parlour was genial enough, accompanied by warm smile and affable hand shake.

K. Aayyappan Ramesh had dressed himself in a simple tee shirt for the visit. He had tried to blend in with the ambience of sobriety, but some of the corporate gloss crept through uncovered entrepreneurial cracks. Telltale little signs in the slight exaggeration of the smile, the hesitant extra shake of the hand, in his shiny bald head that added a couple of thousand volts to his perpetual beam, conjuring a halo of importance.

"The dream job," the top boss smiled.

Sandeep nodded.

"Tangible peanuts replace virtual carrots. I was lucky in a way. Ripples of the financial crisis have unsettled the scholastic world as well. The Principal was overjoyed to have an ex-student who would multi-task as a Maths, English and Physical Training instructor while turning up on Thursdays and Sundays to take the Karate classes. It amounts to having three and a half teachers for the price of one and a half."

Ramesh sat down, his shiny head bobbing up and down.

"And they say that exploitation is the monopoly of evil corporations. So this is the school where you and Pritam studied?"

Sandeep laughed.

"Yes, here is where it started. The strange story that binds us to each other and to you. There were three of us. Pritam, me and a dumb guy called Aveek. We are still remembered in some circles as the three musketeers."

K. Aayyappan Ramesh took in the comfortable parlour with a patronising sweep of his eyes.

"I understand moulding of the minds has its attractions ..."

"In the strictest non-brain washing sense."

The great man smiled.

"Do you really need this job?"

Sandeep shrugged. "Do you really need the Nobel Prize or whatever you are dreaming of? The truth is that it is the dream of many to teach in schools. And thanks to the arrangement with you, I can afford it for the time being. I get plenty of time to do some writing. My own as well as your stuff."

Ramesh pursed his lips.

"I was a bit curious about what you were doing with yourself. So, I decided to visit Kolkata on the way back from Bangalore. I had a day to spare ..."

"Why did it sound like someone running out of comfort feel?"

Ramesh was too poised to react sharply, but nevertheless his eyes dwelled on the younger man for a considerable while.

"I fully believe that you will keep your commitment, Sandeep. You have never missed your manuscript updates – not one fortnight in these four months."

"Thanks."

The Vice President sighed.

"I agree that management by comfort feel is the typical Indian way of doing things. Everyone is insecure and profoundly ignorant of what is actually going on, resulting in half baked products. But, I wonder whether I really fall into that category."

Sandeep reached for the bottle of water. His eyes rested behind Ramesh, at the show case displaying the trophies won by the school in various extracurricular events.

"I guess that was uncharitable. But, I must admit I was a bit surprised when you announced your visit. What can be so important that cannot be discussed over cables and satellites in today's connected world? Kolkata, with all its attractions, is not really a halt on the way to London from Bangalore."

The dignified chuckle was reassuring. "I am collaborating with you on what is one of the – or *the* – most important work of my professional life. Doesn't it justify one meeting in a quarter? Moreover given that you dismissed my invitation to Bangalore with a couple of casual sentences, I really did not have a choice."

Sandeep shook his head.

"I was quite explicit, Ramesh. I have had enough of corporate circus to last me a life time. Besides, it was impossible to come over for the Thursday to Sunday jamboree ..."

"Corporate Event, Sandeep. Best Practice sharing. You are mixing up the two worlds."

"There is no second world, Ramesh. Look at your employees, a bunch of overgrown school kids craving for the supervisor's appreciation, and prizes at the end of the year. Take away genuine respect and dreams from schools and you have a perfect approximation for the corporate organisation. Besides, I teach Karate on Thursday and Sunday, have seven classes to take on Friday and Saturday and a weekly gathering to attend at Birla Mandir on Sunday mornings."

"Professor Lal's *Mahabharata* readings?"

Sandeep nodded. "So it must be palpably clear that I don't have time for workplace whims."

The famed face in front of him became grave.

"You must be aware that I have a team in place, handpicked people who look at your material and package the contents into abridged and impactful presentations, web content and press releases."

"I was not aware, but all the glitzy stuff you do with it is your business. You have the copyright. As long as I don't get wind of it, I am okay ... soon all this will be over."

Ramesh got up and walked to the window. Outside, beyond the trimmed garden and impressive courtyard, the colourful Kolkata street life greeted his eyes.

"Have you looked at *Axiom's* corporate web site in recent times, Sandeep?"

He turned in time to see the smirk.

"Well, you know, what with this thing and that, I kind of ... To be very honest Ramesh, it never occurred to me. I doubt if I will ever take a look."

The wise man nodded.

"I understand you get a kick out of irreverence. But, there is a new flash movie on the opening page. It talks of the success of our paper and gives a brief overview of what the innovation is all about."

"Indeed?"

"There are interesting graphics. Which kind of merges the new cyber-age with traditional knowledge."

"Temporal cocktail."

"Take a look at this."

Ramesh produced a glossy A4 sized poster from his laptop case. A team of graphic designers had worked on it. A computer generated image of a number of zeros and ones formed a chariot with Krishna and Arjuna in their familiar Bhagavatgita setting, the latter with his bow drawn and arrow poised to be shot, the arrowhead formed into the flowing A logo of *Axiom*. On the side of the digital chariot was the slogan "*Axiomatic Wisdom to Combat Crisis*"

"This logo is fresh from the oven. It is already on several websites, billboards, company buses and strategic corporate paraphernalia. Tee shirts, bags, pens, mouse pads. We have a blog and twitter campaign, posting all over the corporate and finance conscious cyber-world, promoting discussions about the methodology. A lot of propaganda is taking place, about the paper and the book. If you see the word cloud on some of the popular..."

"Have been busy, haven't you? Leaving nothing to chance."

"That's not all. I have been to all the locations of *Axiom* around the globe promoting the idea, developing internal awareness. We have taken up a couple of pro bono system design and business consulting projects for The Gita Foundation. In return a scholar is visiting the premises of our offices and also conducting web-conferences to increase the general awareness of the Gita. We want our employees to talk the talk, develop traits. At the same time, we are developing a consciousness of our roots, of the knowledge that we had chosen to forget. There is a cultural change we are bringing about, Sandeep. We are starting with *Axiom*, but by the time the book hits the stands, we will have the whole country and a large part of the world speaking our language."

Sandeep looked at his research collaborator.

"Are you serious?"

"I am, Sandeep. The Communications team is working on a series of cartoons to popularise the concepts of Hindu philosophy. Great work is being done, my friend. We are already having talks with the Astha and Yoga channels, for special 30 minute slots. Press releases are going around in small filler articles, in business and entertainment sections. I have been invited on CNBC, CNN and Business Now prime time. We are even thinking of *Axiom* sponsoring the Asian Archery championships in Thailand, promoting the Arrowhead on the ..."

"Why not have some of the brand essence tattooed on the forehead of the staff? You can use symbols like ohm overriding the euro and dollar together."

Ramesh focused his beam on the cynicism.

"Ah, but you know what? Nike has beaten us to it. Not on the foreheads, but on the calves. Their swoosh had been tattooed by some employees. But I do have something pretty rare. In all corporate events from now on, people will take these away as keepsakes."

He produced a small plastic packet from the laptop case. Sandeep fingered it apprehensively. Inside was a metallic manifestation of the arrow with the *Axiom A* as the head.

"What are these? Body piercings?"

"Actually they are lockets."

"Wow. But, why not piercings? You could make it mandatory for lady employees to wear these next to their navel. Symbolising womb of knowledge or mother of all wisdom. But, on second thought, it is better this way. With the Madhu Debs and the Laharis, you would require a metal detector to find the piercing. But, why are you telling me all this?"

Ramesh let his calm eyes linger on Sandeep's impatience.

"I owe it to you, Sandeep. You can say I am stricken with guilty conscience of making you slog without involving you in the excitement."

"You can hardly think of a greater favour."

Ramesh put his hand on Sandeep's shoulder.

"This is one of the biggest things, Sandeep. You can use the publicity. We will be promoting this as a cross disciplinary venture – where economics, consulting, business, psychoanalysis and creative storytelling come together. What if I hired you back?"

Sandeep started. The big boss of the corporate world had just made him an offer.

"Back?"

Ramesh chuckled.

"Well, not exactly back, but what if I hired you as the Chief Creative Consultant of the *Axiomatic Wisdom* drive? This time under your own name."

Sandeep leaned back in the sofa and smiled.

"You need me, don't you?"

Ramesh nodded, his face earnest.

"Let me be very frank, Sandeep. I have a team of creative talent – designers and artists – for this drive. They are good, but not great. Not imagineers, if you know what I mean. Besides, I am afraid that in the transition from your manuscript ideas to their funky presentations, matter is getting lost, or misinterpreted. I want to take no chances, Sandeep. I want this to be the very best."

Sandeep laughed.

"Ramesh, at least you should remember that we ourselves speak of in built opposite. Along with our always having a choice."

For just a small fraction of a second, Ramesh looked perplexed. But, the beam soon returned to its position.

"Well, I will leave you to think about it."

"I have thought about it, Ramesh. And the answer is no. If I indulge the ghost writer in me anymore, I will lose touch with my real self. I have work to do in my life time. I cannot devote too much time to being god."

Ramesh smiled.

"I have left that idealistic part of me behind somewhere on the riverbanks of time. But, I respect your decision. The work will go on, but maybe it will lose just a bit of the edge because of your refusal. Let me tell you something else. If you like sticking around with students, we can make that option available."

Sandeep groaned.

"Ramesh, I am fed up of dishing out chapters of the Gita to unsuspecting cubicle creatures."

"I was not talking about them. We are having talks about launching a branch of the *Axiomatic Wisdom* program for the student community. To spread awareness of our roots, the philosophies, the wisdom. We are thinking of sponsoring college fests, arranging logo designing competitions and even marketing contests for the MBA students. We may launch it in the schools too. In fact if we can get into schools with promotion of wisdom and heritage, sponsoring their computer education program, designing their websites and blogs ..."

"And you were telling me about the lures of moulding minds?"

Ramesh smiled patiently.

"There are lots of ideas floating about, and it's a win win situation. There is no evil corporation here, Sandeep. We are promoting awareness. We have faced some problems. For example there are always these idiots who will keep mixing up philosophy with religion. They are screaming themselves hoarse about our being non-secular, not catering to the minorities and all that sort of rubbish. But we are finding ways to counter it. Operation Integrated Evangelisation has taken off. If you join us, you can also contribute there by making the model sound more religion agnostic ..."

"Would you be terribly heartbroken if I decided to sit at home and write without joining this group of self appointed messiahs?"

Ramesh looked at the strange man in front of him. He had known him as a consultant, author, showman, impostor, ghost blogger, investigative journalist and now a school teacher. More than that just crazy and obstinate.

"I guess it is entirely up to you."

There was a soft knock on the door. They turned to find themselves looking at a shy fourteen year old.

"Akash. Please come in," Sandeep's cheerful voice greeted him with warmth.

The boy was hesitant. He stole a glance at Ramesh and approached Sandeep with tentative steps.

"I have closed up."

"You locked the games room?"

"Yes. The key is with Stephen."

"That was not necessary. I would be locking up anyway. You want to leave?"

"Yes, please. Will you be dropping by tonight?"

"Tonight? Probably not. I'll be working on a great hoax. Tomorrow perhaps."

The boy smiled shyly and walked out, casting another hesitant look at Ramesh. Sandeep's eyes followed him with affection.

"You drop by at your student's place?" Ramesh asked.

"That's my godson," he smiled. "He is the adopted son of my friend."

"Adopted?"

"Yes. He lost his parents in the Gujarat riots. Was adopted from the orphanage by a well to do family. My friend, Kailash Nayak, used to work with me at that time. We used to run an investigative journalism agency. He found out that the assholes were actually using him for cooking and cleaning, the most blatant violation of child labour laws. He threatened to haul their backsides over slow media fire, and they settled for the alternative of compensation and the pulling of required strings to transfer the legal adoption rights to him. Since then, the boy has been with Kailash. When I joined the school, he requested me to use my influence to get him admitted here."

Ramesh opened his eyes wide.

"That's quite a story. And noble. Your friend must have had a sensational story for print."

Sandeep laughed.

"Well, he did not write the story."

"Someone else did?"

"No. He did not publicise it. The kid has had enough trauma to last him a lifetime. Further media glare is not exactly what he requires for a while."

Ramesh nodded.

"I understand that. But, as a journalist, it is definitely a great opportunity ..."

A smile touched Sandeep's face.

"Ramesh, there is something that I have realised. The people who really work to change the world are too busy working to launch a branding campaign for themselves. *Karmanye vadhikaraste ma phaleshu kadachana, ma karma phala hetur bhurmatey sangostva akarmani.*"

Ramesh laughed.

"You are caustic. And I am human. The paradox is that both of us strive for godliness in our own ways," he got up. "No one can say with absolute certainty whose way is better."

LXIX

The day wanes. The sun is down and haze filled night sky reigns.

I stretch my tired legs. Two games of football with seventeen year olds take their toll, no matter how fit you try to keep yourself. Age can be slowed, but however sluggish the trickle, the years pass under the dam of strictest self discipline.

The dishevelled sofa in my book infested living room beckons me with bewitching promise, to soothe the raven's sleeve of care, to shine the light of other days that fond recent memories bring around me. But, then, I have promises to keep. The laptop waits like troubled conscience, for my fingers to furnish fantastic forgeries.

There is fascination in watching the false forests fill up with fabrication. My soul gives the harness bells a shake, wondering if there is some mistake. It must find it queer that I am standing here in this lowland of lies without any signs of fulfilment near.

I have to finish this quickly, it keeps me from writing truth in my form of fiction ... while I type away fables in the guise of reality. I am tired.

What would I not give at this moment for a refreshing cup of hot chocolate? The rich warm Nederlandse chocomel, sweetened with the kiss of uncertain love and flavoured by the slagroom of conversation. The sweetness of the meaningful nothings, of the fulfilling frolic with frivolously weighty words – and now the bitter pangs of sour separation.

Miles and miles of empty space between us and the internet cannot stand in for one smile. Can technology substitute tactile contact? And why do we touch to feel and feel when we are touched? Why are mind and body so intricately entangled to be beyond the solution of the modem? Why cannot a bicycle creep up on an electronic fietspad and bump into the small of my virtual back as I walk along with you half enfolded in my arms, blissfully unmindful of the universe.

~ ~ ~

"Hello."

"May I speak to Professor Lal please?"

"Speaking," the aged, gravelly, tranquil voice seemed out of place as people rushed about in the mismanaged commotion of the Netaji Subhash Bose Airport.

"Professor, it's a pleasure speaking to you."

A soft laugh in response.

"That's good, but who do I have the pleasure of speaking to?"

"My name is Ramesh," propelled by immediate habit, he added double-o-seven style, "Aayyappan Ramesh."

"The Vice President of *Axiom*?"

Ramesh was thrilled.

"It's flattering to be recognised, Professor."

"You must thank a young friend for that. I have heard a lot about you from Sandeep Gupta. You seem to interest him immensely. And I must warn you that in my experience, such keen interest often results in later manifestations in print."

The Vice President laughed.

"I just hope I don't have to invoke the libel laws. Professor, it is from Sandeep that I got your number and the assurance that it was okay to call you directly."

"Well, I don't have a secretary to screen my calls. All I have for a personal assistant is a Godrej filing cabinet."

"Ha ha ... Professor I have a proposition for bus... er ... collaboration. I wonder if you will be interested."

"Indeed? There are lots of things that interest me. The spirit continues to be willing, but the body lets me down more and more with passing time. Before you proceed I hope you know that I am eighty."

"I do. Believe me, that is positive. Do you know of the paper on Indian Wisdom to tackle Financial Crisis that I presented in an economic conference held in Los Angeles?"

"I do indeed."

"I am flattered. Our idea is to prevent future financial crisis based on some lessons taught by ancient Indian philosophy. Including *Gita* and the *Upanishads*. As an organisational drive I am also ensuring that all my employees become trained in the basic concepts of Indian philosophy."

"That's commendable. However, Indian philosophy is a vast ocean and even the basics may take you into very deep waters."

"Ha-ha, we are doing the best we can. But, I intend my senior managers to be absolutely confident about the Gita ..."

"Well, I must say that's a contradiction in terms. The Gita is not to make people confident. Confidence comes from personal interpretation and choice. Gita raises more questions than answers."

"Well Professor, would you agree to give our managers some lessons on the Gita? Maybe one session a week for the next three months? Or one session for each canto? You will be the best person to decide the frequency."

The public broadcast system coughed to life, with the longwinded multilingual announcement of a departing flight. Ramesh walked towards the toilet to hear clearly.

"Hello ..."

"I am still here, Mr. Ramesh, but I require some time to absorb the magnitude of your proposal. Are you asking me to become an external faculty for your organisation?"

"Absolutely, Professor. We will be honoured if you join us."

"But, young man ..."

"I am past fifty, Professor."

"Well, you are still young to me. I am eighty. It is somewhat late in the day for me to join the corporate bandwagon. I am almost a career span beyond the normal retirement age."

"Professor, I assure you it will be absolutely painless ..."

"There is no painless way to learn Indian philosophy. Even less when you try to teach it."

"What I mean Professor is that you don't have to take any trouble at all. I will ensure that the latest videoconferencing equipment is set up at your place. You don't need to step out of your study."

There was a pause as Ramesh ventured out of the toilet and walked back towards the waiting lounge.

"Well, this proves that even at four score you haven't seen it all. Tempting as it is to have an inside view of the fascinating brouhaha of the corporate world, I must decline citing age as excuse."

"But Professor, we have not talked of the terms and conditions."

"True, we haven't. But, my health has been discussing them with me at length. I have this lecture at St Xavier's, the Mahabharata readings every Sunday and am also working away at the completion of the Mahabharata – which has occupied me for the last forty years. Add to that the intermittent supervision of the Workshop. I know that I can just about manage all these. Anything more will be like the futility of the man in Tolstoy who ran from morning to evening."

"Professor, this is going to be a very big venture ..."

"And your intentions are very noble too. But you need young legs to pull you along. Mine are ancient. I am already resting on a bed of arrows, unable to call it a day till the Mahabharata comes to an end. There is no space for another arrowhead."

"Arrowhead? I see that the propaganda has reached you, Professor. With the kind of publicity that is in the offing, Professor, there could be a lot of mileage for the Workshop and for your Mahabharata venture."

"My chariot wheel is already sinking, my friend, and the inevitable archer is aiming at me. Mileage can do me little good at this stage. I am sorry, but I wish you all the best in your great venture. If you think I can be of any help, please feel free to give me a tinkle and drop in. We can discuss new ways in which the Gita can be interpreted. You are always welcome for a dialogue."

Ramesh waited for a while. The trip was turning out to be a lesson in rejection. It hurt the long unused receptors of refusal in his vice president's psyche. Besides, the declined ideas had immense potential, held plenty of promise for everyone. Yet, the people around whom the ideas revolved were too dreamy to wake up to the opportunities.

"Professor, thank you for the offer. I would have loved to have you wor ... er ... be the honorary philosophical consultant for us. In fact, I was thinking of a sizeable retainer with the designation *Acharya* ..."

There was a gravelly chuckle.

"Intriguing. But, no thanks."

Ramesh sighed.

"Professor, I will definitely respect your decision. But, I do have another small request."

"Well, I can't wait to hear it."

"I would like to present a corporate gift to all the employees during our annual day that is due in a month. I have been a fan of the Writers Workshop volumes ever since I saw your clothbound Bhagavat Gita in Sandeep's possession. Will it be possible for us to purchase copies of the Gita for all the employees? It will make an excellent gift."

"How many copies are we talking about?"

"Well, there are fifteen thousand employees in India and another five thousand distributed around the world. Twenty thousand in all."

There was another pause.

"I don't want bulk discount or wholesale prices. At hundred rupees a copy it comes to around twenty lakhs. Add the shipping costs..."

"I must say this conversation has been full of surprises, and in the space of a few minutes I have been subjected to offers I would have never thought possible. But, much as I would have liked to say yes, I'll have to disappoint you. Twenty thousand copies? For a month I can ask the binder to stop everything else and work solely on your order, but the maximum number of copies I can promise you is two hundred and fifty."

"What?"

"You heard me. We are not Walrus. And even they would struggle to fill in such an order. All the books are bound and stitched by hand, by a family of artists. Even if I want to, I can't grow any bigger without erasing the signature of the Workshop, the cloth bound volumes."

"What if I arrange for the labour, the facilities?"

"My friend, it is no doubt cheap labour, but not the kind which can be reproduced in bulk and sold to the customers. Each of the volumes is the result of the craft of an artist. Art cannot be ordered wholesale. I am sorry not to oblige, but I have not the means."

The back to back to back refusals sat unfavourably on the great man.

"But, then ... well ...," he bit back on the brink of asking the aged publisher how he hoped to run a business this way. A man hurrying to catch his flight brushed against him, and he followed him with his eyes, the perpetual beam giving way to a glare. Inside him was growing an uncontrollable urge to Midas touch the no into yes, something he had always excelled in, the talent that had made him an entrepreneur to reckon with.

"Professor, I think I have to change my plans in that case. Could I interest you in selling five hundred copies within a month?"

"It is not my interest that counts. The spirit, as I say at the risk of repetition, is willing. But the means is what I lack. In this case, it is not humanly possible for my printer. I cannot commit more than two hundred and fifty."

"What about four hundred? I will distribute them only to the middle managers and above."

"Well, you need to come up with a more exclusive group, because I cannot promise you more than two hundred and fifty."

Ramesh flopped down on a reclining chair.

"Okay. Two hundred and fifty then. I have just been struck by an idea of a Wisdom Contest and these can be early bird prizes. Thank you Professor. I think you could teach our senior management more than Indian philosophy. You could teach them to say no to customers. We have forgotten the philosophy, and have never learnt to say no. Okay, I will send you a cheque tomorrow. This is about as much rejection that I can digest in a single day. Have a good night."

There was a trademark chuckle on the line as the Professor signed off. "Okay, good night."

∾ ∾ ∾

Mail from Amrita to Sandeep

I don't even know if you read the mails. You take pleasure in not answering. If that gives you satisfaction, then that is what I will accept.

However, even without being there, you continue to play a role in my life. In my new company, there is a shrewd looking guy called Rajan – a crony of our old mutual friend Gunjan. He has gone around the company, stopping by each interested Indian ear, and even some local ones, entertaining his audience with the spicy stories of my affair with you.

But, then, even as the gossip lovers laugh at me behind my back, I am happy. Even if it is in slander, my name is linked to yours.

Mail from Kailash Nayak to Sandeep

Hi Sandeep,

Interesting outcomes of my pro-bono investigative journalism.

Axiomatic Wisdom is sponsoring Krishna on ATNTV.

Also, there are talks on with FabIndia about ethnic wear bearing the Axiomatic Wisdom theme and with Incredible India tour operators about a semi sponsored Ethnic India tour, which might also cover Cambodia and Thailand.

They are also contemplating entry into niche schools, with essay competitions on topics like Modern Applications of Ancient Indian Heritage, to be submitted electronically at a specially created website, powered obviously by Axiomatic Wisdom. The website will have ancient wisdom, secularly distributed across religion and ethnicity, in the form of comic strips, videos, arrow shooting games.

Talks are also on with a couple of media and entertainment channels, so very soon you can expect articles on the power of Axiomatic Wisdom sprouting across newsprint in apparently innocuous ways – a hint here, a drop there, whetting of appetites, comparisons, full interviews and simplified description boxes. I wonder whether FM channels are going to play a part as well. Plenty of investment, some pretty hush hush synergies must be in the offing ... I wonder how even with all the cash richness and the status of the lodestar in the dark clouds, Axiom could pull off such a lot of venture capital for this initiative.

Mate, your ideas are already being used for several consultancy projects. Big investment opportunities envisioned. Why aren't you rich? More surprising, why are you not in chains?

K.

Part XV:

Flight to Quality and Futures

LXX

Blog of Simple Simon
Tags: Cannabis Conference

In this post, I bring to you the proceedings of the first online Cannabis Conference. There have been discussions about a separate website for the future developments and thought sharing blogs of this exclusive club. However, till such a thing matures, I will be logging the discussions directly into this weblog, using the tried and tested practice of copy and paste.

First online Cannabis Conference – on GTalk (the abbreviations and short forms commonplace in the world of the internet have been replaced with the normal English words as far as possible to facilitate easy reading – easy, that is, for people over fifty)

Participants:
Shruti Rattan – location Amsterdam
Simon van der Wiel – location Utrecht
Suprakash Roy – location Leiden
Sandeep Gupta – location Kolkata

Start of conference: 16:38 GMT , 17:38 Amsterdam, 22:08 Kolkata

Sandeep: Sorry, I am late. Somehow the BSNL connection needed more than the normal prodding.
Suprakash: Ah, the sweet memories of home
Sandeep: Home-LANned!
Suprakash: Good one
Simon: Do we all have the respective intoxicants ready at hand?

Suprakash: Yes

Sandeep: Yes

Shruti: Yes

Simon: For the record and meeting minutes, please state your poison

Shruti: Mine's vodka with lime

Sandeep : Rum and Cola

Suprakash: Ah yes. Excellent multi-purpose drink and disinfectant.

Shruti: Disinfectant?

Sandeep: The doctor is referring to my now famous act of pouring half a bottle of Captain Morgan over Pritam

Shruti: Did you really pour rum over him?

Sandeep: Yes, I confess I did

Shruti: My hero

Sandeep: I have bowed low in response, to e-kiss your e-hand. Am getting back on my chair. Hard to type while on the knees.

Suprakash: Whiskey and Soda

Simon: Red wine for me

Sandeep: It should be stronger, Simon.

Simon: I am into my fourth glass, waiting for you all this while

Shruti: So finally, the first electronic Cannabis Conference.

Simon: After two false starts. But, we have solemnly agreed to have this on the last Thursday of each month. God and BSNL willing.

Suprakash: My role as you all know will be that of a participant as well as an observer of the web world. Interesting that even we have fallen prey to it.

Sandeep: And this one was spurred by sensational developments I have reported to you, the chain of incredible events triggered by our first cannabis conference.

Shruti: For the record, *Axiom*, ably spearheaded by Ramesh, have launched into serious promotion of the *Axiomatic Wisdom* campaign.

Sandeep: Aayyappan Ramesh. The promotion, as reported by the best investigative journalist I have been privileged to know, is something beyond the wildest frontiers of my normally far-reaching imagination.

Simon: They are branding it as if there is no tomorrow. I have already come across several banner ads, flash demos, with the logo of Axiomatic Wisdom hitting you between the eyes every time you unsuspectingly open a company mail. Axiomatic Wisdom is the new incarnation of the *Axiom* brand.

Sandeep: It surprises me on multiple levels. One, the book that will contain the so called Body of Knowledge of the whole Axiomatic Wisdom bandwagon is only about twenty five percent complete. Whatever I have written has been haphazard, far away from the real product. I am still waiting for some of the pioneering psychometric tests which will drive bank regulations, which have been volunteered by our fellow member, the psychiatrist. And they are promoting it already as if their despicable lives depended on it. They have even poached a brand manager for this.

Sandeep: Secondly, my arrangements with Aayyappan Ramesh are purely verbal. There is no binding contract other than a secret sealed by being partners in the impersonation drama. If such gargantuan investments are taking place, isn't it important for me to come under the banner of *Axiom* or at least have a bond writ in blood, with a pound of flesh for the taking if I quit? Apart from the half hearted attempt at winning me over at my school, the big man has not made any serious endeavours to get me shackled to his gilded caravan of entrepreneurship. What if I give him the royal ditch and disappear? With my track record as an impostor specialising in cross border counterfeit and my versatility at multiple occupations how can he show such cavalier trust? What if I become an apprentice Tibetan monk at a remote Himalayan monastery? Or do the ultimate disappearing act by migrating to South America as a member of the Cartel, leveraging on my Cannabis experience? Or become a member of Greenpeace, asking unsuspecting people of the Atacama Desert to pay through their noses for the survival of Beluga Whales? I know Indian business is often built around hawala, but why this unfathomable belief in my feeble honour when the stakes are skyhigh?

Simon: I think I know the answer to the first question.

Sandeep: That's where the four glasses of wine comes into play.

Shruti: And I think I can elaborate on Simon's answer and work out an explanation for the second.

Sandeep: I am speechless – in reverent awe of your intellect. Cannabis conferences are always a class apart.

Suprakash: Let's hear (or should I say read) the two of you, and then I'll see if I have anything to add.

Simon: What we are witnessing here is a branding exercise. A drive to make the tag *Axiomatic Wisdom* recognisable and identifiable. With related connotations across all spheres of life. It will be there when the family sits down for breakfast, gawking at them from the morning papers. It will be there on the billboards and the internet, in school and college competitions, the media reports, the TV channels broadcasting news, sports, advertisements and philosophy. There will always be a ladder to the concept of philosophy and wisdom which binds all the promotion. Ultimate objective of the idea is to make the brand synonymous with wisdom.

It is not that it is promoting philosophical wisdom, it is *the* wisdom. Whenever people will see anything to do with ancient wisdom – be it television serials, comic strips – they will associate *Axiom* with it. So, in these circumstances, what is important is creating public consciousness of the soul of the brand. Whatever the brand sells is actually secondary. Once the brand is sold – the product behind it will sell itself. So, the energy is totally concentrated on brand building. And the product comes in as also ran in terms of importance. Sorry buddy, but that is the truth.

Sandeep: What happened to the glorious traditions of sugar-coating?

Shruti: Bitter pills, Sandeep. I completely agree with Simon. The paper did create some stir among the financial media. There were some important market watchers who spotted potential, or were sold the concept by Ramesh.

Sandeep: Aayyappan Ramesh

Simon: I am actually impressed by Axiom or rather by Mr. Aayyappan Ramesh. He was cut to the quick when Dave de Boer famously taunted his Indian ego. Now he is showing the world that the Indian is right up there. Now, it is the developing countries where McDonalds opens stores for the dark skinned teen-age clientele, who wear Nike and sway to the electronic beats of the iPod, each of the mega brands cashing in on the world walking the American way, culture aping the great capitalists. He is trying a subtle turn of tables, whereby a fad of back to the ancient wisdom will be created slowly, which will actually be creating a culture around itself – the culture of *Axiom.*

Sandeep: And you say the product has little value. If, for instance, I decide to lie incognito in Tahiti from tomorrow, creating Gauguin on Photoshop, the trend will carry on?

Simon: Right, buddy. It will. I don't know what it is that Ramesh wants to pitch on the public, but he is making a market ... and your work is just a minor necessity. Does it matter that the small family run restaurant next door serves tastier, healthier stuff at half the price? People will keep craving for the yellow arch and change culinary preferences to burgers and fries. It becomes an essential cultural symbol. Can you think of a kid not being in McDonalds, or not watching Disney? Quality is secondary. What is important is the spirit of the brand. The esoteric philosophy that marks up the price.

Sandeep: Wow! The soul of the capitalists. Where does that put me? Am I already a target for left wing fundamentalists?

Shruti: It's like the shoes for all the great sneaker companies. Most of them are put together in remote sweatshops of Thailand or Vietnam. You are cheap labour, my dear.

Sandeep: Hang on. So what I have put down to the collaborative genius of the Cannabis Conference is actually expendable cheap labour?

Shruti: The first part was not so. The paper itself was a work of combined intoxicated ingenuity. But, now, the brand has taken over. You provided the corporation with a hazy product that can be easily extended into the esoteric brand spirit Simon mentioned. The rest can be easily manufactured by struggling authors in Bangladesh or Cambodia, and sent across the Internet. You are nice to have with your originality, but other than that, there are so many talented writers waiting in the wings – their shelf space usurped by the spiralling Pran Mehras of the world. It is easy to get the book done real cheap.

Sandeep: So, when Ramesh gave in to my demands and arranged for a retainer, he was actually playing me like a multi stringed instrument. I was in fact selling myself dirt cheap.

Simon: That's what happens, buddy.

Sandeep: It happened twice, Simon. First with that bootlicking baboon called Ajay Yadav and then this Ramesh. My self-respect has come down to the level of my shoelaces. I really need cannabis to get high again.

Simon: I understand you are incensed. You have even managed to drop Aayyappan for the first time in months. You, my buddy, are brilliant when it comes to writing, thinking, and dare I say, innovating. As a martial artist you are right up there with the best. When it comes to the use of hidden cameras, you have no parallel. As an imposter, you are the very one I would chose to bluff for my life. But, pitting your political wits against either stalwart entrepreneurs or ass kissing cubicle creeps is not really your forte.

Shruti: But, tell me, dear. Did you actually want a better deal?

Sandeep: I guess not. Now that I think of it, this is really the dream job for me. But, what I can't stomach is that after coming up with the idea, I can't stop them from bombarding *Axiomatic Wisdom* on school and college kids, even with the threat of my walking out.

Shruti: It will pass Ramesh by as gentle wind which threaten him not

Sandeep: So, all I can do is sulk?

Shruti: Can J.K. Rowling walk away from Harry Potter if she does not like the theme shops? She has become an industry. With fame, choices get limited.

Sandeep: Inbuilt opposite.

Suprakash: Why do you think the brand promotion is such a bad thing? After all you can look at the positive side. A generation that is growing up on Bollywood and Facebook have a way of knowing that there is something called Indian philosophy, which predates Karan Johar.

Sandeep: Doctor. You have been silent so long that I was starting to wonder if whiskey had taken over the psyche of the psychiatrist. But this is packaged Indian philosophy, sold like candy floss. Branded and pulverised into a commodity by *Axiom.* And the way they are going about it, there is no way for the kids not to be influenced.

Shruti: That's true everywhere, isn't it? From *educational* visits to soft drink company factories to drawing circles following shapes of particular chocolate biscuits. In the United States there is consciousness, making School boards and parents organisations speak out against these brain-stamping tactics. But, in India, I don't see too many protests taking place.

Simon: Can a kid escape Disney or Pokemon? How many kids know Mark Twain? They all know Princess and the Pauper. They come to know of The Three Musketeers and Aladin from Disney. They are bombarded more and more.

Sandeep: Kids get to learn about Sachin Tendulkar from the ridiculous 20-20 IPL

Shruti: Exactly, and IPL is branding itself into a life style.

Suprakash: Have you noticed the ex-stars, people who a few days back lambasted 20-20 to preserve the purity of Test Cricket? They now queue up to fill the commentary boxes, do pitch reports and write articles on the tournament and its cheerleaders in newspapers and cricket websites. Find ways to pretend 20-20 is good for the game.

Shruti: IPL is marketed through free channels on YouTube. Desperate to become a pattern in the fabric of life.

Simon: More so, with the school and college work going digital. My niece does her homework online, on the school blog. Online world is without embargo, without borders. It is easier to control the minds of children online. Bombarding them with fads and fashions.

Suprakash: The entire generation is being systematically controlled.

Shruti: You mean through the Internet?

Suprakash: Can I allude to anything else? I am obsessed.

Shruti: I know there are lots of things wrong with the internet. Terrorist groups, child pornography. But, is it really a mechanism of controlling thought? Why, the internet is also the gateway to emancipation, from the fetters of regional control. The power of publishing thoughts and thereby sharing it electronically.

Suprakash: I beg to differ, young lady

Shruti: And I from you, dear doctor. There is a theory that it was the digital computers which made it possible for information sharing leading to the fall of the Berlin wall. It is the internet which allows people in the third world countries participate in forums, make their voices heard, earn money. The fascinating concept of the citizen journalist. It is one medium that has danced around censors of governments. Iranians, North Koreans and the Slavic countries have been able to reach out to the world, report atrocities.

Simon: I agree with you to an extent, but there is a great amount of truth in what the Doctor says. The content of the internet is such that branding becomes easier. Sites, zines, newsletters can be built around products or concepts and at minimal cost. Unbridled marketing.

Suprakash: It cuts out the human liberty of choice.

Shruti: Come on! The internet by definition unleashes the power of choice. Everything is available for the discerning surfer

Suprakash: The key word here is discerning. Let me ask you something. Is too much choice a good thing?

Sandeep: Harking back to the theme of the wish fulfilling tree?

Suprakash: Project Gutenberg. When I was in school, I used to take home one book a week from the library. Something by Dickens or Poe or Stevenson. Not all of their works were available and the books were too expensive for a middle class Bengali to purchase. How I wished that I had all the books in a home library. Now, the internet provides all the classics, free of cost. Tell me, does that increase our reading?

Sandeep: The wisdom of it all. If you have what you want, you have had it. Now, the books are there. Available. We can always go back to read them. And since that is not hard to do it is hardly done.

Shruti: Where is the Life we have lost in living? Where is the wisdom we have lost in knowledge? Where is the knowledge we have lost in information?

Sandeep: T.S. Eliot. Circa 1900 or so. Rings much more true in this day of free information.

Suprakash: Information at fingertips is a dangerous thing. It makes people stop thinking and Google or wiki it out. Playing into the hands of people who want to manipulate thought.

Shruti: That sounds too much like conspiracy theory

Suprakash: Is it? You walk into a bookstore and go over some books. What if a fellow who comes in the next day and tells you the names of the books you have leafed through, shelves you have looked at? Doesn't it sound quite like something that might have taken place in an Eastern European country before the fall of the Berlin Wall? The Stasis – big brother watching? And here we are in the internet age, Amazon and Barnes and Noble.com being our bookshops. Everything we browse, every item we touch remains recorded in the corporate database, carefully stored, digital fingerprints analysed for pattern recognition. Information trails left for powers that be to latch on to. Doesn't it sound quite like the East Germans? With unfailing and efficient systems replacing human spies? Spies who know everything about your habits, interests, the sites you Google, the ebooks you read, the blogs you visit.

Shruti: This sounds scary

Suprakash: Welcome to Corpocracy, dear. Let me give you other examples of thought manipulation. Recommendation of products by purchasers. This is an easy internet phenomenon. Think about it, and deduce how easy it is for people to use the apparently unbiased recommendations that are easily available without having to work for it. Will they think? Will they bother to choose for themselves?

Shruti: There is the choice that one can make. Whether to choose himself or go ahead with the choice of others.

Simon: I agree with the doctor. There is a slow but steady reduction of choice till it becomes a given ... to use another word, an axiom of sorts to possess something recommended by peers. A Nike or an Adidas ... or a recommended product on the web.

Suprakash: Twitter. The next big thing after Facebook and Orkut. What is it? To bombard the human race with continuous stream of consciousness?

Sandeep: Is it the universal consciousness? The whole world connected with a single stream of thought? The oneness of cosmic world? Or have I had a glass too many of Rum and Cola? More rum and less cola with each additional glass?

Suprakash: Twitter ... reminiscent of the birds. The birds are great subjects of cognitive study in the animal world. When they migrate, there is a general combined intelligence based on the formation. Each bird individually has little idea where it is supposed to go, but is guided by the formation of the group. I wonder if human choice is slowly turning into a group phenomenon, a kind of electronic flock of birds.

Shruti: You mean to say human individuality is being suppressed by the openness of the web?

Suprakash: The pseudo openness. Yes. Have you ever witnessed a mob in action? Felt the strange involuntary reactions while participating in a group activity? Wasn't individual thought channelled into collective decision in each case? And now, think of the millions of surfers, iPhone and Blackberry users connected together in a chain of curious consciousness. Can't you feel the incredible psychological interactions that are taking place? A solid chunk of humanity with common receptors and involuntary reactions. Can you imagine how easy it will be for manipulation of conscience? Or how easy it already is?

Simon: Hear hear ... or read read! For mega sized corporations, manipulating thought and creating cultures become so much easier with general social networking and twitter. An idea needs to be repeated often enough to be sellable. And these sites, aided by spamming and advocacy workforce made up of technology and human resources, makes repetition so much easier and wide spread. The power of printed word multiplied by a million.

Sandeep: You are talking of manufactured consent powered by technology, rushing across international boundaries, encroaching the free space of human thought.

Suprakash: To many children of today, Wikipedia is the all purpose text book. Just think of the implications if this project is taken over by a power with vested interest.

Shruti: You are changing my world view

Suprakash: Lady, it has already changed. I am opening your eyes.

Simon: Sandeep just dropped out.

Shruti: Maybe he found the insignificance of quality a bit too much to digest.

Sandeep: I am back. The whims of the BSNL connection.

Simon: We were wondering if you found the situation too scary. The insignificance of quality and the control of choice.

Sandeep: Not really. Manny Manekshaw, Mayank Manhas and the lot have shown me that quality is expendable. I have seen how mutual recommendations, hype and repeated harping generate aura of recommendation, even consented greatness. How lousy songs become hits by repeated airings on FM Channels. The internet – especially the modern innovations of the twitter and networking groups – make eavesdropping and propaganda so much easier, legal and subtle.

Shruti: Orwellian

Sandeep: Right. Yet we cannot deny the uses of the net. The freedom of speech, the treasure of information available to everyone, the scope of collaboration, the ability to bypass middle men, publish oneself ... In fact, some of my co struggling authors believe that the best writing available today are on the blogs. And again on the other side, there are the dangers of collective thought manipulation. A terrifying world of thought monitoring and control. In the end there we come back to the last chapter of the Gita. Following one's own choice, however flawed, is better than following someone else's, however pure.

(Sandeep is typing a message)

Shruti: Way too long to type a message

Simon: I guess he has lost connection yet.

Shruti: I wonder if we should call it a day.

Simon: I think so. Sandeep seems gone for good this time

Suprakash: He is waiting for the green lights of the modem. I know the feeling.

Simon: I will prune and formalise the session and post it on our Cannabis Conference blog site

Suprakash: Can people follow us on twitter?

Simon: Not yet, but the day is not far.

Shruti: I missed Professor Lal's inputs this time.

Simon: I will mail him a copy of the blog and ask for his comments.

Suprakash: Whiskey and Soda time

Simon: Cheers

Shruti: Cheers and Bye.

Suprakash: I think the appropriate expression is GNSD

Shruti: ROTFWL

LXXI

Mail from Professor Lal to Shruti Rattan and Sandeep Gupta

Dear young ones,

The tale of packaged philosophical nuggets, to be served after frying in the hot current fad, is fascinating. Lord Krishna works in miraculous ways and may be this is a new vahana of his lasting leela.

You have wondered how in this kali-yugic times one can count on his teachings to show us the right way? Will the lessons taught when the world was mistaken to be flat become warped in a world that is maha-connected to rediscover flatness?

But young ones, my old senses tend to detect seeds of doubt that stem not only from the wired-weird way of the world, but from the discontent-disconnect of the ways of your mutual selves.

Let us put our foot forward to the step of time and pretend to be beyond the reach of the four old Sanskrit words of dharma, artha, kama and moksha. What does the universal binding language of English tell you?

It is a language that thrives on irony, the ideal medium for sarcastic cynicism. Yet can you find a single word that translates itself into diametrically opposite senses? Think about it. My e-literate grand-daughter says that such cerebral teasers should be followed by the phrase 'scroll down for the answer', whatever that new age expression may contrive to mean. Unfortunately I am a relic of times devoid of such axiomatic wisdom.

Think of cleave, young people. The word that at once implies clinging on with desperation as well as a severing blow leading to separation.

The etymology of the universal language shows the path as well. Choices point, as ever, towards contradictory courses. The freedom of selection is yours.

Article from Financial Times

AxiomConsulting and Kphon Inc. together announced the launch of the new cell phone handset christened Wisdomdial.

The digital keypad of the phone – which includes mp3, email, internet and fm radio features – resembles the shape of a chakra.

"It may take some time for consumers to get used to the keypad, but once hooked, it will be a major style change," a spokesperson of Kphon informed.

The digital display has several wallpapers showcasing mythological and modern backdrops which have come to be the hallmark of Axiomatic Wisdom. The default ringtone is om bhur bhuva swaha performed by the band The Dharmabums.

Mail from Simon to his mailing group
Sub: Reactions and Returns

There have been a lot of responses to the minutes of the first online Cannabis Conference. Even in the microcosm of the small band of followers of my blog, I have detected reactions that stretch across the various possible planes with almost uniform distribution.

Some have revelled at the new points of view presented, especially by the good doctor; some have joined their cyber-voices with him to raise palpable concern. There have been an equal number who have hinted at drug induced conspiracy theory at work, the same psychiatrist's views being labelled the regressive imaginations of a pessimistic mind.

The truth, as always, lies somewhere in the middle, and is precariously balanced on the razor's edge – so much so, that a whiff of unthreatening emission from the global machinery can topple it into the space of the doctor's presumptions. This incidentally is my opinion.

Most of the readers have been regaled by our discussions revolving around branding and corporate bashing, and requests have come in thick and fast.

Why not have a dedicated website for Cannabis Conferences? Why not newsletters? Why not an entire Cannabis movement, akin to advocacy groups? Why not take on the corporations and try to change the world?

Added to this is a plea to me to resume regular postings, something that had become a regular diary of sorts and then slipped back into the dormant and sporadic spluttering of incoherent thoughts.

The departure of my buddy from the scene of action has definitely made posting difficult. No one screens Woody Allen's 'What goes on in the body during an Orgasm' any longer as corporate presentation on teamwork. The most eventful of happenings has petered down to being the relentless grumbling of Gunjan. The corporate journalist has had precious little to report.

However, having said that, some interesting winds are drifting through the workplace. After a few months of licking the wounds to her private parts made dangerously public, and carefully removing the mud of slander from her manufactured armadillo's fur, Madhu Deb is slowly getting back to being her debonair self. She has started mailing more often – and *Sur-Soiree,* for the last few months left in the capable but cribbing hands of Lahari and Gunjan, has been blessed with the return of the nurturing mother. Her mails, re-starting tentatively with official circulars, are gradually working themselves to the old fanfare attracting frenzy.

The theme of the next *Sur Soiree* will be Ancient India. It is quite clear that this will be launching the *Axiomatic Wisdom* theme across the Dutch corporate world. There are already volunteer seeking mails which hint at this being a watershed event, taking *Soiree* to the next level, opening it to the business landscape of the Netherlands. Aayyappan Ramesh is supposed to grace the event with Dave de Boer in tow. As usual, I don't expect the philosophical wisdom to be refined with adjustments for the rich Dutch background of liberalism, Calvinists and Protestants. It will remain an idea template hatched in a deadline meeting corporate cubicle, implemented with hasty trimmings across the world.

Madhu Deb has also been the champion of the new *Axiom* logo. She has been doing rounds, sneaking up on unsuspecting bankers and expounding the principles behind the charioteer and warrior depicted. The personal differences she may have had with some of the key figures behind the *Axiomatic Wisdom* thought have been crushed under the chariot of Corpocracy. Her sole problem is that the moment she encounters me – physically or in the virtual world of emails – her recaptured vibrancy is dampened and the exchanges become sobered by dollops of formality. It seems ridiculous to add a pseudo professional air to something that already reeks of profound fabrication, but the corporate world is a conglomeration of the farcical.

I had plans to quit this summer, but the new wisdom linked juggernaut whets my appetite to continue a while and experience the esoteric levels of branding that can be achieved.

The other tiding of joy is that the minor character in this drama, the apple cheeked Trisha, has utilised the post pandemonium lull to get pregnant. She has shared the good news with customary joy that goes with the traditional Indian girl on the verge of achieving her sole purpose in life.

I had not really interacted with her for the last few months, and when I met her in the canteen, I congratulated her warmly. She blushed according to the demands of the traditional writ and thanked me. The thickness around her midsection now has roots in reasons other than strong interests in current affairs, but I was not uncharitable enough to say so. In any case, when I had once mentioned the mail of my buddy, touching upon the subtle exchange of positions of the broad mind and the narrow waist, she had looked innocently baffled adding that she did not know what I was talking about. The load of innocence she pretends to carry around seems heavy enough to be discouraged during prenatal periods. However, it is good to see her basking in the newly discovered joys of legitimate pregnancy, the fulfilment that comes from being righteously impregnated by one hallowed member of male-dom.

Lastly, I received by post – that outdated mode of communication – a scintillatingly beautiful invitation. It has come from the land that has raised in me so many conflicting emotions and interest, from a living legend I have come across so often in the last few months.

In exquisite calligraphy, the handcrafted card summons me to join the auspicious occasion of the celebration of fifty years of Writers Workshop, a function that will also launch the first collection of Audio CDs of the readings of the Mahabharata sessions by the selfsame Professor P. Lal. The artwork on the card has been designed by his daughter, the artist Srimati Lal. The only problem with the invitation is that the event will be held half a hemisphere away.

Mail from Kailash Naik to Sandeep

Hi Teacher,

Talked undercover to a queer breed of people called book packagers. I was posing as a new novelist, a pretty ordinary talent. For a hefty fee, they can interview the 'author', take his/her ideas forward through 'germination process', use hack writers to package a book, follow it up by arranging deals and ultimately make it a best seller. The degree of talent is irrelevant. Remember Kavya?

As you can make out, I am in the old game of planning an expose, but if you are interested in using their services, let me know and I will put you in contact with some of them, off the record :-)

Speaking of plagiarists, our Uproar management is standing solidly behind Mayuri. They have always been supportive of new Indian talent – to the extent of dragging that dammed Booker winner, one of their founder members, to pen her praises after the twenty five grand deal with Walrus International. This queered the pitch for them once Virginia Mandrian came up with the plagiarism charges. However, our friend, Soma Chatterjee, wrote a plucky defence of the defamed girl. 'In the age of Google', she reasoned, 'what are a few lines lifted from another work?' Voice of the people dealing with public issues. That is Uproar.

It's great to know that Akash is making new friends. Since you are doubling up as a martial arts and games teacher as well, I hope you will make sure that he develops the skills to keep from being bullied. Much as we romanticise about childhood innocence, the little ones can be some of the cruelest tribes around. Golding was not really kidding in Lord of the Flies.

Regards
K.

Mail from Madhu Deb to Axiom-HMH

The time has come for us to let our hair down again, but this time with a significant difference. While the spirit of the next Sur-Soiree event will continue to be to enjoy a nice evening of togetherness, the focus will be on spreading the Indian culture in a BIG way among HMH as well as the rest of our Dutch clients.

As an organisational initiative, top quality artists are being showcased for the event, some of whom will be a nice little surprise. The indi-pop group The Dharmabums will be performing the opening theme.

Ramesh will be gracing the occasion and Dave de Boer has confirmed his presence. Hence all of you are requested to turn out in full numbers. Please maintain the dress code of the freshly distributed FabIndia shirts with the new Axiom arrow head logo.

Here's looking at a wonderful evening.
Madhu Deb
Senior Manager
Axiom-HMH

Mail from Ajay Yadav to Axiom-HMH members

All,

As Madhu says, this is a business need. Hence, all of you are requested to turn out in full numbers. Please

Thanks and Regards,
Ajay Yadav
Account Manager Axiom HMH
Director Operations Axiom BV

Mail from Simon van der Wiel to Lahari

I guess you can make out the second sentence and the ephemeral third are actually copy and paste.

Mail from Lahari to Simon

:-)

Mail from Pritam to Sandeep

Hi Sandeep,

Thanks for the write up on the wretched subject. I really appreciate it, but must confess I have neither the time nor the patience to make sense of the complicated philosophical approach. I am pretty sure no one does and that is something that has worked well for you in getting all the rave reviews.

However, you need not worry about my not really knowing the details. As long as I know a few buzz words it is fine. Neither my bosses nor the level of people I meet from the client organisations have sufficient time, patience or capability to go deep into what supposedly made my fame. I need to claim that I can bring them esoteric benefits and they are more than satisfied. Quizzed by some unrelenting asshole, I can always fall back on the ethical prop of the Non Disclosure Agreement and IPR.

So, it does work for me and I am reaping the benefits of whatever it is you presented. Hope you are enjoying yourself in your own peculiar way.

Cheers,
Pritam

Mail from Amrita to Sandeep

I am not sure whether you read these mails or not. Probably all my life I will have to write to you as one speaks to god, knowing that he is there without really sensing his presence. But, I have chosen my path and will not deviate from it, no matter how arduous it may be. It has always been known to me that I was meant to suffer, and if the suffering has a personified cause I can identify with, it becomes meaningful.

I wonder how god was kind enough to find me the job even when I kept worshipping someone whose heart is made of stone.Why is it that you treat me like this? Is it because I have been the one to say I love you? Do you understand that you are moving me to the edge? I wonder how long I can hang on before falling into the void that my destiny is.

~Love
Amrita

LXXII

"I am here to talk – to the small handful of adhering people who have not yet tired of hearing me," the tall octogenarian, dressed in spotless white, spoke in his trademark gravelly voice. "If you want to know the *indiquy dans l'horaire* you must ask the young lady you see near the door. This is her baby."

Sandeep smiled as the other man reeled under the strain of the French expression and managed a polite smile to get away.

The 'young lady' in question was in her forties, a genial, sophisticated, erudite woman from Bangladesh called Rubana Haq. She stood near the door of the auditorium of the ICCR centre on Ho Chi Minh Sarani. Engaged in researching small publishers in the two Bengals, she had played a pivotal part in archiving and indexing the workshop's massive collection of publications. She had also edited a selection of writings called *The Best of Writers Workshop* – a compilation of published pieces across the last half century. As their eyes met, she smiled and beckoned him.

"Sandeep Gupta, I presume?" she asked.

"Yes, ma'am."

"Call me Rubana, or didi if you want to respect my advancing years. The only one who deserves pedagogic address in this gathering is the professor. He has been extremely lavish in his praise about you," she smiled.

"He is too kind."

"He encourages. For the last fifty years he has been encouraging authors. But he is also reserved in his accolades. I can tell that he considers you to be in his precious ten percent."

People were filtering into the hall. A curious expanse of audience from the well dressed aristocratic elite and dishevelled, rough hewn intellectuals, with all manner of age and dress sense in between. Assembling together, guided by the lamp of culture.

The governor was scheduled to arrive at any moment. A couple of television crews took up positions, eyeing the optimal camera locations to best capture the television and cinema star Shivani Khede. She was there with her husband Siddharth Khede, a theatre personality who had had two plays published by the Workshop in the early seventies.

"Ten percent?" Sandeep scanned the crowd. At the far end of the hall, he could see Jed Bickman from the Brown University, a research scholar currently engaged in a thesis on the Workshop. He was talking to a very decked up Shuktara Lal, the fair hand behind the eloquent emails.

"The professor has this theory of ten percent. Among all the authors he comes across, ten percent produce something worthwhile," the lady explained. "In fact, here comes another one of them." A tall young couple walked in, a smiling woman in a smart salwar suit accompanied by a formally dressed man whose clean cut features were distorted by obnoxiously long and curly hair. Rubana smiled at them.

"Ah, new look. Suits your artistic temperament, I must say."

The curls bounced as the newcomer laughed.

" So, you must be Rumela?"

The woman in the salwar suit nodded, smiling.

"Are you *bowled over*?" Rubana asked and the couple laughed. "Before anything starts, go and meet the man of the moment. He will be very glad that you could manage to come."

"The guy behind the website?" Sandeep asked as the two moved away towards the front row where the aged professor sat with his wife.

"Yes, and he has a few books under his belt. Like you he keeps shuttling across the world."

"I guess I am done shuttling for the time being."

"You can never say for sure these days. Excuse me," the cheerful lady moved towards the door to greet another guest. Sandeep chose a seat and soaked in the atmosphere as the events of the evening commenced.

The governor was exceptionally erudite for someone belonging to that comical collection known as Indian politicians. Taking the stage, he thumbed through the beautiful cloth bound volumes with the unmistakable glee of a true book lover. Rubana offered a vote of thanks and asked him to say a few words.

"Even in these days of glossy paperbacks and misleading recommendation in blurbs – which lure us towards the fatal error of judging books by their cover – the Writers Workshop sticks to its own quirk. It continues to stay off the glitz of DTP processed covers and makes the book as much a work of art as the contents within. It is testimony to the dedication of a single man, who has encouraged and continues to encourage generations of writers who for a number of reasons decide to voice their opinions and tell their tales in the English language."

The professor himself got up to speak, the television cameras following him as and when they could take the focus off the smile of Shivani Khede.

"It is true that I have been publishing for the last fifty years. A half century is quite a long while and there have been several articles and compilations whose authors have stood ready to incorporate last minute changes, lest I pass away just as it went to press."

The auditorium reverberated with laughter.

"And yet, I continue to live. There have been some close shaves, one back in 1989 resulting in *Lessons*. Others more recently, when under the illusion of being Purushottam, I decided to ignore the better senses that accompany one's better half and proceeded to a feverish holiday in Puri a couple of years back. But, I live on. I am the Bhishma Pitamaha who cannot retire while the Mahabharata is incomplete.

"People ask me why I took on the self imposed exile from many attractions of life to concentrate on the line by line transliteration of the epic. They attribute it to my vocation, my dedication, my constancy of purpose, my mulish obstinacy and adamant refusal to see reason. All of them are right to a certain extent. However, the truth is much less dramatic. The reason I started and still keep translating the immortal work of Vyasa is that I want to understand it. In today's fast world, people skim through books without really comprehending them. As a transcreator, I am forced to understand the many dilemmas and questions raised and left open or unanswered by the work. As a tome of compilation, it is a grand treasure trove. Once you get lost in it, there is no coming back. And I have been lost in it for the last forty years of my life.

"During the delights of unravelling the puzzles of the pages of Vyasa, I have been fortunate enough to help the cause of numerous writers who have struggled to have their works see the light of day in the all encompassing darkness that pervades commercial publishing in boom time India. However, I must say that the claim that I have done so single handedly is more than farfetched. There are over 6000 small presses in Kolkata alone, run in small garages or in the corners of rooms. They are run by young, idealist Bengalis to inspire people, to promote culture and instil literary values. These volumes are sold at low prices. I am proud to be in a city that promotes literature.

"The modern dispatches that one can receive through the wonder of the Internet have made me aware of the global presence of such small presses and their continuing struggles against the nexus of commercial publication worldwide. With the coming of the Internet, I am probably seeing a new era of publishing and I hope I will live another few years to follow the course of history of writing that is being written now. It is gratifying to see that even as the US Consulate building across the street beckons you to the world of modernistic marvels, *you* have managed to gather here to celebrate the occasion of an old timer raising his bat on completion of a half century.

"During the course of our mutual journey across the treacherous terrains of publishing, there have been young authors who have wanted to give in, to bow to the nepotistic workings of the book dumping industry and relinquish the gift of producing literature that they have been blessed with. For them I have one story from the Mahabharata.

"When Yudhistira, seeing the land full of dead warriors after the battle of Kurukshetra, wanted to commit suicide, he went to his foster father. He is the Dharma-putra, and his foster father was Vidur, who represented Dharma through wisdom. Vidur agreed with Yudhistira's proposal, but asked him a brain teaser – something today's netizens tell me should be followed with the curious phrase – scroll down for the answer."

The entertained audience laughed again.

"Well, the question was to find out the similarity between *nadi* – the river, *stree* – woman, *taruvar* – tree and *prithvi* – the earth. Yudhistira came back and said that he understood. What did he understand?

"River, tree, earth and woman – they continue to provide even when they are abused, they carry on living after destruction, they bring forth fruit, children, harvest and crops even after being plundered. I would request each aspiring author to remember that. Fruits of labour cannot be stopped by the rape of culture."

Sandeep sat back and closed his eyes. The words spiralled through his mind, running through the strained senses of the past year. His fingers itched for the keypads of his laptop. Was it rebirth? Or was it detoxification?

The professor had branched off and was talking about the four pillars of the Gita now, the multiple interpretations of dharma, artha, kama and moksha. Sandeep smiled and opened his eyes. His refreshed gaze fell on a solitary body hunched over a tape recorder a couple of rows ahead of him. The form and the gestures were oddly familiar.

Listening to the Professor's favourite theme he moved across the seats to get a clearer view of the man. He could make out the line of the jaw, the crop of thinning black hair, the more than necessary layers in the midsection. The fellow was just too familiar to ignore.

"I say," the irritation in the voice behind him made Sandeep squirm apologetically. He looked back to find himself standing directly in front of the guy with long, curly, unkempt hair who had been greeted by Rubana Haq.

"Oh, I'm sorry," he said, and manoeuvred his body to allow a clear view of the stage.

"I'm not worried about the speech, I've heard this part on at least six of my last eight visits to the Workshop," the guy whispered. "It's just that you are standing on my toes."

Sandeep hastily removed his feet and dropped into the seat next to him.

"Sorry."

"What were you looking at anyway? I thought Shivani Khede is sitting on the other wing."

"Eh?" Sandeep chuckled. "It's not that. And I don't find her particularly attractive. The guy you see sitting there seems maddeningly familiar. I just can't see his face."

His new friend squinted at the bloke with the tape recorder.

"I wouldn't be so eager to look at his face if I were you."

"But you are not me."

"True. You have a point there. I'm sure he isn't a celebrity."

"I'm sure of that too. At least the television cameras haven't focussed on him. I just think I know him from somewhere and know him very well."

The curly haired fellow thought about it.

"Maybe I can help you."

"Eh?"

"Focus on him."

With a disinterested look towards the stage, he curled his middle finger under his thumb, positioning a small crumpled paper ball. The next moment he had ejected it carom style and accompanied by a gasp from his companion, the girl called Rumela, the ball hurtled across the brief space to land on the ear of the bulky man. With a seated jump, he turned back and Sandeep saw his face. Bewildered and choleric, a paunchy face with vacant eyes sunken in pudgy cheeks. The streams of recollection overflowed. He smiled widely.

"Thanks, mate. My name is Sandeep," he offered his hand.

"Arunabha," the engineer behind the recollection replied. "And if anyone asks, neither of us knows who threw that piece of paper."

Sandeep laughed. "No one will know."

He walked out into the aisle and the paunchy face followed him, a smile making its way across the jowls.

"Sandeep!"

"Aveek!"

Friendship formed in school may be dampened with time, but once rekindled, it does not take long to hit the peak. The two friends of the famed triumvirate of old embraced in the lobby.

"Been a tremendously long time."

"You can say that again."

"You have hardly changed."

"You have changed for the two of us."

It was a while before Aveek laughed. He had never been quick on the uptake.

"Someone told me you were in the papers."

Sandeep nodded.

"For a while I was a journalist, yes. But not for any paper. More of a freelance team ..."

Aveek shook his head.

"I mean someone saw your name in the papers. The bio seemed to hint that you were you, if you know what I mean. Did you write a book?"

Sandeep nodded a bit evasively.

"Yes, I did. Just had to get it out of my system."

"System?"

"Yes, well, you know, like the circulatory or digestive ..."

"Oh yeah, I know what you mean. Who were the publishers?"

"Well, a small publishing agency called Amphibian Books."

"Amphibian?"

There was a note of recollection in Aveek's voice which startled him. Last time he checked, the reading habits of his friend had been limited to the Drinks section of menu cards. The puzzle did not end there. A function of Writers Workshop was by far the last place on earth where he would have wagered a reunion with this dear friend of his. What was he doing here?

"What on earth are you doing here?" he asked.

Aveek smiled through the jowls.

"I am here for an interview."

"Interview?"

"Yes, you see, I am also a journalist. I work for the Literature section of *Calcutta Times.*"

Sandeep laughed aloud.

"You've really developed a sense of humour in the years. What do you do, really?"

Aveek looked confused.

"I told you. I am with *Calcutta Times.* I am in the Literature section. Most often I write the Book Review column on Fridays, but tonight I am here for an interview."

Sandeep squeezed his eyes tightly and opened them again. The apparition was still there, smiling grotesquely.

"You review books?"

"Yes. Unfortunately I did not get a chance to review yours, but if you can give me a copy I can pull some strings ..."

Sandeep asked him to stop. He asked for a glass of water from the caterers who were preparing the snacks.

"You review books. I ... I must say I'm surprised. I had no idea that you were much of a reader, apart from menu cards and the wall graphitti in the urinals ..."

Aveek smiled.

"It's not that difficult. We don't have to do too much reading. The books come with a summary along with the editor's flag saying whether it is to get a good, average or poor review. It depends on the relationship with the publisher, you know what I mean... And all I have to do is to choose the appropriate template and include a couple of paragraphs. I'm actually pretty good at that. Tell you what, I think I can get you a pretty good review ..."

"Woman, river, earth and tree ..."

"What's that? The name of your book?"

"No. The name of the book is *Doppelganger Days.*"

"Doppel what?"

"Forget it. I am thinking of giving up fiction altogether and limiting myself to truth. But no one would believe me."

Aveek nodded sagaciously.

"I would recommend it if you moved to non-fiction. It is easier."

"You would recommend...?"

"Yes. You see, for a while I had worked as a Reader for Walrus India ..."

"What?"

"I said that I worked as a Reader for Walrus India ... ouch ... why did you pinch me?"

"I just wanted to find out if you were real."

"What's that supposed to mean? As I was saying, the job as a reader was very demanding. You see, all these manuscripts would come in, and it was the company policy to respond to each of it."

"Indeed?"

"Yes, a lot of work. All manuscripts which came without recommendation were put in a tray, and by the end of the day you needed to have a rejection slip posted to each one of the authors. And people wrote such a lot ... manuscript piles were unmanageable."

"Er ... did your job as reader involve reading?"

"Not really. The job description was to find out the name of the work, fill in the rejection letter template and print it out. Only a few manuscripts that came with recommendations of the chief or long standing authors and so on, they were sent to the editorial department. That is why I said, I know. Non-fiction is a better deal. There are not so many manuscripts and you have a chance that your summary letter will be read and someone will find it interesting."

"And you are now here to interview Professor Lal?"

"Professor Lal?"

"Yes, you know ... the one who is giving the speech ..."

"The old guy? Come on. Who will be interested in his interview? I have a meeting with this young girl. A most promising poet. She is also an activist for the Dalits. Incidentally, she was also first published by Amphibian Books."

"Indeed? And is she here?"

"She is supposed to be. She has said that she draws heavily from the condition of the tribal people in ancient epics, so these are events that are tuned specifically to her interest. She generally asks questions that makes waves."

"Waves? As in sound waves? Or is it cyber waves now?"

"Tina Balachander. Have you read her?"

"I haven't even heard of her."

"Strange. Boss says she has written some of the best stuff since ... since ... well, I have forgotten who it was since, but I have it in my notebook. At least that's what I am supposed to write in my interview."

"Really? Has your boss read her?"

"Are you kidding? If the editor of a book review department started to read stuff sent to him he would never sleep."

"They're that bad?"

"He won't have the time. Anyway, this girl comes with excellent recommendations from some of the most respected poets of Southern India. In fact Kamala Subramanium's recommendation stopped her Wikipedia page from getting deleted."

"Her Wikipedia page?"

"Yes. The editors had marked it as an article for deletion because it supposedly did not suit the required notability criteria. And she went ahead and got

Kamala Subramanium's certificate in *The Hindu* proclaiming her to be one of the most notable poets to have come out of modern India. In the discussion page of Wikipedia, it is noted now that Tina Balachander is one of the most notable young poets in South East Asia, and one needs to consider very carefully before deleting. I tell you, she has all the makings of a famous poetess. She has already created a brand for herself. That's what matters."

Sandeep looked up at the ceiling. From the walls, Rabindranath Tagore stared back at him with helpless eyes.

"I better get back inside," he mumbled.

"It was great meeting you, man. What are you doing these days?"

Sandeep shrugged.

"Clutching on to my sanity."

"Eh?"

"Well, a little bit of this and a little bit of that."

"Remember the book. Here, I'll give you my card. Just mail it to me and I will ensure a good review."

Sandeep smiled and patted his old friend on the shoulder.

"Thanks, buddy. But, I think I will pass the offer. Good luck with your interview."

"Hey, what's your cell number?"

"I've got your card. I'll give you a call."

He walked back into the auditorium, where the white form of Professor Lal was nearing the end of his speech.

LXXIII

The world – roll of a casino dice
Now marked up, now half price
Work baby work, slog all day
Think not profit, just get away
Amsterdam to Copacabana
Ma faleshu Kadachana

There was one slightly raised eyebrow in the countenance of K. Aayyappan Ramesh as the lead singer of the *Dharmabums* group got the evening rolling with the revolting rap. He looked around at the audience, mostly bankers winding off after a tough day. They were smiling, tapping their feet to the music. Even Madhu Deb swayed her ample form to the rhythm. The visionary started smiling.

"Why is it that even as the two armies stood there, only Arjuna saw what Krishna wanted him to see? Why did none of the others see the Visvarupa darshan, the magic that Krishna ultimately had to resort to? Was Krishna just a voice in Arjuna's head, or was it a battle between Arjuna's baser and better senses? There are so many questions that remain unanswered. Unlike the Greek classics, the Mahabharata is simple and is still lived out in the modern day. Never more than the crisis ridden present world with the chakravyuha of the internet."

As Sandeep made his way back to his seat, Professor Lal took questions from the audience.

"You maintain that Duryodhana is actually named Suyodhana. Does it mean you consider a lot of the things written about Duryodhana are actually fiction?"

"This is a legend and the boundaries between truth and fiction cease to exist in mythology. However, if the Kauravas had won the war, who knows what Yudhistira may have been known as? Rama won the war of the Ramayana, and Ravana and his followers were branded Rakshashas. Were they actually demons? No way. They were Rakshaks – the guards ..."

There was a click in his mental chain, the connection of a couple of links. The same words spoken in another distant land. The chess bar, the walk down to Chinatown, the Vietnamese dinner, the exchanges ...

A feminine voice of curiously high pitch jolted him out of his fond memories, unbinding the chains connected by links, standing in front of the light of other days.

"Don't you think the Gita is nothing but a piece of dialogue between two great womanisers?"

Sharp intakes of breath integrated into a combined gasp, and cameras swung towards the young dark girl who had asked the question. She stood there in a yellow salwar suit, having risen from her seat, challenge thrown into the look she cast at the old man on the stage. Sandeep placed her somewhere in her mid-twenties.

The Professor almost chuckled.

"The Indian gods and heroes traditionally have feet of clay, young lady. Mahabharata is set in the real world. Arjuna is a troubled soul, searching for answers in a conflict ridden world. He is not like his brothers who are satisfied with the conventional answers. So, he has doubts even while his kshatriya warrior's duty asks him to fight. So, he seeks answers, just like a twentieth century hero does. Through restless contemplation and search for sexual satisfaction. He is very human."

The girl started to speak even as the last words were leaving the professor's lips.

"I'd rather say that he is very much like a man. The archetypical man. Who plunders women because he knows that women, like the trees, river and earth will continue to serve, no matter what abuse one puts them through. The same with his friend, the sorcerer Krishna. The two womanisers have a session of self justification between themselves before they wage war – that other exercise of destruction men excel at."

The professor smiled.

"I cannot deny that. The Mahabharata is very much a doomsday epic, depicting a moral collapse so very contemporary to us. However, we cannot afford to ignore that Arjuna, with all the shortcomings of the *man* in him, is also a pacifist – probably the first in mythological history. He is a humanist, while the one who does not don weapons at all in the war is a militarist. Mahabharata is full of contradictions, young lady. It is fascinating. Even in the context of the modern world."

"So, in your opinion, we need to indulge in genuflection to two womanisers, who even indulge in severe discrimination against the lower caste, as can be seen from the story of Ekalavya. To them, women and the untouchables are both to be exploited and suppressed."

A bored groan drifted in over Sandeep's shoulder. His new found benefactor with long hair was biting down an enraged yawn.

"Who is this compulsive activist?" he asked in a bored voice.

"That's Tina Balachander," the answer was sudden and both Sandeep and the couple beside him looked up with a start to find Aveek seated immediately behind them.

The Professor's voice was calm as he answered.

"Wouldn't it be worshipping *avidya* if we disregarded Simone de Beauvoir for her complicated sexuality and nonconforming relationship with Sartre? What we are looking at is the wisdom and the intriguing questions we can find in the epic. Glorifying the individual characters of the work is a personal choice and we should leave that to individual *swa dharma*."

"How is it that Eve Ensler is listed among the 100 ... ," her next question began almost immediately, with rehearsed spontaneity, but at this moment the Governor got up to leave with his entourage. The television cameras moved to follow the departure of the dignitary. The question died a premature death as the focus shifted from the argument.

Shyamasree Devi, the wife of the Professor for fifty four years, asked the concluding question from the front row.

"So, do you agree that by association women are untouchables?"

A gleam of mischief flickered through the otherwise deadpan expression of the scholar.

"No, they are very touchable. It depends on where and how."

"There are refreshments outside," Rubana Haq smiled at Sandeep as he approached the door. "The tradition of Bharata and Mahabharata."

"I am already refreshed," Sandeep replied.

"I know what you mean. But, it is a sublime occasion, with mythical epics in the air. There might be more surprises in store," she shot a mysterious look and hastened towards another guest.

Sandeep walked out and froze.

The gentle buzz of the curious collection of invitees, the movement of the people under the soft lighting of ICCR, the zooming crowd gathering beside the table displaying the editions of the different *parvas* of the Mahabharata – the elegant dresses and the sparkling jewels, all spiralled into a kaleidoscopic visual din. In the foreground of the disjointed shreds of fuzzy colourful activity stood an apparition from the past, a hallucination borne out of a day fluctuating between truth and illusion. He blinked to make it disappear, but stay it did – adamantly refusing to flitter away into the dreamlands across time zones. He frowned. Already, there had been a flickering shadow of a hope-filled youthful past projected onto the un-really real wall of the scary present. He had had his fill of visions for a night. Extending his hand he pinched.

"Ouch," said the spirit.

"Oops," Sandeep blinked. The kaleidoscope had changed the patterns of time space around him.

"I thought you would welcome me by taking me in your arms, not a part of me in a couple of your fingers? Is that a cost saving thing that you picked up from your research into financial crisis? Or are you still obsessed about my skin-fold thickness?"

Sandeep stood there, scared to twitch his lips into a smile – lest he be stirred awake from the waking dream.

"If you are a dream, please go away ...," he stuttered.

Shruti laughed. The lights, shades, people and paraphernalia around them returned to recognisable patterns with the report – that magical tinker imprinted in the cognitive map of his happiest moments. But, rationality eluded him.

"Have you taken up telekinesis as your new hobby?" he managed to ask.

"I used the chimney with the hot chocolate mugs as portkey."

"The auditorium is that way."

"I know. I had been listening to the professor for a good part of the evening. But, isn't it over?"

"Precisely."

"I don't follow you."

"P.D.A."

"The electronic gadget ? Oh I see ... public display of affection. You are not in Kansas anymore. Nor Amsterdam. In that case I do follow you. And will follow you if you lead the way."

Sandeep nodded. "I want to make it certain that you are real. Every part of you."

"Where is Simon?" Madhu Deb's keen eyes scanned the audience. People seemed to be enjoying the vocal renderings of *om bhur bhuva swaha.* A sense of accomplishment gushed through her. She had screened the musical talents from the pool of *Axiom* resources across Europe to rehearse and present the very cream. The performance churned out by her young protégés had been worth the effort.

Some of the discarded singers had not taken it well. One was so caught up in the imagined oodles of his talent that he had laughed at her face and accused her of being tone deaf throwing her managerial weight around to judge music. But, then, you could not please everyone. She had her job to do, and she had done it well.

"Don't forget to have enough fruits and water," she beamed at Trisha. "One tends to get carried away at these events, but the growing little one needs all the nourishment."

Trisha nodded with a contented smile. She was getting bigger every day.

"Have you seen Simon?" the good lady asked.

Trisha shook her head. "I haven't really looked for him, but I haven't seen him either. I don't think he is here."

Madhu Deb frowned. It had been mentioned very specifically that attendance was mandatory. Why, even Ramesh and Dave de Boer were attending. She did not believe in victimising people, but if the guy took unrestricted amount of liberties, she could not help him in any way. This was a big event for *Axiom* and if he did not understand it after so much evangelisation, it certainly smacked of attitude problem. One thing was for sure. The guy was no team player. And the core message of *Axiomatic Wisdom*, borrowed from ancient Indian philosophy, was collaboration, without the sense of self.

"My writing has been called a lot of things including political and polemical. So the obvious question people ask is why I am using poetry as a form of expression. It's not that I have not dabbled in other literary genres and I chose poetry very consciously. Firstly, because poetry has a special relationship with language, and since language is the site of all subjugation and oppression, I think poetry is unique in the power of being extremely subversive."

Aveek, face expressionless as he held his tape recorder in front of Tina Balachander, stole a glance at Sandeep. He nodded back with an encouraging thumbs up sign.

"On several levels it can challenge a language, its patterns of thought, its prejudices, its enshrined, encapsulated inequalities. Though languages may have their hierarchies firmly in place and though they tend to be degrading to women and Dalits in the Indian context, they are a level-playing field. I can offer my resistance through language. We can announce our revolution through poetry. Secondly it offers me point-blank range. I have to be far more subtle if I were to convey the same through fiction, and very often, there are chances that my subtext is glossed over. And third, a real poet can never escape her politics."

The Professor was cutting a portion of pastry with a spoon when they approached him. He looked up.

"Ah, the cannabis couple," he greeted.

They laughed.

"I wonder if that is flattering," Shruti said.

"Place a couple of intellectual rebels in Amsterdam, and it is expected," Professor Lal's tone was a nonchalant shrug. "And it is not unique in the world of Literature as well. One can look at Huxley and Kerouac ... William Burroughs even sold heroin in Greenwich Village. And going by the number of literary souls who make up the populace there, he had a ready clientele."

Sandeep put his hands up.

"Professor, we are hardly what you would call addicts."

"True. For you the drugs are more of anaesthetics, a counter measure for the social hallucinations – the antidote to *avidya.* Perhaps that is one way to see things clearly in the modern world with hundreds of tools to muddle the doors of perception."

"In fact now people say they can write much better with a word processor. A while back they used to say the same thing about drugs. But have you ever tried hallucinogens yourself, Professor?" Sandeep asked.

"You want to know whether the character of an old man is like the characters of his calligraphy or not? Let me tell you this, young man. Once the Mahabharata gets into your veins, you need no other sauce to get high. And I am too old. So, whenever you need me, I will be there as an honorary member of the exclusive club. And as far as word processors are concerned, I cannot start to define the term. However, it is good to see the two of you together in the real world – as opposed to the nebulous net."

Sandeep agreed. "It sure is. I have no idea what she is doing here, but I am not complaining."

"She hasn't told you yet?"

"No, we just met about fifteen or so minutes back and since then I have been experiencing the truth of your last words on stage."

The Professor smiled as the edge of Shruti's right foot landed with stinging sharpness on Sandeep's ankle.

"Well, even in the illusory parallel worlds of today, we sometimes get the opportunity to come in contact of our own truth. We must make full use of it."

Was there a hint of mischief in the wise eyes? They were not too sure.

"Gwendolyn Brooks and Langston Hughes taught me that poetry was resistance. Apart from them people who have influenced me are Toni Morrison for recreating the magic of a downtrodden section of humanity and Virginia Woolf for showing me my womanhood, to rejoice in my femininity," Tina Balachander continued, as Aveek held the taperecorder, the stifled yawn causing quaint ripples across his jowls.

LXXIV

Mail from Ramesh to Sandeep

Received your latest instalment. I have not really had the time to go through it fully, but it seems to be in the proper direction.

You have recommended Tina Balachander as a member of our initiative who will ultimately take over the portfolio of writing sequels and additional papers/books from you once we disengage at the end of our agreement term.

It is good to see you thinking of the big picture. However, my brand manager has done some background check on the lady, and we are of the opinion that her principal USP combining Dalits and Feminism is not in line with our mission of spreading Indian wisdom.

I would like to take this opportunity to ask you to consider continuing on the assignment beyond the year. We can get you a formal contract. I know you have shared your views on this subject in no uncertain terms, but I cling on to the hope that circumstances may change and you may reconsider.

Till then, keep up the good work.

Just one word of concern. Let us not get too carried away with innovation.

Your essays on the Mahabharata continue to be fascinating, but I cannot really project the Krishna Leela of stealing sarees of the milkmaids as example of Bearish Strategy. Draupadi's vastraharan is too provocative a parallel for the technique bearing fruit during a crisis. I appreciate your imagination, but there are occasions when we need to keep it in check.

K. Aayyappan Ramesh

Mail from Pritam to Sandeep

Aveek a book reviewer for Calcutta Times? Is it another of those things that happen only in India?

Well, yesterday we sold a consulting model to a financial institution – which is still tottering from the crisis. The point that clinched the deal was my supposed expertise in the new panacea – Axiomatic Wisdom – which is touted to deliver us from financial troubles.

So, I am not really surprised by anything.

Wonderful to hear that Shruti is in Kolkata. Hope you have a nice time discussing the socio-political texture of West Bengal. With the colourful public figures there, you will have plenty to talk about.

Incidentally, I have done some marketing for you. I have ordered copies of your Doppel-whatever Days from Amazon and presented them to two of my friends who recently celebrated some auspicious occasions. I have absolutely no doubt that neither will ever read it, but I hope you get some royalties.

Cheers,
Pritam

Mail from Amrita to Sandeep

You are not even moved if I say I will die. I wonder what your reaction will be if I say I will go public with whatever we have had together, your wife coming to know about us.

But then, please don't think I am threatening you. You know I won't harm you in any way.

Please write me one word . . . one . . . please please. . . . Don't you have pity for me?

"I wonder whether that was a good idea," Sandeep wondered.

The rain had come down in accelerating torrents. Streaks of colourful lightening tore across the dark evening sky. The two of them had sprinted to the slip-shod shelter offered by a tarpaulin precariously perched on a brace of bamboo poles. The school building they had left after the afternoon football practice was barely visible through the tropical downpour.

"Not checking the forecast?"

Sandeep shook his head.

"Your joining the football game. We are trendsetters in iPhone proliferation, but the young generation is still not used to damsels dribbling in the football fields."

"Haven't your students watched *Bend it like Beckham?*"

A motorbike skidded past them, carelessly indulging in a dangerous game of chance.

"They have, but movies in this country were never meant to mimic real life. You were expected to giggle, stumble and miss. These guys are athletes, studs. They did not expect being dribbled, outrun and scored against by an Indian girl. Half of them think it's weird and rest are in love."

"That's quite peculiar when you think of all the women heads of states that countries of the subcontinent have produced."

"And yet, a country where Serena Williams hardly raises an eyebrow, there has been no female president. The world is a curious place. So is a Roman Catholic School. I wonder whether their image of liberal education will keep the Father from having something to say about you being a part of the game."

A couple of pedestrians joined them under the sheet. They cast curious glances at the sweating couple, sleeves and jeans rolled up, shoes muddy.

"It's difficult to spend a large part of your formative years in Netherlands and not develop ball sense."

"India is a different ball game. However, I am still curious about the change in your playing field. What exactly is your new research on? You told me in ICCR but I was too caught up in stream of consciousness, it didn't register."

"The effect of the EU policies on the South East Asian conflicts."

A couple of hand pulled rickshaws stopped in front of them. The pullers perched inside, taking refuge from the downpour in the makeshift retreats of their ramshackle vehicles. The fast large drops ricocheted off the streets, the tarpaulin and the plastic sheets of the rickshaw in a mixed medley of beats.

Shruti continued, "I am working on the correlations of major EU events with terrorism figures from the MIPT and GTD2 databases."

"Why does it sound contrived?" Sandeep asked.

"Because it probably is. Your paper has ravaged my lofty idealism in academics."

"Call it our paper, comrade in arms."

"I have done my own private research on academic papers since then. The results are not too encouraging."

A pair of headlights bore through the rain and a blaring blast of honking sounded in its wake. In the lines of thunder following lightening. One of the rick-shaw pullers jumped down from his vehicular shelter to move the rickety contrap-tion. The Maruti Omni moved in to park in the vacated space at a nearly obtuse angle.

"So, is the idealist discouraged?"

Shruti shook her head.

"For me it is better to be rafting in the troubled sea of thought than to be anchored in the safe waters of nonsense. I still believe that I can do useful work. The research is just a vehicle. If required I can get off it. The end will justify the means."

"Why India?"

Shruti looked into Sandeep's eyes. Cynical, yet filled with that compassion that seemed to trace loving lines on her cheeks.

"Why Netherlands?"

Sandeep looked serious.

"Subramanium and Wolfgang would like to open a school in the Netherlands. It may be interesting if I get to teach there. It is a fertile place for a novelist."

They looked at each other and burst out laughing.

In front of them a street kid, homeless and happy, jumped into the quickly filling puddles in front of the cyber cafe. The gust of wind carried his joyful gibberish into the enclosure along with the rain.

"I have never had steady income and stability in life," Sandeep said, looking at the kid. "And to look at it from the point of view of the inbuilt opposite, I am not threatened by the lack of them either. But ..."

"But?"

"Can the volatile be linked? Even wordsmiths run out of conversation. What will happen then?"

Shruti held up her hand.

"Quiz question. The old story of Bollywood numbers being lifted from Western music. Which is based on Mozart's 40th?"

"Well, I'm not that much into music ..."

"I will hum the tune for you."

As soon as Shruti started, Sandeep burst out into a loud song, ridiculously off tune. The two men who had been sharing the tarpaulin with them made a move on sighting a bus.

"Don't murder the song. You have scared those men away. The tune may be lifted, but it is beautiful."

"Extend not your love in vain, for drifting clouds I remain;

How any can I sustain, poor and free from gilded chain."

"Wonderful."

"Now I count from one to ten, wait for your reverse refrain."

"That's why do I adore you, the drifting cloud you remain;

Star crossed are we across lives, I am drizzle of sweet rain."

"Wow."

"Let's see if you still stay vain, taunting me with mock disdain."

"That'll never happen again, I'm drenched let's check in a den."

Smiling through the pins and needles of wind laden showers, the two of them looked for a doorway. There was none open. The establishment they stood in front of looked like a sweet shop, but the shutter was pulled down.

Sandeep knocked loud and hard. Shruti squirmed.

"Come on, it's closed."

Sandeep winked and knocked harder. Disgruntled footsteps greeted their ears through the din of the rain hammered orchestra. An irritated face peeped out of a small opening under the steel shutter.

"What is it?" the gruff voice demanded in Bengali.

"Is this a sweet shop?" Sandeep asked.

"It is closed."

Sandeep agreed. "Technically you are right. But, it's raining."

"What can I do if it rains?"

"Can you provide a couple of drenched souls with tea and *singara*?"

"We are closed."

"Sandeep, stop it."

"Brother, she's from Holland. A guest from abroad. And soaked. Won't you make an exception? Think how much she will appreciate the tea and *singara*."

"She's from Holland?"

"She is. From the land of Gullit and Van Basten."

"We don't have *singara*, but there may be some *aloor chop*."

"Almost as good."

" I am opening the side gate. Come in."

Sandeep looked at Shruti with triumphant eyes.

"Indian service. Business with a heart. Try that in Starbucks."

In front of them the street kid continued his jubilant dance in front of the cybercafé. He sensed Shruti's eyes on him, and something about her told him that she was not from here. For her benefit, he added a special routine to the show, putting his arm around a lamp post bearing posters of XML training and leaning towards the street.

"The Indian Gene Kelley."

"Whatever works," Sandeep remarked. "All places are interesting."

LXXV

Blog of Simple Simon

Tags: Tai chi, Life, Corporations, Choice, Gita, Internet, Cosmic Wisdom, Decisions

For days I have had little to write. I wonder if the readers of my blog still come back to check for new posts. However, to make up for the long periods of silence, I have sat down to key in a comprehensive one. It was not premeditated. Through sheer chance, a lot has happened at once.

It all started when I was sipping beer in the lap of the Black Forest, shoulders and legs aching with the rigours of nearly twenty hours of training. That was when I heard the magic word.

"Travel," the remarkable man was seated in front of me sipping the recommended Bavarian beer. From our place on the porch behind the youth hostel, we could see the lush green football grounds where the Brazilian world cup soccer team had trained during the 1974 tournament. The sun shone down brilliantly and the Herzegenhon Mountain eloquently beckoned adventurous trekkers to its horn shaped peak. However, I had decided to decline the spirited invitations of Stephanie and some other hardy German souls to join them in scaling the peak, preferring to sit it out with chilled beer. My shoulders were sore with a considerable part of the last three days being spent in going through complicated forms wielding heavy, traditional Chinese broadswords. Never since the departure of my buddy-sifu had I had so much fun, fatigue and fulfilment doing *tai chi*.

The invitation had been emailed by my buddy himself, sitting thousands of miles/kilometres away in his school in Kolkata. Sifu Wolfgang Schmidt would be the principal teacher and the master of my master, the diminutive Subramanium, would be a part of the training camp. I had jumped at the opportunity.

It had not been all smooth sailing, though. On landing at the Freiburg-Basel-Mulhouse airport, I had switched on my cell phone to a nasty text message from my senior manager.

"I am surprised. It was made pretty clear that attendance was mandatory for this edition of SurSoiree." It referred to a musical evening in which ancient Indian wisdom was to be pandered to the Dutch clients.

I had sent a polite reply mentioning that I was in Freiburg and would be travelling to Barental for a *tai chi* camp. Besides, I had added, the foremost knowledge of Gita was the power to choose and I had chosen not to be there in the holy hoodwinking hullabaloo. A pity I was not there to witness the reaction of the good lady on receiving my response on her Blackberry.

But, then, with the arduous delight of the three following days, I forgot all about her and the epoch making evening involving the *Dharmabums.* In the same mail that he had sent across to invite me to the camp on behalf of Sifu Schmidt, my buddy had pointed out that by some serendipitous quirk, it was an aptly named band to play at the occasion. His convoluted reasoning derived that we were celebrating the fantastic product of our own hallucinations, a chain of events drafted with our cannabis driven experience, now being championed by a band that derived its name, knowingly or unknowingly, from one of the works of Jack Kerouac, a key advocate of narcotics.

However, I was on a different psychic plane. The slow, hypnotic movements by the two masters had soon transformed the entire long weekend into an ethereal experience.

Whenever Wolfgang and I conversed, it was in English, a fact that perpetually surprised Subramanium.

"Isn't it true that once you know German and English it is easy to understand Dutch?" he asked.

Sifu Schmidt pointed out that it was easy enough to understand, but speaking the language was a different story. To us, it was even more surprising that Subramanium and Sandeep communicated in English.

"India is a strange land," Subramanium explained with a smile. "There are so many states. The moment you move from one to the next, you encounter different cultures, religions, languages, food and even looks. English has given urban India a common language to converse in. Something good in return for all the subjugation of two hundred years."

Well, my past few months of interaction with Indian philosophy has made me a staunch supporter of the karmic cycle. The karma is now definitely being reworked in India's favour as they reap the benefit of the English language, leading the off-shoring and outsourcing world by some distance.

Now, relaxing after the final day's lunch, the teacher was urging me to embark on journeys.

"The forms and the applications vary from place to place, country to country. Things like temperature and economy, body types and facilities, everything influences how people adapt a martial art to their system. To find the right form that works for you, you need to venture out. A dedicated martial artist has to travel. And in you I see a lot of thirst for real knowledge and disregard for the regular supply of nay-sayers that accompany any out of ordinary pursuit. I also detect a curiosity about India. You won't learn about India from National Geographic. You need to visit the land, be there and immerse in the spirit."

I had tried to look up Subramanium on the web before our meeting, but apart from a small write-up about the Karate classes he conducted for a software company in Bangalore, I had not found much else. I knew that he came to Germany each year to teach Yoga and train in Taichi.

I asked him whether he had thought of a website.

"I am too busy learning the arts and teaching them. If someone is interested in making such a site for me, I guess it would help people to find me. But, then, you know, I have found out that some things need to be found with effort, to really benefit from them. A lot of the people from whom I have learnt yoga are not even well known in their villages. But, as a seeker of the arts, I have always managed to find them. If you log on to the Internet, you will find a lot of touristy yoga centres. Some of them are good, some bogus. But, that is available to all the populace. To go beyond mediocrity, you have to take the next step."

I am thinking of moving on for quite a while now. Ever since a certain fiasco, I have kind of fallen out of love with *Axiom* in particular and the entire corporate world in general. I have thought quite a lot in the last few days of taking a few months off, maybe travel around a while. Subramanium might have been reading my mind.

"Travel," he said. "See the world. See the styles, and the martial arts. Write to the kwoons across the world, with Wolfgang's and my references. Sandeep is also pretty well known in some schools around the world. In a lot of these places you will be given accommodation at the kwoon or in the home of some student of the art. Besides, with the crisis ridden world being what it is right now, you will be getting cheap ticket deals. Now is the time to leverage on it."

I mentioned that what he said made immense sense. In professional jargon it was known as turning threats into opportunities.

"All Martial arts concepts are based on that," he mused. "Take judo – pull when you are pushed, push when you are pulled. Aikido – turn when you are pushed, enter when you are pulled. But, aphorisms aside, think about it. You may never again be able to travel at such rock bottom prices."

I said that I had in fact thought about it for quite some time. He was on the verge of making a possible *tai chi* route across the world when my cell phone rang. The number was Indian.

"Greetings, buddy. Could you log in to the *Axiom* conference bridge in a couple of minutes? Here is the pass code ..."

I was too surprised to respond and Sandeep quickly logged off. I excused myself to Subramanium, explaining that my buddy wanted me to join a conference call.

"Sandeep? Sometimes I feel he gets a kick out of surprising people. That is both his source of sustenance and undoing. Live by the sword and die by it sort of a thing in a ridiculous way," he laughed. "Go ahead, we have the entire journey back to Amsterdam on our hands."

When I logged in using the bridge numbers he had supplied, I was greeted by the cheery voice of Shruti.

" Welcome back, Simon. All our Cannabis Colleagues have joined. For the record we have Dr. Roy from Leiden, Simon from Feldberg, Germany and Sandeep and me in Lake Gardens, Kolkata."

Sandeep took up the vein.

"Seated with us is our honorary member, Professor Lal. In fact, Shruti and I are currently in his room in 162/92 Lake Gardens. It could have been called a drawing room if there were places to sit visible to the naked eye. However, *study* is more than appropriate, since the book cases, sofas, tables and floors are all piled with books, books and more books. This is an impromptu follow up session of the second Cannabis Conference, and I don't know about you guys in Europe, but we are already intoxicated by the heady fumes of knowledge that seems to exude from the volumes around us."

Shruti's voice broke through again.

"It is a mark of the times that a transcontinental knowledge sharing session has started off with our journalist friend mimicking an ESPN announcer."

"Thanks for the jibe, Shruti. Just for the record, do you guys have any intoxicant handy?"

I remarked that I did have a few bottles of the best Bavarian beer.

"Excellent. What about you, doctor?"

"Well, all I have with me is a Freudian cigar. Do you want me to get something stronger?"

"Not really, Sup-da. You can double your dose the next time. We have briefed the Professor about the discussions during our last conference, and he did have some observations. So, we decided to call this ad hoc session. Now, without much ado, it is over to the Professor..."

The wise gravelly voice came on line.

"At four score, I am experiencing new frontiers of technology. Every day opens my remaining eye wider with wonder. Connection to people in three different countries with a phone that can be concealed in a palm, what will we have next? Transport of the actual person through space transcending cable paths? It seems that even as we speak, technological waters are flowing under this virtual bridge. I don't know how I can thank you young people for bridging the gap between my ancient ways of the calligraphic pen and next generation communication."

"Professor, not all of us are young. I will be forty any day now," the doctor's voice sounded a touch morose at the inescapable eventuality.

"Well, my boy, in that case you have to go through it all over again from scratch to reach my age. To me you are a slip of a youth, while I am sure my grandson will find you positively geriatric. Life is like that."

Just an hour back, when Subramanium had spoken of training in *taichi* for the last thirty seven years, I had remarked that it was a long, long time. His reply was, "At your age it seems a long, long time. But to me, it is just a part of my life." Different sources, the same flavour of wisdom.

Much of what follows is directly taken from the wav file sent across by Sandeep. He continues to polish his skills as a clandestine correspondent, never knowing when his mercurial professional life will flip him back into one.

The Professor continued.

"You have had some most interesting discourses during your last session. Sandeep had been thoughtful enough to bring me the printed version of your dialogue.

" I see that the mender of minds was insistent that the entire mass of humanity, or rather a large chunk, is being transformed into a shoal like organism, both in terms of collectivism and shallowness, open to orchestration by subtle waft of the wand wielded by powers such as corporations and imperialistic nations. While the beautiful young lady currently sitting next to me was adamant that information exchange is a thing of overreaching optimism, where thoughts and ideas are shared without meddling of middlemen, where citizen journalism is a force to reckon with and great conceptions are powered by the combination of myriad minds. Well, young people, what is there to say? There is no simple answer to the arguments. Both seem so conclusive."

Shruti's voice was heard next.

"We have seen how instant communication of information, instant pictures taken by mobile phones communicated to the news agencies, the open communication of ideas and ..."

The psychiatrist was not too far behind either, "And we have seen how seeds of fear of terrorism sown into mass consciousness, deliberately, with absolute intent, has allowed war mongering states to ..."

I put forward my ideas of how the financial crisis had been triggered, first by the cyberfinance, the lack of inhibition in selling of CDOs, mortgage linked instruments and SIVs, trying to leverage profits from own liabilities – and how later panic had spread across the electronic world to topple the entire system as people refused to trade in instruments.

"All these lines of argument are known to the Professor," it was quite funny that the man who had been a bundle of opinions during his stay in *Axiom* had suddenly turned the neutral host during the course of this interaction. "Now let us hear what he thinks about it all."

The Professor chuckled.

"What I have to say will be ignorant to a great extent, with the parallel world of the Internet being for the large part Yarrow Unvisited to me, and if visited, by proxy, leaning on the able young clicks rendered by my granddaughter. Or as in the case of the Writers Workshop, helped along by Arunav and now, by Rubana. But, what I see in front of me, in the conflicts and confusion of this group of intelligent, intoxicated, young people is very intriguing.

"*Avidya* – anti knowledge – as referred to by the Upanishads, is the suppression of the real nature of things and to present something illusory in its place. In traditional philosophy, the term stands for that delusion which breaks up the original unity, the non-duality that is the real nature of the world and portrays it as subject and object, differentiating between the doer and the deed, the self and the other. It is not ignorance due to lack of erudition, but attributed to the limit of the human sensory or intellectual apparatus. In fact, in many canons, it is put down as the main cause of human misery. The Advaita Vedanta even says that the eradication of *avidya* should be the goal of humanity, leading to the realisation of the self.

"And now, with the internet and the networked souls, what we have been discussing is supposedly creating an illusion of non-duality. A *Mayajal* which apparently disperses the difference between self and other, but does so in an illusory way, a way that can be manufactured and manipulated. It presents dangers of finding pseudo salvation. An illusion of eradication of illusion. This is definitely a complex problem.

"However, as in any path, there is inbuilt positive and negative. As the doctor will no doubt agree, while collective reaction can often be seen in the psychology of the mob, history is not absolutely devoid of the integrated human thoughts working towards the good."

"Fighting the sea in the Netherlands," I offered.

"True. And as our young lady here says, a lot of this can be leveraged for the benefit of humanity. In the end it boils down to the same concept that we stumble upon over and over again. It is the power of choice. We can choose how to look at, interpret and use the Internet, social networking and the rest of it. Just as we can decide whether to ponder over the Gita alone, in a group of likeminded people driven by the goal of knowledge, or tap our collective feet to the rhythm of *Dharmabums* at *Axiomatic Wisdom* concerts.

"As I always say about Gita. It raises more questions than answers. And that is true about the general world. I cannot answer for all of you. I can raise more questions and point my finger. What the finger means in context of each one of you will have to be your own interpretation and choice."

The conference call came to an end. In front of me, the sun still bathed the Herzegenhon peaks. The flowers painted the mountainside in prismatic patterns. A couple of paces away, the globetrotting *tai chi* master sat contentedly sipping his amber drink, patiently waiting for me to resume the conversation if I wanted to.

I had made my decision.

You see folks, on my return to the Netherlands, I will be asking *Axiom* for a year-long sabbatical. If they say that it is not the company policy, I will quit. There is too big a world out there, with too many treasures. I want to see it all. The kwoon hopping idea seems enticing. In the course of my journeys, I may as well stop at the wonder that is India and other mystical nations, in all probability including a visit to 162/92 Lake Gardens. So, what started out as a blog where I put down my ramblings about the corporate world has diverged into a placeholder for my search in life.

And then again, if I follow the Professor correctly, it is the same picture presented in two different ways. What is *artha*? Money or meaning? I hope to find out.

After a year, when I come back, I guess the crisis will have sorted itself out. The job market will be booming yet again. Hopefully I will find a better occupation, where it will take a few more years to realise that things actually continue to suck.

"Is it a continuation of your studies of the negative influences of EU on the Balkan nations?"

Shruti laughed. "It can be presented as a logical continuation. In the end, it is just a job opportunity."

The Professor nodded.

"So, have you already received the grant?"

"I am still waiting for the decision. Quick decision is not exactly the Dutch forte. I wanted to use the time to pay a visit," she smiled. "India is full of interesting nuggets and hidden treasures. If the grant does not go through, I have a lot of choices, some of it can be here."

"And you are looking for ways to become Dutch?"

Sandeep looked up from the Writers Workshop publication he was leafing through – *Holmes of the Raj* by Vithal Rajan.

"I have never had stability in life. I have never settled down. And one of the inbuilt opposites of instability is that I'm not scared by it. I can continue here. I am enjoying the job in the school. Or I can migrate to Amsterdam. I love the canals, the cycles, the pretty old buildings which lean at different angles. I love the greenery built into the city, the dogs, the people, the houses with book cases, spiral stairways and glass windows, the hardy girls with earrings through which an agile cat can easily leap through. Subramanium has hatched a plan with Wolfgang Schmidt to open a *taichi* studio there. Something that whets my appetite. The small liberal land doles out visas to both spouses and partners. Well, we have to decide what to do. Either way, there is a lot of paperwork. The one thing that binds the Indians and the Dutch."

The Professor nodded. The world was getting smaller, connected and different.

"Well, marriage is nothing but a partnership. As long as you are mentally aware of the reasons of togetherness, and the reason does not limit itself to what is inscribed on a legal document."

"In this case legalised, authenticated and apostilled," Sandeep completed. "If we are flexible, lots of choices will pop out. I have made some money from my deal with *Axiom* and Ayyappan Ramesh. Nothing much, but enough to carry me for a while. Maybe I will take a fresh look at renewal of the deal, with caveats, conditions. Walking on the razor's edge. To experiment with life and keep writing."

The Professor looked at Shruti.

"And what about *your* writing?"

"It will continue ... in the unrestrained, unstructured, unclassifiable way. Sandeep has decided to set time bound limits for agents and publishers to respond to each of his works and then go for internet based publication – making use of the self publishing companies available to print on demand and sell on Amazon and countless other websites."

"It is cleaner. No middlemen, no nexus. And the books are still available after a decade, unlike some of the immediate best sellers. There will be a select group of readers – maybe the ones entranced by Cannabis Conferences. There are some independent review companies available as well. Probabilistically a better option to be discovered than by adding to the slush-pile."

The Professor smiled with remembrances of things past.

"When I started Writers Workshop, no one was willing to review our work. So, we took turns to review each other, publishing the critiques in *Literary Miscellany*. Kewlian Sio, Anita Desai, Don Moraes, Jai Rattan ... all of them. I have slowly developed my select group of readers."

"Whenever you go to Amazon pages of little known books, you find an electronic parallel being played out. Self published authors urging others of their tribe to mutually review each other. The internet has eliminated some of the middle men, but things are still far from perfect. However, the last year and a half has taught me many things, and the most important lesson has been to go ahead, and live life to the fullest. I have the curse of a writer. I will be harangued by angst throughout my life. The only way out is to write. And write I will."

Shruti patted his hand.

"I will perhaps go for a combination of Writers Workshop and the Amazon for the time being. I will be writing a lot of stuff for my papers as well."

"It is like cooking," the professor smiled. "What if people don't turn up to sample your food? Preparation with the seasoning and the ingredients and the stirring is what makes it worthwhile. The thing to remember is that often one may have to wait beyond a lifetime. But, never lose heart. Remember, Bernard Shaw had to send his work to sixty one publishers before it was accepted. And *Waste Land* ..."

They were interrupted by a knock. The caretaker of the Book Nook kiosk entered to hand over the keys and the bill books.

After a brief exchange, the Professor turned to find the two young people engrossed in a volume of the Mahabharata.

Shruti was reading a piece softly and Sandeep was listening. His eyes rested on her, the look stripped of the cynic, full of the wonder of sharing. He let them continue, pausing to turn a page of the Writers Workshop volume that lay on the table near him. A picture of two birds greeted him from the first page, with a quotation from the *Svetasvatara Upanishad.*

"Who is happier?" he whispered to himself and smiled.

∾ ∾ ∾

Made in the USA
San Bernardino, CA
15 December 2012